SAGARA

BOOK THREE OF THE TYRO SERIES

LUKE MITCHELL

"Life is not a problem to be solved; it is a mystery to be lived."

SOREN KIERKEGAARD

1

EIGHT MILES HIGH

April first, 2005, somewhere over India.

Badoom... Badoom... Badoom... A bass drum thumped out a repetitive beat. Electric guitars weaved a hypnotic rhythm. A deep male voice sang a mysterious song. *Let me tell you a story. It's about this man I know. He could be your best friend. He could be your foe...* Something sharp digging into my neck. A man with a pock-marked face and rotten teeth was pressing a bayonet's tip into my throat. His twisted grin was repulsive. I had to get away from him. *Now!* I couldn't move, super-glued into a moment in time. My heartbeat thudded in my head. *There's a reason for my not being able to move. What is it? Why do I have to keep still? It's vitally important that I don't move. Why?* The hideous man with the pointed blade vanished. I looked up at a full moon haloed by moisture. A dog howled. A hermit crab scuttled across fine sand. I was on a beach in Cambodia. I remembered why I was petrified. I was sitting on a landmine. *Oh, God, no! I'm going to die. This is it. This is the end.* The moon went down. A blazing sun rose, its heat intensifying rapidly. I was hot and thirsty. A faint trace of Chanel №5 drifted on the humid air. A twig snapped behind me. *Jean?* I twisted around and saw my wife, hair hooked behind her ears, squatting on a flat rock, ready to pounce. I glanced up at her bright, mischievous eyes. I knew what she was about to do. 'No!' I screamed. Too late. She leapt and slammed into me. I tumbled off the landmine. *Boof!* The mine exploded with a dull thud behind us.

'Ugh!' I awoke from the nightmare to find myself sitting in the business class section of a passenger jet. 'What the...?'

I turned to my right and stared out of a porthole. A silver disc floated above the clouds. I wondered if I'd ever be able to look at the moon again, without thinking about the night I'd spent sitting on top of a landmine in Cambodia. *Probably not,* I thought with a shudder.

The aircraft's fuselage juddered as it passed through a patch of turbulence. The cabin lights went out. The captain's apologetic voice came over the intercom. The lights flickered on. I looked away from the sky, fastened my seat belt and studied my wife. Her seat was fully reclined. She was fast asleep and still had black plastic headphones on from watching an in-flight movie. My lips teetered on the edge of a smile, recalling how Jean had said half an hour earlier, 'Isn't George Clooney smashing?' She'd nodded towards the grinning Hollywood star, framed by the small screen in front of her. I reached over, tightened Jean's seat belt and kissed her gently on the forehead.

'Excuse me, sir. Something to drink before dinner?' asked a female voice.

I looked up into the Thai air hostess's narrow eyes. They glistened black in the dim light and seemed completely unrelated to her cherry-red smile. 'No,' I replied. 'I'm fine, thanks.'

The stewardess bowed from the waist and continued along the aisle. *The Thais are strange folk*, I thought, watching the woman's attractive figure sashay into the kitchen, narrow hips swaying under a tight skirt. *You never really know what's going on behind their friendly mask.*

I picked up a news magazine, flicked through its glossy pages and, when I came across a photograph of George W. Bush, stared at it with grim fascination. The Chief Disaster Orchestrator of the United States was grinning at the camera like a chimpanzee, his left arm draped over a Vietnam veteran's stooped shoulders. The man looked old and senile. His wire-rimmed spectacles were tilted at a precarious angle. Upon his head was a baseball cap, emblazoned with the words GOD BLESS AMERICA.

I turned the page and began to read an in-depth article about the war in Iraq. It made me feel sick to the stomach. As you are, so is the world and I wasn't feeling very well.

The multiple courses of strong antibiotics I'd been taking for the past six weeks had worked well, as far as wiping out bacteria went, but the powerful medicines had exacted a price. I was run down and had an unpleasant chemical taste in my mouth. I also missed the daily morphine injections that had suddenly stopped a week ago. Doctor Davuth, the elderly Cambodian orthopaedist who'd removed the large piece of shrapnel from my right shoulder and nineteen metal fragments out of my back and legs, had warned me I might feel a little anxious and shaky when the morphine drip was finally removed from the back of my bruised left hand. A little anxious and shaky were major understatements. Hunger gnawed at my stomach, yet just the thought of food made me nauseous. My hands were shaking and I found it impossible to focus my attention on anything for more than a few minutes. I missed the warm rush of morphine as it streamed into my bloodstream and the attentive staff at Sihanoukville's General Hospital, who'd helped nurse Jean and me back to relatively good health.

As far as hospitals go, the place had been hopelessly under-equipped. What it lacked in medical facilities was more than made up for by the selfless dedication of the people who worked there. I had given a generous donation to the infirmary the day before we'd left, knowing it was only a drop in the ocean compared to what they needed.

Jean's recovery had been remarkable. No doubt because her athletic body was so strong, coupled with her indomitable willpower. Everyone in the hospital had fallen in love with her. Doctor Davuth's last words came back to me. *You've no idea how very fortunate you are to have a wonderful woman like that by your side.* I studied my wife's sleeping face and was overcome by emotion. *It's a miracle,* I thought. *We're still alive.*

The plane banked. Turning once more to the oval porthole, I shielded my eyes with my hands and looked down into the darkness. Clusters of tiny lights sparkled far below. Wondering where exactly our plane was, I switched on the mini television screen set into the back of the seat in front of me. I used the remote to skip through the various entertainment channels. When it came to a satellite map with a red line delineating the aircraft's course, I leaned forward and read the names of the cities it was flying over. Jaipur, Ajmer, Udaipur, Pushkar... *Pushkar!* Although only three months had passed it already seemed like a lifetime ago since the morning I'd sat with Angus, my twin brother, in Sri Lanka and, throughout a prolonged breakfast, listened to him narrate a personal story, about what happened to him in 1975, when he visited the small town of Pushkar in Eastern Rajasthan. I stared blankly at the small television screen. The background hum created by the Airbus A320's twin Rolls Royce engines changed pitch. Jean opened her eyes. I could feel her gaze resting on my haggard face. I was acutely aware of my physical appearance. My skin was the colour of mouldy goat's cheese. My jaw hung slack. Dark shadows circled my eyes.

A sigh escaped from Jean's lips and she said to me, 'You look so sad. Is something troubling you?'

'What? Oh, you're awake, are you?' I asked absently, looking away from the screen to face her. 'Troubling me? Aye, well, you could say that. We nearly got killed by a bomb. I've just spent five weeks in hospital with a bloody morphine drip keeping me comfortably numb on Cloud Nine. I miss my fags since I stopped smoking because you threatened to leave me if I didn't. A tsunami washed away my twin brother and his wife.' I nodded, my chin jutting aggressively. 'Aye, Jean, you could say something's troubling me.'

'Oh, for Christ's sake, Hamish, lighten up will you?'

'Lighten up,' I echoed. 'Lighten up? What the bloody hell do you mean, *lighten up?*'

'Well...for a start, you can lower your voice and stop swearing,' she whispered. 'You never stooped to using coarse language in public before you began hanging around with your crazy brother.'

'Don't speak about Angus like that.'

'Listen, Hamish, there's something I'd like to get into that thick skull of yours.'

'What?'

'I thought Angus was a great guy and Lara was my pal. I miss the pair of them to the extent that I feel like something's been ripped out of me and it hurts like hell – right here.' She patted her left breast to lend emphasis to her point. 'What you have to let into your stubborn mind is the fact that they're gone and they won't be coming back. That's how death is — final.'

'You don't know for sure that they're dead. Jeeps told me—'

'Jeeps!' Jean exclaimed, her voice rising. 'How can you take anything that little nutter said seriously?'

'Angus thought he was enlightened.'

'Aye, right, just like the Dalai Lama. You're starting to sound as wacky as your brother. I liked the Wee Man, but he's as mad as a hatter. Do you know what he said to me just before we left Sri Lanka?'

'No. What did he say?'

'I asked him for his email address and he says, 'What's an email address?'' She shook her head. 'If that's not out of touch with reality, what is?'

'Jean, even taking into account that the man lives in a cave, I suspect he was probably pulling your leg. Anyway, he wasn't the only one who believed Angus and Lara are still alive. That old age pensioner also thought they'd somehow manage to survive the tsunami.'

'Maybe so. But, if you ask me, anyone who wants to leave England to retire in a third world country with Tamil Tigers prowling about in the jungle has lost the right to be taken seriously. You're going to have to learn to accept the fact that Angus and Lara were swept away by a tidal wave and that's it.' Jean glanced at the map on the small screen. 'What's so interesting about Rajasthan? You were staring at that wee telly like it was a crystal ball.'

'I was thinking about how Pushkar was the place where Angus's life took a major turn in a new direction.'

'When was this?'

'Back in Nineteen Seventy-Five.'

'For someone who claimed to live in the here and now, your brother talked a lot about the past. So, what happened?'

'Did Angus ever tell you the story about how he met his first real guru?'

'Guru? Oh-oh, here we go. You mean one of those softly spoken Indian con men with a long beard, hypnotic eyes, wandering hands and a fat Swiss bank account?'

'Not exactly. Don't be so cynical.'

'What you mistake for cynicism is the fact that my critical faculties are still functioning properly. Besides, you know perfectly well what a big deal your brother made out of his private breakfast talks with you in Sri Lanka.'

'Was that a problem for you?'

'No, I was all right with that,' answered Jean, but the tone of her voice revealed that it hadn't been all right with her, not at all.

'Did Lara never tell you anything about Angus's past?'

'A wee bit, not much, just enough to let me know he'd made a lot of money selling drugs and that he was a scheming opportunist who thought life was an illusion. Whatever that's supposed to mean.'

'There was a lot more to my brother's life than that.'

'As I said, Lara didn't go in to elaborate descriptions about the past. That's something most men aren't aware of. Women are more grounded in the present. It's a body thing. If you'd ever given birth to a baby, you'd know what I mean.'

'Aye, right, just like you'll never understand what it means to run a building company with fifty employees, who always think they are not getting paid enough, no matter how big a bonus they receive.'

'Well, my working-class hero, let's not argue about it.'

'Why? Is it too close to home for you?'

'How come you're so aggressive?'

'I'm not being bloody well aggressive. I'm just being honest and direct, that's all.'

'Oh, I see. *Honest and direct,* is it? You grumpy old shit that you are. Well, you listen to me. If you think bringing up our three daughters wasn't hard work, you've got your thick head stuck right up your hairy arse.'

'You bitch, don't you dare speak to me like that. I saved your life when that mine exploded.'

'Yeah, sure, Lord Hamish, your medal for valour is in the post. *Idiot!* You wouldn't have had to save anyone's life if you hadn't parked your arse on a bomb in the first place.'

'You ungrateful bit—'

'Excuse me, sir. Is there a problem?'

'No,' I said, looking up into the air hostess's narrow eyes for the second time in twenty minutes, 'we're just having a... a wee discussion, like.'

'I'm sorry, sir. I have to request that you tone your discussion down a little. Some passengers have complained about the noise.'

I sat up in my seat and glanced around the dimly illuminated deck. Half a dozen people glared back at me from the shadows. I took a deep breath and let out an exasperated sigh. 'I didn't realise we were disturbing anyone. We'll speak more quietly. Sorry about that.'

'Thank you, sir. Is there anything I can fetch you and Madame?' The hostess peeped over at Jean but looked away quickly in case the searing heat streaming out of Madame's furious eyes blistered her centimetre-thick layer of makeup. 'A drink to cool down, perhaps?'

'No thanks,' I said, raising a glass tumbler of Perrier water to my cracked lips. 'Really, we're fine.'

'As you wish, sir. I'm at your service. Dinner will be served in an hour.'

The hostess strode off. I tasted bile in my mouth. Jean hissed a whisper in my left ear. 'Dinner will be served in an hour, *sir.* You're no sir. You're a foul-mouthed lout. That's what you are.'

I felt jets of compressed steam whistling out of my ears. I tried to focus by fixing my tired eyes on the small screen in front of me. We were now in Pakistani air space.

Ten guilt-ridden minutes passed. I turned to my wife and said, 'I'm really sorry, Jean.' I placed a reassuring hand on her knee. Her nose crinkled. She shoved my hand away as if it were a piece of rotten fish and picked up a copy of *Hello!* Magazine, obviously content to let me stew in my caustic juices for a while longer.

I put on a pair of headphones. *Bu...bu...bu...babe, you ain't seen nothing yet...* Bachman-Turner-Overdrive stuttered against my eardrums. The Red Hot Chilli Peppers were next, singing 'Give It Away'. When the recorded backwards guitar solo kicked in, I unplugged the headphones. My head ached from the pressure of too many thoughts. Listening to rock music didn't help. I turned once again to Jean and, with a mouth stuffed with humble pie, said, 'Listen, I'm very sorry. I'll admit it. I lost my rag.'

She raised her magazine to hide her face.

'C'mon, Jean, don't be like that.' My voice began to crack. 'We... We've both been through hell during the last weeks. Please forgive me.'

Jean lowered her magazine. She was grinning like a lottery jackpot winner. 'Okay,' she said, 'I'll forgive you if you tell me that story.'

'What story?'

'Are you getting Alzheimer's or something? The story about what happened to your brother in Pushkar. Remember?'

'Aye, right. Now I'm with you.'

Jean raised her dark eyebrows.

'Aye, well, mind,' I said, 'it's a long story.'

'So is life, and I was enjoying that until you spoiled it for me.'

'Don't rub it in. Are you sitting comfortably?' Jean screwed up her face. I gulped back a mouthful of aerated water, burped and continued. 'Then I'll begin.'

'For God's sake,' complained Jean, 'this is getting boring. Will you just get on with it?'

'But,' I protested, 'every good tale has to have a wee preamble.'

Jean picked up her magazine.

'Okay, okay. Angus had been eight miles high all—'

She asked, 'What does eight miles high mean?'

'I'll start again,' I said, shaking my head in annoyance. 'But this time don't interrupt. Angus had just come down from a very strong LSD trip. He'd finally managed to fall asleep in his hotel room in Pushkar when something banged against the door.'

'I knew he'd taken too many drugs when he was young.'

'I said don't interrupt.'

'Sorry, darling.'

'Okay, here we go.'

2

SHOT DOWN IN FLAMES

The Lake View Hotel, Pushkar, Eastern Rajasthan, 4:00 a.m., May, 1975.

'What the fuck's going on now?' Angus grumbled, just as he was about to cross the threshold of sleep. He sat up. His gaze focused on a bright strip of light below his hotel room's door.

He fumbled around in the dark, searching for his Zippo lighter. A key turned in a lock and the room's door handle squeaked as somebody tried it. Angus called out, 'Hold on. I'm coming.' He found his lighter and lit the short stub of a candle. Dim yellow light suffused the room. He stood up and then bent down to pick his crumpled trousers up off the damp tiled floor. Tying the drawstring on his cotton trousers, he staggered over to the door, unbolted it and pulled it open. He found himself eye to eye with a six-foot-tall woman. Her black hair was cut short. Shaped like a parrot's beak, her hooked nose stopped her face from being beautiful. Her dark eyes seemed too large for her narrow head. She was as thin as coat hanger wire and dressed in skin-tight, pink leather trousers and matching jerkin. Mantis Woman's left hand clutched a red crash helmet. In her right was a key.

She tweaked her nose, looked Angus up and down and said in American-accented English, 'Oh, I'm sorry, did I wake you up?'

He replied, 'Oh, no, not at all, I was just in the middle of feeding my pet rhinoceros.'

She stood on her tiptoes and peered over his shoulder into the dimly lit room. 'You're joking, right?'

'And you're an American who used a crash helmet to bang on my hotel room door in the middle of the night, right?'

'Oh, I'm sorry, did I wake you up?'

Angus looked right and left. He made a puzzled expression. 'Unless I'm mistaken, there's a thirty-second delayed echo in this corridor.'

The woman let out a deep-throated burst of laughter and said, 'Hey, you're funny. I like you.'

Angus tossed his long, dark-brown hair away from his face, gave a wan smile and said nothing. They locked eyes in a spontaneous test of wills. She broke the silence by saying, 'You're Scottish, aren't you?'

He glanced down at her feet. She had on a pair of scuffed snakeskin boots. He answered with a question. 'How did you guess?'

'What's your name?'

'Angus. And yours?'

'Kali.'

'That's an easy one to remember.'

'And a hard one to forget,' she said, stepping forward to stand so close he could feel the heat radiating from her body. 'Listen, Angus, I was just thinking...' She trailed off.

Trouble, he thought. *Do not get involved with her.* 'Thinking what?'

'Never mind,' she murmured. 'It doesn't matter,' she said, examining the keyring in her hand. 'Is this room ten?'

Angus made a show of looking at the black plastic number eight screwed on to his room's white-painted door and then answered, 'No, this is number eight, the presidential suite.' He nodded towards the door on the opposite side of the corridor. 'That's number ten Upping Street over there.'

'Oh,' she said, 'that means we're going to be neighbours.'

'Yes,' Angus agreed, 'I suppose you could say that. We can have a chat over the garden fence when we're hanging out the laundry.'

Kali turned away from him, raising the red crash helmet in her hand, signalling their conversation was approaching a stoplight at a crossroads. 'I think it's time for some shut-eye. Maybe see you later,' she said, crossing the hall.

'Perhaps.' He shrugged. 'Goodnight.'

Angus went into his room, closed the door and bolted it. 'What the fuck was that all about?', he muttered to himself, sitting down on the edge of his creaking bed. As though responding to his question, the candle by his bedside sputtered and extinguished itself.

He lay down and stared up into the darkness, thinking about Kali, wondering as he drifted towards nothingness if, when he awoke in the morning, he would find that she was just a figment of a strange dream. Sleep came as a brass temple bell rang out, heralding the dawn.

Angus was sitting under a tattered sun umbrella in a rooftop restaurant. While waiting to order a late breakfast, he looked out over the Pushkar Lake in search of inspiration to lift his spirits. He was feeling edgy.

The previous afternoon, during a powerful acid trip, he'd decided to pursue a more healthy and spiritual lifestyle. As a direct consequence, he'd left his hashish, tobacco, rolling papers and pipe in a small cave out in the desert. He was missing them now but was determined to stay clean.

A gang of residual LSD molecules was banging around in his brain's synaptic channels and playing mischievous tricks with his neurotransmitters. Reminiscent of comics he'd read as a kid, two word balloons appeared in his head. The one on the right belonged to an angel with a golden halo. She whispered, 'Be good, my son, stay away from dangerous drugs and wicked tobacco.'

The word balloon on the opposite side of Angus's head was attached to a little red devil with black horns and a lashing pointed tail. He jabbed his trident at the angel and shouted, 'Don't listen to that uptight bitch or you'll end up in heaven with all the rest of the boring spiritual people.' The little devil puffed on a cigar. 'Hit the street, score some dope, get wasted and have a good time.'

The angel's wings gave a startled flap. She cried out, 'Get thee behind me, Satan. Don't let temptation get the better of you, Angus, because if it does that evil little beast will steer you onto the highway to Hell.'

The red devil yelled back, 'You stupid Vestal Virgin, go and get fucked!'

'Can I be bringing you something, sir,' enquired a male Indian voice.

'Huh! Oh, yeah,' said Angus, looking up in surprise at a waiter, dressed in a moth-eaten yellow robe. 'I'll… I'll have a pot of coffee and a slice of banana cake.'

'Black or white, sir?'

'What? Black or white banana cake?'

'No, sir, will you be liking to be having black or white coffee, is what I am most humbly asking, sir.'

'Oh, right. Black, please. By the way, Rama, I've been coming here every day for over a month now, so you can call me Angus, not *sir*.'

'No problem, Angus, sir, I'm going to be fetching coffee and cake right away,' said the waiter over his shoulder as he shuffled off towards the kitchen.

India, thought Angus. *I love it.*

Angus looked down at his clasped hands and his memory did a fast re-wind of some visions he'd had during the previous day's psychedelic trip, in particular the ones concerning his dead girlfriend, Jenny, and his closest friends, Raj and Murphy. His thoughts became anxious.

'Hi, mind if I join you?' Kali asked as she approached Angus's table.

'Oh, hi. How's it going?' Angus said, shifting position on his hard chair. 'Grab a seat. I can do with a bit of company.'

She placed her crash helmet beside a potted palm and pulled up a plastic chair. 'What's happening? You look kind of worried. Care to share your thoughts with me?' she said, leaning over to give him a peck on his hairy cheek.'

Like a man lost in a desert, mistaking a mirage for an oasis, Angus imagined that he saw tenderness in Kali's dark eyes. He threw caution to the wind and narrated how he'd cremated Jenny, on a funeral pyre inside a rented house in Nepal, after she'd died from a drug overdose.

'Far out,' said Kali, who despite the heat looked cool. 'That's what I call going out in a blaze of glory. What an amazing send-off to give someone you loved.'

'I'm glad you think so. I thought the same thing, but now realise it wasn't such a smart move.'

'How come?'

'Well, a couple of months back, in Goa, I ran into an old friend of mine

4

called Acid Mike. He told—'

'Interesting name,' commented Kali.

'Yeah, well anyway, Mike tells me that the police are looking for me because I'm their number one suspect in a drug-related murder.'

'You mean the cops think you killed your girlfriend?'

'Exactly. And now I have to wait it out in India until Mike returns to Goa in December with a false passport for me.'

'Holy guacamole, that sounds like deep shit.'

'You can say that again.'

'Okay. Holy guacamole, that sounds like—'

'Hey, come on, Kali, this isn't funny.'

'Seriousness is a disease,' she said with a knowing smile. 'I've contracted it many times and I never want to catch it again. Seriousness can be deadly.'

Angus flashed on how his friend, Murphy, had murdered a gangster in Glasgow who'd ripped them off for half a million pounds. He nodded in agreement and said, 'Maybe you're right.'

'Hey, Baba,' Kali shouted towards the waiter, 'any chance of some service over here.'

Rama shambled over and delivered Angus's cake, a cracked mug that might have been white a century ago, and an aluminium pot of black coffee. He looked at Kali as if she were a demon from a Hindu hell world. 'Yes, Memsahib,' he said, 'what is it that you are wanting?'

'I am wanting scrambled eggs on toast with a big pot of Nescafé,' she replied, employing an exaggerated Indian accent. 'If it is not causing you too much bother, that is.'

'No bother at all, Memsahib. Nescafé all finished.'

'No problem, local coffee will do.'

'We are having local coffee.'

'Very good, Baba, could you be bringing me a pot full of it?'

'Yes, yes, I can be bringing.'

'Today?'

'Yes, Madame, today.'

'Off you go then. *Jehldi, jehldi.*'

'Thank you, Memsahib.' The waiter performed a half-hearted bow and then ambled off.

Kali turned to face Angus. 'So, you're a wanted man?'

'Yes, but there's more. My two closest friends were busted with half-a-ton of Nepalese hashish when driving Rolling Thunder, our customised Mercedes bus, into Iran.'

'Tough shit,' said Kali, helping herself to a mouthful of Angus's banana cake. She mumbled, 'What did they get for that?'

'Twenty years.'

'Holy cow, that's a lifetime.'

'Yeah,' agreed Angus, scratching his chin through his thick beard, 'that's why I'm going to go to Iran to help them escape.'

'That should keep you out of trouble for a while,' said Kali, helping herself to Angus's coffee. 'So, how do you propose to go about busting your amigos out of the can?'

'That's the part I haven't figured out yet.'

'I'd sure be interested to hear how that story pans—'

Just then, a loud commotion rose from the street. Angus and Kali rushed to a rusty railing and leaned over to investigate. They looked down and saw an emaciated brown cow munching on a bunch of bananas it had filched from a street stall. A turbaned man was screaming at the bovine marauder and whacking its skinny hindquarters with a bamboo cane. Passers-by were shouting at the irate fruit vendor for striking the sacred animal. Angus noticed a gleaming, bright-red motorbike parked directly below him. He turned to look at Kali's helmet on the floor. It was the same colour as the motorbike. 'Hey, man!' he exclaimed, glancing first at the bike and then at Kali. 'Is that yours?'

'That's my baby,' said Kali, chuckling. 'Want to go down and check her out?'

'What about your breakfast?'

'I'm no longer hungry,' replied Kali, returning to the table to grab what remained of Angus's banana cake. 'Let's go.'

Angus settled the bill. Kali stood beside him, swinging her crash helmet like a bowling ball. They went downstairs and walked over to the bike. She patted a polished stainless-steel chimpanzee head bolted between the handlebars. She looked into Angus's eyes and said, 'Let me introduce you to The Monkey.'

Angus fired off everything he knew about Indian motorbikes in one simple question. 'It's a Royal Enfield, right?'

She turned to him and said, 'Well, yes and no. The Monkey was a brand-new three-fifty Enfield when I bought it in Bombay six months ago. Since then I've bored out the cylinder to zero point forty,' her long-fingered hands drilled holes in the air in front of her, 'fitted a new piston and high-performance camshaft, to boost torque response, and added—'

'Hold on,' said Angus, 'what do you mean, *you* bored out the cylinder and fitted a new piston?'

'Didn't I tell you I own a motorcycle repair shop that specializes in Harleys, in Santa Fe, New Mexico?'

'No, you didn't tell me that,' replied Angus, glancing down at her long fingers. Kali's hands did not resemble those of a mechanic. 'How could you forget that you hadn't mentioned that? We've only spent about ten minutes in each other's company.'

'Well, I'm mentioning it now. I've loved motorbikes since the day my dear old pop took me for a ride on the back of his Harley Davidson along the Oklahoma Panhandle. Anyway, what are your plans for today?'

Angus shrugged, suspecting Kali was making up her story as she went along. 'I don't have any plans for today. What about you?'

Kali glanced at the crowd of inquisitive onlookers, who'd gathered round to stare at them. 'I don't know about you, but I for one have had about enough of this here one-cow town. I figured on maybe hitting the trail and hightailing it back to Pune.'

'Pune!' exclaimed Angus. 'Don't tell me you're one of Rajneesh's sannyasins.'

Kali pulled a string of black wooden beads, with a dangling plastic locket, containing the bearded guru's picture, out from beneath her leather jerkin and said, 'Of course I'm a sannyasin. Where the hell do you think I got the name, Kali? Mom and pop back in Ponca City?'

'You'll be telling me next that if you hold the locket you'll be in direct contact with your spiritual master.'

'Angus, if you believe that bullshit, you'll believe anything.' She patted the centre of her bony chest. 'Bhagwan lives here in my heart and he's with me all the time. He's a spiritual anarchist. If you're a true rebel you'll come with me to Pune, take the jump and become a sannyasin.'

'I don't think Bhagwan Shree Rajneesh is my cup of tea.'

'Your cup of tea,' she sneered, 'how very British. You're full of shit. How the fuck do you know that if you've never met him?'

'People call him the Sex Guru and say he's only in it for the money.'

'Do you believe everything people tell you?'

'No. Only the stories about two-headed aliens stealing old ladies' Zimmer frames.'

'Man, where do you get those lines?'

'My parents thought I had an overactive imagination.'

'They were right.'

'Maybe.'

'Anyway—'

'Anyway, nothing, I don't feel drawn to this Rajneesh guy. He sounds like a phoney to me.'

'Bull-fucking-shit!' Kali spat on the concrete pavement. 'You don't know what you're talking about. Get out of your narrow Scottish mind and listen to your heart. I'm offering you an opportunity to come and meet the man for yourself. Do you want to come to Pune with me? Yes or no? I won't ask you again.'

Angus looked around at the crowd of spectators, who were following his and Kali's every move with distrustful curiosity. They were becoming more excited and pressing in closer as the two foreigners' discussion heated up. Their rapt faces were concentrated on them the way a magnifying glass concentrates sunlight. Angus looked at Kali's narrow face and was surprised to see it wasn't blistering from the heat.

'Well?' Kali asked, punching him lightly on the shoulder.

'Ooooogh!' A collective gasp of astonishment rose from the gawkers' slack mouths at the sight of the tall, skinny, white women in a pink leather outfit striking the long-haired hippy in the street.

Angus glanced up into the clear blue sky and saw the vapour trail from a jet aeroplane's engines as it cut through the earth's troposphere heading west.

I tapped the flat television screen in front of me. 'And that's how it happened, down there somewhere, that Angus came to make a decision that would change the course of his life forever.'

'Don't tell me he joined a religious cult,' said Jean. 'I remember watching a documentary about the Bhagwan on the telly. If I recall rightly, he changed his name to Osho and had to sell his ninety-nine Rolls Royces, when he got kicked out of America. Didn't some of his lot get thrown in prison for poisoning people in Oregon?'

'Yes,' I answered, 'Osho's sannyasins carried out the only successful biological attack perpetrated on American soil in the history of the United States. That was in the eighties, so we're getting a bit ahead in the story.' I picked up my bottle of Perrier water and, seeing it was empty, turned to Jean and asked, 'Fancy a wee drink of something stronger?'

'Aye,' she replied, 'but I don't fancy the hangover that comes with it. You know alcohol doesn't agree with my constitution.'

'Come on,' I coaxed. 'You only live once.'

'Not according to Angus,' quipped Jean.

'So, what'll it be then?'

'A double gin and tonic with ice,' she replied. 'Remember, though, if I have a sore head when we arrive in Heathrow I'll murder you.'

Five minutes later, Jean and I clinked our glasses together and wished each other good health. She sipped on her long drink, while I knocked back my double whisky in one gulp, gasping as the alcohol burnt a fiery liquid trail from my gullet to my guts. 'Agh,' I sighed, 'ye cannae whack it.'

'Take it easy. You're still on painkillers.'

'I don't give a flying fuck.'

'For Christ's sake, watch your bloody language.'

'Right then, back to Angus's story. You're going to love this part because this is when things really get going.'

Jean swirled the ice cubes around in her glass. 'I'm sure that Kali women is going to turn out to be bad news. So, let's hear it.'

'Fuck it,' said Angus, looking away from the vapour trail in the sky into Kali's dark eyes, 'I'll come with you.'

'Cool, let's get the hell outta here, I'm feeling claustrophobic.' Kali raised her voice. 'Excuse me, folks,' she said, pushing her way through the five-people-thick crowd.

Angus returned to his hotel room and packed what few possessions he had into a black canvas rucksack. *What have I gotten myself into now?* he wondered, retrieving a tightly sealed plastic bag, containing 25,000 American dollars in hundred-dollar bills, from inside the toilet's rust-stained water cistern.

Down on the street, Kali was sitting astride her motorbike, strumming her fingers on the bee sting-shaped petrol tank. Angus walked up to her. 'You want to wear this,' she asked, holding up her red crash helmet.'

Angus shook his head. 'No thanks. It'll be too hot.'

'I agree,' said Kali, tossing the helmet into an open sewer. 'It's time to rock-and-roll. Hop on.'

Man, she's crazy, Angus thought, turning to see the red helmet sink into a stagnant pool of green gunk. He was destined to think a lot about that helmet during the next three days.

The heat from the Enfield's black vinyl saddle roasted his buttocks in under five seconds. 'Put your arms around my waist and hold on tight,' Kali instructed, turning the ignition key. He did as he was told and could feel the curve of her ribcage. She kicked down on the starter pedal. The engine coughed, spluttered, exhaled a puff of grey smoke and died. She pushed down on the starter pedal again, twisted the throttle and The Monkey roared like a gorilla.

Kali manoeuvred her motorbike between what little traffic there was on Pushkar's dusty streets. Soon they reached the open road. She gave the thirsty carburettor a big drink of gas. The Royal Enfield shot off like a surface-to-surface missile, throwing Angus's head back. His cervical vertebrae crunched together and his mouth twisted into a whiplash smile.

It took ten seconds to reach seventy miles per hour. Kali dropped into third gear as she approached a long gradual bend in the road. The motorbike wobbled. She throttled back, slowed to fifty and shouted over her shoulder, 'Hey, Angus, move in closer to my body and just be a sack of potatoes or we'll come off.'

She twisted the throttle. The engine howled, and they thundered off along the desert highway. Two minutes and three miles later, Kali steered onto the centre of the road and shot between two lumbering Ashok Leyland trucks, moving in opposite directions. *Jesus fucking Christ!* Angus's mind screamed. *This crazy bitch is going to get us killed.*

Eastern Rajasthan flew by in a dun-coloured blur. The Enfield wound its way up a two-lane asphalt ribbon, threading its way between forested hills. Kali was leaning so low when entering the road's curves, Angus was beginning to worry about how life would be minus a kneecap. They slowed up when they entered a town called Mount Abu. Kali stopped in front of the Arbuda Restaurant, a white-painted building with a large, open-air terrace. Angus stood on the pavement. His legs were shaking.

'I'm starving,' said Kali, pushing the motorbike up on its stand. 'How about you?'

Angus's belly rumbled out a hungry response. 'Yeah,' he replied, 'I could do with something to eat.'

Kali glanced at him. 'You're looking a bit shaky on your feet. Are you alright?'

'Apart from feeling like I was going to shit myself for the last few hours, I'm fine.'

Kali chuckled, took his arm and said, 'Come on sweetheart, it's chow time.'

They sat at a circular table on a terrace, ordered masala dosas and watched the sunset's colours reflected on a small lake, where Indian tourists were working up a sweat in swan-shaped pedal boats. The food was delicious. They ordered two more dosas with extra coconut chutney.

Dinner over, they sat drinking ice-cold London Pilsner beer. Kali produced a small, conical, pink packet containing Ganesh beedies and offered one to Angus. 'I told you, I stopped smoking tobacco and dope.' He raised his hands palm up in front of her. 'Don't tempt me.'

She struck a match, lit her cheap cigarette, blew a cloud of blue smoke in his direction and said, 'Please yourself.' The beedie smelled like a gardener's fire.

Kali informed Angus that Mount Abu was where her guru, Bhagwan Shree Rajneesh, had first taught his cathartic meditation techniques.

'I did the kundalini meditation twice when I was in Goa,' said Angus.

'And?'

'It was okay.' He thought for a moment and then added, 'I liked the dancing part. That was fun.'

'Is that all?'

'As far as I can recall, yes, that was about the extent of it.'

Kali stood up. 'Let's go.'

'Where to?'

'Well, honey, I don't know about you, but I sure as hell don't plan on sleeping under the stars tonight.'

They checked into a spacious double room in the Lake Palace Hotel. Angus went out onto a small veranda and sat in a deckchair, while Kali used the shower. When she returned to the room, she seemed unselfconscious about her nakedness. *I hope to fuck she isn't going to try to get me into bed,* thought Angus, as he studied her body from behind a sliding glass door. She had pancakes for breasts, pimples for nipples, and steel buns that looked like tan-coloured cannonballs. *Nice ass,* he noted.

'Hey, man,' she called, looking directly at him, 'what are you staring at? You some kinda Peeping Tom pervert, or what?'

Angus headed for the bathroom, saying, 'Put some fucking clothes on if you don't want me to look. I'm a man, remember?'

When Angus returned to the room, Kali was sitting cross-legged at the end of her bed, staring at a candle in a saucer. It was the only source of illumination in the room, and she was naked except for the wooden beads and locket strung around her slender neck. The light bathed her sharp-featured face, arms and flat chest in a soft yellow glow.

'What's up?' Angus asked. 'Saying your prayers to Bhagwan?'

'No, I'm not, smart ass,' she replied. 'I'm getting ready to practise a meditation technique with you.'

Oh, oh, here we go, he thought.

'Keep your clothes off and come and sit here with me,' she said, pointing to the opposite side of the bed.

Angus did as she instructed and asked, 'Now what?'

'Sit up straight and use your left eye to look into my left eye,' Kali replied, adding, 'and try not to blink.'

Angus sniffed the air. 'Hey!' he exclaimed. 'Did you smoke one of those stinking beedies in here when I was in the shower?'

'Shut up and stare into my left eye like I just told you to do.'

He complied.

Five minutes later, his eyes were watering. He kept looking into her left eye. Slowly, her face morphed. Angus watched Kali change from a wraith to a voluptuous goddess. She turned into a wise old Chinaman, a leering drunk, a red Indian squaw, a Buddhist monk, a hatchet-faced harlot, a hare-lipped Harridan, Lady Madonna with a baby at her nonexistent breast and on and on through a multitude of different archetypical personas.

Wow, Angus reflected, *this is a bit like acid.*

'Don't blink,' said Kali.

Tears ran down his cheeks as he strained to keep his eyes open. After a while, the discomfort faded — along with Kali's physical form. The room broke down into lightwave patterns. Out on the street, a dog howled. The thoughts in Angus's mind stopped their incessant chattering. Time stood still and silence filled the room.

Angus rubbed his eyes. The candle had burnt down to a flickering stub. Kali lay curled up like a foetus. She was sound asleep. He placed the candle on a bedside table, blew it out and stretched out on his bed. The events of the day did a fast rewind on the screen of his mind. The last thing he recalled was how the wind had roared in his ears as The Monkey shot along the road, his hands gripping the backrest.

It was still dark when Kali and Angus pulled into a petrol station on the outskirts of Mount Abu. By sunset, they'd reached a small hill resort called Lonavla, a hundred kilometres southeast of Bombay (Mumbai).

It had been a long and gruelling ride with dozens of near misses. Kali had handled her machine like a champion and Angus was suitably impressed, along with his backside, which was suffering from a serious bout of pins and red-hot needles.

As they ascended a flight of steps leading up to a small hotel with pink-painted walls Angus hooked an arm around Kali's slim waist, pulled her close and said, 'I'll say this much for you, you're the best motorcyclist I've ever met.'

'Thanks, sweetheart,' she chuckled, 'I was born to ride.'

Angus looked into her flinty eyes. There was something hard and distant at play in them that made him feel attracted to her, not like a bee to honey, more like a geologist to a curiously formed rock face.

That evening, Angus and Kali made love for the first and last time. It was a strangely mechanical coupling, totally lacking in emotion, and therefore Angus only controlled the ejaculatory urge to a point that was just a little way past what seemed respectful.

'Well,' said Kali, lying at Angus's side in the darkness, smoking a beedi, 'I'm glad we got that out of the way.'

'What do you mean?' he asked.

'Sex has never been a big deal in my life,' she replied. 'To be honest, I don't enjoy it.'

'How come?'

'I can't say for sure. A small part of me wishes that I enjoyed it, but a bigger part of me is content to stay the way I am because it makes me more independent. What I don't like about sex is that it makes me feel like an animal.'

'I think there is an animal in all of us.'

'Speak for yourself, tiger.' Kali reached over Angus to stub her beedie out in a bedside ashtray. 'I'm not an animal. I'm a free spirit trapped in an animal's body.'

'Well, I enjoyed shaving the pubic hair off of your animal's body.'

Kali giggled in the darkness. 'I thought you might.'

After a late breakfast, Angus and Kali made a brief detour to visit the nearby Karla and Bhaja caves. Nestled in lush, jungle-clad hills, the rock temples had been carved out two thousand years before by Buddhist monks and artisans. The Karla cave's main roof was ribbed by curved wooden beams. The place retained a little of its ancient glories in the form of large stone elephants, lacking tusks, and broken pillars, most of which had toppled over. Off to one side were smaller caves. Angus and Kali tried chanting and experimenting with the various resonating sound waves each stone cubicle produced.

Kali hummed like a dynamo for some time, fell silent for a few minutes and then commented, 'I think the monks must've made these caves so that they could activate their chakras.'

'You think so?' Angus asked.

'Of course, I do, you dummy. Why else would someone go to the bother of gouging a cave out of hard rock? You think the Buddhist monks were running souvenir shops here at the time of Christ, or what?'

'Who knows? Maybe they did.'

'Are all Scottish people as cynical as you?'

'Well, put it like this, they're not as gullible as Americans.'

'Fuck you, Angus!'

'You did last night.'

Kali gave him a hard punch on the shoulder. 'Yeah, I did, and I'm already wondering if it was a mistake.'

'A mistake?' Angus echoed, turning to face her. 'What's that supposed to mean?'

She glared into his eyes and said nothing.

Kali took it easy on the last seventy-kilometre stretch of road that brought them to Pune's outskirts. When they were stopped at a customs checkpoint, Angus said a silent prayer to Goddess Laxmi, requesting that she have a quick word with her divine counterpart, Lord Narayan, who runs the universe's financial resources department. Angus's plea seemed to work because, after spitting a jet of blood-red betel juice over the dust-covered Enfield's front wheel, a khaki-clad police sergeant smiled to display his stained teeth and they were allowed to proceed, without Angus's dollar stash being discovered.

'Fucking asshole,' muttered Kali from the corner of her mouth, as she kick-started her trusty steed into life. They headed for the east of the city.

Angus and Kali drove into a garden compound with a sign over the gate declaring that this was the Sundar Lodge. Angus waited outside, while Kali entered a white bungalow to talk to the management. He looked around. There were washing lines with many items of orange-coloured laundry dancing in the breeze, building up as the sun dropped towards the urban horizon.

'We're in luck,' said Kali, approaching him with a pair of tarnished brass keys in her hand.

They wandered by a line of adjoining whitewashed brick shacks with corrugated tin roofs until they reached one with a green wooden door. The number thirteen was written on it with runny, red, gloss paint.

'Home sweet home,' said Kali, standing aside, after she'd unlocked a brass padlock to wave Angus in with a flourishing gesture of her right hand.

Angus stepped inside and looked around. 'This is a bit of a dump, isn't it?'

'Pickers can't be choosers in Pune,' replied Kali. 'Accommodation is scarce so close to the ashram, so don't start to complain. 'That's your bed there,' she said, pointing to a soiled single mattress on the floor.

He threw his rucksack on the stained mattress. A couple of cockroaches scuttled for cover. 'The place doesn't even have a window. It's hotter in here than it is outside.' He looked up at the rusty roof. It was full of holes. 'If it rains we'll get wet.'

'Listen, you grumpy Scotsman, if you don't stop complaining you can fuck off on your own and try to find another place.'

Angus raised his hands, palms up. 'Okay, okay, calm down, Kali. I get the fuckin' message.'

There was a small open shower stall. Angus stripped off his dusty clothes. He used a plastic pot to pour lukewarm water over his head from a conveniently placed aluminium dustbin.

Angus sat on his bed and sorted through his rucksack's contents. He opened the plastic bag containing his money and peeled off a couple of hundred-dollar bills. Kali glimpsed the large bundle of notes in his hands and whistled. 'Did you knock over a bank or something? That's a helluva lot of cash.' She glanced around the small room. 'You better stash it somewhere good.'

'Why?' A profound sense of unease filled Angus's guts. 'The door will be locked when we're out, won't it?'

'Listen, man, the locals around here are making a fortune ripping-off Westerners.' She pointed to the dustbin. 'Stash your money under the water container.'

Angus did as she said, but not before peeling off another handful of bills and putting them in a zippered, leather wallet that hung from his neck. *Not good to put all of your golden eggs in one basket,* he reasoned, squeezing the plastic bag containing the rest of his money under the heavy aluminium dustbin. The tension in his guts left as quickly as it had arrived. He turned, crouching, and looked up at Kali, standing with her hands on her narrow hips. 'You know where I can change money?' he asked.

She shrugged on her crumpled, pink leather jacket and answered, 'Sure. No problem. We can do that after we go for some chow. You ready to hit the street?'

Angus nodded. 'Yeah, let's go. Don't forget to lock the door.'

She looked at him like he was an idiot and handed him a small, brass key. 'Here, this is yours.'

They dined at the Bund Garden Café. Like the Sundar Lodge, it was a one-star establishment. The chapattis and yellow lentil soup were delicious. Kali said little as she puffed on a digestive beedie and sipped on a fresh lime soda. Angus checked out the local clientele. At a neighbouring table, a boisterous and noisy group of Iranian students, from the nearby technical college, were entertaining themselves by slapping each other on the back of the head. Everyone else, except the languid Persian waiters, were sannyasins, dressed in shades of orange. Nobody paid him the slightest bit of attention.

'I was just thinking,' said Kali, interrupting his observations, 'there are a few things I have to take care of tomorrow morning. If you want to go to the ashram, you'll have to make your way there on your own. Bhagwan will be giving a discourse at eight o'clock, which means you'll have to get up early.'

'Oh, yeah, right, Bhagwan's discourse, how could I forget?' said Angus, wafting a cloud of Kali's foul-smelling beedie smoke away from his face with a laminated menu card. 'There's only one little thing you're missing. I don't have a fucking clue where the ashram is.'

Kali stood up from the table. 'Don't worry. You can take an auto-rickshaw. Let's go. It's been a long day and I'm dead beat. We can change your dollars into rupees back at Sundar Lodge. They give a better rate than the banks.'

When Angus walked out onto the Bund Garden Road, the sky was lightening in the east. Birds sang and crows cawed in the banyan trees. He stood by the side of the road, near to a small herd of cows feasting on a pile of organic rubbish. It soon became apparent that he would not find an auto-rickshaw standing where he was, and therefore he began walking towards the sunrise. He arrived at a street corner and asked an old man for directions.

'What country?' asked the man, peering into Angus's eyes through a pair of inch-thick spectacles.

'Ashram, Baba, I want to know how to get to the ashram.'

'What is the purpose of your visit?'

'For fuck's sake,' muttered Angus. 'I want to go to the Rajneesh Ashram.'

'Rajneesh!' exclaimed the Indian. 'Rajneesh very bad man. He is a charlatan.' The old man pointed towards a narrow street. 'Go there,' he said, turning from Angus and walking away.

Angus wandered along the tree-lined street and met a young woman wearing a bright orange robe with a string of black beads around her neck.

'Excuse me,' said Angus, 'I want to go to the Rajneesh Ashram.'

She smiled at him and pointed at a small round badge pinned above her left breast. On it were printed the words IN SILENCE.

'Oh,' said Angus, 'I understand.'

The woman continued to smile, took hold of his hand and led him back in the direction he'd just came from. They crossed the Bund Garden Road, walked along a rutted lane strewn with rubbish, crossed a busy road, where truck drivers honked their horns at them, and eventually entered a relatively quiet street. The closer they drew to the ashram, the more orange-clad sannyasins began to appear. By foot, on bicycles or in buzzing three-wheeler rickshaws, they were all headed in the same direction, like bees returning to a hive, the only difference being that this particular hive had a king bee instead of a queen.

Angus experienced a peculiar blend of feelings: excitement, curiosity, awkwardness and the sensation that he was a little boy, being led to school for the very first time in his life. He reasoned that perhaps holding the silent

15

woman's hand was creating this impression. He turned his head, glanced at her and realised that, even though unattractive in physical terms, there was something beautiful about her, although he couldn't quite figure out what it was. Innocence perhaps.

They approached an ornately carved wooden gate with polished brass studs set into it. Overhead, a white marble beam had big black letters set into it. SHREE RAJNEESH ASHRAM. Angus's silent guide let go of his hand, gave him one last heart-warming smile, and wandered away. 'Thanks,' he said, although she couldn't have heard him because of the crowds of people chattering beside the gate.

The ashram, composed of many buildings, was set among trees, towering stands of yellow bamboo and well-tended gardens. Women, dressed in flowing saffron, peach or maroon robes, walked by clutching cushions and blankets. Some of the men who accompanied them also had on ankle-length robes. Others wore long shirts and trousers, all dyed in orange or red hues. Everyone seemed to know where they were going. Everyone except Angus. He felt like an outsider in a strange land. He looked down at his faded black shirt and matching baggy pants and realised he must be sticking out like a charred tree stump in a poppy field. He began to feel like a shadow among all these gaily dressed people as they talked, laughed and embraced each other.

After paying ten rupees for a ticket, Angus joined a queue outside of Lao Tzu House, the large two-storied bungalow where the master resided. The gardens surrounding the building looked like a tropical jungle. People spoke in whispers and fell silent as the queue filtered into a pillared, circular auditorium, hemmed in by thick verdant foliage. The hall was already packed with seated sannyasins. Angus found a space at the back, sat down and looked over a sea of hairy heads. It was then he realised why people were carrying cushions. The marble floor felt like a block of ice through the thin layer of cotton forming the seat of his pants. He shivered, looked up at the high ceiling and noticed a massive, glittering, crystal-cut chandelier. *Profits showing,* whispered his cynical mind.

The auditorium was now so silent you could have heard a mosquito sneeze. Somewhere a peacock called. A steam locomotive let out a lonesome wail in the distance and began to chug. Moments later came the sound of rolling stock, concertinaing into each other as they were shunted together.

Angus felt a tickle in his throat. He coughed. People sitting near to him fired off a volley of disapproving stares. Their hostile attentions were diverted when a door opened and a little man with a bald head and a long, stringy, black beard appeared. He was wearing a white turtleneck robe, a small blue towel draped over the crook of his right arm. He sat down on a high-backed executive chair, positioned on a marble dais. The master scanned the auditorium for a few moments. Even at a distance of twenty metres, Angus could feel the power of Bhagwan Shree Rajneesh's unblinking, mesmeric gaze.

The guru picked up a clipboard, glanced at it, then spoke into a micro-phone. His amplified voice was delivered from an array of speakers. His voice wasn't loud, but it was clear and like his eyes contained a lot of vital-ity. Angus couldn't understand a word the man was saying. The master was speaking Hindi.

What the fuck's this? Angus asked himself.

'Nirvana,' said Rajneesh, uttering the only word that Angus recognized for the next two bum-numbing hours.

Towards the end of the discourse, Rajneesh's voice grew louder and more intense. Angus wondered what he was raving on about and wished the guru would shut up so he could get out of there and go have a cup of hot tea.

The master eventually laid his clipboard to one side, stood up, did a long *namaste*, raising his hands prayer-like in front of his smiling face, and then disappeared through the same door through which he'd entered, leaving a sort of vacuum behind him.

Thank God for that, thought Angus. *I'm dying for a pee.* He stood and merged with the procession of people snaking towards the exit. He then joined a long line of people queuing up for the toilet.

Angus was sitting in the ashram's Vrindavan Restaurant, sipping on an overpriced cup of cardamom-flavoured *chai*. A familiar voice called out, 'Hey, Angus!' He looked up and saw that it was Shanti Deva, a sannyasin he'd befriended a few months earlier in Goa. Even though Angus was pleased to see him, he still had a bone to pick with the Englishman. Shanti had disap-peared with Angus's two Scottish lovers, Alice and Nina.

'Shanti, sit down, man. It's good to see you again.'

Shanti sat down on a low wooden stool. 'The feelings mutual. Man, I didn't expect to see you here.'

Angus gave the Englishman a sideways look. 'I'll bet you fucking well didn't.'

Shanti ran a hand through the fringe of his shoulder-length black hair and looked directly into Angus narrowed blue eyes. 'What do you mean?' he asked. 'Are you pissed off at me about something?'

'Aye, you're damned right I'm pissed off about something,' replied Angus. 'You ran off with my girlfriends when I went down to Palolem on a diving course.'

'Oh, that,' said the Englishman, making out like it was nothing.

'Aye, *that!* It was a sneaky thing to do. What have you got to say for yourself?'

Shanti looked over from the opposite side of the small, wooden table. 'Well...well, it wasn't quite like that.'

'Oh, it wasn't, was it?' Angus said, working hard at suppressing a grin. 'How was it then?'

'Well, the girls wanted to go to Pune and I went along for the ride.'

'I'll bet you did, you randy fucker that you are. Where are Alice and Nina now?'

'For a start, they're called Rupa and Subha now.'

'What?'

'They took sannyas... Let me see. ...six weeks ago it must have been.'

'And where are Rupa and Subha now?'

'Last I heard, they went off to Rajasthan with a couple of Italian swamis.'

'For fuck's sake,' Angus cursed. 'I just left Rajasthan four days ago.'

'You did? How did you get here? By train?'

'No, I met this crazy American chick called Kali who—'

'Hold on. Did you say Kali?'

'Yeah, I did. You know her?'

'Tall, skinny bird with a nose as big as a traffic cone. Rides an Enfield, right?'

'That's the one. So what's the story?'

'The story is Kali is banned from the ashram and the office wants her mala and locket back.'

Angus felt his guts churning. 'How come?'

'Kali's a thief. She's ripped off a lot of sannyasins.'

'Oh, man,' Angus groaned. 'Don't fucking tell me.'

'Why? You haven't left any money or valuables around that she knows about, have you?'

Angus rose slowly to his feet and said, 'I left twenty-two thousand dollars in a room I'm sharing with Kali back at the Sundar Lodge.'

'Shit!' Shanti sprang to his feet, grabbed Angus's arm and said, 'C'mon, what are you waiting on. Let's go.'

'Hold on a sec,' said Angus, 'I have to go to the toilet'

'I'm not surprised,' said Shanti.

When Angus returned, he was tying the drawstring that held up his black cotton trousers. 'I'll say this much for your guru's ashram,' he commented, 'it has the cleanest toilets in India.'

Shanti headed for the gate and called over his shoulder, 'Will you stop farting around and hurry up?'

Soon, they were speeding along Koregaon Park Road in the back of a rickshaw. *'Jehldi! Jehldi!'* yelled Shanti Deva to make the bleary-eyed driver go even faster.

The rickshaw skidded to a sideways halt outside Sunder Lodge. Kali's motorbike was nowhere in sight. Angus paid the rickshaw driver with a crumpled ten-rupee note.

Shanti and Angus hurried into the lodge's compound and ran towards room number thirteen. The door was padlocked. Angus searched in his pockets for the key Kali had given him the previous evening. He found it and tried to turn it in the lock. It didn't fit.

'Fucking shit,' hissed Angus, turning to Shanti, 'how could I have been so dumb?'

It took a lot of persuasion on Shanti's part to convince the puzzled manager to come and open the door with a spare key. When Angus finally entered the room, the first thing he noticed was that Kali's things were gone. He didn't have to look under the aluminium dustbin to know the money was gone also. He looked anyway, and his suspicions were confirmed.

Angus sat on a mattress, let out a long sigh and said, 'I don't believe that I trusted that rotten bitch. She's burnt me big time. I feel like I've been shot down in flames. If I get my hands around her scrawny neck, I'll strangle her.'

'No you won't,' objected Shanti, squatting down beside him. 'You'll forgive her.'

'Forgive her,' echoed Angus. 'Why the fuck should I forgive her?'

'Because,' answered the Englishman, 'forgiveness doesn't make the other person right. It sets you free and that's what living around Bhagwan is all about — freedom.'

Angus thought about it for a moment, smiled as understanding dawned, nodded, and said, 'Maybe you're right.'

'Was that all of your money?' asked Shanti.

'Most of it,' replied Angus, pulling out the leather wallet from under his shirt. 'I've still got about three grand in here.'

'Rupees?'

'No, dollars.'

Shanti exclaimed, 'Three thousand dollars!'

'Yeah, what's the big deal about that?'

'Angus, man, you're loaded. I'm down to fifty quid.'

'What, you're in India with only fifty quid to your name?'

'Forty, actually.'

Angus felt inspired. He unzipped the wallet. 'Here,' he said, handing the Englishman a couple of one hundred dollar bills, 'take it.'

Shanti hesitated. He asked in a shaky voice, 'A... Are you sure?'

'Take it, man, before I change my mind.'

The Englishmen reached out for the money, folded the bills, and deposited them in his faded orange shirt's breast pocket. He patted the pocket with his right hand and chuckled. 'I'm rich. I'm rich,' he repeated, unable to believe that such good fortune could come out of his friend's misfortune. 'I'd like to invite you to dhal, chapattis and special *chai* at the Café Bund. What do you say, Angus, my friend?'

Shanti's joy was infectious. Angus slapped the grinning Englishman on the shoulder and said, 'You're on.'

Ten days passed before Angus met Bhagwan Shree Rajneesh for the first time. The meeting took place on a small porch outside of the master's house. It was early evening. The atmosphere was so rarefied Angus would not have been surprised if someone had handed him an oxygen mask. There were fifteen other people in attendance at the *darshan* (Lit. 'Sight'. Seeing a holy man.) Dressed in a simple white robe, Bhagwan sat on a high-backed chair, one leg crossed over the other, a position he maintained throughout the ninety-minute exchange of energies. To his left, sitting cross-legged on the floor, was Shiva Murti, the master's bodyguard, whose duties included telling people not to cough or fart in front of the master. One only had to look at his big-boned, ruddy-complexioned, freckled face, his long ginger beard, and wavy hair tied in a ponytail to know that Shiva was a Scotsman.

Three other well-known ashram personalities sat amongst the small congregation on the floor, gazing at their master with beatific smiles upon their calm faces. Bhagwan's personal secretary Laxmi, a frail-looking Indian woman with dark shadows under her eyes. According to rumour, she lived on rice crackers, which, going by her skeletal appearance, was easy to believe. Laxmi was the only person Angus ever met who spoke in the third person when speaking about herself. To her right sat Mukta, a blissed-out, middle-aged Greek heiress. She had a lion's mane of black hair cascading over her shoulders. Mukta worked as a gardener in the ashram's grounds. Angus had already talked to her briefly on a couple of occasions, and he'd taken an instant liking to her. Next to her sat Ma Yoga Vivek, the master's companion, and caretaker. Angus had to stop himself from staring at her. Her long light-brown hair was cut in a fringe and her elfin face peeped out from under it like that of a seductive fairy princess. Angus didn't recognize anyone else, but that didn't matter because the scene was set.

Angus looked on from where he sat cross-legged on the cool marble floor, slightly to the left of a semi-circle of orange-clad sannyasins and a couple of nervous-looking potential converts. Bhagwan sat silently and gazed at each individual in turn. His was no ordinary gaze, for it carried the power to lift people into an exalted state. His eyes were radiant crystal balls, the kind you see your soul in when the light is right. Angus's heart skipped a beat, his thoughts evaporating in the sizzling moment the master's attention focused on him.

Like many a charismatic, Bhagwan spoke with a gentle, hypnotic voice and had a golden tongue that dripped honey and drew out the letter 'S' at the end of words to produce a gentle hiss.

'Yessss, Sadhana,' said Bhagwan, motioning with a graceful hand for an attractive young woman to sit at his feet, 'something to say to me?' Master and disciple chatted like old friends until Bhagwan ended the exchange by saying, 'Very good, Sadhana. This is how life moves. Good.' The woman raised her hands in a *namaste* and then returned to where she had been sitting previously, visibly happy with her reflection in the mirror that did not lie.

It was one of the newcomers next. Bhagwan smiled at him, chuckled and said, 'Yessss, I've been waiting on you.'

The balding American was built like a bulldozer. He uttered a few unintelligible syllables. His broad shoulders shook, and he burst into tears. Bhagwan smiled like a benevolent father, leaned forward, dropped a string of wooden beads with a brand new locket containing an image of himself over the big man's head, and said, 'Sit under a tree. This will be your new name, Swami Prem...'

Angus thought about a couple of things Shanti had told him. He'd said that the idea of using a new name, especially a Sanskrit one, holds great appeal for spiritually adventurous people because it delivers the possibility of developing a personality to fit it. Shanti, whose name meant 'Peace', had gone on to explain how Bhagwan Shree Rajneesh must have been well aware of this because he'd gone through a few name changes himself during his life. Chandra Mohan Jain was born in 1931 in Madhya Pradesh. As an afterthought, his parents added Rajneesh to his name. In the sixties, he was called Acharya (teacher). By the early seventies, Rajneesh began to call himself Bhagwan, an honorific title that means 'The Blessed One' or 'God'.

Angus's felt anxious. His mind began to panic. *Shit, shit, shit, it's going to be my turn next,* he thought, glancing around nervously. *I like my name. I don't want to change it. I wonder what name he's going to give me. Hold on, what am I thinking about? Let me out of here!* His mind crashed to a sudden, silent halt when he heard Bhagwan address him.

'*Angussss,*' hissed the master, 'come closer.'

Angus slid his bum across the shiny floor and parked himself in front of the guru's well-manicured tootsies. He looked up into the master's inscrutable eyes. His olive-coloured face was as smooth as the polished marble floor. They sat together like this for some timeless moments. There was something distinctly out-of-the-body about Bhagwan's presence. Angus sensed that the man's spirit was hovering above his body, attached by a fine thread, as fine and tenuous as a strand of spider's web. Angus experienced several bewildering sensations, but more than anything else he felt like a naughty little schoolboy who'd been hauled up in front of the headmaster for smoking cigarettes in the toilets. He could not prevent himself from smiling. Bhagwan could read a person's mind as easily as most people read newspapers. He must have enjoyed reading Angus's at that moment because he let out a warm-hearted chuckle. In the very same moment, Angus knew without a doubt that the beautiful man seated in front of him somehow accepted him in his totality. There was no logic to this realization; he simply felt it in his heart. Bliss swept over Angus like a tidal wave. 'Wow!' he gasped. Mild laughter came from some of those seated around him. He glanced at the guru's bodyguard. Shiva had a pained expression on his face like someone had let off a rotten egg fart. Angus smiled again. Bhagwan chuckled again.

'What have you been doing with your life?' enquired the master.

Angus didn't need to think about his answer. 'Travelling and taking a lot of psychedelic drugs.'

'Hmm,' intoned the master, as if bemused. 'Very good.'

Very good, thought Angus, *this guy is really far out.*

Bhagwan raised an eyebrow and nodded as if acknowledging the thought. 'You've seen the peak of the holy mountain,' he declared, 'but every time the effects produced by a drug wears off you are back in the foothills, perhaps lower down than from where your trip began. If you wish to remain in the Himalayan peaks of consciousness, you will have to meditate. It is too simple to think you can find God by ingesting a drug. Start doing my dynamic and kundalini meditations every day, and begin to wear orange.'

Angus had dressed in dark blue for the occasion.

Bhagwan used a solid gold pen to write something on a sheet of white silk paper attached to a clipboard. When he'd finished writing, he returned his attention to Angus and handed him the sheet of paper, saying, 'This will be your new name, Swami Anand Loka'

Anand Loka? Angus was finding it difficult to believe what he was hearing.

The softly spoken guru continued, 'It means world of bliss. This will be your new work; to create a blissful world, and the way to do this will be found through meditation.'

Angus looked around and blurted out, 'I feel like I've come home to my spiritual family.' There was a brief burst of gentle laughter behind him.

The master chuckled. 'You have come home.'

Bhagwan was a force, a positive emotional magnet drawing Angus towards him. Angus loved the vibe. He bowed his head. Bhagwan slipped a wooden mala around his neck, dabbed him lightly on the crown of his head, and said, 'Your energy is ready — just a little push, and you will go far. Good, Loka.'

Shanti Deva was waiting for Angus at the ashram's main gate. As soon as he saw Angus had a string of beads around his neck he punched the air and shouted, 'Yeah!' Drawing closer he asked in a more subdued tone, 'What's your new name?'

Angus was so buzzed out he could hardly speak. He looked at the sheet of paper the master had handed him and stammered, 'S-Swami... A-A-Anand...' He handed the paper to Shanti.

'Great,' said the Englishman after he'd read the name. 'So, Loka, what did you think of Bhagwan.'

'He... He's the most amazing person I've ever met in my life.'

'Fantastic!' Shanti hugged Angus and said, 'How about heading down to The Blue Diamond Hotel and cracking open a few bottles of ice-cold Kingfisher beer to celebrate?'

'Shanti, my friend, that is an brilliant idea. But first I'd like to sit down for a minute. My legs feel like they're made out of jelly.'

Nothing was said, but it was clear from the moment they sat down at the bar that Shanti Deva was out to prove a point – an Englishman could drink a Scotsman under the table any day of the week. Fifteen bottles of beer later, Shanti was not feeling so confident. In fact, he wasn't feeling anything at all. He'd passed out in the men's toilets after vomiting the contents of his bloated stomach into a urinal. Scotland staggered home to an eight-seven victory, although, apart from the final score, Angus couldn't remember any of the match's details.

It was mid-afternoon when Angus woke up the following day and found he had company. Iva Brainhaemorrich, the mother of all hangovers, was stamping around in his throbbing head. Iva had used a sledgehammer to batter his cerebral cortex into pulp. Angus groaned, swore he'd never drink alcohol again for as long as he lived, and spent the rest of the day in bed.

The following morning, at 6 a.m., Angus was in the Rajneesh Ashram, doing the dynamic meditation for the first time. 'The Dynamic', as sannyasins called it, was an amalgamation of hyperventilation, bio-energetics, cathartic therapy, traditional meditation and dance.

A bare-chested sannyasin, resembling Jesus Christ a month into a grain-of-rice-a-day diet, encouraged the hundred or so pre-dawn meditators, assembled under the ashram's corrugated iron-roofed Buddha Hall, to be as total as possible.

The skinny Son of God hit the play button on a cassette tape player. To the sound of amplified rhythmic drumming, broadcast through a pair of big rock-and-roll speakers, Angus began the first stage of the dynamic meditation — a ten-minute session of chaotic breathing through the nose. His arms began pumping like pistons on the Bombay Express. Snot flew from his nostrils.

A gong signalled that it was time to move into catharsis, a state of 'let-go', the hallmark of many Rajneesh meditation techniques. The percussion shifted into staccato overdrive. Angus started shouting and screaming, along with everyone else who was present, most of whom were wearing orange blindfolds or black sleep masks. It registered in the back of Angus's mind that the neighbours must have been freaking out at the horrendous racket erupting out of the ashram. He bellowed at the world and the seeming injustices it had heaped upon his shoulders. He yelled at his stepmother, who'd given up on him as a teenager, the judicial system that had locked him up in borstal, Kali for stealing his money, and generally expressed negative emotions. He shed tears over the loss of his beloved stepfather on Iona and Jenny's death in Nepal.

The brass gong sounded again. Stage three begun. Time to jump up and down and continuously shout Hoo! Hoo! Hoo! Angus felt like a pogo stick undergoing an identity crisis. Just when he thought his legs were going to buckle from the pressure, the 'Stop!' command signalled it was time to freeze on the spot. Angus stood like a statue, determined not to move a muscle.

The dense silence in Buddha Hall was broken when an uplifting, acoustic melody began to strum out of the loudspeakers. Angus's body picked up on the rhythm and he began to dance without restraint. He watched as the first light of day filtered through the tall stands of bamboo surrounding the hall. Birds began to sing in an apparent accompaniment to the music. It all seemed so perfect. He kept on moving. It felt great to be alive. He continued to dance. A feeling of gratitude filled his heart. He raised his hands in front of him and brought them together prayerfully. The meditation ended with a period of silence. Stillness embraced all and everything.

After a warm shower, Angus paid ten rupees and went to Bhagwan's morning discourse. He found a vacant space on the floor about seven metres from the master's empty chair. He kept his eyes closed until Bhagwan entered Chuang Tzu auditorium.

A door opened. The master appeared to float over to his high-backed chair. He sat down, closed his eyes and, for a few moments, remained silent. He opened his eyes, glanced at the clipboard his demure secretary had handed him and began talking in Hindi. Angus realised it was not the content of the master's words that was important but the silence separating them. A silence so profound it hummed in his ears like a swarm of nectar-producing bees. Bhagwan communicated a lot through silence, and the silence he emanated was infectious.

Two hours passed like ten short minutes. The master rose from his chair in a practised, fluid movement. He then performed a slow-motion *namaste*. His unblinking eyes peered out from behind his joined hands in an unfaltering gaze, sweeping over the congregation seated before him like a searchlight's beam. The master then lowered his hands and disappeared back into the privacy of his house.

The moon was full. The ashram became alive with even more creative activity than usual. The spiritual community's ranks swelled with the arrival of hundreds of Bhagwan's Indian followers. They'd come to commemorate their master's enlightenment on Guru Purnima, a full moon festival day traditionally celebrated by Hindus to honour their spiritual teachers.

Angus helped out in the ashram's kitchen by using a wooden rolling pin to make thin chapattis to feed the visitors. The Indian sannyasins were a breed apart from Bhagwan's western disciples, in that they fitted more into the traditional framework of how one normally envisions spiritual seekers to behave. Relaxed, gentle, present, meditative, open. Many of them were wonderful people. Some elderly ones looked as enlightened as the man they'd paid homage to.

For most, the day was spent singing lively *bhajans* and eating food served on banana leaf plates, stitched together with wooden toothpicks. The festivities ended with the highlight of the day — a mass *darshan* with the master.

24

Angus stood in a long queue for an hour, waiting to bow down at Bhagwan's feet. Many of the Indians were by now in a state of agitated excitement. Old ladies were swooning at the thought of being so close to their beloved spiritual master. Young Indian men were turning cartwheels and doing the pogo with their arms raised above their heads.

As Angus drew closer, he studied the master. He was sitting in a stuffed armchair, in front of a blue sheet with a golden flame embroidered on it. The whites of Bhagwan's eyes were showing. Some of the Indians became hysterical in his presence and had to be dragged away by security personnel. Like a peaceful island in the centre of a cyclone, the guru sat in Samadhi, unaffected by the surrounding chaos.

Finally, it was Angus's turn. He bent down, gently touched the master's sandaled feet and nearly toppled over from the charge of psychic energy that pulsed through his body. He glanced at Bhagwan's delicate hands, held in a fascinating mudra. Once again, Angus had the impression that the man was attached to his body by a gossamer thread. Although it was a boisterous and noisy celebration there was, as Angus experienced it, an air of profound depth and silence infusing the occasion. Bhagwan appeared vulnerable, yet, simultaneously, there was a great strength in his vulnerability. The master had embraced what almost everyone is afraid of; being completely open and exposed. Standing before him, Angus felt like he was hanging around the gateway of eternity, not quite plucking up the courage to take a transcendental leap into totally letting go of everything, including his self. He trusted that what Bhagwan had said to him on their first meeting was true: just a little push, and you will go far. Angus was waiting for that push.

It was late afternoon on the fourth of July. Angus picked up a telephone in an international call centre, on Pune's busy Mahatma Gandhi Road. The receiver on the other end of the line rang several times before someone picked up.

'Is that you, Angus?' asked a Glaswegian voice.

'Aye, it is.'

'Okay, pal, I'm glad you remembered.'

Static howled out of the telephone.

'Can you hear me?'

'Aye, Jimmy, I can hear you loud and clear.'

'Right, pal, listen up. I want you to come and meet me in the main lounge at The Taj Mahal Hotel in Bombay. Do you know it?'

'Yeah, sure, it's in Colaba.'

'Good. I'll be there on the seventh at one o'clock in the afternoon. You got that?'

'Yeah, no problem, I'll be there one o'clock sharp.'

'You better be, because I'm counting on it. How're things with you?'

'Fine, Jimmy, I've been going through a few changes but nothing I can't handle.'

'Well, that's life, isn't it? I'm looking forward to seeing you. Remember, though, this is business, not pleasure.'

'Yeah, I figured that.'

'Right then, Angus, that's that then. See you on the seventh.'

'One o'clock sharp.'

'That's my man. Don't forget your toothbrush.' Jimmy's laughter crackled in the phone's loudspeaker.

'I won't. See you in Bombay.'

'Right pal, see you soon.'

'See you, Jimmy.'

'See you, pal.'

Click!

3

HUBBLE BUBBLE, TOIL AND HASHISH

A moment after I'd finished describing Angus's telephone conversation with his old friend, Jimmy Bradley, the in-flight attendant asked, 'Would you care to order something for dinner?'

I glanced up at the air hostess. 'I'll have the lamb brochettes.'

'Madame?'

Jean looked up from the menu card. 'I'd like the green chicken curry with basmati rice.'

The hostess glanced at our seat numbers and then jotted the orders down on a notepad. 'Something to drink?'

'Same again,' said Jean, a gold-ringed finger running around the rim of her empty glass.

'Sir?'

I held up a cut-glass tumbler. 'I'll have another one of these, please.'

The stewardess consulted her notepad. 'So, that's lamb, chicken curry, a double gin and tonic, and a double scotch.'

'That's right,' sneered Jean, 'what a good memory you have.'

The hostess shot Jean a poisonous look.

'Thanks,' I said, looking up into her glaring eyes, 'you're most helpful.'

The stewardess walked away and Jean said, 'Most helpful, my Scottish arse. At over a thousand pounds a ticket she should be down on her knees giving you a...' She smiled. '...shoeshine. Anyway, who is this Jimmy character? He sounds like he was up to no good.'

'Aye, Jean, you're right. Jimmy Bradley was a right crook.'

'Who was he?'

'An old friend of Angus's from his teenage days in Glasgow. He was a bit... How to describe it? ...accident-prone.' I let out a spluttering laugh.

'What's so funny about that?' Jean asked.

'Well, the first time Angus met Jimmy he was sitting on a pavement with a piece of wood sticking through his nose. They were close friends for a while until Jimmy's father, who worked for customs and excise, moved with his family from Glasgow to Dover when he was promoted. Very ironic, as you will see as the story unfolds. Anyway—'

Jean cut in. 'No spoilers please.'

'Oh, aye, sorry about that. Anyway, Angus and Jimmy hadn't seen each other for ten years. Then they met by chance in Goa in 1974. Jimmy was in trouble, as usual. He'd gone nuts after some French hippies fed him an omelette laced with datora, a dangerous hallucinogenic drug. Angus and his two girlfriends, Alice and Nina, nursed him back to health. Jimmy sent Angus to the south of Goa to meet some German bloke called Manni. He was a divemaster, and he taught Angus how to scuba...'

The flight attendant appeared with food and drinks on a silver tray. Once she'd served us, she wandered off back to the galley.

'So,' said Jean, 'I take it this guy Jimmy had a reason for sending your brother to do that, besides the good of his health and saying hello to the sharks.'

'Aye, to say the least,' I said, taking a bite of lamb. 'The thing is,' I continued, mumbling through a mouthful of food, 'Jimmy didn't tell Angus why he wanted him to learn how to dive. All he told him was that if he did it, he'd make a lot of money as a result. So, Angus, being the enterprising young man he was, learned how—'

'For God's sake, Hamish, will you stop talking with your mouth full. You're sitting in business class and behaving like an Irish navvy.'

We finished our meal in silence. Jean took a sip of her drink, burped and asked, 'What exactly did Angus have to do to make this money?'

'That's the next part of the story,' I replied, knocking back my single malt whisky in one throat-searing swallow.

Jean shook her head. 'Will you please ease up on the alcohol? You'll be blootered by the time we get to London.'

I laughed offhandedly, a snake of whisky-powered confidence slithering off my tongue. 'Ach, away with you, what's a wee dram to a highlander?'

'A highlander?' Jean retorted. 'Who are you trying to kid? You've drunk a lot more than a wee dram tonight,' she continued, her own drink beginning to make her feel affectionate. 'You saved my life, darling. I just want to take care of you.' She leaned over and gave me a lingering kiss on the lips. She sat back and glanced at her solid gold, pink-faced Rolex. 'Time's fairly flying by, at this rate we'll be landing before we know it. So then, Angus is off to Mumbai to meet his dear auld pal, Jimmy from Glasgow. Then what happens?'

The Taj Mahal Hotel, July 7, 1975, Bombay, India.

Angus glanced at his new plastic and chrome diver's watch, bought especially for the occasion. It was one minute to one. He wandered up to the bar and looked around. People were staring at him.

'Angus!' A familiar voice called out.

He turned and saw Jimmy rising out of a chair over by a wide, tinted glass window. Angus threaded his way between tables, extended his right hand and said, 'How's it going, Jimmy?'

Jimmy laughed loudly, ignored Angus's proffered hand, drew him close and gave him a bear hug.

'Great to see you, pal.' Jimmy's breath reeked of strong drink.

They sat down on upholstered chairs. Jimmy ordered a couple of beers from a passing waiter. He then focused his brown eyes on Angus's bearded face and asked, 'So, what's with the orange robe and the wooden necklace? Don't tell me you've teamed up with the Rajneeshees.'

'I have that and my name isn't Angus anymore, its—'

'Shut it, pal, I don't want to know,' said Jimmy without hesitation. 'You'll always be Angus to me.'

'Suit yourself, Jimmy. What's in a name anyway?'

'Quite a lot if you ask me, pal. By giving someone the power to change your name, you automatically cast that person in a role usually filled by your ma and da. Is this Bhagwan your new—'

'Listen, Jimmy, my parents died on the day I was born. I'm not interested in your fuckin' judgemental attitudes.'

Jimmy swallowed a mouthful of beer and chuckled. 'The judgement that it's better not to judge, sounds a wee bit ironic to me.'

'You're getting very intellectual in your old age,' commented Angus.

'Aye, maybe you're right,' agreed Jimmy, who was twenty-seven. 'And you're getting dumber by the minute. Look at the state of you. You look like a fuckin' holy man. You stupid-looking bam.'

'Look who's talking. Jimmy Bradley, the chubby wee shite in an off-the-peg business suit. You look like Elton John with a new toupee...minus the daft specs. You fucking wanker that you are.'

The two old friends burst out laughing, leaned forward, and slapped each other on the back like they were on fire.

'You want another pint,' asked Jimmy, finishing off his beer.

'No, I'm fine with this one,' replied Angus, glancing at his half-full glass.

'Right then, pal,' said Jimmy, signalling a waiter for another beer by holding up his empty glass, 'the first thing we're going to do is go out and buy you some decent duds. Second thing—'

'What's wrong with what I've got on?'

'You're sticking out like a lost cock in a barrel of fannies. The second thing you're going to do is get a haircut and a shave.'

'No fucking way,' protested Angus.

'Listen, pal, I'm serious about this. Cutting a low profile is the name of the game. If you play your cards right, you'll make five thousand dollars for a couple of hours' work tonight, and that's just for a kickoff.'

Angus stared out of the window and focused his thoughts. He could see the basalt arch of the Gateway of India. Crowds of brightly clad pedestrians passed under it to take in the view of Bombay harbour. Directly outside of the hotel, a motley band of beggars accosted smartly dressed foreigners leaving the building. *Five grand,* he thought, *I could do with that.* He turned back to Jimmy and said, 'Okay, you're on.'

Jimmy glanced at his Ultra-Thin Patek Philippe watch, stood up and said,

'Let's move it. We've got to be back here at five to meet someone.'

Three hours passed. They were back in the Taj Mahal Hotel and Angus felt like a new man. He had on a cream-coloured lightweight suit, white shirt and dark blue tie. His beard was gone and his hair was the shortest it had been in years. It felt strange but also invigorating.

He was seated beside Jimmy. Across from them sat two similarly attired Indian men, who appeared to be in their early thirties.

Jimmy did the introductions. 'Angus, I'd like you to meet Chidvilas and Amritananda. Chid and Amrit for short.'

They shook hands across the glass tabletop.

'Check it out, lads,' said Jimmy, nodding toward two shapely young women in short skirts, chatting up a couple of hook-nosed Arabs at the bar, 'I wouldn't mind giving them one.'

Chid and Amrit sighed in appreciation. Angus recognised the women. 'Man,' he said, 'I've seen those chicks in Pune.'

'You sound surprised,' commented Amrit, toying with his solid gold arm bracelet. 'Here in Bombay, it is well known that some of the Rajneesh's female disciples are prostituting their lovely bodies to be making a few chips.'

'They are costing a lot more than a few chips, Amrit,' said Chid, rubbing a thumb and forefinger together. 'Somebody was telling me they are charging five hundred dollars for a night. I've also heard that the rich Arabs like them to keep their malas on when they are doing the fuck-fuck.'

'Yeah, well maybe I'll do a wee bit of fuck-fuck with one of them later on tonight when we've finished the job,' said Jimmy, glancing nervously at his watch. 'Right then, it's time to get busy.'

One hour later, Angus was standing on the sun-bleached wooden deck of a small, black-painted tugboat. The *Shiva-Shakti* was tied fast to a small pier, beside a somewhat dilapidated warehouse in a fenced-off compound in the Sassoon Docks, south of Bombay's main harbour. The air was rank with the smell of diesel, solvent, two-component epoxy and fish. In a neighbouring yard, a welder worked at the top of a ladder, sending showers of brilliant sparks in a cascading flow that bounced, hissed and died in an oil-slicked puddle below him.

'So, Jimmy,' said Angus, 'I'm finally going to find out what this scam of yours is all about.'

'Aye, pal, you are that,' said Jimmy, raising a pair of powerful binoculars to his eyes. The binoculars' lenses glinted and reflected the sunset's orange colours. He handed them to Angus, pointed out to sea and said, 'See that big container ship over there with the blue and white Greek flag flapping at the stern?'

Angus focused the binoculars and looked at the ship. It was sitting low in the water about seven kilometres away from the shore. 'Aye,' he said, 'what about her?'

'That, pal, is where we're going to be heading in...' he raised his left arm and looked at the time, '...about two hours and forty-five minutes.'

'What for?'

'Come into the wheelhouse and I'll show you.'

'Hey, you two,' shouted Jimmy to Chid and Amrit, who were now dressed in dark-blue boiler suits and smoking cigarettes on the wharf, 'shift your lazy arses and bring a container on board.'

The two Indians fired off quick mock salutes, then hurried by the white Ambassador car they'd arrived in, before disappearing into the warehouse's shadows.

Minutes later, Amrit and Chid staggered up the narrow gangplank. They were struggling for balance as they carried a black, four-foot-long, wedge-shaped, fibreglass container with stainless steel handles bolted onto its sides.

'Bring it in here,' ordered Jimmy through the wheelhouse's open sliding door.

The two men did as they were told. Then Jimmy said, 'Might as well fetch the other three while you're at it.'

'Aye, aye, captain,' said Amrit, grinning to display a set of perfect white teeth.

'Let me guess,' said Angus, patting the black container, 'we have to deliver this to that container ship.'

'Right and wrong, pal. It's a wee bit more complicated than that. You see this?' Jimmy asked, pointing to a red lever at the side of the streamlined container.

'Aye,' said Angus, squatting to take a closer look at the foot-long metal lever.

'When you pull that down, it activates a couple of powerful magnets. Our job—'

'How do the magnets work?'

'I knew you'd ask me that,' said Jimmy. 'The answer is, I don't fucking well know.' He added, 'What I do know is this: it's our job to attach those boxes to the hull of that container ship.'

'Does the ship's captain know about this?'

'Does he fuck, but some friends of mine in Southampton do.'

'What's inside?'

'Fifty kilos of number one Afghani hash. That means we'll be doing two-hundred kilos tonight. You get twenty-five dollars a unit. In two weeks we'll be doing half-a-ton.' Jimmy winked. 'Are you into it, pal?'

'Sure,' said Angus. 'It sounds like a dawdle.'

'Let's see how much of a dawdle you think it was once the job's done. Come on,' said Jimmy, walking out onto the deck. 'It's time for you to check out the diving gear. The containers weigh eighty kilos, so I want you to learn how the specially designed buoyancy vest works. They hold more air than normal ones.'

Angus followed him. 'This operation must have required a lot of financing and organization. Who set it up?'

Jimmy turned to Angus and looked him squarely in the face. 'Listen, pal, that's the first and last time you're ever going to ask me that question. The answer is you don't want to know.'

Angus raised his hands, palms up. 'Anything you say, captain.'

The *Shiva-Shakti* dropped anchor half-a-kilometre to the seaward side of the container ship. The tug's running lights had been switched off. There was no moon. A swell had built up. The boat's rocking motion was making Angus feel seasick. He sat down on the deck beside Jimmy and asked, 'Now what?'

Jimmy jammed a cigarette into the corner of his mouth before answering. 'We wait a while until things settle down a bit.'

'I'm roasting inside this thing,' said Angus, pulling down the zipper on his thick neoprene diver's suit.

'Is that you complaining already? You'll be glad you've got it on once we're in the water.' Jimmy cupped his hands and lit his cigarette with a plastic lighter. 'I'll run a few of the important points past you one more time. You will not switch your torch on until we are under the ship. You got that?'

'Yeah, I'm not deaf.'

'Just answer yes or no, smart-ass,' said Jimmy, pretending to swing a punch at Angus's chin. 'We go down to five metres and swim slowly so we don't use up too much air. You tug on the lifeline three times if you're in any kind of difficulty.' He paused, stared at Angus and asked, 'Are you listening?'

'What? Yeah, yeah, sure, man.'

Jimmy shook his head and continued. 'Whatever you do, don't touch the lever that activates the magnets. After we've done the second box, we swim back here and strap on a fresh oxygen bottle. Hey, pal, are you feeling alright?' He asked, peering into Angus's eyes.

Angus groaned. 'I feel like I'm about ready to throw up.'

'Go to the side and get it out of you,' Jimmy advised.

Angus stuck his fingers down his throat and vomited his stomach's contents into the sea. 'Agh,' he sighed, 'that's better.'

Jimmy handed him a small plastic bottle of water and began to put his flippers on. He then nodded at Angus. 'Come on, pal. It's showtime.'

Angus spat in his mask to stop it fogging up, although he needn't have bothered because the sea was so dirty he wouldn't be able to see his hands in front of his face. Once they'd strapped on their air bottles, Jimmy and Angus sat with their backs to the water. Jimmy reached over and attached a thin wire cable to Angus's belt. It was three metres long and served to keep them in touch with each other when submerged in the darkness. Jimmy nodded to Angus and they tumbled backwards into the water. They adjusted their buoyancy vests by filling them with compressed air. Amrit and Chid lowered a container into the water. Amrit gave a thumbs up hand signal.

Jimmy and Angus grabbed the handles. They let the air out of their vests until they levelled out at five metres below the surface. Angus was terrified. He couldn't see a thing but he could hear the pounding rhythm of his heart over the sounds of his breathing and the air bubbling out of his regulator. His right arm felt like it was being wrenched out of its socket by the weight of the box. He remembered Jimmy's advice to take it easy. He concentrated on his breathing and began swimming towards the container ship. Of all the bizarre drug experiences he'd had in his life none of them could match what he went through in the fifteen minutes it took to reach that ship. It made no difference if his eyes were open or closed, because of the intensity of the Stygian darkness surrounding him. Colour flashed through his brain in time to the beat of his pulse. He kept waggling his flippers and heading in the direction indicated by Jimmy, tugging on the line with his free hand whenever he veered off course. He knew immediately when he reached their destination because the top of his head bumped against the ship's hull. His teeth nearly bit through his vulcanized rubber mouthpiece.

Jimmy switched on his torch and pointed it at the hull to illuminate a few barnacles stuck to a dark orange surface. Angus used both his hands to swing the container into position. Jimmy pulled the metal lever. Clunk. The wedge-shaped container was now stuck fast to the ship's hull. Angus tried pulling on it. It would not budge. He unclipped his torch and, after switching it on to the red beam, he shone it at Jimmy's facemask. Jimmy winked at him, nodded, switched off his torch and began swimming back to the *Shiva-Shakti*.

They reached the small tug and bobbed on the filthy water's surface. Jimmy grabbed Angus's arm and said, 'How's it going, pal?'

Angus spat out his mouthpiece. 'I'm shitting myself.'

Jimmy laughed. 'One down and three to go, are you ready for another one?'

'Am I fuck,' replied Angus. 'Let's do it, man.'

Another thumbs up from Amrit, and they were on their way again. When they were once more under the container ship's hull, Angus's switched on his torch and saw a condom floating in front of his facemask. It had a big tear in it. *Bloody hell,* he thought, *no wonder they've got a population explosion in this country.* A big turd floated by at eye level. *Fucking shit!*

When Angus and Jimmy returned to the tug for the second time, Chid and Amrit hauled them out of the sea. There was no conversation as the divers strapped on fresh oxygen bottles.

It was after midnight by the time the job was done. Angus lay spread-eagled on the heaving deck. His thigh muscles felt like they'd been injected with sulphuric acid.

The tug weighed anchor, and the diesel engine chugged into life. Half-an-hour later, they tied up at the wharf.

Chid drove Angus, Jimmy and Amrit back to the Taj Mahal Hotel. After Chid parked across the street from The Gateway of India in Apollo Bunder, all four men got out, stood on the pavement, exchanged a few words, shook hands and bid each other good night.

The Indians returned to the car. Chid honked the Ambassador's horn, did a high-speed u-turn and, with a squealing of tyres, sped off along Strand Road with Amrit waving an arm out of the passenger's side window.

Jimmy turned to Angus and commented, 'Solid as Ben Nevis those two. Come on, pal. You did well. It's time for a nightcap.'

Ten days later, Angus met up with Jimmy, Amrit and Chid again. That night they attached half-a-ton of hashish to an oil tanker's hull. A month later they attached a ton to another container ship. Thus began a monthly routine that continued for some time. Angus was in the money.

The monsoon rains came and went. Mid-October, 1975, Angus moved out of The Sundar Lodge in Pune. He'd built a bamboo house on the edge of a field to the east of Koregaon Park. The land belonged to Arun Wankhade, a sugar cane farmer who could not believe his good fortune. Bhagwan Shree Rajneesh was becoming famous. Spiritual seekers from all over the world were flocking into his ashram in droves. As a result, there were drastic rises in the price of local accommodation. Bamboo hut villages were beginning to spring up in the rural areas surrounding Koregaon Park.

In between his trips to Bombay, Angus visited the ashram daily. Every morning he rose before dawn and cycled to Buddha Hall to do the dynamic meditation. He attended Bhagwan's lectures, no matter whether they were in Hindi or English. Every word the master said in public was taped and then transcribed into books. Literary critics around the world began to acknowledge some of the publications' excellence. Bhagwan Shree Rajneesh spoke books, hundreds of them. Viewed in a certain light, it could have been perceived as miraculous.

If one had the vision to see it, miracles were an everyday occurrence in Bhagwan's 'commune', as the master was beginning to refer to the community that was quickly expanding and developing around him. People would arrive at the ashram crippled inside and, within a few days, they would be laughing and dancing joyously. Rumours began to spread that Bhagwan restored sight to the spiritually blind and resurrected the psychologically dead, who he then persuaded to celebrate existence.

Apart from the morning lectures and evening *darshans*, the master lived the life of a recluse; a life that very few knew anything about. Bhagwan spent his days in a cold, air-conditioned, white marble room where, according to insider reports, he would speed-read a dozen books a day. The master claimed, among other things, to be an ordinary man. Angus found this difficult to accept because there was absolutely nothing ordinary about him.

Once a week, Angus sat at the master's feet in *darshan* and bathed in the guru's powerful aura. He watched on as Bhagwan used a penlight torch to shine on peoples' third eye and subtle energetic centres, but couldn't help wondering if this was some sort of gimmickry. He wrote his suspicion off as a projection of his made-in-Scotland sceptical mind, a mind that the master described as a prison created by the past. Angus began to tow the party line that prevailed in the ashram. Any conflict Bhagwan's sannyasins had about submitting to the master's supreme authority was viewed as a form of resistance, a shadow of the ego or an unwillingness to let go of obsolete mental programs. Angus had to admit that the act of surrendering his judgmental mind brought with it extremely positive feelings. He felt like an innocent child, living moment to moment in a world where everything would be taken care of.

During the evening *darshans* he attended, Angus noticed that many disciples, rather than enquire about spiritual matters, asked the master questions about their relationships. Bhagwan listened like a patient father and never failed to inject an element of humour into his verbal response. When it was Angus's turn to speak, he'd tell Bhagwan about how his meditation practices were going and, if he were fortunate, he'd bow down and be touched on the crown of his head. 'Very good,' the master would say, as Angus felt his heart filling with boundless joy.

Mid-December. Jimmy and Angus were sitting in The Oberoi Towers' Hotel's main bar polishing off a bottle of Chivas Regal. It was late. Earlier that evening they'd attached eight-hundred kilos of hashish to the hull of a British freighter called The Northern Star. The operation had run as smoothly as a well-oiled sewing machine.

'So, what are your plans for the near future?' asked Jimmy, clinking whisky glasses together with Angus.

'Why are you asking?'

'Because tonight's job was the last one we'll be doing for a wee while.'

'How come?'

'The team on the other end needs to do a bit of restructuring. The last load we sent was busted.'

Angus shifted uncomfortably in his leather armchair. 'What happened?'

'Some bozo got done for speeding on the M One. The bobbies who stopped him had a gander inside the back of the van and earned themselves an overnight promotion.'

'Will the driver keep his mouth shut?'

'He will if he wants to keep living,' said Jimmy matter-of-factly. 'Anyway, we're on holiday till next March.'

'That's cool with me. I'm thinking of heading for Goa. I've—'

'Shit!' Jimmy exclaimed, interrupting him. 'I nearly forgot. I've got a message from Acid Mike for you. He's got your new book, and he said he'll meet you—'

Angus interjected. 'In Joe Bananas for Christmas.'

Jimmy nodded. 'Exactly. Mike mentioned it would be unlikely that you would forget.'

'That's good news,' Angus said. 'I'm looking forward to seeing him. I can't wait to get my hands on a new passport. How's he getting along?'

'Mike? He's fine. The old rogue has been shifting a lot of the gear we've been sending over.'

'It's a small world.'

'It is that, pal, and it's getting smaller every day. By the way, how are Alice and Nina doing?'

'You mean Rupa and Subha?'

'No, I don't mean *Rupa* and *Subha*,' said Jimmy, leaning forward in his seat and raising his voice slightly. 'I've told you before, I'm not into all this changing names shite.'

'Okay, Jimmy, keep your fucking hair on. The girls are fine. I met up with them last week. They're taking care of my place in Pune.'

'So, they've moved back in with you again, you jammy bastard that you are.'

'It's not like that. They've become *Brahmacharis* and—'

'Brahma fucking whats?'

'They've taken a vow of celibacy.'

'Fucking hell, don't tell me,' said Jimmy, pouring the last of the whisky into their empty glasses. 'I thought this Bhagwan geezer of yours was supposed to be a sex guru.'

'You need to wise up and stop believing everything that you read in newspapers. Bhagwan is a Buddha who says yes to everything. He—'

'Aye, right, especially off-shore bank accounts.'

'You're full of it, Jimmy. Let's change the subject.'

Jimmy lit a cigarette and blew a jet of smoke across the table. He let out a bark of a laugh. 'What's the matter? Water getting too hot for you?'

'Is it fuck,' replied Angus. 'You think getting married and having kids is where it's at. I don't. But that doesn't mean I need to get on your case about it.'

Jimmy drew heavily on his cigarette. 'Point taken,' he said, exhaling another cloud of smoke. 'You're right. I am full of shit.' He chuckled. 'But so are you, pal. How about drinking another bottle of whisky to celebrate our full-of-shitness?'

'For fuck's sake, I'm already drunk,' complained Angus.

'I thought you just told me that your guru was a man who said yes to everything.'

'He is, but—'

'Fuck off with your *but*. Are you a hypocrite or a man of principle?'

'I'm neither,' replied Angus, beckoning with a hand to a liveried waiter, who promptly approached their table.

'Yes, sir,' said the waiter, bowing from the waist.

'Bring us another one of these,' requested Angus, holding up the empty Chivas Regal bottle. 'A full one.'

Two days and a massive hangover later, Angus caught the ferry to Panjim. The last time he'd been on the steamer he'd slept under a lifeboat; now he was berthed in a first-class cabin. The second-class deck was crammed with hippies heading for the party season on Goa's golden beaches. Angus wandered among the freaks, immune to the stares directed his way because of his knee-length orange robe, wooden mala strung around his neck and short hair. It struck him that an 'us and them' attitude was beginning to develop between the Goa freaks and Bhagwan's sannyasins.

Angus soon tired of watching chillums being lit to cries of 'Alack! Boom Shanker'. *Been there, done that to the point of excess,* he thought, climbing the companionway stairs to the first-class deck.

He stretched out on his narrow bunk and began reading *The Book of Secrets,* a Bhagwan hardback he'd picked up in the ashram's bookshop. He came across a passage where the master described how sex can be a door; a door one can pass through to eventually transcend sex.

Angus put the book down, sat on the edge of his bed and thought about what he'd just read. In the past months, he'd made love with dozens of beautiful woman. Rather than going beyond sex, he was becoming more obsessed with it. He toyed with the idea of going downstairs and picking up a hippy chick. A tanned beauty had caught his eye. *Why not?* Angus thought. *You've got to get into it if you want to get out of it.*

He shaved, showered and returned to the swaying second-class deck.

It was early evening on Christmas Day, 1975. Angus wandered into Joe Bananas chai shop on Anjuna Beach. He saw Acid Mike straight away. He couldn't have missed Mike's trademark tie-dye trousers, shirt and headband. The acid dealer rose when he noticed Angus approaching his table. They embraced, stood back, gazed into each other's eyes and laughed.

'Jimmy told me you'd turned orange,' said Mike as he sat down on a rickety wooden chair. 'I was surprised to hear that.'

Angus smiled and said nothing.

Mike pulled a brand new British passport out of his shirt pocket and handed it to Angus saying, 'You'll have to grow your beard back.'

Angus looked at his photograph in the passport and asked, 'Who's James Sheridan.'

'You are. James Sheridan was killed in a car accident six months ago and he's been reincarnated as you.'

'Brilliant, man, I owe you a big one,' said Angus, flicking through his new passport's blank pages. 'Wow!' he exclaimed when he came across an India entry stamp dated the first of December. 'How the fuck did you manage to get this together?'

'Piece of cake, matey.' Mike chuckled. 'You want to order something to eat and drink.'

Over king prawn curry and rice, the two friends brought each other up to date.

'Now for the bad news,' said Mike, knocking back half a bottle of ice-cold Kingfisher beer.

Angus looked up from his plate. 'Raj and Murphy?'

'Yes. Your old mates are not having an easy time of it in Iran. In fact, according to what I've heard, they're in very bad shape. They—'

'What kind of bad shape?'

'Torture, jaundice, sexual assault—'

'Sexual assault! What the fuck does that mean?'

'In this case, it means our mutual friend Murphy has been raped repeatedly by some bastard who's got it in for him.'

'Jesus fucking Christ,' gasped Angus. He stammered, 'H... How did you find this out?'

'If you don't mind, I'd like to keep that little bit of information to myself for the time being.'

'Whatever you say, Mike. What else did you hear?'

'I know where the prison is that they're locked up in and know if we don't get them out of there soon they'll be dead.'

'What do you mean we?'

'You know what I mean.'

'You mean we're going to Iran to bust Murphy and Raj out of prison?'

'Yes, Angus, my old son, that's exactly what we're going to do.'

4

JAILBREAK

'I'll say this much for your brother,' said Jean, 'he knew a lot of very strange people.'

'Yes,' I agreed, 'Acid Mike was quite a character. He—'

'I'm not referring to him. I'm talking about Bhagwan and that drug-smuggling gangster, Jimmy Bradley.'

'Oh,' I said, turning to my right to glance out of the window. I leaned over Jean and looked down through the clouds. I could see the lights of a city glowing in the darkness below. 'I'll get back to Jimmy and Bhagwan later.' I studied the small-scale map on the screen in front of me. The plane was passing over the Islamic Republic of Iran. I pointed to the little red dot that represented Tehran and said, 'That's where Angus rendezvoused with Acid Mike in February 1976.' I paused for a moment. 'But first, I have to fill you in on a few details before I go into the story of how Angus and Mike went about breaking Raj and Murphy out of a maximum-security hell-hole in Iran.'

Jean leaned over from her reclined seat and kissed me on the cheek. 'I'm all ears, darling.'

'No way José,' chorused Alice and Nina when Angus asked them to travel with him to Iran.

'I'm not asking you to do it for nothing,' protested Angus. 'I'll pay you for it.'

A thick silence enveloped the three of them as they sat on the wooden floor of Angus's comfortable bamboo house in Pune.

Nina finally broke the silence by asking Angus, 'How much?'

Angus paused before he answered. 'Twenty-thousand dollars each.'

Alice exclaimed, 'Twenty-thousand fucking dollars!'

'Yeah, that's what I said. All expenses paid.'

'I'll do it,' said Alice. She looked at Nina. 'What about you, Subha?'

'Why the fuck should we help those two egotistical idiots?' Nina asked, referring to their ex-boyfriends. 'I can still remember their smiling faces when they stood on that platform in Peshawar's railway station, steam blasting upwards as they waved a not-so-fond farewell to us. The selfish fuckers couldn't wait to see the back of us. That bastard Murphy used me like one of those inflatable sex dolls.'

'Come off it, Subha,' said Angus to Nina, 'you loved Murphy and we all know it.'

'It's true, Subha,' Alice concurred. 'I don't mind admitting I loved that big Indian galoot, Raj.'

Nina began to cry. She stammered, 'That... That rotten shit, Murphy, broke my heart.'

The girls lay on the floor and cried their beautiful eyes out.

Once Nina and Alice had pulled themselves together, Angus rose and his bare feet padded on the varnished floor as he wandered through to the kitchen. He stood watching the kettle come to the boil on a gas ring. He stroked the stubble on his chin, hoping the girls would drop their vow of celibacy. *The sooner, the better,* he thought, pouring boiling water into a red ceramic teapot.

Angus returned to the living room and poured jasmine tea into three waiting mugs. He glanced up and said to Alice and Nina, 'So, are you two going to help me or not?'

'Rupa and I had a quick discussion while you were in the kitchen,' said Nina, 'and we've decided to come to Iran with you.'

'Great news,' said Angus, smiling with relief.

'With two conditions,' said Alice, running a hand over her short dark hair.

'And they are?' Angus asked, studying her sharp-featured face.

'We want twenty-five thousand dollars each for whatever it is we have to do.'

Angus tilted his head. 'That's a lot of money.'

'It is,' agreed Nina, 'but that's how much Rupa and I will have to pay if we want to get a room in the ashram.'

'Okay, you're on. What's the second condition?'

Alice and Nina rose to their feet. Like creatures in a hurry to shed their skin, they peeled off their robes, threw them to one side, pointed to Angus's unmade bed and said in unison, 'You fuck us right now.'

Angus looked at their beautiful tanned bodies and said, 'Alright, I will.'

Nina and Alice giggled, and they both got on all fours. Alice turned and looked over her shoulder at Angus. 'Come on then,' she said. 'What are you waiting for?'

In the five seconds it took Angus to remove his clothes, his cock shifted gear from semi-erect to iron bar hard. He heard Bhagwan's voice echo in his head. *Sex is not an act: you are sex.*

Angus enjoyed the flight from Bombay to Tehran. It was the first time he'd ever travelled by plane.

After they'd passed through customs and immigration in Tehran's international airport, he took Alice and Nina into a clothes shop in the terminal building and bought them black, ankle-length burkas.

'It's roasting inside this bloody tent,' moaned Nina through her face slit.

'Don't start complaining,' admonished Angus, 'you haven't even begun to earn your money.'

Alice muttered from beneath her head covering. 'You still haven't told us what we have to do.'

'That's because I don't know,' said Angus, opening a yellow taxi's back door. 'Come on you two, get in.'

That evening, Angus allowed Alice and Nina to wear Western clothes when they went to meet Acid Mike in the Al-Zahra Hotel's lobby. The foyer seemed to be a meeting place for the affluent. European business-men in smart suits chatted with bearded clients, whose western-clad wives hovered in the background like colourful butterflies. There were large photographs of the Shah on the walls. Mike showed up bang on time. He'd tidied up his beard and tied his long, greying hair into a neat ponytail and stuffed it down the back of a blue cotton shirt's stiff collar. Mike's self-con-scious manner made it obvious to Angus that his friend felt uncomfortable in his creased, navy blue, pinstriped business suit. The four of them went up to the rooftop restaurant on the twelfth floor and ordered dinner.

Within minutes of sitting down at the table, the meeting turned into a heated argument. Mike declined to address Angus, Alice and Nina by their sannyasin names. Alice began referring to Mike as that 'arrogant asshole' and Nina refused to stop telling him he was full of shit. Angus looked out over downtown Tehran and listened to the hum of traffic rising from Shahid Malee Avenue. When he noticed that some of the restaurant's pa-trons were firing off volleys of aggravated looks in their direction, Angus put up his hands and said, 'Cool it, you guys, or we'll get tossed out of here. Mike, you can call us what you want.'

Nina started to protest. 'But I don't want to be called—'

'Shut the fuck up,' snapped Angus.

They ate their meal in a thick and loaded silence.

Mike pushed his empty plate to one side, wiped his mouth with a red serviette and started the argument up again by saying, 'You know, I was reading a Rajneesh book on the flight out here. I have to say that for some-one who is supposed to be beyond it all, your spiritual master likes to slag off the competition in the guru world.'

Oh, oh, thought Angus, *here we go again.*

Alice swallowed Mike's bait, hook, line and mantra. 'What the fuck do you know about it? Bhagwan is the master of masters. He's come down into this world to lead us out of the darkness.'

'That's what Jesus Christ was supposed to be doing,' said Mike, 'and two-thousand years down the line, the lights still haven't come on.'

'You're a cynical shit,' said Nina. 'Really attached to that big fat ego of yours, aren't you?'

41

Mike fired back. 'And you're not?'

Nina replied, 'I've surrendered my ego at Bhagwan's feet.'

Mike chuckled. 'What a load of bollocks. You guys are completely naïve. I suppose you also believe that all the free love that's happening in the ashram has got something to do with enlightenment as well.'

'Bhagwan says yes to everything,' said Alice, 'except repression, which is something no other master has ever done before.'

'That's what you think,' asserted Mike. 'There's nothing new in what Rajneesh is doing. In fact, he's playing the oldest game in the spiritual book.'

'What do you mean?' Angus enquired.

'Gurus employ various tricks to ensure their disciples' allegiance towards them,' explained Mike. 'To control a person's sexuality is to have great manipulative power over an individual's life.'

Angus protested. 'But Bhagwan lets us do what we want.'

'You don't honestly believe that, do you?' asked Mike.

Nina backed Angus up. 'Of course, he does. We all do.'

'Well, I don't,' said Mike, his face transforming into a mask of seriousness. 'Celibacy and promiscuity have one thing in common when it's happening around a so-called spiritual master.'

'And what's that?' Alice asked.

Mike answered. 'They minimise the guru's followers' possibilities of forming deep emotional bonds with each other. As a result, the emotional energy that would normally go into bringing up children is redirected towards the guru which is exactly what they want. On that level, gurus are no different from Mick Jagger.'

'Mick fucking Jagger?' said Nina, her eyes drilling holes into Mike's. 'What's he got to do with Bhagwan?'

Mike replied, 'Rock stars, charismatic gurus and influential politicians are power junkies, who need a regular fix of adulation to keep them smiling. If you don't believe me it just means you've never been to a good Stone's concert and experienced the massive outpouring of emotional energy directed at the stage. The fans get off on the energy also. Some even imagine themselves to be experiencing love. On a more subtle level, a guru's disciples make him feel like he's the centre of the universe.'

'What a load of shite,' declared Alice in a strong Glaswegian accent. 'Unlike Mick Jagger, Bhagwan doesn't have an ego.'

Mike asked, 'How the hell do you know that?'

'Hey, you guys,' said Angus, waving the palms of his hands in front of his friends' angry faces, 'in case you've forgotten, I'd just like to remind you we're in Iran and that we're here for a reason.'

'This wanker's on a big ego trip,' said Alice, raising her pointed chin towards Mike.

'Yeah, you think so? Well, fuck you! You stupid, gullible bitch,' snarled Mike, his voice rising in anger.

Angus shook his head, not quite willing to believe what he was hearing.

42

'Fucking hell, Mike, you should know better than that.'

Mike took in a deep breath, let out a long exasperated sigh and, after a momentary pause, said, 'I'm sorry, Angus.' He turned to Nina and Alice. 'I apologise. Alice, please forgive me for behaving in such a churlish manner. Nina, I can honestly say I deserve a slap on the face for my behaviour.'

Wallop! Nina punched Mike in the mouth.

Mike gasped, 'What the fuck?'

The maitre d' rushed over to their table and spoke quietly to them.

Angus, Alice, Mike and Nina looked up and stared blankly at the immaculately dressed headwaiter. None of them understood a word he said, although there was no mistaking the expression of ill-disguised contempt on the man's face. Mike, whose split bottom lip was dripping blood onto the white tablecloth, resorted to his old public schoolboy persona to inject a spot of decorum into the rapidly deteriorating scenario. 'I say,' said he, smiling across the Persian Gulf into a pair of bulging eyes, 'be a good chap and bring us a bottle of your best champagne.'

The head waiter glowered at Mike for a moment and then fired off his entire vocabulary of English words in one unambiguous shot, 'Please leave — *NOW!*'

It was just after dawn. Angus, Alice, Nina, Mike and his fat lip stepped out of a taxi in northern Tehran's Chamran Road. They checked into two double rooms on the twentieth floor of a five-star hotel that towers over a commercial area known as Evin.

Mike went for a cold shower and Angus pulled the curtains open so he could look out of the wall-to-wall window. Central Tehran spread out below him like a neon-coloured gridiron carpet. Across the street was Mollat Park, a vast, sun-parched expanse of ground, crisscrossed by asphalted walkways and dotted by tall cypress trees. The common was also home to the International Fair, a children's amusement park with gaily-painted rides. Over to his right and through the candy-coloured smog he could just make out a line of snow-capped peaks belonging to the Alborz Mountain Range.

Mike returned to the room. He was naked and drying his thinning, long hair with a dark-blue bath towel. Angus couldn't help noticing he had an exceptionally long penis.

'I could do with a bloody drink,' said Mike, 'those Scottish birds of yours bug the hell out of me.'

'Alice and Nina are two of the best people I know' said Angus, unlocking the mini-bar. 'Shit, there's only a bottle of water in here. I thought this was supposed to be a luxury hotel.'

'That's Muslim society for you,' commented Mike, pulling on a pair of white cotton trousers. 'Let's pick up the shrews and go check out the rooftop teahouse.'

◆ ◆ ◆

'Right then,' said Mike, looking across a wooden table at his three companions as they sat drinking iced coffee on the hotel's rooftop terrace, 'it's time to get down to brass tacks.' He ran a hand over his swollen bottom lip and glanced over to an extensive fenced-in compound, home to a dozen or so grey concrete buildings. The place was about two kilometres away. 'Over there is where Raj and Murphy are locked up.' Angus, Nina and Alice turned in unison. 'For Christ's sake,' hissed Mike, 'don't all look at the same time.' He shook his head. 'That's Evin Prison and by all accounts, it's a bloody hell hole.'

'So what's the plan?' Angus asked.

'First off,' replied Mike, 'I want Alice and Nina to nip out and get some passport photographs taken.' He glared at the young women. 'Now!'

'No problem,' said Alice, rising to her feet, 'keep your fuckin' wig on.'

'Pushy bastard,' mumbled Nina over her shoulder as she sauntered away from the table.

Once they'd disappeared into the elevator, Mike turned to Angus. 'They're beautiful, but talk about hard-boiled, man!'

Angus had to smile. 'Don't worry. As I've told you already, they don't come any better than Alice and Nina.'

'Are you absolutely certain we can trust them?'

'Hundred and one percent,' answered Angus, nodding his head thoughtfully. 'So break it down for me. How do you propose to go about busting the lads out of Evin prison?'

'The first thing we have to do is go out and buy a small van and a fast car. Did you bring the bread as I told you?'

'Yes sir, Colonel Mike, thirty grand printed in America.'

'Good, that'll be more than enough. Time for a scout about.'

Four hours later, Mike and Angus parked a white Peugeot van and a red Ford Mustang in an anonymous side street, fifteen minutes walking distance from their hotel. The Mustang's coachwork was showing a lot of rust, but its V8 engine was still producing the same horsepower and exhaust growl it had the day it rolled off the production line in Detroit a decade earlier.

Next, it was time to visit a hardware store. Mike ticked off the items on a shopping list that included a couple of conical straw hats that looked like they'd been made in China, two shovels, two pickaxes, four pairs of workman's gloves, a hammer, nails, a screwdriver and long screws, brass hinges, a saw, pliers, aluminium steps, a two-part ladder, industrial bolt cutters, three tubs of adhesive, ten cartons of candles, a jumbo-sized plastic funnel, four 50 litre plastic water containers, thirty pinewood planks, a dozen electric torches, twenty boxes of D size alkaline batteries and a twenty-metre length of thick nylon rope.

After they'd loaded their purchases into the back of the van, they drove north out of town towards the Alborz mountains. Twenty-five minutes later, Mike turned left along a little-used dirt track.

'Where the fuck are we going?' Angus asked.

Mike answered, 'I haven't a bloody clue. I'm letting my intuition guide me. Hey, follow your feelings. Isn't that what Bhagwan told you to do?'

Two kilometres down the track they arrived at a dead end. Mike parked the van by a massive limestone boulder. The sun was at its zenith and it was becoming hotter by the minute. They climbed to a high vantage point, sat down and scanned the deserted landscape with a pair of Nikon pocket binoculars.

'Perfect,' said Mike, when he was satisfied that there was no one else around.

'Now what?' Angus asked.

'We start digging,' replied Mike, jumping to his feet.

'In this fucking heat?'

'Listen, Angus, we're planning a jailbreak, not a Sunday school outing. If we get caught we'll be fucked, and I do mean fucked, as in Iranian sausage up the arse.'

'Thank fuck we bought gloves and hats.'

'Yes, matey, nothing quite like a bit of coordinated and careful planning.'

Eight hours, five tons of earth and broken rock later, Acid Mike was back in his hotel room. He was sitting at a desk, stooped over a pair of British passports, glueing Alice and Nina's photographs into them. Angus was in the bathroom, lying in a tub, soaking his aching body in roasting hot water.

There was a loud knock on their room door. Angus held his breath and listened to Mike speaking to a man who spoke with what sounded like a Yorkshire accent. *Who the fuck is that?* Angus wondered, getting out of the bath and turning on the cold water as he stepped under the shower.

He dressed and went into the bedroom. Mike and the stranger were sitting and drinking whisky at a small desk. They both stood when he entered the room.

'Angus,' said Mike, 'I'd like to introduce you to an old friend of mine. Detonator Dick, this is my good friend, Angus.'

Detonator Dick, thought Angus. *How does someone get a name like Detonator fucking Dick? Sounds like something out of a war comic.*

Dick stepped forward and offered a hand as broad as a frying pan, with gnarled knuckles the size of chestnuts. Angus shook it, half expecting to have his fingers crushed. Dick's grip was firm but gentle. He was an exceptionally tall man, around about six-foot-six, Angus estimated, with shoulders like a bull, a head like a breeze block, a nose that had been badly broken and not quite set right, and eyes like bullet holes. He had SAS written all over his scarred face.

'Pleasure to meet you, man.'

'Mutual, Angus.'

Angus hadn't a clue what Detonator Dick was doing in their hotel room, but he knew for certain that he wasn't the kind of man who was in Tehran to visit an archaeological museum — unless he intended to blow it up.

Angus left Mike and Dick to pore over an ordnance survey map that Dick had produced from a patch pocket on his dun-coloured combat trousers. It was Angus's job to deliver Mike's instructions to Alice and Nina, a task he wasn't looking forward to.

When he entered the women's room, it was obvious they'd been out on a little shopping spree, spending money they hadn't yet earned. There were bolts of orange, red and peach-coloured cloth splayed over their beds. Angus sat down on a chair by the window and explained to them what they had to do.

'No fucking way, Angus,' said Alice, standing in front of a mirror checking out how she looked, wrapped in blood-red silk. 'If you think we're going to wander up to a maximum-security prison and ask the governor for an appointment using fake passports, you've got another think coming.' Her voice had become strained, almost hysterical.

'What the fuck did you expect you were going to have to do to make the kind of money being offered?' Angus asked. 'Feed the ducks in the bloody park?'

'We're not stupid, man,' said Nina, rubbing her short, dyed-blonde hair with a white bath towel. She was wearing a pink miniskirt and matching blouse, revealing more than it covered. 'But if we get caught breaking the law in Iran, it won't only be Raj and Murphy who are banged up in prison.' She threw the towel on the floor, sat down on the edge of her bed and began biting her lacquered nails. 'We won't do it,' she mumbled from behind her right hand.

'Man, this is crazy!' Angus rose from his seat with an audible sigh, stood by the window and looked down at Chamran Road. There had been a cloudburst. Speeding cars were throwing up clouds of swirling spray behind them. 'I'll give you fifty grand each if you do what I ask of you.'

The two women turned towards Angus. From their perspective, it looked like he was staring out of the window. He wasn't. He was watching their reflection and observing their body language closely. Nina and Alice glanced at each other. Nina gave a slight nod to Alice. Alice nodded back. *Got them,* he thought.

'Missus Gupta, Missus Anderson, please be seated,' said Yusuf Rahimi, the governor of Evin prison. He motioned brusquely for the pair of beautiful women, who'd just entered his well-appointed office, to sit down on two functional wooden chairs, designed to make the user's backside go numb within the space of ten minutes. He rose to his feet and handed the foreigners their passports, having barely looked at them. 'What can I do for you?'

Alice explained, crossing her legs to expose slender tanned thighs.

'Impossible,' said the governor, after a moment's reflection. 'Visits to foreign prisoners must be arranged with the assistance of an Iranian lawyer. That is, unless...' He trailed off and left the situation open without committing himself.

Nina stood up and shrugged off her grey plastic raincoat to display full breasts, spilling out of a plunging neckline. She sat down again, sighed, opened her red leather handbag and placed a wad of crisp one-hundred-dollar bills on the green, leather-topped desk in front of her, beside a life-sized bronze bust of – Nina glanced at the head – Yusuf Rahimi. The man was vain. She ran her right hand through her long, extravagant blonde wig which, like the black dress she was wearing, had been purchased especially for the occasion. She raised her pretty face and fired a seductive smile across the quickly shrinking bureaucratic chasm that ran between her and Mr Rahimi.

The governor smiled back. He was a grey-bearded, middle-aged, stocky man who'd gone bald on top. He wore a spotless white shirt and green tie. His dark eyes peered out through a pair of uncommonly thick-rimmed glasses. Looking down the nose of his sharp-featured face at Mr Rahimi, from a framed portrait hanging on the wall behind where he sat, was Muhammad Reza Pahlavi, the Shah of Iran, a man who, like the underling sitting below him, was capable of ordering the execution of problematic people to maintain his grip on absolute power.

Mr Rahimi cocked his bushy eyebrows. His leather chair creaked as he leaned forward. He grabbed the money and made it disappear into a locked drawer quicker than it takes a conjurer to say a magic word.

The governor smiled broadly at the two young women and made no effort to avert his gaze from Nina's luscious, tanned cleavage. 'Well now, ladies, if you'll be so kind as to have a few minutes patience, I'll go and see what can be arranged. Oh,' he said, as if suddenly remembering something important, 'perhaps you could grant me a small personal favour.' He fixed Nina with a penetrating stare, began unbuttoning his fly, nodded and leered obscenely.

The air grew hotter and the walls of the room seemed to shrink as Nina and Mr Rahimi stared at one another. She groaned inwardly and licked her lips.

That evening, in Angus and Mike's hotel room, Alice and Nina were in tears when they described in detail what sort of condition Raj and Murphy were in.

Mike was dressed in a long, grey, cotton robe, one of four that he'd purchased earlier that day. 'Who the bloody hell is Dirty Ali?' he asked when the girls fell silent.

Angus took a slug from a pint-sized bottle of Irish whisky he'd paid eighty dollars for in Tehran's thriving black market. It tasted of charred wood. 'We smuggled Ali Khatib into Afghanistan on the bus back in seventy-three.'

'And?'

'Yeah, well...Ali was an Iranian opium addict who wormed his way into our confidence. He tried to rip us off in Mazar-e-Sharif. We caught him running away with our money, tied him up and dumped him in a pine forest. I had to haul Murphy off Ali to prevent him from murdering the rotten fucker. I'm surprised to hear the sleazy bastard is still alive.'

'Murphy told us that Dirty Ali lost an eye,' added Alice.

'That's something I'm not surprised to hear,' said Angus. 'Murphy booted him in the left side of the head and smashed his eyeball.'

Mike shook his head and rubbed his temples with his fingers. 'And now this Dirty Ali is working in the prison?'

Alice and Nina nodded like those cheap, bobble-headed dogs in cars' rear windows.

'Not only that,' said Alice, 'it was Ali who tipped off the customs about the bus's stash compartment.'

'And Ali's had Murphy tied to a table and fucked him up the arse at least a dozen times,' added Nina.

'Jesus fucking Christ!' Angus stood up and paced the room. 'We've got to get them out of there.'

'Easier said than done,' said Mike. 'How's Murphy handling all this?'

'Bit of a sore bum,' said Nina, 'but apart from that and losing a lot of weight he's as full of piss and vinegar as he ever was.'

'Good old Murphy,' said Angus.

'And Raj?' Mike asked.

'He's really fucked up, man,' replied Alice, beginning to sob. 'He... He can hardly walk. Ali's b-b-been battering the soles of his feet with an electrical cable.'

Mike grabbed the whisky bottle out of Angus's hands and poured himself a stiff drink. 'What are the chances of them getting a job outside of the prison buildings?'

Alice and Nina shrugged.

Mike looked thoughtful. 'That means you'll have to go back and talk to the governor again.'

Nina spat on the hotel room's carpeted floor. 'I'm not giving that slime-bag another blow job.'

'I'll do it if it helps to get Murphy and Raj out of there,' volunteered Alice. She turned to Angus. 'By the way, darlin', you don't need to give us the extra fifty grand. We'd do it for nothing if we had to. Wouldn't we, Subha?'

Nina didn't look so sure about that, but she nodded towards Angus in agreement.

Angus sat down on a padded armchair and held his head in his hands as if it weighed fifty tons.

'Come on, matey,' said Mike, patting him on the back, 'stiff upper lip and all that.' He picked up the phone and dialled a three-digit number. 'Hello, this is room twelve, zero, five.' He paused and listened. 'What do you mean you don't understand English?' He listened again. 'If you don't have two bottles of excellent champagne up here in the next five minutes, I'll have a word with the management.' Mike slammed the phone down. 'Idiot was taking the piss.'

Three minutes later, there was a gentle knock on the door.

Thanks to five thousand dollars and the suction power of Alice's pleasure-giving lips, Murphy and Raj were given an outside job four days later.

Raj was kneeling by a line of lettuces, pulling out weeds. He looked up at Murphy, leaning on a shovel as he puffed on a cheap cigarette. 'Do you really think they're going to bust us out of here?'

Murphy tossed a smouldering dog end on the freshly watered earth and ground it out with the heel of his rubber boot. 'Dead fucking right they are. Three days to go and we're outta here and the first thing I'm going to do is stop smoking. That shit's bad for your health.'

'You haven't told me much about your visit from Nina.'

'Yeah, that's because I've been thinking a lot about it,' said Murphy.

'I'm more interested to know how you feel about her visit.'

'She looked good enough to eat. No prizes for guessing where I would have started. I also felt shit about the way I'd treated her on our overland trip. How about you?'

'How about me, what?'

'How do you feel?'

'My feet are killing me.'

'Hey, Raj, so are my Himalayan piles. But you don't hear me complaining about it, do you? So shut the fuck up and stop moaning about your bloody feet.'

Raj took off his rubber boots and examined his feet. They were so swollen and bruised they looked like a pair of overripe aubergines. Raj began to weep. 'I... I was thinking of hanging myself last week.'

Murphy winced at the sight of his Indian friend's injuries. He thought about Sergeant Ali Khatib, the man who'd inflicted the damage with a thick electrical cable. 'I'm going to murder that bastard,' he swore to himself, 'if I get half a fucking chance.' He glanced at the lice crawling around on Raj's closely cropped head. 'Hey, man,' he said, 'if I ever hear you talking about suicide again, I'll kick your fat arse until it's the same colour as your purple feet.'

Raj said nothing.

'Do you fucking well hear me?'

'Aye, Murphy, I hear you. I'm no' deaf.' Raj replied, sounding more Glaswegian than he had in months.

A movement caught Murphy's eye. About fifty metres away, a guard in a grey uniform with a sub-machine gun slung over his left shoulder was walking along the side of the four-metre high, razor-wire-capped, sand-coloured perimeter wall. 'Look busy, Raj, here comes that piece of shit, Barzin. He'll be hustling me for a fag next.' Murphy grabbed his shovel and began turning over the sandy earth. 'Three days to go, Raj, three days to go.'

Angus, Acid Mike and Detonator Dick were sitting in the red Ford Mustang, across the street from Evin Prison's blue-painted, sliding steel gate. There was a broad grey sign above the gate written in four languages, one of them English. It said, EVIN HOUSE OF DETENTION. The place looked more like a warehouse from the outside than the hellhole it was reputed to be. Angus felt the misery seeping out through the walls like dampness in a dungeon. He gave an involuntary shudder.

'They're going to need a new front door in a couple of days,' said Dick, turning to face Angus in the back seat. Dick's face split apart in a wicked smile. He had more gold-capped teeth than a Chinese gambler.

'So, Dick, what's the story with these things?' Mike asked, picking up a black plastic walkie-talkie.'

'Right then,' said Dick, 'the one marked with the red tape is for the gate over there.' He glanced over at the prison's main entrance. 'The blue is for the watchtower and the green is the one you use during the getaway.'

'What does the green one do,' asked Angus from the back seat.

'It's a surprise, mate.' Dick chuckled over his left shoulder. 'Now, listen carefully. You turn these radios on by clicking this switch here.' Dick used a finger that was as thick as a German sausage to show what he was referring to. 'You detonate the explosives by punching in three numbers. One, one, one, is red. Two, two, two, is blue. Three, three, three is green. Don't press the green until you're well clear of the water tower.' He turned to Mike, gave him a conspiratorial wink, which was returned, and then asked, 'You got all of that?'

Mike nodded. 'Loud and clear, old chap.'

Dick ran a hand over the stubble on his square chin and added an afterthought. 'Whatever the fuck you do, don't switch these bloody things on until after you've dropped me off at the airport.'

'Don't worry, we won't,' assured Mike. 'Listen, Dick, is it alright if I square you up when I get back to Blighty?'

For a moment Dick's expression became thoughtful, and then he flashed a twenty-three caret golden smile. 'Your word is good enough for me, mate.'

The Mustang caught the attention of an armed guard, standing to one side of the prison gate. He raised his sub-machine gun and began to amble across the street. Mike drove away.

Detonator Dick caught a flight to London the following morning. On Wednesday afternoon, Angus and Mike drove the girls to the airport. They were booked on a Kuwait Airways flight to Bombay. After Alice and Nina checked in their baggage, the four of them stood in front of passport control.

Alice turned to Angus and said in an affectionate voice, 'So, swami, see you back in Pune.'

They embraced each other for a long time.

Nina looked at Mike. 'Sorry about punching you.'

'I deserved it,' said Mike, running a finger over his split lip. 'Anyway, it will serve as a fond memory until it heals.' He added, 'Angus was right, you two are wonderful women.'

Nina stepped forward. 'And you've got iron balls, Acid Mike.' She kissed him full on the lips. She stepped back. 'You'd make a great sannyasin.'

Mike grunted. 'You're bloody well joking!'

Nina let out a little laugh and walked off.

Angus was behind the Mustang's wheel as they drove back into Tehran. It was a warm day and all the windows were down.

'You know, matey,' said Mike, over the sound of rushing air, 'I feel like I made a mistake with Alice and Nina.'

Angus took his foot off the accelerator, pushed the clutch to the floor and shifted up a gear. 'Don't worry about it, man,' he advised. 'At least you've got the guts to admit you were wrong. We learn from our mistakes, right?'

Mike smiled and wrapped a black cotton scarf around his head. 'Yes, I suppose that's a sensible enough way to look at it.'

Angus fumbled in his shirt pocket and produced a cassette tape. It was the Rolling Stone's 'Exile On Main Street'. He jammed the audio tape into the Mustang's dust-covered player. The speakers were cracked, but 'All Down The Line' still sounded fantastic. Backed by the sound of a hot brass section, Jagger's famous lips blew out the song's lyrics, while guitarist Mick Taylor laid down a sizzling slide solo, which rang in the riders' ears like the call of the wild.

'Right on!' Mike hollered.

Lets open up the throttle, yeah...

Angus stepped down hard on the gas. The Mustang roared, fishtailed, straightened out and shot along the Haghani Modarres Highway.

By early evening, the last job of the day was done. Angus and Mike had filled the car's boot with provisions and stashed them in the hideout in the foothills of the Alborz Mountains.

The pieces were in place. Angus and Mike had an early night. They were getting ready to rock and roll — big time.

Murphy and Raj were pretending to be hard at work in the vegetable garden. Nearby, Barzin, their regular guard, was sitting on an oil drum. He was staring at a Playboy magazine with his jaw hanging slack. Close at hand was Barzin's semi-automatic rifle. The wooden-stocked weapon was leaning in an upright position against the prison's perimeter wall.

Murphy and Raj didn't have a watch but, when they heard a thunderous boom, they knew it was bang on five o'clock. They looked south to the prison's administration block. A thick column of black smoke was mushrooming up into the clear blue sky.

'Holy *ssshit!*' hissed Raj.

Murphy turned to him. 'Get ready to run for your fuckin' life.'

Barzin dropped the magazine, sprang to his feet, grabbed his rifle, glanced over to Murphy and Raj, shouted something incoherent and began hurrying away in the explosion's direction. The guard stopped at a group of prisoners, standing with their mouths open about a hundred metres away. Once again Barzin shouted and continued on his way, accompanied by a co-worker. His pace quickened when a concrete watchtower at the far end of the compound was rocked by a loud explosion. The prison was under attack.

'Now' barked Murphy, starting to sprint towards the wall.

Raj was hot on his heels, hobbling along as fast as his battered feet would carry him.

Angus's head bobbed up from behind the prison wall. He cut through a spiral of concertina razor wire with bolt cutters and lowered a knotted rope. Raj and Murphy grabbed a hold of it and clambered up the wall. The other prisoners began running towards them. When Murphy climbed down the ladder, leaning against the outside of the wall. He glanced at Angus, and said, 'Hi, long time no see.' He then grabbed the cutters and headed back up the ladder.

Angus shouted, 'What the fucking hell are you doing?'

Murphy called back over his shoulder, 'Souvenir hunting.'

Mike was gunning the Mustang's engine. Raj dived into the back seat. Murphy snipped off a length of razor wire and then helped two skeletal Iranian prisoners over the wall.

Angus screamed, 'For fuck's sake, Murphy, come on, man!'

Half a minute later, the Mustang was rocketing down a dirt track, leaving clouds of dust to billow up from its back wheels. Over the howl of the straining V8 engine, Angus could hear automatic gunfire. Bullets stitched a line of round holes across the boot. Spurts of dust kicked up in front of the car as some unseen guard blazed away at them with a machine gun.

'Get your bloody heads down,' hollered Mike as he rammed the gear stick into third.

The Mustang careened sideways into a street and Mike spun the worn, leather-covered steering wheel to his left. Sirens wailed behind them. Pedestrians on the concrete pavement turned and stared. The car sped by a massive water storage tower with reinforced concrete legs.

'Angus, get the walky-talky marked with green tape out of the glove compartment,' ordered Mike.

Angus did as he was told. 'Now what?'

'Punch in three, three, three and then hit the send button.'

Angus obeyed. Nothing happened.

Mike glanced at him. 'Pull out the bloody aerial, you fucking clown.'

Angus pulled out the metre long telescopic antennae, punched in the three digits, pushed the button and *boom!* Detonator Dick's surprise manifested itself.

'Wow!' Raj shouted from the back seat. 'How the fuck did you pull that off?'

Angus stuck his head out the open window, looked back and saw a waterfall pouring out of a huge hole in the water tower. In minutes the street would be transformed into a flowing river. Traffic, moving in the tower's direction, was coming to an abrupt halt and quickly being engulfed by rushing water. People were screaming and running. Mike overtook a bus. The Mustang's left wheels slammed against the pavement's kerbstones. Metal screeched. An aluminium hubcap flew off and smashed through a shop window.

Angus turned to his left and looked at Acid Mike. His friend's jaw was clenched. Sweat was pouring down his face. He was gripping the steering wheel as if his life depended on it. It did.

The Mustang swerved into a wide road with very little traffic. Mike accelerated away, hard. The bonnet was high, tail low, wheels spinning and pouring smoke. The V8 engine was roaring. Angus glanced over at the speedometer. The needle was off the clock. A strong smell of petrol fumes hit his nostrils. Murphy yelled from the back seat, *'Yeeeee haw!'*

Mike pulled into the dirt track that led down to the excavated hideout. He dropped Angus, Murphy and Raj off and sped away. He turned left onto the highway, drove for five minutes, turned right onto a deeply rutted trail, continued down it for another kilometre and then parked facing a deep ravine. Mike switched off the engine and stepped out of the car. He went around and opened the boot. There was an eruption of gas fumes. A fifty-litre plastic container had been punctured by bullets. It was still half full of petrol. He screwed the round top off and doused the car with hi-octane fuel. He dashed back to the driver's side of the car, opened the door and tossed the empty canister into the back seat. Bending forward, he disengaged the hand brake. Returning to the vehicle's rear, he began to push until the car's front tires were level with the edge of the gorge. Mike was gasping for breath. Quickly evaporating petrol fumes were rising up and making the hot air waver like a desert mirage. He took off his headscarf and tied it so it covered his mouth and nose. After removing the car's petrol cap, he stepped back a few paces, struck a match, set the matchbox on fire and tossed it through the open passenger's side window. The fuel ignited with a hissing whoosh and singed Mike's eyebrows off.

The car was burning like a red Ford Mustang covered in flaming petrol. Mike shielded his face with his arms and, using his booted right foot, sent the Mustang to its final resting place. It disappeared over the edge of the ravine. Hot metal shrieked. Acid Mike sprinted away. There was a dull thud. The Mustang had breathed its last. Behind him, thick black smoke rose from the gully.

Mike reached the main road, hid behind a boulder and watched a white police car shoot by with blue and red lights flashing. It took him an hour of ducking and diving behind bushes to reach the trail leading down to the hideaway. He walked backwards for a hundred metres and used a piece of brushwood to cover tyre tracks and footprints. The sun was setting when he knocked four times on the hideout's camouflaged roof. Angus pushed open a hinged trapdoor. Mike dropped into the shadows. The overhead door was pulled shut and it became as black as an undertaker's hearse.

The first part of Angus and Acid Mike's rescue mission had been accomplished successfully, but it was still a long way from over.

Jean unbuckled her seat belt, stood up and brushed food crumbs from her dark blue cotton dress. 'I'm dying to go to the toilet,' she said to me. 'I'll be back in a wee minute.'

I turned and watched Jean make her way down the aisle under the dim illumination provided by the business class section's recessed lighting. I then focused my attention on the small television monitor in front of me. The red line tracking the aircraft's course had now entered Turkish airspace and would soon be passing over Ankara. I leaned over Jean's empty seat and peered out of the portal. The plane was passing through a patch of turbulent air. All I could see were the aircraft's wing lights cutting a swathe through grey vapour. The aircraft wobbled, an electronic chime rang and then the red 'Fasten your seatbelt.' sign came on above my head.

Jean staggered back along the aisle. I stood up to let her pass. She flumped into her seat. 'Bloody hell,' she complained, tightening her seat belt, 'it's like being on the deck of a ship in high seas. So,' she said, turning to face me as I sat down beside her, 'Angus and his pals are hiding out in a hole in the ground. I like that Mike bloke, he sounds like a real man to me. As for Detonator Dick...' Jean let out a spluttering laugh. 'Are you sure Angus wasn't having you on when he told you all this back in Sri Lanka? I mean to say, Detonator Dick could be the name of a character in a kid's comic book.'

A smile slowly formed on my lips. 'I know what you mean,' I said with a chuckle, 'Detonator Dick sounds like Desperate Dan's brother. The thing is, Angus, showed me a photograph of Dick.'

'What did he look like?'

'A bit like a jug-eared Arnold Schwarzenegger with a broken nose.'

'But that could've been a photo of anyone. If you ask me your bloody brother wasn't beyond telling a few whoppers to beef up his stories.'

'I've told you before; don't speak about Angus like that.'

'Alright, alright, keep your hair on.' Jean made a point of glancing at my balding head. 'At least what little hair that you have left.'

'That's hitting below the belt. Baldness is a sign of virility.'

'Not in your case it isn't. There's been very little action from below your belt since we were blown up. Your dick hasn't exactly been detonating lately.'

'Don't rub it in, Jean. I'm all too aware of that. It's all those painkillers and antibiotics I've been taking.'

'Well if it keeps up — or down to be more precise — it's a different kind of medicine you'll be taking when we get back to Oban. I'm talking about those wee blue pills you can buy cheap on the internet.'

'I don't need to take Viagra to get an erection.'

'Aye, that'll be right. That's what all the middle-aged husbands say.'

'And how, might I ask, would you know about that.'

'Women don't just cook, bring up the kids and spread their legs; we use our tongues to communicate with each other — in case you haven't noticed.'

I stared at Jean, genuinely shocked. *'Spread your legs?* What kind of a way is that to be speaking?'

'The down to earth one,' she replied, leaning over to give me a fresh lipstick peck on the cheek. 'Anyway, what about Angus and the lads, how did they manage to get out of Iran? The whole country must have been looking for them.'

'You're right in assuming that. The thing is, Jean, they stayed in their hole in the ground for three weeks.'

5

RAZOR WIRE NECKLACE

'Three fuckin' weeks!' Murphy exclaimed, when Mike informed them how long he thought it necessary to remain in their underground bunker.

'In a couple of days,' Mike added by way of consolation, 'I think things will have settled enough for us to nip out for a breath of fresh air under the cover of darkness.'

Angus looked towards a sudden flare, as Murphy struck a match to light a cigarette. 'I didn't know you smoked.'

Murphy cleared his throat. 'I'll stop when this packet is finished.'

Angus lit a couple of candles with a plastic lighter. He reached into a cardboard box and pulled out a bottle of Johnnie Walker Black Label. 'Fancy a wee bevvy?'

Murphy's face crinkled into a big smile. 'Does the Pope say prayers? I've been dreaming about this moment for months. Pass me that bottle and I'll sing you all a real song.' He nudged Raj with a rubber-booted foot. Raj was curled up on the floor. 'Hey, Gunga fuckin' Din,' said Murphy, 'wake up. It's time to drink your medicine.'

Raj groaned, sat up and grunted, 'My feet are killing me.'

Murphy's eyes rolled upwards. 'Here we go. I've been listening to this guy complaining for months.'

The bottle went round twice and then, suddenly, Mike hissed, '*Ssssh!*'

The sound of an approaching vehicle with a clicking diesel engine filtered through the sand and brush-covered wooden roof. Mike blew out the two candles, plunging the hideout into darkness. The four fugitives sat in complete silence and listened. The diesel engine was switched off. Car doors slammed. Men's gruff voices argued. Heavy boots crunched on gravel. Somebody took a long piss on the roof. It was so quiet Angus heard the man grunt in relief and pull up his fly's zipper. Paranoia infected Angus's mind like a rampant germ. *Fucking hell,* he thought, *if that bastard stands on the roof and realises its hollow underneath, we're fucked.*

A quick burst of radio static, a shout, hurried footsteps, the grumble of an engine starting, car doors slamming, and then the vehicle drove away. There was a communal force-four sigh of relief. Silence reigned in the darkness. Minutes seemed to last an age. Mike said, 'That was too close for comfort.'

'Where's the whisky bottle?' Murphy asked.

'Here,' said Angus.

Glug, glug, glug.

'Hey, take it easy on the firewater,' cautioned Mike's voice. 'We've only one full bottle left.'

Murphy smacked his lips. *'Mmmh,'* he hummed, 'delicious.' He let out a loud satisfied belch. 'Where did you pick this up?' he asked, shaking the contents of the almost empty bottle.

'Bombay duty-free,' answered Angus. 'We've been saving it for a special occasion.'

Murphy chuckled, *'A special occasion?* Is that what you call this?'

Raj groaned. 'My feet are on fire.'

'Don't you start,' warned Murphy.

Angus asked, 'Are you two still not married?' The alcohol he'd consumed was making him drowsy. He lay down and stretched out in his corner of the bunker. On the edge of sleep, he heard someone pass wind with a wet bang.

Murphy's voice spoke out in the darkness. 'For fuck's sake, Raj, what a bloody hum, are you trying to gas us to death?'

Raj made a whoopee cushion sound.

Mike laughed first, and then they all did.

Thus began their first night in the hideout.

Forty-eight hours passed. The underground refuge was stinking like a blocked toilet. The fugitives had been using an aluminium funnel to channel their human waste into a fifty-litre plastic canister, which Raj had knocked over a few hours before when nature called.

Acid Mike stood up and banged his head on the roof. He pushed the trapdoor open with a shovel. Cool air rushed in, bringing welcome relief from the pong. Angus held the aluminium steps and Mike clambered out of the hole. The Englishman's head appeared haloed by starlight. 'I say chaps, the coast's clear. Anyone care for a game of croquet?'

There was a rush to get out of the cramped pit.

The four friends sat around under a clear, star-speckled sky. To the south, lights twinkled and a neon glow rose from downtown Tehran. It was cold. Angus dropped down into the hideout and handed what blankets they had up through the trapdoor.

Murphy tapped Mike on the shoulder and asked, 'What about opening up the second bottle of whisky?'

'Sorry, Murphy, I think it would be wise to save it for an emergency.'

'A fucking emergency? I'm freezing my nuts off out here.'

Angus sat down between them. 'Mike's right, Murphy, don't argue with him.'

'But I'm—'

'Hey, Murphy,' said Raj, looking away from the heavens and scratching his shaved head, 'if it wasn't for these two, you'd still be eating mouldy bread for breakfast, lunch and dinner, so shut the fuck up.'

Angus, Mike and Murphy began doing callisthenic exercises to keep warm. Raj folded a blanket, sat down on it and proceeded to bend his body into a variety of difficult Hatha yoga *asanas*, followed by *pranayama* breathing techniques. This became the four fugitives' nightly routine until the time drew around for them to move on.

The long days in the hideout were spent playing poker, eating, sleeping and holding endless discussions about all and everything. Angus's involvement with Bhagwan Shree Rajneesh was a hot topic. Mike stuck to his hardline anti-guru stance. Murphy thought the idea of an ashram full of beautiful women, who wanted to fuck their way to enlightenment, was a brilliant one. Raj wanted to go to Pune to check out Bhagwan for himself. Angus had described his first meeting with the master in great detail, as though needing to reaffirm it in his mind — so far away did such a beautiful experience seem to him in his current situation.

Raj and Murphy gave vivid accounts of how they'd been busted after driving into Iran from Afghanistan. Murphy told how Ali Khatib tipped off the Iranian customs about the bus's secret stash compartment. Raj explained the legal process that led up to them being sentenced to twenty years in prison and portrayed the inhumane hardships they'd endured at the hands of Sergeant Ali Khatib.

Angus asked, 'How the hell did Dirty Ali, an irredeemable opium addict, get a job as a sergeant in Evin prison in the first place?'

Murphy shrugged. 'Fuck knows. What does it matter? All I know is that he did, and we paid for it.'

For the first and only time in his life, Angus saw Murphy break down and cry as he described being sodomised by Dirty Ali. When Murphy's sobs reached the point of making his words incomprehensible, Raj took over.

'We met this teenager called Nasser,' began Raj. 'He was done for car theft. They locked him up with us and about twenty other guys, mostly political prisoners, in a cell that was built for four inmates. We had to take turns sleeping on the floor because there was so little space. Everyone had to shit and piss in buckets. Anyway, this kid Nasser was sentenced to five years. He'd been banged up with us for a week when one day Dirty Ali opens the cell door. Ali grabs Nasser by the ear and hauls him off to a place called 'The Infirmary'.' Raj shook his head, remembering. 'Nobody in our cell slept that night because we could hear Nasser screaming his fuckin' head off. We never saw or heard of him again.'

'So you think this Sergeant Khatib did away with the boy?' Mike asked.

Murphy had by now reigned in his emotions. 'Of course, he did. He's a murdering bastard.' He picked up the length of razor wire he'd cut as a souvenir from the top of the prison wall. 'That piece of shit, Ali Khatib, is going to get what's coming to him one day soon.'

A thick silence fell upon the four friends. Something was stirring in the back of Angus's mind, an elusive darting thought that, when he tried to focus in on it, faded away like an unsettling dream. He glanced over at Murphy. His old friend's eyes glinted like a cat's in the candlelight. There was something in that reflection that Angus both loved and feared. *Murphy's killed before. Is he planning to do it again?* Angus asked himself. He shivered. 'Hey, Mike,' he called, 'how about opening that second bottle of whisky?'

Mike had been busy with his thoughts. He let out a long sigh and turned to face Angus. He nodded in such a way as to signal to him he too knew that something wicked was percolating in the murky shadows of Murphy's vindictive mind. Mike passed the full bottle of whisky to Angus and said nothing.

A full moon rose into a cloudless sky. The fugitives had now been in hiding for nineteen days. Familiarity does not only breed contempt in regards to people, it also works in the same way with one's surroundings — no matter how dangerous they are.

Murphy had constructed a semi-circle of large rocks. 'It would make a perfect place to light a fire,' he suggested to the others. When he registered their silent resistance to the idea, he said, 'Come on guys, it's fucking freezing. I'm not saying we should light a bonfire, just a wee campfire to heat our hands.' He nodded towards the curved pile of rocks. 'If we do it over there nobody will notice.'

Murphy's persuasion won out and soon the four of them were seated around a small campfire, rubbing their hands and staring into the flames. The situation would have been ideal had it not been for the fact that they were fugitives.

Half-an-hour passed. Nature called by applying pressure to Angus's bladder. He stood up and walked over to a nearby bush to relieve himself. While pulling up the zipper on his jeans, he looked over in the road's direction. He was shocked to see a car's headlights moving down the dirt track. He rushed back to the campfire. 'Fucking hell,' he shouted, 'there's a car coming!'

Everyone jumped to their feet and kicked sand over the fire. They ran over to the hideout, dropped into it, landing on top of each other. Angus pulled the trapdoor shut with a nylon rope. A car drew into the clearing about five metres from where they were located.

It wasn't the police. It wasn't the army. It was a pair of backseat lovers. They were soon going at it like wild animals. Shrieks and grunts began to erupt out of the car, rocking and bouncing on its springs like a carnival ride. At what sounded like the peak of a celebration of unbridled lust, Murphy stood on the foldable steps and peeked out from under the trapdoor. He dropped the hatch and spoke into the darkness. 'Can't see a thing. The windows are all steamed up.'

Twenty minutes later, the car started up and, after what sounded like a six-point turn, the engine noise faded into the night.

◆ ◆ ◆

The following afternoon, the sun was barely visible through an arid haze that had moved in from Tehran's direction. It was agreed that it was time to make a move. They would travel in pairs. Mike would go with Raj and Angus with Murphy. Four matches were drawn to decide who left first. Raj pulled the short match.

Mike rubbed light brown vegetable dye into his pale bearded face and hands. Then he and Raj put on long grey robes. They wrapped black scarves around their heads to form slipshod turbans. Mike bowed from the waist and with a flourish of his hands said, *'Assalaamu aleikum.'* (Peace be unto you.)

'Wa aleikum assalem wa rahmattulah wa barakatuh.' (And upon you the peace and mercy of God and his blessings), chorused his friends, delivering their word perfect, well-practised response.

'Right then,' said Mike, 'we'll meet up in Turkey, outside of Ankara's main railway station. Let's make it nine o'clock every morning right in front of the main entrance,' he suggested. 'If, after two weeks from today, nobody shows up, the other two head back to England. We can meet up at my place in Notting Hill Gate. What do you say?'

Everyone present agreed.

Under the cover of darkness, Mike and Raj set off on the first leg of their journey west.

The next day, Angus and Murphy sat around in the hideout, preparing for their departure in the evening. Angus packed his rucksack with dried fruit, biscuits, bottles of water, money and the false passport Mike had provided him with. Murphy used pliers to twist the ends of a length of razor wire round two pieces of wood. Angus knew what he was making, but said nothing.

Early evening, Angus and Murphy stood outside their underground refuge facing each other. They were both wearing identical grey cotton robes, their bearded faces tanned with vegetable dye.

Murphy stood back from Angus. 'You look like Ali Baba.'

Angus chuckled. 'Aye, right, and you look like one of the forty thieves.'

Murphy kicked the trapdoor shut, slapped Angus on the back and said, 'Let's get the fuck outta here.'

It was 3 a.m. when they reached Tehran's northern outskirts. The few pedestrians they passed on the street paid no attention to them. They entered a deserted building site and took shelter in a half-finished office block that had rectangular holes for windows.

Murphy sat down on a pile of bricks, lit a cigarette, leaned back against a freshly plastered wall and studied the electric wires sticking out of a hole in the ceiling for a minute or so. He then turned to Angus and said, 'You don't have to go through this with me, you know.'

'Through what with you?'

'Come off it, man. Don't play dumb with me, because you're not very good at it.'

Angus ran a hand across his short beard. 'Listen, man, I've come this far with you and I'm not going to back out of it now.'

Murphy spoke slowly and deliberately, considering each word before it was uttered. 'Even if it means killing that dirty bastard, Ali Khatib?' The glare from an orange street light filtered into the room, making his eyes glow like fireballs. He tossed his half-smoked cigarette into a disorderly stack of rusty scaffolding poles, nodded towards Angus and enquired, 'Are you fucking well sure about this?'

The air hung heavy with the smell of damp cement and plaster. Angus looked away from his friend's intense gaze and remained silent. A tingle of dread crept over his scalp and a cold wind passed through the building, chilling him to the core.

Evin prison's main gate hadn't changed much in appearance, despite Detonator Dick's two charges of Semtex plastic explosive having blown holes in it three weeks previously. The replacement gate was painted the same light blue colour as its predecessor.

It was exactly six in the evening. Angus was leaning against a brick wall, approximately one hundred metres away from the prison gate. Its steel wheels rumbled as it was pushed aside. About twenty grey-uniformed personnel filtered out of the prison and dispersed along the street.

Angus peeped out from behind the newspaper he was pretending to read. He hadn't seen Ali Khatib in over two years, but recognized him immediately. Ali still had the same shuffling walk. He'd put on weight and his left eye's empty socket was covered by a black leather patch.

Murphy nudged Angus with the leather-bound copy of the Koran, which he'd purchased earlier that day from a shop selling religious paraphernalia. They proceeded to follow Ali at a discreet distance. Sergeant Khatib walked a block, crossed Chamran Road, wandered past the amusement park and then entered Mollat Park. He ambled along a straight asphalt pathway and stopped to pat a little boy on the head who'd kicked his football into a duck pond that looked like a swamp.

It was getting dark by the time Ali exited the park. He crossed a busy traffic intersection and entered a narrow street, lined by four-storey apartment blocks. He pushed open an unlocked door on the fourth building to the left. Angus and Murphy quickened their pace and arrived outside the grey, cement-rendered edifice in time to see a light go on in a third-floor window.

Murphy turned to Angus and flashed him a wicked smile. 'Our wee birdie's come home to roost.'

Angus looked up and down the quiet street, lined by parked cars. 'Now what?'

'We go back to the park,' answered Murphy, 'and feed the fucking ducks.'

'What with?' Angus asked.

'I don't know,' replied Murphy. 'You can read the Koran if you get bored.'

'But it's written in Parsi.'

Murphy looked at Angus with squinted eyes. 'For fuck's sake, man, I'm joking.'

It was nine o'clock. Murphy and Angus returned to the apartment block and walked up three flights of stairs. Murphy pushed the brass handle down on Ali's front door. It clicked open. He took his razor wire garrotte out of the cloth satchel strapped across his chest, glanced at Angus, nodded and tiptoed into the flat. Angus followed close on his heels. The first thing he noticed was the smell of opium smoke.

Ali Khatib was settling down for the evening. He took a long draw on his faithful opium pipe and then set it down on a conveniently placed brass coffee table. He kicked off his curly-toed leather slippers and leaned forward to switch on a small black and white television set. A great admirer of royalty, he'd probably been looking forward to watching this programme all day long. It was a documentary about Britain's royal family. To the sound of 'Land Of Hope And Glory', the Queen of England appeared on the screen. She was wearing a glittering crown on her head and speaking Parsi. The documentary had been dubbed especially for this broadcast. Tears came to Ali's eye at the splendid sight of Her Majesty the Queen going about her royal duties. Ali Khatib believed that in a previous incarnation he'd been a monarch himself, and that's why he always cried when viewing royal personages on television. When he heard the familiar click of his front door's lock, Ali slowly began to turn in his armchair, reluctant to take his attention away from the TV set. Bewilderment creased his face when he looked up at a tall man with strangely coloured skin, wearing a black turban and a grey robe. There was a cold metallic look in the stranger's eyes, like those of a nocturnal predator.

'Good evening, Sergeant Khatib. Just thought I'd pop in for a surprise visit, like,' said Murphy, smiling like an old friend.

Ali Khatib muttered something incomprehensible. 'Shoma ahleh koja—'

Something slipped over Ali's head and cut into his neck before he uttered another word. It was a razor wire necklace.

Ali thrashed like a hooked salmon. He clawed frantically at the garrotte as it tore into his windpipe. He tried to scream, but all that escaped his lips was a horrifying gurgle that sounded like a blocked drain. His legs began jerking wildly in a death jig. As his brain burnt off the last of its oxygen molecules, a military brass band blared from the television as they marched past London's cenotaph in Whitehall on Armistice Day, playing a rousing version of 'God Save The Queen'. The last words Ali Khatib heard before he left the earthly plane were delivered by Murphy. 'God isn't going to save you.

You evil fuckin' bastard.'

Weakened by months of meagre rations, Murphy still had the strength in his arms to pull the barbed wire through Ali's neck cartilage. Had it not been for the cervical vertebrate, Murphy would have decapitated his persecutor. When the job was done, he left the garrotte embedded in Ali's ruined neck. Murphy stepped forward, knelt in front of Ali Khatib and looked into his right eye. It was bulging out like that of a putrid fish. Light reflections, cast by the blaring television, flickered on its glassy surface. Ali's purple tongue protruded about three inches out of his wide-open mouth, upper dentures hanging at a lopsided angle. His face was twisted into a permanent gargoyle's grimace. Thick blood oozed down the front of his grey cotton shirt.

Murphy glanced over at Angus, whose face was as white and blank as a sheet of paper. He was leaning slack-jawed against the room's doorframe. Murphy lit a cigarette, blew a cloud of smoke into the room and smiled, although the corners of his mouth barely moved.

Angus smelled the ammoniacal tang of old man's urine. Terror-stricken, Dirty Ali had emptied his bladder during his final moments alive

'Switch that fucking shite off,' said Murphy, nodding towards the television, where The Queen was tapping an aged man in a military uniform on the shoulder with a shiny sword.

Angus did as requested and then, moving like a zombie, approached the living room window. The Venetian blind was drawn closed. He prised horizontal plastic slats open with a finger and peeped outside. Apart from a stray dog, cocking a leg against a lamppost, the street was deserted.

Murphy returned to the hall, locked the front door and entered the narrow kitchen. Angus followed closely behind.

Murphy sat on a black leather barstool and said to Angus, 'Check the fridge. I'm fucking starving.'

'How can you be hungry at a time like this?'

'Stop fucking around and do what you're told.'

'Fuck you, man,' said Angus over his shoulder. 'Stop ordering me around. It was me who bust you out of prison — remember?' He pulled the fridge's white-enamelled door open. A repulsive stench assaulted his nose. He let out a choked cough and then slammed the door shut. *'Fuckin' shit!'*

'What?'

'There's somebody's head in the refrigerator.'

Murphy hopped off the barstool and opened the fridge door. He stared for a moment then emitted a bitter chuckle. 'Hi Nasser,' he said, 'we were wondering what happened to you.'

Angus had forgotten the name. 'Who the fuck's Nasser?'

Murphy gently closed the fridge door. 'Remember, the kid Raj told you about? The one Ali hauled out of our cell a few months ago.'

'Jesus Christ,' gasped Angus, 'Let's get the fuck outta here.'

'What's the hurry?'

'*What's the hurry?* We're in an apartment in Tehran with a dead guy in the living room and a human head in the fridge. That's *the fucking hurry!* As if we're not in enough trouble already.'

Murphy picked up a set of car keys from the kitchen table. A Mercedes star dangled from the metal ring. 'We should check this place out first.'

'What the fuck for?'

'These for a start,' answered Murphy, dangling the keys. 'They might be our ticket out of here. Besides, it's getting late. We should wait till dawn before we move.'

Murphy found a wad of hundred dollar bills and a roll of Iranian rials in a drawer. Angus discovered a walnut-handled Colt .45 in a scarred black leather holster hanging inside a wardrobe door.

'Gimme that,' said Murphy when he caught sight of the revolver. Electric light glinted off its five-inch blue steel barrel. He clicked back the hammer and spun the chamber clockwise to check the action. The ratchet whirred and clicked like a rattlesnake throwing a tantrum. He looked closely and noticed the six lead-tipped bullets had a cross cut into their snubbed noses to ensure that they quartered upon entering a body. 'Dum-dums,' declared Murphy. 'The nasty bastard loaded his gun with dum-dum bullets.' He returned the well-oiled relic to its holster, pulled up his robe, strapped the thick leather belt around his slim waist, tightened the brass buckle, turned to Angus and said, 'Check it out, Tonto. I'm the good, the bad and the ugly all rolled into one.'

Ribald laughter rose from the street outside.

Angus stared at his friend, thinking that Murphy hadn't changed much. As selfish as ever, there was an air of brutal ruthlessness about him, thinly veiled by his nonchalant attitude.

They sat in the kitchen. Murphy chain-smoked. Angus grew increasingly impatient to leave.

Dawn was not far off. Murphy gently closed and locked the apartment's front door. He broke the key off in the lock.

The sky was lightening to the east. They quietly walked down the street, stopping at a white Mercedes saloon with rusty bumpers and a broken oblong headlight. Angus unlocked the driver's side door. He ducked his head and slid onto the worn leather seat. He quickly racked the seat back and adjusted the rearview mirror. He leaned over and opened the passenger door. Murphy got into the car and sat down beside him. Angus stuck the key in the ignition, switched on the wipers to clear condensation from the cracked windscreen and turned the key. The engine wouldn't start.

Murphy looked at the dashboard, tapped an orange light with a white coil printed on it, and glanced at Angus. 'You fucking nig-nog, it's a diesel. You have to preheat the elements before the car will start.'

'Oh, right. Never driven one of these before.' Angus turned the key halfway, waited twenty seconds until the orange light went out and turned the ignition all the way. The engine grumbled and coughed. The exhaust popped and sputtered. And then the engine began chugging away as though holding a monotonous conversation with itself. Angus glanced at the fuel gauge. 'The tank's almost full.'

'Great,' said Murphy, 'drive carefully and stick to the speed limit.'

'How am I going to do that?' Angus asked as he pulled away from the curb. 'I can't read the road signs.'

'How about driving slowly?' Murphy suggested.

'Why didn't I think of that?'

The two friends chuckled and headed west out of Tehran.

Thirty-six hours and a thousand kilometres later, Angus parked the Mercedes outside of a white mosque in a quiet side street in Bazargan, a small town close to the Turkish border. He left the key in the ignition in the hope a thief would notice it and steal the car. Angus stood looking up and down the street. 'Last time we were here there was snow on the ground.'

Murphy wiped sweat from his brow with a dirty rag. 'Yeah, things have changed in the past couple of years. We're headed in the opposite direction and our good old magic bus is history.'

'So what are we going to do now?' Angus asked.

'Well,' replied Murphy, 'I don't think Santa Claus and Rudolf the red-nosed reindeer are going to show up to give us a ride on their sleigh, so I suggest we get the fuck out of here. Let's go.'

Angus and Murphy walked along a stretch of road, lined by parked trucks. They soon found themselves on the town's outskirts, heading in a westerly direction. They were approximately twenty kilometres from Turkey. All that stood between them and freedom was the high mountain range forming a natural border between the two neighbouring countries.

During their car journey, they'd stopped off at roadside shops to purchase provisions and items necessary for a mountain trek. These were carried in rucksacks strapped to their backs. They had jeans on under their rumpled robes and wore workman's boots. They'd crossed the language barrier and one police checkpoint by pretending to be pilgrims who'd taken a vow of silence. The big black Koran that Murphy carried with him at all times had added credence to their ploy. Their deception was wearing thin because they'd run out of vegetable dye. Pale skin was showing through their streaky makeup jobs.

By early evening, they'd reached the foothills. Angus sat on a dry stone dyke and began to undo his bootlaces.

'My feet are—'

'Don't start,' said Murphy, cutting Angus off. 'I had to listen to Raj moaning about his sore feet for months. So, you're just going to have to grin and bear it, because any complaints on that level will be falling on deaf ears.' He pointed to a sparse pine forest about two kilometres away. 'Keep your boots on until we reach those trees over there.'

Angus sneezed. 'Come on then. We better arrive there before it gets dark.'

They passed a dilapidated farmhouse where a little boy was chasing a clucking red rooster around a cobbled yard. The dark-haired child looked up when the strangers walked by and ignored Angus's wave. From somewhere inside the house a man's voice called out, prompting the fugitives to quicken their pace.

The sun was setting when they reached the edge of the forest. They continued walking for another twenty minutes until they came across a small clearing sheltered by granite boulders. There was a small circle of blackened rocks where previous visitors had lit a fire. Angus sat down by it and took off his boots. Murphy gathered a bundle of dry branches and acorns. He dumped it at Angus's blistered feet.

'Start breaking these up,' said Murphy. 'It's going to get cold. I'll collect some more wood and then we'll get a wee fire on the go once it's dark.'

Half an hour later, the two friends were sitting by a small blaze, waiting for tin mugs full of water to come to the boil to make tea.

'Ah,' sighed Murphy, 'the outdoor life, you cannae beat it.'

Angus coughed and wiped his nose on the sleeve of his dirty grey robe. 'I think I'm coming down with the flu.'

'Better get something hot inside of you,' suggested Murphy, using the end of his turban to lift the bubbling mugs away from the fire. 'Maybe you should take some of those antibiotics Mike gave us. We can't afford for you to get sick.'

Angus coughed again. 'I don't want to take antibiotics. They make me feel weak.'

'Suit yourself. You're going to need all of your strength to cross those mountains.'

'You're not joking,' said Angus, huddling closer to the fire. 'They didn't seem so big from a distance. Now we're closer to them, they look massive.'

'I reckon some of the peaks are over twelve thousand feet,' added Murphy.

'How will we get over them?'

Murphy shrugged and tossed a small log into the fire. 'We'll find a shepherd's path and follow it into Turkey.'

'How can you be sure that we'll find a path?'

'Hey, Angus, there's very little you can be sure of in this life. We got this far, didn't we? I thought that fucking guru of yours told you to live in the moment.'

Angus nodded, sipped on his tea and stared into the fire.

Murphy was right. It was just after dawn when they found a narrow path that wound up into the mountains. He'd been wrong in assuming that it would bring them over the mountains into Turkey. By midday, it entered a narrow chasm that led to the foot of a sheer cliff.

Angus looked up at the towering wall of rock, shook his head, sneezed, turned to Murphy, who was scratching his head, and asked, 'Now what?'

'Don't look at me like that,' said Murphy.

'Like what?'

'Like I'm some kind of fucking idiot.'

Angus started to retrace their steps.

By late afternoon, they'd been walking along another path for two hours. It began to ascend through a broad gulley that cut between two steep-sided mountains. Up ahead, snow-capped peaks glowed orange as the sun neared the horizon. There were very few trees. They collected any small pieces of firewood they came across.

Angus dropped his pile of wood when they reached a bend in a small stream. 'I'm finished,' he declared. 'Let's call it a day.'

A fire was lit and Angus began to cook porridge in an aluminium pot. The breeze changed direction and blew smoke into his face, bringing on a fit of chest-wracking coughs.

'Man,' commented Murphy, 'that doesn't sound so good.'

Angus spluttered. 'It doesn't feel so g-g-good either.' He let out a shuddering sigh.

'You want some antibiotics?'

Angus shook his head at Murphy's offer and stirred the porridge, wishing he had a bottle of whisky.

Darkness descended. A chilling wind began to howl along the gully, prompting the two friends to use up their firewood supply in a relatively short time. They only had a woollen blanket each to stave off the cold. They sat huddled together, gazing into the fire's dying embers until Angus lay down on the hard ground and fell into a fitful sleep. He woke up in the middle of the night. The fire was dead, and he was feverish. He curled his body into the warm stones to stop his body from shivering. It didn't help.

As soon as it was light, they strapped on their rucksacks and headed up into the mountains. By midday, every bone, muscle, tendon and ligament in Angus's body was aching. He paused and looked up ahead. Murphy was a grey dot set against a steep, greyish-brown incline composed of gravel and sediment. The air was still. Even though he was half-a-kilometre away, Angus could hear the small avalanches of stones tumbling away from Murphy's skidding boot soles as he scrambled over the moraine. Angus estimated that if he caught up with him, they'd reach the snowline in approximately two hours. He coughed up a big gobbet of phlegm. His lungs felt like they were coated in sandpaper. The thin air made him feel light-headed. He gritted his teeth and began to scramble up the steep slope, using his hands to pull himself upwards.

After a hard day in a mountainous hell world, Angus clambered over a rise and was confronted by a small lake, backed by snow-capped peaks. The lake's waters were motionless and reflected the scenery as perfectly as a mirror. Murphy was sitting beside a dead tree and waved when Angus came into view. Despite feeling feverish and exhausted Angus could still appreciate the grandeur and beauty of his lofty natural surroundings. A long way off in the distance to his right he could see the conical peak of Mount Ararat in Turkey. He stumbled in Murphy's direction and flumped down beside him.

'How you doing?' asked Murphy, lighting a cigarette with a match.

Angus let out a spluttering cough. 'I thought you said you were going to quit smoking.'

'I will when we get to Ankara. Anyway, it's your health that we need to be concerned with right now. You look like shit.'

Angus wiped a sheen of sweat away from his brow with the back of his right hand and said, 'I feel like shit.'

Murphy looked around. 'This tree is the only thing that will burn around here. We should find a sheltered spot, make a fire, cook some grub, wrap you up and sweat that fever out of you.'

Angus smiled weakly. 'I'm glad somebody's in charge of the situation.'

They set up camp beside a small cave about a hundred metres from the lake's shore. The fissure was not very deep and there was only enough flat space for one person to lie down. As soon as they were out of direct sunlight it became bitterly cold.

'You make a fireplace,' said Murphy, 'and I'll see what I can do about busting up that dead tree.'

Angus began to form small rocks into a circle. He could hear Murphy chopping at the tree with a hatchet. Angus stood up and watched his old friend at work. Murphy was going at it like a clockwork lumberjack. All that was missing was a large key in his back. When Angus saw there was enough wood to be collected, he wandered over to the lakeside. He was feeling weak at the knees.

'Come on, man,' said Murphy, 'pull yourself together and get a fire on the go. I'm starving.'

Arms loaded with firewood, Angus stumbled back to the campsite. He used a page out of Murphy's Koran to set light to the kindling. There was no text on the sheet of crumpled paper, but he knew that if Murphy saw him tearing a page out of his holy book he'd throw a fit. Murphy was beginning to view his leather-bound copy of the Koran, embossed with gold leaf script, as some kind of lucky talisman.

The fire caught and wisps of smoke rose into the thin air. Angus returned to the lake with an aluminium pot in hand to collect water. He called out, 'Do you think this water's safe to drink?'

Murphy didn't answer Angus's question immediately. He dropped his axe, wiped the sweat from his brow, turned in a circle, checked out the pristine landscape, rubbed his bearded chin thoughtfully, tilted his head, smiled sardonically and said, 'There doesn't appear to be any obsolete atomic warheads and nerve gas dumps around here, or any leaky nuclear power plants for that matter. You never know, though. Damn it, old fruit, I wish I hadn't left my Geiger counter behind in Evin prison.' He raised a hand to shade his eyes and scanned the rocky shoreline with a raptor-like gaze. 'I say, there's not an oil tanker wreck in sight. Tell you what; I think we should risk it. So be a good boy scout and get the fuckin' tea on, will you?'

Twenty minutes later, Murphy leaned back against a pile of splintered wood and gorged himself on half a pot of porridge. After he'd scraped the cooking pot clean he burped and patted his stomach. 'When this is over, I don't care if I ever eat porridge again for the rest of my fucking life. Be a nice fellow and pass me a mug of tea.'

Angus did as requested and then sneezed. His nose was dripping and his face was sweating. Murphy rummaged in his rucksack and handed him some white pills and yellow capsules.

'What's this?'

'Ampicillin and codeine.'

'I'm not—'

'Hey, Angus, has anybody ever told you that you're a stubborn bastard?'

'But... I—'

'Fucking well take them!'

Angus knocked back the pills with a mouthful of sugary tea. Soon, he was fast asleep, the codeine acting as a sedative. Murphy covered him with both of their blankets and spent the night watching the fire's flames dance and die.

Angus woke at dawn. He was damp from sweating. His fever had broken. He lay silently and observed Murphy, prodding at the fire's smouldering embers with a stick and staring at them like they were the last ones on earth.

Angus broke the silence. 'Man, I went out like a light and slept like a pharaoh in his tomb.'

Murphy blinked. 'Who the fuck's Daniel?'

'My dead stepfather. Why?'

'You were talking to him in your sleep.'

'What was I saying?'

'Something about smashing some windows in a church.'

Angus ran a hand over his lips. 'I feel a lot better. I'm as thirsty as a fish in a desert.'

'I'm fucking well knackered. So don't ask me to make the tea.' Murphy nodded to his left. 'There's a flat ledge behind that boulder over there. Give me one of the blankets. I've got to crash.'

'When do you want to get going?' Angus asked.

Murphy studied the soot-blackened palms of his hands. 'We've got enough wood to last us another night. There's plenty of food, so I reckon we can hole up here for another day, while you get your strength back.' He pointed to a split between two cliffs. 'Unless I'm mistaken, we'll find a way through there and after that, it'll be downhill all the way to Turkey. What do you say?'

Angus nodded in agreement. 'Sounds cool to me, man. Go get some rest.'

Murphy stood and picked up his rucksack. Angus uncoiled a woollen blanket from his damp body and handed it to him.

As Murphy walked away, Angus called to him. 'Hey, Mister MacMurphy.'

Murphy turned. 'What?'

'Thanks for watching over me.'

Murphy smiled and shook his head. 'All things considered, I still owe you a big one.'

'Thanks anyway.'

Murphy raised a hand in farewell and disappeared behind a grey granite boulder.

Angus broke off some dry splinters of wood from a cut branch and returned life to the fire by blowing air at a few glowing charcoals that he found under the ashes. Once he had a small blaze on the go, he brewed a mug of tea. He found that if he didn't think too much about his situation he was actually enjoying himself. He held his damp blanket in front of the fire. Soon, steam was rising from it. When the blanket was dry he folded it to use as a pillow. He'd picked up a second-hand copy of Hunter S. Thomson's *Fear and Loathing in Las Vegas* before leaving Pune. After he'd retrieved the paperback from his rucksack, he settled down for a campfire read. Head propped on an arm, he picked up on the story from where he'd left off. Raoul Duke and Doctor Gonzo were driving a red shark through the desert and hallucinating bats; hardly surprising considering the amount of mind-altering drugs they'd taken.

Angus nodded off somewhere in Nevada. When he woke up, there was a sharp pain in his throat. He opened his eyes and found the source of his discomfort was a rusty bayonet. It was being pressed into the flesh above his Adam's apple by a man wearing a wolf's skin cap and some kind of fur coat. Going by the malicious leer on his pockmarked face, he was a wolf in wolf's clothing.

'What the fu—' Angus tried to sit up, but was kept prone by increased pressure on the point of the long rusty blade. With a trembling right hand, he touched the spot where the bayonet was digging into his throat. His fingers came away with sticky blood on them.

The man's face split apart in a broad smile. What few teeth he had embedded in his gums were toffee-coloured. His breath smelled rotten. Malevolence flared from his bloodshot eyes. The hill bandit turned to his left and barked something unintelligible.

Angus's eyes looked to the right and saw another man, dressed in a brown woollen coat, baggy jeans and mud-splattered rubber boots, rummaging through his rucksack. He waved Angus's black leather wallet in the air above his bald head, turned to face his buddy and grinned. It was obvious they shared the same dentist, the one who died of mouth cancer thirty years ago.

Angus was brought to his feet by none-too-subtle prodding from the bayonet. The guy in the brown coat walked over. He was munching on a biscuit. He winked lewdly, grabbed Angus's right buttock and gave it a hard squeeze. He pumped a filthy fist in front of Angus's terrified eyes and then delivered a slobbering, biscuit crumb-loaded kiss to his mouth. The two men laughed. Angus read their faces like the instructions on a packet of rat poison he'd swallowed by mistake. He could see the packet's skull and cross-bones warning flashing in their eyes. His fear was mounting by the second and constricting his windpipe. His intake of breath felt abrasive. The blood drained from his face and his heart pounded against his ribcage.

The bandit with the bayonet tugged at the zipper on Angus's jeans, while his biscuit-munching mate returned to the rucksack and proceeded to empty its contents onto the ground. Angus studied his antagonist's face and tried to find something human in it. It was a mask of pure evil. Angus heard Murphy's voice call out from somewhere behind him. 'Hey, you! Shit face!'

Bayonet man looked up. His eyes widened. There was a loud crack. Angus felt the breeze of a bullet as it zipped by his left ear. It hit the man in front of him in the right eye, sounding like an egg being thrown against a concrete wall. The bandit's head snapped to the right. The long blade fell from his hand and clattered on the rocky ground. His body spun like a drunken dervish until he tripped over a rock and hit the dust face first. The back of his head was missing.

The other man shouted in alarm. He dropped Angus's rucksack as he raised his filthy hands in the air. Angus followed the direction of his horrified stare and turned to see Murphy standing with his legs apart on top of a flat boulder. He was sighting down the blue steel barrel of Ali's Colt .45. There was another loud crack. Murphy's second shot thudded into the biscuit muncher's chest. The man's hands dropped to his sides. He grunted, staggered backwards against a boulder and crumpled to his knees. For a brief moment, silence enveloped the scene. The bald man put his hands to his breast and, when he saw they were covered in blood, proceeded to bleat like a newborn lamb. His eyes were directed upward as if beseeching Allah for mercy. Unfortunately for him, the all-merciful one must have been pre-occupied with preparations for the Hajj in Mecca. It was Murphy the unmerciful who was calling the shots.

Murphy leapt from the boulder and landed on all fours, the heavy revolver clutched in his right hand. He stood up, dusted himself off, blew down the pistol's barrel as if clearing it of smoke, looked into Angus's astonished eyes, winked and said, 'Dirty fuckin' Harry is out of a job.' He twirled the Colt around a finger like Billy the Kid.

Angus stammered. 'J-J-Jesus—'

Murphy, impressively calm, strolled over and shook his shoulder. 'I say, old chap, are you alright?'

'M-M-Man,' stuttered Angus. '*O-O-Old fucking chap?* Are you out of your mind? I've got to t-take a s-s-shit right n-now.'

Murphy chuckled. 'Don't let me interrupt nature's call. Haste ye back.'

When Angus returned from his urgent mission, Murphy was standing over the wounded bandit, who had collapsed on to his left side and lay curled like a foetus in a pool of blood and piss. His legs were jerking.

'What the fuck are we going to do with him,' asked Angus.

Murphy's non-verbal response was to lean over the dying robber and place the Colt's muzzle against the man's right temple. The bandit's eyes rolled up so only the whites could be seen. He tried to sit up. A choked sob escaped from between his cracked lips. Murphy pulled the revolver's trigger and let the snubbed nosed bullet do its work.

Angus saw the bandit's brain splatter on the ground like a bag of fatty minced beef with chips of bone in it. The pistol's report cannoned of boulders. There was a smell of singed hair. Only then did it fully register in Angus's mind that Murphy had just killed his second human being that morning. *Fuuuck!'* Angus let out a throaty roar and then shouted at Murphy. 'What the fucking hell did you go and do that for?'

'I just did the world a favour by getting rid of some nasty genetic mutations. Human vermin. You know, cleaning up the gene pool. Taking out the garbage.' Murphy looked up at the clear blue sky and then back to Angus. 'Besides, what did you expect me to do? Call a fuckin' ambulance?' He pointed the revolver at Angus and said, 'That's you and me quits.'

Murphy's twisted logic was lost on Angus. He was speechless, so he did what came to him. He laughed in relief, knowing without a doubt that those two men lying dead on the ground would have cut his throat after sodomizing him. Still shaking with shock, Angus stared at Murphy over the second bandit's bloody corpse and — here is the truth of it — he understood at that moment that, even though Murphy was a stone-cold killer, he would never be able not to love the man who stood before him.

Murphy pulled up his dirty grey robe and holstered the Colt. 'Man, I don't know about you, but I'm dying for a cup of tea and a fag.'

Angus coughed and asked, 'Where are they? I could do with a cigarette myself.'

'Oh, you could, could you?' said Murphy. 'Well, you're not getting one. So don't ask me again.'

When tea break was over, Murphy and Angus buried the two corpses in a small ravine under a pile of rocks.

Murphy stood on top of the shallow grave and clapped his hands to clear them of dust. 'Okay, man, after you've said the prayers for the dearly departed, I suggest we get the fuck out of here in case any of their hillbilly pals come looking for them.'

Angus spat on the grave. 'Fuck the prayers, let's move.'

Three days later, they stepped out of an intercity bus in downtown Ankara.

It was five minutes to nine. Angus and Murphy dodged morning traffic as they crossed over the busy street in front of Ankara's main railway station. They saw Raj before he saw them. He was standing outside of the station's three-storied, red sandstone building, checking out the young ladies in headscarves hurrying by on their way to work. Their Indian friend was dressed in a stonewashed denim outfit with its short jacket buttoned up to his chubby neck. He'd shaved his beard off and was digging into a poke of roasted chestnuts.

Murphy crept up behind Raj and slapped him hard on the back.

Raj nearly choked on a half-swallowed mouthful of nuts. 'You stupid knob head,' he spluttered, 'what a fuckin' fright you gave me.'

'How ya doin', Raj?' asked Murphy.

'Fine, until you showed up. Where's Angus?'

Angus wandered over. 'Hey, Raj, how's it going?'

Raj coughed and then nodded towards Murphy. 'That idiot gave me a right scare. I nearly choked on a chestnut.'

Murphy pointed towards the station's main entrance. 'There's a complaints box over there.'

Angus hugged Raj and asked, 'How are your feet?'

The Indian Scotsman looked down at his newly purchased, military surplus, black leather boots and said, with a puzzled expression, 'My feet?'

'Yeah, your feet, earthling. They were in a bit of a state last time I saw you. Remember?'

'*Awww, my feet.* Yeah, man, the swellings gone down.' Raj gave a goofy smile. 'Hey! You like the boots?'

Angus peered into Raj's bloodshot, light-blue eyes. 'Are you stoned or something?'

Raj laughed. 'Yeah, yeah, had a wee smoke after breakfast. Turkish hash is pretty tasty if you ask me.'

'Nice to hear you've been sampling the local delicacies,' commented Murphy. 'Anyway, you been waiting long?'

'Three days,' answered Raj. 'Where the fuck have you guys been?'

Murphy replied, 'We crossed the mountains between Iran and Turkey on foot.'

'How was that?' Raj asked.

Murphy glanced at Angus, smiled and said, 'Nice scenery, nothing much to report. Wrote a few postcards to friends and family. That sort of thing.'

Raj sensed immediately that there was a good story to be told but he didn't pursue it. Instead, he informed his friends how he and Mike had managed to escape out of Iran. 'We got smuggled out in the back of a fish lorry. Mike paid the driver a thousand bucks and it took us three days and half a dozen bottles of arak to get the stink out of our nostrils.' He screwed up his brown-skinned face in disgust. 'Put me off fish suppers for life.'

'So, where is he?' asked Angus.

Raj looked around. 'Where's who?'

'For fuck's sake,' Murphy cursed. 'Mike, of course.'

'Awww, right. Mike's a funny bugger,' declared Raj. 'When I woke up this morning, the first thing he says is, 'They're here.' Don't ask me how he knew, he just did. I think he's a bit psychic or something.'

'Psychic my arse,' said Murphy, looking away from a couple of beautiful young women's swaying backsides. 'I wouldn't be surprised if our very own Acid Mike was a fuckin' CIA agent. The guy produces false passports like Tommy Cooper pulling bunny rabbits out of a top hat.'

'If it wasn't for Mike you'd still be in Evin prison,' said Angus. 'So how can you say that?'

'Easily,' answered Murphy. 'The CIA controls most of the world's illegal drug markets. Man, it was Mike himself who told me Timothy Leary might have been working for secret agencies within the American government.'

Angus shook his head and looked at Murphy. 'You're away with the psychedelic conspiracy fairies.'

'If anyone's away with the fairies look no further than Peter Pansy here,' said Murphy, nodding towards Raj.

'Anyway,' Raj picked up from where he'd left off, 'Mike's inside booking tickets for the train to Istanbul. It leaves at noon.'

'Shit,' said Angus, 'I was looking forward to checking out Ankara.'

Raj rubbed the back of his thick neck. 'You're welcome to do that if you want,' he said. 'But you can count me out. Just don't ask me to come to the funeral after you die of boredom.'

Mike had booked six first-class seats, allowing them plenty of space to relax and the privacy of a compartment all to themselves. The locomotive's pistons hissed and the train lumbered out of the station. Gazing through a dirty carriage window, they watched Ankara's outskirts slowly recede. The train clattered over some points and began to pick up speed. The four friends swayed in unison. The wheeze of compressed steam faded and was replaced by the repetitious click-clack of steel wheels on the tracks beneath them.

Five hundred kilometres, two bottles of arak, a large bag of pistachio nuts, a heated argument between Mike and Murphy over the killing of Ali Khatib, six stiff joints, a few stoned conversations and nine hours later the four friends walked out of Istanbul's Haydarpasa Station. They strolled down to the Galata Bridge, the main conduit running between Istanbul proper and the densely populated eastern district of Galata. Night had descended, turning the city into silhouetted shadows dotted and streaked by electric light. They stood looking out over the Golden Horn in the direction of the Sea of Marmara. Dozens of small boats' red and green running lights glinted on the Bosphorus River. On the nearby suspension bridge car headlights strafed through clouds of mist. Rain began to fall. Raj and Mike dug their hands into their jacket pockets and started walking back in the direction from which they'd come. Murphy glanced around. When he was certain that he was unobserved he tossed his leather-bound Koran into the river. He then pulled up the denim shirt he'd bought from a street vendor in Ankara and unfastened the leather holster strapped around his narrow waist. He gave the Colt .45 a quick wipe with a hanky, then threw the revolver and its holster into the water. He tweaked his nose and then, turning to Angus, said, 'What a fucking waste, there were still three bullets left.'

'Man,' said Angus, turning to face Murphy, 'how do you deal with that shit?'

'What shit?'

'Killing people.'

Murphy turned his back on the bridge's iron railing and rested his elbows on it. 'I don't think about it,' he said. 'When you're dead, you're dead. End of fuckin' story. I'm not into all that karma and reincarnation stuff like you and Raj. All those so-called spiritual ideas are just ways of conveniently labelling, what is, in reality, pure chaos. You do what you have to do in life, and it's better not to hang out too much in the past. Tomorrow never comes. It's always today.' He paused for a moment to study a young couple passing by. The pale-faced man had a bushy moustache and was pushing a pram, its passenger a squealing infant. The woman wore an ankle-length dress and a floral-patterned scarf covered her hair. She paused for a moment to comfort her child by muttering something in Turkish, and then they continued on their way along the bridge. Murphy looked away from the passing scene, returned his attention to Angus and continued. 'If you think about it, you die every night, when you fall asleep. You lie down, drift away, maybe never to return. Not so bad, is it? Nothing to worry about. So, it's been my job to send some serious villains into the big sleep. No big deal.' He grinned. 'In a weird kind of way, I enjoyed giving those nasty fuckers the sort of send-off they deserved. We're a predatory species.'

Angus shook his head. 'Man, don't you have any sense of what's right and what's wrong?'

'Yes,' replied Murphy, 'of course I do.'

'I'm listening,' said Angus.

'What removes suffering is right and what creates suffering is wrong.'

'And how the fuck does that tie in with murdering people?'

'In my case, by putting people out of their misery. Like shooting a horse when it breaks a leg.'

Angus understood that one has to be extremely careful in life in regards to telling people what one thinks of them. But Murphy wasn't people. He was his closest friend. He told Murphy the truth. 'You're a fucking headcase, you know that?'

Murphy laughed. 'Thanks for the compliment. Does that mean you're finally welcoming me into the club?'

Angus slapped his friend on the shoulder. 'C'mon, psycho,' he said, 'let's find something to eat.'

A fifteen-minute walk later, Angus, Murphy, Mike and Raj left the prosperity of downtown Istanbul behind as they wandered into the narrow streets of a less affluent area. Ragged children huddled in doorways broke off their excited conversations to stare at the four foreigners passing along the cobbled alleyways. Rainwater gurgled in rusty drainpipes, runoff from the slanted roofs of houses with cracked walls, missing large patches of plaster, exposing red brick. They came to a small, dimly lit square, little more than an intersection of alleyways with a bubbling cast-iron fountain as its centrepiece. They crossed the street and entered a steamy-windowed eatery, whose dozen or so patrons glanced over at them tolerantly and then refocused their attention to the big plates of steaming, yellow soup set before them on red and white checked table cloths. There were no menus, only a blackboard with something scribbled in white chalk in Turkish script. When a young waiter in a long, white apron, with a dark red fez tilted on his close-cropped head, approached their table, Mike pointed at the blackboard and held up four fingers. There was the sound of crockery in the background. The waiter gave a wan smile, nodded and returned to the kitchen. Nobody was surprised when he returned with four plates of butterbean soup and a small basket of neatly quartered flatbread. He plonked down four shiny spoons, wrapped in paper serviettes. Before disappearing, the young man looked down his long nose and said in perfect English, 'Enjoy your meal. If you need anything else I am at your service.' He received a communal chuckle from the four foreigners seated round the table.

During and after the meal, they discussed their next move.

'There's no fucking way I'm going to try and enter England with this book Mike gave me,' said Murphy, fiddling with a white paper napkin. 'Even a blind immigration officer could see that it's a fake passport.'

'I'm sorry about that.' Mike smiled apologetically. 'It was a bit of a rushed job.'

'No problem, man,' said Raj, patting Mike on the shoulder. 'Me and Murphy are forever in your debt.' He glanced over the table at Murphy. 'Right, Murph?'

Murphy nodded in agreement. 'I'll never forget what you've done for us, Mike. I've said it before and I'll say it again, it's an honour to call you a friend.'

'I think this calls for a wee drink,' said Angus, beckoning to the waiter, who promptly informed him that the café did not serve alcohol.

Over four small glasses of thick Turkish coffee, it was agreed that Raj and Murphy would head for Amsterdam, Mike would return to London, and Angus would fly back to Bombay and then on to Pune.

'Here's to Bhagwan,' was the last toast of the evening. Acid Mike remained silent and failed to raise his glass in a gesture of respect.

'Cabin crew, take your positions and prepare for landing,' crackled the captain's voice from the speaker above our heads.

I looked out of the portal. The plane was descending through a thick layer of cloud. It was light outside and raining. Moisture rippled across the window and my ears popped from the decompression. Down below, England was gearing up for another busy day. Endless lines of vehicles were queuing in traffic jams between neatly ordered residential areas and sprawling industrial estates.

'If you ask me,' said Jean, 'Angus and his criminal pals should have been locked up in prison for the rest of their lives.'

My wife's reaction to the story came as no surprise to me. I knew her for what she was, a true blue conservative, who thought Britain's Labour government was far too lenient, especially when it came to dealing with career criminals like Angus and his friends. 'Well,' I said, 'I suppose it all depends on how you look at it.'

'Oh, does it now?' sneered Jean, scorn dripping off the end of her pointed tongue. 'I didn't realise that. Perhaps you'd care to enlighten me with a little more of your penetrating insights into the true nature of reality. A little discourse on quantum mechanics, perhaps. Or, even better, a concise description of the human genome's mapping concerning chromosome architecture and epigenetic inheritance. You've forgotten I have an 'O' Level in biology.'

I had to laugh. 'I love it when you speak like that.'

Jean flashed me a seductive smile and played dumb. 'I've no idea what you're talking about, darling.'

'Well, in regards to Angus and his criminal buddies–'

'Murderers!'

'What?'

'That guy Murphy was a murderer and your brother Angus just stood by and watched him kill people.'

'But Murphy saved his life.'

'That's beside the point. We're Christians and the Bible says it's wrong to take human life.'

'Oh, aye, does it now? What about taking an eye for an eye?'

Jean remained silent.

'Think about it.' I continued, 'Right now, British troops are in Afghanistan and Iraq. Like it or not, they're our soldiers sent by our government and because of their armed aggression thousands of innocent people are being killed and a lot of their relatives are really pissed off about it.'

'Haven't you heard? There's a war against terror going on.'

I shook my head. 'I think the American government, or whoever's pulling the strings in The Pentagon, are the real terrorists.'

Jean narrowed her eyes. 'What on earth are you talking about, now?'

'Angus told me he thought the war on terror was a device created by the American government, to reduce their own citizens' civil liberties, create an excuse for the deployment of their armed forces in the Middle East and cut lucrative arms deal with Saudi Arabia. The Americans also want more control over the oil supplies their economy is so reliant upon.'

'That's preposterous.'

'Is it?' I asked. 'Well, Angus didn't think so, and I'm beginning to think he was right. He said the next thing that will happen is that America will declare war on Libya, then Syria, and then go for the bullseye — Iran.'

'I loved your brother but I'm relieved he's gone from our lives because it's clear to me he's had a very negative influence upon you.'

Anger rose from my guts. I shouldn't have indulged in drinking so much strong alcohol. I took a few deep breaths to exert control over my conflicting emotions. When I'd calmed down enough to speak without losing my rag I said, 'Please, Jean, I don't want to have to say it again. Don't speak like that about Angus. I know he used to be a criminal, but he was also many other things besides that, not least of which was an extremely generous, kind-hearted man who had the guts to live his life and not the one dictated to him by the society he was born into.'

The plane bounced once and, with a squealing of tyres, touched down on Heathrow Airport's main runway.

'Please remain seated until the aircraft is connected to the terminal building,' requested Captain Hugh Armstrong's voice via the cabin's intercom.

6

THE HOLY FIRE

He wore wire-rimmed bifocals and a dark-blue, pinstriped business suit, a fresh white handkerchief tucked into its breast pocket. As he stood in a glassed-in box examining my passport, the pinch-faced immigration officer had the look of a meticulous solicitor. After leafing through the passport's pages he looked up and enquired, 'Mister MacLeod, what was the purpose of your visit to Thailand and Cambodia?'

It was a simple question that set me on the wrong foot. 'Nothing. I mean nothing illegal,' I answered, sounding like a complete idiot. 'I was on holiday with my wife.'

The immigration officer peered through his specs at me. 'Mister MacLeod, you don't appear very certain about that.' He swiped my passport through a slot connected to the Home Office's central computer, monitoring the comings and goings through Great Britain's numerous entry and exit points.

'What exactly do you mean by that remark?' I blustered.

The immigration officer smiled as if he were privy to information about my life that I was unaware of, which he probably was. He then handed over my passport and said, 'Welcome back to the United Kingdom, Mister MacLeod.'

'What was that all about,' asked Jean when I joined her. She'd been watching the brief exchange from the other side of the yellow line that demarked where the outside world ended and not-so-Great Britain began.

'If these bastards get their way, it won't be long until we have bar codes printed on our wrists and silicone ID chips inserted under our skin.'

'Mind your bloody language,' scolded Jean. 'It's for your own good. We need a secure border to help fight the war on terror.'

'The war on terror,' I sneered. 'If you ask me, the only bloody war that's going on in this country is the war against people's privacy.' I glanced up at the white-panelled ceiling. 'Look at this place. There are more bloody cameras in here than there are on a Hollywood film set.'

We stood by a luggage carousel, waiting patiently for our suitcases to appear on a conveyer belt running up from ground level. Nicotine addicts stared at strategically placed 'No Smoking' signs, reminding me that I'd quit the habit and was gasping for a fag. I focused my attention on a pair of blue-uniformed policemen, wearing bulletproof vests with sub-machine guns slung over their shoulders. 'What are they supposed to be doing?' I asked half to myself. 'Getting ready to shoot people who can't resist the temptation to light up?'

'Here they come,' said Jean, alerting me to the fact that our luggage had arrived.

'Excuse me, sir,' said a young man in a blue cardigan, white shirt and red tie, as I passed through a partitioned customs hall. 'Where have you arrived from?' he asked, glancing at the baggage tag with BK printed in big letters attached to the handle of my Samsonite suitcase.

'Bangkok,' I answered.

'Mmmh...' The official hummed and nodded as if I'd just said something that aroused suspicion. 'If you don't mind, sir, I'd like to examine the contents of your luggage.'

I groaned inwardly, lifted my black suitcase onto a rubber-topped table and unlocked the combination lock.

The customs man began rummaging through my personal belongings. He glanced up at me and said, 'Meet any nice young ladies over in Bangkok.'

That did it. Something snapped inside of me. I leaned over my open suitcase and, struggling to control my voice, said, 'Listen, you pimply-faced, little prick, just do your fucking job and mind your own business.'

The young man's face turned scarlet. He looked over to what was obviously one of his superiors and nodded his head. The overweight man marched over, a laminated ID card fastened to a chain bouncing off his wobbling belly, his rubber-soled shoes squeaking on the grey linoleum floor.

'What seems to be the problem,' asked fatso in a stiff baritone voice.

I pretended to be pleasantly surprised by his sudden arrival. 'Oh, good morning officer,' I said, 'no problem at all. Why, I was just saying to your subordinate here, what a fine job you chaps are doing by keeping illegal drugs out of our country.' I glanced at the young man, who was in the process of stuffing my shirts back into the suitcase. 'Weren't we, *son?*'

Son slammed the suitcase closed, bit his lip and nodded.

We wound our way through the crowd waiting at the stainless steel barriers in the arrivals hall. Drivers held makeshift signs at chest level. Expectant families and anxious lovers searched for that special face. Nobody was waiting for us.

I used my Visa Debit card to pay a Polish immigrant worker for two first-class tickets on the Heathrow Express to Paddington, thinking that the money just spent would have kept Jean and I fed for a week in a top Bangkok restaurant.

Outside of the train's steamed-up windows, London suburbia shot by in a wet, grey blur. I glanced around the compartment. My fellow passengers looked ill. It wasn't so much that their skin hadn't been in direct contact with the sun for quite some time, in fact, some of the people were African and Asian. It had more to do with a weariness in their tired eyes as if they were all suffering from some kind of sleeping sickness. Nobody looked at anyone else. Some had high-tech headphones jammed into their ears, listening to music that made them nod their heads like somnambulistic zombies. Others stared and tapped at mobile phones, or had their noses buried in paperback books with glitzy covers or tabloid newspapers with headlines like, 'Our Boys in Basra'. Better heeled individuals raised pink-coloured business newspapers in front of their anonymous faces, making sure the left cuff of their freshly pressed shirts were pulled up to reveal the glint of gold or the stainless steel strap of an overpriced Swiss watch. The social ambience was one of 'don't bother me and I won't bother you'. I was struck by the difference that existed between South-East Asia and the UK. Had this train been travelling in Thailand the air would have been full of life, the buzz of conversation, laughter, curious glances and, most importantly of all, children kicking up a fuss while adoring parents looked on with love in their eyes.

I turned to Jean. She was reading a society magazine. I asked, 'Are you looking forward to getting home?'

'I'm looking forward to eating something decent. Even in business class, that swill they serve you isn't fit for human consumption. That chicken I ate had probably never been outside in its steroid-filled life.' Jean held up a glossy, full-page picture of two rosy-cheeked young men. I didn't recognise them. She said, 'Look at how handsome Lady Diana's sons have turned out.'

I ran a hand over my unshaven cheeks and looked out the window. The train was pulling into Paddington Station.

Our rubber-wheeled luggage made a plaintive rumbling against the platform. We converged with the throng at the turnstile. Towards the station's main entrance we stopped off at a sushi bar, sat on high stools, and selected a few sashimi dishes that were being trundled around for display on a mini conveyer belt. We moved on to Starbucks for cardboard beakers of coffee, so strong it caused a caffeine-fuelled dispute over who would visit the lavatory first. Jean won. The deal was sealed with a kiss. I tasted the bitter flavour of roasted coffee beans as our tongues touched for an instant.

Outside, it was pelting. We stood in a long queue waiting for a taxi. My fault entirely. I'd insisted on it. I couldn't have stomached a journey on the Tube, even a relatively short one.

'We should have caught the flight to Glasgow,' complained Jean, who was wearing a thin cotton dress and sandals. 'I'm bloody well freezing.'

Half an hour passed, the minutes dragging by.

'Kings Cross Station,' said Jean to the pasty-faced cab driver who picked us up.

The black Hackney cab soon had us on Marylebone Road, joining the flow of traffic headed in an easterly direction towards Euston Road. I peered past the raindrops on the window, thinking that there were too many cars in Britain. 'Can you imagine what it's like living in this all the time?' I asked Jean, who was touching up her eye-liner in a compact mirror.

'Sure,' she replied, 'it's just like Bangkok but colder and wetter. If London's good enough for the Queen, it's good enough for me.'

The taxi pulled up outside Kings Cross railway station and we had to run to catch the train to Glasgow, due to leave at midday.

The train picked up speed on the outskirts of the metropolis. The English countryside flew by and I began to settle into the situation and enjoy myself. That is until I got around to switching on my mobile phone and discovering it contained over thirty text messages, most of which were work-related. I jotted down notes in my leather-bound agenda. The buffet trolley clattered down the aisle towards me. I decided I needed more caffeine to boost my concentration. Text messages had located my mind in several places at once.

By three-thirty, the sun had broken through the thick layer of cloud blanketing the North of England, transforming the overcast day into a bright afternoon. It was springtime. Fresh leaves were beginning to sprout on trees and bushes. Squadrons of flapping crows hung and swooped above chugging tractors, ploughing their way along furrowed fields, dark brown from rain, squares and oblongs of damp fertility, delineated by moss-covered, dry stone dykes. Flocks of black-faced sheep dotted verdant hillsides and green fields. *Spring comes and the grass grows by itself*, said a Zen thought.

After a brief stop in Carlisle, the electric train sped towards Scotland and the passengers became more animated. An oil worker, making his way to Aberdeen, sat down on the seat opposite to me and sparked up a conversation. He handed me a green can of Heineken beer and we began a discussion about Scotland's chances of qualifying for the next world cup. A six-pack later, we both agreed that the Scottish team might well win the international football tournament which, if nothing else, goes to show that the Dutch brewer makes a strong alcoholic beverage that can produce in the drinker's mind idiosyncratic beliefs that are not in accordance with what is generally accepted to be reality. In other words, ridiculous delusions.

Jean and I checked into the Thistle Hotel on Glasgow's Cambridge Street. While we were standing at reception waiting for a bellhop to pick up our suitcases, a crowd of noisy men entered the red-carpeted foyer. I figured they were either guests attending a wedding function, or Americans belonging to a clan club, because, apart from the odd eccentric, they were the only people in Scotland who would be daft enough to wear kilts in Glasgow. Sure enough, loud American-accented voices burst into song as they approached the reception desk. I could hear echoes of 'Flower of Scotland', following us along the corridor that led to our fourth-floor room.

The following morning, at ten o'clock sharp, a sleek, silver, four-door Jaguar X-Type pulled up on the street in front of the Thistle Hotel and Jean and

I slid into the blue leather back seats.

'Morning, Charlie.'

'Good morning, Mister MacLeod,' said the ginger-haired young man in the driver's seat, twisting around to face his passengers. 'Hello, Missus Mac-Leod, did you enjoy your holidays?'

'Yes, Charlie,' replied Jean, giving a brief, dismissive snort, 'we did, thank you. Can we get going now?'

'Oops, sorry,' said Charlie, turning back to face the street. He pulled away from the pavement, made a left turn and drove west out of town.

'How was the journey down, Charlie?' I enquired, when the car stopped at a traffic light that seemed to have an aversion to the colour green.

'Not bad, Mr MacLeod,' answered Charlie, absolutely chuffed to be driving his boss's, my partner's, brand new car. 'The roads are always quieter on the weekends.'

We were driving on the outside lane of the westbound carriageway of the M8. Over to my right, I looked north and caught fleeting glimpses of Trinity College's towers, a famous landmark that Angus once told me he had used as a navigating reference point when he first arrived in Glasgow as a teenager and began to explore the city's streets. I gazed out at the passing scene and it struck me how many parts of the city had taken on a very modern appearance. Yet, the brown sandstone tenement blocks looked much the same as they ever did and, yes, there was still a pub on almost every corner. I noticed that Glasgow was flashing by just a little too quickly for my liking. I leaned forward, peeped over the apprentice electrician's shoulder, looked at the speedometer's red needle, edging past 80 mph, and said quietly, 'Take it easy on the gas, Charlie, or you'll be losing your licence if the bobbies catch you driving at that speed.'

The car slowed to a more sedate fifty and drove over the River Clyde via the Erskine Bridge to join the A82. The grey-green mass of Dumbarton Rock passed on our left. The further west we travelled the more beautiful the scenery became. For the first time since we'd left Bangkok, I began to feel a sense of homecoming stirring in my heart. The faces of my five grandchildren passed by the window of my imagination. A knot of emotion tightened in my throat.

Two hours and a short coffee break later, the Jag pulled up outside of our two-storied house on Ardconnel Road in Oban. After Charlie had taken our luggage up the flight of granite stairs that led to the front entrance and deposited the suitcases on the doorstep, I slipped him a crisp fifty-pound note.

Charlie looked at it in mock surprise. 'You don't need to...'

'Och, away with you,' I said. 'Treat your girlfriend to a Chinese.'

Charlie, who Jean suspected was gay, blushed. 'Thanks, Mister MacLeod.' He turned to Jean. 'Welcome home, Missus MacLeod.'

Jean ignored him, walked up the stairs, unlocked the solid oak front door and disappeared inside.

I smiled contritely. 'I'll see you at work on Monday, Charlie.'

The young lad raised a hand in farewell. 'Aye, right you are, Mister Mac-Leod, cheerio now.'

The Jaguar sped off down the street. I stood for a moment and stared up at the house and wondered, like I always did, if it might be a good idea to have the white gloss paint removed from the sandstone walls and return the building to its original condition. I noticed that the living room's blue velvet curtains were drawn behind the bay window and wondered absently why that was.

I walked up the steps, closed the front door behind me and smelled lavender scented furniture wax. I looked down at the polished parquet floor. There wasn't a speck of dust to be seen. The cleaner had been in. I smiled and thought, *Jean, will be pleased.* I carried our luggage upstairs and then entered the master bedroom. I placed the cases on the carpeted floor and went over to the window, where I stood for a few minutes looking out over the small town's rooftops and Oban Bay to the Isle of Mull in the distance. A wave of weariness settled over me.

Jean's voice called from the kitchen. 'Tea's ready.'

I turned away from the window, made my way downstairs and met Jean in the hall. She carried two white mugs of steaming, hot tea in her hands. One of the mugs had I LOVE OBAN printed on it in black and red glaze.

'Let's sit in the living room,' she suggested.

I turned the porcelain doorknob and, for no obvious reason, felt a shard of anxiety pierce my guts. *Strange,* I thought, pushing the door inwards. I looked up and was extremely surprised to find over twenty men, women and children smiling at me.

'Welcome home!' they cried.

I heard Jean gasp in shock and then the mugs of tea smashing on the floor behind me. I leaned against the doorframe for support. Moira, my eldest daughter, stepped forward and embraced me. She whispered in my ear, 'Hi, Dad, welcome home. You've lost a lot of weight.'

Dressed in blue and white Glasgow Rangers football strips, Moira's two little boys began tugging on my trouser legs, chanting, 'Fitba', fitba' fitba'.'

Tears of relief and joy welled up in my eyes. I was so overcome by emotion that I remained speechless for some time. We'd been through hell, survived, and finally returned home to tell the tale.

Like a king and queen in their castle, Jean and I sat down on leather armchair thrones in the centre of our living room and drank in the fruits of everything we'd laboured for in our lives.

By the time everyone left, it was late evening and Jean, exhausted, staggered off upstairs to bed, leaving me alone in the sitting room with only my thoughts for company.

Being surrounded by so much life had built up the momentum of my inner pendulum. It was now swinging in the opposite direction, towards death.

For the first time since it had happened, I accepted the fact that my twin brother, Angus, and his beautiful wife, Lara, had perished when the tsunami had thundered into Unawantuna Bay in Sri Lanka. Tears rolled down my flushed cheeks as I turned a glass of whisky in my trembling hands. I set down my drink and lit a large candle in the centre of a white marble coffee table. I then rose, walked over to the door and switched the lights off. I returned to my armchair, sat down and crossed my legs eastern style. The house was silent. Somewhere in the distance, a ship's horn blew. The candle sputtered and grew brighter. I stared into the flame and strained to keep my eyes from blinking. Soon the room's contours dissolved until all that was left was the light and the awareness of its existence.

Quietly at first, I heard voices. They were singing. As the men and women's voices grew louder, I recognised the song. Angus had sung it for me when I sat with him on the beach in Sri Lanka, watching a beautiful orange sunset over the Indian Ocean. 'There is so much magnificence. Waves are coming in. Waves are coming in. Jump into the holy fire. Jump into the holy flame.'

July 1976. Angus had just returned from Bombay. He entered his bamboo house in the sugarcane fields behind Koregaon Park in Pune and found Alice and Nina sitting cross-legged on the wooden floor, staring at each other across a lit candle.

After warm hugs and a few kisses, Angus narrated how Mike and he had successfully broken Raj and Murphy out of prison. When it came to recounting how he and Murphy had escaped from Iran, he failed to mention that Murphy had killed three men. Angus had already decided that what they didn't know could not harm them. Even without the gory details, it was quite a story and the girls were suitably impressed.

'Where are they now?' Nina asked.

Angus tilted his head. 'Who?'

'Murphy and Raj, of course,' she answered.

'*Of course?*' Angus repeated questioningly. 'Even taking into consideration that you were both instrumental in helping bust them out of prison...for a lot of money, I have to add, you were calling them assholes not too long ago.'

'Come on, man,' coaxed Alice, 'tell us where they are. We're curious, that's all.'

'They've gone to Amsterdam.'

Alice and Nina exchanged a meaningful glance. Angus stood up and went through to the bedroom, closing the door behind him. He opened a hidden trapdoor and retrieved the locked metal box where he stored his illicit earnings. He unlocked it, counted out two neat stacks of hundred dollar bills and then, with a neat bundle of money in each hand, returned to the main room. Nina and Alice were in the midst of a hushed discussion but fell silent when he sat down beside them.

'Here you go', he said, handing the girls their payment for helping out in Iran.

They took the money, counted it out and, when Nina realised he'd given them ten thousand dollars each more than the fifty thousand he'd originally promised them for doing the job, she asked, 'Are you sure about this?'

Angus nodded. 'Of course, I am. A deal's a deal.'

'But...but...you don't need to give us—'

Angus interjected Nina, 'An extra ten grand? I know I don't, but that way you'll have some money left after you've paid for your rooms in the ashram.'

Alice and Nina exchanged another meaningful glance.

This time, Angus decided he'd like to appreciate what it signified. 'What's going on with the pair of you? You're up to something. I know it.'

Nina was their spokeswoman. 'We're not going to move into the ashram, even if they let us.'

Angus studied both of their faces in turn. 'How come?'

Nina answered excitedly. 'Because we're going to Amsterdam to catch up with Murphy and Raj.'

'You're joking.'

'No, we're serious.' Nina turned to Alice. 'Aren't we, Rupa?'

Alice nodded mutely.

Angus noticed tears in her eyes. 'What about Bhagwan?'

Nina replied, 'We both wrote to him and asked him what we should do?'

'And?'

'And he wrote back and told us we should follow our feelings.'

'We love them,' blurted Alice, bursting into tears.

Alice and Nina left for Bombay to catch a flight to Amsterdam. Angus didn't think too much about it. He had other things on his mind. His sleep pattern was being disturbed by nightmares, centred on Ali Khatib's murder and the slaying of the two mountain bandits. Even during the day he was having flashbacks of Khatib's purple tongue hanging out and the razor wire garrotte embedded in his bloody neck. The Turkish hill bandit's right eye would superimpose itself onto people's faces when Angus was talking to them, then wink at him before it was transformed into a blood-red crater. In an effort to erase these horrific images from his mind, Angus began doing the dynamic meditation twice a day, once before dawn in the ashram and in the evening at home. After two weeks, he'd finally managed to enjoy a night of uninterrupted sleep. The daytime flashbacks were to continue for months until they eventually receded into the darkness of his unconscious mind.

Angus attended Bhagwan's discourses every morning. During this time, the master talked a lot about saying 'yes' to everything in life and how saying 'no' to anything brings in an element of conflict from which the shadow of the ego rises like a spectre. Try as he might, Angus found it extremely difficult to say 'yes' to the fact that he'd been an accomplice to murder.

Everything in the ashram was growing bigger. To accommodate the droves of seekers flocking into the ashram, Bhagwan's morning talks now took place in Buddha Hall, his evening *darshans* in Chuang Tzu Auditorium. The master was no longer driven to his morning talks in a gold-coloured Chevy sedan but in a black Rolls Royce. He was a small man seated in the back of a big car. Everyone loved it, especially the media.

As money poured into the organization's coffers from wealthy sannyasins' bank accounts, the ashram's precincts began to expand. New buildings were going up like those in the centre of a thriving town.

Bhagwan's chairs grew larger. His stuffed armchairs had become a thing of the past, replaced by ever more stylish executive swivel seats. Dressed in a tailored robe and wearing an exotic hat, the maestro conducted his orchestra of willing souls in the performance of a polymorphic symphony, composed of radical spiritual teachings, anecdotes and Mullah Nasruddin jokes. As the months passed, Bhagwan's humour became more irreverent and outrageous to the point of being distasteful. Some mornings he would tell more dirty jokes in a two-hour discourse than a drunken Irishman attending a stag party. Some jokes were funny. Many of them were not, but everyone in attendance laughed. What was hilarious was who was telling the comic stories and how he delivered the punch lines. Bhagwan had mastered the knack of tying in the culmination of his jokes with whatever it was he was expounding. Bursts of ribald laughter became part and parcel of the morning discourses as the master poked fun at various respected personages. Jesus was a crackpot who was trying to save the world but couldn't even save himself. Mother Teresa was a social vampire, feeding off the needs of the poor. Mahatma Gandhi was a violent man. The President of the United States was an imbecile. The British monarchy formed the ugliest family in the world, and so on and so forth. Such verbal attacks produced the desired results; Bhagwan Shree Rajneesh's name spread like wildfire. He became fond of quoting Brendan Behan's saying, 'There's no such thing as bad publicity.'

Angus, like the rest of the sannyasins in Pune, fell ever more deeply in love with Bhagwan, to the point of being blind to anything that did not equate with their guru being the greatest mystic of all time. If for some reason Angus missed the eight o'clock morning discourse, he spent the rest of the day feeling like a hungry man who'd missed breakfast. The lectures were a minimalist stage from which Bhagwan delivered a daily non-stop virtuoso performance. The Buddha Hall transformed into a huge, communal, magic carpet ride that flew over the mountains and valleys of a spiritual Utopia where, every now and Zen, one was introduced personally to ancient Chinese masters, Sufi saints, tantric yogis, dancing Bauls from Bengal, laughing Buddhas, Hindu sages and a new vision of Jesus Christ, a man who enjoyed to drink wine with his disciples, make love with Mary Magdalene, and was a yoga adept who managed to walk away from his crucifixion and went on to live to a ripe old age, before he died and was buried in Kashmir.

Despite its almost fluffy exterior, the ashram was not a school for the faint-hearted or men and women who lacked guts. Like the road to truth, it was full of pitfalls, hard knocks and penetrating insights. Every day you went through a personal examination and you either passed it or flunked it.

Bhagwan tied in Western psychotherapy groups with the cathartic meditation techniques he'd devised. Angus enrolled in a primal therapy group, with the idea in mind that it might help expunge the guilt he felt in his heart over what had transpired in Iran. Instead, he spent a week in a padded room, wearing a giant nappy and crying his eyes out about never having known his real mother and father. He did gestalt therapy where he was encouraged to be aggressive and see how ugly a Scotsman can be. He took part in a tantra group, where consciousness was awakened through the ancient technique of collective masturbation, thus enabling him to get a firm grip on his inner wanker. He made love with women whose ages ranged from late teens to late sixties. When he could no longer sustain an erection, he kissed and cuddled bearded men, and ascertained that he was not inclined towards homosexuality. He sat in a Zazen group for a week, breathing into his belly, while he stared at a white wall, watching his past project itself, dance in its death throes, fade away and merge in the Ocean of Non-existence. He did rebirthing sessions and was flabbergasted to find that hyperventilating could bring him into an altered state of consciousness similar to that delivered by LSD.

It was in a group called Enlightenment Intensive that he was introduced to the practice of asking himself the question 'Who am I?' It seemed a simple enough question to ask but, after three days of enquiry, the only real answer he was coming up with was that he did not know who he was. The group drew to a close, leaving him with a feeling of peaceful emptiness that remained with him for a week. Angus sensed that there was no actual need to sweat the big things in life. All would somehow be taken care of and, if there were to be conclusions, their nature would be benign.

When Angus wasn't taking part in a therapy group, he meditated and went to Sufi dancing in the mornings. He enjoyed this dance group immensely. It was led by a lively sannyasin woman called Anita. Her bearded boyfriend played acoustic guitar and sang simple songs. Everyone was encouraged to sing along. The songs' lyrics were often no more than spiritual nursery rhymes, so corny that Angus's teeth hurt when reciting them, but that was unimportant. What mattered to him was the opening that happened in his heart when he sang like his life depended on it. 'Jump Into The Holy Fire' was a firm favourite. When he sang about there being so much magnificence, he meant it. Unlike the Buddhist practice of viewing life as an illusion replete with endless suffering, Angus perceived life as an ongoing miracle, full of illuminating blessings. When he sang, 'Waves are coming in,' he felt waves of invigorating cosmic energy washing over his soul. When he sang about jumping into the holy fire, it wasn't some pie in the sky; it was a burning existential blaze that burned away the ego. Jumping into the holy flame meant leaping into the master's energy field, a force so tangible and powerful that many times Angus had looked on in amazement, observing hard-boiled egos, melting like butter in Bhagwan's elegantly gesturing hands.

Months flew by. Angus found peace in his heart and slowly but surely his mind calmed down until it became as reflective as a highly polished mirror. He also found he had more money than he knew what to do with. Due to his ongoing work with Jimmy Bradley and the international drug-running mules in the form of tankers, freighters and container ships that unwittingly delivered loads of hashish to ports around the world, Angus's treasure chest was overflowing.

Angus celebrated his twenty-sixth birthday with Jimmy in December 1977 in the main bar of the Taj Mahal Hotel in Bombay. Earlier that evening, he'd made a thousand dollars for every year he'd lived, by attaching thirty fibreglass containers to a Japanese car transporter's steel hull. Therefore, Angus was paying for the expensive drinks, poured from a bottle of Moët & Chandon Cuvée.

Miles Davis's 'Kind of Blue' played at low volume in the background. 'Cheers,' said Jimmy, clinking his glass of bubbly against Angus's upraised champagne flute. Jimmy then set his glass on the table, fished a packet out of his waistcoat pocket, handed it to Angus and said, 'Happy birthday, pal.'

Angus unwrapped his present and opened a small leather-bound box. Inside shone a stainless steel Rolex Submariner with a black face. 'Wow!' he exclaimed. He began to slip the armband over his left hand.

'Hold on, hold on,' requested Jimmy. 'Check out the inscription on the back before you put it on.'

Angus held the heavy watch up and read the words engraved on the back of the casing out loud. 'To Angus MacLeod from the Deep Dive Corporation.' He looked from the watch to his old friend. 'Thanks, Jimmy, that's the most beautiful thing anyone's ever given me in my life.'

Jimmy smiled, revealing that he'd had all of his uneven front teeth replaced by pearl-white porcelain caps. 'Glad you like it, pal,' he said, summoning a waiter in a high-necked maroon jacket to bring another bottle of champagne.

'Any word from the lads?' Angus asked.

Jimmy clipped the end off a fat Cuban cigar, lit it with a Dunhill lighter, blew a cloud of steel grey, pungent smoke into the crowded lounge and answered, 'Yeah, I had lunch with Murphy and Raj in The Dam last week.'

'How are they doing?'

'Raj is putting on the beef and Murphy's as mad as ever. You know, I sometimes wonder about him. There's a glint of something in that guy's eye that

I find disturbing. Then again, when it comes to cutting a deal, Murphy's as solid as the Rock of Gibraltar. So, I'm not complaining.' Jimmy took a long drag on his Havana and let smoke slowly filter out through his nostrils. The blue smoke drifted up into his short wavy hair, creating the illusion that his head was smouldering. 'Anyway, they said to tell you that business is booming and they won't be able to make it over to Goa this year, because they're set to make a packet over the Christmas season.' He paused briefly, remembering something. 'Oh yeah, the girls said to say 'Hi' and give you a big kiss.' He blew a smoke-laden kiss over the table. 'That's all you're getting.'

Angus chuckled. 'How are they getting along?'

'They're both pregnant.'

'What?'

'Nina's due in a month and Alice in the spring.'

'Jesus! That's a turn up for the maternity books. How are the lads handling that?'

'Raj is chuffed and Murphy's shitting himself.'

'Which reminds me,' said Angus. 'of how I felt when that tanker cruised by tonight. I thought we'd had our fish and chips.'

'I have to admit,' said Jimmy, blowing at his cigar's glowing tip, 'for a moment there I was a worried man myself. I nearly let go of the container. Oh! I almost forgot.' He handed Angus a cream-coloured business card and said, 'Here, keep this in a safe place.'

Angus examined it and enquired, 'What's this?'

'That's my address in the UK. I want you to have it in case anything ever happens to me.'

'Happens to you?' Angus felt the hair on the back of his neck bristle. 'Like what?'

'Like getting run over by a hundred thousand tons of tanker steaming out of Bombay harbour.'

'That's—'

'Mind if we join you?'

Angus and Jimmy looked up at a pair of young women wearing micro skirts and high-heeled sandals. Angus had noticed them sitting at the bar, firing a string of smiles at him and Jimmy since they'd sat down in the lounge an hour before.

'Not at all ladies,' said Jimmy, smiling at the tall blonde who'd popped the question. 'Sit down.' He glanced over at a waiter and beckoned with a hand. The liveried man came over. 'Bring us another bottle of champagne and two glasses.'

Angus fired off a couple of questions at the woman who sat next to him. 'Don't I know you from somewhere? Have you ever been to Pune?'

She swept her exceptionally long, silky, light-brown hair to one side, doled him out a coy smile, painted with black gloss lipstick, and answered, 'Maybe.' She searched in her orange-coloured, patent leather handbag and pulled out a packet of cigarettes. She offered a slim-line coffin nail to him and asked, 'Smoke?'

Angus turned down her offer to voluntarily gas himself by shaking his head. Her accent was so pronounced that he'd recognized immediately that she was from the North of England, probably Newcastle. There was something in the firm set of her mouth that told him that her role as hotel lobby hooker was not an easy one for her to play. Her dark-blue, high-necked blouse was semi-transparent and he could not resist peeping to check out what was thinly concealed beneath it. Quite a handful from what he could gauge.

The bevelled, gold hoop earrings dangling from her pierced earlobes, beamed light reflections. Her almost nonexistent skirt whispered on her tanned thighs. Her thick makeup implied that her face was a mask and that he was in the presence of someone trying to hide her identity. Then he remembered where he'd seen her before; serving chai from a stainless steel container in the ashram's Vrindavan Restaurant. She noticed Angus's look of recognition, turned away and said something hollow to her giggling friend, who was sitting on the arm of Jimmy's leather chair with her legs open. Angus got an eyeful of the orange G-string that was cutting into the woman's shaved crotch. He checked out Jimmy, filling four flutes with bubbling white wine to the point of overflowing. Jimmy glanced up, winked across the table at him, grinning like a moron.

'Cheers,' said everyone as they raised their glasses to their smiling lips. Angus spilt champagne on the table, laughed self-consciously and realised he was drunk.

Angus woke the next morning, with the long-haired hooker snoring beside him, a head full of jagged thoughts and the sensation that he'd been trampled by a herd of stampeding horses. He groaned, staggered over to the window, pulled the thick curtains apart and gasped when strong sunlight speared into the room and stabbed into his bloodshot eyes. He opened the window and glanced down at the huge swimming pool in the hotel's courtyard. A draught pulled the window closed with a bang. The hotel prostitute moaned a complaint, blinked an unfocused eye and turned away from the light.

Angus stumbled into the blue-tiled bathroom. Ten minutes under a cold shower brought him back to the world of the living. A sharp burst of pain cut through the centre of his brain. 'Fucking alcohol,' he cursed, staring at his fuzzy reflection in a steamed-up wall mirror above the sink.

When he returned to the bedroom, the hooker was kneeling on all fours on the carpeted floor, frantically searching for something. Her pendulous breasts were swinging to and fro, reminding him of a cow's wobbling udder in need of milking. She turned around and presented him with an eyeful of a pinched rectum and a pink pussy.

He pulled on his white cotton trousers and asked, 'What is it you're looking for?'

From under the bed came the muffled reply, 'I can't find my bloody fags.'

Angus couldn't wait to get out of there. The women crawled back up onto the bed. She had a bent king-sized cigarette stuck in her mouth. The black lipstick smudged on her drawn cheeks made her appear like she'd been beaten up. She found a book of matches in a glass ashtray and lit her fag. She coughed, exhaled a long jet of blue-grey smoke in Angus's direction and asked, 'Where are you going in such a hurry?'

He buttoned up his light-blue poplin shirt. 'I've got a train to catch.'

'Not before paying me first, you haven't.'

He'd been waiting for this moment to arrive. 'How much?' he asked, curious to know what the damage was.

'Five hundred.'

'Rupees?'

'Dollars. What the fuck do you think I'm doing in Bombay, working for a charity organisation?'

'Did I actually get it together to fuck you?'

She raised a sceptical plucked eyebrow. 'Twice. Once in the shower and once over there.' She nodded towards an overturned armchair beneath a small acrylic painting of the Taj Mahal, hanging lopsided on a cream-coloured wall.

'But we're sannyasins,' complained Angus jokingly, opening his bulging black leather wallet and extracting a few hundred-dollar bills.

She leaned over and tapped her cigarette against the ashtray. 'That's true,' she agreed. 'But it's also true that business is business. I mean to say, you and your smarmy mate don't exactly give off the impression that you're tour guides.'

'What do you mean?'

'Rolex, expensive lightweight business suit, fat wallet, neat haircut, you've got dope smuggler written all over your Scottish mug.'

Angus glanced in a full-length wardrobe mirror. *She's right,* he thought, walking over to the bed. He dropped the paper money on the rumpled sheets.

Her right hand shot out like a cobra snatching a mouse. She counted the money and said, 'You've given me seven. I only asked for five.'

He stepped closer, bent forward, kissed her on the crown of her head and then said, 'Yeah, well, that's for the wonderful service, even though I can't remember it.'

The tension hanging in the room's atmosphere eased as soon as the financial aspect of their relationship was settled. For the first time, she gave him a genuine smile. She grabbed his wrist, glanced at his watch and said playfully, 'Check out's not for a couple of hours yet.'

Angus felt a hangover hard-on stirring in his pants, but the sharp pain emanating from the centre of his bruised brain won the morning and made him decline the offer. 'Thanks, maybe some other time.' He picked up his small canvas bag containing his orange robe, rubber flip-flops and toiletries. He headed for the door.

'Hey!' she called from the bed. 'Next time it's for free.'

Angus stopped, turned and said, 'The giver should be thankful, right?'

She laughed, sprang to her feet, walked over to Angus, hugged him, purred a little, stood on her tiptoes and whispered in his ear, 'If you give, you get.'

He held her at arm's length and looked into her smiling eyes. He saw his reflection waiting to greet him.

Walking along a dim corridor, he realised they hadn't exchanged names. He stopped outside room 307 and pressed an ear to the wooden door. He heard faint grunts and yelps and reckoned Jimmy had a more pressing engagement on his hands than bidding him farewell until their next job together.

He pushed open a fire exit door and walked down echoing stairs. The physical movement made his head throb. He wished he'd waited for the lift. He passed through the marble foyer, crammed with tourists and smartly-dressed Indian businessmen. Outside, Bombay's humidity hit Angus in the face like a hot, wet towel. He looked up when a passenger jet flew overhead and was blinded by the sun's glare. He hailed a black and yellow taxi and slid into the back seat. The Ambassador car smelled like the driver had shit his pants.

'Where you go?' asked the turbaned man, turning to face Angus.

'VT Station.'

'Fifty rupees, okay?'

'No, it's not okay,' replied Angus, who was not in the mood for haggling. 'Switch your meter on.'

The driver, complied, mumbled a curse, tooted his horn and pulled away from the kerb to join the chaotic flow of traffic heading towards Flora Fountain. The streets were thick with cars and smoke-belching buses. India's ever-present, faceless, urban throng was flowing over the uneven pavements, their existence as inconsequential as that of ants.

On the express train to Pune, Angus nipped into the toilet. The lavatory was splattered with intestinal waste and stank of urine. He held his breath and quickly changed clothes.

Four hours passed. The train pulled into Pune's central station. Hunger gnawed at Angus's stomach. He crossed a busy street and headed for a restaurant that he knew served good clean food. He sat down at a table that had a Thumbs Up soft drink ad printed on it and ordered a rice plate and *kulfi faluda* ice cream.

Dinner over, he returned to the street, jumped into the back seat of a three-wheeled, motorized rickshaw and asked the scraggy driver to take him to Koregaon Park. Weaving its way through traffic, the rickshaw's horn buzzed like an aggravated bumblebee in a tin can.

The rickshaw drew level with the Blue Diamond Hotel. Angus tapped the driver on the shoulder and pointed towards the six-storied, concrete building. The driver performed a sharp right turn into the hotel's forecourt. Angus paid the fare, slung his bag over his shoulder and, having decided he needed to stretch his legs, started walking. He entered the two-lane road that led towards the ashram's precincts. Illuminated by late evening sunlight, orange-clad sannyasins, mostly riding bicycles, passed by in both directions, some, like himself, making their way home.

'Hey, Loka,' called a tall man, stick-thin legs showing from beneath the knee-length hem of a pink robe. 'Haven't seen you in a while. How's life?'

At first, Angus wasn't sure who he was. After exchanging a few words, the Englishman's deep voice stirred memory banks into action. They had met one morning, waiting in the queue for one of Rajneesh's discourses, and shared a laugh, while checking out some of the attractive women standing in their proximity. His name was Vedant.

'Hi, Vedant, what's new?' Angus enquired.

'Oh, well, I finished a Vipassana group last week and I'm just taking it easy. Going to the discourse in the morning and generally going with the flow.' He turned and pointed back up the road. 'Just passed a big fire at the edge of the sugar cane fields. Somebody's bamboo house burned down.' He sniffed at the sleeve of his pink robe. 'Can still smell the smoke on my clothes.'

'*Shit!*' hissed Angus.

'What?' asked Vedant. 'Do you live in the fields?'

'Yeah, man, I do. In a bamboo house.' Angus patted the Englishman on the shoulder. 'I better get going and check that my place is okay.'

'Yes, yes,' said Vedant, 'I understand. Alright, so see you around, Loka.'

Angus hurried off toward home. An evening breeze carried the smell of scorched bamboo. Angus took off his flip-flops and quickened his pace to a gentle jog.

He reached the spot where his house should have been. All that remained was a blackened, smouldering rectangle on the ground. His major concern was for the money that he kept secreted under the wooden floor in a metal cash box. The floor was gone. His rubber flip-flops melted as he searched for the box. He found it under a pile of hot ashes. The aluminium padlock attached to the cash box had been transformed into an unrecognisable lump. The box was welded shut. He blistered his hands when he tried to pick it up. He used a scorched length of bamboo to nudge the box clear of the ashes and hammered it with a rock to force it open. 'Fucking Shit!' Angus gasped when he saw what remained of well over a hundred thousand dollars in cash. What had been paper money was now a formless pile of grey ash threaded with fine strands of partially melted silver.

Angus stepped a few paces back from the charred rectangle. He lay down on his back and stared up at the sky. Fluffy white clouds drifted by, tinged orange by the setting sun's last rays. He sat up and noticed one of the bamboo house's teak support poles was still standing upright. Wisps of smoke rose from its base. Halfway up the wooden pole hung a framed photograph of Bhagwan. It was the only thing that hadn't been affected by the fire. The master had a floral-patterned towel draped over his shoulder. There was a hint of mild amusement on his face. His wide-open eyes stared at Angus as if to say, 'Shit happens.'

Angus sat studying the photograph until darkness set in. He went through moments of sadness, resignation and disillusionment until he finally reached an inner space of deep acceptance where he could embrace what had happened. He stood, stumbled through the ashes and unhooked the framed picture from the rusty nail it was hanging on.

I watched the candle go out in the living room of my home in Oban. I sat in the darkness and smiled as the details of a happy memory became more vivid.

'Here,' Angus had said, a week before the tsunami had crashed into Unawantuna Bay in Sri Lanka to take him and Lara away, 'I want you to have this.'

'What is it?' I had asked.

'My most treasured possession,' Angus replied with a smile.

My twin brother's most treasured possession was now in a suitcase upstairs. I went to fetch it.

Jean moaned in her sleep as I entered the bedroom and slipped out with my case in hand. I returned to the living room, switched on a reading light and retrieved the photograph from the bottom of my Samsonite suitcase.

Time had done its work and faded the picture to a sepia colour. I sat down in an armchair and studied the master's face. The staring eyes soon unsettled me. I turned the picture around and for the first time, I realised that my brother had written something on the back of it. 'Jai Bhagwan.'

I turned the photo over and looked at the guru's face one more time. Despite the bald head and streaks of grey in the long black beard, it was a curiously timeless face that encapsulated perfectly the classic image of how an Eastern wise man might look. The wide-open eyes no longer seemed unsettling but rather surprised, a bit like how my own must have looked earlier that evening when I'd opened the door of the room I was now sitting in and discovered over twenty people were waiting to greet Jean and me.

It struck me that I had a lot to be grateful for. For the second time that evening, tears welled in my eyes. There was no logic to it, yet, inexplicable though it might have seemed, there was no doubting the strong sense that told me that my life was about to begin moving in a new direction.

7

SOUL SURVIVORS

Monday morning. I rose out of bed at dawn. I showered, shaved, dressed and managed to leave the bedroom without waking Jean. She usually got up to make my breakfast and returned to bed to read when I left for work but, on this particular morning, she needed to catch up on some sleep after our intercontinental air journey.

I went down to the kitchen and cooked eggs and bacon in a frying pan, boiled a kettle of water for coffee and switched on the radio. Tony Blair was still the prime minister and his voice filtered into the room, explaining why he thought there was a need for troop reductions in Iraq. I'd been a loyal Labour Party supporter for most of my adult life. I began to ruminate about how Blair had shown so much promise when he was voted into power, but in the end, turned out to be a puppet for the Americans and dragged Britain into an unpopular war. Saddam Hussein's weapons of mass destruction had turned out to be non-existent, but somehow the trumped-up excuse for invading Iraq in the first place had been swept aside and replaced with the war on terror. Next it was Gordon Brown's turn. His deep voice spoke about a long-term vision for Iraq and the need for stability in the region. *Fat chance of that happening,* I thought. I hoped he'd do a better job of steering the Labour Party's ship when he took over the helm from his predecessor, although somehow I doubted it. At least Gordon Brown's a Scotsman. I'd voted for the Scottish Nationalist Party last time there was a general election. I smiled to myself, thinking that Jean would throw a fit if I told her that I hadn't voted for the Tories.

Dressed in a black leather jacket and brown corduroy trousers, I stood on my front doorstep and looked down the street towards Oban. The town was shrouded in mist. I inhaled a deep breath and caught a whiff of fish. One of my neighbours was frying kippers for breakfast.

I pressed a button on a remote control device and the garage's automatic door opened. I entered the garage and reconnected the batteries on my metallic-grey BMW X5 and Jean's white Toyota Celica. The BMW's four-litre engine sparked into life at the first turn of the ignition key. I edged my vehicle up the ramp, turned left along Ardconnel Road and pushed my right foot down on the accelerator. The automatic gearbox shifted smoothly into second and the BMW surged down the street.

I'd washed down my greasy breakfast with two mugs of strong coffee and the caffeine in my system made me crave nicotine. I struggled with the uncomfortable sensation for a couple of minutes and then leaned over and opened the glove compartment. I was in luck. There was a packet of Marlboro Lights with one cigarette remaining in it. The ashtray flipped open and I used the cigar lighter to ignite my quick delivery nicotine tube. I gave a satisfied sigh as I blew my first lungful of tobacco smoke in six weeks out the open window. I switched on the radio and Joe Cocker's Sheffield steel voice came on singing 'Respect Yourself'. I sang along to the remake of the Staples Singer's 1971 crossover hit and found I was enjoying myself for the first time in weeks. 'It's a brand new day!' The few pedestrians on the pavement stopped and stared as Joe and I shot by in style, singing our duet at high volume. Boy, did that brass section sound great. I felt a wee bit dizzy from the nicotine rush. I pulled into a petrol station and bought two packets of cigarettes and six packets of spearmint chewing gum.

MacLeod and Mann's business premises are situated on the outskirts of Oban in a small industrial estate. I drove into the fenced-off compound and parked my X5 next to my partner's gleaming Jaguar.

Dave Mann was standing in the office's doorway with a lit fag in his smiling mouth, waiting to greet me.

'The wanderer has returned,' was the first thing he said as we shook hands.

We went into Dave's private office, sat down on high-backed chairs and began filling each other in on what had been going on since we'd last seen one another five months before.

'What do you mean, you sat on a bomb in Cambodia?' Dave asked, already flabbergasted to hear that I'd survived the tsunami in Sri Lanka and that my brother and his wife had been swept away in it, their bodies never recovered.

I went on to explain about my endless night, sitting on a landmine, and how Jean had crept up on me and knocked me off it, almost killing us both in the process.

It took over an hour for my narrative to arrive at the present moment. When it did, Dave lit a cigarette from the stub of his last one, shook his head in incredulity and said, 'The pair of you are lucky to be alive.'

I raised my eyebrows. 'In this world, you never know what's a blessing or a curse.'

'What's that?' Dave asked, his brow creasing in puzzlement. 'I didn't quite get that.'

'It doesn't matter,' I said, peeling the cellophane from a packet of Marlboro Lights. 'It's not important. It's your turn to talk. How's business?'

'Never been better,' answered Dave, his face brightening.

He went on to explain how he'd managed to sign a lucrative contract to construct two blocks of residential flats for Fort William's town council. I studied him as he enthusiastically described how he planned to make twice as much out of the deal as he was supposed to in the contract.

Dave Mann hadn't changed a bit since I'd last seen him in November. A confirmed bachelor, his appearance was as dishevelled as ever. His thin fair hair looked like it hadn't seen shampoo in a month. The collar of his white shirt was bent out of shape and lined with grime. His nicotine-stained right hand constantly pushed his wire-rimmed glasses up on his greasy nose in a nervous gesture that was particular to him, and he chain-smoked. Dave loved money above all else and he was in an exceptionally good mood that morning because, when it came to the bottom line, he and I were well on our way to making a fortune.

'That's absolutely brilliant,' I said after Dave's explanation about how we were going to make more money by the end of the year than we'd done in the last five, 'I don't know how you do it.'

Dave gave me a smug smile, thumbed his smudged spectacles up onto the bridge of his long nose and said, 'Hard work and determination.'

'How about taking a break from that hard work?' I asked. 'I'm sure you could do with it.'

Dave stubbed a dog-end out on the edge of a metal ashtray and added it to the molehill he was in the process of constructing that morning. He said, 'I was hoping you were going to say that. I'd like to take a month off and go visit some friends down in London.'

I was under no illusions concerning the nature of the *friends* Dave was referring to. They were prostitutes who plied their trade around the capital's Edgware Road. He collected the postcards that the West End hookers stuck in telephone boxes on Oxford Street and, when he returned to Oban, glued them into photo albums. He ranked the sex workers with gold stars after he'd visited each one in turn, sometimes half-a-dozen in the space of a day. One star was awarded to the slappers who made him wear a condom. Five went to the ladies that allowed him to have anal sex and finish him off by letting him come in their mouth — without the barrier of a condom to desensitize the erotic experience. Dave used Viagra to power his sordid adventures. He ordered the pills in bulk from a Chinese wholesaler in Shanghai. They were charging him a dollar a hit for a hundred-milligram pill that looked exactly like Phizer's number one product but contained enough amphetamine to keep a Motorhead fan speeding for a week. Dave was playing with the Ace of Spades and he knew it. One rainy afternoon, he'd gotten completely carried away with himself and swallowed five diamond-shaped blue pills. The following morning he'd had to visit a Harley Street urologist to have an injection to reduce his painful permanent erection. I knew all this because, every Friday after finishing work, Dave and I would sit in a sauna at our health club and I'd listen to him divulge the explicit details of his sexual exploits in London. Dave Mann had the biggest penis I have ever seen and I pitied the poor women who had to put up with it. Dave liked to call it his Loch Ness Monster.

'You horny old devil,' I said, waving a hand to disperse the cigarette fug hanging in the office. 'So, when do you want to head down to the big smoke?'

The word 'smoke' prompted Dave to light up his eighth Benson and Hedges since I'd entered his office that morning. He coughed violently and spoke through a blue cloud. 'I reckon, if I leave this coming weekend, you'll have had enough time to get used to being back behind the wheel.'

I rose from my seat, walked over to a double-glazed window, opened it to let some fresh air into the stuffy room and said, 'That's fine with me, Dave.' I turned to face my partner and asked, 'Have you ever thought about giving up smoking?'

Dave exhaled a cloud of smoke, coughed and answered, 'No, never. But I can see that you are trying to.' He chuckled ruefully. 'Mark my words, though, Hamish. You're a long way from being free of it yet.'

Three busy weeks passed. I was sitting alone in my office, cogs turning in my head. I was thinking too much and feeling edgy as I went about performing my executive duties for MacLeod and Mann, the builders. I toyed with the notion of sending the tea girl out for a packet of fags, but dropped the idea. I was determined to rid my body of its nicotine addiction.

I experienced the troubling impression that everything taking place around me was a shallow farce. I felt destabilised, because I could see clearly that everything I was doing was part of a fiction, a pretence that I had thought to be myself. My logical mind told me I should be pleased to be doing so well in life, but my heart said otherwise. My guts were churning, and I was plagued by the hollow sensation that all was not well in my life. The more I had it together on the outside, the emptier I felt on the inside. Middle age had marooned me on a superficial island of my own making, leaving me with the unsettling feeling that I'd completely missed life's deeper and more meaningful currents flowing below the surface.

Like most people, I'd been conditioned to believe that the more money I had, the more my happiness would increase. The truth was quite the contrary. It was a bewildering experience to realise that the more I had the unhappier I had become. I sat staring out of the window at the falling rain. It had been raining for the past week. *I'm bored,* I thought. *I wish something unusual and challenging would happen.* I shifted uncomfortably in my high-backed, black leather chair and looked around to knock on wood three times because I didn't want to tempt fate — too late, as it was to turn out. Morrígu, the Celtic Goddess of Fate, had heard my wish and was already arranging life's events in such a way as to fulfil it.

Meanwhile, those mental cogs in my mind continued to turn. *Where have I gone wrong?* I asked myself, after thinking for some time about my current role in life. The previous weekend, Jean and I had driven over to Glasgow to pick up a brand new Mercedes 500 SLC sports car. My wife now had something she'd wanted for years, the beautiful driving machine parked in our garage. Now that Jean possessed the Mercedes, it, in turn, possessed her. She'd become a slave to the streamlined German beast and constantly fretted about it being stolen. A small scratch on the driver's side door had sent her into a tantrum and she'd cried herself to sleep the night she'd discovered that some jealous person had ripped a key across the flank of her cherry-red, German wonder car. The very thing that she believed would bring her joy made her lament and cry. The illusion created by a conditioned conceptual belief system began to make itself clear in my mind. It was plain to see that material things — or rather people's attachment to them — were the root cause of so much suffering in the world. *I should write all these contemplative thoughts down,* I thought. Then the idea came to me that I needed a creative outlet. I'd always fancied having a crack at writing. One associative thought led to another until one asserted itself as being superior to all the others. *Write the story of my life and my twin brother's.* I wrote a reminder note to purchase a new PC. *I'll buy it online from Amazon and, while I'm at it, I can order a few self-help books on creative writing,* I thought. *I'll keep it a secret. I won't tell anyone, especially not Jean, at least not until my manuscript is finished.* My mind began to shift into overdrive, visualizing myself tapping away on a new laptop's keyboard.

My runaway train of thought was brought to an abrupt halt when the phone on my desk rang. I picked up the receiver. It was my secretary in the office next door. I listened for a moment and then asked, 'What do they want?' A brief pause and then I said, 'You better send them through.'

Even had I not been informed who they were, I would have recognized them immediately as plain-clothes police officers. Their haggard pale faces, suspicious eyes, anonymous cheap suits, blue shirts and ties, and, more importantly, their thick-soled shoes were a dead giveaway.

I stood and shook hands with the two men as they went through the formalities of introducing themselves.

'Please, gentlemen,' I said, repositioning myself behind the security that my desk provided, 'pull up a chair and let me know what I can do for you.'

The two men glanced at each other and did as requested. Detective Inspector Dunn, the eldest of the two, nodded at me and said, 'Mister MacLeod, perhaps you should also sit down. I'm afraid my colleague and I are the bringers of unfortunate news.'

I did as the detective suggested and thought, *Jesus Christ, something's happened to Jean. That bloody Mercedes.*

The savvy inspector looked over at my drawn face and said, 'It's not your wife if that's what you're thinking.'

I felt the expression on my face change instantly into one of relief. 'What is it then? What's happened?'

Detective Sergeant Grant, the younger policeman, answered, 'We're here because of your business partner, Dave Mann.' He produced a packet of cigarettes and a lighter from his jacket pocket. 'Mind if I smoke?'

I shook my head. 'Go ahead. D-D-Dave?' I stammered. 'What happened?'

The two policemen glanced at each other again and then the inspector said, 'I must inform you that Mister Mann is dead.'

'Dead?'

'Yes, Mister MacLeod,' confirmed the sergeant, 'and we have to ask you a few questions because Mister Mann died under suspicious circumstances.'

'What?' I found it hard to believe what I was hearing. I clasped my hands in front of me on the desk to prevent them from shaking.

'Cigarette?' asked the sergeant.

I took one of the young detective's fags and jammed it between my quivering lips. The cop leaned over the desk and lit it for me. I exhaled a cloud of smoke over the heads of the two stony-faced men, sitting staring at me. I asked, 'What happened exactly?'

Inspector Dunn cleared his throat and answered, 'Mister Mann was found dead in a Bayswater hotel...' He consulted a small notebook in his left hand. '...at eleven a.m., yesterday morning. The deceased was found in a state of undress, a leather collar with metal studs on it around his neck. The collar was attached to a water pipe in the bathroom by a stainless steel chain. It appears that the cause of death was heart failure, although the coroner's report hasn't been filed yet. The previous evening, Mister Mann was seen entering the building with a well-known local prostitute. The hotel reception had received two complaints about the disturbing noises coming out of Mister Mann's suite during the early hours of the morning.' The policeman raised his eyes thoughtfully while I listened on in silence. 'Our colleagues in London, upon searching the room, discovered a number of controlled substances, including cocaine and amphetamine.' Dunn glanced from his notes to my face without missing a beat. 'Mister MacLeod, did you know that your partner was a drug user?'

I was flabbergasted. 'Me? Ehm...well, no...I mean yes.'

'Yes or no?' queried the sergeant, a tinge of impatience in his voice. 'Straight answers will help speed up our enquiry.'

I studied the two policemen for a brief moment and wondered if they enjoyed their work. I reasoned that no harm could come of telling what I knew about Dave's private life, seeing as how my partner was now dead.

'Yes,' I said. 'I knew that Dave used amphetamine from time to time when he visited prostitutes in London.'

'And cocaine?' asked the sergeant.

I shrugged. 'Dave never mentioned to me that he sniffed cocaine.'

'What about injecting it into his penis with a syringe?' asked the inspector, his tone brusque and businesslike.

'Certainly not,' I answered, wondering where this was going.

Inspector Dunn raised a sceptical eyebrow. 'Are you sure about that?'

'Of course, I'm—'

The sergeant cut me off by saying, 'That's a very expensive new car your wife is driving.'

I sensed immediately that this unexpected statement was intended to throw me off balance, but I managed to retain my equanimity and responded by saying, 'You're being ridiculous. What kind of car my wife drives has absolutely nothing to do with my business partner's death.'

Inspector Dunn delivered the sceptical eyebrow treatment again. 'Doesn't it?'

'Of course not.'

Silence. I took a last drag on the cigarette and stubbed it out in an ashtray.

'Mister MacLeod,' said the inspector, leaning forward onto the desk and looking directly into my eyes, 'you've just returned from a very long journey. Am I right?'

'Yes, but... '

'During that time you visited your brother's luxurious home in Sri Lanka. Am I correct?'

'Yes, but how do you know—'

'Mister MacLeod, with all due respect, I would like to remind you that I am a detective inspector of police and you are the subject of a police enquiry. Please answer my question.'

I felt a bottomless pit open up where my stomach should have been. 'Yes,' I said, 'I stayed with my brother and his wife in Sri Lanka for three months. But they were both killed in the tsunami there last year.'

The two cops' bulldog faces brightened, and they shared a knowing look. Inspector Dunn produced a black-and-white photograph and pushed it across the desk towards me.

'What's this?'

'Look at it, Mister MacLeod,' ordered the inspector.

I picked up the grainy photo and studied it. Angus and Lara were standing on wet cobblestones, facing two men who had their backs turned to the camera that had taken the shot. All four of them were wearing raincoats, and Lara was holding a closed umbrella in her right hand. Her left arm was blurred, suggesting movement. Angus was laughing and Lara was scowling. I looked from the photograph to the inspector's inscrutable grey eyes and said, 'So?'

'So, do you see anyone in that photograph that you recognise?' asked the inspector.

'Of course, I do. That's my twin brother, Angus, and his wife, Lara. But, as I informed you already, they were killed last year in the tsunami.'

The detective sergeant took over by saying, 'You're lying, Mister MacLeod. That photograph was taken in Amsterdam a month ago by an undercover police officer from Europol.'

I rose out of my seat. 'That's impossible. They're dead.'

'Sit down, Mister MacLeod,' said Sergeant Grant, lighting another cigarette.

I did as ordered, my legs unsteady.

The sergeant smiled cynically and blew a jet of smoke into my face. 'What I am about to ask you is off the record. At least for now.' He pointed his cigarette's burning tip towards me. 'Do you know your brother is a big international drug smuggler, a money launderer and possibly a murderer?'

'Now hold on a minute.' I caught the other cop rolling his eyes. 'What has all this to do with the death of my business partner?'

'Please, Mister MacLeod,' said Detective Inspector Dunn, drumming his right hand's fingers on the edge of the desk, 'answer my colleague's question.'

I leaned back in my chair and struggled to come to terms with the fact that, if what the sergeant said was true, Angus and Lara were still alive. The realisation followed how it might appear that I had something to hide. Angus as well. *Jesus,* I thought, *that's an understatement. Angus has a lot to hide.* I regained my composure by taking a few deep breaths. I finally said, 'Gentlemen, if you wish to ask me any more questions I'd like to have my lawyer present, Malcolm Robertson. Perhaps you've heard of him.'

It would have been impossible for them not to. Malcolm Robertson QC was well known by the police as being an incorruptible senior barrister, who'd rarely lost a case. Just the mention of his name put the long arm of the law in a sling.

For the first time since the detective inspector entered the room, his pallid face showed a lack of confidence. The exchange changed character at that moment. 'Well, if you want to adopt a stance like that—'

It was my turn to cut someone off. 'A stance like what exactly? Like the stance of a law-abiding citizen, who paid over a hundred thousand pounds in taxes last year to keep you and people like your *colleague* here in well-paid jobs? Now then,' I continued, 'as I've already said, if you have any further questions to ask of me I will only answer them if I have my lawyer present. Am I making myself clear?'

The two detectives stared at each other. Their faces were pensive and troubled.

I rose from my seat, picked up the cordless phone, punched in a number, waited a moment and then spoke into it. 'Doreen, would you be so kind as to come through to my office and escort my two visitors off the premises.' I tossed the phone onto my desk and stood with my back to the detectives, staring out of the window.

The two cops stood up. The detective inspector coughed to draw attention to himself. I turned and glowered at him.

'We'll be back,' said the inspector.

'Not without my lawyer being present, you won't,' I assured him.

The man stepped forward and offered his right hand. I ignored it, straightened my red tie and turned once more to look out of the window. It had stopped raining.

The door opened behind me and I heard my secretary's voice say, 'This way, gentlemen, please.'

I watched the detectives cross the asphalted car park, get into their dark-blue Ford Mondeo and drive away. I strode through to my secretary's office. She looked up from a computer screen. I pulled an office chair over, sat down and looked across the desk at her. Doreen sensed something serious had happened. She removed her reading glasses and carefully placed them on top of a pile of invoices. I took a deep breath and exhaled slowly. 'I'm sorry, Doreen. I've just heard some very bad news.' I paused. 'Listen,' I said, my voice quavering, 'I know this will come as a great shock to you, but I'll give it to you straight.' I hesitated. Doreen stared at me, mouth slightly open. 'Dave Mann passed away yesterday morning down in London.'

'Oh, no.' Doreen groaned, put her elbows on the desk and covered her face with her hands. She began to sob.

I rose from the chair and went around the desk to comfort her. I placed a hand on her back and waited until she'd cried herself dry. When her breathing returned to normal, I said, 'Take the rest of the day off, Doreen. Tomorrow too, if you need a bit of time to recover.'

She began to protest. 'It's okay, Mister MacLeod. I'm fine. I don't need—'

'Come on now, Doreen. I'm not going to argue with you. Away home with you. This will leave us both shaken up for some time.'

'Aye, alright, Hamish. You're probably right.' She looked up at me, her face flushed and swollen.

'Doreen, that's the first time you've addressed me by Christian name in over twenty years.'

'Oh, Mister MacLeod, I didn't mean to be rude. I'm awful sorry.'

I shook my head. 'There's no need to feel sorry, Doreen. Now, away home with you. I'll see you when you're ready to return to work. Take your time.'

'Thanks, Ham... I mean, thanks, Mister MacLeod.' She dabbed at her eyes with a tissue. 'Poor man. Was it the cigarettes?'

'Pardon me?'

'Did Mister Mann have a heart attack from all those fags he smoked?'

I nodded. 'Aye, aye, he probably did, Doreen,' I lied. 'Off you go now.'

I gave her a weak smile and returned to the privacy of my office. I slumped into my leather chair and rummaged in a desk drawer, hoping to find a packet of cigarettes. I didn't find one but popped a piece of nicotine chewing gum into my mouth instead. I wasn't ready to dwell too much on Dave's unexpected departure from the world. It was just too sudden, too strange. The news that Angus and Lara were still alive was even weirder. I needed to focus my thoughts on something mundane. My mind returned to what I'd been thinking about before my unexpected visit from the two police detectives. I went online and began browsing Amazon's website for a laptop. It took me five minutes to decide on a Toshiba. I placed my order and then checked out books on creative writing. I ordered half-a-dozen. I went to the checkout and punched in my credit card details. *There, I've done it*, I thought, relieved to have momentarily escaped more demanding realities.

I put my feet up on the desk and clasped my hands behind my head. I closed my eyes and Dave Mann's tired face appeared. 'No!' I wasn't ready for that. My eyes sprang open, and I noticed the detectives had left the photograph behind. I did not need to examine it again to verify its authenticity. It was real. There could be no doubt about it. Two thoughts started spinning round in my mind. One of them was an affirmation. *One day soon I will begin writing all this down.* The other was a question. *How the hell had Angus and Lara survived the tsunami?*

Unawantuna Bay, Sri Lanka, 8:50 a.m., December 26, 2004. When Angus and Lara reached the four European teenagers, standing on an exposed coral reef at the north end of Unawantuna Bay, they ordered them to take their flippers off and run towards the beach as quickly as possible. The sea had by now receded from the shoreline to a distance of seventy metres. As soon as they reached what had been, ten minutes before, the normal shoreline, everyone jogged towards a narrow wooden bridge, which crossed a small stream running past a white-painted Buddhist temple. They came to a halt by the rivulet's sandy bank. There was an eerie silence in the air.

Lara took hold of Angus's right arm and said, 'Look, somebody is sleeping on the beach in front of the dive centre.'

Angus spun around and looked to where she was pointing. 'Shit,' he said, running a hand over his shaved head, 'so there is. You take the kids and I'll go wake whoever that is up.'

Lara shook her head. 'No way am I going to leave your side at a moment like this.'

Angus checked the look in her adamant dark-green eyes. 'Jesus, Lara, you're as stubborn as I am.' He turned to the four teenagers, who were staring at him like frightened rabbits. 'You lot run like hell,' he ordered, gesturing in the direction he wished them to go. 'When you reach a steep tarred road on the left, keep going until you reach the village. You got that?'

The teenagers nodded in unison.

'What are you waiting for then?' he asked, raising his voice. '*Go!*'

The kids broke into a run. Angus didn't take his eyes off them until they'd sprinted by the Blowhole Restaurant. Then, he and Lara dashed over to the person lying on the beach. There was a loud, watery hiss coming from the ocean's direction. Angus and Lara turned in time to see the tsunami beginning to rise from the water. He grabbed Lara's hand and pulled her in the direction of the deserted two-storey dive shop. She glanced at the person sleeping on the sand and began to protest. 'What about—'

Angus almost pulled her left arm out of its socket. He shouted, '*Come on!*'

They ran into the deserted grey building's open front and hurried up the concrete stairs. Angus grabbed two life jackets off a peg on the way up. 'Here,' he said, thrusting an orange life vest into Lara's hand, 'put this on.' Lara and Angus were struggling into the vests when the daylight flooding into the oblong room via an open window was dimmed by the fast-approaching tsunami. Angus grabbed Lara's left hand. The ten-metre-high tidal wave crashed into and over the two-storey building. They were slammed against a brick wall by the onrush of filthy water. Lara was knocked unconscious. The dive centre collapsed. Angus clung to Lara's body as they were plunged into a swirling torrent. His left shoulder dislocated when it thudded against the trunk of a coconut tree. He swallowed a mouthful of brackish water as they tumbled head over heel in the murk. His head broke to the surface and he gasped for air. He hauled Lara up into the light. He caught a glance of her chalk-white face as the frothing sea dragged them further inland. There was a livid gash on her left cheek. They were whisked past a bellowing water buffalo, struggling to save itself. Its front legs thrashed at the water. The buffalo was tethered to a tree. It was being choked by a nylon cord tightening around its neck. The terrified beast's bulging eyes looked pleadingly at Angus before its horned head disappeared. Lara was sucked below the surface. Angus drew her to him. They had been washed about two hundred metres inland. The water was suddenly still and then slowly began to recede, dragging Angus and Lara out to sea. They were sucked down. Angus's right thigh was ripped open by a submerged barbed-wire fence. He clawed his way to the surface and once again pulled Lara's unconscious body towards his own. The back of his head banged against something solid. It was a refrigerator. Using his dislocated left arm, he grabbed the white oblong box's shiny aluminium handle. He screamed and almost passed out from the pain.

It seemed to Angus that it took forever to haul Lara out of the water and lay her limp body across the refrigerator's semi-submerged door. She'd lost her bikini top and life jacket. The sight of her goose-pimpled breasts unleashed a shockwave of terror into his mind. He drew in a deep lungful of air to try and calm his frantic thoughts. His throat felt swollen and coarse. He kicked to stay afloat. The muscles in his calves began to cramp. He positioned himself at one end of the fridge, hauled himself halfway out of the sea, held Lara's nostrils closed with one hand, forced her mouth open with the other and then blew breath into her lungs. He could sense her spirit slipping away from the earthly plane.

'Nooooo!' he cried, looking up into the cloudless blue sky. He shouted, 'No, I say! If you have to take one of us take me, or else take both of us.'

High above, Angus saw two buzzards coasting on thermals. He turned back to Lara and continued blowing air into her collapsed lungs. He smashed a clenched fist down on her breastbone in frustration and yelled, 'Don't you fucking well leave me!'

Lara's body jerked. Her eyes sprang open. She gasped and then vomited seawater.

By sunset, Angus and Lara were floating five kilometres off the southwest coast of Sri Lanka. They could see Galle Fort in the distance. When it grew dark, there were very few lights to be seen.

'Something terrible has happened,' said Lara staring over at the coastal town's shadowy outline from where a lighthouse's beam flashed every twenty seconds.

As they were to discover three days later, six thousand people's lives were snuffed out in less than a minute when Galle was engulfed by the tsunami.

Angus and Lara quenched their thirst by drinking cans of Coca-Cola they found in the fridge. On the second afternoon, Sri Lanka's coastline disappeared below the horizon. Angus could feel the strong current that was pulling them out into the Indian Ocean drag against his legs. Towards sunset, a black dorsal fin cut above the water's surface. A shark began to circle them, perhaps attracted by the scent of blood seeping from the deep festering wound on Angus's right leg. Angus and Lara shook cans of Coke and then opened them under the water to produce bubbles, knowing from their experience as scuba divers that sharks were spooked by the sight and sound of bubbling air. The black fin disappeared under the surface and the shark swam away.

Just before dawn, Angus and Lara gave two Sinhalese fishermen the fright of their lives when they swam up to their twin-hulled boat and Lara said, 'Ayubowan (hello).'

The fact that Lara was fluent in Sinhalese, to the point of being able to speak the local dialect, had a very positive effect on the fishermen, who were unaware that a massive tidal wave had hit the coast. The fishermen had been at sea for three days and didn't have a radio. They hoisted their tattered brown sail and headed northeast. Four hours later, they came ashore on the beach fronting a popular tourist resort called Hikkaduwa. The scene that greeted them was one of devastation. The beach was covered in rubbish and most of the small shops and restaurants that had once lined the coastal road were gone. The fisherman beached their boat, hitched it to a boulder and then, after a hurried farewell, ran inland in search of their families.

Angus and Lara walked across the beach hand in hand. There were many dead bodies and animal carcasses strewn amongst the debris. The putrid smell was overpowering. Lara began to retch.

They reached the main road only to discover that the highway to the south was mostly gone, as were the railway tracks and the packed trains that had once run along them to and from Colombo.

The capital was one hundred kilometres north, a journey that normally took three hours. That day it took Angus and Lara nine hours by taxi at ten times the normal price. It was midnight when they unlocked the front door of the small apartment in central Colombo that they used when they had to visit the city to attend to business matters. The flat also served as a bolt hole, in case the police showed up in Unawantuna with an international arrest warrant with Angus's name on it. Hidden behind a removable cupboard, there was a combination safe set into a kitchen wall. The steel safe contained over fifty thousand American dollars in various denomination notes and the same again in euros. There were also half a dozen British passports, various rubber stamps to produce exit and entry visas, credit cards in different names and gold bullion in case the global economy went into permanent freefall.

First thing in the morning, Angus and Lara visited a local doctor's surgery to have their injuries treated. Relocating Angus's shoulder caused him to howl in agony.

Wounds stitched and bandaged, they sat around in the apartment, smelling of antiseptic and discussing their next move.

Two weeks later, they caught an LTU flight to Düsseldorf, from where they travelled by ICE train to Amsterdam.

When they showed up unannounced at the front door of a luxurious top-floor apartment in Amsterdam's Prinsengracht, Raj, Murphy, Alice and Nina were relieved and overjoyed to see Angus and Lara.

It was a rainy Sunday afternoon. Lara and Angus had lunch with Raj and Murphy in the Café Luxemburg on the Spui, a cobbled square in the heart of the city. After coffee, all four of them went outside. It was then that Raj remembered something that he'd been meaning to ask Angus for days.

'Does your brother and his wife know that you guys are still alive?'

'No,' answered Angus, 'I want to give him a surprise.' He glanced at Lara, who was frowning, nodded at her and then commented, 'Lara's not very happy about it.'

'I'm not surprised,' commented Raj.

'I think it's a fuckin' brilliant idea,' said Murphy.

Angus laughed and Lara punched him on the shoulder. It was at that precise moment that an undercover cop pressed the shutter button on his Nikon digital camera with a 500mm telephoto lens attached.

Angus noticed the man with the camera, leaning against a lamppost outside a newsagent's shop. 'Hey,' he said, nodding towards the man in a black anorak with the hood up, 'that guy over there just took a photo of us.'

Murphy glanced over his shoulder. The man hurried away and merged with the crowds strolling through an open-air art market on the square. 'Och,' he commented, 'probably some twat who thinks he's David Attenborough photographing Amsterdam's wildlife. Nothing to worry about.' He turned back to his friends and said, 'C'mon, let's hop on our bikes and go for a game of pool.'

'And a big fat joint,' added Raj.

Dave Mann was buried on a blustery Monday morning. I was appointed one of the pallbearers. After a brief church service, we carried the coffin into the cemetery. I was surprised at how many people showed up for my business partner's funeral. Over two hundred mourner's crowded around as I helped lower Dave's casket into the grave by holding on to a thick nylon rope. When Dave's body was laid to rest, I returned to my wife's side. Jean had bought a black suede coat for the solemn occasion. She had on a matching floppy hat with a veil attached that hung down to cover the top half of her face, like a widow in Francis Ford Coppola's *The Godfather.*

We stood silently, listening to a stony-faced minister waffle on for ten minutes. I imagined Dave in his coffin, having an ironic laugh about the lengthy sermon. Until that morning, he'd never entered a church during his fifty-nine years upon God's earth.

After the ceremony, I had a quick word with my lawyer, Malcolm Robertson. The QC and Dave Mann had been on very good terms. They'd shared several things in common. Malcolm and Dave had been in the same class in secondary school, played golf together and shared the same taste in prostitutes. Over the years, the old school friends had often travelled to London together to sample what various ladies of the night offered in the way of extreme titillation. Malcolm and I arranged to meet at the Ballachulish House golf course near Fort William on the following Sunday morning.

Malcolm worked the course with more skill than I possessed. We played eighteen holes. He won to the extent that it made me look like a novice. Afterwards, I sat down at a table in the Ballachulish House restaurant. I had changed my shoes in the car park but kept my golf clothes on, a pair of black jeans and a green Polo shirt. Malcolm, a fastidious dresser, had disappeared for ten minutes into the men's room and reappeared in a lightweight, dark-grey suit, a freshly pressed, light-blue cotton shirt and dark-blue silk tie. His thick silver hair was long for a man of his profession and combed straight back from his broad forehead.

We ordered lunch and, over plates of braised Perthshire beef in a delicious port wine sauce, washed down by two bottles of Châteaux Margaux 1990, I narrated the story about the police's unexpected visit to my office.

Malcolm listened in silence and shook his head in disbelief on a couple of separate occasions. When I fell silent, Malcolm cleared his throat and said, 'I know Inspector Andy Dunn from way back. So did Dave. We used to play football together when we were youngsters. Andy was always a bit of a bully, but his bark's a lot worse than his bite. He's a mason.' The QC glanced at me and waved his fork in emphasis. 'I'll have a wee word with Andy about harassing a well-respected citizen like yourself, Hamish. Silly bugger thinks he's Inspector Rebus.' He winked. 'Besides, from what you've told me, it's clear that you haven't broken the law. Even if you had, it's always the unwritten law that prevails over the written. One small piece of advice, though. That brother of yours... Angus is it? ...if he is still alive, he sounds like trouble so—'

I cut across him. 'That's what my grandfather said about Angus when he was a baby.'

'Robert MacLeod,' said Malcolm. He shook his head remembering my paternal grandfather, who'd been close friends with his father. 'A wee bit of a nippy sweetie, as they say, but a more direct, honest and reliable man you could not ask for. Aye, they don't make them like Rab anymore, may he forever rest in peace. Along with our dear friend, Dave. I will miss him, and I'm certain you will also.' Malcolm placed a liver-spotted hand on my right arm. 'Anyway, as I was saying, if that brother of yours shows up, stay well clear of him. There's no smoke without fire and, by the sound of what DI Andy Dunn said to you, it might well be the case that your brother's past is catching up with him, and it would be a mistake to be in close proximity to him when it finally does.' Malcolm gave me a curt nod and removed his hand from my lower arm. 'Now then, Hamish,' he continued, 'I've got a wee bit of news that may well come as a pleasant surprise to you.'

'And what's that, Malcolm?'

'Dave Mann made up a new will last year.'

I felt my brow crinkle in puzzlement. 'Aye, I'm listening. Go on.'

'As you know, Davey didn't have any close family relations left. And, as you are also doubtless aware, there were no flies on our Davey boy when it came to money matters.'

'I think everybody knew that about Dave,' I commented.

'Aye,' concurred Malcolm, 'but what nobody knew, except me up to now, is that Dave Mann left everything he owned to you.'

'What!' I exclaimed. 'I don't believe it.'

'Aye, well, that's understandable enough.' The senior barrister stood up, straightened his suit jacket and then offered his right hand. 'Mister Hamish MacLeod, let me be the first to congratulate you. I'm pleased to inform you that you are now a very wealthy man, indeed.' He paused for a brief moment and reflected on what he'd just said and then added, 'Or perhaps it's more correct to say wealthier.' I stood up and shook hands. The barrister leaned in close and spoke in a hushed whisper. 'Hamish, I'd like to level with you. Man to man, so to speak. I'm aware that you're not a Mason. I do believe it's time for that to change.' He stood back from me, gripping my hand in a peculiar manner. 'What do you say, my brother?'

I said nothing. But I did see a picture in my mind of myself as a *brother*, wearing a goatskin apron with my trouser legs rolled up. It wasn't an image I liked.

On the drive back to Oban, it began to rain. I switched on the BMW's sidelights and wipers. My thoughts swung back and forth between the unexpected occurrences that had taken place during the last week. Until that moment, I hadn't informed Jean about my disturbing visit from the police or the news that Angus and Lara had somehow survived the tsunami. I decided to let it remain that way for a little while longer, especially now that Angus was the prime target of an ongoing police investigation.

I asked myself why Angus hadn't contacted me to let me know he and Lara were still alive. My brother was a sensitive and intelligent man and would easily have understood the grief I would undergo due to their apparent deaths. Then again, Angus had told me that two British undercover policemen had been snooping around, making what they mistakenly believed were discreet enquiries about him in Sri Lanka. Perhaps the tsunami had provided him with the perfect opportunity to drop below the radar. *Knowing Angus*, I reasoned, *the bloody idiot's planning some kind of big surprise for me. Yes, he's crazy enough to just appear one day out of nowhere and behave like it's nothing out of the ordinary.* I chuckled at the thought of it.

The rain intensified. I clicked the wipers onto high speed. Their motion, coupled with the afternoon's strong wine, began to make me feel drowsy. I lowered my window a little and fresh air streamed into the car. I switched on the radio. *It's raining men! Hallelujah!...* I was tired, but not that tired. I pushed a preset button, tuned to an FM station playing classic rock. *I saw him dancin' there...* I caught Joan Jett and the Blackhearts kicking into 'I Love Rock n' Roll'. I thumbed the plus on the steering wheel's volume control, pressed down on the accelerator and the car shot forward.

Twenty seconds later, I drove into a tight curve at 65 mph. The X5's tyres squealed in protest as the four-wheel-drive strained to retain traction on the slippery asphalt. '*Shit!*' My car skidded off the road, careened down a fern-clad embankment, and then, with a resounding crunch, bounced off a pine tree on the driver's side. Airbags popped. The white bag, released from the steering wheel, threw my head back with considerable force. The car then somersaulted over a ditch and landed upside down on the bank of a swollen stream. Joan Jett's voice mashing with the engine's high-pitched whine is the last thing I remember before blacking out.

'Hamish...Hamish...Hamish.' A female voice was whispering my name. I couldn't recall who the voice belonged to or remember how to open my eyes.

'Hamish, Hamish, please wake up,' the voice pleaded.

My tongue felt thick as I muttered through my cracked lips, 'Jean...Jean, is that you?' My sleep-encrusted eyes blinked open.

Jean, sitting on the edge of my hospital bed, screeched, 'Jesus bloody Christ!' She jumped to her feet and then said more quietly, her voice quivering, 'I... I was beginning to think you were never going to wake up.' Tears rolled down her cheeks as she sobbed, 'I... I thought I'd lost you.'

'W-W-What?' I stammered. I tried to turn my head towards her but couldn't.

Jean looked down and nervously straightened the folds in her black dress. 'How could you do this to me?'

'D-D-Do what to you?' I realised my wife was furious. Black mascara was smudged all over her face. She looked like a witch who'd fallen into a fire.

Jean ran a hand across her furrowed brow. 'What did you do to me? You got drunk and nearly kill yourself in a stupid car accident. First, it's a bloody landmine and now this. Anyone would think you had some kind of death wish.'

I had a flashback of what had happened. I recalled the simultaneous pops of the airbags that had in all probability saved my life. I felt the impact of the BMW as it bounced off a tree trunk, a disorientating spinning motion, loud rock music, a very unhappy car engine and...and then nothing.

'How long have I been here?' I asked.

'Two and a half bloody weeks,' was Jean's angry answer.

'What? Where am I?'

She shook her head in frustration, dabbed at her cheeks with a paper hankie and answered, 'You're in the Western General Hospital in Edinburgh, you blithering idiot that you are! You were strapped to a stretcher and airlifted here in a helicopter.'

Airlifted in a helicopter? I thought. *How could I have missed that?* I put a hand to my aching head and realised for the first time that it was swathed in bandages. I tried to sit up and discovered that I couldn't move. Dumbfounded, I asked, 'What's wrong with me.'

'What's bloody well wrong with you? You've got multiple fractures in your right leg, four broken ribs, two fractured cervical vertebrate and enough stitches in your thick head to darn a pair of bloody socks.' Jean sat down on the edge of the bed and took my right hand in her own. Her tone softened. 'I've been worried sick about you. The doctors have been worried too, about your bruised brain. I was surprised to hear that you have one.'

'But why can't I move?' I enquired, feeling suddenly nauseous.

Jean tightened her grip on my hand. 'Hamish, the surgeons must have used up a whole Meccano Set to join your broken bones together. Your neck was the worst. You now have two wee hinges and eight wee screws in there, and a four-inch incision scar on the back of your neck to prove it. I'll never forget the afternoon you came out of the theatre following that operation. Your head was swollen and your face looked like a Halloween pumpkin. In a way, you are a very fortunate man. I've been informed that the fractures in your neck were millimetres away from being fatal. Something to do with severing nerves that control your lungs or something along those lines.' Jean slackened her grip on my hand and continued. 'So the reason you can't move is due to your injured neck, and because you're strapped to the bed. They can't say for sure to what extent you're going to recover, or how long it will take. Maybe eighteen months before you can walk properly again. Anyway, I'll be by your side whatever the case may be. I'm just glad you are alive.' She stretched over to the end of the bed and detached a plastic catheter bag from a rail. She dangled it in front of my face. 'Well, at least you won't need to get up for a pee during the night. Aren't you the lucky one?'

The daylight in the room was beginning to hurt my eyes. Before I closed them, I looked into my wife's bloodshot eyes. I saw something there that I hadn't seen in what felt like a very long time — tenderness. I asked, 'Did you drive down from Oban?'

'Oban,' she echoed, 'I haven't been home since the accident. Your daughters have been out of their minds with worry. Moira was here yesterday. I'm staying at the Bannockburn Hotel on Craigleith Road.'

'I'm sorry,' I said, because I did not know what else to say. 'I didn't mean to cause so much trouble.'

Jean leaned over and kissed my lips. 'I know, darlin',' she said, her eyes brimming with tears, 'I'll away down the road now.' She sniffed. 'Get some sleep and I'll be back tomorrow afternoon. You just...'

I lapsed into unconsciousness.

I woke up in the middle of the night. The back of my neck felt like it was in the grip of a steel vice. Then I remembered where I was. My mouth was dry. I reached over for a small plastic bottle of water, conveniently placed on a bedside cupboard. I took a sip, lay in the darkness and listened. In the distance, a police siren wailed like a lonesome ghost. The muffled sound of rubber-soled shoes squeaked in the corridor outside of my private room. Rain pattered against the window. The situation was unreal, like a dream I couldn't wake up from. Car accidents, I ruminated, they happen every minute of every day all over the world. Everyone is aware of that. I'd taken pride in my driving skills, lending me the illusion that I would be safe, that serious car crashes were tragedies that belonged in other unfortunate people's lives, but not mine. I was mistaken. Thanks to my bad driving, I was strapped to a hospital bed with a drip feed in my arm. Just like the bumper sticker says, SHIT HAPPENS!

And then, bubbling up from the past, I recalled something Angus had said to me: hospital, prison and your grave are the three best places to find out who your genuine friends are.

Your grave? I thought. *What made him come to such a morbid conclusion?* I looked up to my left and studied the plastic drip-feed bag, suspended from a metal stand. It glowed lime-green in the dark, illuminated by a small screen, monitoring my vital signs. *They put sedatives in there,* I figured. *No wonder I feel drowsy. What was I just thinking about? Oh, yes, finding out who your friends are when you are dead. Typical Angus.* A Woody Allen quote that I'd read somewhere, popped into my throbbing head. *I'm not afraid of death; I just don't want to be there when it happens. Yes,* I reflected, *but sometimes maybe you are there.* My mind drifted into the slipstream of the past.

8

THE BUDDHAFIELD

'God is not for sale', were the last words Angus could remember before Bhagwan Shree Rajneesh said, 'Enough for today,' and then, raising his hands as if in prayer, the guru stood to salute the thousands of orange-robed sannyasins sitting before him. From Angus's position, at the back of Buddha Hall, it appeared like the master was floating on air. Bhagwan dropped his hands to his sides and carefully stepped down from the marble podium and drifted into the back seat of a waiting Rolls Royce.

The gleaming black limousine's tyres crunched over gravel as it slowly circled the auditorium. As the car drew near, Angus turned and *namasted* to the master as he was driven by. Bhagwan was dwarfed by the Roll's Royce's immensity. From the back seat the guru peeped out from behind his hands, once again held prayerfully, and for the briefest of moments, his playful eyes smiled at Angus. This was all that was needed to fill his heart with joy and keep him buzzing on a psychic charge for the rest of the day.

Angus watched as a number of the guru's devotees threw themselves down in front of the master's empty executive chair and kissed the marble where his sandaled feet had rested minutes before.

God is not for sale. Bhagwan's words reverberated in Angus's mind. *God might not be for sale but everything else is,* he thought. The ashram had become a centre of commercial activity. There were now boutiques selling the latest trends in spiritual clothes, all dyed in a spectrum of orange and red colours. A bookshop sold the guru's books, one of which was published every month. For a spiritual master extolling the practice of dropping the past and living in the moment, his ashram's bookshop was doing a roaring trade, selling his past moments captured on videotape and cassette. This did not appear to be raising any sceptical eyebrows. *That is,* Angus reflected, *unless you are a member of the sensationalist international press, ever on the prowl in search of some juicy piece of nonsense to hype up and sell as ground-breaking news.* The journalists, who visited the ashram, were easy to spot in their drab clothes. They were no different from anyone else in the place; they usually found what their hearts and minds were in search of. Bhagwan's commune was, amongst many other things, a hot-bed of scandalous gossip. Rumour mongering was actively encouraged to add a little extra spice to community life. Tittle-tattle about Bhagwan's penchant for groping sannyasin women with big breasts was rife as were stories about sex orgies and international drug smuggling scams financed to help fill the ashram's coffers. Angus knew the latter was true, although not in the way the newspapers contrived to make it appear.

Life in Rajneesh's ashram was, in relation to the rest of India, expensive. Sannyasins needed money to remain there unless they were an *ashramite* with a room and a food pass. During that time, good quality hashish was dirt cheap in India, providing a tempting commodity for making quick money, by packing a false-bottomed suitcase with a few kilos and flying with it into London, Los Angeles, Sydney or Tokyo. Angus was aware of the fact that the ashram's administration knew drug smuggling was going on but, although turning a blind eye to it, this lucrative illegal activity wasn't actually condoned by those running the commune. Most of the sannyasins who smuggled drugs to finance their stay in Pune were not criminal by nature. They were energy junkies, hooked on Bhagwan's limitless supply of cosmic vibes, in no way wishing to be cut off from the source of their addiction. Some of his disciples, planning such an illegal business trip, would ask the master in *darshan* if it was a good idea for them to head West for a short trip. If he gave them his blessing, the dope run was on and, as if by divine providence, was almost guaranteed to be a success. Angus, tuned into the international runner's grapevine, knew what *almost guaranteed* actually meant. Smuggling scams were going down almost every week. The number of sannyasins locked up in prisons around the world was slowly increasing, to the extent that international anti-narcotics agencies were beginning to focus on the Bhagwan's western followers.

Seeds of cosmic consciousness, celebration and meditation were not the only crops being sown in Bhagwan Shree Rajneesh's *Buddhafield*, as the guru was now calling his quickly expanding spiritual community. It was clear to Angus that the ashram was inadvertently providing a convenient meeting place for certain small groups of like-minded individuals to become acquainted. As in any other business career, social connections play an important part in the world of cross-border drug smuggling organizations. The internationalism of the sannyas movement unintentionally put in place a global network of people willing to distribute illegal drugs to make substantial amounts of quick money. The fact that very few of those individuals knew each other's legal names was an added plus. Anand Loka was one such individual. In the eyes of his fellow sannyasins Angus Mac-Leod had ceased to exist; something he experienced no difficulty in accepting. It suited his purposes perfectly because he needed a cloak of invisibility.

Angus continued to periodically visit Bombay to help Jimmy Bradley attach magnetic fibreglass boxes to the hulls of international cargo ships. After his bamboo house burned down, he set about building an even bigger and better one by the side of a stone-lined irrigation well.

The fields behind Koregaon Park and along the banks of the Bund River were filling with hut villages, home to various sannyasin tribes. Angus rented a small patch of land from Arun Wankhade, an overweight and jovial farmer who was partial to Scottish whisky. The farmer was becoming a rich man. He owned hectares of farmland in the area. Arun worshipped Rajneesh almost as much as his followers, but for a different reason. The now internationally famous guru had become an indirect source of previously unimaginable wealth to the sugarcane farmer. As a result of the money that was coming his way, Arun began to drink more bottles of expensive imported malt whisky and buy bigger and more powerful motorbikes.

Angus was developing a friendship with Arun Wankhade and his chattering wife, Archana. On the first day of every month, he visited the farmer to pay his rent. On the first of January, he was surprised to find Arun sitting in his farmhouse's living room with his left leg encased in a white plaster cast.

'Happy new year. What happened to you?' Angus asked, noticing that the latest addition to the farmhouse's interior was a brand-new air-conditioning unit purring in a corner.

'Something very, very, good,' answered Arun, beckoning for Angus to sit down beside him on a red sofa sheathed by a transparent plastic cover. 'I was going into town on my new Honda motorbike with my wife when, suddenly, her sari is becoming caught in the back wheel. I crashed on the bridge near to your house and broke my leg.'

'Is Archana okay?'

'Yes, yes, she is feeling fine. A few cuts and bruises, but apart from that she is almost being as happy as I am.'

Angus turned and studied the farmer's flushed, chubby face. 'I don't understand. Why are you so happy about breaking your leg?'

Arun pushed his white Gandhi cap back on his head, poured himself a glass of whisky, beamed a satisfied smile and said, 'Karma.'

'*Karma?*' Angus repeated, justifiably bamboozled. 'What's breaking a leg got to do with karma?'

'Everything. Karma is having to do with everything. Lord Brahma is everywhere, and he is making us all play our roles according to our karma,' explained the farmer, swallowing a mouthful of Scotland's finest. 'If something is not destined, it will not be happening, no matter how much effort we are making. When something is destined, it is bound to be happening. This is the law of karma and there is nothing we can be doing about it other than to be accepting it.' He studied his glass for a moment, chuckled and concluded, 'This is why I am a lucky man. Breaking my poor leg means I won't be having to deal with any bad karma for many years to come.'

'Oh, right, Arun,' muttered Angus, thinking that perhaps Mother India had been so named because many of the adults in her vast family had a childlike outlook.

Two months later, Angus had a chance meeting with Arun on the small stone bridge where his motorbike accident had taken place. The farmer had his plaster cast off by this time and was gripping a wooden walking stick in one hand and a plastic bag full of, what appeared to be, fresh meat in the other. Angus nodded towards the transparent bag and said, 'I thought you were a vegetarian.'

'You are being correct in your thinking,' said the farmer, hoisting the bag in front of Angus's eyes, close enough for him to see that it contained blood-ied cow's intestines.

'So, what's with the holy cow guts?'

'This is an offering to the mischievous demon who caused my motorcycle accident. You see, he is living under the bridge.'

Angus's new bamboo house was located fifteen metres from the bridge and he hadn't noticed any horned monsters in the vicinity. 'What demon?'

'I'm already telling you. The one who is living under the bridge.'

Two days later, Angus remembered his meeting with Arun and went under the bridge to investigate. He was shocked to run into an aggressive, ten-foot-long rock python living there. It let out a loud hiss when he ap-proached. Curiosity satisfied, Angus beat a hasty retreat.

By mid-April, temperatures were soaring and Angus's compound became a popular meeting place for his friends. The circular irrigation well beside his two-storey, Balinese-style bamboo house was eight metres in diameter, twelve deep and full of crystal-clear water, home to tropical fish, turquoise crabs, turtles and the occasional amphibious snake. There were many co-bras in the sugar cane fields, but they were too preoccupied with evading vicious mongooses' sharp teeth to pose a dangerous threat to the humans who'd set up camp in their territory.

The well was surrounded by tall eucalyptus trees. Their smooth grey branches were used as diving platforms, from where the daring could plunge into what had by now become a communal swimming pool.

During the evenings, discussions took place around a campfire. Some-times heated, these talks were often centred on what Bhagwan had been ex-pounding in his current series of morning discourses. This particular night, J. J. Cale's laid-back guitar twanged from a battery-powered cassette player, while Angus and a small group of friends sat around and discussed the hip-pie movement.

'Bhagwan says he's the original hippie,' proclaimed Shanti Deva who was warming a drum skin by the fire. 'The sannyas movement is a revolutionary party, but not just an all-nighter, this party is going on for the rest of our lives, until we are liberated from the chains the ego binds us with.'

'Bull fuckin' shit,' said Atom, a dark-skinned English hippie with dread-locks and a contagious toothy smile. He'd travelled up from Goa by bus to check out the women in the ashram during the hot season.

'Shanti's right,' agreed Angus. 'Bhagwan said that he is the ultimate drop out. Remember, Atom, I was a hard-core hippie before I took sannyas. Don't take it personally, man, but nowadays when I see Goa freaks, most of them look washed out and they've got grey auras. The difference between Bhagwan's commune and the hippies' alternative life-style is that his commune works.'

'How can Rajneesh say he's a dropout when he's being driven around in a flash Rolls?' Atom retorted. 'That's pure bullshit, man. He's a bread head.'

Angus tossed a log on the fire. 'What's wrong with owning a Rolls Royce?'

'It's an ostentatious capitalist symbol, that's what's wrong with it,' answered Atom, raising his dimpled chin. 'If you ask me, I think your so-called enlightened master's a big ego tripper. And you lot are on an ego trip about dropping the ego.'

Angus and Shanti exchanged a knowing look and glanced up through the eucalyptus trees at the sky. It was clear, with not a cloud in it.

'You know, Atom,' said Shanti, tapping his bongos, 'you just don't get it, do you?'

'Get what?' Atom jeered, looking over the campfire's flames at Shanti with narrowed eyes.

'That you're a stupid asshole. Who do you think you are, calling a beautiful man like Bhagwan a fucking ego tripper?' Shanti spat in the fire. 'You're lost, that's what you are. Can't you see it's peoples' attachment to material things that causes trouble, not the actual things? Bhagwan teaches us non-attachment. He'd be just as enlightened if he were living in a Himalayan cave instead of an air-conditioned room.' He glared at Atom. 'If I ever hear you talking like that about Bhagwan again, I'll knock your teeth down your bloody throat.' Shanti's upraised right fist underlined his aggressive declaration.

During this exchange, Angus had been observing Shanti Deva. Apart from Shanti's threat of physical harm towards Atom, Angus was not sure if what the angry Englishman proclaimed was entirely true. He backed Shanti up anyway, by saying, 'What you have to understand, Atom, is that Bhagwan's presenting us with a new vision for humankind. The old man has fucked things up big time and now it's time for the new man to be born and take over before life on this planet is destroyed by an antiquated material value system, based on warfare and greed. The name of the new man is Zorba the Buddha, and he's the man that says yes to everything, except violence.' He flashed a look of disapproval at Shanti. 'Atom, my friend, your perspective belongs to the old man, in that you equate spirituality with poverty. The new man will be the integration of the earthy part of our nature with the most spiritual.'

Atom laughed scornfully. 'Zorba the fucking Buddha,' he sneered, 'sounds like a drunk Greek with a beer belly.'

Mudra, the fourth member of the campfire circle, had been sitting silently, watching the three men firing off their opinions. She was a Russian Jew and one of the founding members of an underground sannyasin cell in Moscow. Earlier on in the evening, she'd explained how she and her fellow Muscovite comrades met once a week on Red Square before locking themselves in a cellar to listen in secrecy to Bhagwan tapes. The campfire's shadows danced across the angles of her high cheekbones and her thick henna-dyed hair, hanging from her head like an outlandish Eighteenth-Century wig. Angus thought she looked like a witch.

Mudra spoke when the men fell silent. 'Up to a point,' she began, employing the tone a headmistress might use when addressing an unruly class of school children, 'Loka is right in what he said.' She smiled at Angus, who she'd met for the first time that afternoon when he'd invited her round to the well for a swim. 'Where he goes wrong is in assuming that Zorba the Buddha is a man. Zorba the Buddha is an incarnation of the feminine. A non-aggressive, receptive intelligence that accepts existence moment to moment as it unfolds and manifests before her enlightened eyes.' She chuckled, obviously pleased with her command of the English language. 'In case you didn't notice, women hold all the key positions in the ashram. That's because the master knows that men are ruled by their penises and that, sooner rather than later, they always manage to fuck things up. Unfortunately, women still haven't learned to live without men, because they still come in handy from time to time.'

Mudra was suddenly inspired by the music playing in the background. When J. J. Cale started asking his crazy mama where she'd been so long, Pune's one and only crazy Russian mama leapt to her feet and pulled her dark red robe up over her shaggy head. She stood naked, swaying in front of the fire with the equivocal bearing of a street fighter. Her long shapely legs were held slightly apart, bare feet firmly rooted in the soft earth. She ran her hands up her body from thighs to breasts. She cupped her breasts with her hands and jiggled them, a provocative gesture of presentation. Mudra gazed up at the stars, sparkling brightly behind the porous canopy formed by the overhead branches, raised her outstretched arms towards the sky and declared in a husky voice, 'I am Zorbina the Buddha.' As if in response to Mudra's proclamation, a woman in the throes of sexual orgasm cried out from somewhere in the sugar cane fields.

The fire goddess looked down to her three astonished male companions. They were staring up at her ecstatic face, full breasts, narrow waist and wide hips. Mudra's powerful physical presence was as big as a telephone box. Angus and his two friends sat with slack jaws, as if afraid to look away for fear of being transformed into pillars of salt by a flourish of the Russian witch's long-fingered hands.

'Now then,' she purred, casting a hypnotic spell upon her three dumbfounded admirers, 'which one of you men has the phallic capacity to satisfy my sensual cravings?' She angled her body towards the fire and waggled her ample breasts over the flames. 'Come now,' she continued, giving her erect nipples a tweak with thumb and forefinger, 'who among your lusty ranks will accompany me down to the riverbank and fuck me like Lord Shiva under the heavens.'

Atom scratched his dreadlocked head with perplexity, smiled like a donkey with an erection, and nodded mutely.

'Come, my Adonis.' Mudra reached for his right hand and pulled the muscular, dark-skinned man to his unsteady feet. She slipped on her robe and said to Angus and Shanti, 'Goodnight, brothers, see you in the Buddha Hall tomorrow morning.' She led Atom along the winding garden path.

Three days later, Atom bowed down at Bhagwan's feet and became Swami Anand Atom. All thoughts of the guru being an ego-tripper now reduced to dust in the wind.

Angus rose before dawn and cycled along the poorly lit road that led to the ashram. Upon arriving in Buddha Hall, he stripped down to his orange underwear and, when the staccato music came on, proceeded into the four stages of the dynamic meditation.

By eight a.m., he was sitting three rows away from the podium in Buddha Hall waiting for Bhagwan to begin his discourse. Within the space of half-an-hour, the master touched on the subject of the new man's evolution. When he said the words 'Zorba the Buddha', he paused for a brief moment and bestowed a glance in Angus's direction, signalling to him that he'd probably picked up on the previous evening's campfire discussion.

The master went on to describe how occult powers were like cufflinks to an enlightened man. He spoke about the many well-known phoney Indian gurus, like Satya Sai Baba, who claimed to have these *siddhis* (supernatural powers) and how they duped gullible seekers into believing they were witnessing the performance of miracles when in reality they were nothing more than conjuring tricks. Upon hearing Bhagwan's words, many of those present nodded in silent agreement. By sitting in front of their master with an open heart, they knew without a doubt that they were in direct contact with someone producing miraculous transformations in their lives simply by being near to him. Bhagwan's vast presence had the power to lift everyone around him onto a higher plane of consciousness without any effort on their part, other than simply being there.

'The centre of the cyclone is the most ecstatic experience...' Angus began to tune into the silent spaces between the master's words and the next thing he knew Bhagwan was saying, 'Enough for today.' The same phrase he used every morning to conclude his talks.

After the discourse, Angus popped into the ashram's Vrindavan Restaurant. As he stood in the queue, waiting to pay for his cup of scalding hot tea and a fresh croissant, he noticed that the woman taking the money at the cash register was the sannyasin hooker he'd spent a drunken night with in

Bombay. She had an orange scarf wrapped around her head that made her look like an Apache squaw. He handed her a ten-rupee note and said, 'Hi'. When the cashier gave him his change, she made a point of not even bothering to look at him. Angus chuckled, placed the coins on the counter, said, 'Keep the change,' and walked away from her without a backward glance. He knew all too well the contradictions involved in leading a double life.

Outside, under the shade provided by a circular straw roof, Angus sat down at a table and was joined by Mad Max. Swami Max was one of the few Scottish sannyasins in Pune with who Angus was on friendly terms. He knew him from his hippie days in Glasgow, where Max fulfilled the role of DJ at acid-fuelled parties. Max had a thick mop of frizzy hair, a very long beard and a pirate's shifty-eyed face. He tended to lean into a person when he felt he had something important to say to them, especially if they happened to be an attractive woman. Like Angus, Max was involved in the hash smuggling business. His speciality was flattening out kilos of Manali hashish with a heavy steel rolling pin and then fitting the compressed cannabis resin into the sides of suitcases. He charged fifty dollars a kilo for his skilled work. According to Max, he was making approximately five thousand dollars a month from his clandestine activities.

Toddlers wove between the chattering breakfasters' tables, their exited shrieks and laughter adding to the already lively atmosphere. Angus knew, from talking to some of the ashram kids, that many of them disliked the bright orange clothes their parents forced them to wear.

Max sparked up a brief conversation about current affairs in and around the Koregaon Park area. 'The cops busted somebody down at Mobos Hotel last night,' he said in a hushed voice, leaning into Angus close enough for him to smell the spearmint gum he was chewing.

'Anybody we know?'

'Naw, I don't think so,' replied Max, glancing around the packed outdoor café. 'I heard it was a couple of French junkies from Goa who were selling stolen passports. Hey!' Max exclaimed, suddenly remembering something. 'Did you hear about the Samurais beating the shit out of the Iranian students over at the Café Delight the other night?'

The Samurais was the name Bhagwan had given to the ashram's security guards, most of whom were trained in the martial arts. They worked out every afternoon in Buddha Hall under the tutelage of an American karate expert.

'What was that all about then?' Angus enquired.

Swami Max looked away from a fat blonde with enormous breasts straining against the confines of her pink cotton blouse. She was giving him the third eye from a neighbouring table. He whistled through his teeth and said, 'What a pair of beauties.' He leaned into Angus again. 'What happened is this,' he said, returning to Angus's question. 'Last week, some of those Iranian fuckers from the technical college kidnapped a sannyasin chick over by the river and used her for a gang-banging session.'

'Fucking hell!' Angus gasped.

'Yeah, real heavy shit, man. So Laxmi gets word of this and sends the Samurais over to the Café Delight to teach those shites a lesson. I heard a few bones and heads were broken in the process.' Max looked at his plastic wristwatch. 'I'm out of here. I've joined the theatre group. We're rehearsing *Waiting for Godot*.'

Angus asked, 'Who is Godot?'

'Man, have you never heard of Samuel Beckett's *Waiting for Godot*?' Max asked in astonishment. 'It was voted the Twentieth Century's most significant play. It's a story about two guys, wearing bowler hats, who are waiting for a man who never arrives. We're going to stage it in Buddha Hall. You'll love it because in many ways sannyasins are also waiting on Godot in the form of enlightenment. And guess what? Like the playwright's elusive character, enlightenment still hasn't shown up.' Max stood up and said, 'I'm playing music tonight at a wee bash over in Laxmi Villas. Come over for a boogie, if you feel like it.' He raised a hand in farewell. 'Catch you later, swami.'

Angus watched as Max stopped by the big-busted blonde. She rose to her feet, hugged him, said something to Max and then he quickly scribbled on a paper napkin. He handed her the white serviette and then, sensing Angus eyes on him, glanced over his shoulder and flashed him a wink.

Angus sipped on his now lukewarm tea and took in his surroundings with a sweep of his head. It struck him that Bhagwan's spiritual commune was turning into a Club Med-style, non-stop swinger's party. Sannyasins were swapping sexual partners as casually as other people exchanged greetings. Sexually transmitted diseases, herpes, gonorrhoea and occasionally hepatitis were also being traded freely. The latter was taken by many misguided sannyasins as being symptomatic of resistance to the master's transformative energies, rather than one's immune system's incapacity to deal with an acute viral infection of the liver. Jaundiced yellow eyes were becoming as common as broken relationships in the ashram. Angus had also had his share of illnesses, which included gonorrhoea, dengue fever and amoebic dysentery. The fact that local farmers sprayed their crops with massive amounts of pesticide certainly didn't help anyone's health. The ashram's well-equipped medical centre had run a chemical analysis of vegetable produce sold in Pune's main market and found that the greens, potatoes and tomatoes on sale contained dangerously high levels of sodium cyanide and DDT.

By 1978, Angus was doing six hours of Bhagwan's meditation techniques a day and having the time of his life with dozens of readily available sannyasin women, only too willing to help him fulfil every sexual fantasy he'd ever entertained.

The intensity of Angus's meditation practice coupled with his promiscuous lifestyle was yielding results. He felt like a young god. In yoga, the base of the spine is considered very important because not only is it the foundation of our corporal frame it is also the seat of kundalini, the mysterious serpent force which binds the physical to more subtle bodies. It is said that, when the power of kundalini is awakened, etheric energy floods the brain, the third eye opens and the yogi has visions of spiritual realms. Angus was not having visions of spiritual realms, but he did believe he had entered paradise. Then, during one of Bhagwan's morning discourses, the master said something that alerted Angus to the fact he'd made the same mistake that many who'd gone before him had made — believing that the elevation of the serpent of kundalini is illumination, when in fact, it is only the beginning of initiation rather than the end of it.

Angus felt fortunate to be living under the direct guidance of a man who understood such matters. Otherwise, he might have been tricked by the power of kundalini into believing he had attained spiritual enlightenment. Bhagwan had already made it clear to him, on two separate occasions, that his journey towards truth was a long way from over, and that it was most important that he stand back from what he took to be himself and witness whatever was taking place in his inner world, in the knowledge that whatever he could witness was not who he was. His last *darshan* with the master had ended when an unsmiling Bhagwan said to him in a firm manner, 'You are not who you think you are.'

Due to the massive influx of seekers vying for the master's attention, it was becoming increasingly difficult to gain a personal audience with Bhagwan. Angus was now only allowed to speak once a month with him and then only for a few minutes. In May of that year, he once again found himself sitting on the marble floor in front of the master, staring up directly into his unfathomable brown eyes.

Bhagwan raised a curious eyebrow. *'Mmmm,'* he intoned, introducing enormous gravity into the single syllable. 'It is time for you to begin cleaning the toilets.' He paused, smiled and then added like a doctor giving a prescription, 'Enter into the work totally.'

Angus bowed down at the master's sandaled feet, stunned. The idea of working as a toilet cleaner in India did not appeal to him. Outwardly he had surrendered to and accepted the master's suggestion but he was completely resistant to the idea. It would take a little more time before Angus realised Bhagwan had prescribed the correct course of action. All talk of psychic powers and yogic terminology had been cast to the wayside to avoid inflation of the ego and replaced with the requirement to perform physical work to keep grounded. The ashram was an explosion of activity, not because Bhagwan Shree Rajneesh was building an empire with himself as the self-proclaimed king, but because his disciples needed physical labour to keep them connected to their body and out of their mind. In the search for a new spiritual identity, beyond the boundaries of the limited ego-self, it is necessary to cross an inner no-man's-land that produces a loss of personal identity. At the heart of meditation, there has to be a willingness to let go of absolutely everything and enter a state of not knowing. Angus was unsure if he was willing to face this. The master's account of what he went through before enlightenment was hardly reassuring. It sounded like a nightmare from which there was no escape, although some tried. There had already been several suicides in Pune's sannyasin community. No one was more aware of the tremendous psychological damage that could be done by the powerful psychic energy pouring forth from every pore of his body than Bhagwan himself. He understood it was necessary to channel that energy in a constructive direction to avoid negative consequences. He was also no doubt very much aware than the stubborn young Scotsman sitting before him was completely resistant to the idea of working as a toilet cleaner, and that life would have to teach him a hard lesson to jolt him out of his defiance before he would heed his wise counsel.

'*Hmm?*' Bhagwan intoned questioningly. He smiled, leaned forward a little in his black, high-backed chair, touched Angus lightly on the crown of his head and concluded the exchange by saying, 'Very good.'

Instead of signing up at the ashram's employment exchange, Angus enrolled in a week-long encounter group intensive that began the next day.

Ten days later, he took a four-hour taxi ride to Bombay. For a few days, he lay around in the sun by the side of the Breach Kandy swimming pool, waiting for Jimmy Bradley to arrive in the city. He used this time to try and assimilate what he'd been through in the previous week's therapy group. He'd careened through heaven and hell and back again, accumulating a few minor injuries on the way, including two black eyes. It was on his third day in Bombay that he connected with a long-legged Australian air hostess, called Angela. They met by the pool and spent twenty-four hours together in an air-conditioned hotel room. Angela got it into her head that she had finally found what she was looking for — her soul mate. Battered and bruised though Angus might have been, a man in the throes of a kundalini experience can seem charismatic and irresistible to women. For his part, Angus liked her but recognized their brief relationship for what it was — a sex-fuelled chance encounter, destined to go nowhere. He was honest enough, or blunt enough, to let the Australian women know how he felt. A flood of tears, a barrage of angry words, and a bit of door slamming later, a broken-hearted Angela stormed out of the hotel room and hurried off to join a Qantas flight bound for Sydney.

A string quartet was playing chamber music in a large, wood-panelled dining room in the Taj Mahal Hotel. Seated in the main lounge, Angus listened absently to the baroque melodies drifting on the air, tinted blue with cigarette and cigar smoke. He glanced distractedly at his black diver's watch. Jimmy Bradley was over an hour late.

'Hello there, pal,' said Jimmy as he approached, a pint of beer in his left hand. 'How's it going?' He smiled apologetically, shook Angus's right hand as if he were pumping a car jack, and then sat down on a stuffed leather chair on the opposite side of a small glass table. 'Sorry to keep you waiting. I had a couple of things to take care of.' He glanced at Angus's face and noticed that he was sporting a pair of bilateral periorbital hematomas. 'Man, what's with the black eyes? You look like you did a round with Muhammad Ali.'

'I picked them up in an encounter group,' replied Angus, smiling to reveal the absence of two front teeth.

Jimmy shook his head. 'Has your guru integrated kung-fu fighting into his meditation techniques?'

Angus put on a pair of sunglasses. 'Last time I saw him he told me that I should start cleaning toilets.'

'For fuck's sake. You've got to be joking.'

'I wish I was. Anyway, what's new?'

Jimmy swallowed half a glass of lager in one long gulp, smacked his lips and answered, 'What's new is that tonight's job is the last until after the monsoon. The good news is that we have to attach two tons to a container ship bound for merry old—'

'Two fucking tons!'

'You'll make sixty grand for eight hours hard graft. Are you into it, pal?'

'Could Jimi Hendrix play the guitar with his teeth?'

'Hey, Joe, you bet your hairy Scottish arse he could.' Jimmy drained his beer glass, stubbed out a half-smoked cigarette in a white marble ashtray, studied his slim-line watch for a moment and then said, 'Listen, I'll be going straight to the airport when we finish tonight.' He added. 'The missus is expecting our third any day soon.'

'You've been busy.' Angus leaned over and punched Jimmy lightly on the left shoulder. 'Congratulations.'

'You're a bit early with that, but thanks anyway. It hasn't been an easy pregnancy. I swear it's the last.' He smiled at the thought of it. 'You've no idea how much work it is bringing up kids.'

'I can imagine.'

'Yeah, I'll bet you can, but maybe not in the right way.'

'What do you mean *not in the right way*?'

'Well, I'll put it like this. When I listen to your stories about surrendering to Bhagwan, I just think to myself that you don't understand how much surrender is involved in bringing up kids.' Jimmy looked into his eyes and asked, 'You ever think of settling down?'

126

Angus thought about it for a moment before supplying an answer. 'Sure I have. Thing is, I can't see myself playing dad.'

Jimmy laughed. 'It will never happen as long as you're thinking about it. Take my word for it; you'd make a great father.'

'I love kids.'

'I know you do, that's why I'm saying it.' Jimmy let out a short laugh, stood up and straightened his tie. 'C'mon, let's go up to my room. I'll give you your money now, so there's one less thing to do. Maybe we can catch a bit of kip this afternoon.' He started to make his way towards the elevators in the foyer and commented over his shoulder to Angus, following closely behind with his cream-coloured suit jacket in hand, 'It's going to be a long night.'

Angus lay in the darkness of his hotel room. His eyes were closed. He wanted to sleep, but couldn't. He was too keyed up. Jimmy Bradley had given him a 25,000 dollar bonus. *Eighty-five thousand dollars,* he thought, an air conditioning unit humming in the background. *Many people in this country won't make half that much money in their entire life, and I am making it for eight hours of work. Incredible!*

The frenetic din of Bombay's mid-afternoon traffic penetrated through the drawn curtains and double glazing. Angus lay spread-eagled on his bed, watching the flow of his breath. His excited thoughts began to diminish. He entered a state of deep relaxation. Sleep was on the point of taking him when there was a rapid knock on his door. It was time to go.

At precisely six in the evening, Jimmy and Angus exited the hotel, pushed past a small crowd of aggressive beggars and got into the back of a waiting Ambassador car. Chid and Amrit turned to face them, welcoming their British counterparts with toothy grins and loose handshakes. Angus was by now familiar with the two Indians. The more he got to know them, the more he respected them. Always positive, they seemed fearless and treated the dangerous business they were involved in like it was a schoolboy's prank.

'Next stop, Sassoon Dock,' called Amrit as he pulled away from the pavement. His wrists were home to about a half kilogram of gold bracelets, chains, and lucky charms.

Chid leaned forward and patted a small, eight-armed brass statue of the female Hindu deity Durga glued to the dashboard. The fierce-looking goddess is invoked for her sometimes violent assistance against demons, terrors and disasters. Durga sprang into immediate action by making Amrit stamp down hard on the brake pedal, preventing a collision with an excited brown cow that ran in front of the car. The white Ambassador skidded to a halt and missed the big, horned, holy beast by inches. Chid twisted around in his seat and smiled knowingly as he said, 'Durga, number one flaming goddess,' and then gave a thumbs-up sign with both hands.

Amrit managed to navigate through Bombay's congested streets without further incident. By the time they reached Sassoon Dock, it was almost dark. Chid got out of the car. He unlocked the metal gate to a fenced-off yard with a warehouse and small wooden jetty. The *Shiva-Shakti* was tied up to a pair of rust-encrusted, cast iron bollards. There was a strong smell of fish wafting over from the nearby fishing fleet.

All four men changed into dark-blue overalls and busied themselves with their respective tasks. Amrit and Chid carried fibreglass containers from the warehouse and began stacking them up on the black tug's foredeck. Jimmy kept watch with a pair of high-powered binoculars. Angus set about checking the diving gear, making sure that the twenty matt-black aluminium oxygen bottles lined up outside the wheelhouse were all full and their valves functioning properly.

When Amrit and Chid had finished bringing the containers on board, they threw a black tarpaulin over the conspicuous oblong pile. Angus stood looking at it and wondered how on earth they were going to manage to attach what weighed over two-and-a-half metric tons onto a ship's hull.

Jimmy approached him from behind and said, 'Don't worry, pal, we'll manage.'

'Man,' said Angus, 'you picked up on my thoughts.'

'Just goes to show that your guru isn't the only one with psychic powers.' He called to Amrit and Chid, who were sitting on the prow and laughing as they shared a joint of sweet-smelling Kerala grass. 'Hey, you two, stop farting about and go bring out our new addition to the operation.'

The two Indians disappeared into the warehouse's shadows and proceeded to haul a two-wheeled, metal-framed trailer out into the compound. On it was a six-metre long, semi-rigid, Zodiac. Like the rest of the operation's equipment, it was matt-black. Its eighty horsepower Evinrude motor was encased in black foam rubber to muffle its sound. Angus and Jimmy lent a hand to wheel the trailer down a concrete ramp into the water. The Zodiac was then secured to the tug's stern with a length of nylon rope.

'C'mon lads,' said Captain Jimmy Bradley, 'it's time for a wee booster.'

The four men congregated in the wheelhouse. Jimmy used a Gillette razor blade to chop up two grams of cocaine on a shaving mirror.

There were now a dozen thick lines of sparkling crystalline powder on the circular surface. Angus lowered his head and used a rolled-up hundred-rupee note to sniff one of them up. The coke hit his brain like a bullet of light. He gasped.

Jimmy chortled. 'That, pal, is ninety percent, pure Bolivian boo.' He looked at each of his comrades and asked, 'Are you ready to rock 'n' roll.' After his three companions nodded he raised his clenched right hand above his head and said, 'Let's do it.'

Angus staggered to his feet. The coke rush felt like he'd just drunk ten litres of strong black coffee.

Amrit started the tug's engine. A thick cloud of black diesel smoke rose into the muggy night air. After he'd untied the mooring ropes, Chid jumped onboard. Jimmy took the wheel and manoeuvred the *Shiva-Shakti* away from the dock. Angus sat on the deck and pulled on his neoprene diver's suit. He'd never felt so wired up in his life. He could taste the coke on his tongue. He spat a mouthful of bitter phlegm over the side as the boat picked up speed.

Halfway between Bombay and Elephant Island, Jimmy cut the engine and Chid tossed a stern anchor into the water. A chain clattered. The sea was calm and lapped gently against the tug's hull. A kilometre away was the biggest container ship Angus had ever seen. She was haloed by the bright light cast by halogen floodlights mounted on her massive superstructure. Men's shouts were carried on the breeze from her vast decks, where cranes lifted and shifted multicoloured cargo containers, stacked six high like giant Lego bricks.

'Looks like she's about ready to head out to sea,' commented Jimmy, a lit cigarette jammed into a corner of his mouth.

'The first load's ready to go,' said a breathless Chid, after helping Amrit lower ten fibreglass containers into the Zodiac.

Jimmy glanced at the black dinghy. 'Jesus,' he commented, 'she's sitting a bit low in the water.'

'No problem,' assured Chid. 'If we are taking it easy, she will be fine.'

Amrit, Jimmy and Angus got into the Zodiac. When the semi-rigid was just beyond the circle of light surrounding the container ship, Jimmy and Angus pulled down their Perspex masks and tumbled backwards into the water. Although Angus was by now familiar with this procedure, the first moments, when he found himself submerged in murky water, always came as a shock to him. He took a few deep breaths to slow his accelerated heart-beat and adjusted his buoyancy vest.

Ninety minutes later, the first five hundred kilos were securely attached to the underside of the container ship's hull. Angus had used up two bottles of air, and every muscle in his body felt like it was on fire. They headed back to the tug and collected another load along with four aluminium oxygen bottles. Then Jimmy and Angus were back in the water with the combined weight of a container and hashish straining between them, threatening to wrench their arms out of their sockets.

Second cargo done and dusted, Angus and Jimmy lay sprawled on the *Shiva-Shakti's* swaying foredeck. A swell was beginning to build up. Thick cloud was rolling in towards Bombay.

Jimmy looked away from the sky, turned on his side and said to Angus, 'Fucking shit, pal, I think there's a storm brewing. We better get a move on.'

After a quick wheelhouse stop for another line of coke, Amrit, Jimmy and Angus were once again headed for the container ship. The tide was turning and beginning to produce a current that made swimming more strenuous. Both Angus and Jimmy ran out of air on their way back to the Zodiac for the last magnetic box. On the short return trip to the tug, Angus caught a glimpse of forked lightning out to sea.

When they were once more back on the tug's rocking deck, Jimmy said to Angus, 'We better take three bottles each for this one.'

Angus grabbed onto a side rail to keep his balance. 'Fucking hell,' he gasped, 'maybe we should save the last eleven boxes for another time.'

'*Another time,*' echoed Jimmy. 'There is no fucking other time. I told you already, this is the last job until the monsoon season is over.' He tweaked his nose. 'Another line of Charlie will do the trick.' He tilted his head and looked into Angus's worried eyes. 'You up for it, pal?'

Despite the paranoid thoughts ripping through Angus's mind like cut-throat razors, he nodded and said, 'Why not?'

Two hours, six aluminium air bottles and ten boxes later, Amrit lowered the last fibreglass container into Angus and Jimmy's waiting hands. The Indian had just let go of the handle when he tumbled over backwards into the sea.

Jimmy pulled the breathing apparatus out of his mouth and called to Angus, 'Jesus fucking Christ! Go and get hold of him. The daft bastard doesn't know how to swim.'

Angus did not need to hear anything else. He dived under the Zodiac, kicked his fins and collided with Amrit's thrashing body. He couldn't see a thing under the water but somehow managed to haul the non-swimmer up to the surface. He pulled out his air regulator and shouted, 'Calm down! Calm down, Amrit.'

His words got through and the Indian nodded as his eyes came back into focus. 'Okay, okay, I'm okay,' he gasped with a trembling voice. He retched and then said, 'Please, Angus, man, help me to get out the water.'

Angus did as requested and then swam round to the other side of the Zodiac, where Jimmy was straining to keep a firm grip on the box as waves threw him against the reinforced rubber hull.

'Grab the fucking handle,' cried Jimmy.

Angus took a firm hold of it. Jimmy let go and used his left hand to grip the handle on the tilted container's underside while shaking his right arm to boost circulation.

It began to rain heavily. Thunder boomed overhead. The two divers went down five metres and began swimming towards the ship.

The ocean-going behemoth's overhead spotlights illuminated the water as the divers drew closer. Beneath the surface was a uniform moss-green universe, home to myriad squiggling microorganisms, feasting on Bombay's untreated sewage.

It was pitch black under the ship until Jimmy and Angus switched on the waterproof torches strapped to their heads. The swell was strong enough to make the ship shift position. The motion made Angus's job of scraping barnacles and hairy algae from the steel hull with a rubber-handled knife more difficult. His right hand strained to retain its grip on the fibreglass container's handle. His thighs were burning from kicking his flippers to maintain his position. Once the small section of orange-painted steel was more or less smooth, Angus and Jimmy hoisted the heavy load into position. When it was flush with the hull, Jimmy pulled on the foot-long metal lever to activate the powerful electromagnets that would secure the box. Instead of hearing a reassuring clunk, they heard nothing but their laboured breathing. It felt to Angus like every strained breath took with it a fragment of his life, gone forever. Jimmy began jerking the lever up and down like he was desperately trying to win the jackpot on a one-armed bandit in an underwater gambling arcade. The extra exertion quickly burnt off the remainder of his air supply. Jimmy ran the index finger of his rubber-gloved right hand across his throat. Angus gave a thumbs up to acknowledge that he understood this most vital of hand signals.

Jimmy let go of the handle and kicked off towards the surface. The added weight pushed down on Angus's shoulders. He could feel his air supply thinning. His hamstrings began to cramp as his flippers thrashed at the water. He reached around and pulled down on the metal leaver. *Clunk!* It worked. The last fibreglass box was stuck fast to the ship's hull.

Angus didn't waste time hanging around to admire his handiwork. His oxygen-starved brain was making him feel dizzy. He headed for the surface. He looked up and saw Jimmy's silhouette, hovering in a semi-circle of green light. An oblong shadow rapidly increased in size as it descended towards his partner and engulfed him. There was a loud boom. A shockwave of pressure hit Angus's body. His mind screamed, *What the fuck was that?*

While being slotted into a secure position on the ship's deck, a container had broken a crane's cable and tumbled overboard. Angus bobbed to the sea's surface. He sucked in desperately needed air and gagged on a mouthful of filthy saltwater. He looked up and was dazzled by the glare of floodlights being redirected towards the semi-submerged container, floating in the waves five metres away. Alarmed shouts shot down from above. Angus and Jimmy had been spotted. Angus swam towards his partner, who was drifting away from him face down in the water. He grabbed hold of Jimmy's lifeless right arm. Jimmy had taken a direct hit from the container. Every bone in his body must have been broken. There was a flattened stump of mashed pulp where his head should have been.

Angus heard a yell. 'Come on!'

He looked away from Jimmy's battered corpse as the Zodiac pulled up beside him. Amrit reached down and pulled him into the dinghy. The Indian turned towards the idling motor.

'What are you doing?' Angus shouted.

Amrit hollered back over the suppressed roar of the motor. 'We've got to get away from here.'

'What about Jimmy?'

'He's dead. Leave him.'

Angus pulled his flippers off, jumped up, grabbed the Indian by the throat and screamed into his shocked face. 'No fucking way. That's my oldest friend floating in the water. Cut the fucking motor or I'll throw you into the sea.'

Amrit did as he was told and then began helping Angus haul Jimmy's lifeless body on board. When the Indian saw what little was left of his boss's head, he fell to his knees and threw up. A siren howled. Angus gunned the Zodiac's motor and sped beyond the reach of the ship's lights.

'Where's the fucking tug?' Angus yelled.

'C-C-Chid will be taking her b-back to the dock,' stammered Amrit.

Ten minutes later, the Zodiac overtook the Shiva-Shakti as she ploughed through the waves towards the Sassoon Dock. Angus waved to Chid, turned to Amrit and said, 'Take over. I haven't a fucking clue where we are.'

The two men sat with the vibrating motor between them as the semi-rigid thudded over the sea. Amrit reached over and touched Angus's left knee to gain his attention. They exchanged a meaningful look in the gloom. The Indian nodded, acknowledging that he'd panicked and Angus had done the right thing by hauling Jimmy's body on board.

Angus stared at the lifeless lump encased in a neoprene diver's suit as it wobbled on the deck. There was an eyeball dangling from the bloody pulp that had been Jimmy's brain. 'It'll take more than a smack on the head to kill me.' Jimmy's words from long ago, when they were kids on the streets of Glasgow, echoed over the ocean of time.

'Fucking shit!' Angus cursed, remembering something Jimmy said to him less than twenty-four hours ago. *The missus is expecting our third any day soon.*

An orange sun rose over the sprawling slum villages on Bombay's outskirts. Amrit drove southwest out of the city, heading for Lonavla. Approximately five kilometres from the small town, he turned left onto a narrow dirt track, no more than a rocky furrow gouged into the hillside. He carefully steered the white Ambassador down the rutted slope and parked the car under the shade provided by tall eucalyptus trees. Amrit, Angus and Chid got out and looked around.

'What do you think?' Chid asked, puffing nervously on a cigarette.

'It's as good a place as any,' replied Angus. 'I'll carry the shovel and you guys can carry Jimmy.'

Angus opened the Ambassador's boot and picked up the black-painted spade he'd bought thirty minutes earlier from a roadside ironmonger. His two Indian companions were left to struggle with Jimmy's cumbersome corpse, by now wrapped in a sheet of black plastic. Angus walked into the forest. When he came to a stand of yellow bamboo, he sat down on a moss-covered rock and took in his surroundings.

A gurgling sound came from a nearby stream. A cuckoo bird called in the distance. Crickets whirred in the background. Sunbeams slanted through the overhead foliage, dappling the scene with blotches of brightness. Amrit and Chid's voices grew louder as they drew closer.

Angus rose to his feet and began to dig a grave. The two Indians appeared out of the woods. Their backs were bent by the heavy load carried between them. They dropped Jimmy's body, flumped onto the leaf-covered ground, lit cigarettes and watched Angus labour at his task.

It was hot and humid. Angus stripped down to his underpants, threw his muddy suit trousers and blue cotton shirt to one side and continued to dig. The Indians sensed rightly that Angus didn't want assistance.

By noon the oblong hole in the ground was five feet deep and slowly beginning to fill with water. Amrit and Chid hauled Angus out of the soggy pit. Then all three of them lowered Jimmy's body into its final resting place.

The Indians filled in the pit while Angus sat on a rock, looking on in silence. When the work was done, everyone gathered leaves and broken branches to cover their handiwork. They stood by the grave and each said their final farewell to a friend they'd loved and respected.

While Amrit and Chid muttered Hindu prayers, Angus remembered the first time he'd met Jimmy in Glasgow and how as teenagers they'd had so much fun roaming the city streets.

'I'm going to miss you, pal,' he said out loud. 'You'll always be a part of me.'

Jimmy's voice whispered in the back of his mind, *'Keep this in a safe place.'* Jimmy had said that when he'd handed Angus a business card in the lounge of the Taj Mahal Hotel.

The memory prompted Angus to walk away from the grave and return to the car to check if the card was still in the inside pocket of his lightweight suit jacket. It was. Once he'd retrieved it and put it in his wallet, he tossed the jacket into the bushes. He would no longer need it. His double life was over.

The sun was sinking behind the hills surrounding Lonavla. Angus, Amrit and Chid sat down for a rice plate at a roadside transport cafe. It was a noisy spot. A stone's throw away from where they sat an endless line of motorized transport roared by in both directions on the two-lane asphalt road. The three men were in a state of shock. They sat outside around a dusty plastic table and ate in silence. The carbohydrate-rich food restored their spirits and over a strong pot of coffee, Angus told a few anecdotes from his and Jimmy's teenage years in Glasgow. He concluded his narration by saying, 'So, now you know, Jimmy was always a bit accident prone.'

'Hold on,' said Amrit. 'You mean to say the boss had an axe stuck in the crown of his head and was living to tell the tale?'

Angus let out a short laugh. 'Yeah, he did. I'm surprised it didn't damage his brain, but he turned out to be one of the smartest guys I've ever met.'

Chid commented, 'That story about those sister-fuckers down in Goa, who were giving the boss an omelette laced with datora, is one I'll never forget. Did you ever hear what happened to them, after force-feeding them all those drugs?'

Angus shook his head. 'No, man, I didn't, but I wouldn't be surprised if they went insane. A taste of their own very bad medicine, one could say.'

'Yes,' Chid agreed. 'That's karma for you. It always gets you in the end.'

Chid's words succeeded in stopping the conversation in its tracks. They were all thrown back to the tragic loss of their friend. Karma, the tangle of cause and effect that everyone lays down in the course of their life, had certainly got Jimmy in the end.

'So, what are you guys going to do now that the boss is gone?' Angus asked, breaking the thick silence that had enveloped them.

The two Indians glanced at each other and shrugged.

'Will you be wanting us to be driving you to Pune?'

'Thanks for the offer, Chid,' replied Angus. 'I appreciate your asking, but you don't need to do that. I'll catch a taxi.'

'Tell me, Angus,' said Amrit, looking directly at him, 'this Rajneesh fellow, what kind of a man is he?'

Angus paused and reflected for a few moments before answering. He wiped his hands with a paper napkin and said, 'Well, the Bombay press has dubbed him the sex guru and the sceptics say he's a charlatan. As far as I'm concerned, he's the most remarkable man I'm ever likely to meet in my life.'

Chid asked, 'Have you ever talked to him?'

'Dozens of times.'

'What did he say to you?'

'Last time I spoke to Bhagwan, he said that it was time for me to start cleaning the ashram's toilets.'

Chid looked puzzled. 'And?'

'I'm going to sign up for the job as soon as I get back to Pune.'

All three of them burst out laughing.

Amrit toyed with a thick gold bracelet on his left wrist, looked over at Angus and said, 'You saved my life last night. I'll never forget that.'

Angus gave him a wan smile.

Amrit's eyes filled with tears. 'I am feeling very sorry that I wanted to leave the boss in the sea. It...' His voice broke. He sniffed, regained his composure and continued. 'It was a terrible thing to do. I—'

'Hey!' Angus interrupted, raising a hand, palm facing Amrit. 'There's no need to beat yourself up about that. It's gone. Over. Let it go, man.'

'But—'

'But nothing,' Angus said. 'We were both frightened and shocked. You can make a wrong call in such a hellish predicament. I was shitting myself.'

'You were?' Chid asked, who had been listening intently.

'Of course, I was,' Angus confirmed. 'For fuck's sake.' He laughed. 'Who do you think I am? Superman, or something?'

Chid lit a cigarette and then said, 'We don't really know who you are,

Angus. But we both really like you.'

'A real stand-up guy,' added Amrit.

A car transporter whined past, spewing out a filthy cloud of exhaust smoke that engulfed them.

When the smog cleared, Angus said, 'I appreciate the compliment. I've enjoyed working with you two. I'm going to miss our wee adventures on the high seas. You alright for money?'

Both Indians nodded and Amrit said, 'We were paid in advance.'

Chid changed the subject. 'Listen, there is something I've been meaning to tell you about for some time, but never found the right moment.'

'No time like the present,' said Angus.

'Right,' agreed Chid, after taking a long contemplative drag on his cigarette. 'So, it's like this. I come from a very religious family. My mother is worshiping at the Ganesh temple every morning and my father visits his guru once or twice a month.'

Angus's ears pricked up.

Chid went on, 'My father's guru is called the Beedie Wallah.'

'*The Beedie Wallah?* What kind of name is that for a guru?' Angus asked.

'As I understand it,' said Chid, 'he used to be running a cigarette shop near to Bombay's red-light district. But that is beside the point, other than to explain how he got his name. You see, my father is a deep and spiritual man, who claims that his guru is a *jnani*, a sage. My father is often requesting me to come and have *darshan* with the Beedie Wallah. But I've never been interested in such things.'

'Then why are you telling me all this?'

'Because, Angus, I think you might appreciate what the Beedie Wallah has to offer.'

'But I already have a master,' protested Angus.

'Yes...yes, I am knowing that,' said Chid. 'But Amrit and I have been discussing this and we think that you might have been tricked by this fellow, Rajneesh.'

'*Tricked?*' Angus blustered. 'How would you know that? You've never met Bhagwan, but think you can pass judgement on him?'

'I told you that's what he'd say,' said Amrit to Chid, lifting a white coffee mug to his smiling lips.

'Okay, Angus' said Chid in a humble voice, 'it's up to you. I just thought I would be mentioning this to you. No harm is being done in doing that. Now, is there?'

'No,' agreed Angus. 'I don't suppose there is.' Something in Chid's reserved manner struck a chord in Angus's curious mind. He enquired, 'So, saying it happened that I wanted to meet this Beedie Wallah guy, how would I go about it?'

Chid let out a short laugh.

'What's funny about that?' Angus asked.

'I'm not going to tell you how to find the Beedie Wallah,' Chid answered.

'That is something you have to discover for yourself.'

It was Angus's turn to laugh. 'What a fuckin' wind-up,' he said, in between chuckles. 'You get me interested in the Beedie Wallah, and then you won't tell me how to find him.'

Once more all three of them joined together in laughter, Jimmy momentarily forgotten.

When Chid got his breath back, he said, 'That's how we do things in India. If you are meant to be meeting a real *jnani*, the way will be made clear to you.' He smiled self-consciously. 'I picked that up from my father.'

Angus glanced at his watch, signalling to the others that it was time to go their separate ways. They stood and shook hands.

Angus never saw or heard of Amrit and Chid again.

'Are you ready for your breakfast, Mister MacLeod?'

My reverie was disturbed by a young nurse's voice. I looked away from the square of cloudy grey sky, framed by my hospital room's window, and answered, 'No thanks, dear, I'm not hungry.' I could smell the distinct scent of carbolic soap.

She clucked like a chicken, checked the drip-feed, changed the colostomy bag at the side of the bed and glanced at the monitor screen. 'Now that you're on the road to recovery, you have to build up your strength.'

Ten minutes later, I had a bib on and was making a bad job of spooning thick, putty-flavoured porridge into my mouth. Sucking through a thick plastic straw, I washed the lumpy gruel down with orange juice. It tasted like it had been watered down with battery acid. The same straw was used to drink weak coffee that made me think of cigarettes. To distract myself from the idea of inhaling nicotine-loaded smoke, I used a remote control to switch on a small television set fixed to a metal bracket in a corner of the room. The early morning news came on, showing pictures of a burning armoured car in Basra. According to the commentator, the war in Iraq was not going well.

The televised images set a line of associated thoughts spinning in my mind. Angus had told me that when he first watched film footage of planes flying into the World Trade Centre on CNN, he'd immediately thought that the incident had been manufactured.

Angus said, 'The USA's ace manipulators have learned their trade from past masters of the political chessboard. When I saw the Twin Towers collapse I thought about how Adolf Hitler had pulled off a similar stunt.' He explained, 'In 1933, the great dictator staged a phoney attack on his own parliament building in Berlin. Communist fanatics were blamed and Germany's armed forces began a string of pre-emptive strikes on countries purportedly supporting terrorists, all in the name of homeland security. Sound familiar to you? It should.' As if to add credence to Angus's remembered words, George W. Bush appeared on the small screen. The presidential puppet of the United States of America was bungling his scripted lines, as usual, self-righteously declaring that it was his mission to restore democracy to the Iraqi people. *Democracy,* I thought, *has to be the worst thing that ever happened to the Iraqis.* I pressed the red button on the remote and the TV picture imploded.

I closed my eyes and lay listening. The silence was broken by a knock on the door. The newspaper lady entered. 'Morning, Mister MacLeod. Would you like a paper?' she asked, brandishing a tabloid newspaper with a naked pin-up girl on the front page under a headline proclaiming that the troops would be home for Christmas.

'No thanks,' I answered.

'How about a lottery ticket,' she persisted. 'There's a roll-over jackpot this Friday. Forty-six million pounds! Now, don't tell me you wouldn't like to win that,' she said, patting her beehive hairdo.

'I don't do the lottery,' I said, wishing that she'd go away and leave me in peace.

'Oh, but you must,' she insisted, sitting down on the edge of my bed and waving a National Lottery coupon under my nose.

I could smell her cheap perfume. The lavender scent reminded me of the air freshener that Jean used in the toilet at home. 'I don't know how to fill it in.'

'No problem, Mister MacLeod, I'll help you.'

I crossed numbered squares I couldn't see because I didn't have on my reading glasses.

When I thought I'd finished, I handed her the coupon. Her forced cheeriness was grating on my nerves. She snatched it out of my hand and glanced at it. 'Why don't you fill in another box and make it an even five pounds?'

Pushy bitch, I thought, asking, 'Could you be so kind as to fill it in for me?'

'Aye, sure,' she replied, eager to leave the room now that she'd sold me something. 'I'll bring you the receipt this evening. Would you like to order a Sunday Mirror? I think they're giving away a free CD of the Spice Girls Greatest Hits.'

'Thanks,' I said, 'but I think I'll give that a miss.'

She shook her head as if to say I must be an idiot to turn down such a great offer. 'Suit yourself.'

'My wallet is in the drawer.' My bandaged head moved towards the bedside cupboard. 'Just take whatever I owe you.'

She did as requested, said, 'Have a nice day,' and closed the room door behind her.

I lay staring up at the white ceiling, wishing I could go home.

9

CREMATION GROUND CROSSROADS

August 2007, Oban, Scotland. My journey back to full health was a long and arduous one. I spent two months in hospital, during which time I filled in a National Lottery coupon every week and somehow succeeded in not winning a penny. I spent the better part of a year learning to walk again. My aluminium walking sticks were now hanging on a hook in my garage, a grim reminder of the potentially dangerous consequences of driving too fast on a wet road. I still had a bit of a limp and, when it rained, as it often does in Oban, my right leg ached. My neck had healed well, although I would never again be able to rotate my head to the extent that I could before the accident. My broken ribs had been the least serious of my injuries, but every once in a while, when I exerted myself, I felt a twinge of pain in my right side. Life goes on and I had adapted to the changes that had come about because of my misfortune. To coin an expression, I'd often heard Angus use, it was a steep learning curve. Angus! I still hadn't heard from him, but I felt in my heart that it would not be much longer before I did. I was looking forward to that day. I missed him.

One recent development that arose out of this difficult period in my life was that it had provided me with the time to jot down notes and begin organising them to prepare for writing a book about my life and my twin brother's escapades. I was not sure what form all this was going to take but, slowly but surely, it was shaping up. I'd even wrote the opening lines to the story. *Click! I froze. The sound of the spring-loaded triggering mechanism propelled me into a concentrated moment, crammed with disbelief and fear. A paralysing chill coursed through my body.* Overdramatic, but I felt confident that anyone reading that would wish to continue, which was the whole idea. I'd been doing my homework, studying the writer's self-help books I'd ordered from Amazon.

It was late morning and I had just returned from the gym in a good mood. I'd broken my personal record on the treadmill. I was sitting sipping on a cup of tea and gazing out of the kitchen's open window at bumblebees gathering pollen from a pink rose bush. A brilliant sun shone over the back garden. It was hot and I was sweating in my black training suit. I'd just begun munching on a slice of burnt toast, slathered with butter and marmalade when I heard the front door open and close. Keys rattled on the telephone table in the hall. High heels click-clacked on oak parquet tiles and then Jean entered the oblong kitchen. I spun my rotating stool around so I could look at her. She'd had her hair cut to shoulder length, the fine streaks of grey dyed out. It looked like she was wearing an exotic black helmet composed of shiny silk thread.

'I like your new hairstyle, darling.' I felt like laughing, but suppressed the feeling, knowing Jean might take offence. As she aged, she was becoming increasingly touchy about everything that concerned her physical appearance. 'Very modern,' I added.

'Did you have a good workout?' Jean asked, switching on the electric kettle.

'Aye, not bad,' I replied. 'I managed to do five sets on the bench press with a hundred-kilo load.'

Jean approached me and pushed her hips between my bent knees. She curled her hands around the back of my neck and kissed the crown of my balding head. 'Joining the gym was a great idea.'

I agreed with her but said nothing, thinking to myself that our sex life had never been better. During the last fortnight, we'd made love almost every night.

The kettle came to the boil and shut down with a click. Jean poured hot water into a mug containing two heaped teaspoons of decaffeinated coffee granules.

'So, what gossip did you pick up down at the hairdresser?' I asked, returning my eyes to the view outside of the broad window.

Jean perched herself on a stool next to me, hooked her black leather boot heels on a stainless steel spar, and cradled her mug of unsweetened coffee against her pointed chin. Steam drifted up to her face. 'Och, nothing much. Sheena Lynch is pregnant again.' She ran a hand over her glossy hairdo. 'Oh aye, I just remembered, Maureen Baxter, the new assistant that did my hair this morning, was saying that some idiot in Edinburgh won seventy-two million pounds on the lottery eleven weeks ago. Nobody has claimed it… Can you believe it? …and if they don't come forward in the next week, the prize money goes to charity. Makes you wonder why some people bother to buy a ticket in the first place.'

The thought of so much money made me think about something I'd wanted to discuss with my wife for months, but couldn't pluck up the courage to broach the subject. Even though I knew it would cause trouble, I decided that this was as good a moment as any to run it by her. 'Jean,' I said, 'I've been thinking—'

'I thought I could smell burning,' she commented, interrupting me.

'I've been thinking,' I persisted, 'that I'd like to sell the business.'

'What?'

'You heard what I said.'

'You'll do no such thing,' she declared, slamming her coffee mug down on the black granite tabletop.

'Why not?'

'Because you're only fifty-five and we don't have enough to retire.'

'Don't have enough?' I repeated as if it were nonsense. 'Well, you're wrong there, going by my estimates. If I sell the business and convert to cash everything we own, we're worth over twelve million, and that's not including this house or that tract of land I bought up in Aberdeen back in the seventies.'

'That's what I mean,' said Jean, as though I'd just stated an obvious fact, the meaning of which was beyond my comprehension. 'Twelve million pounds today will be worth two million in ten years. By the time we're seventy, we'll be poor and plagued by financial problems.'

'Problems!' I exclaimed, realising that my arguments were making about as much impression on my wife as a drop of rain would on Ben Nevis. 'Our so-called financial problems are beyond most people's wildest dreams.'

'Don't you bloody well start,' said Jean, stabbing an accusatory finger at the tip of my nose. 'Besides, what would you do if you retired? Mope around the house all day long?'

'Well, for a start, I was thinking we could do a bit of travelling.'

'Travelling!' Jean pronounced the word as if it were an unspeakable obscenity. 'In case you've forgotten, the last time we went *travelling*...' She wiggled her index fingers above her indignant head to lend emphasis to the word. '...you nearly got us killed by sneaking off to smoke a cigarette and sitting down on a bomb. It's a bloody miracle we got out of Cambodia alive.' Her tone softened as the memory surfaced in her conscious mind. 'Anyway, Hamish, my love, where would you want to go?'

'Well, maybe we could start by going to India.'

'*India!* You mean to say, you want to drag me away from one of the most beautiful places in the world to visit a Third World country, where starving people are raking through the rubbish to find something to eat? What would we do in India?'

'We could visit Varanasi for a start. Angus told me—'

'Angus! For Christ's sake!' Jean stood up and started pacing around the kitchen. 'I might have guessed he was behind this. The bugger's come back from beyond the grave to haunt us with his mad ideas.' She paused, then said, 'Listen, I've told you before that you're going to have to learn to accept —'

'Jean,' I said, cutting her off, 'there's another thing I've been meaning to speak to you about.'

'What?'

'Angus and Lara are still alive.'

'Oh, no, don't start,' she groaned, returning to her stool. 'I've told you—'

'Yes, I'm aware of what you've told me,' I said, cutting across her again, 'but there are things I haven't told you that I should have mentioned ages ago.'

'Like what?' Jean asked, standing up.

I blew out a long breath that whistled between my teeth. 'I think you better sit down again and listen to what I have to say.'

Pune, India, October 1978. It was almost midnight. Angus asked the taxi driver to drop him off at the burning ghats on the banks of the Bund River. Overhead, large fruit bats screeched from their perches in tall banyan trees. Angus walked down a short concrete road. He sat down by an oblong pit under a corrugated tin roof and watched wisps of smoke rise from a funeral pyre's smouldering ashes. Tears came to his eyes. Jimmy Bradley had just been killed the night before and for the first time, Angus allowed himself to vent his grief by crying and sobbing. He fell silent when it struck him with stunning clarity that he hadn't realised how much Jimmy meant to him and that one never really knows how much another person has become part of one's life until they disappear from it. Angus had valued Jimmy not only as a friend but also as a link to his past. Now that he was gone forever, it felt like the past was drifting beyond the vast ocean of time's horizon, leaving him in the eternal present with only himself for company. For the first time in years, he felt lonely.

 Angus began to contemplate death and what it really meant. He concluded that in life death is the only certainty and without those two extreme opposites neither of them could exist. He picked up a short stick and poked at the smoking ashes. Encircled by darkness, he gazed into the glowing embers before him, thinking that only a few hours before those red-hot coals had been a human being. He saw that his grief was not so much connected to Jimmy's demise but rather to his ego's insistence that it should not have happened to somebody he loved, that he didn't want this form of separation. He'd listened to Bhagwan depicting death as something to be celebrated. It had sounded like a wonderful idea in the Buddha Hall when Angus was surrounded by life, but now, faced with the existential reality of losing someone close to him, rejoicing about it wasn't as easy as it sounded.

Angus was in the midst of such thoughts when he heard gravel crunch underfoot behind him. He was beginning to turn his head when a female voice called out, 'Hi, Swami, mind if I sit down beside you.'

He recognized an Irish lilt in her accent, looked up at the woman's shadowed face and replied, 'Sure, I could do with a bit of company.'

She sat down on a concrete block about three feet away from him. 'I love it down here at the burning *ghats*. It's the crossroads where life and death meet.'

Angus glanced at her and said nothing, thinking that this was typical sannyasin rhetoric.

'I know it sounds clichéd,' she continued, as if in response to his unspoken thought, 'but it also happens to be true. Life and death are locked in an eternal dance called constant change. Family and friends will meet again and again, for we are fellow passengers on life's journey that every once in a while passes through death's dark tunnel and emerges into the light on the other side. You never meet anyone in this world by accident.'

Angus was only half listening to her words but, when she said her last sentence, something clicked in his mind. He turned to look more closely at her face. It was too dark to see anything much. The woman produced a candle from a cloth shoulder bag, lit it with a match and held it in front of her. On the first take, she appeared to him as strikingly beautiful. Thick, shoulder-length, dark hair framed penetrating almond-shaped eyes, high cheekbones, a broad forehead, a smiling mischievous mouth and a strong chin. He had a sudden flash of himself, holding her close and kissing her passionately like Humphrey Bogart in an old black and white Hollywood film. He didn't follow through; he felt like an actor in an unscripted movie and didn't want to ruin the scene by saying the wrong lines.

She laughed. 'You don't recognize me, do you?'

Angus continued to look at her. 'No, I can't say I do. Should I?'

'Well, put it like this, I remember you.'

'Who are you? Have we met before?'

'You really don't remember me, do you?'

'No, I don't.'

'Well, Swami, I'll tell you who I am and maybe that will refresh your memory.' She raised a hand to her unlined forehead and pushed a lock of hair to one side. 'My name is Ma Deva Lara and I'm the women who has been waiting for a very long time to meet you.'

'W-Wh-What?' Angus stammered, incredulous.

Lara said nothing. She answered his question by standing up and walking away. Her perfume lingered on the warm air.

He sat watching her wander slowly up the concrete track that led to a tar road until her robed form vanished into the night.

Such exchanges were commonplace in and around Bhagwan Shree Rajneesh's ashram. A feeling of connectedness existed between the master's disciples that manifested in various forms, from thinking about someone and they appeared moments later in the flesh in front of your astonished eyes, to the guru himself using something you'd said the evening before in the following morning's discourse. Be that as it may, Angus had not the faintest idea who Ma Deva Lara was or why she said that she'd been waiting a long time to meet him.

He returned his attention to the dying embers in the cremation pit and tossed Lara's candle onto the hot coals. The wax hissed, quickly melted, and burst into flame. He sat in the darkness, staring at the bright blue and yellow flames as they danced before his eyes. He watched his mind drift into the past to the last time he'd taken LSD. The peak of that psychedelic trip had taken place in a small hillside cave in the desert just outside of Pushkar in Rajasthan. He smiled, remembering how he'd hallucinated Satan calling his name. *I must have completely lost it,* he thought. During the acid trip he'd had many visions, one of which was host to a mysterious woman with green eyes. She'd been sitting beside a smouldering fire, just like the one he was sitting beside now. She'd said something to him. *What was it she said?* Angus asked himself, wracking his brain to remember. *I've been waiting for a very long time to meet you.*

'Holy fuckin' shit!' His pulse began to beat in great jolts. Shock coursed through his body like electricity as he underwent some kind of déjà voodoo. Angus grabbed his bag, jumped to his feet and ran up the rough concrete track. The road was deserted. 'Oh, no!' He spun around like a ball of confusion. After a couple of disconcerting minutes, he accepted that Ma Deva Lara was gone. He decided it was time to head home. He'd only taken a few steps when Lara stepped out from behind a bush.

Angus stopped dead in his tracks. 'What the...'

She burst out laughing and asked, 'What took you so long?'

He stepped forward and pulled her close, wrapping both arms around her, eliminating any possibility of escape. Slender, she was nearly as tall as he was. 'Got you,' he said playfully. His flesh tingled, as if close to an electric power source. From somewhere deep inside, Lara gave a faint, almost sexual sigh. They sought each other's lips and kissed. Tentatively at first, and then stronger. He felt her tongue flicker. Her fingers dug into the back of his neck. His erection was a rigid pounding presence, as painful in its hardness as the erections he'd had as a teenager. Lara giggled. 'Oh, oh, kundalini rising.'

Angus held her tighter and whispered in her ear, 'I still don't remember who you are, but it doesn't matter. We've found each other, and that's what counts.' He buried his face in the curve of her warm shoulder and breathed in her flowery scent, sensing beneath it something passionate and intimate.

Over the years since Jenny's death, a longing had been developing in Angus's heart, an unfulfilled desire to have his being confirmed by a woman, not just any woman but one who he loved, cherished and respected. During the time he'd spent in Bhagwan's spiritual community, he'd been involved, to a greater or lesser extent, with many beautiful women, some of whom, in his own chimerical way, he'd imagined himself to be in love with. Longstanding relationships were a relative rarity in those wildly promiscuous times. The sannyasins lived like bees and butterflies, flitting from one fascinating flower to the next in a blossom-filled garden of sexual delights. Sex, for Angus, had turned into a sport. He found it difficult to bond deeply with a female partner. Enticement was always lurking around the next corner, calling like a siren from the rocks of temptation, strewn with the wreckage from the many relationships that had floundered against them, before sinking in a sea of lonely hearts. In effect, this communal trend caused people to surrender to Bhagwan rather than each other, something nobody in the ashram seemed in the least bit concerned with, too preoccupied with worshipping the very air their guru breathed and having the licentious time of their lives.

On the night they met, Angus took Lara home and made love with her under a clear sky filled with sparkling stars. When clouds glowed orange in the east and a red sun peeped over the horizon, heralding the arrival of a new day, they fell asleep in each other's arms.

Over a late breakfast by the well in front of his house, Lara explained how, a year earlier, Sola the Gypsy had used tarot cards to divine that one evening Lara would meet the man she'd been waiting for by a smouldering fire.

'Who is Sola the Gypsy?' Angus asked, dropping breadcrumbs into the clear water to feed a pair of carp, cruising beneath the surface in search of a titbit.

'She's a seer who lives in Laxmi Villas,' answered Lara. 'Would you like to meet her?'

Angus looked away from the white, rose and orange-coloured fish, smiled at Lara, shrugged and said, 'Why not?'

Ten minutes later, they were sitting in the back seat of a noisy motorized rickshaw, filling each other in on their backgrounds. Lara had been born in Dublin. When her Irish father was offered a job in a civil engineering architect's office in Aberdeen, he'd moved there with Lara and her mother.

Angus had visited the grey granite city on Scotland's northeast coast. 'Aberdeen is a bit of a bleak place,' he commented. 'If you ask me, the locals up there are a dour lot.'

Lara nodded in agreement. 'I know what you mean. They can come across like that at first. Once you get to know them, though, the Aberdonians are some of the kindest and most generous people I've ever had the pleasure of meeting.'

'I find that a bit hard to believe.'

'Take my word for it. It's true. Anyway, by the time I finished at Gray's School of Art on the bonnie banks of the River Dee, I couldn't wait to get out of there. The winters up there are terrible and seem to last forever.'

Angus chuckled. 'Now that's something I find easy to believe.'

The rickshaw skidded to an abrupt halt outside Laxmi Villas. Angus paid the beedie-smoking driver and then walked with Lara between black metal gates, flanked by a pair of rusty wrought iron cannons mounted on wooden wheels. Angus was familiar with Laxmi Villas because, after the ashram and the burning *ghats*, it was one of his favourite places to visit in Pune. Surrounded by a sprawling overgrown garden, the main building, various outhouses and newly constructed bamboo huts were home to about two hundred of Bhagwan's followers. The place was run by a rabble-rousing sannyasin called Anand, an old friend of Angus's, whom he'd first met in Herat in Afghanistan when the dread-locked Guadeloupian was calling himself Claude. Anand was involved in an ongoing conflict with the ashram authorities. They viewed him as a troublemaker, who liked to throw open-air parties, where clouds of hashish smoke ascended into the sky, signalling to the local renegades that high times were to be had by one and all. Apart from the occasional complaint from the ashram's policymakers, Anand got away with his all-night celebrations; he was one of Bhagwan's favourite rebels.

During the Rajneesh ashram's early days, disillusioned Goa hippies had formed a large contingent of the hard-core of individuals who'd helped lay the foundations of the spiritual community. Under the bright orange banner of rebelliousness, raised by a man deliberately setting out to destroy any preconceived notions about how an enlightened person might behave, there were still some pockets of resistance in the land of surrender. All this ran through Angus's chattering mind as he walked through Laxmi Villas.

'This way,' said Lara, leading him by the hand along a dark corridor in the heart of a building, which in another era had been the servant's quarters in a maharaja's palace.

They came to a bright red door. Lara used the knuckles of her right hand to knock lightly upon it.

'Come in,' called a woman's voice in response.

'I've been waiting for you,' said Sola, when the couple entered the candle-lit room. 'Please be seated and make yourselves comfortable.'

Angus and Lara sat on cushions placed on the small room's white marble floor tiles. The air was thick with sandalwood incense smoke. The square living space was bare except for nine things: a single mattress, a broomstick wedged in a corner with two orange robes hanging from it, the round wooden table Angus was sitting beside, three threadbare cushions and, hanging on the mould-stained wall he faced, a large black and white picture of Bhagwan in a floppy hat. The master's indecipherable face stared back at Angus and something he'd heard him say recently popped into his mind. *The whole world is a madhouse where everyone is competing with each other. In reality, there is really no need to prove that you are better than anyone else. Nobody is superior and nobody is inferior. Everybody is who they are and all comparisons are simply stupid.*

Bhagwan's words provided Angus with the nerve to look the seer directly in the eye. The energy field surrounding the plump lady, wearing gold hoop earrings, was intimidating. He could have sworn there were waves of sky-blue energy pulsing from her like electrical charges. The seer gazed back at Angus with dark eyes that gave little away about who was looking through them. She flashed him an enigmatic smile and returned her attention to shuffling a pack of Aleister Crowley Tarot cards.

'Now then, what have we here?' she said, fanning the cards out face down on the black velvet cloth that covered the circular table. She closed her eyes, ran her gold-ringed fingers over them and plucked one out at random. She placed it on the table facing the couple. It was one of the most fundamental cards in the Tarot – The Lovers.

Sola glanced over at Lara. '*Mmmmh,*' she hummed, 'you may well find reason to smile, my dear,' she said with a cultivated American accent. 'It would seem that you've found the one you've been waiting on. But look here,' she said, pointing an index finger's long tapering fingernail, coated with shiny purple varnish. 'Twins. I sometimes think that this particular card should have been called The Brothers, rather than The Lovers.' The seer glanced at Angus, whose bullshit meter was going into the red. 'Do you have a twin brother?'

Angus shook his head vigorously. 'No.'

'Strange,' muttered Sola, 'the cards say otherwise. The sword is for the most part an engine of division. Perhaps you were separated from him when you were too young to remember anything about it. I'm intrigued.' She pulled another card and placed it directly in front of Angus. 'Turn it over,' she instructed.

Angus stared at the image on the back of the oblong card. It reminded him of the Celtic crosses he'd seen as a child on Iona. He found himself reluctant to touch the card.

Sola noticed his hesitation. 'There's nothing to be afraid of,' she assured him.

'I'm not afraid,' snapped Angus.

Sola raised a sceptical, painted eyebrow and said nothing.

Angus flipped the card over and there was the Grim Reaper, scythe in hand, reaping death's harvest.

'Oh, my condolences,' said Sola. 'I see you've lost someone very close to you.' She turned another card. 'Recently, it appears. There is an element of water involved. Life moving through water, to be more precise.'

Angus felt a knot of emotion expand and constrict his throat. Lara sensed this, took his right hand in her left and clasped it tightly. A runaway tear trickled down over his cheek. Sola turned over four more cards. They were The Juggler, The Prince of Wands, Queen of Swords and the Ten of Disks.

Sola studied the cards intently for some time with half-closed eyes. She asked Angus, 'Has the master told you to do something that you have not followed through on?'

'Yes,' replied Angus, 'The last time I talked to him, Bhagwan told me to begin working as a toilet cleaner in the ashram.'

'And?'

'I didn't do it.'

'Why not?

'I have better things to do than clean toilets.'

Sola tapped The Prince of Wands. 'Fate dictates otherwise. Why play at surrendering to the master, if you are not willing to act on his suggestions? He will steer you in the right direction if you allow it. One of the pitfalls of ascending the spiritual ladder is to become absorbed in the psychic realm. Something, I might add, that I've fallen prey to frequently doing what I do. The master puts his disciples to work in order to ground them in their meditation. Otherwise, they will be little more than metaphysical hedonists.' She reached over and gave him a motherly pat on the cheek, the corners of her eyes wrinkling with a knowing smile. 'You must learn to overcome that stubborn Scotsman who lives in your heart. Throw him out of the house of your soul, along with all the other innate tendencies dwelling within you. It will help if you follow the master's wise advice. You'll need a toilet brush to clean all that bullshit out of you.'

All three shared a few moments of laughter and then Sola said, 'There's no need to worry about your rebelliousness because, when the prodigal son returns to his father, it's his homecoming that is celebrated the most. When it happens that a human being liberates his consciousness from the trap of the animal body, the angels in heaven always throw a big party. Now then,' she said, returning to the cards, 'I see that you will have a lot of material wealth made available to you. Lara, you must always have the last say in the joint business ventures I see the pair of you embarking on in the not too distant future. As for the distant future, Angus, pull a card.' Once again, she fanned the deck of cards face down on the velvet cloth. Angus let his right hand hover for a moment before he drew out the Queen of Cups. 'Mmmh,' hummed Sola again, glanc at the card. She then returned the card to the pack, shuffled the cards for what must have been about a minute, and then once more fanned the cards across the table in front of Angus. 'Pull a card,' she said to him. He took his time over it and, when he chose a card, was astonished to see that it was again the Queen of Cups. 'Yes,' said Sola, 'there can be no doubt about it. The queen sits at the edge of the shoreline, yet her feet do not touch the water. You must both be very respectful to large bodies of water, especially the ocean.' She nodded at Angus. 'Pull another.' He did as she asked and chose the Three of Swords. 'My goodness,' she commented. 'I will be frank with you. The combination of these two cards signifies heartbreak and loss. My intuition tells me that, although I see you both love the sea, as all Celtic people do, the sea will often work against you both in the future, if it hasn't done so already.' For the second time in ten minutes, Angus found his thoughts returning to Jimmy Bradley.

Sola asked Angus to pull one more card from the deck spread before him. He turned over the Ten of Swords. The seer became thoughtful, closed her eyes for a few moments and then said in a solemn voice. 'I foresee great difficulty ahead, a painful rite of passage, some kind of disease, life-threatening...' She broke off. 'Please, Lara, draw a card. I don't wish our session to end on such a gloomy note.'

Sola gave a forced smile. Angus studied her face and wondered what she'd seen behind the veil. Lara pulled The Lovers again and the seer's smile once more became genuine.

She picked the card up and said, 'Now that you've found each other, you are duty-bound to take care of one another. As long as you remain together things will always work out for the best, which doesn't mean that it's always going to be easy. I see difficult times ahead. You, in particular, would do well to remember this,' she said, skewering Angus with a piercing stare, 'for your tendency towards obstinacy will one day bring your life in danger. So,' she concluded, 'listen to Lara when she offers up advice, even if it's unasked for because it is Lara more than you who will be the guiding light of your relationship.'

Over the next few weeks, everything Angus had ever thought he knew about women receded into the mists of the past to be replaced by the dawning of a new, more profound understanding. For the first time in his life, he felt true love.

The whole time Jean had been listening to me narrate the story of how Angus and Lara first met and their subsequent visit to Sola the seer, she'd remained silent. She suddenly laughed and said, 'Sounds like a load of black magic, mumbo-jumbo to me.' She looked at me, with a puzzled expression upon her face, and said, 'I don't get it.'

I asked, 'Don't get what?'

'The reason behind why you told me all that nonsense about what that fortune-teller said.'

I stood, stretched my arms above my head, sat down and smiled at Jean.

She asked, 'What are you looking so smug about?'

'Angus and Lara are alive.'

'I've told you a hundred—'

'Listen, Jean…' I quickly moved on to how the two police detectives had visited me at work, the questions they'd asked and the photograph of Angus and Lara they'd shown me.'

'Unbelievable. Are you sure it was them?' Jean asked.

I nodded. 'One hundred and one percent.'

'If they are alive, why the hell haven't they contacted us?'

I shrugged and scratched my head. 'I've been asking myself that very question for over a year now. Knowing my brother, I am sure he has his reasons. Just don't ask me what they are.'

'Why on earth didn't you tell me about this before?'

'Ehm…eh, I forgot.'

'Forgot? My Auntie Nellie's arse!'

'I wanted to surprise you.'

'Well, you've succeeded most admirably,' said Jean, cupping her head in her long-fingered hands. Her expression became thoughtful. 'So, tell me, how does this tie in with what a gypsy woman said to Angus and Lara? What was it, about twenty-eight years ago?'

'Yes, that's about right. Well, you see, everything Sola told them eventually happened.'

'I know they made tons of money drug-dealing but—'

'Dope dealing.'

'What?'

'Angus said he wasn't a drug dealer. He described himself as a *dope* dealer.'

'Is there a difference?'

I shrugged. 'Beats me. Angus seemed to think so. He made a point of explaining it to me in detail. Didn't make much sense at the time. Still doesn't, now that I think about it.'

Jean twisted her lips into a sardonic smile. 'I can easily imagine him explaining the kind of details that made him come out of it smelling of roses instead of cannabis resin.'

'Angus dealt in other illegal drugs. Not just hashish.'

'I'm not surprised to hear it,' Jean commented. 'So, this Sola lady said something about some kind of disease. What was that all about?'

'That's the next part of the story.'

'You know this, you're starting to sound more and more like your brother every day.'

'Is that a bad thing?'

'No, it's a fact. Anyway, you've got me curious now. Is it a long story?'

'Long enough to fill a chapter in a book,' I replied.

'You're not answering my question by saying that,' said Jean, looking out of the window. 'Come on. Let's go out for a stroll on a lazy Saturday afternoon. It's a beautiful day. We can walk and talk.'

Five minutes later, Jean and I were outside our house, walking arm in arm along the pavement, heading for Oban harbour. Overhead, gulls wheeled and cried as they coasted on the breeze. A ship's klaxon called out in the distance.

'So,' Jean said, 'I'm listening.'

'Okay. It was like this. The morning after Angus and Lara visited—'

Jean said, 'I love the sound of your voice.'

'What?'

'I said I love the sound of your voice, it's so deep.'

'You're joking?'

'You think so?' Jean asked, stopping dead in her tracks. She put her arms around my shoulders and began kissing me passionately. After a few moments, she broke the embrace and said, 'Did that feel like I was joking?'

I chuckled, feeling self-conscious about behaving like a couple of lovesick teenagers in public. 'Jean,' I said, facing the person I loved most in the world. 'I really don't know what's going on with you...' I paused for a heartbeat. '...but I like it.'

We waited for a fish lorry to speed by and crossed the street. I took hold of Jean's left hand and returned to the telling of what happened to Angus and Lara after they met with Sola, the Tarot Reader.

10

RUDE AWAKENING

Two days after they'd visited Sola the seer, Angus and Lara rose early, put on fresh robes and cycled to the ashram. Angus paid the twenty rupees entrance fee. A bearded Indian sannyasin gave him a toothy smile as he handed over two tickets. Angus joined Lara in a long queue outside Buddha Hall. Soon they were seated in a sea of orange in the oval-shaped auditorium, listening to Bhagwan deliver an exceptionally interesting discourse. Every once in a while, the master employed bawdy jokes to poke fun at everyone and everything. His audience responded with howls of uninhibited laughter. About half-an-hour into the talk, Bhagwan got around to discussing Tarot card readers and astrologers. Angus's ears pricked up as the master described how people turned to such sources of divination when they lacked significance in their lives. Angus's logical mind reckoned a lot of the people around him must lack meaning in their lives because the ashram's officially sanctioned set of Tarot cards were selling like hot chapattis in the bookshop. His soul soaked up Bhagwan's words like a dry sponge, while his mind rattled like a can of dry peas.

Towards the end of the discourse, Bhagwan's voice grew more intense and urgent. 'One should be completely surrendered to the river of life, completely surrendered to the river of existence. In deep surrender, the ego disappears. When the ego is gone, you become that which has always been there.'

Yes, Angus thought, opening his eyes. He glanced around at the blissed-out expressions on Lara and his fellow listener's faces, and it occurred to him that nobody he looked at was enlightened. Everyone seated around him appeared content just to pursue enlightenment, rather than reach the ultimate goal. *Am I just like them,* he asked himself, *forever destined to be a seeker instead of a finder? Am I kidding myself? Setting myself some lofty spiritual goal because it helps define my life more than the quest for money or power? ? Or have I fallen into some kind of trap, baited with something that tastes so fantastic I'd have to be crazy not to want it?*

Angus's reflections drew to an abrupt halt when Bhagwan said, 'Enough for today.' The master laid his clipboard to one side, rose to his feet in a graceful motion and namasted reverently to all who sat before him. He turned and slowly walked towards the back of the hall, where a gleaming, black Rolls Royce awaited him, a rear door held open by a bearded Samurai guard.

People began to disperse. Angus and Lara sat in silence for some time, breathing in the air of peace that permeated Buddha Hall. Eventually, they too rose to their feet and headed for the exit.

The previous afternoon, Angus had applied for a job as a toilet cleaner. He'd managed to convince himself that he must be drawing close to enlightenment because that very morning he was going to ascend the last rungs of the ladder that leads to nirvana, with a lavatory brush in his right hand raised in salute to the all-encompassing transcendental state.

After a hurried breakfast and a long goodbye hug with Lara, Angus rushed off to work in the therapy area toilets. Wearing nothing but a pair of shorts and rubber gloves, he began scrubbing away at an already spotless line of porcelain lavatory pots as if his spiritual awakening depended on it. As the day wore on, more and more people began filtering into the long, white-tiled room to use the gleaming toilets. Most of the transient visitors were naked. Many were participating in the therapy groups taking place in the basement's padded rooms and were often in a state of high anxiety or bewilderment. Angus watched in amusement as primal therapy groupies unfastened jumbo-sized safety pins and pulled down their oversized cotton nappies before sitting down on a plastic toilet seat to evacuate their bowels. Others simply vomited the contents of their stomachs into a vacant lavatory pot or, if they couldn't control themselves, into a convenient sink. Angus surrendered to the situation and, without so much as a word of complaint, either wiped or mopped up the disgusting mess.

Bhagwan's voice rang out in Angus's head. *The lotus of consciousness grows out of the mud of human existence.* Through the residual pong of human excretion, Angus could smell the lotus flower of enlightenment's sweet fragrance, prompting him to bow down in front of a gurgling cistern.

Squeals and grunts rose from a glass-partitioned shower stall as an amorous couple made love under jets of steaming water. Angus had heard Bhagwan say, 'Let celebration be the only rule,' and everyone in the commune seemed to be taking his words sincerely as opposed to seriously — that is, apart from a handful of female individuals called Zen Mistresses.

Angus had been working for a fun-filled week in the group room toilets when he was caught having a friendly chat with an attractive, naked brunette from Canada, sitting on a freshly disinfected toilet to relieve her bladder. The main door burst open and in stormed Deeksha, the Sicilian dragon who ran the ashram's main restaurant with an invisible Zen club in one hand and a huge slice of chocolate cake in the other. She was a fat lady with a big hooked nose who spoke strongly Italian-accented English. Her best feature was her eyes, perfect shiny brown almonds. They sent out a semaphore alarm message by blinking rapidly.

'Whaddya thinka you're a doing here, Swami,' she asked Angus, who looked away from the Canadian woman with an expression of shocked puzzlement on his face.

'I-I-I'm cleaning the toilets,' stammered Angus.

'No a you're a not a cleaning the toilets. You're a resistant.'

'Resistant,' said Angus, justifiably perplexed. 'Resistant to what?'

Deeksha glanced around the long oblong room with an indignant look upon her chubby face. 'You're a resistant to the master's work.' She turned to the tall balding man behind her. He was holding a clipboard. 'Sagar,' she ordered, 'write a this swami's name a down and give him a toothbrush first a thing tomorrow morning.'

Sagar nodded his head, asked Angus his name and scribbled it on a sheet of paper.

'What do I need a toothbrush for?' Angus asked.

The Italian Zen Mistress glared at him as if he'd just asked her if she enjoyed anal sex. 'None of you're a fucking business.' She pulled up her red robe, sat down on the toilet next to the naked woman from Toronto, turned to her and asked, 'What a the fuck are you looking at.'

The Canadian shrugged, closed her gaping mouth and said nothing.

Deeksha farted loudly and looked up at Angus. 'You stupido Scotsman, you will a find out what a surrender is all about tomorrow morning.' She stood, pulled up her XXXL, black scanty panties and said to her assistant, 'Come on, Sagar, enough of this a nonsense.' Sagar looked up at the ceiling barely able to conceal the grin that was threatening to dislocate his jaw.

Deeksha and Sagar spun on their heels and whirled out through the open door like twin tornadoes.

Angus glanced down at the Canadian woman, who was shaking her head in disbelief. 'What the fuck was that all about?' he asked.

She looked up at him and replied, 'I can't stand that power-tripping fascist bitch, she's full of Italian—'

Deeksha reappeared in the doorway and shouted, 'Don't you stupidos dare a talk a bad about a me behind my back.'

The following morning, Angus was handed a brand new toothbrush and ordered to scrub the spaces between the floor tiles.

It was December. Angus had been cleaning floors with toothbrushes for six weeks. He'd recently attended a *darshan*, where Bhagwan had said that a man who is aware becomes the source of his roles in life, which left Angus wondering what on earth he was doing down on his grazed knees, scrubbing a spotless floor with a nylon toothbrush. He didn't recognize it at the time, but he was going through an intentionally brought on identity crises. He was in the midst of the painful process of discovering that he was not what he thought himself to be, that he was a nobody rather than a somebody. Large chunks of his personality were being flushed away. It was a void-like experience, a psychological death. The master had not been joking when he'd proclaimed that his whole effort was to lead his disciples into nothingness, a spiritual vacuum that requires them to die to everything they'd erroneously believed themselves to be. This crux is when the husk of superficial personality is stripped away to leave the authentic spiritual essence naked, dropping the seeker into a psychological no-man's-land, where the faint-hearted fall to the wayside and only those grounded in the need to experience the truth that lies behind all material and mental forms will pass through it.

Deeksha, who'd made it her mission to get on the stubborn Scotsman's case and drag him over the many barbed wire fences strung across no-man's-land, burst into the toilets and interrupted his contemplations. 'You fucking stupido man, why don't you try a putting some a love into what you're doing?'

Angus, who'd by now become inured to the Zen Mistress's jibes and insults, looked up at her from his kneeling position on the floor. They stared into each other's eyes in silence. Angus could not fathom the fire-breathing dragon who harassed him daily. He also could not bring himself to hate her, because he sensed that she saw and understood something about him that he was unaware of.

'I don't know anymore what it is that I'm supposed to be doing,' said Angus in a voice strained by the effort of trying to keep it calm. 'So how the fuck am I supposed to put love into it?'

Deeksha must have been studying her Bhagavad-Gita earlier on that day because in response to his question she fired off a quote from it. 'For aspirants who wanta a to climb the mountain of spiritual awareness, the path is a selfless work.' Pleased with her erudition, she tilted her head and smiled down at him like a fairy godmother.

Angus glared back at her. 'What the hell has climbing a spiritual mountain got to do with scrubbing a floor with a fuckin' toothbrush?' He shouted at the Zen Mistress in frustration. 'The fucking floor's not even dirty. I...' A lump of emotion lodged in his throat.

Deeksha said gently, 'Let it out.'

He began to cry. Deeksha knelt beside him, placed a comforting hand on his shoulder and said, 'I'm amazed that you haven't a got around to telling me to shove that a toothbrush up a my a fat Italian arse.'

Angus's angry tears ceased. They shared a hearty laugh. Deeksha snatched the worn-out toothbrush from his hand. 'No more a cleaning. Tomorrow morning, after discourse, you go down the town and start a to bake a the bread.'

The ashram's bakery was in a narrow lane off Pune's main commercial strip, Mahatma Gandhi Road. The premises were owned by a Muslim businessman. His two employees worked at night, baking buns and biscuits. During the day, half-a-dozen sannyasins took over the wood-fired oven and baked good quality bread.

Bhagwan's ashram might have had the cleanest toilets in India but, in the beginning, they had the filthiest bakery. Thanks to a group of hard-working sannyasin cleaners, it didn't remain that way for long. It took a week to clean the place up. The only dirty thing left in the bakery was one of the Muslim bakers, who never washed and, during the afternoon, slept in a rust-stained bathtub.

By March, outside temperatures were soaring towards thirty-five degrees centigrade. Inside the bakery it was closer to fifty, due to the heat generated by the brick oven. To combat dehydration a large aluminium kettle, full of lemongrass tea, was simmering all day long. Angus was drinking at least five litres of this tea every day. Due to mineral deposits in the municipal water supply, used to brew the tea, he developed kidney stones. It was a painful experience. Fortunately for him, they left his body a fortnight later when he urinated them out after drinking several glasses of sugarcane juice. His penis was left in a traumatized state, due to the small stones' abrasive passage, a sensation somewhat akin to peeing broken glass. Angus's short-lived career as a baker came to a sudden end.

While Angus was lying in bed convalescing, nursing a bruised and swollen penis, padded with an icepack, he and Lara came up with a new idea.

During the evenings in the ashram, when *darshan* was taking place on Bhagwan's porch, Buddha Hall hosted a free-form dance group. The community was blessed with many talented musicians, who jammed for up to two hours, while hundreds of people sang and danced around them whirling into ecstasy. When *darshan* was over, the music group finished and the ashram's gates closed. The result was that a large number of people were out on the street, dressed up in orange with nowhere to go. Angus and Lara thought that this social vacuum could be filled if they opened a nightclub.

Once the inflammation in Angus's penis had healed, he and Lara put on fresh robes and went to the ashram's Gateless Gate reception desk to make an appointment to see Laxmi, Bhagwan's personal secretary.

When Angus and Lara entered Laxmi's air-conditioned office, she was seated in a bright-orange executive chair, dwarfing her diminutive physical presence. She listened patiently while Lara outlined their plan to build an open-air nightclub. When Lara had finished, Laxmi interlocked her hands in front of her narrow face and remained silent for a few moments while she considered the proposition. When she finally spoke she did so in the third person, as was her custom. 'Laxmi thinks that this is a good idea. Bhagwan wants his sannyasins to dance their way to God and, as long as there is no drug use, Laxmi gives you her permission to proceed with your plan. If your dance club proves to be a financial success, Laxmi will be pleased if you bring a weekly donation to the ashram office.' Her dark eyes scanned their faces briefly. 'Is there anything else you wish to ask Laxmi?'

Angus and Lara glanced at each other and then he asked, 'Does Laxmi have a suggestion as to what we should call our nightclub?'

Laxmi's thin lips parted in a smile to display two rows of small teeth. She adjusted the position of her orange hat and answered, 'Yes, Laxmi suggests that you call your club 'Caravanserai'. After all,' she added, 'that is what this world is — a stopover for the night.' She nodded, hinting that their short meeting was drawing to a conclusive end, and then said, 'You have Bhagwan's blessing.'

Angus and Lara walked hand-in-hand towards the ashram's back gate. They were so happy to have the master's blessing for their project their feet barely touched the ground. They hailed a passing rickshaw and were quickly transported to Arun Wankhade's farmhouse. Arun invited them in and, after pouring himself and his two guests large shots of whisky, he listened to the couple's proposal.

'Arun, would you be willing to rent us a piece of land to build a dance club?' asked Angus.

'Yes, I am most happy to be doing that,' replied the farmer, draining his whisky glass.

Lara enquired, 'Do you think you might like to help us buy the materials and help us build it?'

The farmer poured himself some more whisky. 'Yes, I am thinking this could be a most profitable business and, if you are willing to supply the rupees, I will be helping you most earnestly.'

Angus said, 'Arun, man, this whole scene will be totally illegal. If we supply the money, will you take care of bribing the police?'

Arun held his glass up to the light and studied its amber-coloured contents as if the whisky were a portal into the disclosure of future realities. 'Yes,' he said, after a few moments of contemplative silence, 'I will be taking care of paying the baksheesh to police *wallahs*.' The farmer looked at the glass in his hand again, smiled and looked into Angus's eyes. 'Police commissioner for whole of Pune is my cousin.'

Work began the following morning and thus the foundation was laid for the Caravanserai Discotheque, the first commercial enterprise of its kind to be officially sanctioned by the ashram.

The site on which the nightclub would be built was on the extremities of Arun Wankhade's land, situated to the east of Koregaon Park. A field of mature sugar cane was cut down by machete-wielding farmhands, then ploughed and flattened by bullock-drawn contraptions that looked like they'd been constructed by carpenters during the Fourteenth Century. Sections of bamboo matting were fitted into thick wooden frames and then fastened to upright telegraph poles set into concrete holes. A rectangular compound was formed that measured fifteen metres by forty metres. On one end a wooden stage was erected and on the other a roofed enclosure that would house the bar. Around the edges of what was to become the dance floor, raised seating areas were constructed from wooden planks.

Above the bar enclosure, a wooden platform was built. Once in place, a small bamboo hut was constructed on the platform, with a large open window overlooking the dance floor. This was to be the DJ booth. There was much debate about what materials should be used for the dance floor's surface. In the end, the most expensive option won the day. The following afternoon, a truck, loaded with smooth teak planks, pulled up outside of the discotheque's main entrance.

Lara busied herself with designing cushions and upholstery for the seating areas, a task that required daily trips in and out of the city's commercial areas. Angus rented a large van with a driver and disappeared into the hubbub of Bombay. Two days later, he returned to Pune with almost a ton of big, black loudspeakers, amplifiers, electric cables, lighting equipment and the notion that the project was growing too big for him and Lara to handle. They needed another partner.

A week later, after Bhagwan's morning discourse, Angus and Lara were standing outside the Ashram's main gate in a small enclosure called the 'Beedie Temple'. Bhagwan had declared that smoking tobacco was childish stupidity, but had also said that it was okay to smoke if it was done in a state of awareness. Angus tossed a half-smoked beedie into a clay ashtray, turned to Lara and said, 'Man, those things taste awful.'

Lara shook her head. 'I don't know why anyone would want to smoke them. It's such an unaware thing to do and they make your breath stink.'

Angus cupped his hands and blew into them and sniffed. 'I can't smell anything.'

'I'm not surprised.'

'Okay,' conceded Angus, 'I get the message. I'll brush my teeth when we get home. That's the last beedie I'll ever smoke.'

She looked Angus in the eye. 'You promise?'

Angus smiled. 'Yeah, I give you my word.'

Lara hugged him and whispered in his ear, 'I love you.'

Angus was uncertain if he could resist the temptation to smoke and therefore decided a quick change of subject was needed. 'Man, that was a great discourse, wasn't it?'

'It was amazing,' said Lara, nodding in agreement. 'The old man was in great form this morning. I loved what he said about being a pure hedonist. Oh yeah, and how we should dance our way to God. Perfect! By opening the Caravanserai we are doing the right thing at exactly the right—'

'Hi, guys!' Swami Max called from behind them and gave Angus a hard slap on the back.

'For fuck's sake, man,' cursed Angus, turning to face his fellow Scot. 'What did you eat for breakfast this morning, a can of spinach?'

Max performed an impromptu jig, singing, 'I'm Popeye the sailor man...'

'Good to see you, Max,' said Angus. 'I've been thinking about you a lot recently.'

Max scratched at his chin through a thick layer of beard. 'I wondered why my ears were burning. So, how come you've been thinking about me?'

'Well,' Angus said, 'we're opening a disco back in the fields on Wankhade Farm. It's going to be called—'

Max cut across him. 'Caravanserai.'

'You heard?'

'Loka,' said Max, using Angus's sannyasin name, 'everyone in Koregaon Park has heard about what you guys are up to.'

'They have?' Lara asked.

'Yeah, of course, they have. I even heard you got Bhagwan's blessing for the project. Fantastic! Anyway,' Max continued, looking away from Lara to once again face Angus, 'how come you've been thinking about me? Nothing erotic, I hope?'

Angus laughed. 'That'll be right. We need a DJ.'

'Yeah!' Max punched the air with a raised fist. 'Now you're talking. My answer is yes, yes, yes. I just picked up a box of cassettes from the post office yesterday. Tons of great new sounds. Iggy Pop, Sex Pistols, Fleetwood Mac, Aerosmith, Bob Marley and the Wailers, Peter Tosh, Rick James, Earth, Wind and Fire, B52s—'

'B52s?' said Lara. 'Never heard of them. They good?'

Max looked at her in mock surprise. 'Good! Good isn't the word. The B52s are fuckin' fantastic. Can't believe you haven't heard 'Rock Lobster'. Really groundbreaking. Iggy Pop's new album is pretty far out—'

'Okay, okay, Max.' The sun was getting hot and Angus knew from experience that once Max started raving about music, he could go at it for hours. 'How about you come by the Caravanserai this evening and check it out, man?'

'Far out!' Max exclaimed, looking around in amazement.

He, Lara and Angus were standing at the centre of the Caravanserai's teak dance floor. The sun was setting. A breeze was picking up and overhead, squeaking fruit bats were heading out into the clear sky to forage for food.

'You think this looks good,' commented Angus, 'wait until we switch the lights on.' He took hold of Max's right arm. 'Come on. I want to show you something.'

They went into the bar and ascended the wooden ladder that led up to what had become the control tower.

'Shit, man, this must have cost a fortune,' said Max, studying the rack of industrial power amplifiers, stacked to the side of a low table that was home to two cassette decks and a mixer. 'What's that?' he asked, nodding to a board inset with black switches, plastic knobs and slider controls.

'That's how we will control the lighting,' answered Angus, sitting cross-legged on the floor. 'Check it out.' He turned two dimmer switches. They both looked out of the wide window frame to see the wooden stage bathed in red and violet light.

Max shook his head. 'Wow! I don't believe this is happening.' He leaned into Angus and placed an arm over his shoulder, pulling him close. 'I'm going to feel blessed to be a part of this. Man, this place is going to be written into sannyasin history. Hey, what about the most import thing of all? The sound system.'

Angus turned to his right and clicked the red plastic power switches on the bank of amplifiers. A faint electrical hum rose from the dance floor. Angus twisted the knob on the mixer's master volume control and hit the play button on one of the Sony cassette decks. The sound of Jerry Rafferty's 'Baker Street' erupted from the Caravanserai's array of loudspeakers. Lara began spinning on the dance floor like a whirling dervish.

You're going home... To the soaring crescendo of a multiple guitar break-out, whining and whooshing like musical rockets, the song drew to a close.

'Man, I love that sax solo,' said Max, 'even though there are places in the song that sound a wee bit out of tune. Great sound system, though.' He turned to Angus. 'So, when are we opening?'

'Saturday,' answered Angus.

Max counted on his fingers. 'That's only five days from now.'

Angus nodded in agreement. 'You better start getting your set organized. Are you sure you can handle it?'

Max rose to his feet and dusted sawdust from his dark red jeans. 'Handle it? Of course, I can handle it. It's going to be a blast. Any special name for the event?'

'Yeah,' replied Angus, 'we were thinking of calling our opening party 'Saturday Night Frenzy'.'

Max offered a wry grin. 'Sounds like the Bee Gees on acid. It's going to be a trip, man.'

Saturday night rolled around with over a thousand sannyasins showing up for the free entrance opening party. Six people were working behind the long, wooden bar, selling drinks as quickly as they could pour them.

The party kicked off with a live band called Bhagwan's Bauls. The frontman was Arihanta, an old friend of Angus's, who he'd first met in Goa some years before. A quintessential rebel sannyasin, Arihanta loved smoking hashish in a chillum pipe and singing rock 'n' roll songs. There were eight members in the band, most of whom could not be described as professional musicians, with an additional three female vocalists delivering out of tune choruses. The one seasoned player in the group was the lead guitarist, Michael Mustard. He'd learned his chops playing in underground rock bands in Sixties London. The band's sound was a mash-up of classic rock and blues standards, heavy on percussion with extended guitar solos from Michael Mustard, whose favourite pedal was a fuzz box. Arihanta delivered the lyrics like he was out to incite a riot. All in all, Bhagwan's Bauls sounded two short steps away from awful, but they received a reception like The Rolling Stones on a good night.

'Bo Diddley, done had a farm,' Arihanta hollered at the top of his voice. 'Hey, Bo Diddley,' echoed the screeching chorus girls, causing the speakers to distort by singing too close to the microphone.

Up in the control tower, Max, who could hear a bad note before it was played, turned to Angus and said, 'Jesus, man, where did you find this lot. They gotta be the worst band on the planet.'

Angus laughed. 'I think you might be right. But check out what's happening on the dance floor.'

They both looked down to the writhing mass of dancers. Several hundred men, women and children, dressed in a spectrum of orange and red, appeared to be performing a human re-enactment of a volcanic eruption. Screams of joy were cutting through the thunderous noise produced by the band. Michael Mustard took centre stage and delivered a blistering solo that somehow managed to merge with an unexpected turnaround, executed by a band of amateur musicians who'd probably never heard of the musical term. The effect on the dancers was visible. They were pulsating like a wild red beast at a musical feast. Everyone present voiced their enthusiasm in a communal roar that Bhagwan must have heard a kilometre away in his air-conditioned room.

Arihanta was having the time of his life. Sweat glistened on his bearded face as he delivered the song's last line. 'Slipped on me like a Cadillac-eight.' The chorus girls, unaware that the song was supposed to be drawing to a close, began chanting 'Hey, Bo Diddley ' like a hypnotic mantra. The percussionists did their best to make something out of it until, after a chaotic five minutes of pandemonium, Michael Mustard held his guitar in front of a large speaker cabinet, producing a howl of feedback that silenced everyone except the crowd, cheering like it was the best music they'd ever had the good fortune to hear.

The vocalist did not pause to catch his breath. 'I'm gonna tell you how it's gonna be.' The crowd hollered back, 'You're gonna give your love to me!'

Max slapped Angus on the back and shouted in Angus's ear, 'I told you this was going to be a trip. Incredible!'

'You're not kidding, man,' Angus shouted back. 'I better go down and check out how the bar is going.' He ran his hands through his thick wavy hair. 'Last time I looked, it was chock-a-block. You cool with the sounds when it's your turn?'

DJ Max patted the two-channel analogue mixer. 'I can't wait to let it rip, man. I'm going to open my set with the B52s' 'Rock Lobster'. Most of this crowd probably never heard of the B52s.'

Angus descended the wooden ladder that led down to the bar. When his head was level with the floorboards, he called out to the DJ, 'Give it everything you got, Swami Max!'

159

The bar was mobbed. Over two hundred people were squashed up against each other. The noise level was high. People were shouting, cheering, laughing, screeching and trying to get the attention of someone behind the bar. The air was humid. The half-dozen sannyasin bartenders were overwhelmed, their clothes soaked through with sweat. Money and foaming Kingfisher beer bottles were being exchanged rapidly.

Angus entered a small storeroom, off to one side of the long bamboo bar. 'Shit!' he cursed. The two thousand bottles of beer, delivered that morning by a lorry, had almost disappeared. He glanced through the open door, towards the opposite end of the bar, and saw a steadily growing mountain of empty brown beer bottles. He talked out loud to himself. 'Man, the place has only been open for two hours and we're nearly out of beer. Shit! Shit! Shit!' He began ripping open cartons, containing bottles of cheap alcohol called Country Liquor. It was a desperate decision. He'd bought twenty cardboard boxes, each containing twelve bottles of the clear alcohol when they'd fallen off the back of a lorry, the same lorry that delivered the beer earlier in the day. At five rupees a litre, it was a steal.

He turned and shouted to Lara, busy stuffing paper money into a black plastic bag under the bar. She didn't hear him. He hurried over, took hold of her arm, guided her into the bamboo-walled storeroom and closed the door behind them.

Lara pulled thick strands of hair from her sweating brow and then studied Angus's face. 'You okay? You look kind of worried. This is supposed to be our big night.'

'I am worried,' said Angus, nodding towards a half dozen cartons of Kingfisher stacked in a corner. 'We're running out of beer.'

Lara placed the point of her index finger on her smiling lips. 'And?'

'I'm going to mix up two hundred bottles of Country Liquor with fruit juice and ice to make a cocktail.'

'A cocktail made with Country Liquor!' Lara exclaimed. 'You better call it a Molotov.' She pulled a pint bottle from a cardboard box, screwed off its metal top and took a swig. 'Phew!' She spat the clear liquid onto the cement floor. 'Gaddy gook! This stuff is lethal. It tastes like napalm. People will get paralytic drunk drinking this shit!'

'Yeah, yeah, I know,' Angus agreed. 'We won't charge for it. But we have to give people something to drink. And they don't want water.' A roar of applause rose from the dance floor. 'Listen to that. We've got over a thousand Zorba the Buddhas out there and they want to party.'

Staccato music ricocheted through the bamboo walls. *It was a rock lobster... Eww... Ahh...* The B52s were taking off.

Angus rolled an aluminium drum into the bar and began filling it with Country Liquor, orange juice, chunks of ice, slices of banana, watermelon, pear and mango. By the time the barrel was full, the beer supply had run dry. Word soon went round that the drinks were on the house. Nobody seemed interested in what the sickly sweet concoction was that they were drinking. The fact it cost nothing, tasted fiery and was orange-coloured appeared to have shut down everyone's early warning systems. Two glasses of Molotov down the hatch and any vestiges of common sense took a nose dive into a murky pond of rotgut alcohol.

Max fought his way through the crowd to Angus, now serving drinks behind the bar.

'I'm dying of thirst,' shouted Max.

'Here,' said Angus, handing over a full glass of his brain-melting concoction. It had steam rising from it.

Max gulped a mouthful. 'What the hell is this?' he spluttered. 'It tastes like fucking paraffin with sugar in it."

Angus laughed. 'It's called a Molotov.'

Max staggered as the crowd pushed in from behind. 'Man, you better give me three Molotovs. Getting here was crazy.'

Nothing comes my way... Iggy Pop's jaded voice delivered a complaint to the packed bar.

'Hey,' said Angus, handing over two more high-octane cocktails, 'Aren't you supposed to be taking care of the music?'

'I'm on it,' said Max, turning away to make his way through the crowd, three glasses of steaming Molotov balanced in his hands.

Angus returned to serving drinks to thirsty people.

J. J. Cales 'After Midnight' drifted in from the dance floor, prompting Angus to look at his Rolex. Midnight was long gone. So were all the drinks, except for water and Coca Cola. He told the bartenders to put everything liquid up on the bar. Lara busied herself with stuffing plastic bags full of paper money into empty cartons in the storeroom.

Angus entered and closed the reinforced door behind him, enabling them to talk without having to shout.

'How's it going?' Angus asked.

Lara stood up and shook her head. 'I can't believe how much money we've taken in. Ten boxes full of rupees.'

She placed her hands on his shoulders and gave him a sweaty kiss.

'Yeah,' said Angus, still holding Lara close. 'Funny how, no matter what we are up to, we humans always get a kick out of making money.'

Lara stood back from him. 'Do I detect a hint of guilt in your voice, Swami?'

He gazed into her green eyes. 'Guilt? Maybe a wee bit. After all, we are all family here and it feels a bit strange to be making money off my friends like this.'

'Och, away with you,' Lara joked. 'Sounds like the puritanical spirit of a Presbyterian upbringing is still retaining a wee bit of a grip on you. You're making money because you put in weeks of hard work to make this happen. So why on earth should you feel a wee bit guilty about it? Don't forget, Bhagwan charges ten rupees for his discourses every morning. I agree with what he says about people not fully appreciating something unless they pay for it.'

Angus felt his spirits lift. 'You're right. I drank half a glass of Molotov. Must have been demon alcohol speaking.'

'Talking of which,' said Lara, reaching up to retrieve a ready rolled joint from a shelf, 'how about a wee smoke?'

Angus shook his head. 'Man, I haven't smoked a spliff in ages.'

She waved the cone-shaped joint in front of his nose. 'It's a special occasion.'

'What is it?' he asked.

'Fresh Kerala grass,' she answered.

I feel love... Donna Summers seductive voice beckoned from outside.

'Light it up,' said Angus.

Lara and Angus disappeared in a cloud of marijuana smoke and reappeared in the middle of the packed dance floor. Barry Gibbs' falsetto gave voice to the Bee Gees' 'Stayin' Alive' as the crowd sang along. Angus caught Saturday Night Fever. His head was spinning. He focused on his legs to keep his balance. The music began to phase. *Somebody help me...* He reached for Lara as he blacked out.

The sun was high in the sky when Angus regained consciousness, lying on a pile of cushions to one side of the Caravanserai's dance floor. He propped himself on his elbows and looked about. Lara was lying face down beside him. At least twenty other people were crashed out around him. The after-effects of the Molotov Cocktails had kicked in. Dishevelled revellers were sitting up, groaning and holding their heads in their hands. Over in a corner, a naked man with a long beard and semi-erect penis was vomiting into a plastic bucket. Angus was feeling rough himself. He lay back against a cushion and watched two buzzards in the sky as they glided on a thermal.

11

PRELUDE TO A DREAM

Jean and I stopped for a moment at a metal-ringed quay and watched a small trawler deliver its haul of fresh, sorted fish to a waiting white van. I turned around and the green sign over Drifter's Bar caught my eye. 'Fancy a drink?'

'It's a bit early in the day for that,' Jean said, looking up from the trawler's open hold.

'Not that kind of drink,' I said. 'I mean like a coffee or something.'

Jean took my hand. 'Come on then. I've never been to that place before, but I've heard the food's good.'

We crossed the road, walked along the pavement and entered Drifter's Bar. We were greeted by the sound of bagpipe music, played through a sound system at moderate volume. A young couple were just leaving. We sat down in the seats they'd vacated by a large window.

Jean looked out over Oban bay. Sea birds coasted on the breeze. A car ferry was heading out to sea. 'Nice view,' she commented.

'What'll you have?' I asked her.

'Whatever you're having,' she replied.

I wandered over to the bar and ordered two cappuccinos from a young barmaid with pink cheeks and a charming smile. 'I'll bring them over when they're ready,' she said, using a remote to change the channel on a silent wide-screen TV, fixed to a cream-coloured wall.

'Thanks,' I said absently, momentarily distracted by a cry of delight and a clatter of coins. An old codger in a kilt had just hit the jackpot on a one-armed bandit.

I went back to our table and sat down beside Jean.

'So,' she said, returning to Angus and Lara's story from where it left off. 'How long did this Caravanseria Discotheque in Pune last?'

'Not long,' I answered. 'A few months, if I remember correctly.'

'During which time they made a fortune, knowing them,' said Jean.

'Well, I would not say a fortune. But they made quite a bit of money and had a lot of fun doing it, according to what Angus told me, anyway.'

'And then what happened?' Jean asked.

'Quite a lot, to say the least,' I said, luring her into the next part of the story.

'Like what?'

'Ehm... Well, like training to become a therapist. Travelling to Mumbai to visit a mysterious guru. Oh, yes, I almost forgot...' I trailed off and made a premeditated pause.

Jean stared at me for a moment and then said, 'Here! Are you deliberately trying to wind me up, or something?'

'No,' I lied.

She tilted her head and squinted her eyes at me. 'Come off it. Who are you trying to kid?'

I let out a sudden laugh, reached over and patted her hand.

Jean pulled her hand away and examined the Chanel red lacquer on her long fingernails. 'I know you,' she said glancing away from her fingers to my eyes. 'And don't you ever forget that, Hamish MacLeod. You wind-up merchant that you are.'

I laughed again. This time, with ironic self-recognition.

'Here ye go,' said the rosy-cheeked barmaid, delivering two giant cups of milky coffee to our table.

I looked up into the young woman's unlined face and handed her a crisp ten-pound note. 'And here you go,' I said. 'Keep the change.'

The barmaid giggled. 'Oh, thanks very much, sir,' she said, turning to walk back to the bar.

As soon as the waitress was out of earshot, Jean remarked, 'I see you're getting a wee bit over-generous in your old age.'

'Come off it, Jean,' I chided. 'What's the use of money if you can't share it? We can afford to be kind to people.'

'Aye, well, you certainly seem to think so. Anyway,' she continued, 'Angus and Lara had a successful night, got pissed drunk and high on pot, then what?' Jean made a wide-eyed questioning expression, with her mouth partly open, as if she were in for a surprise. She was.

With the arrival of the monsoon rains, the Caravanserai closed. Angus, Scottish Max, Arun Wankhade and a gang of his farmhands dismantled the structure. India was way ahead of the world in those days, everything was recycled. A local building contractor bought most of the materials that were of any commercial value. Sheets of bamboo matting, telegraph poles, wooden planks, electrical cables and also the sound system and lighting were loaded into the back of an open lorry and driven away. Anything left over disappeared into the farm labourer's homes; ramshackle hovels with rusty, corrugated tin roofs that were dotted around the edges of the sugar-cane field.

The damp earth smell of rain hung heavy in the humid air. Lightning lit the edges of billowing grey clouds as Angus, Lara and Max stood studying the bare rectangle of ground that had been home to the first sannyasin discotheque. Thunder boomed in the distance and a light rain began to fall.

'I can't believe it's gone,' said Lara, opening an orange umbrella.

Max chuckled and adjusted his tattered red baseball cap. 'Aye, well, that's life, isn't it? Here today and gone tomorrow.' He draped his arms over Angus and Lara's damp shoulders and pulled them close. 'You can't stand in the same part of the river twice. Life just keeps flowing on and on.'

Angus nodded in agreement, running a hand over his wet hair. 'Aye, you're right, Max. But we had a blast, didn't we?'

Max dug his hands into his bright-orange dungarees' pockets. 'You're not kidding. Remember the night we had a barney with those Iranian students because we wouldn't let them in?'

'How could I forget?' Angus asked. 'I still have an ache in my ribs from that fat guy booting me when I was down.'

'Right,' concurred Max. 'You took quite a kickin' that night.'

Lara joined them on their stroll down Memory Lane. 'I'll never forget the run-in with the cops. The time when they said ten thousand rupees wasn't enough baksheesh. Greedy buggers! Then they threatened to lock us up.' She shivered. 'I really thought we'd had it that time.'

'Me too,' Max agreed. 'I have to admit that I was shit scared. Touching cloth, as they say.' He paused, remembering, and then added, 'Still, everything worked out in the end. That was the night we poured water out of the ice barrels over all the people who'd passed out in the bar from drinking...'

'Molotov Cocktails!' all three cried out in unison.

Angus looked up at the thick blanket of dark-grey cloud. It was getting dark. The rainfall was intensifying.

Lara turned to Max. 'What are you doing now?'

Max looked around the empty field, walled in by swaying banks of sugarcane. He shrugged and asked questioningly, 'Talking to you guys?'

Angus chuckled in the gloom. 'I knew you were going to say that. You want to come back to our place and dry off. Maybe have a bite to eat?'

Max didn't need a second invitation. 'Let's go,' he said. 'I could eat a holy fuckin' cow all on my own.'

The three of them set off over the field, dodging puddles on their way to the asphalt road.

Wrapped in a bath towel, Lara lit a gas ring to boil a pot of water for pasta and cobbled together a meal. Angus and Max got out of their soaking wet clothes and dried off.

Half-an-hour later, three plates of pasta spirals with pesto sauce had been devoured with relish.

'That was delicious,' declared Max, leaning back on a blue velvet cushion. He looked over the low wooden table at Lara. 'You're a superb cook.'

'Thanks,' said Lara, putting a lighter flame to three thick candles on the centre of the teak table.

A shower of hailstones ricocheted off the aluminium and tar-sheeted roof. Thunder rumbled in the distance.

'So, Max,' said Angus, pouring green tea from a white ceramic teapot into three waiting glasses, 'any plans for the future?'

Max removed the cellophane from a fresh packet of Camel cigarettes. 'Mind if I smoke?' he asked Lara.

'Go ahead,' she said, weaving her damp hair into a braid.

He leaned forward on the table to light his Camel from a candle flame. Resting back on his cushion he savoured a long drag on his cigarette and then, after blowing a long jet of smoke up into the yellow bamboo rafters, Max returned his attention to Angus. 'I'm thinking of going to Bombay for a few days.'

'What for?' Angus enquired.

'I feel like a bit of a change,' said Max, continuing to draw on his king-sized smoke. 'And I also want to check someone out.'

'Don't tell me,' joked Angus, 'some Indian bird in a sari with big bazookas.'

'Angus!' Lara hissed.

'What?' Angus smiled. 'Everyone who knows this guy knows he loves triple Ds'

'It's true,' admitted Max. 'But that's not who I'm going to see.'

'So,' said Angus, placing a glass ashtray in front of his friend, 'who *are* you going to see?'

Max stubbed his cigarette out in the ashtray. 'The Beedie Wallah.'

'Who?' Lara asked.

'Hold on,' said Angus. 'I think I've heard of him. He's some kind of guru. Right?'

Max nodded. 'That's right. A couple of people I know have said he is a really special master. So I just thought I might as well check him out for myself.'

'What about Bhagwan?' Lara said.

'What about him?' Max asked.

'Well, isn't he supposed to be your master?'

'Yeah, sure,' Max said to Lara. 'But it doesn't do any harm to go and check out the competition. Anyway, according to Bhagwan, seriousness is a disease, So, why should I take all this masters and disciples game seriously? Isn't that part of the illusion as well?'

Lara shrugged. 'Yes, you have a point there,' she conceded. 'It's just that, according to tradition at least, you are supposed to stick to the master you chose.'

'Okay, I've heard that too,' said Max. 'But breaking away from the whole idea behind tradition is what sannyas is all about. I mean to say, Bhagwan's got us all running around in orange clothes. Saffron is the traditional colour of renunciation and all things holy in Mother India. Think about it. Western chicks parading up and down Mahatma Gandhi Road in orange mini-skirts, without a bra under their skimpy tank tops. That's an outrage in this country. I'm not complaining about it, but the locals certainly are. So,' he concluded, 'who gives a fuck about tradition?'

'All right, Max,' said Angus, 'we get the picture. Where does this Beedie Wallah live in Bombay? Does he have an ashram?'

Max let out a spluttering laugh.

'What's so funny about that?' Lara asked.

Max reached for a glass of green tea and took a couple of sips before answering. 'The Beedie Wallah doesn't have a fancy ashram like Bhagwan. He holds informal *satsang* (Lit. Association with the true and the wise people.) in a small attic of his house, which is near Bombay's red-light district.'

'What?' Lara exclaimed.

'Sounds like my kind of man,' continued Max, without skipping a beat. 'Oh, yeah, and Beedie Wallah is just a nickname. His proper name is Sri Nisargadatta Maharaj.'

'Maharaj,' echoed Angus. '*Great king*. That means he's the great king of Bombay's red-light district.'

Max smiled. 'Sure. Why not? A bright light of consciousness slap-bang in the centre of the maya.' He paused and studied Angus and Lara's faces for a moment, then asked, 'You guys want to come to Bombay with me to visit Maharaj?'

Angus shook his head. 'Thanks for the offer, but Lara and I have other plans, starting next week.'

'Like what?' Max asked.

Angus answered, 'Like enrolling in a few workshops and eventually working as individual therapists in the ashram.'

'Good way to spend your hard-earned money,' said Max. 'If you ask me, this whole meditation and therapy fusion taking place here in Pune will go global one day. Big bucks to be made.'

Lara disagreed. 'It's not about making money. It's about finding a platform to work from and putting something wholesome back into life in gratitude for what you have received.'

Max gave a knowing chuckle. 'Can't fault you on that one, Lara. You're a fine woman. I wish you both the best of luck.' He glanced at his watch and rose to his feet. 'I have to get going.' The sound of the pelting rain on the roof intensified. Max grinned. 'Oh, oh, here we go. I'll get soaked to the skin by the time I get back to Mobo's Hotel.'

Lara stood up. 'You're most welcome to stay here. No problem to make up a bed for you.'

'Thanks, but I know I'll sleep better in my own scratcher. Besides,' Max added, 'a wee bird told me this morning that I might have a visitor later on tonight.'

'Triple Ds?' Angus asked.

'Double,' said Max. 'But I'm not complaining.'

All three laughed and shared a hug.

Max headed out the door and then, just before entering the pouring rain, he turned back. 'Hey, Lara, if you get fed up with this guy, just give me a shout.'

'That'll be right,' called Lara, walking to the kitchen with glasses and tea-pot in hand.

'Get the fuck outta here,' said Angus jokingly, standing by the table. 'I'll be looking forward to hearing how you got on in Bombay.'

Max raised a hand in farewell, closed the door behind him and was gone into the night, accompanied by an extended roll of thunder that shook the house.

It was a Monday morning. Bhagwan's discourse had just drawn to a close with the master's customary parting words, 'Enough for today.' With great care and economy of motion, he rose to his sandaled feet, acknowledged his disciples with prayerful hands and beaming countenance, and then appeared to almost float above the white marble floor on his way to the black limousine awaiting him on the gravel driveway.

Angus pushed through the throng of people milling around the ashram's imposing wooden gates. He walked along a line of bicycles, parked up on aluminium stands, until he came to the purple one belonging to him. He unlocked a heavy padlock and unwound the thick metal chain, wrapped around the frame and the back wheel's rusty spokes. He set off down the road. Before he'd gone twenty meters he realised the front tyre was flat. It was the third time in a week that had happened. Street urchins were employed by roadside bicycle repairmen to let the air out of tires during the morning discourse. Angus dismounted and pushed his bike over to a thin man, dressed in filthy clothes and wearing a pair of cracked spectacles.

'Puncture repair?' the elderly man asked expectantly.

Angus said to him, 'No, Baba. Pumping, pumping.'

The man wiggled his head Indian style, bent down as if it were agony to do so, inspected the flat tyre for a moment, looked back to Angus and said, 'Acha. Fixing, fixing.' He then attached a foot pump and delivered the compressed air where it was needed.

The repairman straightened his back with a theatrical groan and extended his oil-stained right hand towards Angus. 'Five rupees.'

It was a ridiculous demand. Angus was in a hurry so he paid the man without protesting.

Angus pedalled fast and sped along the banyan tree-lined road, heading in the direction of a colonial mansion, one of many rented in Koregaon Park by the rapidly expanding Rajneesh Ashram.

He parked his bike on the grounds of the large, grey-painted house and ascended black marble steps.

This was the first day of a six-week-long Rebalancing course. It was the first time this new form of physiotherapy was being introduced to students.

Angus entered a spacious white room and sat on a cushion in a circle with eleven other students. Six of them were women. Smiles were exchanged. All present remained silent, awaiting their new teacher's arrival.

A tall man with long fair hair strolled through the door. He had California written all over his tanned face. 'Hi, folks, I'm Daniel. I'm going to be your main instructor in the coming weeks,' he announced, taking his place in the circle.

Everyone present was given a few minutes to introduce themselves, say a little about their life and explain why they had enrolled in the course. Daniel described how he'd learned his profession from Ida Rolf, the woman who'd originally developed Structural Integration, a type of manual therapy that aims to treat the human body as a whole as opposed to dealing with particular symptoms.

Introductions over, the rest of the day was spent studying anatomical charts. Studying on an educational level was something new to Angus in his adult life. He had to fire-up parts of his brain that had lain dormant for years. It was made easier by the great admiration that grew in him towards his new teacher, Daniel. He was an easy man to like. What impressed Angus most about the Californian was his non-serious approach to Bhagwan and the sannyas movement in general. Somehow, without actually saying much about it, Daniel made it clear that everything he experienced in Pune was just a passing chapter in his life; that it was just a question of time before he moved on to something new and, going by his supremely positive attitude, it could only get better. This presented a fresh perspective to Angus, a possible respite from the ashram's principal reality — it's always here and now. Life around Rajneesh was so grounded in the present, all thoughts of possible future realities quickly vanished into nothingness. If renegade thoughts managed to survive in a sannyasin's forward-thinking mind, the scenarios that usually played out were invariably centred around Bhagwan and living in or around one of his increasingly numerous international communities.

There was another aspect of Daniel's personality that drew Angus towards him. Nobody around Daniel was being hurt, let alone murdered. Murphy killing three men in Iran, and the tragic loss of Jimmy Bradley in Bombay harbour were the source of nightmares that occasionally tore Angus from sleep. Therefore, he made a firm commitment to learning everything Daniel was willing to teach him and, in due course, leave his criminal life where he felt it now belonged — in the past.

Meanwhile, Lara too had discovered a new teacher, Meera, a gifted Japanese artist. Every evening, Lara returned home with rolled-up paintings she'd created during the day. Most of her artistic creations were bright watercolours, featuring natural elements within an abstract setting. She was so possessed by her new-found passion that all thoughts of doing anything else fell to the wayside. All she wanted to do was paint and then paint some more.

Towards the end of the Rebalancing course, Angus ran into Scottish Max in the ashram's Vrindivan canteen. Angus noticed him immediately but, at first, did not recognize his friend. Max was sitting on a wooden table in the full lotus position with his eyes closed. He'd shaved his head and face and was wearing a white cotton shirt and trousers. Angus pulled up a chair and sat at the table, looking up at Max's serene face. Several minutes passed before Max registered Angus's presence. His eyes flickered open and a gentle smile lifted the corners of his lips. He remained silent for a short time, during which he gazed down into Angus's eyes. Angus eventually blinked. Max said, 'Hi, man, how are you?'

Angus chuckled. 'Hi, Max. I'm fine. And yourself?'

Max unfolded his legs and got down from the table. 'I'm good' he said, seating himself on a wooden stool an arm's length from Angus.

'And?' Angus enquired further.

'And what?'

'Did you go and see the Beedie Wallah?'

'Yes. I went to see Maharaj.'

'And did you talk to him?'

'Well, through a translator I did. Maharaj doesn't speak English. Well, at least not during his *satsangs*, anyway.'

A beautiful woman in a skimpy dress brushed by them, making her way to a neighbouring table where a trio of equally attractive women awaited her. Max did not so much as glance at any of them

'I see you've changed,' commented Angus. 'Come on, man. What did you learn from the Beedie Wallah?'

Max did not reply immediately. He tilted his head to one side and studied Angus for a few moments. All the time the gentle smile on his lips remained as fixed as the intensity of his brown-eyed gaze. 'You know,' he eventually said, 'all we really are is a bunch of memories held together by attachment. You can step outside of that attachment and let those memories go. If you manage, you might see what you are is something behind and beyond memory. You cease to be that fictional personality, running from here to there, doing this and that. Peace at last. You understand in the depth of your heart that there was nothing wrong at all with the world, just the way you were looking at it. The idea that there is something wrong is the blow torch burning under humanity's blistered ass. I tell you, man, I'm finished with being caught up in the web of desire spun by ignorance. I want to be free. I want to be free of *me*.'

Angus let out a gentle laugh and patted Max on the arm. 'Sounds good, man. I have to admit, I sometimes tire of being me and just want to disappear. So, is that what Maharaj told you?'

Max shook his head. 'No. Not directly, at least. He's a powerful being. Just a direct look from him can knock you into another dimension. A bit like Rajneesh, but different, more intimate.' He nodded as if recalling something. 'I won't be going back there.'

'You won't?' Angus said. 'Why not?'

'There's no need,' answered Max. 'Maharaj told me you don't need to be in close physical proximity to a master to receive his blessings. He said life itself is the supreme guru.'

Angus made a show of looking around the busy outdoor cafeteria. 'So, what are we all doing in this ashram?' he asked.

'That's a good question,' said Max, 'but it's none of my business what everyone else is doing. All I know is that my time here is over. I just came back to collect some personal belongings and say goodbye to a few friends.'

'And then what?'

Max shrugged. 'I'm heading up north to the Himalayas, maybe visit Rishikesh first. I've never been there. It has crossed my mind to join a Tibetan monastery.'

'Is that why you shaved your head?'

Max ran a hand over his smooth skull. 'No. I'm not sure why I did that. I suppose it signifies a new beginning or something like that.'

'So, you're dropping out of the sannyas movement?'

'Yes. I handed my mala over to Laxmi in her office this morning.'

'What did she say to you?'

'She said, 'Laxmi feels that you have Bhagwan's blessings.' She's totally devoted to Rajneesh and I love her for it.'

'Yeah, she's great. Anyway, do you think I should visit the Beedie Wallah?'

Max shrugged. 'You will if you're supposed to. It's hard to explain, but when I first arrived in Maharaj's attic I had the distinct feeling that something beyond my comprehension had brought me there. It's that kind of scene.' He reached into his trouser pocket and withdrew a small piece of folded paper. 'Here,' he said handing it to Angus.

'Nisargadatta Maharaj's address in Bombay, right?'

'Right first time, brother,' said Max, rising to his feet. 'It's not the easiest place to find but, if you get hold of a smart taxi driver, it should not pose a problem. If and when you arrive there, you'll know you're at the right place by the stink. It's unforgettable.'

'What do you mean? What kind of stink?'

Max chuckled. 'You'll find out if you get there.'

Angus slipped the paper into his orange shirt's breast pocket. 'Looks like all roads say adios, amigo.' He stood and shared a long, heartfelt hug with Max.

They strolled together to the ashram gate and, with a parting wave of farewell, walked in opposite directions.

'No bicycle today, sir?' called a familiar voice.

Angus looked in the voice's direction. It was the bicycle repairman he'd recently used to pump up a flat tyre, dressed in his customary dirty clothes and smoking a beedie under the shade of a frangipani tree. 'Correct, Baba. Bicycle is being stolen last night.'

'Acha,' said the rake-thin man, giving his head an understanding wiggle. 'Very bad news.' Behind his spectacle's cracked lenses, his bloodshot eyes widened, as if a bright idea had just occurred to him. 'I can be fetching you almost new bicycle. I will be selling you at a very cheap price.'

'Maybe tomorrow,' Angus said, continuing on his way.

Angus arrived home. He stripped and dived into the well's cool water. A thick bamboo wall surrounded the compound so there was no need to be concerned about upsetting the locals with nudity. Angus was still naked when he wandered into the house. He found Lara in red lace underwear, putting the finishing touches to her latest creation, a watercolour depicting autumn leaves being blown by the wind.

She looked up at him. 'Oh,' she said, 'you're home. What's new?'

Angus sat down on a woven matt, leaned over and kissed her waiting lips. Lara pulled back from him. 'You're soaking wet,' she said. 'Don't you dare drip water on my painting. I've been working on it all afternoon.'

'Oops.' He reached for a towel, hanging over the back of a rattan chair. 'I just met Max in the ashram canteen.'

'Max?' Lara said. 'I'd forgotten about him. How is he?'

Angus rubbed his shoulder-length, wet hair with the white towel. 'Max is in a wonderful space. Shaved his hair and beard off.'

'Did he go to Bombay and meet the Beedie Wallah?'

'Yeah, he did.'

'What did he say about that?'

'Not much. A few words. That's all.' Angus paused and then went on. 'You know, Max has really changed. There was something about him. Something... I can't quite put my finger on it. Like he's dropped a lot of baggage.'

'Is he still chasing after every woman he sees with big boobs?'

Angus shook his head. 'No. Quite the opposite. He said something that stayed with me. Max said, 'I'm finished with being caught up in the web of desire spun by ignorance."

Lara laughed. 'Max said that? Doesn't sound like him at all.'

'No. It doesn't, does it? He also said he wanted to be free.'

'Free from what?'

'Himself'

'Really? And this had to do with going to see the Beedie Wallah?'

'I'm not sure. But one thing is for sure. I'm going to see the man.'

'You are? When?'

'I don't know,' answered Angus. 'As soon as I finish the next Rebalancing course, I suppose. I thought you might like to accompany me.'

'Too far ahead,' Lara said, cleaning a paintbrush in a jar of murky water. 'Let's see closer to the time. Anyway, where's Max now?'

'I reckon he's packing his bags. He said he was heading for the Himalayas and his time with Bhagwan is over. Oh yeah, and he's not wearing orange anymore either.'

'Is that so?' Lara stood up, stretched, and then reached behind her back to undo the hook on her red bra. 'Never a dull moment,' she said, dropping her bra in Angus's lap. 'I think I need to lie down a bit. How about you?' she asked, removing her panties and heading towards the bedroom.

Angus watched her disappear into the shadows and heard the crisp rustling of freshly laundered bedsheets. Lara let out a loud sigh. He looked down at his sexual compass. It was pointing towards the bedroom.

Five weeks passed, and the Advanced Rebalancing Training Course drew to a close. Angus had had every muscle in his body pummelled and every bone in his skeleton manipulated into optimal position. He felt grounded, centred and more at home in his body than he'd ever felt. In a nutshell, he'd been rebalanced.

On the last afternoon of the course, Daniel led Angus outside of the colonial house where the training programme had taken place. They sat together on a cement bench and drank tea in companionable silence.

The sun was setting behind a line of royal palms when Daniel said, 'You're a natural. I'm going to put in a recommendation at the office that you be allowed an opportunity to give individual sessions in the ashram.'

Angus was deeply touched. He steadied his breathing and composed himself. 'That is fantastic news, man,' he said. 'But, Daniel, what makes you say I'm a natural.'

The Californian smiled. 'You just have a way with people. A natural ability that somehow succeeds in making people trust your hands.'

'I do?'

'Don't be so modest. Of course, you do. I wouldn't say it if I did not feel it to be true.' Daniel draped an arm over Angus's shoulder and continued. 'Don't forget, I've been observing you for weeks. That exercise you did yesterday with Devi was textbook perfect. Going through the abdominal wall to get to the psoas muscles like that is a very difficult and sensitive procedure. Yet Devi did not so much as let out a whimper. She just breathed into it as you instructed her to.'

'Yes, but—'

Daniel cut him off. 'Come on. Get out of your own way. You need to open up more to the idea that you have a wonderful gift to share. You just don't seem to comprehend the positive effect you have on the people around you. It will become clearer to you once you begin giving regular sessions.'

Angus nodded. 'Okay, Daniel, I will take what you just said onboard. You are a great teacher, man. Thanks for everything you taught me.'

Jean pretended to cry and dabbed at her eyes with a blue silk handkerchief.

'I'm so touched.' She gave an exaggerated sniff. 'You'll ruin my makeup, dar- ling. Telling me tearjerkers like that. I'm surprised the Vatican hasn't de- clared Angus to be a saint.'

I shook my head. 'You're terrible. You know that?'

'What do you expect?' asked Jean, in no need of an answer. 'Your brother was a bloody drug dealer. It was about time he tried putting something back into life instead of always being on the take.'

I looked around Drifter's Bar. It was relatively quiet. The lunchtime crowd hadn't arrived yet. Nobody was paying us the slightest bit of attention, ex- cept for a periodic fleeting look from the barmaid, checking to see if we wished to order another drink. 'I was just thinking,' I said, glancing at our empty coffee cups, 'maybe we should place an order for something to eat.'

Jean raised her right arm and screwed up her eyes to check the hands of her pink-faced Rolex. 'It's just gone twelve,' she said. 'You could have a look at the menu and order me another coffee.' She stood. 'You take care of that and I'll away to the ladies and tidy my face.'

Jean wandered off. I raised a hand to attract the barmaid's attention. The young woman hurried over to my table by the window. 'What'll it be?' she asked.

I said, 'Could we have two more coffees, please? A wee bit smaller cups would be good.'

'Aye, no problem. Anything else?' the waitress enquired expectantly.

I squinted my eyes and peered over at a small blackboard, hung behind the bar between a long line of malt whisky bottles. *Today's Special. Roast Beef with Baked Potatoes and Vegetables.*

'Today's special sounds good,' I said, returning my attention to the bar- maid's plump face. 'I'll have two servings.'

'I'm sorry,' she said. 'Lunch is served at one.'

'Oh.' I turned to look out of the window. Thick, grey cloud was rolling in over Oban Bay. A few spots of rain had already lodged themselves on the glass. 'It's beginning to rain.'

The barmaid gave a forced chuckle. 'That's hardly news in these parts. Are you on holiday?'

'No.' I smiled up at her. 'I've lived in Oban all my life.'

'Oh, right. Well, I've only been here a couple of months,' she informed me. 'And I'm already thinking of moving back to Inverness. I miss my pals and the nightlife here sucks. Oban is completely dead at the weekends.'

Jean returned to the table and sat down after clearing a few crumbs from her seat. 'So, did you order lunch?' she asked.

'I was just doing that,' I answered. 'Before we began talking about the weather.'

Jean's eyes glanced out the window. 'Nothing like an intense, intellectual discussion to stimulate the gastric juices.'

I ignored Jean's sarcasm and cleared my throat. 'So, dear,' I said to the waitress, 'that'll be two small coffees and two specials when you're ready to serve them up.'

The young woman jotted the order down. 'Right you are, sir. I'll be back in a minute with your coffees,' she said, before walking away.

'It's pelting down,' commented Jean, looking out of the window.

'Trying to start an intense, intellectual discussion to stimulate the gastric juices?' I enquired.

Jean sniggered. 'I'd rather hear what happened to Angus and Lara. I can tell the story's building up to something unexpected.'

I gave a nod of agreement. 'You can say that again.'

'I can tell the story's building up to something un—'

'Stop it!'

'Okay,' said Jean, turning to face me. 'It's raining, the sign outside says that lunch is served from one o'clock and I'm sitting comfortably. So, can we get back to the story, please?'

'Aye, we can.'

Angus did not begin working as a therapist in the Shree Rajneesh Ashram. His innate curiosity drove him to go to Vanamali Mansion, 10th lane, Kethawadi, Bombay to visit Sri Nisargadatta Maharaj, aka, The Beedie Wallah.

Dressed in orange and carrying a rucksack, Angus travelled alone. Lara had decided that she wasn't interested in meeting another master. She'd suggested that Angus was turning into a guru hopper. He didn't like the sound of that and the snide way in which she'd said it. He overreacted. They'd argued, and he'd left the house the following morning at dawn, without saying goodbye.

He joined the crowds walking out of Bombay's VT railway station. It was a hot afternoon with not a cloud in the sky. The city hummed with human and mechanized activity. Just before he reached the taxi rank he nearly stumbled over a corpse, lying across the pavement. Someone had lit a few incense sticks to cover the stench of decomposition. Angus stood for a moment, absorbing a scene he'd never forget. He then caught a taxi to the Colaba district. He got out of the black and yellow cab in front of Dipti's juice bar. He decided to pop in for a cold drink. The sun had passed its zenith by the time he crossed the street and checked into The Rex Hotel.

Angus lay naked on his double bed, staring up at the yellowed ceiling fan, home to the squashed bodies of countless flying insects and flies, who'd breathed their last on the slowly rotating blades. It was the first time he'd been back to Bombay since Jimmy Bradley's unfortunate death. His memory shifted into fast rewind. Images from past events, taking place in and around Bombay, played out on the screen of his conscious mind. Suddenly, a recollection popped up, unrelated to everything else he was thinking about. Angus found himself back in the Rajneesh Ashram's canteen, listening to Scottish Max saying, 'You know, all that we really are is a bunch of memories held together by attachment. You can step outside of that attachment and let those memories go. If you manage that you might see that you are something behind and beyond memory. You cease to be that fictional personality, running from here to there, doing this and that. Peace at last.'

'Peace at last,' Angus said out loud. 'I like the sound of that.'

He reached into his rucksack and extracted a well-thumbed, paperback copy of George Gurdjieff's *Meetings With Remarkable Men.* He read a couple of chapters, detailing the Armenian mystic's travels and adventures in Central Asia, before setting the book aside and falling into a deep dreamless sleep.

Angus awoke, unsure of his location. It was dark. He lay for some time, gathering his thoughts. He got up and took a lukewarm shower with water that reeked of chlorine. He went downstairs. A young woman in a blue sari was fast asleep behind the reception desk. Outside, Bombay was as quiet as it gets.

Angus turned a corner and entered an almost deserted street. A tea stall was ready to do business. The chai wallah was an elderly man, who spoke a little English. He practised his linguistic skills on Angus as he poured steaming, caramel-coloured chai from a flame-blackened aluminium kettle into glasses that would have failed any tests set by a hygienic standards board.

'*Ji,*' said the tea seller, employing the respectful term equivalent to 'sir', 'what country?'

'Scotland,' Angus answered absently.

'What is the purpose of your visit?'

Angus had been subjected to this kind of banal grilling many times before. When the old man reached the 'How many children?' part, Angus patted the old fellow's bony back and retired to the Leopold Cafe's closed entrance to enjoy his over-sweetened tea and sticky bun in peace. The bun tasted like it had been made from vanilla-flavoured paper-mâché and sand. Grit crunched on his teeth. Somebody groaned behind him. He turned and peered into the shadows. Half-a-dozen beggars were sleeping on sheets of cardboard.

A black and yellow Ambassador taxi pulled up beside the tea stall. The driver got out, ordered a chai and lit a cigarette. He was in his late twenties, clean-shaven, dressed in jeans and a smart shirt. Angus liked the look of him. He walked over and said hello to the taxi driver. Showing the young man a piece of paper with Nisargadatta's address on it he asked, 'You know where this is.'

The taxi driver, studied the address for a moment and then smiled at Angus, saying, 'Beedie Wallah, correct?'

Somewhat taken aback, Angus stammered, 'Eh... Yeah... Correct. You know him?'

The driver shook his head. 'Not knowing personally. I have been seeing him in the street. I am living in same neighbourhood. Very wise man I have been hearing.'

'Can you take me there?'

The taxi driver took a last draw on his cigarette, before tossing it into the gutter. 'Sure, *bhai*, I take you. No problem.'

The taxi driver started his meter and pulled out into the street. They sped along Marine Drive, heading in a westerly direction. Angus looked to his left and saw Chowpatty Beach pass in a blur, the sun not quite breaking above the sea's horizon. It took over an hour to reach Vanamali Mansion and Angus knew he'd been taken for a ride. The taxi had crossed the same intersection at least twice and although Bombay was a huge city it was not so big that one needed to travel thirty kilometres to reach somewhere within the city limits. Nonetheless, Angus paid the extortionate fee without protest. He'd enjoyed the driver's company and wished him luck in achieving his ambition to become a marine engineer.

Angus stepped out of the cab, closed the door and looked up at Vanamali Mansion, which did not at all resemble a mansion. It was a small terraced house in a litter-strewn side-street, identical to many streets in the bustling metropolis. Overhead, electric cables and telephone wires cross-hatched to form an irregular angular web. Crows sat on rooftops, cawing to each other as they scanned the streets below in search of a snack. The stench of urine, emanating from a nearby public latrine, was so overwhelming it made Angus's eyes water. He hurried over to the open doorway. There was nobody around and no doorbell to summon someone. He stepped inside and ascended a narrow staircase. The walls, which might have been white a century before, were filthy and peeling flaky distemper. He followed an excited voice emanating from somewhere above. He found himself in the doorway of a crowded attic room, which Angus reckoned to be only thirty square metres. About twenty people were sitting huddled together on the tiled floor, their attention focused on a thin, bald Indian man. He was sitting cross-legged on a covered mattress, wearing the plain, collarless shirt and the matching white cotton trousers of a working man. He was talking urgently in Marathi, Maharashtra State's native language. To his left, a middle-aged man with black plastic-rimmed glasses was trying his best to keep up with the master as he hurriedly translated what had just been said into English. 'Because you want *'to be'* you occupy yourself with talking and all else. To sustain this *'you are'* you carry out various activities. Thus, you keep your mind busy. But, to the realised one, the mind flow is like the release of obnoxious gases from below.'

Nisargadatta noticed Angus standing in the doorway and paused for a moment. The stillness of the master's gaze settled on him for a few seconds. Angus froze on the spot and then Nisargadatta proceeded to talk again.

The translator continued. 'The one who is stabilised in the self looks down upon the mind-chattering as though it were dirty and unwanted, like those gases in the stomach.'

Angus wondered if the master was talking about farting. He edged his way into the room and sat down with his back against the wall, a wall which, going by the sweat stains, had supported countless backs before his. Bombay's noise and squalor suddenly seemed very remote to him, even though street sounds were entering the room via an open double window. To the right of the window, an oscillating fan rattled as it circulated humid air. Angus closed his eyes for a few minutes and focused on the powerful vibration of peace that filled the crowded room. He felt like he was coming up on some kind of drug trip. Over the persistent whir of the fan and the master's excited voice, answering a question posed by an Indian lady seated in front of him, Angus began to pay close attention to the translator's Indian-accented words which, as he was to recall later, ran something along the following lines: 'Ignorance is like a fever. It makes you see things that aren't really there. Karma is like a divinely prescribed medicine. Embrace karma, follow its instructions and you will get well. Once the patient has recovered, they can leave the hospital. To persist on immediate freedom will simply hinder the recuperation process. Accept your destiny and fulfil it. To act from desire and fear is bondage. To act from love is freedom.'

To act from love is freedom. That simple sentence triggered something in Angus's mind, shutting down all other thought. For the remainder of the session, Angus simply sat, leaning back against the dirty wall in Nisargadatta's attic, in a state that defied description.

'You have to leave now.'

Angus's eyes sprang open. 'What?' He looked up into the smiling face of a man of medium height, with thinning grey hair and a thick bushy beard, whose most notable feature was a prominent hooked nose.

The American laughed. 'Here, let me help you to your feet,' he said, offering a hand of support.

Angus rose unsteadily. He looked around the deserted room. 'Wow!' he gasped. 'I must have spaced right out.'

'It happens,' said the man, leading him out the door. 'Come on. You look like you need a cup of hot chai. I know a place just around the block.'

They exited the house. Once again the stench of urine hit Angus like sniffing a rag soaked in ammonia.

His newfound companion gave a knowing chuckle. 'Pretty rich, isn't it? I've been coming here for a year now and my poor nose still hasn't become accustomed to it. I've heard about the lotus growing out of the mud.' He nodded towards the public lavatory. 'I can't imagine anything but disease growing out of a god-damned shit hole like that.'

They strolled along the edge of the street, turned a corner and entered an open-fronted café. They sat down by a table that still had dirty plates on it. A waiter with big false teeth, stained red with betel nut juice, cleared the table and wiped it with a rancid cloth. He took their order for tea, dhal and chapattis.

'What's your name?' Angus asked the American, seated across the round table from him.

'David. David Buschman. And yours?'

'Loka.'

'No. I mean your real name. Not the one Rajneesh gave you.'

Angus took no offence and saw no harm in giving the man his Christian name. They shook hands.

'I'll tell you straight up, Angus. You're making a mistake wearing your sannyasin outfit up at Maharaj's. He threw one of your lot out last week.'

'Why? Does he have something against Rajneesh?'

'No. He doesn't have anything against Rajneesh, or anyone else for that matter. Neither do I. The guy who was thrown out was arrogant and Maharaj does not like arrogant people. He also does not like people who are with other masters to attend his *satsangs*. Don't ask me why? He just doesn't. So, if you go back to Maharaj's for another visit, dress appropriately. Meaning, get rid of the orange clothes and mala.'

'Okay, I get the message. Thanks for telling me, David.'

'I've actually met Rajneesh a couple of times before he moved to Pune. He used to live over at Malabar Hill, back when he was calling himself Acharya Rajneesh.'

'What did you make of him?'

David shrugged. 'I liked him. Big energy. Great talker.' He paused to reflect and then continued. 'In fact, now that I think of him, I found Rajneesh to be a wonderful man. Charming, humorous at times and above all charismatic.'

'But?'

'No *but*. He was one of many Indian gurus I had the good fortune to meet. I spent a few months with Neem Karoli Baba, a very powerful being. I was there when Baba Ram Dass gave Karoli Baba a massive dose of LSD. Baba just smiled and behaved as if nothing out of the ordinary had happened. Incredible!' The American laughed and then went on. 'I sat listening to Krishnamurti, a brilliant and articulate man. I received shaktipat initiation from Muktananda. That was extraordinary. One afternoon, he touched me on the crown of my head with a peacock feather and I lost all contact with my physical body for several light-filled hours. The list goes on. I've spent over twenty years travelling around India and Nepal, visiting holy men and women, ashrams and monasteries. And then, quite by chance, I arrived at Maharaj's feet and my search ended.'

'If you don't mind me asking, how do you manage to support yourself?' Angus asked.

'Wealthy background,' answered David. 'Pop died when I was thirty-three and left me, mom and my two sisters a substantial inheritance. Never got on too well with the old man while he was alive, but I've been grateful to him ever since the day he passed on. I was always the black sheep of the family. I studied medicine in Boston for some years and then the Sixties revolution rolled into town and I dropped out before I graduated.'

Their food arrived. Angus and David ate without saying much.

Angus burped and took a sip of hot tea. 'So, David, what makes Nisargadatta so special?'

'Good question,' said David, using a thin serviette to wipe flecks of yellow dhal from his thick fingers. 'I don't know if *special* is the right word. Sri Nisargadatta is by far the most enlightened individual I've ever met. A true *jnani*. I've felt attracted to Advaita Vedanta for some years now and Maharaj expounds the teaching of self-enquiry better than any other living master I know of. For example, unlike Rajneesh, Maharaj never contradicts himself, never wavers in his approach to finding truth. I like that. I also appreciate that Maharaj remains humble in the way he lives. I know for certain that people have offered to build an ashram for him, but he simply does not want that, because he knows such an institution will imprison him. He is content to walk these dirty city streets, where he worked and brought up a family, without the encumbrances and limitation brought by fame and fortune.'

'I have to admit, from what little I saw of him, Nisargadatta left a strong impression on me.'

'Yes,' said David, 'that is easy to understand. Perhaps it's not the right time yet for you to be around someone like Maharaj.' He paused for a moment and studied Angus's face. 'How old are you? Mid-twenties or thereabouts? I'm going to turn sixty next week. Big number.' He chuckled. 'You have plenty of time left. I suggest you go the course with Rajneesh. It will pass. Everything does.'

Just then, there was a prolonged, metallic crash out on the street. A woman's scream was cut off before it had given full voice to its anguish. A heavily laden oxen cart had collapsed, spilling its load of iron girders onto the pavement, bordering the opposite side of the street. David and Angus jumped to their feet, rushed outside and hurried over to the scene of the accident. A young girl, maybe sixteen, was trapped under a pile of orange-painted girders that must have weighed well over two tons. The girl wasn't dead. Her eyes were glancing around like those of a frightened bird. A crowd began to gather, but no effort was being made to free the trapped teenager.

'Let's do it,' said Angus to David.

The pair of them began to lift the girders piece by piece to the side. It was no easy task. Each four-metre-long beam weighed over a hundred kilos and there were at least twenty of them. Something cracked in Angus's back as he helped lift his fourth iron beam in as many minutes. The pile shifted its weight and the girl shrieked in pain as the weight bore down on her ribcage. Men began to step forward from the rapidly gathering crowd to lend a much needed helping hand. It took almost ten minutes to free the young woman, by then unconscious and lying in a pool of blood. Angus bent forward and watched David kneel and lift her bloodstained dress to examine her thin lower legs with an air of practised professionalism. Thick blood oozed from flesh pierced by compound fractures.

Angus stood up straight and gasped from a sharp pain in his lower back.

David glanced up at him. 'Are you alright?'

'I don't know. I think I've maybe slipped a disk or something.'

'I'll look at it in a minute,' David said, his breath still rapid from exertion. He placed two fingers on the woman's neck.

'What do you think?' Angus asked. 'She looks in terrible shape.'

'I agree.' David rose slowly to his feet to stand beside Angus. 'There are almost certainly internal injuries. Going by her low pulse rate, I'd say she needs a blood transfusion soon to stand any chance of making it.'

Angus looked around. 'I think I heard someone say they'd called an ambulance.'

As if on cue, a siren howled in the distance. A few minutes later, an ambulance with flashing red lights pulled up in the street. A pair of young paramedics wearing shabby white overcoats jumped out of the battered vehicle and walked over to the accident scene. One of them lit a cigarette as he bent down to inspect the injured girl. A couple of khaki-uniformed cops arrived and started brandishing their long bamboo lathis to disperse the crowd of curious onlookers. Angus and his American friend were unceremoniously shoved out of the way.

From across the road, in front of the café they'd just enjoyed a meal in half-an-hour before, Angus and David watched as the injured girl was lifted onto a canvas stretcher and dumped with little care on the ambulance's floor. Doors were slammed shut and then the yellow ambulance with red crescents painted on its side panels slowly edged its way along the busy street, heading east. The sound of its blaring siren slowly faded.

The waiter with red-stained teeth brought them out two large glasses of hot tea. Angus and David sat down on the edge of the uneven pavement. An unexpected movement caught Angus's eye. He looked down and over to his left. A long-whiskered rat peeked up at him from an open sewer before it disappeared from sight.

David glanced at his cheap plastic watch. 'Maharaj's afternoon talk begins in thirty minutes. Do you want to come along?'

'To be honest, I don't feel up to it.' Angus set his tea glass down on the concrete pavement, pushed his shoulders back and then groaned. 'My back is killing me.'

'Oh, my apologies. I forgot about that. Stand up and let me have a look.'

Urban traffic trundled, honked and spewed exhaust smoke at them as David examined Angus's naked back at the side of the bustling street.

David prodded Angus's lower back with his fingers. 'Does that hurt?'

'No.'

'And this?'

'No.'

'Here? Any pain?'

'No.'

'Good,' said David, walking round to face Angus. 'I don't think you've slipped a disk. If I were you, I'd have an x-ray. Just to be on the safe side.'

Angus sighed with relief. 'I'll do that when I get back to Pune.'

'Listen, I have to get back to Maharaj's. He's very punctual and expects the

181

same of everyone who attends his talks.'

'I understand,' said Angus. 'I'm going to my hotel. So I can stretch out flat on my back for a while. I'll see how I feel in the morning.'

'Fine. That sounds like a good idea.' David extended his right hand. 'Pleasure to meet you, Angus.'

'Likewise.'

They shook hands and smiled at each other for a moment, before turning away and walking off in opposite directions.

Angus waved down a taxi cab at a busy street corner. He was outside the Rex Hotel in a third of the time it took on the morning journey and the fare was five times less.

There was a sharp, staccato rap on the wooden door. Angus woke up and looked around his small hotel room. Sunlight was strafing in through an open window at an acute angle. There was another faltering knock on the door. 'Okay, okay, hold on a minute!' he called, checking his watch. It was 11.30. 'Man,' he mumbled to himself, 'I must have slept for eighteen hours solid.'

He rose from the bed, threw on some clothes and opened the door. A barefoot lad in shorts and a blue Fanta tee-shirt stood looking up at him, with three white towels in his arms. 'Towel changing, sir.'

'What? Yeah, yeah, thanks.' Angus took the towels and dug into his pocket for some change. He handed the boy a few coins.

'Thank you, sir.' The young lad gave an impromptu salute and hurried off back along the hotel corridor.

Angus had forgotten all about his sore back. In the shower stall, he dropped a plastic shampoo bottle. He bent to pick it up. A sharp nervous jolt shot along his spine. The shock made him nauseous. He staggered back to bed and lay prone without a pillow until the sick queasiness in his gut subsided. He only ventured out once that day, to cross the street for vegetable samosas and a banana milkshake in Dipti's juice bar. The rest of the day and night was spent reading and sleeping.

Once again, Angus slept in late. He lay on his back, watching the ceiling fan's slowly rotating blades. He turned things over in his mind and decided he wasn't quite ready for what Nisargadatta had to offer, although he wasn't sure exactly what that was.

By midday, Angus had found a taxi driver, willing to drive him to Pune for a reasonable fee. As the kilometres rolled by outside of the cab's tinted windows, Angus began to ponder on what his whole fascination with gurus was all about. He thought, *whether fake or genuine, spiritual masters are always going to remain in some way enigmatic. Unless I actually live close to a guru for years, I'm only going to see stage presence or my own projections screened on the master. The golden carrot that is enlightenment cannot happen as long as 'I' am in the way. How strange. How mysterious,* Angus reflected, slowly drawing around to accepting David Buschman's advice to go the course with Rajneesh. *David was right. Everything passes. Can't argue with that.*

Not far from Lonavla, the taxi passed a steep dirt track, which led down to the place where Angus, Amrit and Chid had buried their mutual friend, Jimmy Bradley, in an unmarked grave. A spasm of pain brought Angus back to the present and on to the future. *Two hours and I'll be home,* he thought.

The sun was dropping towards the horizon. Angus opened the bamboo gate and entered his compound. Lara and two girlfriends were sitting by the well. They were naked and laughing about something. The scene was idyllic. He could easily have imagined he'd landed in paradise but, on this particular afternoon, he simply waved to the women and continued along the short winding path that led to his house. Once inside, he pulled off his clothes, dropped them beside his rucksack on the wooden floor and lay down on bed, feeling completely drained and exhausted.

Lara entered the house. She wrapped an orange lunghi around her body and said, 'What happened to you?'

'It's a long story,' he answered, turning to face her. 'I'll tell you later.'

'Are you alright?' Lara enquired. 'You didn't say hello when you arrived.'

'I'm sorry,' he said. 'No offence meant. I hurt my back in Bombay lifting something and now I feel like shit.'

'Oh, diddums,' Lara cooed, 'Let mumsie-wumsie come and kiss it better.' She hurried over to the bed like a distressed mother attending a distraught infant. She knelt on the bed in front of Angus. Her bent knees, pressing into the coconut fibre mattress, succeeded in pulling her lunghi down far enough to expose her pert, round breasts. 'Oh, dear,' she sighed, cupping her breasts with both hands. 'Look who just popped out to see you.'

'*Diddums?* Where did you dig that one up?' Angus gave a tired chuckle. 'Take it easy, Lara. I'm not up to fooling around. Come here.' He groaned as he pulled her down towards his chest to embrace her.

'You're hot,' she said, propping her head on a bent elbow.

'Aye,' sighed Angus, 'I think I'm coming down with something.'

She placed a cool palm on his sweat-lined brow. 'Wow!' Lara exclaimed. 'You're burning up!.' She sat up on the bed. 'Get under the blanket and I'll bring you a hot drink. You need to sweat that fever out of you.'

Angus complied. By the time Lara returned to the bedroom with a steaming mug of ginger tea, he was sound asleep.

He woke up the following morning. His fever had intensified, and he was a little delirious, unsure of whether he'd just returned from Bombay, or whether he'd only dreamt it. He soon fell asleep again, but this time he didn't wake up. He lapsed into a coma.

'My god, Hamish, what was wrong with him?' Jean asked out of genuine concern.

'That's the next part of the story,' I said, glancing over to the open kitchen doorway in Drifter's Bar. 'Here comes lunch.'

I looked up from a hot oval plate of roast beef and baked potatoes. *'Mmmh,'* I hummed in mouth-watering delight. 'This beef has been cooked to perfection.'

'Don't talk with your mouth full,' Jean scolded. 'It's very bad manners.' She raised a stainless steel fork to her mouth with a yellow slice of potato impaled on it. 'But I have to say, these roast tatties are scrumptious. This is five-star pub grub. They should have this place in the Michelin Guide.'

The rest of the meal was eaten in silence.

Over her fourth cup of coffee that day, Jean enquired, 'So, what happened to Angus? I know he didn't die, but something serious happened. Correct?'

'That's right,' I replied, taking in what was going on in the pub. By this time, the place was packed. The noise level was such that I was forced to raise my voice to be heard. Over the excited chatter of multiple conversations, I could just make out Simple Minds playing through the small sound system. Jim Kerr's voice called out, *Don't you forget about me...* The well-known pop anthem returned my thoughts to my wife's question. 'Jean, I don't think this is the right setting to tell the next part of the story.'

Jean raised a cupped hand to her right ear. 'What?'

'It's time to go.' I rose to my feet and went over to the crowded bar to settle the bill.

'That was fine,' commented Jean, standing on the wet pavement, looking back at the Drifter's Bar's green-painted facade. 'It's great you can find food like that in our hometown.'

It had stopped raining. Jean and I walked along the wet streets. When we arrived home, I suggested I light a fire in the lounge.

'Why?' Jean asked. 'We have central heating.'

'To set the mood for the telling of the next part of Angus and Lara's story,' I answered.

'Oh, aye, alright then,' she agreed. 'I'll away through to the kitchen and get the kettle on.'

'I think something a wee bit stronger might be appropriate,' I suggested. 'What I am about to describe might require some liquid fortitude to dull your sensitivities.'

'Golly, grandad, you're getting very melodramatic in your dotage.'

I shook my head and knelt to set crumpled-up newspapers and kindling in the rough-cut, black granite fireplace.

Soon, we were both seated in front of a roaring blaze. Red and orange-tipped flames shot up the chimney, seeking dissolution in the damp air outside.

'This is cosy,' said Jean, raising a crystal glass tumbler, one-third full with Bruichladdich, twenty-four-year-old malt whisky. 'Cheers!'

'Cheers, Jean. Wishing you good health and a long life.'

We sat back in our armchairs, remaining silent as we gazed into the blazing fire, enjoying the presence of the other.

Jean spoke first. 'Well, then, shall we continue?'

I sat up straight and placed my empty tumbler on a smoked-glass coffee table. 'Aye, we can. No interruptions, please. I need to focus on—'

'Will you please just get on with it. The prelude, if that's what you call it, lasted all bloody morning.'

'Aye, okay, here we go. It was 1980 in Pune. Angus woke up to...'

12

WANG FU

Angus woke up to find himself lying on a bed. A steel-framed bed in the centre of a dingy room. The walls, painted in a sickly shade of green, reminded him of stagnant water. Behind an opaque window to his right, he could see diffused, flickering images of people walking by outside. He looked up to his left and saw a drip feed bag suspended from an aluminium stand. A transparent tube snaked down from a cylindrical flow-regulator. Angus followed the tube's course. It led to his arm, where it was joined and taped to a needle inserted into the back of his bruised left hand. 'What the fuck?' He tried to sit up, but his brain's impulses were not getting through to the muscle groups to make this simple physical movement possible.

A door creaked opened. An old crone entered. She wore a green sari, the same depressing colour as the walls. She raised a broomstick and dustpan in a visual explanation about why she was there. She muttered something incomprehensible, turned around, exited the room and closed the door behind her. A few minutes later, the old woman reappeared and once more repeated the same movements with her cleaning implements. Several repeat performances ensued. Finally, the old hag reappeared with two similarly attired women and, in a joint effort to make the reason for their presence in the room crystal clear to Angus, raised their hands palm up and started bleating, 'Baksheesh! Baksheesh! Baksheesh!'

Angus freaked out. He'd no idea where he was. His tongue felt thick and dry, and he had a terrible headache. He looked around the room for his clothes, but there was no sign of them.

The three women encircled him, their plea for money intensifying. 'Baksheesh! Baksheesh! Baksheesh!' they cried, as if reciting a mantra.

'Out! Out!' Lara's voice cut across the room. 'Get the fuck out of here!' she shouted, shooing the women away with her hands. The cleaning ladies disappeared out the door.

'Thank God you're awake,' said Lara, sitting down on the edge of the bed and clasping Angus's right hand. 'I was worried sick that you weren't going to come back. I've been sleeping here every night.'

Angus glanced at two folded woollen blankets and a pillow stacked in a corner. 'Where am I?'

'Emerald Hall Clinic. You've been here for over a week. You've been in a coma. The doctor had to order some special medicine from Bombay to bring your fever down. You were burning up. Your brain was overheating. One degree Fahrenheit more and your body's motor systems might have shut down.'

'What the fuck's wrong with me?'

'Nobody knows. I had one of the ashram doctors here three days ago. He didn't have a clue either. Said something about it maybe being typhoid but he wasn't certain.'

'Typhoid? How could I have contracted that? I had an inoculation against typhoid before I went to Iran.' Angus tried to sit up again. He couldn't. 'I can't fucking move.'

Lara gave a concerned nod. 'Yeah, I know. That's another thing. There's something wrong with your lower back that is affecting nerve endings. They took x-rays but they couldn't find anything wrong. You don't have a slipped disk. That's for sure.'

Angus hiccupped. 'Man, I'm exhausted.'

'You just woke up.'

'I know. But I feel like I just want to sleep.' He hiccupped again.

Lara let go of his hand and crossed the room to fetch him a glass of water. 'Here drink this.' She handed him a tumbler.

Due to his horizontal position, water spilt over his chest. He looked up into Lara's concerned green eyes. She looked worn out, but somehow she'd never appeared more beautiful and radiant to him as she did at that moment. Tears brimmed in his eyes. 'I love you,' he said. 'You're my guardian angel.'

Lara began to cry. Through her sobs she gasped, 'I... I love, too. It... It feels like we only just found each other. I... We'll get through this.'

Angus fell asleep. Lara slipped off to take care of some errands.

That night, Angus's hiccups returned with increased intensity. Every twenty seconds a hiccup emerged and the repetitive process would not stop. Under the stark light of a naked light bulb suspended above Angus's hospital bed, Lara and he came up with every home remedy they'd ever heard off. Angus tried sucking several glasses of water through a straw, biting a wedge of lemon, getting Lara to tickle him and breathing into a paper bag to increase the amount of carbon dioxide he was taking in. None of these tried and tested cures worked.

After a sleepless night for both of them, Doctor Chopra, the young Indian doctor in charge of Angus's case, knocked and entered the room. Dressed in a white overcoat, freshly pressed trousers, shirt and tie, a black stethoscope hung around his neck, he cast a professional impression.

'Good Morning.' The doctor cleared his throat and ran a hand over his oily hair to check it was in place. After unhooking a clipboard at the foot of the bed, he studied it for a few moments. Looking up, he smiled benevolently at

Lara and then Angus. 'How is my patient today?'

Angus hiccupped. 'I've got the hiccups and they won't go away.'

'Well, Mister MacLeod, that's the least of your problems in my estimation.' He laid the clipboard on the bed and stuck his forefingers in his jug ears. 'Just do this,' he advised. 'You see, hiccups are no more than a reflex. They come when the vagus nerve, which runs from the brain to the abdomen, becomes irritated. They're a minor nuisance, that's all.' Doctor Chopra removed his fingers from his prominent ears.

Angus continued to hiccup; now with his fingers jammed in his ears.

Lara looked at the doctor. 'Anything come back on the test results?'

Doctor Chopra cleared his throat for a second time. 'Thanks for reminding me. Bad news I'm afraid. Your... Your husband?' he said, unsure of the couple's marital status. 'Mister MacLeod has contracted typhoid and hepatitis.'

'What?' Lara gasped. 'How could he have managed that?'

The doctor gave a knowing chuckle. 'In any number of ways: contaminated drinking water, unclean food, unprotected sexual relations and, of course, dirty needles from intravenous drug use.'

The latter made Lara think of the needles used to draw blood specimens from Angus's arm. On two occasions she'd noticed the needles had not come out of fresh packets. They were already attached to the stainless steel syringes. *The bloody clowns have been using recycled, unsterilized needles,* she thought.

Doctor Chopra misinterpreted the anguished expression on Lara's face. 'No cause for worry,' he said brightly, employing a form of English acquired in an expensive fee-paying university somewhere in England. 'We'll soon have Mister MacLeod back on his feet. Modern medicine is a wonderful thing, you know. Well, now, if you will excuse me, I must go and attend to my other patients.' He began to turn away.

'Hold on!' Lara cried out. 'What about his back.'

The doctor tutted, before turning once more to face her. 'Nothing to be concerned about. Muscle strain, a torn ligament at most. Perhaps a mild case of sciatica. Rest will cure that. It's typhoid that's the real problem, but we'll soon have that under control with the correctly prescribed medications. Good day, Mrs MacLeod.' He gave a slight bow.

Lara glared at the doctor's white-coated back as he crossed the room.

Angus hiccupped behind her. He still had his fingers in his ears and had missed the entire exchange.

'For Christ's sake,' she said. 'Am I surrounded by idiots? Take your bloody fingers out of your ears. That's not going to work. That guy's a complete asshole.'

'What?' Angus asked, removing his fingers from his throbbing ears.

Lara glowered at him. 'I said, sticking fingers in your ears won't stop your hiccups.'

'Why? What did the doctor say?'

Lara told him and concluded by saying, 'Listen, this is getting a bit too much for me. I haven't had a wink of sleep all night. I need to go home and rest. Is it okay with you if I come back in the evening?'

Angus hiccupped. 'Yeah, sure. I have nothing planned for this evening.'

She gave a sad smile. 'See you later, sweetheart.'

An unorthodox cure for Angus's hiccups was found two days later. He discovered that if he stuck his fingers down his throat, and vomited into a plastic bucket, the hiccups stopped for twenty minutes, during which time he was able to catch a little sleep. His problem was he had little appetite, so there was nothing in his stomach to throw up. This was overcome by drinking bottles of a soft drink, called Mangola. Over the next two weeks, he managed to heave up twenty-four crates of the sickly sweet, mango-flavoured beverage, putting him off of one of his favourite fruits for many years to come.

Sleep deprivation distorted Angus's sense of time to where he did not know if it was dusk or dawn. Three weeks after first entering Emerald Hall Clinic, Angus stopped hiccupping. He viewed this as a minor victory, returning him to a normal sleep pattern.

One would be justified in wondering why a hospital allowed someone to apply a bizarre remedy like throwing up into a bucket to cure a prolonged bout of hiccups. As long as Angus's paid his bills at the end of the week, nobody among the hospital staff, including Doctor Chopra, was in the least bit interested in him. For each week Angus stayed in the clinic, he paid what a civil servant in India earns in a year. That was the least of his worries.

Since he'd first entered the hospital, Angus had lost over twenty kilos of weight. He did not look like someone who'd just walked out of Auschwitz. He looked like someone who was still in the God-forsaken place. He couldn't walk. He could stand by the side of his bed for a couple of minutes at a time before the pain kicked in and then he had to lie down again.

It was the end of week six when Doctor Chopra walked briskly into the room and proudly announced that Angus was completely cured of typhoid and hepatitis. 'You can go home now,' he declared, before marching off to visit his next unlucky patient.

Angus stood naked at the end of his bed, grasping the iron bedstead for support. The week before, Lara had brought in an oblong mirror to reflect more light into the dull room. It was that mirror he now stood gazing into, and he was horrified to see his reflection. He saw a skeleton covered in pale yellow skin, sagging from his emaciated limbs. His once muscular thighs had been whittled down to the thickness of a pint beer mug. His ribs protruded, as did his sternum. His abdomen was concave. His genitals had shrivelled and retracted. He peered into his sunken eyes to see their whites were yellow and lined by ruptured veins. He collapsed onto the bed, curled up and cried until there were no more tears to shed. He felt sorry for himself, dejected, broken-hearted and utterly depressed. Out of a dismal ocean of gloomy thoughts, one single thought held a faint glimmer of hope. *I have to get out of here.*

Angus used crutches to walk out of Emerald Hall Clinic's main exit. At the bottom of a small flight of broad steps, a taxi awaited his and Lara's arrival. Angus turned around and looked up at the hospital's double glass door. *I should have just let go and died in there,* he thought. The stark realization was dawning that, if he was going to recuperate, it would require every gram of strength and willpower that he had left in his ruined body to travel the long road of agony on the way to recovery. *Shit! I don't know if I have it in me,* was the last thought in his mind before Lara helped him ease into the back of the cab.

Angus could not wait to get home. Every pothole the taxi hit delivered a jolt of pain that shot up his spine like an electric shock. The normal one minute journey from the asphalt road to his bamboo house seemed interminable. Each bend on the slanting path by the well required patience and attention to traverse. When Angus finally made it to his king-sized bed, he lay flat on his back and cried with relief.

Lara was also suffering, albeit in a different way. Her routine life of meditation, celebration, attending Bhagwan's discourses, lovemaking, dancing and painting was quickly being eroded and fading into the past. She was devoted to Angus, but the strain was making its presence felt. She'd already stormed out of the hospital more than once in a fit of frustration. She'd shouted at Angus, ordering him not to indulge himself so much in self-pity. Yet, she rarely left his side.

Over the coming weeks, friends would visit. Upon seeing Angus propped up in bed, there was always the same reaction, horrified shock. His physical condition was deteriorating. Pain never left him for long and his bed sheets were damp with sweat.

Someone had suggested that Angus see a chiropractor.

'I'm finished with him,' announced Angus, one evening at home. He was lying flat out on his bed, as had become the norm.

'But why?' Lara called from the kitchen, where she was preparing supper.

'Because the guy's going to kill me if I keep going there. I'm getting fucking worse, not better. The guys cracked my spine dozens of times and it doesn't help. I'm still fucked. Hey!' he called out, suddenly remembering something. 'Did you get me some more painkillers when you were out?'

'I'm sorry,' she yelled back. 'I forgot.'

'*Forgot!*' Angus said, his voice becoming aggressive. 'How the fuck could you forget. I'm in agony. Look at the fuckin' state of me!' He began to shout. 'I can hardly move! For fuck's sake!'

Lara appeared framed in the kitchen doorway. She had a large saucepan in her right hand, her left fist wedged in her side. 'Don't start,' she warned. 'Stop feeling so sorry for yourself. You have to be strong.'

'*Strong!* Fucking well strong!' Angus yelled. 'How can I be strong when I'm trapped in a fucking corpse. I'm fucked. I know it. You know it. And everyone else knows it.' He jabbed a furious finger at her. 'So why don't you just fuck right off and go to Hell.'

'*Hell!*' she screamed, her voice shrill. 'I'll tell you about Hell. I've been in Hell since the day you came back from your bloody sojourn to Bombay. If you hadn't gone there, none of this shit would have happened.'

'You don't know that,' Angus snarled.

'Don't I?' Lara took a step into the room. She shook her brass cooking pot at him. 'You think you're so spiritual. Asking yourself who you are and all that Advaita nonsense. Well, I'll tell you who you really are. A grumpy, weak-willed Scotsman, who can't even wipe his own bloody arse. You think I enjoy doing that for you?'

Angus shouted from his bed. 'Fuck off! You stupid cunt!'

'*Asshole!*' she screamed, launching the heavy metal pot across the room in Angus's direction.

He didn't see it coming. *Dong!* The pot hit him square on the forehead, almost knocking him unconsciousness. He saw blue stars. His ears were ringing. 'What the...' He shook his head trying to focus.

'I'm leaving,' shouted Lara, grabbing a thin satin jacket on her way out the door. 'There's a party in Laxmi Villas tonight and I'm going to it.' The door slammed.

'Now,' Angus said to the silent room, 'that's what you call a right fuckin' head-banger.'

He ran a hand across his forehead. A hard perpendicular bump was forming under the skin. He checked his palm for blood. There was a red streak. He turned on his side, switched on a bedside lamp and looked at his face in a small oval mirror. 'Shit,' he muttered to himself. 'I look like a baby rhino. At least the whites of my eyes aren't yellow anymore.' A sharp pain throbbed from his lower spine. 'Ow!' He lay flat on his back and gazed up at the bamboo rafters. 'What a state I'm in.' He felt as insubstantial as the dust motes, drifting aimlessly in the cone of light projected upwards from the circular opening at the top of the lampshade. A wave of despair washed over him. His heart sank in a swamp of loneliness.

It was the first time he and Lara had ever had a real argument, let alone a shouting match. He felt twinges of guilt for having cursed at her. The effort of yelling had left him drained, although not quite empty enough to shut down the chatter of his mind. Insecure thoughts wobbled into his head on swivelling steel casters. He imagined Lara in Laxmi Villas, bustin' moves on the dance floor to the Bee Gee's 'Stayin' Alive'. He saw handsome men checking her out and leering at her. *Now's their chance*, he thought. *She'll revenge fuck some guy.* Images ripped into his mind of a muscular stud with a huge erection taking her from behind. *Aw, aw, aw, aw, stayin' alive.* He could hear her moans of pleasure; the same moans he'd heard because of what he was doing to her, not some other man. He broke out in a cold sweat, envisioning this all taking place two kilometres away. His whole life was disappearing, spiralling down the drain. Terrified, he thought, *If I don't get out of my head I'll blow a fucking circuit. I'm cracking up.*

Angus looked over to the bedside table. Lara had left a Rajneesh book there. It was titled *The Shadow of the Whip*. He reached for the hardback, opened it at a random page, then tilted the book towards the lamp. Rajneesh was talking about fear and how it is part of humanity, part of life...something natural. Fighting fear is useless. Accepting fear will help it disappear. Fear is the shadow of death. Accept it! It was exactly what Angus needed to hear. He set the thick hardback aside, closed his eyes and watched his breathing. The vicious thoughts that had been tearing him apart receded. A feeling of peace entered his heart. He listened to the rhythms of the house, creaking bamboo, the whisper of the breeze gently rustling the eucalyptus leaves outside. Wind chimes tinkled in the garden. Somewhere in the vicinity, he could hear a baby crying. A dog barked nearby, and another one answered in the distance. Behind those everyday sounds was silence, the silence that is always there, the silence his raucous thoughts had prevented him from hearing. Angus sank deeper into the mystery of his being. He watched his life unfold before him. How he'd played as a child on Iona. Grown-up in Glasgow. Travelled overland to India. He saw his old friends, Raj and Murphy's laughing faces, and it registered that he would one day see them again and how happy he would feel when that happened. He missed them. Then it came to him that there was a part of his being beyond all the comings and goings of life. For him to see his life unfold, he had to be there to see it. He realized he must have existed before human reality. Or something did. The same something that would continue after his body fell away when it died. It became clear that his physical death was some way off. There were many things that he still had to do in life. Somehow he would recover from this terrible illness that gripped him in its talons. Life's essential purpose burst forth. 'Life is for living!' he called into the silence. And for the first time in what felt like an eternity to him, he laughed. A loud, relieved chuckle. It struck him with dazzling clarity that his moments of darkest despair were the moments that provided him with the most lucidity, helping him see things as they really are, like a curtain being drawn back, allowing bright sunlight to illuminate a gloomy room.

Just sitting up in bed was a painful struggle. Standing up was worse. Walking to the kitchen felt like he'd just broken free from a wooden cross after being crucified. Sweat dripping from his face, he made it to the kitchen. Making a cup of tea was an arduous task. But, come what may, he managed to bring that cup of tea back to his bedside without spilling a drop. The honey-sweetened tea tasted like nectar. Invigorated, he stood up again and shuffled over to a portable cassette player. He pressed the play button. Reggae music. It was a Paul Simon song, called 'Mother and Child Reunion'. Angus had never really listened to it before, but now he gave it his full attention. The lyrics could have been written for the way he felt in that instant. The female chorus came in. *Oh the mother and child reunion...* The song drew to a close. He rewound the cassette and listened to it again. He began to sing along. 'It's only a motion away.' He was in no fit state to dance, but he could hold his arms up. That's when the door opened and Lara walked it. Her jaw dropped. She gasped, 'You're dancing?' Angus's arms flopped down. He shrugged, then staggered towards her.

She switched the music off and helped Angus back to bed. They lay together and, between hugs and soft kisses, apologized to each other for treating one another in such an abusive way.

Lara began crying, hot tears that came from deep in her heart. She wiped her cheeks with the back of her hand and ran a gentle finger across Angus's inflamed brow. 'My God,' she sobbed, 'how could I have done that to you? I'm so sorry. Please forgive me,' she blubbered. 'I didn't mean to hurt you.'

Angus chuckled. 'Och, it's nothing. A wee bump on the head, that's all.'

'A wee bump on the head,' she echoed, incredulous. 'You look like you're growing a horn. Does it hurt?'

He shook his head. 'Not really. Anyway,' he said, 'I deserved it.'

'Don't you ever call me a cu—'

Angus placed a finger on her soft lips. 'Don't say it.' It was a whisper. He'd hurt her and he knew it. He could see her pulse beating in the hollow of her throat. 'I'm sorry I said that. I'll never do it again.'

Her eyes watered and her lips quivered. 'P... P... Promise?'

'Scout's honour,' he said, placing his right hand over his heart. 'How was the party at Laxmi Villas?'

She wiped a tear from her cheek and shrugged. 'Okay, I suppose. Danced for half an hour. I saw—'

Angus cut her off. 'Did they play the Bee Gee's 'Stayin' Alive?"

Lara frowned. 'No. Why? I thought you didn't like the Bee Gees.'

'I don't,' he said, avoiding eye contact. 'I just wondered,' he mumbled, guilty with his lie. 'That's all.' Something in the tilt of her head told him he wasn't fooling her.

'You're hiding something. Anyway,' she said, quickly changing the subject, 'you feeling better?'

He reflected. 'I don't know if *better* is the right word. Somehow your cooking pot connecting with my head knocked some sense into it. I've never been so down in my life. Mental anguish intensifies the pain in my body. I have to accept and adapt to what's happened to me, instead of caving into it. It's all very well thinking you are not the body when you're fit and healthy. It's not so easy when you're in the physical condition I'm in. But one thing is certain; I swear to you, Lara, I'm going to haul myself out of this pit I've fallen into. There is a part of me that understands it's all just some kind of nightmarish illusion. I sometimes ask is there anything in this world that is real?'

'Of course, there is,' said Lara.

'What?'

'Love is real. And there are an infinite number of ways to express it.' She moved in closer to him and kissed the oval bump on the centre of his brow. 'I'll stay by your side. I'll stick it out with you...no matter what.'

Angus gazed into Lara's green eyes, drawing from her the strength and steadfastness he needed. 'If we had a relationship manual,' he said, 'this would all be in the chapter titled 'Making Up'.'

"Making Love' would be a more satisfying chapter,' she said, 'but I suppose 'Making up' will have to do for now.'

It was the morning of June the First, 1981. Angus was home alone, procrastinating over whether or not he should attempt to rise out of bed and shuffle through to the kitchen to make breakfast. Months had passed since he'd first fallen ill and his condition remained unchanged. As those months drifted by, fewer friends visited him. At first, this new development upset him, but eventually, he came to an understanding. The sannyasin community was, in many respects, selfish. Rajneesh encouraged his followers to be selfish, in the sense that selfish means to be yourself. The controversial master taught that the path to authentic altruism involved being only concerned with oneself in the preliminary stages of the process. By being self-centred, the genuine need to share with others would soon arise.

On another level, the Rajneesh ashram, with its madhouse-carnival atmosphere, was like a fun-filled surf party, where everyone involved was riding the waves of change and bliss emanating from the tidal epicentre that was Bhagwan Shree Rajneesh. If one was unfortunate enough to wipe-out and fall into the churning undercurrents, as Angus had, then you had to learn to swim fast. India is a country where life is dirt cheap.

After a week without visitors, Angus was surprised to hear a gentle knock on the bamboo door. 'Come in,' he called from the kitchen.

The door opened inwards. A tall, potbellied man with short, grey hair and wearing a wine-coloured robe entered the living room. He sat down in a rattan chair and looked around, his shifting weight prompting the chair to creak. His name was Yogi and he hailed from Montreal. Angus had become friends with him during his last Rebalancing training. Yogi said, *'Bonjour.'* He watched Angus slowly make his way from the kitchen to his bed. *'Fais chier!'* Yogi exclaimed. 'I heard you were in a bad way but, *merde,* I didn't envisage it would be this bad. You look like shit.'

'I feel like shit.' Angus rejoined with a sigh.

'*Mon Dieu*, you have lost so much weight.'

'Last time I checked,' said Angus, 'I weighed in at forty-seven kilos.'

'*Incroyable*,' said Yogi, patting his protruding belly. 'You must tell me your secret.'

Angus's laughter was cut off by a shock wave of pain.

'You are so pale. You look for all the world like a skeleton with skin stretched over it,' commented the Canadian. 'I am reminded of a skinny Vietnam vet I met in Goa a few years ago. A heroin junkie. Poor guy was held captive in a filthy hut for two years by the Viet Kong. He told me he only survived because he ate worms, rats, snakes, insects and sometimes his own shit, otherwise he would have starved to death. *Merde!* Can you imagine?'

'For fuck's sake, Yogi! Lighten up a bit, man. I'm in a pretty vulnerable state here, in case you hadn't noticed. I don't need to hear disgusting stories about Vietnam vets eating turds. You'll be giving me fucking nightmares telling me shite like that.'

'Oh, sorry, *mon ami*. Perhaps I was being a little... How do you say? ...*insensitive*. What exactly is wrong with you, anyway?'

Angus spent ten minutes explaining. When he'd finished, Yogi suggested they go out for a walk. 'A walk!' Angus gasped. 'I haven't been outside for a walk in months.'

Yogi eyed a pair of wooden crutches set in a corner of the sunlit room. 'You can use those,' he suggested.

'But how will I make it up to the road?'

'Simple. I will carry you.'

Angus sat on the edge of his bed and his voice rose a note in protest. 'The pain will fucking well kill me, man.'

'Lara told me that you are taking morphine tablets. Take one of those and, when it begins to work, we will go for a walk. It's a beautiful warm day outside.'

Twenty minutes later, they were slowly walking down the road, Angus on crutches, eyes focused on the asphalt, so that he did not trip in a pothole. His breath was laboured from the strain. He came to a sudden halt when confronted by a pair of rubber-tipped crutches similar to his own, a pair of shiny black shoes, grey socks, and two spindly legs encased in a web of splint-like metal braces. His eyes moved up across short trousers and a blue cotton shirt and finally came to rest on a young schoolboy's face. He could not have been more than fourteen years old. The face had olive-brown skin, a set of cheap spectacles framing dark-brown eyes, and a mouth that was split in a toothy grin. 'Good morning, sir. What is your name?' asked the young teenager.

'Eh... Eh... Eh...' Angus was lost for words. The lad was in worse shape than he was, yet he was smiling, walking on his own and, of all things, being polite. It was one of the most emotionally punishing moments in his life. Angus began to weep. His illness had opened him up to the full impact of a side of Indian life that he'd become inured to, other people's raw and unadulterated physical suffering.

The cripple, whose wretched physical condition was due to polio, was unaware of the effect his cheery presence was having on the weeping foreigner before him. He enquired, 'What is the matter, sir?'

Yogi intervened and tried to hand the boy a ten-rupee note. The young fellow's eyes creased with apprehension. He shook his black-haired head vigorously and said apologetically, 'So sorry, sir. My mother is telling me not to be taking money from strangers. Will your friend be alright?'

'Yes, yes,' the Canadian assured him. 'He will be fine. A little upset, that's all. Don't you worry about it.'

'Okay, sir. I am going now. Bye-bye.' The boy made a deft movement, spun around on one wooden crutch, and headed off down the road at a rapid clip.

Yogi helped Angus home.

'You should check into another hospital,' Yogi advised Angus. 'You have to find the right doctor to determine what is wrong with you. I hate to say it, but if you don't receive the right medical care soon, you will not be much longer for this world. Do you understand me, *mon ami*. You will die.'

'Yes, Yogi, I understand what you're saying,' said Angus, resting his head on a pillow. 'I appreciate your honesty. I will check out another hospital tomorrow.'

'*Salut.*' The Canadian patted him on the shoulder and exited.

Angus lay flat on his bed. He could not erase the image of the cheerful polio victim on crutches, grinning like his life was perfect, while asking for his name.

'Wake up!' Lara shook Angus awake.

'What? What is it?' he asked, struggling to sit upright in bed.

'Something really weird has happened.'

'So, what else is new?' Angus groaned. The morphine tablet's pain-nullifying effects were wearing off. 'My whole life is weird.'

'Bhagwan has left the ashram!' she exclaimed. 'He was driven away in the back of his white Rolls Royce. Rumour has it he is going to America.'

'What?'

'Somebody said he is going to New Jersey.'

Angus was not nearly as moved as Lara was by this unexpected development. She was almost in tears.

'Someone from the office said he will not be returning to India any time soon. What are we going to do?'

He shrugged. 'That's a good question. First thing tomorrow morning, I'm going to that hospital near the railway station.'

Lara noticed that one of the rattan chairs was in an unusual position. She knew Angus did not have the strength to move it. 'You had a visitor?'

'Yeah. Canadian Yogi was here.'

'The big fat guy? I can't stand him. I met him the other day, and he stared at my breasts the whole time we stood talking.'

'He's okay,' Angus said. 'He made me go out for a walk.'

'He did?' Lara said in surprise. 'How was that?'

'Totally bizarre. Met a crippled kid outside Prem's Restaurant and it completely blew my head off.' Angus reached for his packet of painkillers. 'Yogi told me I needed to find the right doctor because he thinks if I don't I might die.'

'And you believed him?'

'Yes, my love, I did.' Angus popped a white pill in his mouth and washed it down with a glass of water. 'That's why you're going to take me to the hospital tomorrow morning in a rickshaw.'

As soon as he arrived, Angus knew it was a mistake to have even bothered coming to this particular hospital. He set his crutches to one side and sat down on a bare aluminium chair. The waiting room was mobbed with Indians, some in worse shape than he was. Lara found the atmosphere so claustrophobic and oppressive she went outdoors and sat by the side of a busy street.

The only thing that seemed to be functioning correctly in the stuffy room was a large walk clock. Angus watched the slender, scarlet second hand travelling around it until he realised that it was eleven-thirty; meaning he'd been waiting for three hours without seeing a single member of the medical staff. There were still about a dozen people in the room, all of them women. He gazed at the knots on the worn pine floorboards for some time and then shifted his attention to the women, seated around the room in various states of near collapse. Most of them were elderly, with lengths of faded sari cloth draped over their dejected heads. The more he studied the disconsolate faces, the more inhuman they appeared. The women quickly became aware of Angus's curious stare and began to gawk back at him. Soon Angus was the centre of focus for a dozen pairs of cheerless eyeballs, set in the eye sockets of yellow skulls. Canadian Yogi's words flashed red in his mind. *If you don't receive the right medical care soon, you will not be much longer for this world.*

'Shit!' Angus hissed between his clenched teeth.

Lara entered the room as he was struggling to lodge his crutch's black plastic pads under his armpits. 'Have you seen a doctor?'

'No,' he replied. 'I've seen something else, though, and it told me to get the fuck out of India. Bhagwan's not the only one heading West. We are too. Come on!'

That afternoon, they worked out a course of action.

Angus opened his strongbox and started making bundles of different denomination banknotes from various countries. He reckoned there was close to half-a-million dollars worth of paper money, most of which would be stashed in a State Bank of India safe deposit box.

Meanwhile, Lara caught a rickshaw downtown to visit a travel agent, where she booked two intercontinental air tickets, the final destination being Aberdeen's Dyce Airport in Scotland. She then walked to the general post office and made an international call to her mother, who Lara had last seen at her father's funeral in Dublin, four years previously, in 1977. Lara took another auto-rickshaw over to the Mecca Pharmacy on Centre Street, known to be the place to buy drugs normally unavailable over-the-counter without a doctor's prescription. Ten intense haggling minutes later, she exited the pharmacy minus one-thousand rupees, and plus an unmarked plastic bag containing six rubber-capped phials of morphine, six syringes and half-a-dozen needles sealed in cellophane packs.

On the evening of June 5, 1981, Angus and Lara boarded a Lufthansa flight to Munich. Angus had just self-administered his second intravenous vial of morphine that day in a public lavatory's cramped cubicle. He'd almost passed out on a dirty toilet seat from the opiate's powerful rush. Lara had to enter the gentlemen's toilets to haul Angus out, in fear of missing their flight. Angus was so stoned he could not remember any of this, or the flight to Munich, nor the long wait for the connecting flight to London's Heathrow, or handing a British Passport in the name of James Sheridan over at Heathrow's immigration checkpoint, where he was waved through on his crutches without so much as a blink of an eye. He also could not recall passing out with a syringe in his left arm in a men's toilet in Heathrow Airport, or the commotion that took place as Lara dragged him out of the cubicle in full sight of half-a-dozen outraged male patrons.

Angus was lucid enough to take in the last leg of their 7000-mile journey. On its approach to Dyce Airport, their twin-propped passenger plane was buffeted by high winds. There was much muttering of prayers and tightening of seat belts. Angus felt no fear whatsoever. Comfortably numb, he gazed out of the window at the scene passing below him. Patches of cloud over the grey North Sea, white-capped waves battering rugged coastline, the River Don winding its way through Aberdeen's outskirts and then, finally, the runway's tarmac, a screech of tyres, the smell of scorched rubber and the plane's engines being shut down.

Angus's state of anaesthetic-induced euphoria was so complete that he let Lara carry his crutches. He strolled through the arrivals gate, feeling like a skeleton-thin Lazarus raised from the dead.

Lara's mother, Monica Shannon, was waiting for them in the carpeted arrivals hall. Her long brown hair had streaks of grey and was tied up in a loose bun on top of her head. She wore a blue padded anorak and tight jeans, tucked into a pair of black leather riding boots. Angus wandered by her and was on his way to the revolving exit door by the time Lara grabbed his right hand and dragged him back to introduce him to Monica. Mrs Shannon shook his limp hand and said, 'Lovely to meet you, Angus. Forgive me, but

I refuse to use those silly Indian names Bhagwash has been handing out. Please call me Mona.'

'Cool, Mona,' said Angus, his attention focused on a newsagent's shop. 'I could go a can of ice-cold Irn Bru.'

Monica stood back and looked him up and down like an assessor studying a derelict building. 'I don't mean to offend you, Angus, but I have to say that you look absolutely dreadful.' She turned to Lara, standing to her left, smoothing creases in her crimson robe. 'Is he on drugs?' Monica asked in a hushed voice. 'His pupils are like pinpricks.'

'As I told you on the phone, mum, Angus has been ill for months. He had to take very strong painkillers to be able to make it through the journey. He's in a lot of pain.' She tugged Angus's arm to get his attention away from the ceiling. 'Aren't you, Angus.'

'What?' he asked, blinking his way back to the moment.

'You're in a lot of pain,' she repeated.

'Oh... Yeah... Yeah... Right! I was just thinking that I need to visit the toilets.' He began to walk away.

Lara grabbed him by a wrist, stopping him in his tracks. 'Oh, no you don't,' she pronounced firmly, before turning to address her mother. 'I think it's time we got out of here, mum.'

Monica's green eyes were alight and shifted like a pendulum between Angus and Lara. 'Yes, I do believe you're right, my dear.' She picked up a red suitcase. 'Come along, Angus. My car's in the park house across the road.'

Angus's pain was returning. Lara handed him his crutches. She'd noticed him wince twice during the brief exchange.

It was raining. The air was fresh and carried the faint scent of pine. By the time they reached the multi-storey car park, Angus's thin orange shirt and matching trousers were soaked through. Monica's car turned out to be an olive-green, short-wheel-base Land Rover.

The road journey took forty-five minutes. They drove into the picturesque village of Banchory, the main street lined by shop fronts. The Land Rover turned left at the traffic lights, crossed a granite bridge spanning a fast-flowing river and, five miles later, drove into the tree-lined driveway that led to Monica's home. Thick tyres crunched on gravel chips. The Land Rover came to a halt in front of a two-storied, slate-roofed house, its grey granite walls covered by ivy. Angus was in agony.

Once indoors, Monica guided a stumbling and disorientated Angus up a flight of solid oak stairs. She pushed open a door leading into a red-carpeted bedroom with an en-suite bathroom. The room was warm. Water gurgled in a radiator. 'You look like you need to rest,' she said, guiding him over to a double bed with a thick duvet folded over to one side. Angus collapsed onto the mattress and groaned with relief. Monica shook her head. 'I suggest you get out of those wet clothes.' She pointed to a tall, wooden wardrobe. 'You'll find a set of my late husband's pyjamas in there. I'm going downstairs to have a word with my daughter.' Monica left the room's panelled door ajar. Angus listened to the clump of her footsteps descending the staircase. A few moments later, the distant sound of an argument drifted up from below.

He sat up and rummaged in his leather shoulder bag. He removed his belt from his narrow waist and tied it around his left bicep. He fixed a fresh needle onto the end of a plastic syringe and used it to puncture a phial of morphine's rubber cap. Drawing back on the syringe he sucked up the small bottle's clear liquid contents. He gave the syringe a quick squirt and slapped his bruised lower arm to bring up a vein. 'Bingo!' He hit a mainline on his first probe and drew back on the plunger. Blood mushroomed into the transparent plastic cylinder. He pushed down, and the syringe shot the morphine into his arm. The belt was loosened. Morphine flooded his vascular system. A hot flush rushed through his wrecked body. The room wobbled up and down like a malfunctioning TV screen. He closed his eyes. His spinning head flumped back onto a feathered pillow. Angus spiralled down into a vivid dreamworld.

Whoomp! Whoomp! Whoomp! A bass drum laid down a hypnotic beat, guitars crunching and grinding in a synchronized loop. A deep male voice began to sing. *Let me tell you a story, it's about this man I know...* The music sounded like Sixties psychedelic, but Angus did not recognize the song. *He could be your best friend. He could be your foe... Whoomp! Whoomp! Whoomp!* The beat went on and on. The same lyrics repeated again and again.

Angus looked around. He was in a barbed-wire compound. *Let me tell you a story, it's about this man I know...* He remembered who he was supposed to be and quickly slipped into the appropriate personality. He was an American Marine, taken captive by the North Vietnamese during the Vietnam War. Mosquitoes flitted against his face. He was kneeling in thick, wet mud, groping around in the sludge for something to eat. He extracted a long earthworm from the gunk. Slime dripped as it wriggled in the illumination cast by a roving searchlight. The worm was juicy and cool in his parched mouth.

'Hey! You greedy motherfucker!' called a familiar voice. 'I thought the deal was that we shared everything edible.'

Angus swallowed quickly. He gazed up at Corporal Murphy, gaunt, covered in filth and missing front teeth. 'Sorry, man,' Angus apologized, 'but that lousy worm was the only thing I've had to eat all day.' He looked past Murphy, peering around the shadowy compound, noticing stark electric light framed in a bamboo hut's open window. 'Where's Raj.'

'Inside,' said Murphy, scratching at the lice inhabiting his close-cropped hair. 'Jammy bastard caught a rat. Soup tonight and then afterwards we can shoot up some China White for desert. Wang Doo smuggled in an ounce in her snatch this afternoon.'

'Fuckin' great!' Angus exclaimed, standing up and wiping filth from his hands on his mud-splattered camouflage trousers. 'That cheap brown was giving me a right headache.'

'Come on,' Murphy said, throwing an arm across Angus's bony shoulders. 'It's time to eat our first decent meal in a week.'

The searchlight's beam followed them across the quagmire. Angus knew that Binh Dung was on duty in the spindly-legged watchtower. Angus stopped, turned, shaded his eyes with one hand and waved with the other. The searchlight was extinguished. Angus's eyes quickly adjusted to the gloom. Binh Dung's shadowy profile was outlined in the wooden watchtower. He was wearing a bush hat. Dung did not return the wave. A cigarette's ember glowed in the darkness.

Inside the smoke-filled hut, Private Raj sat cross-legged, stirring a bubbling broth in a blackened aluminium pot, simmering over a small open fire. Raj glanced up as his two muddy buddies entered. 'Almost ready,' he announced. 'Found a couple of rhinoceros beetles, a centipede and a baby tarantula to add a bit of flavour. It's gonna be a first-class nosh up.'

'Could have been better,' grunted Murphy. 'I caught Private Angus here munching on a big juicy worm. The greedy bastard that he is.'

Raj looked scornfully at Angus. 'You didn't, did you?'

'Sorry, man,' said Angus. 'I was fucking well starving.'

'We're all fuckin' starving,' mumbled Raj, his attention returning to the rat soup. 'If it wasn't for the smack, I don't think I could cope.'

He could be your best friend. He could be your foe... Whoomp! Whoomp! Whoomp!

'Ugh!' There was a groan from a darkened corner of the hut. 'Is it chow time yet?' asked a gruff male voice in a Texas drawl.

'Coming right up,' answered Raj.

'Sir!'

'Coming right up, Sergeant Fury, *sir!*'

'That's more like it, Private Raj.' Fury pulled his trousers on. His muscular frame swaggered over to the cooking fire. He bent his knees and picked a burning ember up with thick fingers to light the stub of a cigar. He took a couple of contemplative drags and then sniffed the air. 'What the fuck are you using for fuel there, Private. It smells like a goddamned shit house in here.'

'Yeah, sir. I'm not surprised. I'm burning shit that I retrieved from the latrine.' Raj added, 'It took two days to dry it out in the sun.'

'Me hunglee,' called a whining female voice from the corner. 'What cooking? Smell good.'

Raj scratched his shaved head and sniggered. 'Make special for you, Wang Doo. Best rat soup south of Hanoi.'

Wang Doo slinked over to the steaming pot. She was naked. When she bent over to scrutinize the stew more closely in front of Angus, he cringed, turned to Murphy and screwed up his mud-splotched face. Murphy gave a toothless smile and waggled his tongue. 'Phew!' The skinny Asian whore spat on the dusty floor. 'You one clayzee motherfucka if you think I eating that.'

'Shut the fuck up,' spat Fury, spittle flying in her face, a reject pancake with narrow eyes, squashed nose and a red-lipstick smear for a mouth. 'You eat what we serve you. You crazy slant-eyed bitch!' The sergeant slapped Wang Doo's sagging buttocks with a hand the size of a Frisbee.

'Ow!' she squeaked. 'Wang Doo no clayzee bitch! You call me clayzee bitch one more time, then no more sucky-fucky and no more number one smacky-smacky.'

Fury laughed with pleasure. 'Come 'ere, gal.' He pulled Wang Doo down into his waiting lap, where she remained until everyone present had licked their tin plates clean of every last disgusting streak of Raj's rat stew.

'Fucking delicious,' said Murphy, licking his cracked lips in satisfaction. 'All I need now is something sweet.'

Fury pushed Wang Doo from his lap. 'Go get the horse, gal. *Nanh len!*'

'Okay, okay, me hurry.' Wang Doo wrapped a sarong around her waist and shuffled out the door. She returned a minute later with a small, sausage-shaped package. She knelt by the fire's smouldering embers and unfurled cling-film to reveal a glycerine bag containing an ounce of sparkling heroin.

'Get the works over here, pronto,' Corporal Murphy ordered Private Raj.

The tarnished stainless-steel syringe had the same rusty, blunt needle on it that it first had when Wang Doo had smuggled it into the POW camp six months previously.

A bent soupspoon was used to cook the heroin over the smouldering fire. Murphy gave an exaggerated smile, exposing two rows of missing and rotten teeth. He drew up the solution through the thick needle, filling the syringe's transparent glass barrel. Fury's leering face turned reptilian. As was the time-worn custom, the veteran sergeant took the first shot. Wang Doo was next, followed by Murphy, then Angus and finally Raj.

Within a week, the heroin was finished. Wang Doo disappeared from the compound. She returned two days later. Her face was badly bruised but, more importantly, she had a fresh ounce of China White. Business was good. When it was bad, Wang Doo brought raw morphine in the form of sticky pink powder, and then everyone complained, including Wang Doo.

And so the days and months drifted by in an opiate-induced haze. During the hot, turbid afternoons, the junkies scavenged for anything that was in the least bit edible, including dead sparrows and crows at the foot of the electrified perimeter fence. On a lucky day, they collected rotten turnips, thrown over the razor wire by taunting guards in uniform black fatigues. Raj dried faeces in the sun to provide cooking fuel. During the humid nights, they used candle flames on the seams of their clothes in a futile attempt to rid themselves of body lice and injected smack into their festering, scab-covered arms.

Whoomp! Whoomp! Whoomp! Let me tell you a story...

Disaster struck on a wet and extremely windy night. A typhoon had swept in from the South China Sea. Rainwater was cascading into the bamboo hut like an unwanted simulation of Niagara Falls. Wang Doo had finally returned, after an absence of several long days, during which Sergeant Fury and his three-man platoon of skag-head grunts experienced horrifying psychological withdrawal symptoms, muscle cramps and nausea.

'Wang Doo been working double-time,' she declared, sitting down on the compacted earth floor in a dry corner of the leaky wooden hut. 'Me buy Number One from fat Chinaman in Hanoi. Nice Chinaman give Wang Doo real good price. I give Chinaman real good time.' She pushed a cheek out and in with a dexterous tongue, in case anyone was in doubt as to what Wang Doo believed a good time represented.

Under the stark light of a high-wattage light bulb, everyone, including the Vietnamese whore, already smacked out of her head, was eager to sample the goods. Sergeant Fury, desperate for a quick hit, used a blunt penknife to bust up a quarter gram of heroin on a greasy tin plate. He formed four thick lines and snorted two up his crooked nose. 'Oooof!' 'Oooof!'

Wang Doo quickly performed a repeat of the human vacuum cleaner routine. 'Snuuuf! Snuuuf!'

Murphy held a match under a soot-blackened spoon to cook his fix. The rusty needle sucked up the bubbling solution. His face was a mask of filth, eyes gleaming in excited anticipation. He muttered, 'This is what you call a hot fuckin' shot.' He probed for a vein in his emaciated and badly infected left arm. He was just about to push down the plunger with his grubby right thumb, when Angus placed a restraining hand over his comrade's right wrist and calmly said, 'Don't.'

Murphy glared into his eyes. 'Why the fuck not?'

'There's something seriously wrong with that shit. Look.' Angus nodded towards Fury and Wang Doo. The couple were lying on their backs. Sergeant Fury was motionless, water from an overhead leak splashing off his face. Wang Doo's skinny legs juddered. There was a long shuddering exhalation and then she also lay absolutely still...in a puddle of her own urine.

Raj gaped. 'Fuuuuck!' he gasped. 'They're dead. What are we going to do now?'

Murphy stuck a grimy forefinger into the plastic bag containing the heroin. He withdrew his finger and licked at the glistening crystals adhered to it. 'Tastes fine to me.' He took another lick. 'In fact, I'd say this is the purest smack I've ever tasted. I reckon it's pure China White. Maybe three or four times more potent than the last batch.' He looked at the two corpses. 'Those stupid fuckers took too much.'

'Oh, that's a relief,' commented Raj. 'Now all we have to do is deal with two dead bodies in the middle of a fucking POW camp in hostile territory. I'm sure the gooks won't mind us dragging a couple of stiffs around the compound, seeing as how they're such obliging fellows and all that.'

'You're right,' Angus agreed. 'We're in even deeper shit than we normally are.'

'What a pair of wet blankets you two turned out to be,' Murphy said, looking around his soaking environment. 'We'll deal with the bodies tomorrow. Right now it's party time.' He started to mix up a fresh solution in the spoon. 'Or should I say snow time?' Just then, the camp generator ran out of diesel. The light bulb above his head flickered and died. Murphy's voice broke through the silence. 'You know, one of these nights, when the generator shuts down, I'm going to go through the wire and escape.' A match flared in the darkness and the stub of a candle was lit.

Murphy was right; the heroin was the purest they'd ever tasted. Tomorrow arrived three days later, by which time the two corpses had turned lime-green and were giving off a putrid stench.

Angus and Murphy cowered in the hut's doorway like two ashen-faced vampires unaffected by sunlight. The typhoon had rolled by and left the pale-blue sky free of cloud. Far in the distance, they could hear the stutter of automatic gunfire. High above, a squadron of B-52s headed north in a loose V-shaped formation. There did not appear to be a fighter escort. Murphy interpreted this as a good omen. 'The war will be over soon,' he said. 'It won't be long until this dump is liberated.'

'Now that the good news has been delivered,' said Angus, looking away from the sky to face his comrade, 'could we move on to what we're going to do with the two decomposing bodies. You know, the ones we just so happen to be sharing our living quarters with.'

Murphy rubbed at his nose. 'Don't worry about it, man. I have a plan.'
'You do?'

'Of course, I do. We're going to burn the bodies out in the compound.'

'Brilliant idea, Murphy. I don't suppose the gooks will notice us lighting a bonfire with two stiffs on it. Or the strong smell of burnt bacon hanging in the air. Oh, no, how could they? They'll be far too busy making conical straw hats, polishing bayonets, or perhaps writing a letter to Uncle Ho Chi Minh, telling their dear leader what a fun fuckin' time they're having watching their Yankee prisoners cremate each other. They're bound to get a commendation for that.'

'Very funny,' said Murphy. 'But I'm serious. I really do have a brilliant plan.'

Angus gave his genitals a frantic scratch. 'These fleas are driving me nuts. Anyway,' he said, 'let's hear it.'

Murphy talked while Angus listened, nodding in agreement because, within the broad parameters established by Murphy's completely warped logic and standards, the plan was a simple one and likely to succeed.

Whoomp! Whoomp! Whoomp! Let me tell you a story...

Corporal Murphy got word through to the camp commandant, Colonel Giang, that hygiene standards were not up to par in Hut 108, and he feared an outbreak of typhus fever or perhaps cholera. He suggested a bonfire would be the simplest remedy for ridding the camp of contaminated items, including mattresses, clothing and lengths of timber and bamboo rife with woodworm and vermin. The Viet Cong rarely entered the compound and were not in the least concerned about what was going on inside Hut 108, as long as the prisoners behaved themselves and did not complain about their deplorable living conditions. Word came back that, due to its being Ho Chi Minh's birthday, Colonel Giang had kindly given permission for the POWs in Hut 108 to light a celebratory bonfire.

Angus made an arrangement with Binh Dung, the watchtower guard. Binh Dung would leave five gallons of diesel in a fuel canister inside the electrified fence the next time the camp generator packed in, an almost nightly occurrence. In exchange for this Binh Dung would receive Sergeant Fury's military watch and twenty American dollars, a small part of the roll of paper money Murphy had discovered in Wang Doo's urine-soaked panties.

By snorting copious amounts of heroin, Raj was made fit for the grisly task of dismembering the putrefied corpses with a crude blade formed from a sharpened length of corrugated tin. Angus and Murphy discretely added gore-splattered body parts to the growing pile of refuse being built up in the centre of the compound.

There was a strong breeze blowing in from the east. Murphy lit a fuel-soaked rag and tossed it at the foot of the stack of rubbish. The diesel sprinkled over the pile ignited with a dull thud. Thick black smoke billowed up into the sky, to be quickly dispersed by the wind. Bamboo crackled and popped. A bedroll smouldered and burned. Flesh sizzled and fried.

Corporal Murphy rubbed his hands and said gleefully, 'This is just like Guy Fawkes.'

A skull exploded with a sharp crack.

Private Angus was not amused. 'If the gooks find out what we're using for fireworks, we'll be lined up and shot at dawn.'

Sky-blue flames congregated and danced at the centre of the intensifying blaze. An intense shriek could be heard emanating from the heart of the inferno.

'You hear that?' Raj asked. 'That's Fury and Wang Doo, screaming as they fly down the Highway to Hell.'

The blaze took two days to cool. The sun was setting when Murphy came into the hut with a handful of pure white powder. 'Check this out,' he said to Angus and Raj, seated on the floor, studying a bubbling pot with dull-eyed fascination.

'What's is it?' Angus asked, keeping his eyes fixed on the grass-snake stew.

'This,' declared Murphy, 'is something major. There's about twenty kilos of this shit at the centre of the bonfire's ashes. It tastes like smack. I'm going to try it.'

Raj looked up at him. 'You've lost the plot, man. Shoot up ashes and it's your body we will be burning next.'

'Raj, I know I'm crazy, man,' Murphy admitted. 'Although I'm not crazy enough to jack up this stuff. But I am crazy enough to fucking well smoke it!'

Murphy sat down in a corner and used a penknife to knock together a long-stemmed, bamboo pipe.

Whoomp! Whoomp! Whoomp! He could be your best friend. He could be your foe...

He used a match to heat a smidgen of the crystalline powder in the pipe's bowl. To no avail. He tried a second time. He huffed and puffed. No joy. More heat would be required to melt the powder, a product of high-temperature fusion. Murphy lit six matches in one go, held the flame over the pipe's bowl and sucked hard. The crystals vaporised. *'Ouff!'* He blew out an almost invisible jet of vapour with a spluttering cough. 'Oh wow,' was the last thing Angus heard Murphy say before his friend lay back on the earthen floor and closed his eyes.

Angus returned his attention to the evening meal. 'You think it's ready yet?' he asked Raj, who was stirring the watery stew with a dirty stick.

Raj fished out a round chunk of half-cooked snake from the black pot. He blew on it and popped the steaming piece of boiled reptile in his mouth. His jaw muscles worked in his thin face. 'No, not quite cooked to perfection yet,' he finally said. 'It's like chewing on a lump of hot silicone. Another ten minutes at least.'

Twenty minutes passed. Raj used a tin mug to ladle the thin stew into two waiting plates. 'What about Murphy?' he asked.

Angus went over to Murphy's prone body, gave it a nudge with a bare foot and returned to his previous sitting place by the smoky fire. 'Leave some in the pot for Murphy. He'll be back at some point and there will be hell to pay if we eat his share.' He then began to chew on his dinner. 'Not bad,' he said to Raj. 'Not bad at all.'

Raj smiled and removed some fine bones from his mouth. 'Amazing what you can come up with if you put your mind to it,' he said philosophically. 'That woodworm powder I used as seasoning adds a nice tangy flavour. Necessity really is the mother of—'

'Yargh!' Murphy yelled as he sat bolt upright in the corner. *'Wow! Wow! Wow!'*

'What a bloody fright,' Angus grumbled. 'I nearly jumped out of my skin.'

Murphy leapt over and settled by the fire. 'Funny you should say that because I just left my body and went for a float.' He nodded towards the pot. 'Any soup left?'

Raj poured what remained in the pot onto his comrade's waiting tin plate. 'So, what's the story?'

'The story is,' said Murphy, mumbling through a mouthful of foul-tasting snake soup, 'we've hit pay dirt. Somehow — you can call it magic if you want — we now have in our possession twenty kilos of the most mind-blowing and utterly mysterious substances I've ever had the pleasure of sampling in my entire life. I feel fantastic.' He poured his stew back into the empty pot. 'In fact, I feel so good I don't want to swallow another mouthful of whatever the fuck it is Raj cooked today. *'Yeehaw!'* He tossed his plate away, stood up and performed a spur-of-the-moment jig.

Angus and Raj watched Murphy reel around the room. There was a healthy aura surrounding their friend that had not been seen for months.

The conclusion was not long in coming.

Angus took a long draw on the pipe. The vapour tasted of aniseed. He exhaled and heard a rustling crackle. There was a build-up of pressure humming in his head. His surroundings broke down into a fuzzy molecular interplay. His eyes closed and he soared out of his body like a submarine-launched, heat-seeking missile homing in on the sun. He was no longer sure if he had a body or not but, when the thought came to look down, he saw he was high above the jungle. It was dark but he had some kind of ultra-violet night-vision that made the scene below glow in subtle fluorescent colours. It occurred to him that what he was experiencing might be taking place in his mind, or that he might have died. He looked in the direction he took to be up. He was presented with a flabbergasting vision of the Milky Way he'd only ever glimpsed before in astronomy books. Distant galaxies spun and turned in fantastic colour spectrums he had no name for. *Whoosh!* A fighter jet shot by. Angus decided to investigate. He surfed onto one of the twin-engine fighter-bomber's wingtips. He could see two helmeted air-men under the canopy. He drew closer and tried knocking on the canopy's reinforced Perspex, realizing as he did that he didn't have a hand to knock with. When the pilot's dark visor momentarily faced in his direction and then back to his glowing instrument panel and its shivering gauge needles, it confirmed to Angus that he'd been rendered invisible. There was no trace of his reflection in the pilot's reflective visor. He could hear the navigator talking to the pilot via a live mike. They were Americans and cruising at twenty thousand feet. A radio crackled. 'Green Strike,' said the voice of a ground air controller, 'this is King Bee. Bandits at two-ten-oh degrees, thirty miles. Over.' Angus did a backflip and watched the F-4 Phantom's blue-flamed afterburners recede into the distance.

Angus focused on his geographical location. He was hovering high above southwest North Vietnam. The large clearing that housed the POW camp came into focus. He could see roads cut into the glowing jungle, flooded rice paddies and a fast-flowing river of neon-blue effervescence moving south. Hut 108 came into view. *Whooomp!* Home sweet home. 'Man,' he breathed, opening his eyes, 'that was absolutely incredible.'

'I told you,' said Murphy in a singsong voice. 'And there's more good news. I think the stuff has healing properties. I'm not craving heroin and the scabs on my arms have stopped festering. It's a fuckin' miracle, man.'

Angus jumped up and did an impromptu jig, much in the way that Murphy had done earlier on. 'Man,' he yelled, 'I feel wonderful!' Murphy joined him and they spun around arm and arm, yelping and crying out in exuberance.

Raj, who'd also taken a big hit on the pipe, returned to earthbound reality. He leapt to his feet and joined his friends as they danced to the ever-present music that had increased in volume.

Whoomp! Whoomp! Whoomp! Went the big bass drum. *Let me tell you a story...*

The three friends chorused, 'It's about this man I know!'
He could be your best friend...

They pointed at each other accusingly. 'He could be your foe!' They burst out laughing. When they could laugh no more, they collapsed on the floor. *Whoomp! Whoomp! Whoomp!* And the band played on and on and on.

A week and many pipes of magic crystals later, it had become absolutely clear that the substance did indeed hold miraculous curative powers. Murphy's missing front teeth had grown back. All of their eyes were clear and bright. Parasitical insects no longer bothered them. They experienced no withdrawal from heroin abstinence or any compulsion to use the drug again. Although unwashed and filthy, their bodies exuded a sweet sandalwood fragrance and radiated a glow of health. All of their wounds and sores had healed leaving their skin without blemish. They did not suffer from hunger and thirst and therefore did not need food or liquids.

'This stuff is worth millions,' declared Murphy. It was night time and the three comrades were stretched out in the compound, staring up at innumerable stars, sparkling in the clear sky. 'Death is a disease, and we've discovered the cure. If we bring the crystals to Saigon,' he went on, 'we'd never have to work another day again in our lives. Thanks to the stuff we—'

Angus cut him off. 'You know, we have to come up with a name for *the stuff*, as we keep calling it. '

'Yeah,' Raj agreed. 'I've been thinking about that myself, and managed to come up with a brilliant name for it.'

Murphy sniggered. 'Oh, oh, here we go.'

'I think we should call it Wang Fu,' Raj continued, 'after our dearly departed friends, Wang and Fury. May they forever rest in peace. If it wasn't for their cremation and all the smack that must have been in their bodies, I'm quite sure the miracle drug would never have been created.'

'That's true,' Angus agreed, 'but Wang Fu sounds like something out of a Bruce Lee movie.'

'Which one?' Murphy asked. '*Chasing the Dragon?*'

In the end, Raj's suggestion won out. They spent the rest of the night smoking Wang Fu, exploring various alternate realities and dimensions. Upon returning from a midnight flight to Venus, Raj used a slightly adulterated quote that encapsulated the Wang Fu experience perfectly. 'It's like how that Chinese beatnik, Ching Hoo, put it. 'I was so high that I didn't know if I was a man who dreamt of being a dragonfly, or if I was a dragonfly dreaming that I was a man."

Whoomp! Whoomp! Whoomp! Let me tell you a story...

One unexpected development that came out of the Wang Fu sessions was the discovery of the POW camp's exact location and the fact that it was situated near a river. The river flowed in a south-easterly direction towards South Vietnam. South Vietnam meant freedom. The three POWs began to cultivate an escape plan, although Angus did not want to risk it. From what he'd heard while eavesdropping in the cockpits of B-52 bombers and listening to shouted conversations between door gunners on Huey helicopter gunships, the war was at a decisive juncture and would draw to a close any day soon. Murphy was motivated by greed and adventure. If he could bring twenty kilos of Wang Fu into Saigon he reckoned that it would fetch a price somewhere in the region of ten million American dollars. The problem was that if the war ended the GIs would be sent home, leaving no customers to buy the expensive and exotic product. As far as Raj was concerned, he would accompany Murphy because he felt it was only right to watch his comrade's back. A week before their capture near the DMZ, Murphy and Raj had been engaged in a life-and-death clash with the enemy, involving hand-to-hand combat in a muddy trench. A Viet Cong soldier was about to bury a bayonet in Raj's throat. Murphy came to the rescue and stove-in the enemy combatant's head with a golf club. Raj never did find out how Murphy came to be in possession of a 9-wood golf club in the DMZ, but he did know that the man who wielded it on the battlefield that day had without doubt saved his life, and left him forever in his debt.

The night of the great escape arrived. The camp generator sputtered to a halt on a moonless night. The light bulb in Hut 108 flickered and died as it had done on countless previous evenings. Private Raj and Corporal Murphy said a hurried farewell to Angus in the shadows, a ten-kilo waterproof package of Wang Fu strapped to each of their backs. As they shook hands, Angus experienced a moment of trepidation, wondering if he'd made the right decision to stay behind in the POW camp, waiting for the war to end. A prolonged rumble of artillery fire in the distance eased his anxieties. He sat hunched in the hut's doorway, watching his two comrade's shadowy forms crawl beneath the neutralized electric fence's razor wire. Then they were gone into the night.

Twenty minutes later, the camp's diesel generator chugged into life and the light bulb above Angus's head shone brightly. *Raj and Murphy will have reached the river by now,* he thought, imagining the fugitives commandeering a small fishing canoe and setting off downstream. *Good luck to them.*

Winged insects began to swarm around the bare light hanging from the corrugated tin ceiling. The night air was warm. Angus decided to celebrate the occasion by smoking a heavy dose of Wang Fu. He sat outside Hut 108 and struck half-a-dozen matches. The blue-tipped flame was sucked into the bamboo pipe, vaporizing the white crystals in its path. There was no pre-blast-off crackle in his brain. He felt his body flatten on the compound's dry earth. Something was wrong. Very wrong.

Whoomp! Whoomp! Whoomp! Let me tell you— The song that had always been playing suddenly stopped. A siren howled. *Oh, God, no!* Angus thought. *Raj and Murphy must have been captured. It's the firing squad for them. Maybe me also.* Darkness enveloped him. He tried to open his eyes, but couldn't. The siren's howling intensified. He drifted rudderless in a black void. *Am I dead?*

'Angus... Angus...' A pleading female voice called his name. 'Angus...

Angus...'

A shudder of great emotion ran through him.

'Lara?' His eyes sprung open.

Lara shrieked. 'Jesus bloody Christ!' Her face loomed above him, beautiful, concerned, shocked.

The images from Angus's dream vanished like vaporised Wang Fu crystals. He looked from side to side. He was in an ambulance, siren wailing. An oxygen mask enveloped his nose and mouth. Lara was wearing a gauze mask, covering the lower part of her face. Sitting opposite to her was a dark-skinned man, dressed in a black uniform and peaked hat, also wearing a white mask. Sweat glistened on the bridge of his nose.

Angus ripped his plastic mask off and asked, 'What's with the face masks?'

Lara slapped him on the face. 'You bloody irresponsible idiot! How could you have done that?'

'Calm down, Miss,' cautioned the paramedic. 'Your friend's going to be fine. We should arrive at the City Hospital in about ten minutes.'

Angus put a hand to his stinging cheek. 'What was that for?' He noticed tears in Lara's eyes. 'Done what?' he asked.

'Take a drug overdose in my mother's house,' she said, taking his right hand between both of hers. 'Monica brought you up a cup of tea and found you unconscious. You had a fucking syringe sticking in your arm! She nearly had a heart attack, but opted for throwing a fit of rage instead.' She added, 'I've never seen my mum so angry before. She completely freaked.'

The pieces tumbled into place in Angus's fuzzy brain. 'Man, I'm really sorry,' he apologised, his voice close to breaking. 'The... The pain was getting too much for me to handle. I just thought—'

Tyres screeched. The ambulance shot across a busy intersection on Aberdeen's Great Western Road.

Lara said, 'I was sure you were going to die. The paramedic thought you'd stopped breathing. Then you came to and started singing a daft song about some man you knew.' Her grip tightened on his hand. 'Anyway, you're alive and that's what counts. The sooner you're in a hospital bed, the better. I can't take much more of this.'

Angus was overcome with guilt. 'I really am sorry for what I've put you through,' he said, feeling it wasn't enough. 'I... I... I'll make it all up to you one day soon,' he promised, once more feeling his words were inadequate. 'Fuck it! I don't know what to say.' Angus gave it one more try. 'Lara, I love you.'

Lara smiled. 'I love you, too.' She paused. 'By the way, who's Wang Fu?'

It was Angus's time to smile. 'Wang Fu?' He chuckled. 'It's a long story.'

'Here we go,' announced the paramedic. 'City Hospital.'

The siren was switched off and the ambulance's back doors swung open onto what looked like the grounds of an old folks' home. Angus was transferred to a waiting gurney and wheeled into a grey building.

◆ ◆ ◆

Jean drained her whisky tumbler, leaned forward in her armchair, and looked accusingly at me. 'Hamish! That story you just told me is the biggest load of guff I've heard in my entire life.'

'I swear to God, Jean,' I said into the fireplace, taunting embers back to life with an iron poker, 'every word I've told you is true.'

'How can you expect me to believe that?' she asked, pushing her elbows back to stretch her upper back. 'How do you know Angus wasn't making that whole story up when he told it to you in Sri Lanka?'

'I just know, Jean,' I said, sitting back in the armchair opposite her. 'Angus didn't need to make stories up just for the sake of it. Besides, the British Medical Journal wrote an article about his case. Angus was the first person they used some kind of new scanner on at the time. He showed me the magazine.'

'What about all that Wang Fu nonsense? That couldn't possibly be true.'

'Not in real life. It was a dream,' I explained. 'Angus almost died from an overdose of morphine, an analgesic narcotic known to produce hallucinogenic, dream-like states. I mean to say, morphine is named after Morpheus.'

'What? Laurence Fishburne in *The Matrix*?' Jean asked with a playful smile.

I missed the humour in her question. 'Of course not,' I said seriously. 'Morpheus is the Greek god of sleep, with the ability to morph himself into different characters in dreams.'

'Fascinating, *Doctor Hamish*. And why were they wearing masks?'

Jean's jumping from one subject to another threw me off track. 'What masks?'

She sighed impatiently. 'The masks Lara and the paramedic were wearing in the ambulance. It's not as if they were about to be infected by a drug overdose.'

'Ehm... Right,' I said, back on track. 'They were wearing masks because, when Lara dialled 999, she told the emergency services that her friend had just returned from India and that he had typhoid. She did that because—'

'Don't tell me,' she interrupted. 'Lara said that because of the typhoid outbreak in Aberdeen back in nineteen-sixty-four. She thought that by telling them there was a typhoid case in Banchory Angus would receive prompt attention. That's why they rushed him to the City Hospital, because that's where they quarantined typhoid cases back in the Sixties.'

'Absolutely correct!' I confirmed. 'How on earth did you figure that out?'

Jean tapped the right side of her head with a forefinger. 'I've got this thing up here called a brain.' She nodded towards me. 'I'm not as stupid as you look.'

'Very funny.'

'So,' Jean said, moving along, 'Angus ends up in the City Hospital, where, I suppose, they find a cure for whatever it was he had. Then what?'

I rubbed my temples with my fingers. 'Well, it's not quite as straightforward as that. Yes, Angus recovered, but it took a hell of a long time from what I could gather. He didn't go into it in much detail. Funny enough, I was thinking of taking a wee trip up to Aberdeen.'

'Aberdeen!' Jean exclaimed. 'Surely Angus's story isn't so important that you need to go all the way up there to find out about it.'

'That's true,' I confirmed. 'But I have to go to Aberdeen next week to see about finalizing that deal on the sale of the land we own in Tullus. I was hoping you might like to accompany me.'

'You know, Aberdeen is not exactly my favourite place in Scotland. It's grey and miserable and so are the people.'

'I was thinking we could pay a wee visit to Mrs Shannon.'

'Who?'

'Lara's mother. I've heard that she is a remarkable woman.'

Jean frowned. 'I'd be surprised to hear that she ever spoke to Angus again after what happened.'

'They did more than speak,' I said. 'They went on to become close friends. Angus adored her.'

'So, apart from business and going to see Lara's mother, what else is on the agenda for Aberdeen?'

I thought about it and then answered, 'We could do a bit of driving up Royal Deeside, pop in and say hello to The Queen if she's up shooting deer on the Mar Estate, stay in some nice hotels and maybe make a wee honeymoon out of it.'

'*Hmm,*' Jean hummed, as if impressed. 'A wee honeymoon? I like the sound of that. You're on. When are we going?'

'How about the day after tomorrow?'

Jean bent towards me and offered her right hand. 'Deal!'

13

FROM HALLADALE TO SCOLTY

When we landed in Aberdeen, neither of us were surprised to find that it was raining. I picked up our rental car from an office near Dyce Airport Terminal and drove towards the granite city. Evidence of the ongoing oil boom was everywhere. Brand new top-of-the-range cars were queuing up at traffic lights. Articulated lorries, transporting steel pipes and supplies for the oil industry, threw up clouds of spray as they thundered by the strategically placed speed cameras at the side of the dual carriageway. New buildings, neither office blocks nor warehouses but a hybrid of both, were being built on muddy construction sites, under the extended mechanical arms of cranes rotating over chicken-coop housing schemes. Jean was the navigator and, when we took a wrong turn on the congested North Anderson Drive bypass, we laughed about it. The honeymoon had begun. We encountered no difficulty in finding the Marcliffe Hotel in Pitfodels on the western outskirts of Aberdeen. I've never felt comfortable in posh hotels, but I liked the Marcliffe's relaxed atmosphere. We ate lunch and took it easy for the rest of the day.

The following morning, I was up at dawn. The previous day's rain had dissolved into mist. After a quick breakfast, I drove over to the Tullus industrial estate to meet a representative of an international car dealership. He was overseeing the purchase of a tract of land I'd bought in conjunction with my deceased business partner, David Mann, almost thirty years ago. At nine o'clock precisely, a German-plated Mercedes pulled up at the gated entranceway to my land. A tall man, broad-shouldered and bulky in the chest without being overweight, got out of the black limousine. He was wearing an immaculate dark-blue suit. He strode towards me and introduced himself as Herr Klaus Zeidler. We stood by a chain-linked fence and exchanged pleasantries. A twelve-wheeled articulated lorry roared by with its horn blaring. A cloud of squawking gulls rose into the air over the small loch on the opposite side of the road. With a squeal of brakes, a white van drew up and a young man in tight jeans and a duffel coat with the hood up got out and approached us. He introduced himself to Klaus and myself, informing us that his name was Greg Watson and that he was the chartered surveyor, hired to check that the land's measurements were in accordance with what was written on the title deed.

Two hours passed, by which time I was seated beside Klaus Zeidler in a Polish lawyer's office in Aberdeen's Albyn Road. I signed several pieces of paper, shook hands and the deal was done. I'd just made close to a million pounds sterling from an original investment of thirty thousand. The money was to be transferred into my Royal Bank of Scotland account that very afternoon. I couldn't believe my good fortune. Inside my head, I heard Dave Mann's voice speak from beyond the grave. *Next to bricks and mortar, land is the best investment. Every day there is less of it and every day there are more people who want to buy it.*

I enjoyed an early lunch with Herr Zeidler in an up-market pub on Union Street. We shook hands for the fourth time that day and went our separate ways. I couldn't wait to get back to the Marcliffe Hotel to tell Jean the good news face to face. On impulse, I stepped into a jeweller's shop and used a credit card to purchase a solid gold, Cartier, *Juste un Clou* bracelet to give Jean something to add to her collection. On the way back to my car I dropped a fifty-pound note in a street beggar's hat. The bearded man had a ripped sleeping bag wrapped around his shoulders and, when he looked up at me in disbelief, I laughed and handed him another fifty quid. I was in a very good mood.

The following morning, Jean and I checked out of the Marcliffe Hotel. A bellhop loaded our suitcases into the boot of our rented Ford Mondeo.

Jean looked up at the sky. 'It's a miracle,' she declared. 'The sun is actually shining in Aberdeen. I'm dressed too warmly.'

It took us thirty minutes to drive to Banchory, the gateway to Royal Deeside. We drove into the quaint village, turned left at the golf course and then checked into the Tor-na-Coille Hotel, a beautiful converted country house with impressive gardens. I made a brief telephone call to Monica Shannon to confirm we would soon be arriving at her home, only a few miles drive from the hotel.

Back on the road, we drove a short distance before stopping at the Bridge of Feugh. We walked to the centre of a metal walkway and stood watching salmon leaping up a waterfall. The river was in spate and I found myself wondering how a fish could survive the battering it received in the violent torrent of brown water. A busload of Japanese tourists swarmed onto the bridge, prompting Jean and me to move on.

Halladale, Monica's house, was situated at the foot of Scolty Hill. The steep hill's most outstanding feature was a cylindrical stone tower on its summit. Her ivy-clad, two-storied house looked well maintained and rather big for an old woman who lived alone. We parked beside an olive-green Land Rover and walked over to the front door. I tugged on an old-fashioned bell-pull set in the doorframe and heard a bell chiming through the transparent barrier of the wooden door's triple-glazed window panels. One half of the double door swung inwards and there stood Mrs Shannon, waiting to greet us. My first impression was that she appeared remarkably fit and youthful for a women in her eighties. She didn't look a day over sixty. I would not have said she looked beautiful, but there was something attractive and noble in her cheerful face.

Monica stepped aside and beckoned with an elegant hand. 'Come on away in with you,' she said, in a lilting, Scottish accent. 'A pot of tea's brewing in the kitchen and there are freshly baked scones to go with it.' We crossed the tiled vestibule into a high-ceilinged hallway. 'You can hang your jackets there if you wish,' Monica announced, pointing to a shiny suit of armour with metal coat hooks welded to its polished breastplate. 'That's Archie by the way.' She added, 'He doesn't say much and the cat is terrified of him.' As if on cue, a well-fed Siamese cat wandered by, looked up at me with light-blue eyes, meowed once, glanced at Archie, hissed and scampered off into the house's interior. Monica chuckled. 'See what I mean?'

The kitchen was, like everywhere else in the house, spotlessly clean. I glanced up and saw exposed oak beams. Behind a pair of grey marble wash-basins, two arched windows looked out onto a well-manicured lawn, edged by flowering shrubs. A red, white and black-plumaged woodpecker clung to a bird feeder, swinging to and fro in the sunshine. There was an air of peace and solitude permeating the atmosphere, as tangible as the solid mahogany table that I found myself, Jean and Monica sitting around.

We drank tea, ate buttered scones and exchanged small talk for some time. Monica went along with it, but I could recognize by her slightly impatient expression that she was not someone accustomed to indulging in conversations based on life's mundane superficialities. Jean was showing off her newly acquired Cartier bracelet. Monica glanced at it and said, 'It looks like a bent nail.'

I stood up to look more closely at a framed black and white photograph, hung on a tiled wall behind the Rayburn. It was a photograph of Angus and Lara, sitting cross-legged at the foot of a stone Buddha. They were looking into the camera with slightly bemused expressions.

'I love that photo,' Monica called out from her place at the table. 'I still miss their presence in the house almost every day. You know, after Angus was discharged from hospital, they spent eighteen months with me here. I learned so much from them, and I hope they learned a little from me. Your brother is a truly remarkable man.'

I looked away from the photograph and turned to face Monica. Her long, light-grey hair was tied back in a thick ponytail, slung over a shoulder and reaching down to the leather belt circling her narrow waist. Her spine was ramrod straight. 'Do you really think so?' I asked.

'What?' Monica tilted her head in a questioning manner. 'Do I really think Angus is an outstanding fellow? Why, of course, I do. Don't you?'

I shrugged. 'I'm more inclined to describe your daughter as truly remarkable.' I looked at my wife. 'Jean thinks Angus is—'

'Hamish, darling,' said Jean, cutting me off, 'I'm perfectly capable of speaking for myself.' She smiled blandly at Monica before continuing. 'I think Angus is a bit of a troublemaker. Yes, he's a great guy and all that. But he's also completely irresponsible. Do you know, Angus has still not contacted us to let us know that he and Lara, who I love dearly, survived the tsunami in Sri Lanka? We had to have a police inspector pass on the good news to us in Oban. Of course, knowing that *truly remarkable man*, Angus, he'll appear out of nowhere one day to give us a pleasant surprise, and behave as if everything is one big, cosmic, bloody joke!'

Monica laughed. 'I appreciate your honesty, Jean. And I do agree that Angus is a bit of a lad, as they say. But he is also very courageous, wise, adventurous, exceptionally kind-hearted and above all as funny as can be.' I was touched to see that Monica's eyes were getting a bit teary in the process of conjuring up Angus's wild spirit. She concluded. 'You know, I still crack up recalling the last joke he told me when I was over in Sri Lanka.'

'What kind of joke?' Jean asked, her mouth so tense it looked like she was ready to hear a joke in the worst of taste.

'Shall I tell it to you?' Monica asked, obviously eager to do so.

'Please do,' I said, sitting back down at the table and helping myself to another scone.

'Well,' she began, 'It goes like this. A young man is driving his MG sports car along a narrow country road at high speed. A large hare bounds out from under a hedge. It stops in the middle of the road. The young fellow slams on the breaks. Too late. The driver gets out to take a look. The hare is now embedded in the MG's radiator grill. The young driver feels devastated. You see, he just so happens to be a nature lover. He begins to cry. Just then, a red Ferrari pulls up next to him and a stunning blonde in a short skirt and high heels steps out of the gleaming car. 'Whatever's the matter?' she enquires. 'Can I be of assistance?'

The young fellow sniffs and points to the dead hare. 'Look what I've done. Killed a beautiful wild animal. I feel terrible!'

The woman takes a closer look at the dead hare, smiles and says, 'Oh, poor little thing. Don't worry, though, I have just the thing to fix it up as right as rain.'

'Fix it up?' splutters the young man. 'How on earth do you propose to *fix up* an animal that is stone dead?'

The blonde rummages in her shoulder bag and produces an aerosol can. 'With this,' she declares, spraying fine mist towards the dead hare.

All of a sudden there is movement in the car's radiator grille. The dead hare pulls itself together and springs back onto the road. The hare gives the humans a toothy grin, raises a paw in farewell and bounds away.

'Jesus Christ! exclaims the man. 'I can't believe this is happening. This must be some kind of miracle.'

The hare continues up the road. Every few yards it turns and waves to the two motorists, standing in the middle of the road, watching him recede into the distance.'

The young man turns to the blonde and says, 'My God. What is that stuff you sprayed on the hare?'

The woman smiles and hands him the aerosol can.

He reads the label. It says, 'Vitalis Hairspray. Restores life to dead hair and leaves it with a permanent wave'.'

Monica fell silent and looked at us.

Jean and I laughed awkwardly at first, and then wholeheartedly. And then Monica did, too. It wasn't so much that the joke was funny, but rather how it had been told by a dignified old lady. We guffawed until our laughter became all that mattered. That was when I knew we were going to become good friends.

During the afternoon, Monica informed us she'd received several post-cards from Lara during the past year, from various locations. The last card had been posted from Amsterdam. Monica handed me the postcard. I read it. *Miss you, mum. Hope to visit soon. Angus sends his love. Lots of hugs and kisses. Lara.*

On the front was a photograph of tulip fields with a wooden windmill off to one side. I turned the card over and peered at the postmark. March 21, 2009. Two months ago.

Towards evening, we wandered into the garden and sat around a green plastic table, nibbling on savoury snacks and drinking tea. I must have drunk a gallon of strong tea that afternoon. The air was warm. Bees buzzed as they flitted from flower to inviting flower. The sound from the road in the distance was barely audible. The situation was idyllic.

Before we left, Monica invited us to come and stay for a few days. We returned the following afternoon and soon settled into a peaceful country existence. On our third day, we set off on a cross-country hike. Monica had tremendous stamina. Jean and I struggled to keep up with her. We arrived breathless at the twenty-meter tall Scolty monument and went up the stone steps that led up to the observation platform. The view was splendid. The pleasant weather had continued. The air was crystal clear. Spread out below was the undulating green tapestry of the Dee Valley. In the distance, we could see the Grampian Mountains, some peaks still capped by snow. Not for the first time, I was struck by Scotland's great natural beauty.

That evening, we ate a light supper in the kitchen and afterwards we went through to the comfortable lounge where Monica had lit a fire in the grate, creating a snug ambience. She poured three healthy shots of whisky into cut-glass tumblers and we toasted each other in front of a crackling blaze to the sound of a Mozart piano concerto, tinkling in the background. The days were growing longer. Even though it was nine in the evening, it was still light outside. I sat for some time in a leather armchair, gazing out the bay window at pink-tinged clouds drifting behind towering pines. Then I remembered I wanted to ask Monica about Angus's time in the hospital, in the hope that she'd be willing to describe the process that led to his com-plete recovery.

'Monica,' I said, looking over a glass tabletop towards her, 'I was just wondering—'

'Please, Hamish, I've already told you to address me as Mona.'

'Oh, I'm sorry, *Mona*. I'll begin again. I've been wondering if you might describe to us what happened to Angus when he first arrived here. You know, when he went to the hospital after returning from India.'

Monica's chair creaked as she shifted position. Her face took on a pained expression. She shook her head as if to rid it of unwanted memories.

Jean glanced at me like a disapproving granny might do when faced with the prospect of reprimanding an insolent grandchild. She looked away from me, leaned forward in her antique armchair and said, 'Are you alright, Mona? You don't have to speak about these things if you don't wish to.'

Monica raised the palm of her left hand. 'No, Jean, I'm fine. It's... It's just that it was such a dreadful time to witness in someone's life.' Her voice bore a hint of sorrow. She looked directly into my eyes. 'Oh, the pain and suffering that your poor brother underwent. When I think about it, I always wonder where he got the strength to overcome what he had to go through.'

I commented, 'I think it might have had something to do with Lara hitting him on the head with a cooking pot.'

Monica nodded. 'Yes, she told me about that. The poor girl was guilt-ridden. As for Angus, I can easily imagine him needing a good wallop to wake him up to the realities of his plight. He can be such a dreamer. Like he's living on another planet.' She shook her head remembering. 'I'll never forget the first time I met him at Dyce Airport. He really did look like death warmed up. There's no better way to describe it.' She sighed and bent forward to poke at the fire. Her movements were precise and practised. As I observed her, I couldn't help thinking Monica was trying to hide something. Sadness, perhaps. When the fire began to blaze again, she leaned the iron poker upright against her side of the granite fireplace. 'And then there was that incident in the guest bedroom upstairs,' she went on. 'The room where you two are now. The damned fool took an overdose of morphine. It was me who found him unconscious with a bloody syringe lodged in his arm. I thought at first that Lara's new boyfriend was one of those poor drug addicts that you hear about in the news. Of course, I found out later the real reason behind why he needed such a strong painkiller.' Monica drained her glass, sat up straight and entered more deeply into her narration.

Monica described how Angus was kept in a strict isolation unit at Aberdeen's City Hospital. Blood, urine and stool samples were rushed to a laboratory for analysis. The results came back within twenty-four hours, ascertaining that Angus was not carrying typhoid. But his wrecked body was definitely host to something, but nobody could say for certain what that something was.

The man in charge of Angus's case was Doctor D. D. Smythe, a dedicated specialist in contagious diseases. Angus met him for the first time on the morning after the day he'd been admitted into the hospital.

Angus woke up and looked around the room, which, unknown to him at the time, was to become his home for four months. A ceiling fan turned slowly above his bed; ineffective as far as circulating the turbid, over-heated air went. Nothing was hanging on the magnolia, matt-painted walls to break up their stark monotony. He faced a dull green door with a small window at head height, set into a varnished wood frame. A ruddy-complexioned man's face appeared in the window. The door swung inwards. A tall, bulky man in a white overcoat strode into the room. His body language and the expression on his face were vigorous and resolute. Two similarly attired men and two nurses, wearing light-blue uniforms, accompanied him.

'Good morning Mister...' The tall doctor unhooked a clipboard from the foot of the bed and glanced at it. '...Sheridan.' Angus was still going under the name supplied by the passport Acid Mike had given him six years earlier. The doctor frowned. 'My name is D.D. Smythe and I will be in charge of your case until you're discharged. How are you?'

Angus sighed and said, 'I'm accepting my fate.'

The doctor studied him for a few moments and then said, with the slight increase in a Scottish accent that usually indicates annoyance, 'Listen up, laddie, just so we start on the right footing. Don't give me that *I'm accepting my fate* nonsense. I've made it my vocation in life to manipulate fate as much as possible on a daily basis. I can see that you are in bad shape, but I can assure you that I've seen a lot worse. I'll do all that is within my power to bring you back to health. But I won't be able to do that if you lie there like a sack of bloody tatties, meekly telling me that you are *accepting your fate*. Am I making myself understood, James?' Doctor Smythe asked forcefully.

Angus lay looking up at the physician, feeling as if he'd just received a whack on the head from a Zen master wielding a wooden club. 'Ehm... Yes, Doctor Smythe,' he replied, 'I understand you loud and clear.'

The doctor smiled for the first time since entering the room. 'Good. Now then, could you try and sit up, please.'

Angus did as requested. The simple act of sitting up triggered multiple agonies, causing him to cry out.

Doctor Smythe turned to the man wearing a white cotton housecoat on his left. 'Simon, get the patient on a morphine drip immediately. We'll put James here on Septrin for the time being.' Simon scribbled on a notepad and hurried off. Smythe turned to his right and addressed one of the nurses. 'There is no record of the patient's blood pressure. See to it.' The nurse tugged an ear lobe and stood there as if unaware of her physical location. Smythe raised his deep voice. 'If it's not too much trouble, Nurse Ross, I'd very much appreciate if you attended to that immediately.' Nurse Ross gulped then shot out of the open door as if a swarm of angry hornets had just buzzed up her skirt.

Doctor Smythe returned his attention to Angus. 'We'll need more blood samples later today. I'm not yet certain what it is you have. I have my suspicions, but they are not yet confirmed. Some form of bacterial infection. I will have to have your lower back x-rayed.' He glanced at the other man to check that he was taking notes. He was. 'You're obviously in a lot of pain, James, so we'll have you on a morphine drip soon.' He studied the clipboard for a moment. 'I see you were admitted after having overdosed on drugs. Are you an intravenous drug user?'

Angus cringed inside. He felt like a steamroller had driven over his self-esteem. 'No,' he answered. 'I injected the morphine because it was the only thing available that helped me cope with the pain.'

'Alright, I understand. A bit foolhardy, to say the least,' commented the doctor, hooking the clipboard to the end of the bed. 'That's it for this morning.' He started to turn away and then, looking once more at Angus, he said, 'And remember what I told you. Don't just lie there like a—'

Angus completed the sentence. 'Sack of potatoes.'

Doctor Smythe pushed fingers through his thick, grey hair. 'Aye, that's right. Good to see that you know how to listen.' He gave Angus a warm smile that went straight to his heart.

Nurse Ross hurried into the room. A plastic cuff was fastened around Angus's almost non-existent left bicep and inflated. The nurse wrote down his blood pressure on the clipboard. 'It's a fine day,' she said, her voice charged with professional cheerfulness. 'Lunch will be along soon. So, you have something to look forward to today. Mince and tatties, I believe.' And, with her well-meant words still hanging in the air, she was gone. Just the thought of food made Angus feel nauseous. He focused his mind elsewhere. He reflected on his first meeting with D.D. Smythe and felt inspired. It struck him as ironic that he'd travelled to India to meet spiritual masters and now, out of the blue, he'd encountered a master in Scotland. There was no doubt in his mind that Doctor Smythe was indeed a master. The man exuded energy and compassion, an empathic response that can be delivered by a swift stroke from a sharp sword. Master Smythe's words came back to him. *I've made it my vocation in life to manipulate fate as much as possible on a daily basis.* Angus tried to sit up, but found it impossible.

Two weeks drifted by in a morphine-induced fog. Angus swung in and out of consciousness and, if anything, his condition was worsening. He could no longer feel his feet. He'd crossed a new threshold of pain, which came in lightning bolt spasms that lifted him off the bed. He was wheeled out of the hospital and into the back of a waiting ambulance. He was being transported to Aberdeen's Royal Infirmary, to have section-by-section scans taken by a newly developed nuclear scanner. By the time Angus reached the infirmary, a massive pain attack racked his body and left him screaming for morphine. He was sedated and transferred to a bed in a communal ward. When Angus came around, he checked out his roommates in a scene that could have been taken from a film adaptation of Dante's *Inferno*. He reckoned the majority of the two-dozen patients were road accident victims. To his right lay a man with his head encased in a metallic contraption that kept his shaved skull absolutely still; his neck had been broken by whiplash. To his left was a middle-aged man dressed in striped pyjamas.

220

He was sitting on the edge of his bed, smoking a cigarette, its ash almost an inch long. His head was covered in large bumps. He noticed Angus staring at him, and stubbed out his cigarette with fingers stained brown from tobacco smoke. He stood up, arms akimbo. He wobbled towards Angus like every joint in his body was dislocated. He extended a shaky hand and said, 'Craig.'

Angus shook the clammy hand and asked, 'What happened to you?'

Craig gave a lopsided shrug. 'Nothing, pal. I was born like this.'

The gravity contained in the man's simple answer crushed Angus's heart like an ice-cold vice. He looked around and thought about the shocking world he now inhabited, the vast realm of ill-health, filled with misery, terrible ordeals and misfortune.

Angus did not sleep all night. In the darkness, the sick coughed, groaned and cried out in anguish in a choral symphony from Hell. Just before dawn, there was a commotion three beds along from where he lay. Someone had died.

It was late morning when Angus was delivered by wheelchair to a subterranean room with a large scanner as its centrepiece. He was slid into the machine's circular core and requested by a Pakistani technician to remain still. The scanner hummed into action. Angus controlled his breathing in order to hold off a spasm attack that he could feel straining to break out from the base of his spine.

Two more sleepless nights passed in the ward of horrors before word came through that he was to undergo a biopsy. Once again, Angus found himself staring up at strip lights, flashing by on lowered ceilings as he was wheeled by gurney along the factory-like corridors of the National Health Service. He hadn't seen Lara in three days and missed her devoted and reassuring presence.

He was delivered to an operating theatre that smelled strongly of surgical spirit. A surgeon, dressed in blue scrubs, matching hat and face mask, informed him that the biopsy he was about to perform required a long needle to penetrate the stomach walls, to take a bone sample from the inside of Angus's third lumber vertebrate. The gleaming surgical instrument reminded Angus of something he'd seen in a horror film he'd snuck into when he was a kid in Glasgow. The surgeon also explained to Angus that he would receive a general aesthetic from an anesthesiologist. A younger man in similar attire and horn-rimmed glasses stepped to the fore. He said in a Welsh accent, 'Now, Mister Sheridan, this won't hurt at all.' Angus felt a prick in his left arm, an uncomfortable sensation that he was by now accustomed to. The anaesthesiologist nudged his glasses up with a rubber-gloved knuckle and went on. 'I'd like you to count down from ten.' Angus began counting down in his head. *Ten... Nine... Eight... Seven...* Darkness enveloped him. He blacked out like a television in a power cut.

Whoomp! Whoomp! Whoomp! Let me tell you a story... Angus hauled himself out of a spiralling free fall through clouds over North Vietnam. He had no desire to return to Hut 108's nightmarish realities or to smoke any more Wang Fu. His eyes sprang open. He saw the ceiling fan slowly turning above him and realised he was back in his private room in the City Hospital, although he held no recollection of how he'd got there. It was a late-summer morning. The window was open. Curtains billowed from a breeze that carried the pong of rotten eggs, a stink that originated from the nearby coal-fuelled gasworks.

'You're back.'

He turned his head. 'Lara?' he said, taken by surprise. 'Man, the last thing I remember about this world was counting down from ten in an operating theatre.'

Lara smiled. 'How are you feeling?'

Angus shrugged. 'Comfortably numb, I suppose.' It was then he noticed Lara's left hand resting on the white bedcover over his right leg. He could not feel the pressure from her hand. He tried moving his legs. He couldn't. The command signal from his brain wasn't getting through to his lower body. 'Oh, oh,' he said.

'What?' Lara enquired.

'I've suddenly noticed a fresh development in Mister Sheridan's condition.'

Lara sensed something was seriously wrong. Her forehead creased with anxiety. 'Angus, stop fooling around. What the hell is it?'

'Well, old girl,' he said, putting on an Oxbridge accent, 'I'm frightfully sorry to inform you that James is now paralyzed from the waist down.'

'You're joking?'

'I wish I was. But I'm not. I can't feel my legs.'

'Bloody hell!' Lara cursed. 'I thought you were supposed to be getting better, not worse.' Tears streamed over her cheeks and a sob broke from her lips. Soon, she was snatching sharp inhalations of breath between intermittent sobs.

The sight of her distress broke his heart. Angus wept for her, bringing on a pain attack that made him cry out in agony. Lara hit the red emergency button. Moments later, a nurse rushed into the room. When she saw what was taking place, she quickly recalibrated the morphine drip to increase the flow. Angus was soon drifting in oblivion. Morphine does not take the pain away, it takes you to a place beyond the pain.

Two days later, Doctor D.D. Smythe marched into Angus's hospital room. He was alone. It was obvious from his excited expression that there had been a new development in Angus's case. A positive one.

'Good morning, James,' said Doctor Smythe, pulling up a chair and sitting down at Angus's bedside. 'I have good news and I have bad news. Which one do you wish to hear first.'

Angus did not hesitate in answering. 'What's the bad news?'

222

Smythe gave a knowing chuckle. 'That's generally what my patients ask first. I think it must have something to do with the human need to hear the worst because that shifts the survival program into top gear. Gets the old juices flowing.' He pulled out a plastic x-ray sheet from a folder and handed it to Angus. 'This x-ray shows you have swelling behind your third lumber vertebrae. Note the perforations.' Angus studied the x-ray but was not sure what he was looking for. His third lumbar vertebrae looked like a lump of cheese with holes in it. He held the plastic sheet towards the open window. The doctor leaned over the bed and pointed to the spot that required scrutiny. 'Just there,' Smythe said, jabbing a forefinger. 'That is a tumour. The biopsy report shows that it is the result of tuberculosis.'

'But isn't TB a disease of the lungs?' Angus asked.

'Yes, generally it is. But it can also affect other parts of the body. In your case, the spine. Bone tuberculosis is an ancient disease. Research has detected it in Egyptian mummies. What is exceptionally rare about your tuberculosis bacteria is that they are bovine in origin, which means you might have contracted it from drinking contaminated milk in India. The scan you had in the Royal Infirmary found a hairline crack in your L three vertebrae.'

Angus flashed back on when he'd help shift iron girders after a street accident in Bombay.

Smythe continued, 'The TB bacteria have left your lower spine peppered with holes to the extent that they have eaten through to your spinal cord. Hence the paralysis of your lower limbs.'

'Jesus!' Angus gasped, struggling to keep cool as his stomach tensed and knotted. 'Give me the good news, quick!'

'The good news is that there is a tried and tested cure,' said Smythe, his voice unusually pleasant. 'I am confident it will work. I'm going to put you on a course of Rifnah-300. It's a powerful antibiotic that has the ability to kill intracellular and extracellular microorganisms. Rifnah has been associated with liver dysfunction and therefore you will be remaining here with us for some time, so we can keep you under observation.'

'For how long?'

The doctor closed his right eye for a moment before answering. 'It's early days yet, but I'd say at least a couple of months.'

Angus swallowed hard and remained silent.

Three days later, Angus awoke from an afternoon nap to a scene that gave him one of the biggest shocks of his life. Standing around his bed, looking down at him with concerned faces, stood Lara, Monica, Acid Mike, Raj, Murphy, Alice and Nina. Alice and Nina had gained a lot of weight and held babies to their chests. Alice's eyes were brimming with tears. Nina was gnawing at her lower lip.

'Surprise!' They chorused.

Angus thought, *Oh, man, this is it. I'm going to die. I'm on my way out.* His nervous eyes focused on Raj, who nodded and smiled, his big teeth very white in his dark-brown face.

Murphy ran a thumb and forefinger across his bushy moustache and then broke the thick silence hanging in the room. 'Angus, man, you look like fuckin' shit.'

Still in a state of shock, Angus said, 'Hi, Murphy, good to see you, man.' Noting a mischievous glint in his old friend's eyes, he added, 'And, for fuck's sake, don't do anything daft. Laughing could quite literally kill me with pain.'

Murphy pointed two forefingers towards himself. 'Who me? Do something daft?' He glanced around, searching for inspiration. 'Hold on!' he said. 'I've just had a brainwave.'

'That's impossible,' commented Raj, 'because you don't have a brain.'

Angus knew something crazy was about to happen. 'No! Murphy, please, don't do whatever the fuck it is you're thinking of doing. I'm begging you, man.'

'*Aieeeee!*' Murphy yelled as he ran across the room and dived out the open window.

The room erupted in laughter. Angus had a laughing fit and was wracked by excruciating pain as a result. He reached for the morphine regulator and turned the notched, black plastic wheel to the maximum. The drug streamed into his vascular system. A chuckling Murphy clambered back into the room through the window.

The afternoon passed in a blur of conversation, occasional bursts of subdued laughter and, most importantly of all, an outpouring of love and friendship. As far as Angus was concerned, it was just what the doctor ordered.

Acid Mike was the last to leave the room. He sat holding Angus's hand, tilted back his tie-dye headband and said, 'Listen, matey, you look like you've been dragged through Hell and back by a tractor. But, from what Lara's told me, you will soon be on the mend. When you're fit and ready, come to Amsterdam. I'm onto something amazing. It's going to go global.' Mike's smouldering blue eyes were positively glowing. 'I've got my hands on a new designer drug, coming out of California. It's called MDMA and it's going to start a revolution.'

Angus shook his head. 'Sorry, Mike, my dealing days are over.'

'That's what you think, matey,' said Mike, letting go of Angus's hand and rising to his feet. 'Mark my words. You will only need to take MDMA once to change your mind. I've left a dozen sample hits with Lara. You can try it out. Once you're on your feet again, that is.' Mike began walking towards the door. He opened it, then turned back into the room. 'Be strong, my friend. This too will pass.' He raised a hand in farewell. The door closed behind him.

Angus smiled. *Acid Mike,* he thought, *what a man. MDMA? Sounds like an acronym after a doctor's name.*

It was a grey and windy November morning. Lara collected Angus from the City Hospital. He could barely walk and had to use aluminium crutches to reach Monica's Land Rover. He still wasn't used to sitting up straight. Lara drove slowly. When they stopped at a traffic light on Aberdeen's principal thoroughfare, Union Street, Angus stared in fascination at the pedestrians crossing the road in front of him. It struck him how everyone took it for granted that they could walk without support. The traffic thinned on the city's outskirts. They entered the two-lane road to Banchory. Most of the roadside's deciduous trees had already shed their leaves. As they approached the village, Angus spotted Scolty Monument on a distant hill's summit. He asked what it was and Lara explained that it was an old war memorial quite near to her mother's home. Angus declared, 'I swear that when the day arrives that I can jog up there, without stopping for a breather, will be two days before we leave here and head for Amsterdam.'

Lara took her left hand off the black steering wheel, reached over and patted his emaciated right thigh, barely as thick as her arm. 'Step at a time, my darling,' she said. 'Step at a time.'

Angus kept his eyes fixed on the stone tower, a target at which he aimed his will like an iron-tipped arrow. His jaw set in stubborn determination. He'd established a seemingly impossible goal for himself, but nothing would stop him until he achieved it.

Monica, who'd visited Angus at least once a week in the hospital, was waiting to greet them when they drew up in front of her house. Grey smoke was rising from a chimneypot. Angus got out of the four-by-four and took a deep breath. The air smelled fresh and clean with a hint of burning pine. *Freedom*, he thought. *This is the smell of freedom. I love it.* He stood with his crutches, gazing up at the overcast sky as if it were the first time he'd seen it.

Monica took hold of his arm. 'Are you feeling alright, Angus?'

He hobbled towards her and planted a kiss on her worried forehead. 'Never felt better, Mona,' he lied. 'Never felt better.'

Monica shook her head and chuckled. 'I certainly don't believe that for a moment, young man. But I do so very much appreciate your enthusiasm.' She tugged at his arm. 'Come away in with you. You're not used to being out of doors. The last thing we need now is for you to catch a cold.'

And so began Angus's convalescence. Remote, deserted and shrouded by mist, the Scolty Monument stood like a silent sentinel, patiently awaiting his arrival.

Angus and Lara made love for the first time in what felt to him like an eternity. He'd been dreaming about how it might be for too long a time. The sudden realization of how dull and toneless dreams are in relation to the living moment hit him in the testicles like an electric cattle prod. Lara straddled his stiff cock and rode it like she was out to win a steeplechase. When she crossed the finishing line for the third time, she shrieked in ecstasy. Angus's simultaneous orgasm felt like he was ejaculating molten rock. The howl that erupted from his throat was powered by an intense combination of extreme relief and burning pain fused with pleasure. Lara collapsed onto his skinny body and whispered in his ear. 'If my mum heard that she would have broken down the door, thinking we were in the process of murdering each other.'

It took Angus three months to be able to bend his back enough to tie his shoelaces. He began to walk without crutches. The winter was a particularly hard one. Six feet of snow lay outside. Temperatures dropped below minus 10° Celsius, reminding Angus of the cruel winter on Iona that had killed his step-father, Daniel. Angus discovered a book on Hatha Yoga on a shelf in Monica's extensive library. He started practising basic asanas and stretching techniques. By early March the snow had melted and Lara and he ventured into Aberdeen to buy an electric treadmill and a set of dumbbells from a sports shop.

Every morning before breakfast, Angus walked over to a ramshackle cabin at the far end of the garden and switched on the treadmill. On Sundays, he'd raise the treadmill's incline and increase the speed at which the kilometres passed. By the summer's end of 1982, Angus was jogging at ten kilometres an hour on a fifteen percent incline. He could only keep that pace up for twenty minutes, a long way off from his goal of one hour. When the weather permitted, Lara, Monica and he went for long walks in the verdant countryside. In the evenings they cooked, chatted and played card games. Monica did not have a television. She was a great lover of classical music; her favourites were always violin concertos.

On the Christmas holidays of that year, Monica went to stay with friends in Edinburgh for a fortnight, leaving Lara and Angus to enjoy Halladale on their own. It was Christmas Eve and once more heavy snow was falling, the window panes edged by frost. Lara and Angus were sitting in companionable silence in the lounge, their attention focused on the crackling blaze in the granite-faced fireplace. Suddenly, Angus remembered something.

'Hey, Lara,' he said, 'Acid Mike told me he left some pills with you for us to try out. Do you still have them?'

Lara had to think about it for a few moments before she answered. 'Yeah... Yeah, I think I stashed them in an old jewellery box at the bottom of the wardrobe in our bedroom. Why?' she asked. 'Do you want me to go and get them?'

'Yes. Why not? Maybe tonight's the night to take a wee trip to celebrate Christmas and all that.'

Lara disappeared upstairs for five minutes and returned with a small plastic packet. 'Here you go,' she said, tossing it onto his lap.

Angus removed two oval-shaped, white pills from the packet and studied them. He looked across at Lara, who had returned to her leather armchair. 'They look like Paracetamol tablets.'

'What are they supposed to do to you?' Lara asked. 'Knowing Mike, they're probably some kind of psychedelic.'

'I'm not sure,' said Angus. 'Mike wasn't too specific. But he was enthusiastic. Said he thought it was going to be the next big thing or something like that. It's called PMDA, I think. I can't remember exactly.'

'PMD?' Lara sniggered, unzipping her red, Aberdeen University hoodie. 'If it's a cure for premenstrual depression, I'll have two, please.'

'So, you up for it then?'

'Yes. But only one pill. I don't feel like tripping out of my head and imagining a soot-blackened Santa is coming down the lum singing Jingle Bells.'

Lara went into the kitchen and returned with two glasses of water. They washed down a pill each. The mantelpiece clock ticked out the seconds.

Twenty minutes later, Angus felt like he was ascending in a high-speed elevator. 'Phew!' he gasped. 'This... This stuff is strong.' He said, his voice constricted by a racing pulse. 'I feel like I'm coming up on acid.'

Lara said nothing. She smiled at him and closed her eyes.

Angus's sensation of upward acceleration increased until he levelled out on a clear plateau. Unlike the increasing peaks of the LSD experience, MDMA brought him to a lucid high that didn't carry any particularly jarring visions or uncomfortable physical sensations. He simply felt extremely happy to be alive and basked in the pleasure of being in the presence of the person he felt closest to in the world. He looked over at Lara. She still had her eyes closed. Candlelight added a touch of warmth to her face. Her smile was serene. He was inspired by her silent example and closed his eyes. He felt no division between body, mind and spirit, just a natural oneness that encompassed all and everything. He felt an opening in the centre of his chest. The simple act of breathing became a miraculous revelation, divulging profound secrets related to the subtle mechanics of life's give and take process. He only needed to think of a friend and they appeared in his mind's eye, with all their utterly perfect imperfections. This, for Angus, was the drug's most fascinating aspect; its capacity to amplify empathy to a point where you truly understand not only how it felt to stand in another person's shoes, but also comprehend how it might feel to dance a few steps in their feet. He heard Acid Mike's deep voice in his head. *You will only need to take MDMA once to change your mind.* Angus remembered the abbreviated name of the drug he'd taken and he wished he could share how he felt at that moment with all of his friends.

'This stuff is amazing!'

Lara's voice returned him to his physical location. Angus stood and went over to her. He knelt in front of her and stared into her green eyes. An overwhelming feeling of love washed over him. Lara appeared to be the ideal incarnation of all things feminine. He breathed in her sweet scent. It crossed his mind to pull her down beside him and make love with her in front of the open fire. The notion went as quickly as it arrived, everything already seemed so perfect. *Besides,* he reasoned, *the night is young and so are we. Plenty of time for that later.*

'I feel like dancing,' Lara announced. 'Don't you?'

The thought hadn't occurred to him, but it sounded like a brilliant idea. A pain-filled lifetime had passed since he'd last danced. He rose to his feet and went over to a long shelf housing Monica's record collection. It was mostly composed of classical music. Towards the end of the shelf, he found a dozen or so folk albums. He started thumbing through them. Peter, Paul and Mary, Nina and Frederick... Angus turned to Lara and asked, 'How about 'Puff the Magic Dragon'.' Lara gave a theatrical frown. ...Rolf Harris... 'Rolf fucking Harris! Where the fuck did your mother find this shit?' ...Woody Guthrie, Engelbert Humperdinck, Nat King Cole... Angus pulled the record sleeve out and looked at the front cover. Nat King Cole smiled up at him. *Looks like a nice guy,* Angus thought. He slipped the vinyl disc out of its protective cover and placed it on the turntable of Monica's antiquated record player.

Cole's rich and soulful voice crooned out of a pair of battered-looking bookshelf speakers.

'Yeah!' Lara yelled, jumping to her feet and taking Angus's hands.

The music took hold of them. They danced and they spun and they sang along to the chorus. 'Let's face the music and dance!'

The lyrical content of the second track, 'Nature Boy', nailed them to the spot and brought tears of appreciation to their eyes. They stood in the centre of the room hugging each other, until side one of the album drew to a close with 'As Time Goes By'.

Lara suggested they go outside to look at the sky. There was snow on the ground. At first, they hardly noticed the cold on their bare feet. The night sky was clear and speckled by twinkling stars. They stood in each other's arms, gazing northeast towards an undulating translucent curtain, produced by the Borealis, pulsating neon-green and magenta.

'Isn't this incredible?' said Lara, her voice quivering with delight.

'Yeah...' A memory surfaced in Angus's mind. 'The *Northern Lights.* That was the name of my father's trawler. He...' Angus fell silent, the air ice cold against his nose and cheeks. He pulled Lara closer. The sheer magnificence of the heavens and the thought of his father lost at sea on the day Angus was born, brought an emotional lump to his throat.

When the sub-zero temperature began to creep up their legs from their chilled feet, they hurried back inside and made tea. They sat in the kitchen and talked for hours. Angus looked out the window and, much to his surprise, saw Monica's Siamese cat staring through the glass at him, its breath misting a corner of the glass. The cat's ice-blue eyes were the same colour as the lightening sky. A grandfather clock in the hall chimed seven times, prompting Angus to marvel at how quickly the night had passed. He realised he was coming down from the MDMA. They went to bed. The sun began to shine between the snow-shrouded pines surrounding the garden outside. After making slow, sensitive love they dissolved into a profound, dreamless sleep

The next day passed in somewhat of a daze. Lara and Angus did not venture outdoors, preferring instead to sit by the fire, drinking mugs of herbal tea and discussing the finer points of their MDMA experience. Neither of them thought of MDMA's potential as a party drug, viewing it more as a sacred substance for introspection and inner transformation.

Forty-eight hours later, both Angus and Lara experienced a fleeting bout of mild depression, but apart from that, they were both looking forward to their next MDMA session.

Some days after Monica returned from Edinburgh, Lara flew down to London to catch a connecting flight to Bombay and from there on to Pune. Her mission was to collect money from The State Bank Of India to bring back to Scotland.

This was the first time Angus had been left alone with Monica at Halladale for an extended period. Weather permitting, they'd take long walks together along snow-covered paths in the winter landscape. They talked as they walked and narrated the stories of their lives in great detail.

Monica spoke about Des, Lara's father, describing how she'd come to terms with her grief at his sudden and unexpected departure from this world, and how that grief had almost driven her insane in the months after his death in 1977. 'In the end,' she'd concluded, 'life goes on and one just has to adapt to the loss of loved ones. We're programmed to survive. What else can one do? If one needs a philosophy to help cope with life's trials and tribulations, surely the best option is to view life as an extended learning process. In my case, I had to learn to live without the man I'd loved for most of my adult life. It was a hard lesson. At first, life without Des felt meaningless to me. I willed myself to create a new meaning to fill the awful void. Life can be cruel but, if you truly love someone, that love does not die with their disappearance from the earthly plane. It lives on in your heart and you'll carry that love with you when the time comes to leave this mysterious world we live and die in. As for life after death, we know no more about it than people living in the Stone Age. Maybe less. My late husband was an agnostic. I believe everything living — people, animals, plants and so on — live and die and, in some mysterious way, it all moves in circles that are connected with other circles that work together to form the magnificent design of life. If life works like that, one has to remain open to the possibility that death does too.'

'Meaning?' Angus asked, his breath billowing out in a vaporous cloud before him.

'I mean,' answered Monica, trudging through deep snow at Angus's side, 'it's possible that we return to this world again and often meet those people with whom we have been deeply involved in previous lives. Our roles change, but the deep emotional bonds remain in one form or another. Surely it has occurred to you that your closest friends sometimes feel so familiar that the question arises in that curious mind of yours — do I know them from some other time and place?'

The metaphysical ball had rolled into Angus's corner and he kicked it into a long description of his relationship with his two closest friends Raj and Murphy. He described how he'd lost his oldest friend, Jimmy Bradley, in an accident in Bombay harbour, and told Monica about Murphy killing four men. He concluded, 'If Murphy hadn't shot those bandits in the mountains, I would not be here to tell the story.'

Much to his surprise, Monica laughed. 'I loved Murphy; just as I grew to love all of your friends, during that wonderful week last year when they came to stay with me at Halladale. There's no doubt that Murphy is a special case. He has something wild about him that fascinated me. Going by your descriptions, the men he killed sounded downright evil. Human monsters. Makes me think of a pertinent quote from Saint Bernard of Clairvaux. He said, 'A Knight of the Temple, who kills an evil man, should not be con-demned for killing the man, but praised for killing the evil.' I picked that up from a novel I'm currently reading, although I'm by no means convinced that I agree with what Saint Bernard said. After all, different times require different codes of morality. Times have changed.'

'I suppose it's a relevant enough quote,' commented Angus, 'but it's stretching it a bit to cast Murphy in the role of Knight Templar. Rebel with-out a pause more like.'

'Murphy is certainly a rebel,' Monica agreed, taking hold of his hand for support. 'That's a characteristic all of you lot have in common, Lara in-cluded. I adored Mike. Had I been twenty years younger, I might have been tempted to go for him. Such a gentleman, and so intelligent. And those mel-ancholic eyes of his. I get the shivers just thinking about them. Reminded me of Frank Sinatra. Although I can't quite envision Ol' Blue Eyes dressed in a tie-dye outfit.' She chuckled self-consciously and then asked, 'How did you come to know Mike?'

Angus stood for a moment to take his bearings. They were down in a valley by the River Feugh's swollen banks. Scolty Hill stood to the south, its summit shrouded in mist. Snow clouds were drifting in from the northeast. The return trek would be mostly uphill. He figured it would take at least an hour to get back to Halladale, by which time it would be almost dark. He clapped his gloved hands and turned to Monica, saying, 'We better keep moving.' They set off again and Angus told Monica the story of how he became friends with Acid Mike, without omitting any of the good parts. By the time his narration drew to a close, they could see grey wisps of smoke rising from Halladale's chimney into the darkening sky.

'So,' said Monica, as they walked along the tree-lined drive leading to her house, their footsteps crunching in hard-packed snow, 'Mike's the biggest drug dealer of you all?'

Angus digested the question and all that it implied, then said, 'Yeah, yeah, I suppose he is, although my dealing days are a thing of the past.'

'And do you still have any of that MDMA drug that he gave to you?'

'Yes, I do. Why?'

'Well, after Lara told me about her experience, I thought to myself that I wouldn't mind trying it.'

'You're joking?'

'Why do you think that? Let me guess. Old ladies like me don't do things like that?'

'Er... Right.'

'Angus, let me tell you something. This particular old lady will try anything once. If it's as good as my daughter said it was, I might even be inclined to try it twice.'

That evening, sitting by the fire in the lounge, the room illuminated by a dozen candles, Angus and Monica took MDMA together.

It was the first time Angus had ever seen Monica with her hair untied. Her thick, almost white hair hung down to her waist, making her appear like an ethereal Celtic queen, her throne an overstuffed armchair. For a couple of hours, they sat in silence.

The silence was broken when Angus heard Monica ask him something in a quiet voice. His eyes blinked open. 'What? I'm sorry. What did you say?

She replied, 'I said, will you do something for me.'

'Yes... Yes, of course. How can I be of help?'

'Could you come over here and sit beside me?'

'Sure,' he said, rising to his bare feet and padding over the worn Persian carpet.

Monica patted the thickly upholstered arm of her seat. 'Here.'

Angus sat down where she'd indicated and looked down into her glittering green eyes. The atmosphere felt slightly charged. Something was going on that he felt unsure about, but he relaxed into the situation.

A brief, mildly loaded silence ensued, broken when Monica said very meekly, 'Angus, I'm going to ask you to do something and, if you don't go through with it, I'll never live it down.'

She could see a few uneasy thoughts flit across his furrowed brow before he said, 'Okay, what do you want me to do?'

'Angus,' she said, almost in a whisper. 'I've been thinking about Des, and how much I miss him. Physically...I mean.' Her voice broke. She closed her eyes and took a few deep breaths before once again looking up into Angus's perplexed eyes. 'I want you to kiss me. Just once, that's all. I don't mean a peck on the cheek. I mean a full-blooded kiss like you would give Lara after having not seen her for some time.' She gave him a tender smile and studied his impassive face, wondering if he might be pretending to be unfazed. 'Do you understand what it is I need?'

Angus chuckled. 'Sure I do, darling. Come here.' He pushed one side of her long hair back, bent down towards her face, closed his eyes and delivered a passionate kiss to the old women's waiting lips.

The long kiss ended. 'Thank you,' Monica sighed, her eyes still closed, her lips glistening in the candlelight. 'Thank you so very much.' Her eyes fluttered open. 'I am very grateful to you. I know it was a strange request but—'

'It's okay, Monica.' Angus stood. 'I understand. At least I think I do.'

'Good!' Monica said brightly. 'Now off you go. Back to your seat, before I'm tempted to ask you for another bloody kiss. One revelation in an evening is more than enough for me.' She laughed to herself. 'My goodness, this MDMA stuff is absolutely fabulous. I'm sure it's going to catch on.'

'Yes, I think you might be right,' said Angus, a broad grin on his face as he fell into his leather armchair.

'Would you like me to brew us a pot of Darjeeling?'

'Why, Monica,' said Angus, putting on a posh accent, 'that sounds like a capital idea.'

Lara returned a few days later. She was exhausted. Her normally lustrous, coppery auburn hair was lifeless and dull. She'd missed her Air India flight in Bombay and spent an extra two days in the city.

Angus and Lara sat in the kitchen, filling each other in on what had transpired since they'd last seen one another.

'How was Pune?' Angus enquired.

'Busier than ever as far as the traffic was concerned,' said Lara. 'Arun Wankhade, the farmer, sends his regards. The ashram has become a veritable ghost town.' She continued. 'Buddha Hall has been dismantled. I met Norwegian Vasant. He's caretaking the master's house. Thanks to him, I had the privilege of visiting Bhagwan's bedroom.'

'You did? What was that like?'

'Completely frigid. It was like being in a deep freeze made from polished marble. Then Vasant told me to close my eyes.'

'And?'

'And... And the inside of my head lit up like I'd been plugged into the national grid. You could feel Bhagwan's presence. It was as if he were sitting on the bed next to us. Utterly astonishing. The entire house is permeated with his vibes.'

'Did you get the money?'

'Sure, no problem. I still don't understand why you asked me to bring so much. Mister Dilip, the assistant manager at the bank, opened the door for me when I left. Money talks, as they say. And you? Any fresh developments at Halladale?'

'Not really. Spent a lot of time with Monica, walking and talking. Chopped up a big pile of logs.' Angus paused and pretended something had just occurred to him. 'Oh, yeah, I almost forgot. I took MDMA with your mum.'

'You did what?'

'Yeah, we took a wee trip together one night by the fire. No big deal.'

'No big deal? Are you out of your fucking mind? My mother's an old lady. For Christ's sake! She could have had a heart attack or something.'

'Monica? A heart attack? No way. The old girl will probably outlive both of us. We've been marching around in the snow for hours every day like a pair of commandoes on a survival course.'

They heard the front door close and fell silent.

Monica entered, her long hair tied in a thick pleat. She was wearing a knee-length plaid skirt and a multicoloured Fair Isle cardigan. She said, 'Ah, the wanderer hath returned. Good journey?'

Lara rose to her feet, and they embraced. She then stood back and looked her mother up and down. In a tone of mocking sweetness, Lara said, 'I hear you and Captain Fantastic here...' She made a show of scowling at Angus. '... have been sharing some stimulating experiences.'

Monica laughed. 'Oh, yes, by golly, we've been having a high old time of it.' She patted Angus affectionately on the head. 'Haven't we, Angus?'

He gave a guilt-laden smile, nodded and said nothing.

In early April, Angus spotted a classified ad in the *Evening Express.* He and Lara drove over to MSG Motors in Findon, on the coastal outskirts of Aberdeen, to check out a Mercedes 300CE coupe that was for sale. The Land Rover pulled up at a gravelled car lot in a small industrial estate. A tall fat man, wearing an oil-stained boiler suit and a red baseball cap, greeted Angus and Lara. He introduced himself as Jack and spoke Doric, a strongly accented local dialect. 'Fit can ah dae ye fur?' he asked jovially.

Angus stepped forward and shook hands with Jack. 'I called earlier about the left-hand-drive Merc you have advertised in the *Evening Express.*'

Jack said in perfect English, 'Oh, of course, right. Angus, wasn't it?'

'That's me,' confirmed Angus.

Jack smiled and nodded in the direction of a gleaming white Mercedes with tinted-glass windows. 'That's her over there and I don't mind telling you she's an absolute beauty.' He ushered Lara and Angus towards the car. 'Came in last week in a trade-in. Belonged to a bloke in the oil industry. Owned her since she was first registered in Germany. Broke his heart to sell her. But a left hooker is no use in these parts. Useless for overtaking lorries on some of the narrow roads we have up here.' He opened the driver's side door and stood aside to reveal unmarked, cream leather seats. 'Just over eighty-thousand on the clock with full Mercedes service history,' he went on. 'A real topper, even if I say so myself, and an absolute steal at only nine grand.'

'Hold on,' said Angus, turning to face the motor-mouthed car dealer. 'The advert said seven thousand or nearest offer.'

Jack didn't miss a beat. 'That bloody newspaper's always making printing errors. I'll have to get on to them about that. I'll tell you what I'll do,' he said, rubbing thoughtfully at his freshly shaven triple chin. 'I'll meet you halfway. Just been MOTed and she has a brand new set of Goodyear tyres on her. Received a full Mercedes service a month back. New cambelt. New brake pads. The last owner cherished her more than his wife. Top-of-the-range with a twenty-four valve engine. Eight grand and she's all yours. I have a good insurance broker if you need one.'

Angus had to laugh. Jack didn't miss a trick in the hard sell, car dealer's handbook. He stood back and admired the car. 'Can I take it for a test drive?'

Jack patted him gently on the back. 'Aye, no problem at all. I'll just have to put garage plates on her because she's not insured.'

Ten minutes later, Angus and Lara were strapped in and ready to hit the highway. Through the open driver's window, Jack gave a word of warning. 'Take it easy on the dual carriageway. There at more cameras at the side of the road than they have at the bloody Oscars and the bizzies are always around when you don't want them.'

Angus slipped the automatic gear lever into drive, pushed down gently on the accelerator and the car moved off.

'Jesus,' said Lara, 'what a bloody talker.'

'What do you think about the car?' asked Angus, steering carefully into a slip lane.

'I think you will buy it and so does our man, Jack. I could see the pound signs flashing in his eyes.'

'But do you like the car?'

'Hit the gas and I'll tell you.'

Angus clicked a switch by the gear lever to change the gear ratios from economy to sports mode. He floored the accelerator and in fifteen seconds the car was roaring down the highway, doing twenty miles-an-hour over the maximum speed limit.

Over mugs of steaming Nescafé in Jack's cramped office, the car's ownership papers were signed over to James Sheridan. The selling price was eventually lowered to the original ad's price because there was rust on the chassis and exhaust system due to the amount of salt used on Scottish roads during wintertime. On the drive back to Halladale, Angus started planning his first road journey. He eyed the cream-coloured business card he'd placed on the dashboard. He had one last thing to do for his old friend, Jimmy Bradley.

Angus and Lara were sitting in a small café on Banchory's main street. They were discussing the mission Angus would embark on the following morning at dawn.

Lara sipped on a frothy coffee, looked across the table at Angus and said, 'That's an awful lot of money to give someone you've never met.'

Angus nodded. 'I know.'

'So what exactly is it that is compelling you to do this? It's not as if you are a multi-millionaire with money to throw around.'

'I suppose it's a mixture of things. Somehow Jimmy sensed that something was going to happen to him. He didn't exactly say that, but he hinted at it when he handed his address in the West Midlands to me.'

'Do you feel guilty about what happened to him?'

Angus shook his head vigorously. 'Definitely not. We all knew there were risks involved in what we were doing. No, guilt has nothing to do with it. I kind of feel like I'm party to an unspoken gentleman's agreement. I just want to close it by doing the right thing, which is giving Jimmy's wife and kids a good deal of money to compensate for their loss a little. That's it. Plain and simple.'

Lara reached over and held Angus's hand tightly in her own. 'You know, you're a good man, Angus MacLeod. Do what you have to do and I'll see you when you get back. And, for God's sake, please drive carefully.'

It was exactly four o'clock in the afternoon when Angus parked his Mercedes at the end of Albany Road in Harborne, an upmarket suburb on the outskirts of Birmingham. He strolled past a line of Victorian period terraced houses, faced off in biscuit-coloured brick, until he reached the number he was in search of. He glanced around and walked up to a black-painted door with a brass lion's head knocker. He checked the plastic nameplate, K. Bradley. He turned and walked back to his car. He got in, switched on the radio and waited. Thirty minutes passed, during which Angus had decided against writing a note of explanation for what he was about to do.

I'll be watching you... Sting was singing 'Every Breath You Take' when a Ford Granada pulled up in front of Kelly Bradley's house. Angus used a small pair of binoculars to observe a plump woman with straggly blond hair help three young children out of the blue Granada's back seats. *That's her,* Angus thought, remembering a photograph of Kelly that Jimmy had proudly shown him in Bombay. *She's gained weight, and she looks a wee bit older, but that is definitely Kelly Bradley, Jimmy's childhood sweetheart, wife and mother of his kids.* Angus hunkered down in his leather seat and waited for darkness to fall.

David Bowie's 'Let's Dance' was halfway through when Angus switched off the Blaupunkt radio. He went around to the back of the car, opened the boot and retrieved a shoebox wrapped in plain brown paper. He ambled down the street, checking that he was unobserved. When he reached Kelly's front door, he placed the parcel on the doorstep, looked around one last time, pressed the doorbell once and then hurried back up the street. By the time he was back in his car and focused his birdwatcher's binoculars, the parcel was gone.

Five minutes passed. A light went on above the Bradley's front door. Dressed in a dressing gown, Kelly walked over to the pavement and stood with her hands on her broad hips, looking up and down the deserted street. She eventually went back indoors and the overhead light was switched off. Angus thumped the black leather steering wheel. 'Yes!'

Kelly Bradley and her three children were now one hundred thousand American Dollars the richer, thanks to the anonymous driver of a white Mercedes Benz purring past their doorway, accelerating as it headed for the M1 motorway's northbound carriageway.

Angus and Lara spent the summer touring the North of Scotland, camping in the Highlands, and hiking over mountains and glens. A part of them could have stayed on in Angus's homeland, but having just witnessed the passing of two freezing, Scottish winters was a sure antidote to following up on such chilling notions.

One warm August afternoon Angus put on his running shoes and set out to fulfil the first part of an oath he'd made when he first laid eyes on Scolty. He jogged along a rutted dirt track and then turned left onto a sheep track, crisscrossing its way over a hillside stained purple by heather in full bloom. Sweat poured from his body as he ran up a narrow path that cut a line through a pine plantation. The densely planted forest buzzed, twittered and cheeped with natural frenetic excitement. All Angus could hear was his thudding heartbeat. He broke through the tree line onto a highland moor. Recently shorn sheep bleated and scampered off as he ran by, panting for breath. He reached the Scolty Monument and, without a moment's pause, ascended the tower's narrow and spiralling stone steps. He collapsed exhausted on the observation deck, his heart beating against his chest like a rubber mallet. He lay staring up at the puffy white clouds drifting by. Once his heartbeat slowed down, Angus stood and drank in the great beauty of his natural surroundings. He gazed north and recognised mountain peaks he'd scaled with Lara during the past months. A wave of deep emotional gratitude washed over him. His long journey back to health was finally over.

An hour passed before Angus saw Lara and Monica break out of the pine forest. Monica marched some way ahead of her daughter. Angus laughed and thought, *I'm going to miss the old girl.* As if picking up on his thoughts, Monica stopped in her tracks and waved enthusiastically in his direction. Angus waved back.

When Lara and her mother reached the foot of the stone tower, they walked over to a wooden bench, took off their thin anoraks and sat down. Angus joined them. Lara produced a thermos of tea, three tin mugs and a half-dozen tuna fish sandwiches from her backpack.

Monica poured steaming tea into the waiting mugs. 'Oh, I do so very much enjoy a picnic in the Scottish Highlands. Don't you?'

They ate sandwiches and drank tea in pleasant silence. For some time they studied a hawk, hovering high above, scanning the ground for prey. A pair of red deer wandered out of the woods and then disappeared behind a dense patch of bush. Somewhere out of sight, a lamb bleated for its mother.

Monica put her empty tin mug down on the wooden bench with a deliberate clank. 'Unless I'm very much mistaken, I do believe we're entering the season of farewell.'

'Don't worry, mum,' Lara said tenderly. 'You know we'll always return to see you.'

Monica patted her daughter's hand. 'I know that, my dear. But what I don't know is how much longer I'll be here.'

Angus began to protest. 'Aww, come on, Mona, you'll probably outlive—'

'No, Angus, I know what you're going to say,' said Monica. 'Unfortunately, I don't believe it to be true. At my age you just have to take each day as it comes, knowing it may be your last.'

'Mum, you're not becoming a drama queen in your dotage, are you?'

'No, Lara, I most certainly am not.' Monica laughed half-heartedly. 'It's just that recently I've been feeling a little tired. That's all.' She stood up briskly. 'Well then, that's enough idle chatter. Tally-ho! It's downhill all the way. Last one home's a rotten kipper.' Monica marched off in the direction of the pines.

Lara glanced at Angus. 'What was all that about?'

Angus shrugged. 'Who knows? Maybe feeling her age a bit. I wouldn't worry about it.' He stood and brushed breadcrumbs from his shorts. 'Let's go. You heard what she said.' He bent forward and sniffed Lara's hair. 'I do believe I smell a rotten kipper.'

She tried to slap him, but he dodged out of the way and began jogging down the hillside.

Angus and Lara left for Amsterdam two days later. Their parting with Monica was uncomplicated and warm. They stood outside Halladale's front door and hugged in a threesome for as long as seemed appropriate. Monica requested that they pass on her warm regards to their mutual friends when they reached Amsterdam. 'Especially Ol' Blue Eyes, Mike,' she called, just as Angus was opening the car door.

Angus turned around and walked back over to Monica. He embraced her one last time and surprised her by kissing her on the lips. She stood back from him and said, 'You'll never forget that one, will you?'

Angus laughed out loud. 'I'll remember it for as long as I live. Take good care of yourself, Mona.'

Monica was also laughing. 'And you take care of my daughter, Angus MacLeod.'

Angus and Lara drove off. They looked back one last time. Monica was standing with her Siamese cat, cradled in her arms like a baby.

'That's quite a story you've just told us, Mona,' I said, dragging my eyes away from the red embers in the fireplace to face her. She smiled and said nothing. 'So you met Angus's gang.'

Monica seemed amused by the question. 'I'd hardly describe his friends as a gang, Hamish. They are more like an extended family. Of course, they're outlaws, but that's what I loved about them. Just being around them made me feel young and rebellious again.'

'And you liked Mike especially.'

'Well,' said Monica coyly, 'you must have gathered that from what I imparted.'

'And what about that Murphy bloke?' Jean asked from her antique armchair by the fireplace. 'Weren't you afraid of him, after hearing what Angus told you about him murdering people?'

'I'm not in the least surprised that you ask me that question, Jean,' said Monica, tossing her thick pleat of hair behind her back. 'But I am sure you will be surprised to hear that I felt very safe and secure in Murphy's company. That's not to say I'd like to get on the wrong side of the man. I wouldn't. That said, he's a caring father, kind and extremely funny to be around. Much in the way that Raj is.'

'And Alice and Nina?' I asked.

'Oh, the girls were just adorable. A bit New Age... I think that's the expression. You know, dressed in Eastern style clothes, talking about karma and doing yoga in the garden. They caused a bit of a rumpus over in Banchory. They sat down on a wooden bench outside of the church and breastfed their darling babies, just when the Sunday morning service was coming out. Some old bat rang for the police. Mike managed to smooth the incident over and nothing came of it.'

Jean went to the bathroom. When she returned, she said to Monica, 'I was just wondering. Have you and your daughter always discussed the...eh...sexy details in your lives so openly?'

'Why, yes, we have. Well, ever since Lara started having sex, we have. We don't limit ourselves to any conversational level. We've always enjoyed a frank and open relationship.' She looked directly at Jean. 'Why are you asking?'

'Having three daughters of my own,' Jean said proudly, squeezing out a thin smile, 'I'm not so sure if I'd be comfortable going into the intimate details of their sex lives with them.'

'Oh, but Jean, you have no idea what fun you are missing. That story I told you about asking Angus to kiss me when we were high on that MDMA stuff... Well, when I told Lara about it, we didn't know whether to laugh or cry. It was hysterical. Speaking for both of us, I can't remember a time when we'd felt so close to each other.' Monica went on. 'I really missed having sexual relations with my husband after he died. But I got over it; to where I was no longer interested in men on that level. Besides,' she added as an afterthought, 'Lara was so kind as to buy me one of those battery-powered vibrating thingamabobs. I never got around to trying it out, but I did so very much appreciate my daughter's thoughtfulness.'

I took a peek at my wife. Even though there were only a few candles illuminating the room, I could see Jean's face had turned scarlet. She pretended to blow her nose with a handkerchief to hide her embarrassment. I realised the best thing I could do was change the subject.

'So, Mona, you took ecstasy with my brother?'

'It wasn't the first time that I'd taken an illegal drug. I took LSD with Des back in the Sixties. During those times in Dublin, everyone was taking it.'

'How was that?' I asked, keeping attention away from Jean, still trying to compose herself. I thought she was being ridiculous. But then again, women in their eighties talking about their dildos was an eye-opener for both of us.

'Oh, tripping on LSD was wonderful,' said Monica. 'I thought I'd died and been reborn in heaven. But, you know, Hamish, I never experienced the need to try it again. Just that once was enough to last me for a lifetime. I suppose, like many people who took it, LSD showed me we are all part of the same thing. Desmond didn't like the experience at all. Not one bit! I think he had a wee bit of what they call a bad trip if you know what I mean. He never spoke about it much, just mumbled something about being chased around a farmyard by a fire-breathing demon with a sharp sword who wanted to chop his head off because he did not know how to lay an egg. Sounded preposterous to me. Still does, now that I think about it. Who has ever heard of such a thing?' She concluded. 'The one good outcome that resulted from Desmond's LSD trip was that he became a strict vegetarian afterwards. Which just goes to show the different effects those mind-altering drugs can have on people's lives.'

Monica fell silent for a moment, her gaze empty. I'd noticed that she had the habit of cocking her head to one side when thinking, therefore I knew there was something on her agile mind waiting to be expressed. 'You know,' she finally said, 'I was just thinking. I've never believed in all that 'war on drugs' propaganda the government churns out. In fact, I rarely believe anything the government says. If you ask me, British politicians are a cabal of scheming crooks, whose media-powered brainwashing techniques are so pervasive that the masses fail to see what's going on right under their noses. I am compelled to agree with Angus; all drugs should be legalized. Young people are dying unnecessarily due to the likes of MDMA being criminalized. If substances like that were sold in a controlled setting, there would be no chance of people ingesting pills contaminated by God-only-knows-what.'

I found myself nodding in agreement, even though most of Monica's opinions on the subject ran contrary to my own. I felt no need to judge anything she said because I didn't want to trap myself in the limitations of my comparisons. I just wanted to remain open to the new perspectives being presented to me by someone I respected.

The evening wound down and we all retired for the night. The grandfather clock in the hall chimed midnight. I didn't hear it because I was sound asleep.

We left for Oban on a Friday morning. Monica made a favourable impression on both of us, although Jean had her judgements, as she did with most people. For my part I found Monica to be a source of great inspiration. She was a perfect example of being as old as one feels. The old girl was somebody who would feel forever young, even as she exhaled her final breath.

I sat in my office on a dismal Monday morning, methodically working through a mountain of paperwork. My company was involved in several construction projects and, even though I had over fifty skilled tradesmen in my employ, the prospect of hiring more workmen was looming large with the start of a big job for the town council in Fort William in June 2009. I looked at the calendar on my desk. I had the date circled in red. It was only a week away. By midday, I'd pretty much sorted everything out, sent and read a dozen emails and made the calls necessary to keep my firm on the road to ever-larger profits. Business was booming, as they say, but my heart wasn't in it. I felt life was somehow passing me by. All I had to show for it was a bigger bank balance. There was a familiar rap on my door and then my secretary, Doreen, entered my office with the morning's post bundled in her arms.

'Good morning, Mister MacLeod,' she said, her lilting voice bright and optimistic. 'You have an appointment with the Town Planning Office at two.'

'Morning, Doreen,' I said, returning the same greeting we had been repeating for over twenty years. I studied her while she set letters in different piles on my desk. She was so stylishly out of place in a builder's office, in her high heels and neat, light-grey secretary's outfit. She sensed my attention and looked towards me enquiringly. She had dark humorous eyes and a peachy colour to her skin. 'And how's life been treating you, Doreen?' I asked

She let out a restrained laugh and said, 'Och, I'm grand, Mister MacLeod. Me and my man went down to Glasgow for the weekend. We went to see Billy Connelly at the theatre.'

Like most Scots, I loved Billy Connelly. My interest was genuine when I enquired, 'And how was that?'

'It was absolutely brilliant,' she said. 'The Big Yin is no' quite as on the ball as he once was, but he's still the funniest man alive in my books. It only took him five minutes of blathering to get the whole place in an uproar. There was plenty of effing this and effing that. It was a bit overdone at times but the audience fair lapped it up.'

'Good to hear that Billy's still on form,' I said, turning my attention to a stack of letters.

'I'll away then and get on with it,' Doreen said, before gently closing the door behind her.

I went through the letters until I came across a picture postcard. I studied the coloured photograph of a huge motor yacht. The superstructure was painted navy blue. There was an exhaust funnel with four stainless steel pipes sticking out of it and sun decks with cushioned loungers positioned around them. The ship must have been five stories high. It reminded me of the superyachts that sometimes berthed over at Kerrera Marina during the summer, if we were lucky enough to have a summer. *What a beauty*, I thought, turning the card over to see who it was from. I read: *I was wondering if you and Jean would like to go on a world cruise. Sagara is undergoing a refit at present and will be ready to set sail by September. She has ten staterooms and I'm reserving one for you guys. I bet you thought, 'what a beauty,' when you looked at the picture. See you soon. Angus. PS. Monica has signed up for galley duty.*

I looked at the picture again and thought, *This is going to cause trouble.* Truth be told, it was already causing trouble. I felt pissed off, happy, excited and completely puzzled all at the same time. I Googled the word 'sagara'. I found out that it means 'ocean' in Sanskrit. It was a good name for a ship.

That evening, after we'd finished eating a light supper in the kitchen, I handed Jean the postcard. She studied the picture for a moment and turned it round to see what was written on the back. She shook her head and looked at the photograph of *Sagara* again.

'What the bloody hell is this?' she asked. 'Don't tell me you're contemplating taking your brother up on his offer.' She glared at me. 'Are you?'

I had to laugh at her serious expression. 'As a matter of fact, Jean, I am. It would be the trip of a lifetime. I mean to say, look at that ship. Don't tell me you wouldn't like to cruise the world on a beautiful boat like that.'

'*That!*' she blurted. 'has got to be a modern-day pirate ship, if ever I've seen one. Where on earth did Angus get his hands on the money to buy a thing like that? And please don't tell me he borrowed the cash from his auld pal Rupert Murdoch or Sheikh-ur-Booty because I won't believe you.'

'I think it's time to put the kettle on,' I suggested.

'Oh, is it now,' said Jean. 'And why is that?' She raised her right hand, palm towards me. 'Don't say a word! I've already figured it out. Angus made the money selling drugs. Dealing drugs all over the place with that criminal gang of his. Am I correct in my assumption?'

I loved it when my wife played the outraged, law-abiding citizen. 'Yes, darling, you're right on the money as usual. Now, are you going to make tea, or do I have to do it?'

'No, you just sit where you are.' Jean stood, went over to the sink and poured water into the electric kettle. She said over her shoulder, 'Just get on with it.'

'Get on with what?'

She turned to face me. 'Don't play dumb with me, Hamish MacLeod. I know you. Remember? So, just get on with telling me how Angus made his millions.'

I did as I was told.

14

AMSTERDAMED

September 15, 1983. Angus left the Amsterdam ring road via a slip lane signposted Amsterdam Centrum. He drove around a roundabout and steered the Mercedes onto a wide street with double tram tracks running down its centre.

'This is the Overtoom,' said Lara from the passenger seat, a street map spread across her lap. 'Go straight down here to the end and then take a left onto the Nassaukade.'

Angus kept his eyes fixed on the street in front of him. There were cyclists everywhere, electric trams with clanging bells and impatient taxi drivers, behaving as if they owned the road.

'Here!' Lara jabbed a finger in the direction she wished to go. 'Turn right here. This will bring us onto the Marnix Straat.'

She was right. Angus came to a halt at an electronic ticket machine, spoke to a uniformed parking attendant and then steered the car up a spiralling driveway to the highest level of the Europarking building. An electronically controlled metal door rumbled open, and he drove into a secure parking area that could have been a luxury car showroom. He parked at the end of a line of foreign-plated limousines that made his Mercedes coupe look like a banger.

It was one o'clock in the afternoon. The sun was shining. A ten-minute taxi ride brought them to the Prinsengracht. The cigar-smoking taxi driver drove to the end of the undulating one-way street and dropped them off at a corner. They stood looking up to the top floor of a three-storey terraced house, faced off with saddle-brown brickwork. Angus walked up sandstone steps and pressed the button marked 6 five times, as he'd been instructed to do. A voice squawked out of an entry phone's tinny speaker. 'Scottish Embassy.'

Angus chuckled. 'It's me, Murphy. Open the door.'

The voice squawked again. 'Smile, you're on Candid Camera.'

Angus grinned at the beady glass eye of a small surveillance camera bracketed to a corner of the cream-painted doorway. There was a buzz and a click. The thick wooden door opened, sunlight reflecting on its glossy blue paint. Once more, Murphy's voice crackled through the intercom. 'Take the lift to the top floor and take a right.' The front door closed behind them, cutting off the street sounds outside. They crossed a marble-floored hallway and entered an elevator. The lift heaved up. The elevator door thumped open. Lara and Angus stepped out into a carpeted corridor. They turned right, stopped at an open red door and entered a spacious room with a plaster-medallioned ceiling, a glittering crystal candelabra as its centrepiece. Murphy, Raj, Nina and Alice were waiting to greet them. The place had a smell of cooking oil, emphasised rather than disguised by the reek of sandalwood incense smoke rising in front of a six-foot-high brass, Shiva Nataraj statue festooned with blinking fairy lights. From somewhere within the apartment came the sound of someone practising scales on a piano.

Lara was bustled into the kitchen by the women. Angus sat down by a low coffee table, set in front of a large bay window with a view to the tree-lined canal in front of the house. Over to the left, he could see the nearby Amstel River, where various small craft bobbed to and fro, dodging cargo barges, emitting trails of oily smoke from their blackened funnels as they ploughed through the dark water. 'Quite a place you've got yourselves here,' he commented to Murphy and Raj, as they sat down on embroidered cushions opposite him.

'This is my place,' said Murphy, correcting him. 'Raj and Alice live in the neighbouring apartment.'

'We have a view directly overlooking the river,' bubbled Alice, delivering three sweating bottles of Guinness to the table.

'I'm impressed. You must be paying a fortune in rent for two apartments like this.'

Murphy quickly put Angus in the economic picture. 'We don't pay rent. We own these apartments. In fact, Raj and I own the whole building.'

'What?'

'We bought the place eighteen months ago for a million guilders. We must have put another million into getting all six apartments renovated. Gas-fired central heating, new roof, new plumbing, rewiring, solid teak floorboards, a fuckin' lift, you name it, we paid for it. Most of it under the table, of course. We only moved in a couple of months ago. The downstairs apartments are rented to foreigners.'

Angus took in the furnishings. Retro designer lamps, stainless steel-framed Scandinavian chairs, sofas and tables, brass statues of Hindu deities, dark-red Afghan carpets spread across a herringbone wooden floor and a sound system with white speaker cabinets as big as refrigerators. Simple Minds were spinning in the background. Jim Kerr was singing 'New Gold Dream'.

'Profits showing,' Angus commented. 'Aren't you worried about putting the local snoopers' suspicious minds on red alert?'

Murphy smoothed his walrus moustache with a thumb and forefinger and then drank a mouthful of Guinness from a bottle. 'Naw, we're not worried about that in the slightest. We've got that side of things completely covered. Haven't we, Raj?'

Raj looked up from the joint he was rolling in a small brass tray. 'What?

Yeah... Yeah, we have everything covered, man. Mike helped us set up shell companies in Gibraltar. Asshole of the universe that fuckin' place, but great for doing hanky-panky, banky business. No questions asked.'

'What's a shell company?' Angus asked.

Simple Minds played on in the background. *81, 83, 83, 84...*

Raj lit a long, tapering spliff and blew a fragrant cloud of hash smoke into the room. 'Your new education is about to begin, Angus, my man. A shell company, amongst other things, is a front for an illegal business. You need a shell company, or companies in our case, when you acquire something that you don't want the government to find out about for tax reasons. Here in Holland, especially. It's not PC Plod and his mates you have to worry about here; it's the tax authorities that are the problem. If they get onto you, you are fucked.'

'So,' said Angus, after taking a drag on the joint Raj handed him, 'how did you learn about this?'

Murphy answered. 'Mike has been showing us the ropes for a couple of years now. Turns out he's a bit of a financial wizard. Don't know what we would have done without him.'

'Mike?' Angus said. 'Where is he? I thought he would be here.'

'He's in California,' said Raj. 'He'll be back in a couple of weeks.'

'What's he doing over there?'

'He's over seeing about getting hold of some ADAM,' said Raj.

'Who's Adam?'

'It's not who. It's what,' explained Murphy. 'ADAM is what they've started calling MDMA. Mike's convinced that it's the next big thing, but I'm not so sure about that. Nobody is interested in pills. It's cocaine everyone wants. There's a snowstorm of coke blowing through Amsterdam right now. Everywhere you go you're offered a line of coke. We've all sworn off of the stuff. That shit fucks your head up. Only thing it's good for is all-night fucking sessions. And I don't need any help in that department.' He patted his crotch. 'Old Wonder Boy here is always ready to stand to attention. Ask Nina.'

Raj said, 'I don't need to ask Nina about that. I could hear you two last night from next door. It sounded like someone was making a cheapo porno flick.'

Murphy let out a dirty laugh. 'Yeah, I always thought you might have your ear to the wall, listening in on our wee tantra sessions, ya filthy Indian pervo that you are.'

Angus joined their ribald laughter. They began to talk about the past, re-counting escapades, scams and deals gone wrong. The years fell away. They were back together again. The three friends fell silent and introverted as they drifted into their stoned zone. It was the first time Angus had smoked hashish in years and it felt like it. Everything seemed funny, but at the same time, he was experiencing a bout of uncomfortable self-consciousness. He turned back to the window and saw the sun appear from behind a cloud to brighten Amsterdam's rooftops. He looked down. The shadows on the street were beginning to lengthen. A canal tour boat cruised by, looking to Angus like a floating greenhouse packed with tourists. He wasn't yet accustomed to being in a city and after a minute or two decided to go out for a walk to catch a breath of fresh air. He heard the women laughing in the kitchen. He felt unsure about going in there to ask Lara if she wanted to accompany him. Murphy and Raj were both reading copies of *High Times*. In the end, Angus just sat there, gazing out the window, viewing the cityscape through a green haze. *Stoned again,* he thought. 'Wow!' A large seagull landed on the ledge outside with a silver fish in its yellow beak.

Raj looked up from his magazine and nodded towards the gull. 'Hey, man, I think that's the same fucking bird that shat on my head yesterday morning.'

Murphy turned to him and asked, 'How the fuck would you know that?'

Raj studied the seagull for a moment. 'I don't know, man. Maybe it's that 'next time I see you walking down the street, I'm gonna shit on your head' look in its eye.'

Murphy nodded. 'I know what you mean. I think psycho gull has definitely got it in for you. You better start wearing a helmet when you go out. '

'You really think so?'

Murphy nodded again. 'Yeah, Raj, I do. We live in dangerous times. Bird shit can give you brain cancer.'

Raj groaned. 'Oh, no. Don't tell me.'

Angus chuckled. His attention drifted towards the music, thumping in the background. Someone had set the CD player on repeat. Simple Minds kept singing the same song. *81, 82, 83, 84...*

From outside, a low, deep-throated, syncopated engine sound came to Angus's ears. It was the distinctive rumble of a Harley-Davidson motorcycle. He stood to get a better view from the window. He watched a motorcyclist, clad in black leather and wearing a shiny coal-scuttle helmet, steer a white motorbike with gleaming chrome along the street on the opposite side of the canal. The biker took a right, crossed a narrow humpback bridge, took another right and parked the Harley under a tall elm tree, a few doors down from Raj and Murphy's house. Angus pressed his face to the glass but could see little of the motorcyclist because of the elm's thick foliage. He turned towards Murphy and Raj. 'How do you open the window?'

Murphy rose to his feet, stepped by Angus, twisted a lever and pushed the window to one side. 'What's up?' he asked.

Angus gave the facial equivalent of a shrug. 'Nothing. Just wanted to check out who was driving that fancy Harley.'

Murphy stepped aside. 'Don't let me stop you.'

Angus leaned out of the open window and looked down, just in time to catch the motorcyclist taking off the chrome crash helmet. The biker was a tall, skinny woman with short, dark hair, a narrow face and a big nose. Angus recognized her immediately. It was Kali. 'Fucking hell!' Angus exclaimed, turning to face his friends. 'I don't believe it,' he declared, shaking his head.

Murphy and Raj sat looking up at him for a moment. Finally, Raj asked, 'Don't believe what, man?'

'Remember when we were in Iran, hiding out in our hole in the ground, and I told you about an American chick that ripped me off in Poona?'

Raj said, 'Vaguely.'

Murphy said, 'Her name was Kali, right?'

Angus said, 'You have an excellent memory.'

Murphy stood. 'And now Kali just parked her motorbike outside of our front door in Amsterdam?'

Angus was still shaking his head. 'Yeah... Yeah, she did. I don't fucking well believe it, man.'

Murphy chuckled. 'It's karma.'

Raj glanced up from crumbling heated hash into a joint. 'But you've told me dozens of times that you don't believe in karma.'

'That's true, but sometimes, especially in moments like this, my belief system becomes more... How should I put it? ...flexible.' Murphy bent to tie the laces on his Nike trainers. He then headed towards the front door.

Raj called after him. 'Where are you going?'

Murphy called back over his shoulder. 'I'm taking the dog for a walk.'

The apartment's front door slammed.

Raj looked nervously at Angus.

'What?' Angus asked.

'We don't have a fucking dog.'

They both went to the window. Moments later, Murphy walked down the front steps and began strolling along the street, in the opposite direction from where the white Harley Davidson was parked under the elm tree. He turned, looked up, waved to them and continued on his way.

Angus turned to Raj and asked, 'What's he up to?'

Raj took a drag on his joint. 'Fuck knows. But he's up to something. I know it.'

Lara, Nina, and Alice entered the living room. High heels clicking on the wooden floor. They'd decided to go out for a curry at a nearby Indian restaurant. When Angus and Raj said they were happy to stay home, Nina told them she'd bring them back a takeaway. 'Where's Murphy?' she asked.

Angus replied, 'He said he was taking the dog out for a walk.'

Nina screwed up her face. 'Dog? We don't have a fucking dog.'

'That's exactly what I just told him,' said Raj.

'He's probably just stoned,' commented Alice, shrugging on a red leather bomber jacket. 'C'mon girls,' she said to Nina and Lara. 'We're outta here.'

Angus and Raj went back to the window. There was no sign of Murphy. It was getting dark. The street lights came on. Amsterdam by night. Beautiful. A stoned hour drifted by. The two friends left the window open and returned to their seats. Angus refreshed Raj's memory about how Kali had ripped him off for nearly every cent he had back in 1975. Raj rolled another joint, took a long drag and said, 'Man, she sounds like a right fucking piece of work. Makes me wonder how come you got tangled up with a rotten bitch like that in the first place.'

Angus nodded in agreement. 'Yeah, man, wondered a lot about that one myself. Sometimes these things just happen, I suppose.'

Raj looked around as if just realizing where he was. 'Hey, man, it's dark outside. Where the fuck is Murphy. He's been gone for nearly two hours.'

Whoomp! The sound came from out on the street. It was followed by a bright orange flash. Burning leaves crackled.

'What the fuck?' Raj jumped to his feet, hurried over to the open window and looked outside. '*Awww*, for fuck's sake!'

Angus joined him. 'What is it?' He looked down to his right. The white Harley Davidson was covered in flames. The tree it was parked under was on fire. People on the pavements were shouting and running away from the blaze. Cars ground to a halt. 'Wow! How the fuck did that happen?'

Raj ran his hands across his oily black hair. 'You only get one fucking guess.'

'*Murphy?*' Angus gasped.

'Yeah.' Raj gave a troubled nod. 'Right first time.'

Angus gasped again. 'Murphy set Kali's motorbike on fire?'

'This is completely nuts,' said Raj, drumming his fingers on the window-sill. 'Right outside of our fucking house. The cops will be crawling all over the place.'

Right on cue, a police siren wailed from a couple of blocks away. Minutes later, two white Volkswagen Golfs with flashing blue lights pulled up on the bridge.

Vurump! The Harley's petrol tank exploded. A woman screamed. On-lookers, standing at a safe distance, cheered. Flaming petrol and oil floated on the canal's surface. A canal tour boat reversed under the bridge. A second elm tree caught fire. Thick, black smoke billowed by the window.

Raj appeared anxious, his brown face pale. 'Fucking hell! This is starting to look like *Apocalypse Now* around here. Where the fuck is Murphy?'

Angus looked across to the other side of the canal. Someone waved from a recessed doorway. It was Murphy. Angus pointed. 'There he is. Can you see him?'

Raj gave his glasses a quick wipe. 'Yeah. The midnight fucking rambler himself.'

A small fire engine arrived and within a few minutes, the flames had been extinguished. One of the police cars drove away. People began to disperse. The smell of petrol and burnt rubber hung in the air. The apartment's front door slammed. Murphy wandered into the room as if having just returned from a pleasant evening stroll in the Vondel Park. 'Hi guys,' he said, the picture of innocence. 'What's cooking?'

There was an awkward silence.

Raj stood up and glared at Murphy. '*What's cooking?* Are you out of your fucking mind? A Harley-Davidson motorbike and a couple of beautiful trees is what's fucking cooking.'

Murphy raised his hands. 'What are you on about now?'

Angus attempted to laugh, but it caught at the back of his throat.

Raj gave him the evil eye. 'This isn't funny, man.'

A woman's hysterical voice rose from the street outside. Angus, Murphy and Raj hurried over to the open window. Over on the humpback bridge sat a parked police car with its headlights on. Kali had arrived on the scene. She was screaming at two police officers, the shorter of whom was a woman. She'd taken a hold of Kali's left arm and was trying to calm her down. Kali wasn't having it. Her right arm swung up and her coal-scuttle helmet smacked against the side of the policewoman's head. The cop staggered and fell to the ground.

Raj hissed in Angus's ear, 'For fuck's sake. Your pal's in deep shit now.'

Angus turned to him and said, 'She's not my fucking pal, man.'

'I say,' said Murphy is a posh English accent, 'could you chaps in the front stalls quieten down a bit? You're spoiling the show.'

The other cop fumbled with his holster, pulled out his pistol and trained it on Kali's chest. He shouted at her, raising his gun towards her face to emphasize his point. Kali looked around, shook her head and her helmet clattered to the cobblestones at her feet. The cop yammered into a microphone on his shoulder. He bent a knee and stooped to check on his unconscious partner, his gun still pointed at Kali. Another police car arrived on the scene, siren wailing, blue lights flashing. Kali had her hands cuffed behind her back and was bundled into the second Golf's back seat by two burly police officers. An ambulance screeched to a halt and within minutes the downed female cop was whisked away on a stretcher. Two more police cars pulled up, blocking off the bridge, now a serious crime scene. The show was almost over.

Raj turned to Murphy. 'You smell of petrol.'

Murphy smiled. 'Must have been from all that smoke.'

Raj shook his head. 'Smoke my ass. You took the gas canister out the back of our van and decided to play pyro-fucking-maniac.'

'Elementary, my dear Watson.' Murphy rubbed the palms of his hands together. 'Time for a shower after a job well done.'

81, 82, 83, 84...

Murphy looked over to the stereo equipment. 'Man, that song has been playing all day. Who the hell put the player on repeat? Time for a change.' He picked up a plastic case, extracted a disc, cut Simple Minds off mid-song, ejected the CD, tossed it onto a chair, put a different disc in the tray, turned up the volume on the amp and hit play.

A kick drum's bass tones rattled the windows.

'That's better,' shouted Murphy over the sonic blast of Prince and The Revolution's 'Let's Go Crazy'. He strode back across the room and hugged

Angus. 'Welcome to Amsterdam,' Murphy yelled in Angus's ear. 'Great to have you back, man. Oh yeah, and remember, when the girls return, mum's the word.'

Angus chuckled. 'Anything you say, man.'

Murphy went off for a shower. Raj turned the music down and joined Angus by the window. The police cars were gone from the bridge.

Raj said, 'You do realise that Murphy is a fucking headcase, don't you?'

Angus laughed. 'Hasn't changed a bit since the last time I saw him. Would you have him any other way?'

Raj stroked his double chin as if he needed to think deeply about the question. Finally, he said, 'Naw, I don't suppose I would want Murphy any other way. Kinda like the asshole just the way he is. Man, that bitch, Kali, got what was coming to her. Karma, wouldn't you say?'

'You know, in some mysterious way, karma gets everyone eventually,' said Angus. 'No matter who you are, you can't get away with fucking people over. What goes around comes around, as they say. Sooner or later life will serve you up exactly what you deserve. I'm not into revenge, because the people who hurt you one day have to deal with what they have done and, if you are lucky, like today, karma will let you watch. It's a bit like life showing you that just thinking you got away with doing some shit doesn't mean you did.'

Prince sang in the background. *We're all gonna die...* Raj flumped onto a sofa. 'Yeah, man, Prince is right. Better enjoy life while we still can. Great to have you back, Angus. I've missed you. Hey! Fancy another joint?'

'Why not?' said Angus.

Let's go crazy...

A week later, Angus and Lara moved into an attic apartment in the Sarphati Straat, just round the corner from the Amstel Hotel. On their first evening in their new home, Lara called a delivery service and, twenty minutes later, they sat down on a leather sofa and helped themselves to thick segments of oven-baked pizza.

Angus shoved a greasy morsel into his mouth and wiped his oily fingers on a paper napkin. He looked around the spacious room and said to Lara, 'Well, what do you think?'

She placed a hand over her mouth and burped. 'Scrumptious.'

'I'm not asking about the food. I meant this place. Our new apartment.'

'Oh, sorry. Yes, I like it. Not too keen on the trams rumbling by outside but, apart from that, I think we've landed in a comfy spot. Love all the polished marble in the bathroom and the his-and-hers basins. I like the fact that there is a metro station just across the street and that you can be downtown in next to no time. Tea?' She stood and went over to the open-plan kitchen to switch the kettle on. Her voice chimed from across the room.

'Everything is brand new. I can smell fresh paint. Great of our friends to let us stay here for free. Must have cost a bit.'

Angus called back. 'They can afford to be generous. They own this apartment. Bought it two months ago. I think it's called money laundering. Raj told me they are making on average one hundred thousand guilders a week.'

'Wow! How are they doing that?'

'Murphy told me they are sending at least four hundred kilos of good, commercial Moroccan to London every month.'

'Clever boys,' said Lara, placing a tray with a teapot and two mugs on the low wooden tabletop in front of him. 'I don't suppose they're using the Dutch postal service to deliver it.'

'No, they're not. They've got this guy, Dynamite Dick, and some of his ex-SAS pals, taking it across The Channel from somewhere near Rotterdam in a semi-rigid with three two hundred horsepower outboards. The way Murphy described it, I'm surprised the boat doesn't lift off the water and shoot up into the sky.'

Lara poured green tea into the mugs. 'Dynamite Dick? I've heard that name before. Wasn't he the guy who helped you out in Iran?'

'Yeah, that's him. He's not as funny as his name sounds. He has 'deadly serious' tattooed all over his scarred face.'

'And how do we fit into all of this? I presume that's what we are going to do here, fit in somehow. Aren't we?'

'I don't really know. I have mixed feelings about it. Murphy and Raj are carrying on like it's business as usual. They seem oblivious to the fact that I changed in India. Man, I've been stoned every day since we arrived here. I thought I'd said goodbye to all of that. Not to mention dealing.'

'What does your heart say?' Lara asked, joining her long fingertips together to form a steeple and pressing them to her lips.

'My heart's not in it.'

'And your head?'

'My head says go for it. Completely counter-intuitive. Raj and Murphy are offering us a cut of one third from all profits generated from the operation.'

'Us? I don't understand. What would I be doing?'

'It's what will *we* be doing? Murphy and Raj want us to take care of the money side of things. They are busy almost every day buying dope, wrapping and packing dope, and delivering dope to Rotterdam for shipment to England. They also have to meet British dealers here and in London. Every two weeks one of them has to fly down to Malaga in Spain to confer with Moroccan smugglers. The whole operation is becoming too much for them to handle on their own. Month by month it's growing bigger and more complex. Demand is outstripping supply.'

Lara looked over at him from the opposite side of the teak wood table, inlaid with mother of pearl. She sipped tea from a white mug. 'Okay,' she said, 'I get the pretty picture. Business is booming and we have to take care of the financial aspects of it. But what does that entail exactly.'

'That's what I'm coming to. Hold on,' Angus said, getting up from the black leather sofa, 'I just want to put some music on.' He went over to a large portable stereo system and flipped through a small selection of CDs in a plastic folder. He settled for ZZ Top's 'Eliminator'. *Nice car,* he thought, glancing at the picture on the CD's cover of a chopped, 1933 Ford. Billy Gibbons' voice growled out of the speakers. Angus turned the volume down to a level that would not disturb conversation and returned to the sofa. 'So, it's like this,' he explained to Lara. 'I collect the money in London, take it to a moneychanger and then I or Mike drop the changed money off with Dick, so he can bring it back to Holland in his speed boat. Barring a bit of bad luck, there is only a small element of risk involved. You know, like being stopped by the cops for some unforeseen reason, or being in the wrong place at the wrong time. Your job would involve keeping the books here in Amsterdam. Shouldn't be a problem because you have a good head for numbers.'

'Well,' said Lara, 'I'm good at my sums. You could put it like that.'

'Okay, you don't quite have a degree in economics, but near enough. That will come in handy because it's more complicated than it sounds. Money goes out to various dealers in Amsterdam and also to smugglers in Spain. Dick and his crew receive two hundred guilders per kilo transported to England. Meanwhile, in London, I'm changing up the money that comes in into guilders with a bunch of crafty Arabs, who will always try to knock me down a few points in relation to current exchange rates. Doesn't sound like much but, when it comes to converting millions of pounds into Dutch guilders, it's easy to be diddled. It will be your job to keep track of all that with your accounting. Do you think you can do that?'

Lara thought about it for ten seconds and then nodded. 'Sounds straightforward enough. I don't mind doing it. After all, it's only hash that's being traded, isn't it?'

'Yes, like me, Raj and Murphy have never been into selling shit that messes up people's lives. The bottom line is, don't deal in drugs that you would be unwilling to consume yourself. Talking of which, I have to admit that I've been enjoying smoking the occasional joint. I just have to stop feeling guilty about it.'

Lara gave a playful laugh. 'Talking of which, would you fancy a wee smoke?'

'Wouldn't mind a wee smoke, to be perfectly honest.' Angus went over and turned the music up a touch. 'I really love this song.'

'Me too.' said Lara, crumbling Nepali hash into the joint she was preparing. 'Turn it up a bit more.'

Angus sat down again. 'I thought that maybe I should cut my hair and have it styled, so I look more straight. Maybe buy a suit.'

'Ooh la-la,' Lara cooed, 'sounds sexy.'

'So does making lots of money,' said Angus. He began singing along to ZZ Top.

Angus and Lara looked across the glittering tabletop at each other, jabbed their fingers towards one another in time to the music, and sang along to the chorus. 'Cause every girl crazy 'bout a sharp dressed man!'

ZZ Top, that little ol' band from Texas, rocked, rolled, and cruised on into the Amsterdam night.

A suntanned Acid Mike returned from California, where he'd managed to purchase eighty thousand high-quality MDMA pills for a reasonable price. He'd also bought a fully restored '69 Ford Mustang. Ever since the jailbreak in Iran, Mike had adopted the idea that Mustangs were a symbol of good luck. In a month's time, the bright-red sports car, along with the illicit cargo stashed in its chassis and tyres, was to be delivered to Bremerhaven, a large container port on Germany's North Sea coast. An exceptionally tall Italian called Geet, who Angus vouched for because he knew him from Poona, was the one in charge of signing the import papers and driving the car to a garage in Arnhem, where it would be unloaded. When Murphy heard about Geet's involvement in the scam he'd flipped out, because Nina had a brief affair with the Italian in Rajasthan, back in '75.

Angus sat around in Murphy's Prinsengracht apartment drinking bottled beer, and listening to Mike's enthusiastic report about the popularity of ADAM in America's Golden State.

Two days later, Acid Mike and Angus ascended the creaky wooden stairs leading up to Mike's small apartment on London's Portobello Road. They smoked a joint, watched a video copy of 'The Terminator' and laughed at Arnold Schwarzenegger's throwaway lines. *Hasta la vista, baby.*

Angus's first day of work began at nine o'clock sharp the following morning. Sporting a stylish haircut and wearing a brand new Adidas tracksuit and trainers, he lugged a black sports bag on his right shoulder and walked up the road toward Notting Hill Gate tube station. The canvas bag weighed over twenty kilos and had the handles of two squash rackets sticking out of it. This was a ruse he'd learned from Raj's uncle Sulli back in the early Seventies. He looked like he was making his way to a sports centre for a game of early morning squash, although he hadn't a clue if there was such a place in the vicinity.

His destination was a small bureau de change right next door to a branch of the NatWest bank. He found it without any difficulty. It was the kind of place tourists exchanged money and bought telephone credit cards, with a closed glass counter facing a large window that looked directly onto Bayswater Road. He entered the deserted office front and walked up to the counter. Behind thick glass, a chubby man was running twenty-pound notes through an electric money-counting machine. He had pale brown skin and greasy, slicked-back, henna-dyed hair. Angus rapped on the glass. The man looked up from his task with a startled expression on his haggard face. He stepped over to the counter and said abruptly, 'What do you want?'

'I'm looking for Mister Dawoud.'

'I am Mister Dawoud. Who sent you?'

'Mister Michael.'

'*Mmmh,*' the sallow-faced man hummed. 'You have note?'

'Yes, yes, I have a note,' said Angus, dropping the heavy sports bag onto the worn synthetic carpeting. He fished in his leather wallet and produced one half of a torn five-pound note. 'Here,' he said, slipping it through the narrow space at the bottom of the thick window.

Mister Dawoud produced the other half from a metal drawer. He joined the two halves of the fiver together and then did something unexpected. He smiled. 'Please, please, come in,' he said, unlocking a door set to one side of his glassed-in workplace. Angus entered. 'Sit. Sit, please,' said the Arab, pulling over a functional office chair. Angus sat down. Arabic music tinkled from a small transistor radio. 'You have money?' asked Dawoud expectantly.

'Yeah, it's in here,' said Angus, nodding down to the canvas bag on the floor.

'Give, give.'

Angus nudged the bag with a foot towards the standing man.

'How much?' the moneychanger asked. Angus told him half a million and Dawoud said, 'Business good?' Angus was unsure if it was a question or a statement, so said nothing. The Arab unzipped the bag, set the squash rackets to one side, and then dumped the money out onto the carpeted floor. Angus's heartbeat sped up so rapidly it became nauseating. The hairs on the back of his neck prickled. Flashes of panic broke out in his mind. He looked over to the window. People were walking by on the pavement only three metres away. Across the street was an apartment block. He could have sworn he saw a curtain move on the third floor. Dawoud registered his nervousness. 'Don't be worried. There won't be problem. Come back...' The Arab glanced at his cheap wristwatch. '...three o'clock. I have guilders ready then. I give good rate.' He stepped over the pile of multicolored money bricks and unlocked the inch-thick glass door. 'See you three,' he reminded Angus, gesturing for him to squeeze by.

Back on the street, the ordinariness of the day mocked Angus. It was just another sunny Monday morning in London. He walked along the pavement, glancing over his shoulder twice, something that he would do a lot of during the coming years. When he came to a shop window, he stood and checked the reflection for any sign of anything that could indicate a police presence. Satisfied that the police were not in evidence, plain-clothes or otherwise, he breathed a sigh of relief and continued on his way. He sniffed the exhaust-tainted air. It smelled wonderful.

He returned to pick up the changed money at exactly three o'clock. 'Money fifty pounds short,' said Mister Dawoud, as soon as Angus was once again seated in the cramped office.

Acid Mike had warned Angus that nine times out of ten Dawoud complained that the money was a few quid short. Angus did as Mike had instructed and said, 'Oh, I'm sorry about that. It won't happen again.'

Dawoud smiled and handed Angus a slip of paper with numbers printed on it. 'Take,' the moneychanger said. 'You see, I give very good rate.'

Angus studied the calculation. The exchange rate was one-point-five percent less than the banks were offering, which was fair enough. 'Very good,' he said, unzipping the sports bag containing neat wads of newish-looking hundred guilder notes, bound together by thin rubber bands. He placed the squash rackets on top of the money, closed the bag and hoisted it onto his right shoulder. It was decidedly lighter than when he'd first arrived in the shop. He shook hands with Mister Dawoud and said, 'See you tomorrow.'

The moneychanger smiled again. 'Yes, tomorrow, nine o'clock sharp.'

Angus returned the following morning and went through the same procedure, minus uncomfortable introductions and torn banknotes.

The only difference on the third day was that the money he'd handed over was twenty quid too much. Dawoud handed him a crumpled twenty-pound note and delivered an admonition, outlining how Angus should be more careful in the future. Angus, of course, apologized profusely.

On Thursday morning, Acid Mike and Angus joined the rush hour traffic heading in an easterly direction. They were in Mike's white VW Transporter. The vehicle suited Mike's needs perfectly. Anonymous and reliable, it was always transporting something, usually of a highly illegal nature. The cargo hold was filled almost up to the roof with thick sheets of plywood. The bottom half of the pile had been hollowed out to accommodate whatever it was Mike needed to conceal. On that particular morning, the illicit cargo was forty-five kilos of hundred guilder banknotes.

Sixty miles northeast of London, the van drove through Ipswich in Suffolk. *I'm coming, I'm coming, yeah...* Frankie Goes To Hollywood's 'Relax' was playing on the radio. 'I wonder how they got away with that one,' commented Mike, switching off the radio. He made a sharp and sudden turn right. The tyres squealed and the van continued northeast along a two-lane road. They passed a signpost pointing to the village of Orford. A few miles later, within sight of the sea, they entered a furrowed dirt track. They pulled up beside a small farmhouse with a green Toyota Hilux parked outside. A red-painted door opened and, dressed in white tee-shirt and green camouflage trousers tucked into black army boots, Dynamite Dick stepped outside, raising a big hand in greeting.

The interior of Dick's house was tidy and comfortable. There was no sign of a women's presence, but there was plenty of military memorabilia hanging on the walls indicating the nature of Dick's past. A regimental flag depicting a winged sword was pinned on a soot-stained wall above a brick fireplace.

They sat around a wooden table, drank tea, and talked for some time.

'How was it getting out of Iran?' Dick asked Angus, in a thick Yorkshire accent.

'Oh, that was quite a trip,' said Angus. 'Nearly froze up in the mountains we had to cross to get into Turkey.'

Dick gave a knowing chuckle, his jaws moving like nutcrackers. 'The lad's jailbreak got a small mention in a couple of national newspapers over here. Oh yeah, and Mike told me you offed a couple of rag heads over there. Sounds like your mate, Murphy, is a good shot. Met him many times. He's as mad as fuck, if you ask me. A genuine limited edition psycho. That's not to say I don't like the man. I do. Raj is a good bloke too. Heart of gold.' Dynamite Dick glanced at his watch, stood, and pulled on an oil-stained sweater. 'Right then, no rest for the wicked. Time to get a move on.'

The three men went outside. Dick opened the double garage doors, Mike reversed the white van inside and Angus pulled the doors closed. The money had been formed into three blocks, wrapped in black plastic. They were placed on a wooden bench. The empty stash place in the van was then filled with twelve hessian bales, each containing ten kilos of Moroccan hashish.

When the job was done, Dick asked Angus if he'd like to see the *Boomerang*.

'What's the Boomerang?' Angus asked back.

Mike answered, 'That's his bloody six-hundred horsepower rib boat. He rarely stops talking about it.'

Dick grunted. 'She's my pride and joy.' He grabbed Angus by an arm and said, 'Come on, I'll show her to you.' He led Angus across the yard and unlocked a brass padlock on another set of double doors. Angus noticed the long garage had double doors at both ends and figured this made it easier for Dick to haul his boat in and out of the place quickly. The doors swung open to reveal three massive outboard motors, mounted on the back of a black rubber boat that must have been at least eight metres long. The boat was secured onto a four-wheeled trailer. 'That's my baby,' declared Dick, his gravelly voice swollen by pride. 'Hundred-gallon fuel tank, a state-of-the-art navigation system, communication system and, most importantly, a top speed of well over a hundred kilometres-per-hour. Nobody can catch me in this beauty.' Dick turned to Angus, his face split by a grin that displayed his gold-capped teeth. 'You'll have to do the crossing one night with me, mate. It beats the hell out of sex, I'll tell you that much.'

Acid Mike placed a hand on Angus's shoulder. 'Matey,' he said, 'don't believe a word that this crazy bugger tells you in regards to that beast he calls a boat. I went over and back with him one moonless night and I have no desire to repeat the experience. It was insane. I must have thrown my guts up a dozen times. And to top it all, about twenty miles out from the coast on our return journey, Captain Pugwash here...' Mike nodded towards a still grinning Dynamite Dick. '...steers us across a super tanker's wake at a ninety-degree angle and we must have shot about ten feet out of the bloody sea. When I got back to London, I had to visit a chiropractor to get my skeleton realigned.'

Dick gave Mike a friendly slap on the back. 'He's exaggerating as usual,' Dick said to Angus, man-to-man. 'All that LSD Mike swallows has damaged his head. I mean to say, just look at the fucker.' Mike was wearing a scuffed, ankle-length black leather coat with wide lapels and, of course, a tie-dye headband. 'He looks like a flipped-out *Obergruppenführer*, commanding a company of psychedelic storm troopers, marching through the mud-filled trenches at the Glastonbury Festival, singing the Horst Wessel song as they head towards the main stage.'

Mike chuckled. '*Obergruppenführer!* That's a good one. Sounds like you've been rehearsing your lines, matey.'

Dick winked at Mike and returned his attention to the boat. He patted one of its Yamaha engines. He asked Angus, 'You know why she's called the Boomerang?'

Angus thought for a few seconds and then said, 'Because she always returns?'

Dick laughed. 'Right first time, mate. You're pretty smart for a fucking Jock. Joking apart, the Boomerang cost me over a hundred grand and, all things considered, it was a great investment. Wouldn't you agree?'

'I have to agree, Dick.' It was Angus's turn to give an affectionate pat to a massive, rubber-coated engine. 'The *Boomerang* here is going to make us all rich unless I'm very much mistaken.' Angus paused and breathed in the reek of petrol fumes permeating the garage. 'Dick,' he continued, 'one night I'm going to take you up on your offer to join you on a run. I was just wondering, could I bring my girlfriend along?'

Dick's scarred face screwed up as if he'd just swallowed a pint of battery acid. He scratched a nervous itch on the back of his thick neck. 'I'm not so sure about that, Angus. I'd have to meet her first before I decide. Tell me, does she have good sea legs.'

'Well, man' said Angus, 'I don't know if they're sea legs but they are very good ones.'

Dick cracked a wry smile. 'That might do the trick, mate. Let's see. Okay?'

'Okay.'

'Good to see you again, Angus, my lad.'

'Good to see you, too, Dick.'

Mike and Angus drove back to London, retracing the route they'd taken earlier in the day.

And thus a pattern was set that would more or less remain unchanged over the coming two years. Angus flew in and out of London and, by 1986, he'd changed over fifty million pounds at Mister Dawoud's office in Notting Hill Gate. Lara kept the books in Amsterdam and bought herself a brand-new Porsche 911 Carrera with her own hard-earned money. Raj and Murphy continued to buy good quality hashish and deliver it to Dynamite Dick in Rotterdam, where they collected bags of Dutch guilders, which they re-invested in their ever-expanding illegitimate business activities. Alice and Nina gave birth to their second babies, learned to speak Dutch fluently, became Dutch citizens, paying income tax on what they earned from their flourishing interior design business, decorating properties belonging to Raj and Murphy.

Acid Mike continued to deal hash in London and stockpile ecstasy pills in Amsterdam. Mike had smuggled in half a million hits of MDMA from California. He'd only sold forty thousand pills but remained confident that it was only a matter of time until demand increased. As it turned out, he was correct. The ecstasy boom was just around the corner. Angus and his friends were about to shift into overdrive in the financial world. Instead of making millions a year, smuggling and selling hashish, they began earning millions a month, selling illegal designer drugs.

15

MONOPOL'E'

Murphy and Raj's 'office' was located on the Rozenstraat, a narrow street running parallel to the much wider Rozengracht, the main traffic artery that runs through the Jordaan district in central Amsterdam. Raj and Murphy had set up a front to hide their illegal activities. Rembrandt Decoration was a small painting and decorating firm. Rembrandt's employed two professional painters and decorators, Hans and Willem. Rembrandt's had, over the course of three years, earned a good reputation in the Jordaan. The firm's apparent success was due to Rembrandt's excellent work at half the price normally charged by local competition. Hans and Willem were a gay couple, who did not mind working hard for their salaries because they were earning twice as much as anyone else in Amsterdam with similar professional skills. The front business did not make money, but it did give a good reason for the constant comings and goings of the two Renault vans with Rembrandt's name and colourful logo painted on their side panels. Hans and Willem were given the headlines and played along. Their five thousand guilders a month salaries made them utterly loyal to their generous Scottish employers. Rembrandt's had strict working rules. Hans and Willem were prohibited from entering Rembrandt's business premises between ten in the morning and five o'clock in the evening, when the real business behind the front took place. Accessed from the Rosenstraat, a double garage led to a large office, storeroom, kitchen and toilet. Hans and Willem had never entered the storeroom and therefore had never set eyes on the two industrial vacuuming machines, electronic scales, tubs of ammonia solution, parcel tape dispensers, and boxes of plastic bags that are part and parcel of the hash smuggling trade.

It was a sunny afternoon in May 1986. Raj, Murphy, and Angus were sitting around in Rembrandt's office, drinking filtered coffee and passing around a joint of Zero-Zero Moroccan hashish, fifty kilos of which had been purchased in Breda that very morning. Raj was just drawing to a close in his description of accompanying Dynamite Dick on one of his high-speed runs.

'So when Dick sees this blip on the radar heading straight for us,' Raj said excitedly, 'the crazy bastard steers right across the bow of a huge tanker. Man, we must have missed the ship's bow by about five metres. I nearly shit my pants. Meanwhile, Dick's laughing like a fucking madman. I thought we were already going flat out but, when he slams the throttle forward, my hair nearly got pulled out by the roots. Really, man, I'm not exaggerating. The wind was howling in my ears. What a fuckin' speed we were going. The *Boomerang* was skimming over the waves like a low-flying jet. I tell you. I am never going...'

Just then the office door burst open. Everyone jumped up, fearing a bust. Acid Mike strode into the room. He was wide-eyed and slightly out of breath. 'I sold it! I've finally sold it,' he announced emphatically.

'For fuck's sake, Mike,' complained Murphy, 'what a fucking fright you gave us. And all because you sold a bike that you bought in Vondel Park last week from a junkie called Spike. How much did you make? Ten guilders?'

For a moment Mike stood motionless in the middle of the office, unsure of what he had just been asked. 'What?' he said hoarsely.

Mercedes met Benz, Dow met Jones, Murphy, Raj and Angus met Acid Mike and had benefitted greatly from a lucrative partnership with him. They had much to be grateful to him for. A gratitude extending way beyond the point of helping them become wealthy. The Scots viewed the Englishman as part of their extended family. They loved Acid Mike. That said, everyone present knew that Mike was extremely tight with money. His broad philosophy on life included the idea that people do not appreciate something unless they pay for it, as long as it wasn't him. The more the better, as far as he was concerned. In the past, there had been a few heated arguments about the English dealer's penny-pinching attitude. The bottom line was always the same. They cared more about each other than they did about how much money they were making.

The golden penny of understanding dropped into Mike's head. He blinked at Murphy. 'Of course, I didn't sell my bike. For that to happen I'd need to make twenty guilders at least.' Mike smiled broadly. 'But I have sold my entire stockpile of MDMA in one go. Made four hundred percent on what I paid for it.'

Murphy shook his head vigorously. 'I don't believe it. And here's me thinking you'd lost the plot.'

'But you were dead wrong there, matey,' said Mike without an I-told-you-so tone in his voice.

'Congratulations,' said Angus. 'Who bought it off you?'

'Two geezers I know from way back,' Mike replied. 'They own a couple of small dance clubs in Manchester and London. According to them, people are starting to call MDMA, Ecstasy. They also said they'll take all the product that I can come up with. No laying it on either. Cash on the button.'

'Hey!' Raj exclaimed, suddenly remembering something. 'Weren't you supposed to be having another load coming in this week?'

Mike sat down. The enthusiasm drained from his bearded face. Confidence leaked from his voice, replaced in equal measure by solemnity. 'That's the other bit of news I have to tell you lot, and it isn't good by a long shot. Geet got done, driving out of a bonded warehouse in Bremerhaven. The *Zolle* were waiting on him. They must've discovered the stash of pills and hung around until the poor blighter showed up to collect the car. I'm surprised German customs agents didn't tail him to find out where he was going.'

'Ah well,' Murphy said unsympathetically, 'we can thank fuck Geet doesn't have a clue who the fuck we are, or where the fuck we are. I never liked the look of that lanky sannyasin fucker from the minute I set eyes on him. He looked like an orange lampost.'

Everyone frowned at Murphy.

'Come off it, man,' said Raj. 'We all know you don't like the guy because he had a fling with Nina donkeys ago. But he's not nearly as bad as you're making him out to be. He'll keep his mouth shut.'

Murphy ignored Raj's comments and laid a reassuring hand on Mike's arm. 'Given half a chance that skid mark, Geet, would grass us up for sure, man. Take my word for it.'

'The driver's always a weak link,' Mike said thoughtfully. 'Sooner or later they usually get caught and that's why it's important to maintain the maximum distance between them and us.' He scratched nervously at a hairy cheek. 'I suppose I better drop a wad through his woman's letterbox next time I'm passing through Arnhem. The poor girl won't be seeing her man for some time. Geet told me he had a couple of kids with her.'

Murphy maintained his hard-boiled stance. 'Waste of fuckin' money if you ask me.'

'That's definitely the right thing to do,' said Angus to Mike. 'Even though it will break your heart to do so, ya old fucking skinflint that you are.'

Directing everyone's attention to Mike's stinginess had the desired effect. Everyone lightened up.

Once the atmosphere had settled, Mike outlined a new strategy. 'Listen,' he said, 'I've been thinking.' Everyone's ears perked up. When Mike thought about something it usually produced a dividend. 'The real money lies in manufacturing your own MDMA. The problem is getting your hands on the right chemicals, the necessary equipment, and, of course, a couple of technicians with the laboratory experience required for ecstasy production. A couple of weeks ago, I sold some gear to a chap I know from my schooldays. He lives in South Kensington. George is well connected and told me he knows some bloke who runs a textile factory in Poland that uses all kinds of chemicals. I believe it might be in our interests for me to pop up to Warsaw and visit this chappie.' Mike continued. 'While I'm doing that, you lot can start scoping places out to set up a lab. I was thinking along the lines of a small warehouse on the outskirts of town. Angus should do the talking because he is the most straight-looking one amongst us.' He adjusted his multicoloured headband and smiled at Angus. 'That's your payback for having such a smart hairstyle and owning a suit. What do you think?'

Angus contemplated the question for a moment. 'So, Mike, you are certain this ecstasy thing is going to take off?'

Mike nodded. 'Positive.' He paused, realizing he did not sound very convincing. 'Angus, I have never been more certain of a thing in my entire life.'

Angus checked out Murphy and Raj, sitting across the paint-splattered table from him. They both gave barely perceptible nods of the head. 'Alright, Mike,' said Angus, turning back to face the Englishman, 'we'll see you when you get back from Warsaw. Good luck. In the meantime, I'll see if I can find a cool spot to set up a lab.'

A week passed before the four friends were once more seated around the table in Rembrandt's back office. Acid Mike had just returned from Warsaw that morning. It was raining heavily and Mike's grey-tinged blonde hair was wet and pulled back into a dripping ponytail, his beard flecked by raindrops. His leather Gestapo coat was slung over the back of his seat, forming a puddle on the linoleum floor. Coffee was poured and the three Scots sat waiting to hear what Mike had to say for himself.

'Well,' he began, 'there's good news and bad news. I'll give the bad news first.' Murphy, Raj and Angus leaned forward, eager to hear it. 'The bad news is that PMK, the main precursor needed in the production of MDMA, is almost impossible to obtain in Europe. The police authorities know what it is being used for and it is red-flagged, meaning it's a strictly controlled chemical. Secondly, the hardware required for MDMA production, pressure tanks, heating mantles, reactors and so on, are difficult to procure.'

'For fuck's sake, Mike,' growled Murphy, 'can we hear a bit of good news, please. If it's not too much to ask.'

'Patience will be most handsomely rewarded in this case,' said Mike. 'The good news is that this bloke in Warsaw, a Liverpudlian called Paul Harrison, as it so happens, can order as much PMK as he wants from a Chinese chemical company in Shanghai, under the pretext of using it as an agent in textile production. The cream on the cake is that Paul has lab technicians under his employ who have the equipment and the know-how to produce high-quality MDMA and then deliver the finished product in powder form to us here in Amsterdam.'

'Wow!' Raj exclaimed, fired-up, distinctive blue eyes gleaming. 'That is amazing news. But how much will it cost us?'

'That's the second part of the equation,' said Mike. 'Paul can produce a one hundred and twenty-milligram dose of MDMA for a little over fifty cents and, delivery included, he wants two Swiss francs a hit. He insists on being paid COD in Swiss francs, high denomination notes, which means I'm going to have to talk to Mister Dawoud back in London.'

'How much can we sell it for?' Murphy asked.

'It's early days,' said Mike, 'but we can start wholesaling it out at seven guilders a hit and take it from there.'

'And when can this guy in Warsaw start delivering the powder?' Angus asked.

'Paul reckons he can supply us enough to produce a million pills within three months,' answered Mike. 'After that, he will deliver three times as much every month or thereabouts.'

'Man, this is incredible news,' said Angus. 'But how are we going to make pills out of powder?'

'I have that end of things covered,' replied Mike. 'I used to make my acid tabs, so it should be easy enough to make ecstasy pills, a bit bigger than required for hits of acid, but that shouldn't pose a problem. I know someone in Brussels who will supply a couple of automated pill presses, no questions asked. Bloody expensive things, mind you, but needs must be. Oh, just remembered.' Mike faced Angus. 'How did you get on with renting a small warehouse?'

Angus leaned his elbows on the table and placed his hands on the sides of his head. 'Not much joy there. I checked out a couple of industrial estates, but I was treated with suspicion. Being a foreigner is a minus in that department. The Dutch behave like they accept foreigners, but I suspect that many of them might resent our presence here in Holland. Anyway, I came across an interesting place in Amsterdam-Oost, right at the end of the Middenweg. It's in a compound, secured with a metal perimeter fence capped with triple strands of barbed wire. There's a big garage on the ground floor and a few rooms on the first floor. The guy who wants to rent it is a mechanic. He used the place as a BMW service centre. Now he wants to retire. Nice Dutchman. Speaks good English. Smokes dope. We shared a joint as we looked over the place. He wants four thousand guilders a month rent and only wants to declare half of it.'

Mike glanced at Angus with a hint of interest. 'Which end of the Middenweg are we talking about?'

'The one that's a two-minute drive from the Amsterdam ring,' answered Angus.

'You know what I'm thinking?' asked Mike.

'Let me make an educated guess,' cut in Murphy quickly. 'You're thinking that place might be in the perfect location for distributing our MDMA, because it's on the outskirts of town and therefore less liable to have police check-points.'

Mike's smile crinkled the skin around his blue eyes. 'Murphy, you just read my mind. Angus, get in contact with this Dutch guy again and rent the place. Pay the man a year's rent in advance. Get some kind of receipt if you can. If the slippery bugger only wants to declare half what he's earning in rent, that should ensure he won't cause us any grief.'

A month later Angus was in London, changing money. Mike had arranged with Mister Dawoud to change their pounds into Swiss francs. How the moneychanger came up with millions in 1,000 Swiss franc notes was a mystery to Angus. The Arab asked the occasional business-related question but made it very clear that he did not like answering questions of a personal nature. Angus appreciated the fact that Dawoud had never bothered to ask for his name. He'd grown to like the man in a workmate sort of way. He enjoyed his no-nonsense attitude and his secretive ways. With such thoughts in mind, Angus turned a corner, heading for the moneychanger's office. When he drew near he kept on walking. A police squad car and a marked police van were parked outside Dawoud's business premises. He glanced to his left as he passed the plate glass window and caught a flash of two men in white overalls, dusting off the office counter for fingerprints. A uniformed policeman hurried over to the squad car, jabbering into a walkie-talkie. Angus walked a few blocks and, when his pulse slowed down, crossed the road at a zebra crossing. It began to rain heavily. He pulled his blue anorak's hood up and walked back in the direction he'd come from. The police vehicles were still there. Angus now knew for certain that he'd never return to Mister Dawoud's money exchange shop again.

The following afternoon, Mike showed up at his apartment. He'd just returned from a two-week break in Ibiza. His face was tanned and he seemed lighter on his feet. Happy. He already knew about Dawoud's shop being busted, although how he came by that information so quickly was to forever remain a mystery.

'The fuck wit was changing up money for a gang of Nigerian smack dealers,' Mike declared, putting his bare feet up on the kitchen table. 'The bloody clown should have been more careful about what kind of people he worked with.'

'I'm glad it was weeks ago since I last went there,' said Angus.

'Yes, matey, you were lucky. The Old Bill probably had the place under surveillance for some time.' Mike gave him a thoughtful look. 'I wouldn't worry about it. If they'd clocked you, you wouldn't be sitting here with me now. Anyway,' he continued, 'no point in crying over spilt milk. It's time to milk another cash cow. I know this Pakistani chap with a bureau de change office down by Kings Cross Station and he will help us out. He's a young bloke. Goes by the name of Rahim Gurmani. He's not quite as together as Dawoud, in terms of coming up with large amounts of foreign currency fast. I've used his services a few times and he always pulls through in the end. Rahim is honest and reliable, which is worth a lot in this corrupt level of existence we presently inhabit.'

'How was Ibiza?'

'You've obviously never been there, Angus, or you wouldn't be asking that question. It's a wonderful island. There is something magical about the place. I love Ibiza, the fantastic people who live there, the nature, the sea, the beaches, the scene, the restaurants, the clubs, the music... Take my word for it. Ibiza has everything. You and Lara have to come down next time I'm there. I own a beautiful old *finca* in the hills, overlooking the sea. Tons of space. I've been working sporadically on the place for nearly a decade now.

The builders are starting work on the pool next month. I'm going to retire there one day. Not today, though.' Mike pulled on his scuffed cowboy boots. He stood. 'Come on, Angus, let's go. We have work to do, starting with a quick visit to Rahim Gurmani's foreign exchange office. You'd better bring a big bag of money along to get things rolling in the right direction.'

The first shipment of ecstasy powder from Poland was delivered to the garage near the end of Amsterdam's Middenweg on a frosty November morning in 1986. Angus and Mike were eating ham and cheese sandwiches and drinking black coffee in front of a two-bar electric heater. They looked up from the orange glow when a medium-sized truck, with white German number plates, pulled up at the locked wire gate, tooting its horn and flashing its headlights. In the truck's cabin were two burly men, wearing caps and smoking cigarettes.

Angus and Mike pulled on their working gloves and sprang into action. Angus gave the prearranged hand signal by raising a clenched fist. An identical fist shot out from the lorry's passenger side window. Angus unlocked the aluminium chain-link gate and pushed it aside. The truck reversed into the asphalt compound and Mike guided it into the garage. Angus relocked the gate, sprinted into the garage, and pulled down the metal-shuttered door behind him. Steel slats clattered together and slammed against the concrete floor. Mike switched on the overhead strip lighting. The driver cut the truck's diesel engine. He and his mate stepped down from the cab. 'Dzień dobry,' said the driver, who was a good bit shorter than his companion. Handshakes were exchanged but no names. Mike disappeared upstairs to keep a lookout from an office window. The taller of the two men undid a heavy-duty padlock on the truck's double back door. The doors swung outwards to reveal the cargo. Two layers of brown-painted, fifty-gallon drums on pallets reached up almost to the roof. They looked heavy. Angus watched the two broad-shouldered truckers straining to manhandle a steel drum down onto the concrete floor. Sixteen metal barrels had to be removed from the truck's interior before the eight drums with the powder were located. By this time the two Poles were sweating profusely and breathing heavily. Angus offered them coffee. The truckers smiled, shook their heads, and proceeded to reload the sixteen drums back into the lorry. It took them thirty minutes of puffing and swearing, in what Angus presumed to be Polish, to get the job done. After much 'kurwa' this and 'kurwa mac' that, handshakes were once more exchanged. Angus refused the unfiltered cigarette he was offered. The two men smoked in silence, taking long draws and exhaling smoke through their noses. Once finished, their heavy workman's boots ground out the smouldering dog ends on the oil-stained floor.

The two Poles looked at Angus expectantly, reminding him that he'd forgotten about the money he had to give them. He rummaged in a steel locker and produced a large packet of Alpen muesli, containing two thousand 1000 Swiss franc banknotes. He handed the sealed muesli packet to the driver, who nodded and grunted in acknowledgement. The Poles climbed back into the lorry's cabin without saying a word. The diesel engine coughed out a cloud of black exhaust smoke and chugged into life. Angus pushed the shuttered door up, sprinted over to the gate, unlocked it, and swung it aside. The truck rolled out of the garage, accelerated, and shot out onto the narrow street, missing an oncoming car with its horn blaring by the width of a Polish sausage. Angus pushed the gate closed, turned, and gave a wave to Mike, on lookout duty at an upstairs window of the red brick building.

Angus returned to the garage and rolled the metal door down behind him. He ran upstairs. Mike was in the kitchen making filtered coffee.

Angus sat on a high-backed wooden chair. Mike came into the room. He placed two mugs of steaming coffee on a makeshift table made from a wooden packing crate. He sat down and faced Angus. 'Everything alright, matey?'

'Yeah, man, I'm fine. A bit jacked up on adrenaline, that's all.'

'Fancy a spliff?'

'Good idea.' Angus dropped a brown sugar cube into his coffee with a splash.

Mike produced a ready-rolled joint from the bib pocket of his navy-blue boiler suit. 'That was intense,' he said, firing up the joint with a lighter.

'You're not joking. Do you think those guys understood English?'

'Going by the looks of them, I doubt it. Surly pair of buggers. Still, they delivered the goods and that's what matters.'

'Man, I can't believe I just handed two million Swiss francs to those jokers, without even checking out what I bought.'

'Don't worry about it. When I was up in Warsaw, arranging the delivery, I tried a sample. It's the purest ecstasy I've tasted. Wandered around the city's Old Town's market square with Paul Harrison. Good bloke. Family man. He has no reason to cheat us. Making more than enough as it is.'

Angus took a long drag on the joint and blew a jet of blue-grey smoke into the cold room. 'You think we should open a drum and have a look at the powder?'

Mike swallowed a mouthful of coffee. 'Let's leave that until tomorrow morning. The first thing we have to do is get the drums up here.' He nodded towards two industrial pill-pressing machines, shrouded in white cotton sheets and mounted on wooden pallets. 'We have to get those things up and running by tomorrow afternoon. I have an order for two hundred thousand pills that have to be ready and bagged by the weekend.'

'How many pills can those things produce in an hour?'

'About eight thousand, I've been told.'

Angus made a quick calculation in his head. 'So about twelve hours to make up your order?'

'Yes. More or less. I was just wondering what stamp to use. I thought about using the heart.'

'What colour is the powder?'

'Violet.'

'Purple hearts,' said Angus. 'Sounds good.'

'So, matey, you've moved from orange to blue. Somebody was telling me the FBI deported Rajneesh from the States. Your guru is back in Pune now and calling himself Osho. Have you heard anything about it?'

'Yes. I've heard a few things. All of them crazy. Lara and I had lunch with a couple of Danish sannyasin friends the other day. They were in town hoping to score some 'E'. Small timers. Only wanted five thousand, so I didn't mention what I was up to. Anyway, they'd visited the Rajneeshpuram commune in Oregon and were amazed by what had been accomplished there. Hard to imagine, but they told me they even had a sannyasin police force in lilac uniforms, armed with automatic weapons. Then, after a month, my friends left because there were some really heavy trips going down. Weird rumours flying around about the National Guard getting ready to storm the place. Some woman tried to assassinate Osho's doctor. *Sannyasin assassins!* That's a new one. Then a bunch of sannyasins went into a local town, entered restaurants, and sprayed the salad bars with salmonella bacteria. Hundreds of people became seriously ill, including children.'

'What the hell was the point of that?'

'Something to do with rigging local elections. They figured if enough people were laid up in bed, sannyasins could take over the local government and then do whatever they wanted. Sounds completely nuts to me.' Angus went on, 'My friends also heard that Bhagwan—'

'It's Osho now.'

'Oh, yeah, right. Anyway, they heard Osho had become addicted to laughing gas and Valium. I find that hard to believe. As far as I know, he has always maintained a firm anti-drug stance. When I told Osho I'd taken a lot of acid, he suggested it might be wiser to hit it on the head and start meditating. And now here I am, sitting with you in Amsterdam, getting toasted on fresh Manali.'

Mike laughed and coughed out a lungful of hash smoke. 'Yes, this is powerful shit. It's a funny old world. I always wondered about you getting involved with Rajneesh—'

'Hey, Mike, it's Osho now. Remember?'

Mike laughed again. 'Frightfully sorry, old chap. This hand-rubbed *charas* has gone right to my brain.' He tapped the side of his head. 'So, as I was saying, you and that whole orange thing you got into puzzled me no end. I mean to say, hooking up with a spiritual teacher is the most treacherous beast in the jungle. You just never struck me as the type of man to run around like a born-again Buddhist. How do you view your guru trip now?'

'*Born-again Buddhist,*' Angus commented. 'That's a good one. I think that Bhagwan... oops ...I mean Osho, is the most remarkable man I've ever had the pleasure of meeting in my entire life. It's partly because of his influence that I now see that the real guru is life itself. If one personalises the source of what life teaches, you end up with an outer guru. If you tune into life directly, the process is reversed, and the guru works from within.'

'Sounds like something the Beedie Wallah might have said.'

Angus was surprised to hear Mike say that. 'Man, you know about Nisargadatta?'

'Sure. *I Am That* is my favourite bedside read. If I only had one book to take to a desert island it would be that one. Have you read it?'

'No. Haven't got around to it yet. But I've met Nisargadatta.'

It was Mike's turn to be surprised. 'You have?'

'Well, I didn't really meet him in person. Just before I fell ill, I went to one of his talks in Bombay and I caught his eye for a moment.'

'And?'

'I felt out of my depth. When he glanced at me, I felt like a schoolboy, caught with my pants down, playing with my dick. Totally weird.'

Mike chuckled. 'Does the Beedie Wallah actually smoke?'

'When I was there he smoked one fag after another.'

'That is wild. Never could stand cigarettes myself. I like my spliffs, though.' Mike stubbed the joint out and rose to his feet. 'Come on. We better get a move on and see how we're going to get those barrels of ecstasy up the bloody stairs.'

By July 1988, Angus and Lara had a joint bank account in Luxemburg with over ten-million Swiss francs deposited in it. When they left the Banco Zol, Ludwig Bloomberg, the middle-aged banker who looked after their financial affairs, held the door open for them. They then crossed the Boulevard Royal and entered Banque OTT Internationale, where they'd rented a large safe deposit box for stashing gold bars, rare coins, and valuable watches. An hour later, Angus drove his Mercedes coupe, now painted in a dark-blue metallic colour and sporting yellow Dutch number plates, over the border into France.

Angus and Lara were on their way to Paris to meet up with Acid Mike and Murphy to assist in the biggest MDMA deal of their careers, involving the handover of five million ecstasy pills. A five million Swiss franc deposit had already been taken in Amsterdam, the remaining fifteen million was yet to be paid. It was a huge amount of money and Angus and his partners did not want to take any risks, apart from the ones they were already taking.

The sun was setting behind the Eiffel Tower. Angus steered his Mercedes into central Paris. Lara sat at his side, studying a street map. 'Turn right here,' she said, pointing towards a wide avenue in the city's eighth district, within sight of the Arc de Triomphe. They pulled up outside an imposing sandstone building on the Place de l'Etoile and checked the number. 'This is it,' said Angus. 'I'll wait here. You check with the lads about how to enter the underground car park.'

Five minutes passed. Murphy came out of the building, slid into the passenger seat, and guided Angus to a side street. They drove down a steep ramp and parked the car alongside Mike's VW Transporter. An illuminated corridor led to a lift with a polished brass sliding door. The elevator took them up to the third floor, where they crossed a landing and entered a luxurious apartment. Angus looked across a wide room with modern furniture, an antique fireplace, hardwood floor, and wide windows, providing a fantastic view of both the Arc de Triomphe to the right and the Eiffel Tower to the left. 'Quite a place you've got yourself here,' Angus called over to Mike, who was sitting chatting to Lara on a black leather chaise longue.

'It fuckin' well should be,' commented Murphy from behind. 'We're paying more money a week for this place than what your average man in the street earns in a year.'

Angus turned to face Murphy. His old friend was smartly dressed in casual designer clothes and sporting a reasonably short hairstyle. His moustache had also been recently trimmed. 'Everything going alright at this end?'

'Just about,' replied Murphy. 'We're going to have to wait around for a few days. The froggies are having a wee bit of a job raising the cash. Albert says he'll have it together by the weekend. I don't like that guy. The slime ball wears too much aftershave and there's a sneaky look in the fucker's eyes that I'm not comfortable with.' He pulled up his grey Polo shirt to reveal an automatic pistol's black rubberised grip sticking up from behind a brown leather belt. 'I'll tell you one thing. Bertie Boy better behave himself.'

Angus shook his head. 'For fuck's sake. You better watch you don't blow your balls off. Where the fuck did you pick that up?'

'From a wee Bulgarian birdie down in Amsterdam's red-light district. C'mon,' Murphy said, dropping his shirt back in place. He led Angus by the arm into a bedroom. 'Better show you where the gear's stashed, to bring you up to speed.'

Murphy stood in the doorway while Angus looked around the room's Spartan interior, composed of a high double bed, two chairs, and a walk-in closet. He checked the carpeted cupboard and, apart from an assortment of clothes hangers, found it to be empty. Angus shrugged and sat down on the bed. 'So where is it?'

Murphy pointed at him. 'You're sitting on it.'

Lara and Angus took in the sights, explored The Louvre, visited Notre-Dame Cathedral, and ate a lot of croissants in coffee bars. The weekend came and went, but the French dealers were still struggling to come up with the cash. Mike took the precaution of renting the apartment for another two weeks. Enjoying the novelty of their luxurious surroundings was wearing so thin they could see through it and recognize it for the expensive facade it was. It began to rain heavily in Paris. To ward off an outbreak of cabin fever, Murphy nipped out and bought a game of Monopoly. To make the board game more interesting it was decided that it would be fun if real money was substituted for fake. Each player was to begin the game with 20,000 French francs. A mutual fund was established in the bank, which held 10,000 francs to pay out prizes. Mike lit a fat spliff. Dice were thrown. Murphy wound up in jail. He used his 'Get Out of Jail Free' card and rolled a joint of Columbian weed to celebrate. Around and around the board the players went, collecting cash if they passed 'Go' and buying up the streets they were fortunate enough to land on that weren't already owned. An argument broke out between Angus and Murphy over a deal involving the exchange of railway stations for utility companies. The rule book was consulted. It was written in French, which no one understood enough of to make an accurate translation. A peace pipe was passed around and the game continued under a canopy of hash and marijuana smoke. Red hotels and green houses began to line the streets. *Money...* Pink Floyd's 'Dark Side of the Moon' warbled from a portable CD player. Everyone, including Lara, was completely smashed. She stood up and tried to disperse the smoke with her hands. 'Hey, you guys, the stink of dope in here is so thick you could lick it out of the air. We should open a window or something. I'll bet you can smell it out in the corridor.'

Murphy looked up from the Monopoly board and sniffed the air. 'You're right,' he said to Lara. 'Go into the kitchen and heat up that oil in the big pot. You know, the one I used last night to make chips. Leave it on for five minutes. The smell of cooking oil should cover up the pong of dope.'

'Good idea,' said Lara heading for the high-tech kitchen. She turned an electric ring on and pulled the stainless-steel pot, half full with cooking oil, over the quickly reddening element. She hurried out of the kitchen and pulled the door closed behind her. She returned to the game in time to catch Murphy about to throw the dice. 'Stop!' Lara yelled, seeing that Murphy's top hat counter was sitting on Avenue Des Champs-Elysees. Lara owned the French equivalent of Park Lane and had a five-star hotel on it. She studied the relevant property card. Her dark eyebrows arched. 'Murphy, you have to pay me two-thousand francs.'

Murphy, winning the game up to this point, was a very bad loser; the sort of man who finds it infuriating to lose at heads or tails. 'Shit!' he cursed. 'Can I swap you...?'

'No. I don't want to swap anything,' Lara said sharply, cutting off his proposal. 'I want the money.'

Murphy sighed and handed over twenty crisp 100 franc notes. He'd thrown a double so it was his turn again. He shook the dice and rolled them onto the lime green board.

'Snake eyes!' Lara shrieked with joy. Murphy's top hat counter was moved to Rue de la Paix, the French equivalent of Mayfair. She laughed gleefully at Murphy. 'You're owe me another two grand.'

'Fuckin' ridiculous,' Murphy complained, handing over a crumpled bundle of banknotes.

Lara made a show out of counting the money slowly. 'This is two hundred short.'

Murphy gave her a guilty smile, handed over 200 francs, threw the dice again and, when he passed 'Go' and landed on 'Chance', he said, 'Thank fuck for that.'

Acid Mike was, of course, the banker. He handed Murphy two hundred francs for passing 'Go' and asked, 'What does your 'Chance' card say?'

Murphy pulled the top card from the pile, read it, and said, 'I don't fucking well believe it.'

Lara grabbed the yellow card out of his hand, glanced at it, and said, 'Advance to Rue de la Paix.' She tilted her head and gave Murphy the sweetest of smiles. 'Murphy, *mon cherie,* you owe me another two thousand francs.'

Murphy looked into the eyes of his fellow players. 'Are you guys setting me up. This is going way beyond bad luck.'

Mike smiled and said, 'I do believe we have a bad loser in our midst.'

That did it. An argument developed that took twenty minutes to run its course. It ended when Murphy stood up abruptly and threw what remaining money he had onto the Monopoly board. 'I've had enough of this shite,' he declared angrily. 'I wouldn't be surprised if those fuckin' dice were loaded. I wish those French shites would show up with the cash so that we can get the fuck out of here.'

Just then, the sound of police sirens on the street outside filtered up into the room.

Murphy strode over to the wide window and looked down to the tree-lined street. 'Fuckin shit,' he spat. 'There are three cop cars down there and a platoon of gendarmes piling into the building.' A louder siren wailed. 'Here comes the fuckin' fire brigade.'

The doorbell chimed. Everyone sprang into action at once. Mike gathered dope and rolling papers together, hid them under a settee cushion, and tucked his long scraggly hair under a cap. Lara collected banknotes and stuffed them into a drawer. Angus ran into a bathroom, glanced in the mirror, and splashed cold water onto his worried face. Murphy entered the bathroom. He looked even more worried. 'I need to take a shit,' he declared.

Boomp! Boomp! Boomp! Someone was thumping on the front door.

Angus hurried back into the lounge. Lara and Mike were staring at each other, their jaws slack. Lara's face was as white as snow. 'It's a fucking bust,' said Angus, his voice almost a shout. *Boomp! Boomp! Boomp!* 'Lara, you better answer the door.'

'Me?' she gasped, putting her hands to her pale cheeks.

'Yes, you, Lara,' confirmed Angus. 'For Christ's sake, pull yourself together. This is no time to throw a wobbler.'

Boomp! Boomp! Boomp!

Angus pleaded, 'Come on, Lara, answer the fucking door!'

Boomp! Boomp! Boomp! Boomp! Boomp! Boomp!

Lara walked across the room, straightened her dress, and went into the hall to open the front door. A toilet flushed and Murphy rushed over to join Mike and Angus. They sat down on leather armchairs and did a poor impersonation of three wealthy tourists, relaxing on a rainy afternoon in Paris. *The lunatic is under my bed...* Pink Floyd added a surreal touch to an already bizarre situation.

Three uniformed gendarmes barged into the room, followed by a fireman in a black helmet and a shocked-looking Lara.

Mike tried to take control of the situation. 'Good afternoon, officer,' he said calmly, to the man with three white stripes on his arm, most likely the police officer in charge. 'What seems to be the problem?'

The three black-capped cops looked blankly at each other. The police sergeant said something in French, the emphasis laid on the phrase *être en feu*.

A sheen of sweat glistened on Murphy's forehead. He leaned over and whispered to Angus, 'What the fuck's he going on about?'

Angus shrugged, a cold lump of dread spreading out from the pit of his stomach.

Lara spoke up. '*Feu* means 'fire,' she said. 'I think they are here because of a fire in the building.'

Murphy shot out of his armchair and shouted, 'The fuckin' chip pan!' He rushed over to the kitchen door and yanked it open. A cloud of thick black smoke engulfed him.

The fireman yammered into a hand-held radio. The lounge was filling with smoke, making it difficult to breathe. Another two firemen, rubber face masks on, rushed into the room, bright red fire extinguishers at the ready. It was all over in a matter of minutes.

Every window in the apartment was opened to dispel the acrid smoke. The gendarme sergeant asked the foreigners for their passports and quickly jotted down the required details on a notepad.

Fifteen minutes passed, the emergency services departed and the four friends were left sitting around the lounge's glass-topped table, staring into space in shell-shocked silence. The acrid smell of burnt cooking oil hung in the air.

Acid Mike spoke first. 'Whose bright idea was it to leave a bloody chip pan on the cooker in the kitchen?' he asked, voice crackling with suppressed anger. Murphy and Lara exchanged a guilty look, which Mike did not fail to perceive. 'You're a pair of bloody fuck-ups, you know that?' Lara and Murphy nodded glumly and focused their eyes on the floor. 'You do realise that, if it had been discovered that we're sitting on two tons of ecstasy pills, we would have all ended up breaking rocks on Devil's Island or some other godforsaken place for the next twenty years.'

Murphy shook his head. 'Not me. I'd have joined the Foreign Legion.'

'C'mon, Murphy, don't kid yourself, man,' chided Angus. 'That was a really daft thing to do. I think what Mike's saying is we better pay more attention to what we're doing in future. Twenty years banged-up in prison is no fucking joke.'

Mike added. 'We're going to have to foot a hefty bill when the agent works out how much the damage will cost us. The kitchen looks like a bloody coal mine!' He looked like he had a lot more to say, and wasn't saying any of it.

'I'm sorry, man.' Murphy squirmed in his armchair. 'You guys broke me out of jail in Iran. If you were busted due to something I did, I'd never be able to forgive myself. My most humble apologies.'

Lara sobbed, tears rolling over her pale cheeks, some from guilt, others from relief. Angus pulled her close. Mike's mobile phone rang. He checked the caller number, raised the phone to his ear and nodded an apology to everyone present. 'Yes...' He listened. 'Okay...' He stood up, eyes flicking left and right as he took mental notes. 'That's very good news. See you then. I'll have the coffee ready.' Mike returned to his seat by the table. 'That was Marc, Albert's partner. He and his friends have the money and they are coming to pick up the gear. Tomorrow morning at eight o'clock sharp.'

Nobody said a word in response to Mike's announcement. Angus went over to the open window and looked out. The city's constant background hum droned in his ears. The rain had stopped and the sun was setting. The Arc de Triomphe glowed orange in the light cast by oblique rays of sunlight. Thick, swiftly moving traffic circled the monument like a mechanized army in the act of deployment. Angus looked down and realised both his hands were clenched tight into fists. He extended his fingers. His hands were shaking.

Albert and Marc were three hours late. They showed up with two growlers in tow, who looked like they came from Albania or some other remote region in Europe, where Cro-Magnon tribes still live in mountain caves. They reeked of violence. The pair might have been twins, except one of them had big pointed ears like Mister Spock in *Star Trek*. Both of the cavemen had black crew cuts, short black beards, wore black boiler suits and carried two medium-sized black suitcases. Apart from noticing the men's favourite colour, Angus observed bumps under their armpits, suggesting they both carried holstered pistols. Their obvious lack of brainpower was compensated by iron-pumped muscle. After setting the suitcases on the table, the one with the normal ears nodded twice at Angus to demonstrate how far he could count. Noddy turned to Spock, growled something in rapid-fire French, and then they stood well back from the proceedings, their alert eyes scanning the room.

Albert wore a short, tan-coloured leather jerkin and matching skin-tight trousers. His oily blonde hair was slicked back. He reeked of expensive aftershave. Marc, a plump man in a dark business suit, smiled broadly for no apparent reason and ran a hand over his thinning hair, before taking a seat beside his partner, sitting opposite Angus and Acid Mike.

'My apologies for being late,' Marc said, running a nervous forefinger across his light brown toothbrush moustache to make certain it was still there. 'We were held up in traffic and had to make two detours around police checkpoints on the Boulevard Périphérique,' he informed Angus and Mike.

Angus looked over toward Murphy. He was sitting by the window, reading a *Rolling Stone* magazine with a photo of Bruce Springsteen on the front cover. Murphy appeared uninterested in what was taking place in the room. Every minute or so he'd glance down at the street. Lara had left the apartment as soon as the visitors arrived. She was sitting across the street, outside of a bistro, keeping a watchful eye on the neighbourhood. She had an open book on her lap. Mike had told her to place the book on the table if she noticed anything suspicious, unusual police activity or strange people entering the building. Following Mike's instructions, she'd ordered a bottle of the most expensive Sauvignon Blanc the bistro stocked, so the waiters wouldn't bother her. Angus glanced at the hired muscle and felt secure in the knowledge that Murphy had his automatic pistol jammed into the back of his Levi's with the safety off. Noddy and Spock had their eyes glued to the black suitcases, which Mike had just opened.

Mike said to Albert, 'What's all this? I told you we wanted to be paid in thousand Swiss franc notes.'

The Frenchman raised his hands in apology. *'Pardon!* It was impossible to find that amount in thousands. The money's all there. *S'il vous plaît,* count it if you wish,' he said in faltering English, unzipping his leather jerkin. 'We tried the samples of 'E' you gave us. We like it. *Être exagéré.* We also like the Mercedes star logo on the pills. *Très chic.* Our customers will love that.' He sniffed the air. 'Something smells burnt in here.'

'Yes, I know,' said Mike. 'We had a small fire in the kitchen yesterday afternoon.'

Angus switched on the brand new electronic money counting machine he'd purchased in Luxemburg. It gave off a mauve glow from the built-in ultra-violet, counterfeit note detector. He fed in wads of different denomination banknotes and realised how noisy it was. 'Better turn on the radio,' he suggested to Acid Mike. Mike got up and tuned the radio to an FM station. Sylvester's 'You Make Me Feel (Mighty Real)' blared into the room. It was highly inappropriate, but succeeded in drowning out the counting machine's rapid clack, clack, clacking. It took over two hours to count the money. Fifteen million Swiss francs exactly. Angus led Albert and Marc through to the bedroom and hauled the mattress off the bed to reveal the black plastic storage boxes containing the five million ecstasy pills. Meanwhile, much to the consternation of Noddy and Spock, Mike left the apartment with the two suitcases containing the money. He hurried down the fire exit stairs to the underground car park to stash the cash in his VW

Transporter.

It took the French dealers a couple of hours to carry fifty plastic storage boxes downstairs to the garage where they were loaded into a Renault panel van. Noddy and the Vulcan carried electric power tools back and forth to appear like maintenance men. Fortunately, nobody noticed them. After the last box had left the apartment, Marc and Albert returned to shake hands and express their desire for a repeat performance in three months' time.

As soon as Lara saw the black Renault van turn into the street, she summoned a waiter and paid her bill. She removed four hundred francs from her purse and, as an afterthought, added an extra hundred as a generous tip. She staggered across the street, entered the building and said a slurred *bonjour* to the lobby-bound concierge, clad in a grey topcoat holding the glass door open for her. When she entered the apartment's lounge, she collapsed onto a sofa.

Murphy asked her, 'Are you okay?'

Lara tried to sit up. Her brown hair hung down on either side of her fringe. She was as pale as a corpse but much more beautiful. 'Yeah, man, I'm okay. A bit sloshed.' She laughed for no reason, other than being completely drunk. 'I drank two whole bottles of Sauvignon Blanc. La Mont Damne Chavignol, no fucking less. *'Eeeugh!'* She vomited onto the carpet. Angus carried her to their bedroom and carefully laid her on the bed.

An hour passed. The doorbell chimed. Mike answered the door. It was Monsieur Leclerc, the agent who had rented him the apartment. The flush-faced agent had an unpleasant bulbous nose that he constantly dabbed with a stained handkerchief. Leclerc was accompanied by a tall, thin man, introduced as Monsieur Sabot. His presence was required to assess the cost of the damage caused by the fire in the kitchen.

After ten minutes of adding up figures, Sabot came to a bottom line of 32,500 francs. Mike didn't bat an eyelid, counted out the cash on a blackened worktop in the ruined kitchen, and said to Monsieur Leclerc, 'I trust you will accept my most humble apologies and accept an extra five thousand francs to cover any inconvenience caused by my negligence.'

The agent could not hide his pleasure. His big nose glowed like a red light bulb. He was smiling from ear to ear as he stuffed the paper currency into his leather wallet. He consoled Monsieur Mike by telling him that accidents happen and any time he wished to rent another apartment in central Paris he had his telephone number and he shouldn't hesitate to use it.

The following morning, Angus drove back to Amsterdam. Lara lay on the back seat of the Mercedes, nursing a mountain-cracking hangover.

16

A SQUEAKY SHOCK ABSORBER

'Your hands are shaking,' Lara said to Angus, in the bathroom of their Amsterdam apartment.

'I know.' Angus set his disposable razor down on the yellow marble circling the twin sinks. He checked his reflection in the mirror. He still looked tired after a twelve-hour sleep. 'Since our close encounter with the gendarmes in Paris, I'm afraid to pick up a cup of tea in case I spill it. I think I might be suffering from delayed shock.' He wiped shaving foam from his neck with a white hand towel. 'I reckon I need a break from work.'

'A holiday, you mean?'

Angus studied her round breasts in the mirror for a moment, then turned and looked into her green eyes. 'Yeah, a holiday,' he said. 'That's what I need. Mike's flying down to Ibiza next week. He's been asking me for years to visit the island and check out his farm.'

'Sounds like a good idea. Do you want me to book tickets?'

'I was thinking it might be fun to drive down.'

'Only if we go in your car. You know I don't like anyone else driving my Porsche.'

'Yeah, sure, I'm cool with that. I like my old Merc better, anyway. It's quieter. So,' he went on, 'we can drop off some money in Luxemburg, check out the south of France and Barcelona, and then catch a ferry to Ibiza. What do you think?'

'Sounds great.' Lara planted a wet kiss on his lips. 'When are we leaving?'

'I'll need to check with the lads. Shouldn't be a problem. I haven't had a real holiday in a couple of years.' He pulled her closer and hugged her naked body. His chest was alive to the pressure of her taut nipples. He whispered in her ear, 'You fancy going back to bed?'

She stepped back and took hold of his right hand. 'That's a question you'll never have to ask me twice.' Lara smiled, took his hand, and led him into the bedroom.

There was little in the way of foreplay. Lara's cries of sensual pleasure grew louder and filled Angus's ears, but not his head. He was tense, distracted, and unable to let go into total abandonment. He was thinking instead of feeling and realised what he needed was a complete change of environment and lifestyle.

Raj and Murphy were busy vacuum-packing plastic bags full of yellow ecstasy pills in the upstairs office above the garage on Amsterdam's Middenweg. As the Eighties passed, the demand for designer drugs was increasing. Merck, the pharmaceutical giant, had patented the drug at the beginning of the century. They'd contemplated putting MDMA on the retail market as an appetite suppressant. Merck dropped the idea because of insufficient demand for their new product. Times had changed. Angus was in an adjoining room, overseeing the production of ecstasy pills, spilling out of the two pressing machines at the rate of 120 a minute. The yellow pills were embossed with a Mister Smiley logo. This was the last batch of powder to be turned into round tablets for some time; there were almost ten million pills stored downstairs in plastic drums. The building's upstairs section was permeated by the sweet, cloying, chemical smell that a large quantity of MDMA secretes. The next shipment of ecstasy powder from Poland was due in two months. It was time for a coffee break.

Murphy and Raj had their feet up on a makeshift table, munching Kit-Kats between sips of hot, filtered coffee. Angus was puffing on a fragrant joint of Red Leb, a unique blend of hashish imported from Lebanon and becoming an increasingly rare product to get one's sticky fingers on. Angus hummed along to The Stone Roses' 'Fool's Gold', playing on a small transistor radio by the kitchen sink. It was his current favourite song. *Down, down, down, down, da, down, down, down...*

He blew a smoke ring across the table towards his partners in crime. 'I've been considering going to Ibiza with Lara for a wee break.'

Murphy broke off, staring at his scuffed, steel-toe-capped boots. 'No problem, Angus. Right, Raj?' he asked, glancing at Raj.

Raj was somewhere else. 'What? Yeah, right. No problem at all. But how long is a wee break?'

'I was thinking along the lines of a couple of weeks.'

'Two fuckin' weeks!' Murphy exclaimed. 'That's nothing, man. Go for a month and party-hearty with Lara down on the magic island. You need a break, Angus. You haven't been right since Paris. That trip with the cops did my head in as well.'

'Aye,' said Raj. 'You lot must have been shitting yourselves when the bizzies showed up. I'm glad I missed out on that one.'

Angus smiled at his closest friends, suddenly overcome by emotion. 'Hey,' he said, 'do you guys think you get high from handling 'E', even with rubber gloves on?'

Murphy let out a spluttering laugh. 'Are you stupid or something? Of course, you get high from handling the stuff. The place is completely polluted with 'E'. We're breathing the shit. If we had any sense we would be wearing masks. I'm fucking well flying, man.'

'Me too,' said Raj, reaching over to take the smouldering joint from Angus. 'I can feel love vibrations.'

Angus laughed. Ridiculous as it sounded, he could also feel love vibrations. Murphy and Raj were never happier than when they were getting high and, of course, when they were making lots of money.

Fool's gold... The Stone Roses pulsed the airwaves.

Lara and Angus deposited two million Swiss francs in their joint account and stashed three kilos of gold coins in their safe deposit box. They drove out of Luxemburg and headed south on the highway through France. They were pulled to the side at a line of tollbooths just outside Lyon. Too gruff customs agents with unshaven faces and an Alsatian on a leash searched the Mercedes coupe. The dog was barking like its tail was on fire but it found nothing illegal; there wasn't anything to find. The car was clean but in need of a wash and a good going over with a vacuum cleaner.

Barcelona was a sun-drenched city full of life. Angus and Lara strolled hand in hand up and down La Rambla, a kilometre long, tree-lined human river formed of tourists, locals, street performers, buskers, hustlers, and vendors selling everything from newspapers to exotic birds in cages. The narrow alleys leading off the tiled walkway were filled with interesting shops and tapas bars, where you could enjoy delicious snacks and cheap drinks while sitting outside in the shade provided by tenement buildings. They spent two days in the bustling city before catching a night ferry to Ibiza.

Lara and Angus stood on the ship's stern sun-deck watching Barcelona's lights recede into the distance, propellers churning up the sea into a wide wake below them. There was a buzz of excited conversation throughout the ship's interior. Angus and Lara retired for the night to a neat first-class cabin. The bathroom had a leaky showerhead, seeping rust-coloured water into a plastic shower basin, and a stained lavatory pot that looked like it had been salvaged from a shipwreck.

They were woken in the morning by a blaring announcement, emitted from a speaker set into the cabin's ceiling, informing passengers that the ferry would be docking in Ibiza harbour in thirty minutes. Angus didn't want to hazard using the shower. He left Lara to take her chances under a spluttering jet of steaming water and navigated his way along a narrow corridor in search of the wide stairway leading up to the observation deck. It was already hot outside. The calm sea was deep-blue and Ibiza's old town loomed in the near distance. Rising behind the seafront an ancient citadel, built upon a hill, was surrounded by fortified walls. Around the headland and into the harbour, the city's Old Town lay beneath the fortress, a mish-mash of whitewashed residential buildings piled one on top of the other. Several luxury yachts were tied up at the quay beside the ferry terminal.

Angus steered his Mercedes down a steel ramp and swung right onto a broad, natural stone-paved esplanade. Lara consulted a road map spread across her lap. 'Turn right at the end and continue for about a kilometre,' she instructed.

The car's windows were rolled down. The rushing air felt warm and humid. The opposite side of the road was jammed with traffic, queuing to enter the city. Brightly clad tourists strolled along the pavements fronting shops and apartment blocks. Angus circled a roundabout and exited halfway around. The hustle and bustle of Ibiza Town were left behind. A short stretch of dual carriageway took them past a line of commercial warehouses. The traffic began to thin and soon they were driving along a two-lane road, heading north to the village of San Juan. The fields were yellow and parched, lending a stark contrast to the verdant fruit and olive trees dotting them. The further north they travelled, the greener the countryside became. Pine forests blanketed the hills. Angus drove into a small village and parked the car outside of a thick-walled white church. The quaint village had a well-taken-care-of feeling about it. There wasn't a scrap of waste to be seen on the streets or pavements. Mulberry trees hummed with the buzz of bees. The church bell tolled as Angus and Lara strolled down the main road. There was a communications centre, called EKO, in the village square. Angus went inside and asked a German man with curly hair, sitting behind a glass-topped counter, if he could make a phone call. 'Cabin two,' said the man pointing to his right. Angus dialled Acid Mike's number and told him they had arrived. He returned to the counter and asked the German guy how much for the call. He looked up from a newspaper, smiled, and informed Angus that local calls were free. 'Gracias,' said Angus, before walking outside. He and Lara crossed the street and entered the Vista Allegre Café. They ordered milk coffees. The tall man behind the bar had a comb-over hairstyle and wore black-framed glasses. He was talkative, spoke perfect English, and added 'very nice' to the end of almost every sentence he uttered. Angus and Lara carried their coffees out to a porch, sat down at a wooden table, and checked out the café's clientele. They felt right at home, surrounded by what looked like extras from a remake of *Woodstock*, the movie. A sannyasin couple wandered in, dressed in orange clothes with strings of wooden beads looped around their necks. They smiled as they passed, speaking German to each other, as did a number of people at nearby tables.

'Hey, you guys, welcome to Ibiza,' called Acid Mike, coming up the stone steps leading from the narrow pavement. He was wearing tie-dye shorts and a matching tee-shirt, a black turban wrapped around his head. In San Juan colourful clothes blended with the Bohemian character of the place. Nobody paid Mike the slightest bit of attention. They exchanged hugs and left the café.

Mike was driving a black Toyota Four Runner. Lara and Angus followed the dust-covered four-wheel-drive out of the village. A left turn took them onto a steep dirt track. Fine grey powder spewed up in rooster tails from the Toyota's broad back tyres. Angus closed the coupe's sunroof and slowed down to create distance between the vehicles. The track wound its way up into the hills. Over to the left, Angus could see the Mediterranean Sea in the distance and a black and white striped lighthouse on a prominent spit of land projecting from the jagged coastline. White farmhouses peppered hills and valleys. The track narrowed as it ran along the edge of a steep gorge, with no barrier to stop one going over the edge to meet death or serious injury. They passed a bearded man riding a brown horse. He waved. They came to an agave cactus with a five-metre tall candelabra loaded with jagged seedlings, and turned left onto a steeply descending rocky track, bearing a close resemblance to a dried-out stream bed. Angus heard the exhaust pipe scrape against a dislodged stone. Mike pulled up in a large flat circle of parched land, edged by rocks worn smooth by the elements. Angus imagined it had served as a threshing ground in a bygone era, being familiar with such rudimentary agricultural practices from his childhood days on the Isle of Iona. Now here he was on another island with a different kind of beauty from his birthplace. It looked like it hadn't rained in months.

Wendy B. White, Mike's off-and-on girlfriend over the past fifteen years, was waiting to greet them at the wooden gate of a small courtyard that was home to numerous cacti and succulents, planted in large terracotta pots. Wendy had aged since Angus had last met her briefly in Goa some years before. Thick blonde hair piled on top of her head, crows-feet fanned out around her flinty blue eyes, while a lopsided smile hung on her full lips, freshly made up with bright red lipstick. Wendy had big round breasts straining to break free from the constraints of the flimsy, low cut, floral-patterned dress she was wearing. 'How wonderful to see you again, Angus,' she cried in a distinctly upper-crust accent. Wendy pulled his face to hers and gave him a slobbery kiss, smack on the lips. She peeped over his shoulder. 'Oh, my goodness, you must be Lara. Come here, my darling girl, and give old Wendy a hug. My, you're even more gorgeous than Mikey described you.' She put a hand to her mouth in ersatz astonishment. She rushed past Angus to embrace Lara like a long-lost daughter. Angus saw Wendy's rotund buttocks having the same effect on the back of her dress as her bulging breasts did on the front. She was a big woman.

Mike's home was fairly typical of the area, flat-roofed and built to withstand a siege. The whitewashed stone walls were a metre thick, with barred windows too small to climb through. The double front door was made of stout weathered planks, studded with large, iron nail heads. Angus entered the house and found himself in a cool, cavernous room with several doors, a flight of narrow stone steps leading upstairs. Angus glanced up at the high ceiling, formed from sturdy beams of juniper, supporting uniform slats of olive. The place smelled of teak oil. Most of the wooden furniture had been imported from Indonesia, low opium tables, colonial-style chairs, and, over to one side of the rectangular room, a four-poster bed with a thick black mattress and several red bolster cushions. There was a stereo system with a power amp displaying twin fluctuating lines of green LEDs. *A friend of the devil...* The sound of The Grateful Dead was rippling quietly from a pair of floor-standing speaker cabinets. Angus turned to Mike and said, 'Still listening to the golden oldies?'

Mike sat down on a creaky chair. 'Yes, I'm still listening to The Dead after all these years. I think *American Beauty* is one of the best albums they ever cut. Timeless, in my opinion.'

Angus flopped into a teak plantation chair opposite Mike. 'Yeah, it's a great album. My favourite track is 'Ripple'.'

Mike smiled thoughtfully. 'I'd go so far as to say that 'Ripple' is my all-time number one track.' He began singing a line from the song. 'There is a road, no simple highway...'

Angus joined him. 'Between the dawn and the dark of night...'

Neither of them were very good singers. In fact, they were terrible. They burst out laughing.

'Good to see you again, Angus.'

'The feeling is mutual.'

'I was just thinking. If I die before you do and you happen to be around, please make sure that 'Ripple' is played at my funeral.'

'For fuck's sake, Mike. This is Ibiza. I thought this place was all about life, not fucking funerals.'

Mike chuckled. 'Yes, you're right, matey. The strange thing about it is that the more intensely one lives, the more one becomes aware of death hovering around in the background. Although it's perhaps unwise to dwell on the fact overmuch. Anyway, I hear you need a good holiday.'

'That is an understatement. Check this out.' Angus held out his right hand and splayed his fingers. 'My hands have been shaking like this since that weird trip in Paris.'

'Yes, well, it kind of goes with the territory. I felt pretty shaky myself after that carry-on. It will pass.'

'Will it?'

'Of course. Everything does. You just need to kick back while you're here, go swimming... Man, I haven't shown you the pool yet. It will blow that busy mind of yours clear out of the water.' Mike stood. 'Come on, you're going to love this.'

The new swimming pool was at the back of the house. Wendy and Lara were already in the pool, floating naked, face down on plastic airbeds. It was quite a sight. The infinity pool was fifteen metres long. It was faced off in grey slate and had a magnificent view over an undulating valley with the Mediterranean Sea as a backdrop. It was a hazy day and difficult to determine where the sea ended and the sky began. Angus stripped off and dived in. He surfaced and looked around. He'd landed in paradise.

Three roasting hot days later, Angus and Lara attended their first Ibiza full moon party. At midnight they began a long uphill walk. They'd swallowed a hit of ecstasy each. Mike and Wendy had both dropped blotter acid. They were headed for 'Cana Paz', a small farmhouse with a few acres of land on top of a hill. The bright moon illuminated the barren landscape with a silvery light. They began to meet people on the rocky *camino*. Most of the partygoers were high on something, a few so intoxicated they'd given up trying to make it up the hill, deciding instead to let go of their minds where they were and have a good laugh about it. The closer they drew to the party, the louder and more distinct became the thump, thump, thump of a bass kick drum, the beat that defines acid house music. Cars were parked all over the place, some not very sensibly. A battered Renault Four was stuck in a ditch with half a dozen laughing people trying to free it.

The main event was staged in a flat field. The music was delivered by twin stacks of industrial speakers, most of which were bass cabinets. The bass was so physical Angus felt his heart beating in time to the music, a not entirely unpleasant sensation. At 130 beats per minute, it was exciting. Without a moment's hesitation, Angus and his three companions joined hundreds of ravers on the dance floor. It was tribal. Angus felt like he'd been reunited with his clan, and what a wild, crazy, ecstatic, and multi-ethnic clan they were. He hadn't been in a scene like this since Anjuna full moon parties in Goa, and there wasn't a cop in sight. He shouted to Lara, jumping around like her feet were on fire, 'This is fantastic!'

A dust cloud had formed over the dance area. Illuminated by red, blue, green, and yellow spotlights, it resembled a coloured parachute undulating in the air. The DJ wore a black top hat and was punching the air as if battling invisible demons. Old dance classics were sampled, looped, and blended with cutting-edge house beats, provoking the dancers to shout encouragement to the DJ who, in Angus's expanded mind, appeared to be a musical genius. The age of rock stars was losing its sparkle; the era of superstar DJs was dawning. The rave-olution would not be televised.

Angus and Lara levelled out from their 'E' rush and went in search of something to parch their thirst. It was by now firmly established that one of the risks involved with MDMA use was dehydration. They discovered a makeshift tea stall behind some bushes. A tall man with thick curly hair stood behind the counter serving the queue. When it was his turn, Angus asked the man for two glasses of tea and a slice of apple pie. Sheep bleated in the background. Angus looked around. There were no woolly sheep in sight. The man behind the bar glanced at him and smiled. Angus could swear he was now hearing automatic gunfire and police sirens in the distance.

'That will be three hundred Pesetas,' said the tea-seller in heavily Dutch-accented English, placing two glasses of milky tea and a slice of pie wrapped in a paper napkin on the counter.

Angus said to him, 'Did you hear that?'

'Did I hear what?'

'Gunfire and police sirens.'

The Dutchman glanced around. Angus looked up when he heard a helicopter flying overhead.

The Dutchman gave a toothy grin. 'I think it's a jet fighter next.' Jet engines whined from the bushes. There was an amplifier hidden under the wooden counter. When a lion roared, he turned it down. 'Don't want to frighten the kiddies, now do we?' He didn't wait for an answer. 'Do you like Tommy Cooper?'

Just the thought of the British comedian, wearing a fez and performing ridiculous conjuring tricks that always backfired, made Angus splutter with laughter. 'Of course, I like Tommy Cooper. Who doesn't? The man was brilliant.'

'Just like that!' said the Dutchman, offering a hand, which Angus gladly shook. 'My name's Willem by the way.'

'Angus. Nice to meet you, Willem.'

'Enjoy the party,' said the jovial Dutchman, turning to serve a blonde woman wrapped in white gauze, carrying a brass trident in one hand and an enormous teddy bear in the other.

Lara and Angus sat on a slab of yellow limestone, sipping hot tea and munching delicious apple pie. Above them, ragged clouds tore over the moon. 'Man,' said Angus, 'there are some really crazy people around here.' The sound of a football crowd cheering erupted from a nearby bush.

'What the hell was that?' Lara asked, looking behind her with a puzzled expression. Angus explained and when a cuckoo called out at one hundred watts per channel, they both fell over laughing.

Time flew by. Angus, Lara, Mike and Wendy sat on the edge of a clifftop, watching the sunrise over the distant island of Mallorca. The magnificence of the scene defied words. The four friends remained silent, humbled by Ibiza's pristine beauty. There was something distinctly feminine about the landscape. No sharp contours. Like the scent of pine carried up by the breeze from the forest below, there was a stimulating presence in the atmosphere that made one feel grateful to be alive.

'Yeah, mon!'

Angus recognised the voice immediately. He looked up into Anand's smiling eyes. 'Man, I haven't seen you in years. The last time was in Poona. Laxmi Villas if my memory serves me well.' Angus shook his head. 'Man, what are you doing here?

'Yeah, mon, the show must go on,' said Anand, tugging at one of his long dreadlocks. 'This is my place, mon.'

'What? Cana Paz! You own this place?'

'No, mon. I don't own it. I rent it,' Anand declared. 'Money's Babylon, mon. Better not to own anything. Things tie you down. Then you have to build a fence around all that shit to protect it. Pretty soon you're living in a cage. Might be made of gold, but it's still a cage. I love my freedom, mon.' Anand sat on a smooth boulder and lit a spliff. 'How about the flying Scotsman?'

'I'm getting along fine, man. Been living in The Dam for some time.'

'Amsterdam is Babylon, mon. Smoke?' Anand handed Angus a pungent-smelling joint and said, 'You want to get a place on the island, while there are still places to get. Nostradamus said Ibiza will be a safe place to be when the Armageddon comes.'

'Nostradamus said that?' Angus took a big drag on the spliff. His head spun.

'Sure, mon, everybody living around here knows that. The Armageddon coming soon, mon. Babylon be governed by cunning lizard people and the sleeping masses are easily influenced by them. Lambs to the slaughter, mon. Lambs to the slaughter.' Anand nodded his head knowingly and smiled. 'That's one of the life's great mysteries, mon.'

'It sure is,' agreed Angus, unsure of what exactly he was agreeing with.

Just then, another old friend appeared, Atom the woodcarver. Angus had first met him in Goa during the early Seventies. He was sandpapering a wooden hand. 'You like it?' he asked, handing it to Angus. Atom behaved like it was only yesterday since they'd last seen each other.

Angus studied the hand, carved from olive wood. It was a thing of great beauty. He looked into Atom's bloodshot eyes, framed by thick black dreadlocks. 'You've come a long way from carving hairpins down on Anjuna beach, man.'

Atom smiled shyly, a gold-capped tooth reflecting an early morning sunbeam. 'Yeah, I suppose I have. You wanna buy it?'

Angus had anticipated this question. He laughed and asked, 'How much?'

'Five thousand pesetas?'

Angus pulled out a small roll of Spanish banknotes from his jean's pocket. 'I'll tell you what. Make me another hand just like this one and I'll give you twenty and you can keep the change.' He handed over the money. 'How does that suit you?'

'Yeah, man!' exclaimed Atom, giving Angus such a hard slap on the back he nearly knocked him off the cliff.

Angus looked around at his friend's smiling faces and knew that once again he'd found a place he could call home.

The return road journey to Amsterdam was uneventful. It felt like an uphill grind all the way, perhaps because Angus had been reluctant to leave Ibiza. Both he and Lara had fallen in love with the island and wished to return there as soon as possible. The highlight of Lara's first visit to Ibiza had been going with Wendy to 'Ku', a vast, open-air discotheque just off the San Antonio road. She'd been thrilled to find herself dancing next to Grace Jones.

What stayed with Angus was his last conversation with Acid Mike, before he'd flown up to London to take care of business. They'd been sitting outside by the pool, under the shade of a fig tree, when Mike had pointed to a large two-storied farmhouse nestled at the foot of a pine-clad hill. He'd said, 'That *finca's* up for sale. Not cheap, but it's worth every peseta they're asking for it. Over one hundred thousand square metres of land and has its own borehole for water. No electricity, but poles are going up along the side of the road, so it won't be long before power is available. If I were you, matey, I'd consider buying the old place. It will be worth a fortune one day.' Later that afternoon, Angus had wandered by the house. It was deserted. He took the opportunity to snoop around a little. He immediately began fantasizing about what could be made out of the dilapidated farmhouse with the help of a big financial investment. Coming from a humble background, he'd never actually owned much in the way of property. Now that he could easily afford it, working on such a place would be a dream come true.

It was a wet, mid-September Monday morning when Angus returned to work. He strolled into Rembrandt's back office to find Murphy and Raj with their feet up on the paint-splattered table, smoking their first joint of the day.

Murphy exhaled hard, expelling a long stream of hash smoke in Angus's direction. 'Where the fuck have you been?'

'Ibiza, of course,' Angus replied. 'You know that.'

'Yeah, of course, I do. But you've been gone for a long time. Too fuckin' long.'

'Well, it was you who said I should go for a month.'

'Aye, I did. But you've been gone for over six fuckin' weeks, man.'

Raj said, 'You're going to have to get over to London quick, man. There's tons of money waiting to be changed up.'

Murphy added. 'And it's not good to have over ten million eggs in one basket.'

'Here, I brought you both a wee pressie from Ibiza.' Angus handed his business partners two small packages wrapped in a Spanish newspaper.

Murphy quickly unwrapped his gift. When he saw what it was he stared at the wooden hand and asked Angus, 'What the fuck's this?'

Angus said, 'I thought it might come in handy.'

Murphy raised his eyes to the ceiling and said, 'I walked right into that one. Didn't I?'

Raj chuckled. 'You did. I saw it coming from a mile off.'

'How come you're so fuckin' smart all of a sudden?' Murphy asked Raj.

Angus poured coffee for himself, pulled up a chair, and took his place at the table. His two partners proceeded to inform him about new developments that had taken place during his absence. Once Angus was up to date, he rose quickly to his feet and said, 'I'm off to the travel agent to get a ticket to London. See you guys when I get back.' He was heading out the door when he realised he'd forgotten something. He walked back to the table and held both his hands out in front of him palms down. 'Check it out,' he said to his seated friends.

'What?' asked Raj.

Murphy stroked his moustache thoughtfully for a moment. 'Your hands have stopped shaking. Right?'

Angus nodded. 'Right first time, amigo.'

'Nice one,' commented Raj.

On the evening of the same day, Angus landed in Gatwick. He then caught a train to Victoria Station and a taxi from there to Mike's apartment on Portobello Road. Acid Mike said he was happy to see him, although Angus could see he looked decidedly unhappy.

'What's up, Mike?'

'Check this out.' Mike was pointing at a narrow column in a national newspaper.

Angus skimmed the article about an ecstasy bust in Manchester. The city's anti-narcotics squad claimed they'd made a record seizure of MDMA with a street value in excess of a million pounds. Several suspects had been charged, including a well-known nightclub owner. 'Our Product?'

Mike nodded slowly. 'Yes, matey, I'm afraid so.'

'Did we lose a lot of money?'

'That's not the problem, Angus. Charlie Barnes always paid upfront. The problem lies in the fact that Charlie is undoubtedly facing a long prison term for trafficking big time in a Class A drug. I've known him for ages and he knows my proper name, although he doesn't know where I live. I trust the man but, when someone with a wife and kids faces being banged up for years, you never really know whether or not they will grass you up.'

'So what do you think you're going to do about it?'

'I've been thinking it might be a good idea to get out of Dodge. We've had a remarkable run of good fortune over here. My gut feeling tells me it would be wise not to push our luck. Always better to err by playing it safe.' Mike took off his headband and placed it on the centre of the kitchen table. 'Another thing that's bothering me is that the 'E' business is falling into the wrong hands. A couple of kids died in Brixton last week from taking contaminated ecstasy pills. There was a coloured picture of the pills the girls took in the *Evening Standard*. They look exactly like those Mitsubishis we were putting out a few months back. Those weren't our pills, because I know from taking them myself that they are pure MDMA. Someone is copying our product, because our pills have a good name.'

'What's your next move then?'

'I'm seriously contemplating closing up shop here and coming over to Amsterdam to join you lot. The Dam's the perfect place to lie low for a while and let the dust settle. There's also plenty of business to pick up on if I feel so inclined.' Mike gave Angus a droll smile. 'In the meantime, we need to get the money that's here changed up as soon as possible. I have to drive up to

Birmingham to collect a load of cash tomorrow. Apart from that, there are only a few bits and bobs to take care of. Nothing major. If you get Raj or Murphy on the blower before I do, please let them know what's happening.'

All international telephone conversations were made from public call boxes in Amsterdam and the UK, and they were always brief. Different telephones were used on different days of the week, at different times and in different locations in central London. There were only outgoing calls from Amsterdam and only incoming in London. Conditions determined if the calls were answered, but more often than not they were. Of course, there was always the possibility that the police authorities were monitoring international calls held in public phone boxes and call centres. The police weren't stupid. They knew perfectly well what was going on. But what the police didn't have was limitless resources to pursue such time-consuming work. That single fact had so far tipped the scales to the dealers' advantage.

Angus caught a Hackney cab to Kings Cross. These taxis provided an extra sense of security when travelling across central London because the police rarely checked them. Angus sat in the cab's back seat with a sports bag containing a million pounds at his feet. He stared blankly out the tinted glass window, his eyes barely focused on the traffic thronging the Marylebone Road. A deep longing for Lara suddenly overcame him. He pushed the feeling away, thinking it wasn't the right time or place to indulge himself in sentimentality. A simple case of the mind winning out in the constant struggle between head and heart, which prompted him to feel like there was a crowd inhabiting his consciousness. Angus saw clearly he was not one individual. He was many, each entity vying for control, pulling him at times in opposite directions to the extent he felt torn apart. He recalled a quote from Armenian mystic, George Gurdjieff. 'Man's name is legion.' A disturbing notion in his train of thought, quickly shunted aside by a contemplation upon how the word *wealthy* has its roots in *well-being* and is meant to connote not only large sums of money but also a rich and satisfying life. The irony of it was money working to create quite the opposite in his life, leaving him isolated and dissatisfied. Money felt like a chain wrapped around his neck, dragging him wherever it wished to go. He paid the cab driver and the heavy bag of money yanked him into Rahim Gurmani's foreign exchange office.

Rahim was a Pakistani in his early thirties with a squint in his right eye. His neat and tidy business premises were a stone's throw from Kings Cross railway station. Angus always felt relaxed going there. Unlike Mister Dawoud's office in Notting Hill Gate, it had a windowless back room where all illegal transactions took place, well away from the public eye. Rahim thought Angus's name was 'Nathan' and that he'd been born in Dublin.

Rahim always wore a freshly pressed cotton shirt and matching tie. He greeted Angus with a toothy smile and a Cockney accent. 'How are you today, mate. That's a big bag you're carrying, Nathan. That's a good sign. Bees and honey.'

287

'Hi, Rahim, top o' the morning to you,' said Angus, sounding more like a Cornish yokel than an Irishman. 'You're going to be seeing a fair bit of me in the coming days because I have a dozen big bags waiting to visit your office.'

'That's what I like to hear. I have a good connection running in the City of London right now and he needs a lot of merry-go-rounds. Shouldn't be a problem getting my hands on Swiss Francs either. I've got it sorted. Coffee, Nathan?'

'No thanks,' said Angus stepping into the moneychanger's back office and placing the sports bag with the cash on a counter beside two electronic counting machines, lights blinking and ready to roll. 'I'd like to keep moving. There's a million quid in the bag and I can bring the same again this afternoon if you can handle it.'

The Pakistani made a show of looking at his recently acquired solid gold wristwatch. 'If you can make it back here before one, I'll have it sorted by six-thirty this evening at the latest. How's that suit you, mate?'

Angus had to smile at Rahim Gurmani. He was grinning like a hard-working Pakistani about to earn over a hundred grand in a week.

It was after midnight. Dynamite Dick, Acid Mike, Angus and Billy Beard, a clean-shaven man, who said little and had lost the thumb on his right hand, were halfway between the south-east coast of England and Rotterdam. The *Boomerang* was flying across the water like a skimming stone. Angus hung onto a reinforced plastic handle, bolted to the rib boat's centre console, as the boat's triple engines propelled them through a choppy patch of water. The *Boomerang* smacked into the tail end of the wash thrown up by a passing freighter and three stainless-steel propellers whined in high-pitched unison as the boat went airborne for five very long seconds.

Mike yelled in Angus's right ear. 'I swore I'd never do this again and here I am. I must be out of my bloody mind!'

Angus turned and looked into Mike's eyes. It was the first time he'd ever seen fear in them. Angus was enjoying his express ride on what felt like a surface-to-surface missile. He loved the sense of high-speed motion and the vast space provided by the starlit sky and open sea. The only thing he didn't like were the memories being dredged up concerning Jimmy Bradley's death in Mumbai Harbour, the last time he'd been in a boat like the one he was now standing in, knees bent to absorb the shockwaves. Dick shouted something to catch his attention and passed him a half-smoked joint. Angus cupped it in his hand and took a long drag of tobacco smoke flavoured with Afghani hash. He looked over again at Dick. He had both hands on the wheel, face illuminated by a glowing instrument panel, muscular body braced against the thrust. Dynamite Dick was grinning like a chimp who'd just been handed a bunch of ripe bananas. Angus thought he'd never seen a man more at home in his element. There was a marked change in pitch from one of the engines. Billy Beard whistled from behind. Angus turned and Billy signalled with a hand minus a thumb for him to ditch the smouldering joint because he was about to check a fuel line.

In the distance, the cloud base over Rotterdam reflected a dull orange glow. Dick steered the boat in a more northerly direction. Closer to the coast, a low-flying passenger jet passed overhead, wing lights blinking, forward beams strafing ahead into patches of mist as it made its runway approach. The *Boomerang's* roaring motors blotted out the sound of the plane's engines. Angus began to make out the shadowy and angular forms of buildings. He saw a car crossing a humpback bridge, its headlights cutting across the sky like twin lighthouse beams. Dick dropped the speed by half and steered the boat into a narrow channel. A red light flashed in the darkness, three times, four times, five times. The searchlight in the prow remained switched off. The boat veered to the left. Dick cut the engines, then levered them up to protect the props from damage. The hull crunched on gravel and came to a halt in a small beach's shallows. A strong smell of tar wafted over from a nearby wooden boathouse. The silence made Angus's ears ring. His eyes focused on an unexpected movement in the shadows. Dressed in black, Murphy appeared from behind the boathouse. Dick and Billy heaved four canvas bags onto the sand. No return journey cargo. Mike and Angus pushed the *Boomerang* out into deeper water. Detonator Dick gave a thumbs-up. Billy Beard waved a four-fingered hand. The engines thrummed back into life. The boat reversed for a short distance and then, with a roar and a raised prow, she spun on her axis, performed a neat 180° degree turn in the channel, and shot back out to sea.

Five minutes later, Mike and Angus were sitting in the passenger seats of a Rembrandt's van, as Murphy drove them through a sleeping seaside village. A cat's luminescent eyes glinted from the pavement. They passed by dark houses and headed north in the direction of the highway. Murphy drove on, silent, focused, and keeping ten kilometres an hour below the various speed limits all the way. It took a little over ninety minutes to reach Amsterdam's Rozenstraat, where the van was driven into the garage and the doors securely locked behind it.

Acid Mike had rented a top-floor pied-à-terre on the Stadthouderskade in Amsterdam's Oud-Zuid district, near to the De Pijp area, his favourite part of the city. Mike enjoyed nothing more than to stroll along the kilometre-long Albert-Cuyp street market. Regarded as Europe's largest daytime market it is set up and dismantled on an almost daily basis. Towards evening he'd wander into local coffee shops to sample exotic blends of hashish and get stoned with the multi-ethnic locals.

Angus's life became more leisurely. He was able to spend more quality time with Lara. She'd returned to painting and was planning an exhibition of her work in an up-market gallery when she'd completed her collection.

In June 1989, their source of ecstasy powder in Poland dried up. Paul Harrison, their supplier, had received an unexpected visit from two high-ranking police detectives, belonging to Warsaw's anti-narcotics squad. The Englishman managed to explain why the business he managed was ordering large quantities of PMK, the main precursor required in the production of MDMA, and showed them the fabricated paperwork to prove everything was legitimate. The Polish detectives were veterans and had seen and heard it all before. They smelled a foreign rat and did not mince words when they warned Paul that, if they paid him a return visit, it would be to arrest him and throw him in prison for a very long time.

Paul Harrison handed in his notice on the very next day and a week later returned to the UK, secure in the knowledge that he'd stashed away enough money to live comfortably for the rest of his life.

Angus and his partners were not particularly bothered by this new development. They'd had a very good run by anyone's standards and still had over two million ecstasy pills in stock. The face of the business was also changing. Gangs of unscrupulous East European and Asian drug dealers had begun to flood the market with inferior ecstasy tablets, containing very little or no MDMA and a lot of cheap to manufacture crystal meth, or other dangerous chemical concoctions. Acid Mike suggested waiting for a dry spell in the market and then sell their quality product at double the price they'd been charging up to that point in time. It turned out to be a sound business strategy. A shortage arrived in September. By the end of October, there were only 200,000 pills left in storage at the garage near the Middenweg.

Eight o'clock on a Monday morning in November, Amsterdam was shrouded in mist, the temperature a few degrees above zero. Patches of frost glinted on the street. Murphy met up with Angus at a tram shelter near the Amstel Hotel. They set off on bicycles, heading over to the garage to vacuum pack the remaining stock of ecstasy pills for a German customer from Berlin, who wished to buy the lot. They pulled their woollen caps down over their ears to protect them from the bitter wind blowing across the Amstel River. They chatted as they pedalled along a cyclist's lane on the edge of a quiet residential area. Thin ice on frozen puddles crackled under their tyres.

Angus was coasting down a narrow street within sight of the garage, Murphy a short distance behind. A red car indicated and pulled out in front of Angus, prompting him to brake and come to a halt beside a black VW van, parked to the left of him. One of the van's back shock absorbers squeaked, alerting Angus to the fact that there was someone in the vehicle. He glanced through the van's passenger side window. The glass was partly misted from condensation. There was nobody in the cab. Angus felt the insecurity that accompanies sensing something is seriously wrong. The red car drove off. Murphy drew alongside Angus, who spoke quietly but urgently from the side of his mouth. 'Keep peddling. Act normal. Don't look at the garage. I think the place might be under surveillance.'

They cycled at a leisurely pace, turned right onto a cycle lane, and continued over a wide bridge, busy with rush hour traffic crossing the Amstel river. They took another right and came to a halt beside a wooden bench. They dismounted, sat down, and had a quick confab.

'What the fuck was that all about?' Murphy asked, pulling a packet of Drum tobacco from his jerkin pocket.

'Did you notice that black van we stopped beside near the garage?'

'Yeah, of course, I noticed it. I stopped right behind it when the red car pulled out. What about it?'

'There was somebody inside it.'

'No there wasn't. I peeked in the passenger's window when we got going again. There was nobody in the cab.'

'But there was somebody in the back of the van.'

'How the fuck would you know that?'

'I heard one of the back shocks squeak from an increase of pressure.'

'You did?'

Angus gave a worried smile. 'I did. And did you notice the condensation on the windows was on the inside?'

'Fuck!' Murphy lit a roll-up and blew smoke in the river's direction. 'I noticed that van parked there last week.'

There was a long, heavy pause as they considered this distressing fact. Finally, Angus said, 'Man, they're fucking well onto us. We better go back to the office and tell Raj and Mike about this, pronto.'

'Let me finish my fag first.'

'I thought you'd quit smoking.'

Murphy took another quick drag on his cigarette and pushed his woollen hat to the back of his head.. 'Yeah, I did stop smoking. But I just thought I'd buy some tobacco because it's cold.'

'That's a pretty lame excuse if ever I heard one. You'd better roll me one, too.'

They sat on the bench, drawing on their soggy-ended roll-ups and gazing past a line of houseboats over to where the garage was hidden behind a row of apartment buildings. They both knew they'd never return there. Angus spat out a loose thread of tobacco, turned, and studied his friend's tense face, locked in a quandary he couldn't resolve. He could have sworn new lines had appeared on Murphy's forehead during the last half hour. The city hummed in the background as it wound up for another working day. Autumn was running its course. The trees were shedding their withered leaves.

❖ ❖ ❖

Raj cycled over to the garage in the afternoon. He hadn't been there in a fortnight. He kept the hood of his blue anorak up as he passed the black van, still parked in the same place. The air was chilly. He noted the vehicle's windows were completely clouded by condensation on the inside. All the other car windscreens in the street were clear. He turned a corner, coasted to a halt, and chained his bike to a lamppost. Walking back the way he'd come, he saw the beginnings of a muddy footpath at the edge of a patch of woodland with tall birch trees, their yellowing foliage fluttering in the breeze. He wandered along the slippery path, sat down behind a thick clump of nettles, and put his right hand in dog shit. 'Fuck!' he cursed quietly, wiping the offending substance off his hand with nettle leaves.

The black VW van was in sight, but only just. He hunkered down, waited, and watched. About an hour passed, before a man in a light-blue shirt stepped out of the back of the van. Raj jerked his anorak's hood off and raised his pocket binoculars to observe him more closely. The tall man pissed against a conveniently positioned tree. Raj caught a flash of his flaccid penis, his clean-shaven face, and his broad forehead, which had POLITIE written on it in big capital letters. Raj lay back in the grass and the back of his head landed in a soggy lump of dog shit. He lay there without moving, gazing up at the white sun, partly obscured by a thin layer of cloud. Raj was thinking he was in a lot worse kind of shit than the canine brand. When the stink became intolerable, he rose to his feet and slinked back to his bicycle.

It took Raj twenty minutes to cycle back to the Rozenstraat. He took his time chaining his bicycle to an aluminium bike stand, surreptitiously observing the street and pedestrian traffic as he did so. Nothing in sight aroused suspicion. When he entered Rembrandt's back office, Murphy, Mike and Angus looked up at him with concerned expressions.

'Well?' Mike said.

Raj gave a wan smile. 'It's the fucking cops.'

'You sure?' Murphy asked.

'Hundred and one percent. I saw one of the fuckers taking a piss against a tree.'

'*Fucking shit!*' Angus hissed through his teeth.

'Talking of which,' said Murphy, wrinkling his nose, 'there's a terrible stink of dog shit in here. Raj, check your boots, man.'

'I don't need to,' said Raj. 'I didn't step in dog shit. But I do have skittery dog shite plastered all over the back of my head.'

'Fucking hell,' gasped Murphy, a smile spreading quickly across his face. 'I'm not even going to bother asking you how the fuck that happened.'

Everyone, including Raj, laughed, diminishing the tension that had been hanging in the room before the foul-smelling Indian Scotsman's arrival.

Business shut down completely that afternoon. Angus sold his Mercedes coupe the next morning for a quarter of its value. He'd taken his car over to the Middenweg garage two weeks previously to put underseal on it in preparation for winter. The car was no longer registered in his name, but he wanted to get rid of it just in case. He was glad that they'd all obeyed Mike's strict rule to always wear gloves in the garage. Murphy and Raj dumped two industrial vacuum-packing machines into the Amstel River in the middle of the night. Lara searched through Rembrandt's office, getting rid of anything at all that looked in the least way suspicious: notes with lots of big numbers jotted on them, plastic bags, parcel tape dispensers, chunks of hash samples. On Friday morning she sold her Porsche for a good price. Everyone tidied up their apartments, throwing out old airline tickets, baggage bar codes on suitcases, bank receipts, address books, photographs. By the weekend everything had been taken care of and they all sank into the nerve-racking reality of waiting for an unfamiliar knock on the front door, or an unexpected ring on the doorbell.

Every morning for a week, Nina and Alice bought local and national newspapers, scanning the pages in search of a report on the police discovering a large cache of ecstasy pills on Amsterdam's Middenweg. Not a word.

Two weeks passed and nothing untoward happened. A month later, they breathed a communal sigh of relief. They'd gotten away with it.

Murphy and Raj took their families to Thailand for a three-month holiday. Angus, Lara, and Acid Mike flew down to Ibiza. Angus immediately put down a deposit on the dilapidated farmhouse he'd seen on the old Portinatx road. His life as an international drug smuggler, dealer, and money launderer had come to a sudden and timely end. He and Lara had the modern-day equivalent of over thirty million euros to play with. They began to live the kind of life that most people only ever get to dream about.

17

I LEAVE YOU MY DREAM

'My mouth's as dry as a desert,' I said.

Jean was sitting on the opposite side of the kitchen table, head in hands, eyes fixed on my face. 'I'm hardly surprised to hear that,' she said. 'You've been talking non-stop for...' She glanced at the wall clock. '...almost two hours.'

I ran my parched tongue over my dry lips. 'What did you think?'

'A lot of things. But mainly I was thinking that Angus and his pals are a right bunch of scheming crooks. I'd no idea Lara was involved with your brother's shenanigans to such an extent. She never mentioned any of that to me during our time in Sri Lanka.'

'Did you ever ask her about such things?'

After a moment's reflection, Jean said, 'Now that you mention it, I don't recall that I did. I've told you before that women tend to talk more about what's current. Women's things. For instance, Lara told me that she'd had her fallopian tubes tied. She'd been informed by a specialist that she might die if she gave birth. That's why they never had kids.'

'Yes,' I said, 'Angus mentioned that to me in Sri Lanka. Didn't seem to bother him. Said he'd never been the fathering type. Saw himself more in the 'nice uncle' role.'

Jean carried on talking as if she hadn't heard a word I'd just said, a common enough occurrence in my daily life. 'You know, women are not so inclined as men to speak about the distant past in too much detail. We're just more here and now. I've told you before; it's a body thing. It's as simple as that.'

I thought that over for a while because I disagreed with everything she'd just said. It wasn't as simple as that. I'd overheard Jean and our daughters speaking about the past on many occasions. I thought, *maybe men have better functioning memories than women.* But I couldn't remember having ever heard anyone say that.

Jean stood up and went over to put the kettle on. She dropped PG Tips tea bags into two empty mugs. She returned to the kitchen sink, parked her bum against it, crossed her arms across her chest, and waited for the water to come to the boil. 'I was just thinking,' she said. 'How on earth do you manage to remember all those details about Angus's life?'

'What details are you referring to exactly?'

'You know, things like dates, street names in Amsterdam, strangers' appearances, amounts of money, that sort of thing.'

Oh, oh, I thought, *here comes trouble.* 'Jean, I have a wee confession to make.'

Jean's eyebrows shot up. 'You sound like a Catholic. What kind of confession?'

'Well, I've been writing a book about it all.'

'*A book?* What *kind* of bloody book?' The kettle grumbled behind her.

'I'm not sure exactly.' I quickly racked my brain for a more coherent answer. 'I began taking notes after I had my car accident. You know, memories, my brother's adventures and things like that.'

The kettle came to the boil and Jean poured steaming water into the waiting mugs. '*Things?* What kind of *things?*' she enquired, turning to fix her eyes on mine.

'Och, nothing important really,' I said, trying to play it down. 'How I feel about life. New perspectives I picked up from Angus. Stories he told me. *You.*' Oops! I knew I shouldn't have uttered that three-letter word as soon as it left my dry lips.

'*Me?* For God's sake, what have you written about me? I hope to Christ you haven't been writing about the intimate details of our sex-life.'

I pretended to be surprised. 'Of course not,' I lied.

Jean looked reassured. She believed me. I've never been very good at lying.

'Well, thank goodness for that,' she said, visibly relieved. 'So, where is this book of yours? When do I get to read it?'

'It's written in a Microsoft Word document on a laptop I keep locked up in the office safe. It's—'

Jean interjected. 'That's probably a very good idea, taking into account your brother's nefarious past. There would be hell to pay if the police ever got their hands on it. Anyway, go on.'

'Yes, well, the story is almost finished and I'll let you read it when it is. But there's one condition.'

'And that is?'

'I'll only let you read it if you agree to go on the world cruise with Angus, Lara, and their friends.'

I was surprised to see that Jean was smiling at my suggestion. 'I'll consider it.'

'What?'

'I said, I will consider it.' She took the soggy teabags out of the mugs, dropped them into the waste bin under the sink, carried the mugs over to the table, and set one down in front of me. 'Don't sit there grinning at me like a shot fox. I haven't said I'll do it yet. Just that I will *consider* going on the cruise. That's all.'

Emotion constricted my throat. 'I… I'm so happy to hear that, Jean. What made you change your mind? You sounded dead against it earlier on.'

'Well, for a start, I'd like to meet that Acid Mike guy. He sounds like quite a character from what you've described. A right bloody criminal but also a gentleman.'

'*Oh!*' I sighed.

'What?'

'There's something I haven't told you.'

'I'm listening.'

'It's to do with the last part of the story.'

'In that case,' said Jean, 'you better wet your whistle first.'

'Cheers.' We clinked our mugs together. I took a few sips of tea. I returned to Ibiza, picking up on the threads of my story. The details were clear in my mind. A few days previously, I'd written it all down on my laptop, while in my office with a couple of hours to kill.

Angus and Lara moved into their new home in Ibiza at the beginning of February 1989. The *finca* had several rooms, but only one without a leaky roof. Renovation work on the old farmhouse had begun in January and was therefore barely in its elementary stages. The only things about the building that did not need to be knocked down, ripped out and replaced were the metre-thick stone walls, originally constructed over a century before. The builder overseeing the project was Hassan, a chubby Moroccan man. He spoke very little English. Hassan seemed to know what he was doing and most of the time Angus and Lara left him to get on with it. He had half-a-dozen of his fellow countryman under his supervision, involved in various tasks: carpentry, plastering, plumbing, tiling, laying electric cables for the power that would hopefully one day be supplied, and repairing dry stone walls to stop subsidence on terraces overgrown with weeds.

It was cold and damp. Angus and Lara had soon discovered that wintertime in Ibiza was a world away from the summer months. In mid-January, a northeasterly storm system brought low temperatures and it snowed, a meteorological phenomena so rare in the region that it made front-page headlines in the local newspaper, *El Diario de Ibiza*. There was a soot-blackened open fireplace in their one habitable room. One of Angus's daily tasks was to ensure there was plenty of firewood at hand to ward off the cold at night. Angus purchased an old but reliable Land Rover. Each working day of the week he drove into Ibiza Town during the morning with Lara to buy everything from six-inch nails to toilet rolls. Most evenings, Lara and Angus walked over to Acid Mike's nearby house and enjoyed dinner with his old friend and Wendy B. White, a marvellous cook, her speciality Thai curries. Mike had invited them to stay as long as they wished in his comfortable home, but Angus and Lara, enjoying their independence, declined his friendly offer. They'd already begun to love their own house and enjoyed nothing better than lying in bed at night, watching the roaring fire's flames disappear up the stone chimney.

Spring came and the weeds grew by themselves. Angus and Lara began to visit well-stocked garden centres and purchased plants, cacti, shrubs, and saplings to plant around the house. Although the property had a borehole with plenty of fresh water in it, the two-horsepower submersible pump had no electricity to power it. A ten-kilowatt diesel generator was purchased and installed. With the arrival of the summer season, Lara began to water the garden on an almost daily basis. The orchard, now home to orange, lemon, apricot, pear, plum, apple, and persimmon trees was watered twice a week, along with a vegetable garden and a watermelon patch irrigated by furrows. By August it became so hot there was little else to do other than attend to life's necessities, go swimming, and generally take it easy. Angus and Lara loved their afternoon siestas and lay around in their cool room, reading and sleeping. Six days a week the Moroccans laboured on through the sweltering summer. Angus suspected that the workmen intentionally made a lot of noise during siesta time. The constant tap-tap-taping of the stone masons' hammers, cutting limestone to fit into newly constructed walls, was often drowned out by the sound of a cement mixer being cleaned out or a ten-ton truck with its noisy diesel engine chugging outside of the front gate, unloading piles of sand and bags of cement on pallets. Angus didn't mind the noise. He interpreted it as a sign of progress. The house was shaping up. The roofs had all been repaired or replaced.

Angus met an amicable American man, Jerry, in the nearby village of Santa Gertrudis. Jerry owned an antique shop just off the village square. Over coffee at the Bar Costa, Jerry shared some details about his life. He'd grown up in Brooklyn and lived in Bali for many years. Angus asked him if he could help arrange a shipment of Balinese furniture to Ibiza. Jerry said that for a small fee he could easily organize it.

On Christmas day of that year, Angus and Lara caught a flight to Madrid and from there on to Bali. They met up with Jerry in Ubud and spent two weeks visiting various furniture shops and purchasing items they felt would fit into their new home on Ibiza. Angus and Lara liked the Balinese, a people who made something sacred out of even the most mundane of daily acts. Tourists had overrun Bali, but a short detour from the well-beaten track revealed what a beautiful place it had been before rampant commercialization destroyed a lot of its charm.

Angus and Lara booked an Air India flight and landed in Mumbai's international airport on January 15, 1990. They checked into a quiet hotel in the city's Colaba district and spent a couple of days shopping and wandering the bustling streets. While sitting drinking mango *lassi's* in a juice bar, they struck up a conversation with a middle-aged Norwegian man, Dag, dressed in a Tibetan monk's maroon robe. One thing led to another and Angus's ears pricked up when Dag mentioned that he'd spent a few weeks sitting with Nisargadatta.

Angus asked, 'Does the Beedie Wallah still live in the same place.'

Dag chuckled. 'From what I know of Sri Nisargadatta Maharaj, I'd say, yes, he probably does still live in the same place. He died of cancer almost ten years ago.'

'Oh,' said Angus, 'I'm sorry to hear that. Not surprising, taking into consideration he was such a heavy smoker.'

The Norwegian lit an unfiltered cigarette and blew a cloud of smoke at a whirring electric fan. 'The body picks up habits on its journey through life.'

Angus nodded. 'I see what you mean.'

Dag coughed. 'I've just been in Allahabad visiting a master called Hari Sahaj Vichara. He's a wonderful old fellow, and I'd say it would be worthwhile for you to check him out.'

'Why?' Lara asked.

'Because,' said Dag, 'as far as one can gauge such things, he is an enlightened man. I've met many so-called masters who turned out to be fakes. I have to say that old Hariji is authentic. There's no need to draw comparisons, but Hariji bears certain personal characteristics that reminded me very much of Nisargadatta. He makes a point of not allowing people to touch his feet, or make any kind of fuss about him.' The Norwegian took a final drag on his cigarette and corkscrewed it out in an ashtray. A fine plume of acrid smoke rose and stung Lara's sensitive nose. 'Hariji doesn't smoke, but he chews pan.' Dag chuckled, glancing at Angus and Lara. 'I think you two might benefit from what Hari Sahaj Vicharaji has to impart. His truth is singular, unassailable and without contradiction.'

Lara looked deeply into Dag's blue eyes and liked what she saw.

Angus and Lara caught a taxi to Pune on the evening of the following day. When they drove by a dirt track just outside the town of Lonavla, Angus pointed out the open window into the darkness and whispered in Lara's ear, 'That's where I buried Jimmy Bradley.'

It was late at night when they checked into the Blue Diamond Hotel, on the periphery of Pune's Koregaon area. Their reasons for visiting the city were two-fold. They still had over a quarter of a million American dollars stashed in a safe deposit box in a downtown branch of The State Bank of India, and they wanted to visit the Rajneesh ashram. Osho was back in residence after his shambolic expulsion from America and a 'World Tour', during which he was refused an entry visa by over twenty countries.

Angus and Lara did not awaken until late afternoon. They ordered a meal from room service, ate in bed, showered, and then set off walking towards the nearby ashram. The sun was low in the sky behind trees that were filled with squadrons of loudly cawing crows. Trucks, buses and cars honked their horns, vying for position on the busy road. Behind the clamour, Angus and Lara both sensed a strange vibration in the atmosphere. They turned a corner and were confronted by a huge procession of sannyasins clad in orange and white.

'Someone has died,' commented Lara.

They stood to one side and made way for the funeral procession. The body, held aloft on a wooden pallet by many willing hands, drew level with them. It was Osho.

'Oh, no!' Lara burst into tears.

Standing at the side of the road, Angus experienced a strange mélange of feelings. The dominant one was great sadness. Although Osho hadn't figured much in his life during the past decade, there was a part of Angus that always felt he would see the master again one day, but not on the way to the burning *ghats* to be cremated.

Angus and Lara joined the tail end of the procession as it wound its way to the cremation ground on the banks of the Bund River, the place where they'd first met, ten years earlier. Many hours are needed to burn a human body on a funeral pyre. It was almost dawn by the time they returned to their hotel room and lay down on the bed exhausted. Osho had received the kind of sendoff he was most in favour of...a celebratory one, full of song, dance and tears of gratitude.

The following day, Osho's ashes were brought to the ashram's Chuang Tzu Auditorium, where the master had given discourses and met with sannyasins and seekers for many years. His powdered remains were interred under a marble slab, upon which were inscribed words dictated by the guru some months before.

OSHO

NEVER BORN

NEVER DIED

ONLY VISITED THIS PLANET EARTH BETWEEN

Dec 11 1939- Jan 19 1990

It was an intense time. Angus and Lara stayed in Pune for a week. They went to the ashram most days at some point, where they meditated and met up with old friends. One thing that hadn't changed in the ashram was that rumours and gossip were still very much alive. Most sannyasins believed Osho's death had been caused by poison, given to him in food when he was imprisoned for some days by Ronald Reagan's American Government. A few were sceptical about this, believing instead that the master himself was responsible for his own demise, due to his addiction to nitrous oxide and prescription tranquillizers and the subsequent withdrawal symptoms produced when he broke free of substance abuse.

Angus was more interested in hearing how Osho handled leaving his body. The official report said that the master had died of heart failure, after refusing an injection from his personal physician to increase his heart rate. Before closing his eyes and leaving his body in an extremely relaxed manner, Osho delivered his final pronouncement: 'I leave you my dream.'

From the various reports Angus heard he concluded that no matter what criticism Osho's detractors had levelled at him while alive, they would find it difficult to deny that the spiritual master died an enlightened man, one who knew how to face death with grace and dignity.

◆ ◆ ◆

Lara and Angus embarked on a two-day train journey to the city of Allahabad in Uttar Pradesh. The decision to travel to the small city had been a spontaneous one. Osho's death had brought home the stark reality of life's transient nature to Angus, and the idea that it might be beneficial to reconnect with something more eternal. They hoped Hari Sahaj Vichara might be the sort of man who could guide them in the right direction.

It was mid-afternoon. Allahabad was hot and humid, a typical subtropical climate for a city located on the plains of North India. Angus and Lara checked into a modern hotel in the railway station's vicinity.

'You know,' said Lara, fiddling with the controls on an air-conditioning unit, 'it feels a bit strange to be doing this.'

'What?' asked Angus, removing his damp clothes. 'Turning on an air-conditioner?'

Lara shook her head. 'No, stupid. Coming to Allahabad to see another guru.'

Angus sat on the bed. 'What's so strange about that?'

'I feel like I'm somehow betraying Osho.'

'Lara, that is pure bullshit. A guilt trip. Osho never wanted his people to feel guilty about anything. I remember him saying that when he was gone he'd guide his sannyasins to other masters if there was a need for it.'

'I never heard him say that.'

'I can assure you he did.'

'Great,' said Lara, sitting on the bed beside Angus. 'Thanks for telling me that.' She leaned into him. 'Let's make love.'

Lara and Angus spent the rest of the day in bed, chilling out and recovering from their long train journey.

Their first meeting with Hari Sahaj Vichara took place the following morning. Hariji held *satsangs* in a bungalow on Allahabad's urban outskirts. He gave a brief talk, describing in some detail his meetings with his master, the renowned Indian sage, Ramana Maharshi, during the 1940s in Tiruvannamalai, Tamil Nadu. His narration concluded with a brief description of the years he'd spent wandering through India and travelling around the world, before taking up permanent residence in Allahabad. Angus found Hariji's stories both fascinating and revealing. When the master's recounting ended, a questions and answers session began. Most of Hariji's responses were based on the precept that freedom is everyone's birthright. There was an informal ambience throughout the whole occasion. The people attending the *satsang* appeared sincere. A few outbursts of communal laughter diminished the gravity created by the weighty matters being discussed. When the *satsang* drew to a close, Angus and Lara were invited by an elderly Indian disciple to meet the master on a more personal level. They entered a small room and sat down on the carpeted floor in front of a wooden bed, upon which Hari Sahaj Vichara was sitting cross-legged.

Hariji spoke to Lara first, and it soon became clear that the master liked her. There was a tangible energy in the room that was both stimulating and peaceful. When it was Angus's turn to speak to the master, he got off to a poor start.

Hariji asked him, 'Where are you from?'

Angus replied, 'Scotland.'

The master frowned. 'When I was in the army, I was under the command of a Scottish officer. He was a terrible bully who often shouted at me. I could never understand what the man was saying.'

Angus gulped, looked up at the master's bulldog face, and said nothing.

Hariji lodged a wad of pan in his left cheek. 'How long will you be staying in Allahabad?' he asked.

Angus attempted to soften his Scottish accent. 'I haven't thought about it. We've only just arrived here.'

'We?'

Angus nodded towards Lara. 'Lara is my partner.'

Hariji glanced at Lara and then returned his attention to Angus. 'Do you realise how fortunate you are?'

Angus laughed self-consciously. 'Sometimes,' he replied.

Hariji stared at him. 'There is no *sometimes*. Sometimes does not exist. There is only this moment. What comes and goes has no more permanence than the clouds passing overhead in the sky. I am not concerned with any state that is temporary by nature.' The master leaned forward a little, the intensity of his gaze increasing. 'You stay here. Remain silent. Mind your own business and don't gossip.'

Angus nodded and said, 'Yes, Hariji.'

Angus took Hariji's words seriously, meaning that he was seeing things via the distorted reflection presented by his proud Scottish ego. However, no matter how he looked at it, he just couldn't envision himself as a nosey gossip unable to mind his own business. He continued to attend Hariji's talks every morning with Lara, and the more acquainted he became with the master, the more he appreciated him. A week passed before Angus recognised that what Hariji had said to him was simply good advice for maintaining a peaceful life. By remaining silent, minding one's own business, and not gossiping, the mind will naturally become more quiet and still.

Angus wrote a short letter of appreciation to Hariji then, one morning, during *satsang*, the master read it out loud. The master invited Angus to sit at his feet, then bent down towards him and whispered in his ear, 'You have no desire to be in the womb again, isn't that it?' Angus was catapulted back in time to a moment that had taken place forty years earlier, the moment of his birth into this world. It was an unexpected and shocking experience that made Angus realise with absolute certainty he was sitting at the feet of a powerful and wise man. He answered the master's question. 'Yes, Hariji, that is correct. I never want to be in a womb again.'

Hariji let Angus know he was perfectly aware of what had just taken place inside of his being by saying, 'To be born means you have created an imaginary world around yourself with a fictitious you at its centre. This is what everyone is doing. You are no different from anyone else on that level. You have created a world for yourself, a world that you alone inhabit. Ignorance has imprisoned you. Now, if you truly wish to be free, all you have to do is refuse reality to your prison.' Hariji looked deeply into Angus's eyes for a few concentrated moments and then gave a curt nod. 'Yes. Understanding is dawning.' The master continued, 'Do not make the error of asking the mind to confirm what is beyond the mind's comprehension. My words create a distraction for the mind, while that which needs to happen simply happens. Pure experience is the only valid confirmation of what I am directing you towards. Total awareness of life as it happens is the whole point of living.' The master gave a sagacious nod, signalling to Angus that their meeting was swiftly drawing towards a conclusion. 'Good,' Hariji said. 'And remember, as long as there are sheep there will be herders. How many lions do you see being herded?'

Angus replied immediately. 'None, Hariji.'

The sage chuckled. 'Yes, that's the right answer,' he said approvingly. 'Now wake up and let out a roar. Declare your right to awaken. I cannot liberate you. You have to liberate yourself. Now, if the need arises, feel free to come and talk to me. '

'Thank you,' said Angus. He bowed with reverence at the master's feet, stood up, and returned to his place at the back of the small hall.

The master also called Lara that morning. 'Lara,' said Hariji, remembering her name. He patted the empty half of the red sofa he was sitting on. 'Come. Sit here with me.' Lara did as requested. The old man draped his right arm over her shoulders. 'Any questions?' Hariji asked her, a playful smile upon his lips.

Lara shook her head. 'No, Hariji, I don't have any questions. Sitting here beside you answers all of my questions. I am content.'

The master chuckled with pleasure. 'I am happy to hear that,' he said, still chuckling. 'I meet a lot of people who, seeking happiness, live in a state of perpetual misery. It is rare for me to come across one, such as yourself, who says, 'I am content.' Many people, from all over the world, come to see me here in Allahabad. Some stay for weeks, others for months and even years. Ideally, what I have to impart should take root in a seeker's heart within a few days of encountering me, and that is when a person should leave. That way the seed can grow and one day blossom in the sanctity of the seeker's own heart. The fruit must grow out of you,' he said, like a benevolent father explaining something to a receptive child. 'My fruit has already ripened and fallen from the tree. You are the conscious principle. Accept it and then you can forget it. Never allow yourself to become dependent on any authoritarian figure because your unique individuality will not be able to express itself fully as long as there is dependence. There is nothing to seek and find because there is nothing lost. Do you understand?'

Tears streamed over Lara's flushed cheeks. Unable to speak, she looked at Hariji and nodded vigorously. The master nodded back, pulled her closer to him on the sofa, and then he burst out laughing. Through her tears, Lara also began to laugh. In response, the hundred or so people assembled in the rectangular room started laughing also. Angus laughed so hard it hurt his sides. The beauty of it was that he wasn't exactly sure why he was laughing. He'd become laughter itself.

A minute passed and the room fell silent. Lara stood and another woman was called forward. Her hands were raised prayerfully as she sat on the floor in front of the master. She was young and, Angus judged by her effusive behaviour, naive. 'Guruji, I've had a very deep meditation experience and I want to share it with you,' she declared, her voice almost shrill with excitement. Hariji smiled and nodded, signalling for her to continue. 'I've been practising hatha yoga for six months and...' The young woman proceeded to reel off a string of shallow insights that she obviously believed were strong indicators of progress in her quest for enlightenment as she sped along the spiritual path, a path she failed to see she was not quite on. She babbled on about consciousness, awareness, chakras opening, light in her third eye, and kundalini rising out of a bubbling New Age potpourri that amounted to nothing more than a need to impress the master with how spiritually advanced she was. Angus saw clearly that she needed praise for her lofty inner achievements, to reinforce her self-image of being a very spiritual person. Hariji was patient with her, answered her questions, when given a chance, and gave the woman his undivided attention, as he did with anyone he found sitting before him.

Man, Angus thought a little smugly, *the bullshit you have to put up with when you are a guru.* He closed his eyes. The physical realities of the satsang faded as his mind drifted towards the land of the distant past. He began to recall a meeting he'd had on the banks of the Ganges, when he, too, had been young and inexperienced, somehow believing he was a really spiritual person, on a quest to find answers to life's deeper questions. The realization came to him that some of the answers he'd been given at the time were the right ones, but he'd been so preoccupied with his mind that he did not allow them to enter his heart. He felt slightly uncomfortable when he heard his own voice echo across time. *Swami Ram, will you be my guru?* Angus smiled at the naivety of his question. *How easy it is to feel superior and judge others,* he thought, *for that which I have been guilty of myself.* At that moment, Angus understood he was being taught a profound lesson by something bigger than himself, a living presence that is always there but for the most part, goes unheeded. Hari Sahaj Vichara's words to Lara a few moments before echoed in his head. *There is nothing to seek and find, because there is nothing lost...there is nothing lost...nothing lost.* As if in response to Angus's reflections, Swami Ram's gentle voice from long ago spoke in his head. *Never forget, the real guru lives in your heart. All others are merely fingers pointing at the moon. There's no need to become attached to a finger.* Angus nodded and thought to himself, *Swami Ram was right. It's not the finger that's important, it's the moon.*

Lara had by this time returned to her place next to Angus. She sensed immediately he was somewhere else and nudged him gently in the ribs with an elbow. Angus opened his eyes and turned to see her smiling face. She winked at him. He winked back and then returned his attention to the master, who was in the process of bringing the satsang to a close.

'Living is life's only real purpose,' said Hariji, addressing everyone in the room. He spread his arms, the palms of his hands turned up. 'It's that simple.' He smiled, dropped his arms, and concluded, 'Fulfil your eternal destiny by meditating, learning, loving, exploring, discovering, enjoying the company of real friends, and bowing in gratitude to existence for the great gift that is the breath of life.'

A week later, Angus and Lara were in Mumbai airport, boarding a plane that would fly them directly to Madrid.

Angus and Lara returned to Ibiza to find Acid Mike busy with a new project. He'd travelled to Mallorca and bought a *llaüt,* the traditional trawl fishing vessel of the Balearic Islands. It was about eight meters long and looked much too heavy to manhandle. Mike later explained how he'd hired a lorry and had it delivered by ferry to Ibiza. Mike was using an electric sander to remove peeling blue paint from the *llaüt's* wooden hull, supported by cut telegraph poles and blocks of wood. When he sensed someone standing behind him, he looked up from his work. His tie dye headband was soaked with sweat. 'Welcome back,' he said with a dust encrusted smile. 'You guys were away longer than I expected. You were due back three weeks ago.'

'Yeah, I know.' said Angus. 'We made a wee detour and stayed in Pune longer than planned. Osho died the day after we arrived.'

Mike laid his sander on the ground to take a drink of water from a plastic bottle. 'Well, ultimately the same fate awaits us all.' He nodded thoughtfully. 'Quite looking forward to it myself. What did Osho die from?'

'Heart failure,' answered Lara.

'Knowing you sannyasin lot, I suppose there was a big celebration.'

Lara chuckled, 'There was. People were singing and dancing and going completely nuts.'

'Did the old boy say any final words?'

'Yes,' said Angus, 'Osho's last words were, 'I leave you my dream."

'Strange thing for someone to say after a lifetime spent trying to wake people up from their dreams.' Mike wiped sawdust off his cheap plastic watch, peered at it for a couple of seconds, and then glanced up at the afternoon sun. 'It's about time for a cup of tea and a joint. Care to join me?'

'Sure,' replied Angus. 'No joints, though. We've both stopped smoking dope.'

'Sign of the Times, matey. Sign of the tragic, bloody times,' Mike concluded with a sigh, sauntering over to the wooden gate of the courtyard in front of his *finca*.

It was a sunny morning in late June when Mike's *llaüt*, delivered by a truck with a crane to a small sandy cove in Portinatx, was lowered into the water. Legend has it that changing a boat's name invited bad luck. Mike was not the kind of man to be influenced by superstition. He renamed his refurbished boat *Tanit*, the name of a Punic goddess first introduced to Ibiza when the Phoenicians colonized the island 2500 years before. The sight of the *llaüt* sitting in the turquoise-blue water was fit for a picture postcard. Her white hull shone in the sunlight, the eye of Horus painted in black on her prow above her name. Lara, Wendy, Angus, and Mike were all dressed in white shorts and tee shirts. The women had on straw hats. They waded into the sea and climbed aboard, using a folding stainless-steel ladder attached to one side of the boat's stern. The smell of linseed oil rose off *Tanit's* new teak deck. Rigging was wound around the wooden mast, a white canvas sail wrapped around a lowered boom. More decorative than functional, the sail could be raised and unfurled if the engine broke down, highly unlikely as Mike had installed a new, six-cylinder diesel motor into the engine compartment towards the vessel's stern. To the left of the wooden steering wheel and instrument panel, with several dials set into it, were three small steps leading down into the cabin. Everything inside was made from varnished wood, including two single bunks, set against each side of the hull, and a small galley. The *llaüt* was perfect, not just from an aesthetic point of view but in terms of practicality. Most importantly of all, the boat was constructed to resist the adverse weather conditions that often prevail in the Mediterranean Sea.

Mike turned the ignition key. *Tanit's engine* chugged into life. A few puffs of smoke rose from an exhaust pipe in the stern. Mike spun the wheel and engaged the engine. Tanit wound her way between pleasure craft moored in the bay and headed out to the open sea. Music was delivered by a powerful, four-channel car cassette player and heard through several inset waterproof speakers, strategically placed around the deck. Mike had given some thought to what music he was going to play on *Tanit's* maiden voyage. Stephen Still's guitar glided out of the speakers to provide the intro to CSNY's version of the Jefferson Airplane's 'Wooden Ships'. It was pure Sixties music and a perfect soundtrack for a cruise along Ibiza's northwest coastline.

Mike popped the cork off a bottle of ice-cold champagne. He poured bubbling liquid into four waiting glasses. 'Cheers!' The four friends toasted each other as the boat cruised by a spit of land known by foreigners on the island as 'Moon Beach'; its rocky and pitted surface resembled that of Earth's closest neighbour.

Angus and Lara were to remember that day as one of the most beautiful and carefree of their lives. Ibiza is called 'Magic Island' for a good reason. It is truly a magical place, as Angus and Lara were in the process of discovering.

One aspect that Angus noticed about living in Ibiza was that time seemed to fly by very quickly, and it wasn't just because he was enjoying himself. Months passed like weeks. Raj, Murphy, and their families began to visit every summer and Angus cherished each precious moment he spent with his old friends. The house rang with their children's joyful cries, running wild, free from the constraints of urban life. Raj and Murphy had moved into the burgeoning indoor growing business and had opened two grow shops in Amsterdam, supplying everything needed for the indoor cultivation of marijuana. Alice and Nina were much the same as they ever were, a little older and, Angus couldn't help noticing when they had their bikinis on, a little plumper. Their days on the island were often spent down on Benirras Beach, minding their four children as they frolicked in the bay's crystal clear waters.

It was August, 1998. Ibiza had become the clubbing capital of the world. The days of the open-air discotheques were over. Decibel levels were strictly monitored by the Guardia Civil. The full moon parties in the hills were all shut down by the law. The island of the hippies had been commercialised. Rents were becoming so high hard-core hippies could no longer afford to pay them, although the island was still being touted internationally as a 'hippy' paradise. Clubs like the Pacha Discotheque on the edge of Ibiza Town had begun promoting 'Flower Power' nights, where people, who had never dropped an acid tab in their lives, dressed up in designer hippy gear and danced to Sixties music. One balmy summer night, Angus and his friends decided to go check out Pacha's 'Flower Power' night to see how it felt on LSD.

It was after midnight. The discotheque was already throbbing and punters had to join a long queue. Angus talked to a wary-eyed bouncer in a no-funny-business suit at the club's main entrance. He was acquainted with the doorman from previous visits. They shook hands and Angus palmed him a hundred euro note. Angus and his seven companions were allowed to enter without queuing, a good start to the night out. The place was packed and, in true Sixties spirit, The Troggs' 'Wild Thing' could be heard booming out from the main dance floor's powerful speakers. Angus was soaring on the acid Mike had given him two hours earlier. His mind kept looping back to the moment Acid Mike had placed a little orange pill in the palm of his hand and said, 'You'll remember this one from the good old days.' Angus hadn't been sure if he'd wanted to take such a heroic dose of acid and then go out to a nightclub. Mike had sensed his uncertainty, smiled at him and said, 'Why not?' Angus had swallowed the orange pill. *Why not? Why not? Why not?* It was like someone had pressed the rewind button in his brain. The image of the little orange pill in the palm of his hand and Mike's voice saying, *'Why not?'* kept replaying over and over again in his head, usually at the most unexpected of times. *Why not?*

The scene inside the discotheque was surreal. Drunken tourists were wearing cheap, black afro wigs, flashing the two-fingered peace sign in front of his face as Angus squeezed by them. Beautiful women leaned against the walls, looking like Janis Joplin might have done had she had an expensive facelift. The air-conditioning was running on overdrive, but the club felt hot and humid. Surreal morphed into unreal. Angus felt like heading for the exit door although he'd only been there for ten minutes Earth time. Lara sensed his unease and took a firm hold of his hand, leading him through the crowd to the dance floor. Mike and the gang were already there, bouncing around to Creedence Clearwater Revival's 'Proud Mary'. Angus didn't think about what he should do next. He started moving and shaking to the beat along with everyone else in the club. Mike was laughing and moving his arms and legs like he was in an aerobics class. The big wheel of life kept on turning and Proud Mary kept on burning. Mike passed Angus a grass joint. The weed lit up Angus's brain. John Fogerty's voice fired up his imagination and he visualized the band's frontman down in Memphis cleaning dirty plates by a sink in an all-night diner and pumping gas down in New Orleans. 'Rollin', rollin', rollin' on the river!' Everyone sang along to the chorus, including Angus. He was beginning to enjoy himself.

The Stone's 'Gimme Shelter' came on. Charlie Watts was banging on a war drum. Jagger's voice was as sharp as a scalpel and cut Angus to the emotional bone. He felt the world on the brink of an apocalypse. It was all just a shot away. Rape, murder, raging fires and tsunamis, the images flooded his mind. *Love sister...* There was only one positive solution. It was just a kiss away. Angus pulled Lara close and kissed her passionately. She staggered backwards and shouted something. 'What?' Angus shouted back. Lara leaned into him and yelled in his ear. 'That was amazing. I love you.' As Keith Richards played one of rock's greatest guitar solos, Angus felt a lift of excitement. He knew that he was in the right place at exactly the right time.

Up in the DJ booth the master of flower power ceremonies faded out 'Gimme Shelter' and let conga intro to 'Sympathy for the Devil' patter in. Nobody present had to guess the name of this particular man of wealth and taste. After all, Lucifer had been around for many years, stealing men's souls and faith. The crowd cheered and started chanting, 'Ooo hoo, ooo hoo, ooo hoo...' Angus looked around, wondering if he'd joined a satanic cult. *'Ooo hoo, ooo hoo...'* A woman near to him screamed. Angus closed his eyes. Adorned with swastikas, *Luftwaffe* bombers flew along his synaptic channels, clusters of grey bombs falling from their swollen bellies like metal teardrops. A narrow-faced general with a black patch over his right eye looked down from a tank's turret at a vast battlefield, littered with wrecked military vehicles and strewn with stinking broken corpses. Someone shouted out, 'Who killed the Kennedys?' Maybe it was the Chicago mob, but Angus pled guilty in the courtroom of his conscience. He zoomed in on a motorcade making its way along a street in Dallas, Texas. Shots rang out. He looked on as Jacqueline Kennedy clambered over the back of an open stretch limousine, her pillbox hat askew, blood and pieces of her husband's brain splattered all over her pink Chanel suit. The President of The United States had been hit in the head by an assassin's bullet. *Oh, yeah. Oh, yeah!...* Keith Richards' guitar riffs shot out of the thundering speakers like bolts of musical lightning. Angus was undergoing an electronic crucifixion. *'Aaaa-aaaaagh!'* He screamed. Nobody on Pacha's main dance floor noticed. Everyone was yelling. *What's my name?... Ooo, hoo!*

After dancing non-stop for three mind-melting hours, Angus told Lara he was going to the toilet. His clothes were soaked with sweat. The corridor leading to the men's toilets was expanding and contracting like the walls of a birth canal. His perceptual distortion made it appear like he was inside a big circular screen with the images of a corridor being projected onto it. Angus began thinking, not for the first time in his life, that the world surrounding him was unreal, a dream, a fantastic illusion manufactured by his brain working through his senses, now informing him that his bladder was experiencing a lot of pressure. He made it to a urinal. His penis looked weird, a pale soggy sausage. He was bursting for a pee but had forgotten how to activate the brain signals for the most elementary of the body's waste elimination processes. He shifted from manual to automatic. *'Oooooh!'* He groaned with relief. His urine splashed into the porcelain urinal. The sensation was so pleasurable he began giggling to himself like a little boy watching a funny cartoon on television, oblivious of any curious stares being directed at him. He washed his hands at a sink. He couldn't generate enough saliva to lubricate his parched tongue. He cupped a hand under the tap and scooped water into his dry mouth. The water tasted extremely salty. He spat it into the sink, stood up straight, and looked at his face in a mirror. His wet hair hung down to his shoulders, framing his face, which looked like... He leaned in closer to his reflection. ...an Alex Grey painting. A couple of excited gays were making a show of doing coke on the edge of a neighbouring sink. A women's voice moaned in distress behind him. He caught a flash of a floral-patterned dress. Recognizing it, he spun around. It was Wendy. The top of her dress was ripped, exposing both of her breasts, two flesh-coloured basketballs with startled brown eyes. Half-a-dozen guys were staring at Wendy with their mouths hanging open. Angus stepped over and took ahold of her right arm. Wendy glared at him in shock. Eyes ringed by runny mascara, cheeks flushed, tears and sweat had cut runnels through the thick makeup plastered over her chubby face. She looked like a well-fed tribal vampire on the warpath. She did not recognize him and instinctively tried to pull her arm free from his grasp. Angus tightened his grip and jerked her arm. 'Wendy,' he said, 'It's me, Angus.'

'Wendy? Wendy?' she blubbered, amid an ego meltdown. Wendy was a coke-head at heart and not accustomed to taking powerful doses of LSD in enclosed public places. She hugged herself and shivered, even though the air was warm.

'Yes,' Angus said gently. 'You're Wendy and my name's Angus. I'm your friend. We're in the Pacha Discotheque's men's toilets and we have to get you out of here.' He let go of her arm and covered up her breasts with a damp Hindu prayer scarf he had draped around his neck. She tried to kiss him on the lips. 'C'mon, Wendy, pack it in.' She gave him a goofy smile. 'Let's go.' He took her hand and led her out of the toilets into the corridor. Hendrix's 'Purple Haze' was thudding out of the dance floor speakers like a funeral dirge. Angus didn't know if he was coming up or down. The place was heaving with people, a lot of them out of their minds on various drugs. Angus held Wendy's hand as they side-slipped through the crowd, emerging into the more subdued ambience provided by the VIP lounge. Normally Angus detested the whole notion of anything VIP, but that night he was glad someone had come up with the idea. He sat Wendy down on a plush red velvet sofa and ordered water from a passing waitress in a micro skirt. Wendy was gazing around like Alice in Blunderland, her thick blonde hair matted with sweat. Angus glanced at a framed psychedelic poster of John Lennon. John's lips curled up into a warm smile. His granny glasses spiralled with rainbow colours. Angus was tripping strongly, but having to take care of flipped-out Wendy kept his feet firmly planted on Planet Pacha. 'Listen, Wendy,' he said, turning to look directly into her wide-open eyes, 'I'm going to see if I can find some of our friends. You stay here. Don't move from this spot. You got me?' He gave her a quick hug.

Wendy nodded vacantly, like a bewildered village idiot. 'Where am I?' She paused, zoned-out for a moment, and then asked, 'Who am I?'

Angus took her hand again. 'That's a good question, Wendy. Just be a good girl and wait here till I get back. Okay?' He passed her a small bottle of water.

She smiled uncertainly and nodded again, like a four-year-old who'd just been handed a lollipop by a stranger.

Purple haze!...

It was the peak of the night's entertainment. The PA system was cranked up and hitting sonic overload. The small dance floor was packed to capacity, with an extra hundred dancers squashed in to make the atmosphere more sweaty and intimate. Jimi Hendrix's version of Bob Dylan's 'All Along The Watchtower' was thunderous, like the building had been struck by an earthquake. Angus stared into the writhing mass on the dance floor and couldn't see anyone he recognized. He was also experiencing difficulties in seeing *anything* he could recognize; he was standing on the edge of a bubbling pile of multi-coloured lava. *There's too much confusion...* All things considered, one of Dylan's greatest understatements. Angus was swirling around in a state of synesthesia, created by a confusion of sensations between different types of stimuli. He caught a glimpse of Lara's ecstatic face, coated with glistening mercury. She was right in the middle of the crammed dance floor, waving her hand's in the air like she just didn't care. Angus waded into the crowd. Hendrix's guitar zoomed around the club like a squadron of UFOs, travelling at the speed of ultrasound. Angus swam towards Lara. She grinned and gave him a hug. Her body was hot. Angus felt a tingle in the right place at the wrong time. He hollered in her left ear. 'Wendy has flipped out. Find Mike and the others. I'm over in the VIP lounge. Kiss me if you got that.' She cupped his face in her hands and kissed him on the lips.

Angus pushed his way through the writhing mass of people as gently as he could manage. He was elbowed in the ribs a couple of times but, for the most part, everyone was cool. The volume level of the music was earsplitting. It took an eternity to reach the club's VIP area. He found Wendy where he'd left her. She was crying. He sat down on the red sofa beside her. 'What's wrong?' he asked.

'Miiiiiikey!' Wendy brayed. Angus tried to silence her with a stern look but to no avail. 'I don't know where Mikey is,' she bawled, her voice a prolonged sob.

Angus took both her hands in his and held her attention with his gaze. 'Don't worry, Wendy,' he said soothingly, wishing that Mike carried a cell phone so he could call him, but Mike was a man who, unless cutting a deal, derived great pleasure from being unreachable. 'Mike's around here somewhere. He'll show up in a minute,' said Angus, aware of how lame it sounded.

'But I don't know who I am,' she complained, wiping at the tears running down her face with the back of a pudgy hand.

'Listen, Wendy, you took some really strong acid and you're freaking out. Take it easy. Everything is going to be fine. Do you understand what I'm saying?'

Her brow crinkled in puzzlement and she began shivering as if undergoing a malaria attack.

'Wendy, look at me.' She peeked at him shyly, her big white teeth chattering like a flamenco dancer's castanets. There was a fragile helplessness about her that Angus found unsettling in such a public place. 'You are going to be alright,' he assured her again. 'I'll take care of you until you level out. Do you understand?' he asked, spelling the words out. 'Everything is going to be fine.'

The thought seemed to cheer Wendy, if only for a fleeting moment. She nodded as if under a spell. Angus's kindhearted assurance and the tenderness of his expression were getting through to her, making a positive impact on her fractured mind. She edged closer to him and, for the second time that night, tried to kiss him on the lips.

'Well, well, well, boys and girls, what's going on here now? Looks suspicious, if I'm not very much mistaken.'

When Angus heard Murphy putting on his PC Plod voice, he looked up at him and was glad to see Nina standing beside him, holding his hand. They both looked like they'd just walked out of a sauna, with their clothes on. 'Man,' said Angus, 'I'm relieved to see you guys. Wendy in Wonderland here has...eh...lost her way a bit. Disappeared down a rabbit hole, if you catch my drift. She says she doesn't know who she is.'

Nina sat down beside him and said, 'Well, that's something I can relate to. I'm absolutely scoobied myself. On top of that, some poxy asshole stole my bag. Glad I left my fuckin' passport at home.'

Lara, Raj, and Alice hurried over. Lara sat down on the opposite side of Wendy and slung a protective arm around her shoulders. 'How you doing?' she asked Wendy.

Wendy had stopped crying by now. Her cheeks were smudged with mascara, concern etched around her pouting lips. 'I want to see Mikey,' she said in a little-girl-lost voice.

'Yeah, where is Mike?' Raj asked. 'Last time I saw him he asked me if I wanted to take some 'E'. And that was light years ago.'

'He offered me some too,' Alice chipped in, pushing away strands of black hair stuck to her damp face. 'When Mike goes for it, he goes for it big time. That acid he gave us is as strong as fuck.' She knelt in front of Wendy. 'You alright, Wendy, doll?'

Wendy began to perk up a little. 'Oh, hi, Alice, darling. What are you doing here?' She turned to Lara. 'And you too, Lara. What a pleasant surprise. I think this calls for a *wee* drink. Don't you?'

'That's the best fuckin' idea I've heard all night,' said Murphy. He nodded to a round table that four Arabs in white robes, accompanied by two thick-set bodyguards in black suits, had just vacated. 'C'mon, there's an empty table over there.'

The women guided Wendy over to the circular table and they all sat down around it. Raj caught the attention of a waitress in a black bikini top and skintight black trousers. He ordered two bottles of the best champagne in the house, with no idea that might cost him what a hard-working waiter in Pacha earned in a month...including tips.

Drinking ice-cold champagne soon had everyone back in high spirits. Wendy, was quickly slipping back into her accustomed role of a good-time girl, thirty years older than she wanted to be. 'I sa-sa-say,' she stammered, spilling some of her drink into her lap, 'this damned bubbly is going straight to my noggin. I'm starting to feel a *wee* bit tiddly-widdly. I can feel those *wee wee* bubbly-wubblies popping in my brain.'

Wendy sounded so ridiculous, everyone started laughing. Angus laughed so hard he looked down at his flat belly to check it hadn't exploded.

Over on the dance floor, a cheer went up when Canned Heat's 'On The Road Again' drove out of the sound system. Murphy drained his glass and stood up. 'I'm going to see if I can find Mike. Anyone else up for a gander around?'

'Yeah, me, I'll come,' volunteered Raj.

I'm on the road again...

They returned ten minutes later and sat down at the table. Murphy shrugged and shook his head at nobody in particular.

Angus looked over the table to Wendy, studying the reflections in her empty champagne glass with intense curiosity. 'Hey, Wendy,' he called to her, 'when was the last time you saw Mike?'

Wendy looked away from her glass and screwed up her dirty face, trying to remember. 'You know,' she said, 'I seem to recall Mikey saying he was going out for a breath of fresh air, about an hour after we took those Es.'

Angus asked, 'How long ago was that?'

Wendy shrugged. 'I've absolutely no idea. I do believe I became a little confused at some point during the festivities. I fell over and tore my dress. God, I felt utterly wretched. Thankfully, a charming young girl in the lady's room lent me her shawl to cover up my titties and saved me from embarrassing myself.'

'Embarrassing yourself?' said Murphy, his tone mildly mocking. He adopted a posh English accent. 'God forbid you might actually fall foul of humiliation, Lady Wendy, my dear. Lord Woodcock, the Right Honourable Conservative MP for Spunkyton and Fudwrinkle, might take an issue of such grave national importance up in The House of Commons for debate.'

Wendy looked startled. 'Goodness, Murphy,' she said seriously, 'do you honestly think so? My god, I'd never be able to live that down.'

'For fuck's sake!' Murphy chortled and glanced up at a small rotating mirror ball suspended above his head. 'C'mon,' he said, pushing his chair back. 'Flower Power night at Pacha is wilting. I think we better see if we can locate Mike, especially now that it has been established beyond any doubt that *The King* has left the fuckin' building.'

As they headed for the exit, the DJ mixed in The Door's 'Break On Through (To The Other Side)', having decided to end the night's revelry with a bang. Jim Morrison's voice followed Angus out onto the pavement. *You know the day eats up the night...* He looked to his left. The rising sun was hidden behind apartment blocks, spreading beaming rays up into an almost cloudless sky. A passenger jet roared by overhead, wheels down, heading for the Playa den Bossa end of the airport's runway. The seven friends congregated at a traffic light and crossed the road when it turned red. Mike's Toyota Four Runner was parked on a piece of waste ground beside dozens of other vehicles, their roofs and bonnets glistening with condensation. Angus hurried ahead and saw Mike's bare feet sticking out of one of the black Toyota's back windows. Angus ran a finger up the sole of Mike's right foot. There was no response. He looked in the open window. Acid Mike was lying on his back with a smile on his face. Sensing something wasn't quite right, Angus hurried over to the other side of the car and opened the back door. An overhead cabin light came on above Mike's ashen face. He didn't appear to be breathing. Angus placed two fingers on his friend's neck, checking Mike's carotid artery for a pulse. He closed his eyes and concentrated. There was a pulse, a very weak one.

'What's happening?'

Angus opened his eyes and looked across at Murphy, his face framed in an open window. 'Not good, man. Mike's in a bad way. He's alive but only just.'

'*Fuck!*' Murphy cursed.

The others arrived. Wendy saw Mike, picked up on the vibes and freaked out, crying, screaming and babbling. She buried her face in Lara's shoulder. Lara tried as best as she could to calm her grief-stricken friend down, but it was futile. A quick decision was made to take Wendy home immediately. She was bundled into the back of Angus's Land Rover, parked close by. Raj drove off with the girls. Angus jumped into the Toyota's driver's seat while Murphy got in on the other side. Angus went to turn the ignition key. It wasn't there. 'Where's the fucking key?' he said. Murphy found the key in Mike's trouser pocket. Ten minutes later, Angus pulled up outside the A&E entrance of Can Misses General Hospital. He hurried inside and explained as best as he could, to a stressed female receptionist with thick glasses, what had happened. It took five very long minutes before a couple of male orderlies arrived with a rattling gurney. Mike was lifted onto it and whisked away. Angus drove the Toyota around to the car park. Then he and Murphy sat on the floor of a crowded waiting room for over an hour. 24/7, August is the busiest month of the year in Can Misses Hospital.

A bearded doctor in a light-blue top and matching trousers, a stethoscope draped around his neck, appeared in the waiting room's doorway. He consulted a clipboard, looked up and called out, 'James Sheridan?' Angus stood and strode over to the doctor. They walked together into the reception area, where Doctor Roig introduced himself and informed Angus that his friend had been pronounced dead on arrival. Cause of death heart failure. Angus felt nauseous. Sweat prickled his forehead. Doctor Roig registered his shock, took a firm grip of his left arm and led him back to the waiting room. As soon as Murphy saw Angus's drawn face he knew it was bad news. They sat together and looked up at the doctor as he informed them that the Guardia Civil would soon arrive and in circumstances such as these they'd be required to make a police statement. The doctor gave a curt nod and walked off. Angus and Murphy went outside to search Mike's car for some form of identification. Murphy unlocked the glove compartment. He found a British passport and driving licence under the Toyota's insurance papers. Murphy hailed a passing taxi. Angus stayed behind to deal with the police.

Two young cops wearing olive-green uniforms arrived in the waiting room. Angus accompanied them outside to a white van with Guardia Civil decals on its side panels. The police officers were not unsympathetic. They smoked cigarettes and chatted in broken English as they wrote Mike and Angus's details down. Angus reluctantly told them where he lived, shook hands with the two young men, and headed for the car park.

Angus entered the farmhouse's kitchen. Murphy and Raj were sharing a joint by a small dining table. Alice and Nina had taken their kids down to Benirras Beach. Lara was over at Mike's house, taking care of Wendy. Murphy offered the joint to Angus. He refused it.

'Wendy's in a right state,' said Raj.

'Yeah,' agreed Murphy. 'Thank fuck we found some Valium to knock her out. Talk about a comedown. What a fucking way to end an acid trip. I reckon Mike took too much 'E' and it blew a gasket in his heart.' He shook his head slowly. 'What a fucking drag, man.'

Raj blew a cloud of hash smoke over the table towards Angus. 'What did the cops say?'

Angus shrugged. 'Nothing much. They were alright.'

Murphy asked, 'What name did you give them?'

'James Sheridan.'

'You still running on that book?' Murphy said. 'I thought it had expired.'

'It did. Mike renewed it for me, about three years back.'

'Mike was a handy guy to have a-around, wa-wasn't he?' Raj said, trying unsuccessfully to keep his voice from wavering.

Angus placed his hands on the sides of his head, not quite able to take on board what had happened. 'Jesus, man, Mike was a lot of things. I feel like I just had my heart cut out with a hacksaw.' Tears welled in his eyes. 'I can't believe he's gone.'

Murphy sniffed. 'I'm going to miss that old devil.'

Raj's hangdog face was ready to melt and drip onto the stone floor. 'It's a bummer, man,' he declared, his voice little more than a whisper.

Mike's funeral might have been the end of the story were it not for another tragic incident, looming on the near horizon; an event that would alter the course of Angus and Lara's journey through life forever.

Three days had passed since Acid Mike's sudden and unexpected departure from the earthly plane of existence and, much to Angus's relief, there had been no further contact with the local police authorities.

It was a hot afternoon and Angus was alone in the living room of his *finca*. Raj and Murphy had taken their families over to The Jockey Club on Salinas Beach for lunch. Lara had just popped over to Mike's house to see how Wendy was getting along. *Getting along* did not exactly capture the state poor Wendy was in. She had been drinking heavily since Mike's death. She was morose, depressed, and occasionally hysterical. According to the book Angus was reading that afternoon, it was no way to behave when someone close to you died.

The Tibetan Book of The Dead was a book that Angus had been studying off and on for many years. The house was quiet and still. Angus was stretched out on a couch with his head propped up by a thick cushion. He was reading about confronting Dharma-Rāja, the King of Death, and how one must never lie to him because he will know you are being dishonest by consulting the Mirror of Karma, wherein every good and evil act of the naked soul is vividly reflected. A small lizard skittered across the stone floor. Angus looked up from his book. A light breeze stirred the bamboo fly curtain. Wind chimes tinkled in the garden. When Angus heard the front gate close, he laid the book aside and sat up. He was surprised to see Lara enter the room. She'd only been gone for about fifteen minutes. Even though her face was suntanned, it was pale and drawn. He sensed immediately that something was wrong. Lara approached Angus and sat down beside him. She took ahold of his right hand and said nothing.

'What's happened?' Angus asked in a soft voice, a feeling of dread rising from his guts.

Lara pursed her lips, shook her head and remained silent.

Angus exhaled a long breath. 'C'mon, please, Lara, tell me what has happened.'

'She's dead,' said Lara, in a voice bereft of emotion.

'*Wendy? Wendy's dead?* Please don't tell me Wendy's dead.'

Lara tightened her grip on his hand. 'I'm sorry, Angus. She's dead.'

'Fucking hell,' he groaned. 'What happened?'

Lara took a deep breath and exhaled slowly to compose herself. 'I went over to Mike's,' she said as if describing a dream. 'The door was unlocked. The house felt very still and quiet. Wendy wasn't around. I figured she was probably upstairs in bed, drunk or asleep. I thought it would be a good idea to make her a cup of tea and take it up to her. I made the tea, went upstairs with it, and opened her bedroom door. Wendy was lying on her side. She'd been sick. I put the tea on a bedside table and placed a hand on her chest to see if I could feel a heartbeat. I didn't feel one. Then I noticed there was an empty bottle of vodka on the table beside the mug of tea and...' She reached into her pocket and produced an empty blister pack. '...I found half-a-dozen of these scattered on the floor.' She handed the plastic packet to Angus.

He screwed up his eyes, examined the bubble pack, and read out loud, 'Phenobarbital 100mg.' He counted the burst blisters. 'Fourteen,' he said. 'She must have taken enough barbiturates to knock out a rogue bull elephant on a rampage and washed them down with a bottle of vodka. No wonder Wendy is dead.'

They were both in a state of shock. Lara more than Angus. 'What are we going to do?' she asked.

Angus ran his right hand over his freshly shaved face. 'That's the million peseta question, isn't it?'

'Will I go down to San Juan to inform the Guardia Civil what's happened?'

Angus thought about it for a minute and said, 'No. I don't think that's a good idea at all. I'm surprised we heard nothing more from the cops after Mike's death. If we go down to the village and tell them Wendy's dead, they're going to start wondering what the fuck's going on. I mean to say, two of our neighbours dying within seventy-two hours of each other doesn't exactly look like everything is running smoothly in this neck of the *campo*, now, does it?'

'But we had nothing to do with it,' protested Lara.

'Yeah, I know that, but the fucking cops don't. They're bound to start snooping around and making inquiries. What worries me most is them asking me for my fingerprints.'

'Why?'

'Lara, you're not thinking straight. You know why. I told you what happened in Nepal when I burnt that house down with Jenny's body in it. You know that's why I'm still running around on somebody else's passport. Not to mention all the other things we've been doing. If the Spanish police authorities send my fingerprints and a photocopy of my passport up to the British Home Office, I'm fucked. They'll find out James Sheridan died in a fucking car crash fifteen years ago. And that's just for a start.'

'You're right. I wasn't thinking straight. So, I'll ask you again. What are we going to do?'

Faced with managing their own survival, all feelings of grief over the loss of their two friends were shunted aside. They'd have plenty of time for that later, once they'd resolved the precarious state of affairs they now found themselves at the centre of.

'Listen, Lara, thinking about what happened in the past has given me a brainwave. Did you lock Mike's house when you left?'

Lara pulled a set of keys out of a back pocket on her denim shorts and dangled them in front of his face.

'Good. Does anyone else have a set of keys for Mike's house?'

'I don't think so,' answered Lara. 'Wendy told me that Mike sacked that Spanish cleaner they had about two weeks ago. They caught her stealing money. Mike changed the locks. So I'm pretty sure nobody else would have access to the house.'

'That's also good. How would you feel about leaving Ibiza for some time?'

Lara did not have to think about her answer. 'Angus, as long as I'm with you, I really don't care where I am. How does that sound?'

'Great. I feel exactly the same way.'

They sat in silence, holding hands and looking out past the shifting fly curtain in the doorway to the walled courtyard and the sun-baked hills beyond.

Lara spoke first. 'What are we going to do about Wendy's body?'

'I'll take care of it.'

'You'll have to do it soon, or it will begin to smell.'

'Yes, I know. I'll need Raj and Murphy to give me a hand when they get back from lunch over at Salinas. That lot will freak when they find out Wendy's dead.'

'You're not going to tell me your plans, are you?'

'No, Lara, not right now at least. You better let me get on with what needs to be done. Your job will be to gather what you want to take with you before we leave the island.'

'Where are we going?'

'Not sure yet.'

'When are we going?'

'That depends on when they release Mike's body for burial. I was just thinking about that song by Propellerheads, 'History Repeating'. Came out a few months ago. You know it?'

'Yeah, they play it on the radio a lot just now. I love Shirley Bassey's voice. She's been on the go for ages. My dad used to listen to her singing 'Big Spender' when I was a teenager in Dublin. What about it?'

'What she sings about is true,' said Angus. 'It's all just a little bit of history repeating.'

Lara reflected on what they'd been discussing and finally said, 'For crying out loud, don't tell me you're planning to burn Mike's house down with Wendy's dead body in it, are you?'

Angus glanced at Lara and gave a guilty smile.

'For Christ's sake,' she said, raising her voice, 'that's a bloody stupid idea if ever I heard one. Talk about not learning from your mistakes. Surely you can come up with something better than that.'

He looked at her and hoped that he could.

Acid Mike was buried on September 3, 1998, in the San Lorenzo cemetery. Angus and his extended family were the only people in attendance. Mike had been acquainted with many people but, in his private life on Ibiza, he tended to limit himself to a few select friends. There was no priest present. Mike had detested priests of any religion. Everyone standing around the grave knew that, were Mike somehow able to witness the scene in the graveyard from the other side, he'd freak out if he saw a Catholic priest at his interment. There were a couple of grubby-looking gravediggers over in a corner, sitting on a headstone and smoking cigarettes.

Please make sure that 'Ripple' is played at my funeral. Acid Mike's voice echoed from the past inside Angus's head. He pressed the play button on a battery-powered CD player and Jerry Garcia's wistful voice delivered the lyrics of Acid Mike's favourite Grateful Dead song. Angus looked around at his friends and wasn't surprised to see that all of them were pretty choked up. As the song faded, they each threw a handful of red earth into the grave where it splattered onto the coffin lid. Angus changed the CD, pressed the play button again, and another song came on. *Drifting...* Jimi Hendrix's gentle voice and evocative words opened Angus's heart to the unexpressed grief held inside. Angus wept for the first time since Acid Mike had died. Lara drew closer to Angus and embraced him, his body shaking. *Sailing home...* The song ended. Birds fluttered and chirped in the trees. From the direction of the whitewashed church, there came a sudden clattering of wings. A flock of white doves flew overhead. The birds circled the graveyard three times, then headed north, quickly dwindling to a moving white speck in the cloudless blue sky. Murphy shouted a short eulogy, 'Adios, Mike! Fly on, brother! Go for the light!' Everyone cheered.

The Casanova Bar was a minute's walk from the church. Everyone needed a drink. Except for a lone barman reading a newspaper, the place was deserted. By late afternoon, Angus and his friends were pleasantly drunk. Nina and Alice had promised the babysitter they'd be home by six. It was time to hit the road.

Wendy's body had now been wrapped in black plastic bin liners and layers of parcel tape for over two weeks. There was a faint smell of decomposition in the upstairs master bedroom, but nothing to write to the local town council about. Angus's original idea of burning the house down with Wendy's corpse in it had been quickly extinguished. When he'd suggested it to Murphy and Raj, they'd looked at him like he was a mad pyromaniac. Raj made a point of reminding him he was still paying the price for the last time he got carried away with a box of matches, a can of paraffin, and a box of fireworks in Nepal.

'Discretion is the name of the game,' Murphy told Angus. 'Everyone in the neighbourhood knows you were close friends with Mike and Wendy. You guys were in and out of each other's houses all the time. We do what has to be done and then fade into the sunset. End of story.'

Angus, Murphy, and Raj spent a day going through Mike's house in search of anything in need of disposal. All they found worth keeping was a brief-case full of Spanish bank notes. They also came across a couple of American passports with Mike's photo in them, his UK driving licence, Wendy's British passport, a mouldy kilo of Moroccan hashish and a bag of ecstasy pills. They were all thrown in a small fire and burned.

The sun had set. It was beginning to get dark. Murphy and Raj drove in Mike's Toyota behind Angus's Land Rover as it wound its way along the old Portinatx road. They'd taken this particular route because the local police never set up checkpoints on it. When they came to a junction in the small tourist village, Murphy and Raj turned to the left and Angus took a right.

Someone had stolen Mike's dingy. Angus stripped off by a boathouse and swam out to *Tanit* with his clothes bundled on his head. Acid Mike had ex-plained to Angus at least a dozen times how it was most important to open the hidden fuel cut-off tap, before trying to start the diesel engine. Angus had forgotten this and nearly ran the twin batteries flat before remembering what he was doing wrong. He turned the ignition key and waited for the heating elements to warm up. The engine was sluggish and didn't fire up until the third turn of the starter key. It was unsettling for him to be on the small fishing vessel minus Mike's physical presence. Angus had accompanied him many times on boat excursions and the occasional nocturnal fishing expedition. They'd never caught much to boast about on those trips but had both enjoyed each other's company and lying on their backs gazing up into the star-filled sky. Angus unhitched a rope from an orange plastic buoy, attached by a rusty chain to a heavy concrete dead-weight at the bottom of the sandy cove. He switched on the running lights and navigated slowly between the many deserted pleasure craft moored in the inlet. There was a balmy sea-to-land breeze out on the open water. Angus increased *Tanit's* speed a little and she cut smoothly through the calm sea. Twenty minutes later, he was half-a-kilometre out from Moon Beach. He flashed a powerful hand torch three times and seconds later he saw three flashes from the shore. He spun the wheel to his left and edged closer to the land. He knew this area of coastline well but could see little of it due to it being dark. He disengaged the engine close to a rocky outcrop. Murphy tossed a nylon rope down to him and he caught it first time. Two plastic bags landed on the wooden deck. Raj dived into the warm sea and, moments later, clambered aboard using the folding ladder towards the stern.

'How's it going?' Angus asked.

Raj rubbed his body with a dry towel from one of the plastic bags. 'What a fucking job we had lowering Wendy's body down that cliff. She's heavier than a dead horse. The bags she's wrapped in got ripped in places. As you're going to find out in a minute, the old girl doesn't smell quite as good as she did when she was alive. In fact, she fucking well stinks.'

Murphy flashed his torch. Angus said to Raj, 'C'mon, quit complaining and give me a hand here.' Murphy tossed another rope onto the deck and then rolled Wendy's corpse towards the water. There was a splash and moments later Angus and Raj hauled her on board. Raj was right, she was heavy. *Tanit's* prow scraped against rock. Angus quickly engaged the motor and shifted into reverse. Murphy dived into the water.

Murphy's wet head appeared by the rudder. 'I say, chaps,' he called, 'full speed ahead, hop-diggety!'

Angus kept the running lights off. He steered the boat towards the open sea. The dripping, misshapen bundle that was Wendy's corpse lay in the prow. The wind was blowing a putrid stench directly into Angus's face. He felt like throwing up. About two kilometres out, a searchlight appeared to his right. He switched on the running lights. Angus called over his shoulder, 'Something's coming our way. Better wrap those chains around Wendy and get ready to dump her.'

Whatever kind of boat it was, it was heading directly towards them... fast. Whoever was steering it must be able to see them but, just in case they didn't, Angus flashed his torch towards it. A searchlight returned the signal. Angus began to worry it was a custom's boat. He glanced at the depth finder. The sea was 127 metres deep. Deep enough for his purposes. *'Dump* her!' he shouted. *'Now!'* Wendy's corpse tumbled into the sea and quickly disappeared below the surface. The speedboat was about 200 metres away, heading directly towards them. In the last moment, the fifteen-metre-long Sunseeker veered to starboard. Angus heard a blast of rock music. *Woo hoo!* … It was Blur's 'Song 2'. He caught a flash of a woman waving from the boat's prow, her long hair blowing back in the slipstream. A Jolly Roger flapped at the boat's stern. Moments later, the Sunseeker's foaming wash hit *Tanit's* bow head-on and nearly succeeded in knocking Murphy and Raj into the sea. The fishing boat bucked a few times then levelled out when it entered calmer water.

Murphy was furious. He stood on *Tanit's* swaying deck and shouted and ranted in the quickly receding speedboat's direction. *'Fucking assholes!* One day I'll have a fuckin' boat ten times bigger than yours!'

Murphy and Raj flew back to Amsterdam with their families.. Angus and Lara spent over a week in preparation for leaving Ibiza. Lara struck up a conversation with a retired Swiss couple in the Vista Allegre Bar in San Juan. They were looking to rent a house in the area on a long-term basis. The Swiss couple moved into Angus and Lara's house at the end of the week. To this day Mike's house remains uninhabited. *Tanit* sits rotting in a boatyard off the Santa Eulària/Ibiza road. Just another abandoned relic from someone's broken dream.

Angus and Lara caught the night ferry to Barcelona, where they bought open around-the-world flight tickets. They visited Central America, staying in Costa Rica for two months. One morning, Lara awoke to find a large black scorpion on her pillow, flexing its pincers. She decided it was time to move on. They flew to Australia and then on to New Zealand. An earthquake in Christchurch left them badly shaken. After a three-month-long tour of Southeast Asia they landed in Sri Lanka's Colombo airport. Angus liked Sri Lanka a lot: the people, the cuisine, the jungle, the verdant paddy fields, the coastline, the mountains, the Buddhist culture, but most of all he liked the fact that the country was totally corrupt. Sri Lanka was the kind of place that you could get away with almost anything if you had the money available to grease the right bureaucratic palms. When Lara heard about an old Dutch colonial house for sale with a few hectares of land near Galle on the southwest coast, she and Angus went to investigate. It wasn't exactly what they'd been searching for, but it had potential.

The sun was setting over the Indian Ocean. Lara and Angus were sitting in a beachfront restaurant facing Unawantuna Bay. They were in the midst of an intense discussion about the pros and cons of buying a property in Sri Lanka.

'Och, jings, look who the wind has blown in,' said a Scottish voice.

Angus looked up at the bearded man standing beside him. 'Jeeps?'

The Wee Man spread his arms and bowed. 'At your service.'

Angus rose from his seat and hugged his old friend. He stood back from Jeeps at arm's length and said, 'Man, it must be twenty-five years since I last saw you. How's it going?'

Jeeps chuckled. 'It's going. Don't ask me how. It just is.'

Angus laughed. He looked down at Lara. 'Jeeps,' he said, 'this is my beloved Lara. Lara, this is Jeeps, an old friend of mine from the hippy days in Scotland.'

Lara rose from her wooden chair and hugged Jeeps. They sat down and Jeeps commented in a loud whisper, 'Aye, Angus, you were always lucky with the women.'

Angus nodded. 'Well, I don't know about *always* but, as far as Lara is concerned, you never said a truer word.'

Night descended quickly. Angus and Jeeps proceeded to fill in the blanks, while Lara listened on. Six bottles of ice-cold beer later, Jeeps enquired, 'And what brought the pair of you to Sri Lanka?'

Lara explained without giving too much away and told Jeeps about the property they'd seen that afternoon. 'We like the place,' she concluded, 'but we're not a hundred percent sure about it.'

'Fools rush in, as they say,' said Jeeps, lighting a cigarette from a candle. 'I've been living around these parts for five years now and I've seen a few people blow in, all bushy-tailed and wide-eyed, and setting themselves up to land in a shit-load of trouble. This country is a basket case as far as foreigners buying property goes. They change the laws every month. Right now is a good time to buy. But I've heard they're going to slap a huge tax bill on foreigners buying a property in Sri Lanka very soon. So, if you're going to make a move, better do it quickly.' The Wee Man stroked his long beard for a moment. His eyes glistened in the flickering candlelight. 'Tell you what. I think I know where this place is you just described. It's up above the old granite quarry. Let's meet up there tomorrow, towards sunset, and see if I can help you come to a decision. I have a little something for you to try that might clarify the situation. What do you say?'

Lara and Angus nodded in agreement. Waves crashed on the beach as Angus pondered on what the *little something* Jeeps had for them to try might be.

'*Garaguru?*' Angus said, examining the contents of a small plastic bag. 'What the fuck is *garaguru*? It looks like herbal tea.'

Jeeps chuckled. 'Aye, well, it is kind of herbal, I suppose. Neo-aborigine bioneers cooked it up, under the shade of a wattle tree in the dreamtime. Flown all the way from Australia by dragonfly. It's medicinal.'

'But we're not ill,' said Lara.

Jeeps chuckled again. 'Aye, Lara, I can see that. But it's not that kind of medicine. Trust me. If you smoke this, all will be revealed.'

They were seated on the cracked marble steps at the front of the derelict colonial house. Angus looked past a stand of coconut trees to the vast expanse of the ocean. The sun was low in the sky, bathing the scene in a golden light. 'Okay, I get the picture, Jeeps. But what exactly does this garaguru do to you when you smoke it?'

'Well,' said the Wee Man, producing a long-stemmed pipe from his embroidered satchel, 'you've smoked DMT before, right?'

'Yes, I have,' confirmed Angus.

'So, it's a wee bit similar,' said Jeeps, tamping a smidgen of the smoking mixture into the glass pipe's bowl. 'But garaguru is more benign. Gentler. Feminine. The problem with DMT is that the experience can be kind of aggressive and overwhelming to the point of it being difficult to assimilate what happened to you afterwards. Kind of like smoking toad crystals at an extraterrestrial tourist convention on Pluto. I mean to say, if you want to have contact with an alien, why not shake tentacles with a friendly octopus? Anyway, garaguru isn't like that. You come up almost instantly, the veil lifts and...' He trailed off and shook his head. 'Hey, come on, man. Get with the programme. There are lessons to be learned here, and some of those lessons are not for the fainthearted. If you want to learn more, you have to inhale the spirit of garaguru.'

Angus bent forward and glanced at Lara, sitting on the other side of the Wee Man. She looked open and vulnerable. He did not wish to be part of anything that could potentially harm her. He said to Jeeps, 'I'm not sure about this. Is this stuff dangerous in any way?'

'Only if you're afraid of stepping out of the confines of three-D reality for a few timeless minutes.' Jeeps gazed into his eyes. 'Trust me,' he said for a second time.

Angus did. 'Okay, then. Pass me that pipe and I'll try it.'

The chubby Scotsman smiled and nodded. 'If you want to break through, you will need three hits. Draw slowly and hold each lungful of smoke in for as long as you can.' He raised the glass pipe to his forehead and then handed it to Angus.

Angus held a plastic lighter's flame to the bowl. He sucked gently and inhaled smoke. It tasted of mothballs. He held his breath for twenty seconds and exhaled. He repeated the process. On his second exhalation, he heard a faint fizzing in his head. His surroundings began to glow and pattern. He exhaled his third lungful of garaguru smoke and gasped. 'Wow!' Jeeps reached over and took the pipe from Angus's hand. Angus looked over to a pile of brown rocks. They looked like giant toads. A subtle pattern of interlocked triangles blanketed everything. His eyes shifted to the coconut trees, their leaves fluttering and crackling in the breeze. The swaying trees were profoundly beautiful and very alive. Angus detected a subliminal clicking emanating from the trees. He focused on the sound. They were communicating. *With him!* Bizarre as it was, he went for it and sent out a non-verbal response. *What is it? What do you want to say to me?*

The coconut trees sang back with childlike voices. 'We like you. Stay here. Bring us water. We are thirsty.'

Talking trees! A wave of positronic emotion swept over Angus. 'My God!' he gasped. 'This is incredible.' For a few kaleidoscopic moments, there was no residue of ordinary reality. He was tempted to close his eyes, but kept them open a little longer. Everything he looked at appeared to be living artworks in a fantastic exhibition. The poignant beauty of his majestic surroundings bordered on the overwhelming. He closed his eyes and found himself under the vaulted ceiling of a vast psychedelic cathedral, it's surface pulsating with geometric hallucinations. He experienced a moment of panic when the intricately patterned ceiling bore down on him, threatening to engulf him. His eyes blinked open, and the vision was gone. He turned to Jeeps. The Wee Man took a puff on his pipe, nodded to Angus and laughed. Angus laughed as well. It felt like he'd known the man for a thousand lifetimes. 'It's so good to see you again,' said Angus.

Jeeps smiled. 'Likewise.'

They laughed some more.

The shadows were long. The air was balmy. Life's interconnectivity hit Angus full blast. All around Mother Nature hummed, chirped, buzzed, and twittered. Wood pigeons cooed in the background. Jeeps's face was a turquoise skull covered in translucent skin, his shiny eyes jacked directly into a 90 billion neuron-powered brain. Angus experienced existentially how life's creative principle needed human bodies as vehicles to revel in its astonishing creation. His mind and ego drifted away, mere bubbles, floating and dissolving. in the vast ocean of existence. For a few enduring moments, he was pure consciousness grooving in the utter wonder of being. He understood with great clarity the purpose of human life; to share love and delve into the endless mystery of existence to the absolute maximum of his capability. He glanced up and thought, *The sky is not the limit.* There was a deep thump. Angus looked over towards an ancient banyan tree, glossy elliptical leaves flashing myriad shades of green, aerial prop roots hanging to the ground and developing into new trunks. Another deep thump. *Man, is that the banyan's heartbeat I'm hearing?* Angus wondered. *Do trees have hearts?* He'd never hugged a tree in his life. He was thinking now might be a good time to start when he caught Lara's eye. She raised a hand to clear hair from her brow, inclined her head to one side like an inquisitive bird, and smiled questioningly at him. A glorious embodiment of all things feminine, he'd never seen so much startling beauty concentrated in a human face. Her smile melted his heart. He felt tears run down over his cheeks.

Angus began to level out. The awe-inspiring vision of nature's divine symmetry and perfection began to diminish, leaving him with an open sensation in the centre of his chest, gently radiating out to encompass his whole body. He felt cleansed. Purified. He did not wish to speak, sensing that talking might break the beautiful spell. Finally, he said to Lara, 'You have to try the garaguru. It's like coming home. Very familiar. A regular old gift of the gods.'

Jeeps handed her the lighter and the pipe. She fired it up and inhaled a lungful of smoke. She coughed on her second exhalation and handed the pipe back to Jeeps. 'Oh, my God,' she gasped, nostrils flaring. She looked around and shook her head, as if not believing what she saw. She stared intensely at a line of chestnut-coloured ants, marching by her bare feet. Lara nodded to herself, sat up straight on the steps, and closed her eyes. She emitted an orgasmic moan. Jeeps turned to Angus and winked.

Ten minutes passed. Lara opened her eyes. She gave a light laugh and said to Jeeps, 'Your *medicine* is probably the most amazing substance I've ever taken in my life. It cured me in an instant of wishing to be anywhere else other than the here and now. A powerful healing remedy. Thank you so much for presenting me with the opportunity to try it.'

Jeeps went all bashful. 'Och, don't thank me. Thank the spirit of garaguru.' He chuckled self-consciously. 'No' bad, though, eh?'

Lara laughed loudly. '*Not bad!* Jeeps, that has got to be the understatement of the century. I'm thinking of something William Blake said: 'If the doors of perception were cleansed, everything would appear to man as it is. Infinite." She looked over towards the Indian Ocean. The setting sun's orange light created a shimmering avenue on the water. 'God! This place is absolutely perfect.' She joined the palms of her hands together in front of her smiling face and saluted the disappearing sun as it sank below the ocean's distant horizon.

Jeeps began to fill his pipe in preparation for round two. Somewhere below their high vantage point, a temple bell rang out.

Angus and Lara bought the property in January 1999.

'I'll say this much, you've become a great storyteller, Hamish.'

'Why, thank you, Jean. Coming from you, I take that as a real compliment.'

'Aye, well, don't let it go to your head,' she said, resting her elbows on the kitchen table and cupping her chin in her hands. 'Sounds like that garaguru stuff went right to Angus and Lara's heads.'

'Aye, I suppose it did. I have to confess that I've maybe exaggerated a wee bit here and there but, for the most part, everything I've just described is a pretty accurate account of what Angus told me in Sri Lanka.'

'Which means I'm definitely never going to meet Acid Mike.'

'No, Jean, you're not. The poor fellow has been dead and buried for over ten years now.'

'He was a long way from poor by the sounds of it. Whatever happened to all that money he made from selling drugs?'

'Angus never mentioned anything about that.'

'Did he tell you how old Mike was when he died?'

'Yes, as a matter of fact, he did. Angus found out Mike's date of birth from his British passport. He was sixty-four.'

'Did Angus ever find out what exactly he died from?'

'No, not really. He just reckoned Mike took a lot of ecstasy and LSD that night on Ibiza and it was too much for his ticker. So, he probably died of heart failure, like the Spanish doctor said.'

'And that woman, Wendy B. White, didn't anybody wonder where she disappeared to? I seem to recall you telling me her stepfather was a Conservative MP or something like that. Surely he would have contacted the police and asked them to investigate her disappearance.'

'Yes, you're probably right. But Angus never mentioned anything about that either. He would have been thousands of miles away by then. Besides, as far as I know, Angus and Lara never returned to Ibiza.'

'They didn't? But what about their house? It must be worth a fortune by now.'

'I suppose it must be. Angus just said he had to 'let go' of it. His place on Ibiza wasn't so much a financial investment, but rather an emotional one. Besides, he didn't need the money. Before the introduction of the euro, Angus converted half of his fortune into gold and eventually tripled his investment.'

'From rags to riches, as they say,' commented Jean. 'You know, I wouldn't mind trying Ecstasy,' she said, changing the subject with such disconcerting suddenness it caught me unawares.

'What?'

'You heard me. Do you think you might be able to get your hands on some?'

'Oh...eh...sure. I'll just nip down to Oban harbour and see if there are any dealers hanging about on the quay.' I shook my head. 'Have you taken leave of your senses?'

'God, sometimes you're so stuffy. You need to lighten up a bit, *man*. Maybe smoke a wee pipe of that garaguru stuff.'

I chuckled. 'Now it's you who is starting to sound like Angus. What's come over you?'

'What do you expect? I've been sitting here listening to you telling stories about people selling massive amounts of *'E'*, and then you go all conventional about it when I inform you that I wouldn't mind trying the stuff. I was just thinking some of the young lads at work might be able to get some for you. Like that laddie with the red hair that picked us up when we flew back from Thailand. Eh... What was his name?'

'You mean *Charlie*.'

'Aye, that's him. The gay laddie.'

'*Gay*? Charlie's not gay.'

'Aye, right, and neither is Elton John. If you can't see that boy's a homosexual, you definitely need a new pair of specs. Strong ones. Anyway, how about asking Charlie boy to score you some ecstasy?'

I sat forward and stared at my wife. I couldn't believe what I was hearing. 'Jean, will you just pause for a moment and think about what you're saying. You're requesting that I approach one of my employees and ask him if he can *score* me some MDMA?. That's a Class A drug, for Christ's sake. Are you out of your mind?'

Jean let out a spluttering laugh. 'I'm winding you up, you silly bugger that you are. God, what a prude you are sometimes.'

I had to admit it was true. 'You're right, Jean. Thanks for pointing it out to me. To be honest, I wouldn't mind trying MDMA myself. Just once, mind. I don't want to risk getting addicted to it or anything like that.'

'*Addicted?* You don't know what you're talking about. You need to educate yourself about the true nature of drug addiction. I recommend you begin by reading Irvine Welsh's *Trainspotting* for a start.'

'I didn't know that you'd read that. Is it any good?'

'*Good* isn't the appropriate word. It is a brilliant book. Disgusting in places. Hilarious in others. I absolutely loved it. A contemporary master-piece, no less.'

'You're full of surprises tonight.' I stood up. 'I feel like we've been sitting here for hours.'

'That's because we *have* been sitting here for hours. I've enjoyed it, though.' She glanced up at the wall clock. It was after midnight. 'We better away up to bed. You told me you have an early start tomorrow morning.'

'*Shit!*' I cursed. 'I'd forgotten all about that. I have to drive up to Fort William to oversee a load of ready-mix concrete being poured. Fifty thousand quid's worth. I have to be up there by nine at the latest.'

Jean yawned as she passed me. I switched out the kitchen lights before following her upstairs to our bedroom. I brushed my teeth, took off my clothes, pulled on my pyjamas, and was asleep before my head sank into the soft pillow.

18

SAGARA

It was a warm spring morning in May 2010. I was in my office going through a pile of mail when I came across a postcard. I knew immediately it was from Angus. It pictured a ship's dark blue prow, the name SAGARA fixed to it in brass letters. I must admit, I'd kind of given up on my brother. I hadn't seen Angus in over five years, and the last time I'd heard from him was almost a year ago when I'd received a similar postcard, telling me to prepare for a world cruise that never happened. That postcard had caused a lot of trouble between myself and my wife. Jean had capitulated and agreed to go on the cruise, but when we had heard nothing from Angus by last September, Jean went ballistic on me. It passed like everything else in life, but it remained a very touchy subject that I didn't dare broach again. Now, here was another such postcard, and, naturally, I was curious to see what Angus had to say, no matter how brief. I turned the card over. The writing was so small I had to put my reading glasses on to read it. *Dear Hamish, my most humble apologies for not keeping in touch. I know it will have upset you and Jean. I'm sorry. It won't happen again. I feel an explanation is due. Last September, a drunken boy-racer, driving a sports car, ran into Lara when she was cycling home. She was badly injured. She's healed well and is walking again. I had to re-sit a Marine Navigation exam, which I had failed the first time. If everything goes according to plan, we will be over to see you soon. Start packing your bags to prepare for a world cruise. Existence has its timing. I love you like the brother you are. Angus. PS. Lara sends her love to you and Jean.*

I checked the postmark. Amsterdam 22-05-2010. That was four days ago. I quickly re-read my brother's message, picked up my mobile, and called Monica Shannon's number. She answered almost immediately. We spoke for half-an-hour.

Monica had been to Amsterdam twice to visit her daughter, while Lara was in the hospital recovering from the accident. She'd been cycling home one night and decided to take a shortcut through an industrial estate. Unknown to her, this area was used by some young men for car racing. An Audi TT had sped around a corner on the wrong side of the road and collided with Lara. She'd flown over the roof of the car and as a result, was left with broken wrists and a severe compound fracture in her right leg. By the time an ambulance arrived on the scene, Lara had lost a lot of blood. According to Monica, it had been touch and go in the beginning. The Audi was driven by a Dutchman in his early twenties. He was given a breathalyzer test by the police and found to be three times over the legal limit for alcohol consumption. The young guy was sentenced to four years in prison for drunk and reckless driving.

Monica had also been on board *Sagara* for a test run. She'd described the ship as being like, and I quote, 'A souped-up version of the *Royal Yacht Britannia*'. The motor yacht had been moored at a small dock near Rotterdam. Murphy, who now had a captain's license, had informed her that *Sagara* should be ready to embark on her global voyage by the end of June. Monica had sounded very enthusiastic about the prospect of going on such a trip. She'd talked excitedly about how she'd bought two dozen cookbooks, as well as an instruction manual on how to tie sailor's knots, the latter of which sounded absurd to me. She'd then gone on to tell me what wonderful people Angus and his friends were and how heartbroken she'd felt when Lara told her Mike had passed away. The old girl must have been in her nineties, yet she'd babbled away like a teenager in love with the members of a new boy band. Monica's last words, before the call ended, were, 'I do so very much hope you and Jean will be accompanying us on what promises to be a fun-filled voyage around the world. Tell Jean I'm asking for her.'

I sat at my cluttered office desk, undergoing the corrosive effects produced by a seething cocktail of conflicting emotions. My mobile rang. The black oblong device glowed and vibrated on my desk like a radioactive beetle that had landed on its back. I checked to see who was calling. Nobody important. I put the mobile out of its misery by switching it off, thinking there's nothing quite like a smartphone for making people look dumb. I picked up the office phone and spoke to my secretary, informing Doreen that I didn't want to be disturbed for an hour. I then did something I hadn't done in a long time; I closed my eyes and meditated.

When I opened my eyes my first thought was, *I must remember to do that more often.* I stood up and went over to the office safe. I turned the combination lock, pulled the thick metal door open, and removed the PC I used solely for my writing project. I returned to my desk, lifted the black laptop's lid, and proceeded to bring my manuscript up to date with the latest developments in the story.

Rain clouds were scudding across the late afternoon sky when I arrived home. I wasn't at all surprised to find Jean in the lounge with her feet up, engrossed in the latest celebrity news in *Hello!* Magazine. Her hair was wrapped in a damp red towel and she was wearing a black Adidas training suit with three white stripes running down the sides of its legs.

She looked up and peered over the top of her blue-framed reading glasses. 'You're home early.'

'We're going,' I said.

Jean gave me a puzzled look and took off her specs. 'Going where exactly?'

I sat down on an armchair and faced her. 'We're going on a world cruise with Angus and his friends.'

'Oh, for God's sake,' she groaned. 'I thought we'd been through all that. Last time you got me all worked up about it and what happened?' she asked, all too willing to supply the answer herself. 'I'll tell you what happened, sweet Fanny Adams.'

'But—'

'Hamish. I don't want to know about it. End of story. That's it. Over and out!'

'Come on, Jean,' I pleaded to her. 'Don't be like that.'

'Be like what? Like someone who doesn't want to be messed around by a gullible fool and his manipulative brother?'

It was obvious I had my work cut out for me by the devil himself because it was going to be a devil of a job to steer my wife around to seeing things the way I did. I began by telling Jean about the latest postcard I'd received from Angus. When I got to the part about Lara being involved in a serious accident last September, she sat up straight and paid attention. After I filled her in on Monica's description of *Sagara*, remembering to add the key phrase, a *souped-up version of the Royal Yacht Britannia*, Jean surprised me by saying, 'I'll think about it.'

I gaped at her for a few seconds before I found my voice again. 'You will?'

'You know something? I think you imagine me to be a lot less flexible than I am. I'm away through to the kitchen to make a cup of tea.' She stood. 'You want one?'

'Yes,' I said absently, more focused on the excitement bubbling up from my belly. I'd won her over.

'Don't go away. I'll be back in a minute,' she said, closing the door behind her.

I jumped to my feet, punched the air above my head, and yelled, *'Yes!'* just like that kid, Kevin, does in the movie *Home Alone*.

It was an unusually warm morning in late June. Sunlight strafed through our bedroom window, making me hotter than I already was. Jean was lying on top of me, panting after trying to break her record for achieving multiple orgasms. She's going to kill me when she reads this.

Ding-dong. I heard the doorbell chime downstairs. Jean whispered in my ear, 'Ignore it.' The doorbell chimed again... several times. 'For Christ's sake,' Jean hissed. 'Don't they know it's a Sunday morning?'

I said, 'I better get up and see who it is.' Our naked bodies, drenched in sweat, made a sucking sound, like Velcro being pulled apart, as Jean lifted herself off of me. *Ding-dong, ding-dong, ding-dong...* 'Alright, alright, I'm coming,' I mumbled grumpily, shrugging on a dressing gown. I glanced out the window down to the street and saw a new-shape, silver Jeep Cherokee parked outside that I wasn't familiar with. *Ding-dong, ding-dong, ding-dong...* 'For fuck's sake!' I cursed under my breath as I hurried downstairs to find out whose finger was stuck to the doorbell button.

I opened the door. Angus and Lara were standing on the doorstep, grinning at me like a pair of hungry lions who'd just spotted easy prey. I'd been half-expecting them to show up but, as they both must have noticed, I was lost for words upon actually seeing them. 'Oh... Good morning,' I stammered like an inmate in a mental asylum who'd just discovered he could speak.

They both laughed. Angus said, 'Good morning, Mister MacLeod, aren't you going to invite us in?'

'What? I'm sorry. Come in, please. Come in.' I said, standing aside to let them pass.

Jean called from upstairs, 'Who is it?'

'Angus and Lara,' I announced.

There was a high-pitched squeal before my wife hurried down the stairs, scantily clad in black silk panties and a matching bra. She hugged Angus and Lara in the hall, her eyes gushing with tears. I looked on and was struck by how pale and lean Lara had become since the last time I'd seen her on the morning of the tsunami in Sri Lanka. Angus looked more or less the same: shaved head, muscular, a few lines on his face that hadn't been there five years ago. Jean led them into the kitchen, pulling herself together by filling the coffee maker with water and setting cutlery and plates on the dining table. Suddenly becoming aware that she had very little on, Jean dashed back upstairs to dress more appropriately.

I sat down at the table and stared at my brother and Lara.

Angus said, 'What would life be without a few surprises? Eh, Hamish?'

I still don't know why, but his words struck me as highly amusing. I laughed. My laughter soon turned to tears. 'I thought you two were dead,' I blurted through my sobs. 'The police came around asking questions about you, Angus. They showed me a recent photo of you in Amsterdam. And... And... And...'

Angus and Lara got up and came over to me. Angus placed a reassuring hand on my back and Lara kneeled by my side, taking hold of one of my hands. She whispered, 'It's alright to cry, Hamish. We're here now with you and that's what counts.'

I had calmed down by the time Jean returned to the kitchen, dressed in her black Adidas tracksuit. We began filling each other in about what had been happening in our lives since we'd last been together. When Lara described their almost miraculous escape from the tsunami, I thought to myself, *good material for my manuscript.*

Angus announced proudly, 'It's official. I'm now a fully certified marine navigator. But you don't have to address me as *sir*,' he joked. 'Well, at least not yet, not until you're aboard the ship.'

I'd been so preoccupied with what was taking place in the kitchen, I'd forgotten all about *Sagara*. 'Where is your boat?' I asked. 'When do we get to see her?'

'Well,' said Angus, running a hand over his smooth head, 'for a start, she doesn't belong to me. Murphy and Raj paid for her. And *Sagara* isn't a *boat*, she's a *ship*. A great big, beautiful ship that's going to take us around the world.' He paused and studied Jean and me. He said finally, 'You two are going to come, *aren't you?*'

'Of course we are,' said Jean enthusiastically as if there had never existed a shred of doubt in her mind. 'I'll start packing my suitcase this afternoon.'

'Don't forget your sailor suit with the bellbottom trousers,' Angus reminded her playfully.

'So where is the *Sagara*?' I enquired.

Angus leaned forward over the table, interlacing his fingers. He smiled at me and said, 'You'll be happy to hear that she's anchored a little way out from Oban Marina.'

'*What?*' I gasped. 'Over at Kerrera?'

'Aye, lad,' said Angus, 'the one and only Kerrera Island. Lovely place. We had dinner there yesterday evening.'

'We can go over to the ship now if you like,' said Lara. 'My mum's already on board. We have a tender tied up down in the harbour.'

'Give me five minutes to get shaved, washed, and dressed,' I said, springing to my feet.

Jean gushed, 'God, this is so exciting!'

Angus handled the white semi-rigid like he'd been doing it all his life. We shot out past Oban's harbour wall and headed straight over to Kerrera, Jean and I laughing as the tender thumped across the waves. My brother was right. When the *MV Sagara* came into view, I could see straight away that she wasn't a plain old *boat*, she was a majestic ship. A sixty-metre-long luxury motor yacht, to be more precise, with four decks showing above the waterline. She wasn't a particularly streamlined vessel and looked like she'd been designed along classic lines about twenty years ago. As we drew closer, I could see a red, white and blue flag fluttering in a light breeze behind someone waving from an open deck in the stern. It was Monica, dressed in a navy-blue dress that matched the colour of the ship's hull perfectly. Lara hitched the tender to a shiny brass bollard bolted to the ship's lowest stern deck, where there were two wooden staircases to each side, leading up to the second deck. I noticed a healed scar on Lara's lower right leg, which I assumed had come as a result of her unfortunate accident. A heavily built Indian man with shoulder-length black hair and startling blue eyes appeared beside her. He clung to a stainless steel railing with one hand and offered the other to Jean and me to help us aboard. I stood beside him, looking across the water at Oban. He turned to me and said, 'I suppose that big-

mouthed brother of yours has told you all about me. Don't worry, I'm probably not as brilliant as he made me out to be. Angus is always exaggerating.
I won't shake your hand because we've already done that.' He slapped me
so hard on the back I nearly fell overboard. 'Pleased to meet you, Hamish,
hope you guessed my name,' he chuckled. 'I'm the ship's engineer. Welcome
aboard the *Sagara*.' I liked Raj immediately.

Our jaws dropped when Lara led us into the ship's main salon. I thought,
How on earth did they manage to get away with this? Dark-blue oriental rugs
were scattered over charcoal-coloured, wall-to-wall carpeting. Two banks
of light-grey, upholstered seating lined the sides of the room. They were
littered with pastel-coloured scatter cushions to add a sense of homeli-
ness. Cut flowers in ornate vases had been placed by bowls of fruit on four
thick glass tables fronting the seating arrangement. Curved orange-tinted
windows were set into the walls at eye level. There was a bar with high
rotating stools at the far end of the room. Classical music streamed from
concealed speakers. I recognized Vivaldi's 'Four Seasons'. The overall impression was that of luxury, and that is an understatement. The saloon led
into an intimate dining area with a large oval table surrounded by high-
backed chairs. Between elliptical portals hung abstract and impressionist
paintings, mounted in thick gold leaf frames. I knew some of them were
famous works of art, but I didn't know if they were real or good reproduc-
tions. One of them was a small Van Gogh. I turned to Lara and asked, 'Is that
an original?'

She smiled enigmatically and answered, 'I've no idea. Murphy picked it up
somewhere.'

Lara took Jean's hand. 'If you'll come this way I'll show you your suite.'
She led us up a flight of stairs, then along a dimly lit corridor with recessed
lighting. We reached an oak door. She pushed down on a brass handle,
opened the door, switched on the lights, stepped aside, and, with a flourish
of a hand, said, 'There you go. What do you think?'

I didn't know what to think. The cabin looked like a suite in a five-star
hotel. There was a broad oil painting of Ben Nevis hanging behind a king-
sized bed's bamboo headboard. Lara noticed the painting had caught my
attention. 'Angus had that one painted especially for you by a Dutch artist,
who took his inspiration from a few photographs. Do you like it?'

I loved it. The painter had succeeded in capturing the spirit of the Scottish Highlands: majestic, ancient, vast, moody, sad, empty, yet full of life
and beauty. Two bright dots caught my eye beside the artist's scrawled sig-
nature. I put on my reading glasses, looked more closely, and saw two tiny,
identical figures in black jackets and yellow kilts. Twins! For the second
time that morning, I was overcome with emotion. I flumped down onto
a padded leather armchair. My throat muscles constricted. I think I would
have begun crying at that moment had it not been for Jean, running out
of the bathroom, gushing in an excited voice, 'Oh my god, I can't believe it.
There's a bloody Jacuzzi in there, big enough for four people.' She was like a

keyed-up teenager, who'd just been introduced to Michael Jackson. I let out a spluttering laugh.

Once I'd caught my breath, Lara showed us into the suite's office. It was the size of the average person's living room, with a huge plasma TV screen fixed to the wall backing a teak wood desk as big as a ping-pong table. 'Every suite is equipped with Wi-Fi linked to a satellite dish, so no problem if you want to use Skype to keep in touch with your business and personal matters back home,' said Lara, imitating a stuck-up real estate agent laying the hard sell on for some prospective buyer. Laughing, she performed a pirouette in the centre of the room, bowed gracefully, spread her arms, and looked at Jean and me with her beautiful green eyes. 'Tar-ah,' she trilled. 'So, you guys, what do you say? Do you like the looks of your new home away from home? Yes or no?'

Jean and I looked at each other and laughed. Lara said, 'I think that's a yes.'

An announcement squawked out of a concealed speaker. I recognized Monica's voice. 'Lunch will be served on the lower aft deck in fifteen minutes.'

'Where's that?' I asked Lara.

'Downstairs. Come on, I'll show you the way.'

The lower aft deck was as big as a squash court. The far end was open air, but the seating area was covered by a white awning. Large bowls of Thai-style food and smoked fish were already laid out on a rotating tray at the centre of the table. When everyone had arrived Monica said, 'Please help yourselves and get stuck in.'

Raj introduced Jean and me to his wife and their two children. Alice had thick black hair piled up on her head. She reminded me of Amy Winehouse. Whenever she spoke, her artificial eyelashes fluttered like black butterfly wings. She had a strong Glaswegian accent, although she occasionally conversed with her offspring in Dutch, speaking the guttural language like a native. Her son, Adam, looked like he was in his early twenties and her daughter, Gloria, was a young teenager. They both had light brown skin and their father's bright blue eyes. They were remarkably well-mannered. I was surprised to see that Raj was quite a strict father. I'd observed him reprim-anding Gloria twice for speaking at the table with food in her mouth, some-thing my grandchildren did constantly.

I listened in when Jean asked Angus, 'Aren't there any staff on the ship?'

'No,' he said, in between nibbling on a kipper, 'just us lot. The last owner employed sixteen crew members. Raj and Murphy spent a couple of million on upgrading the ship's mechanical side to make *Sagara* almost fully auto-mated. The navigation bridge is equipped with sophisticated electronic gear, making it possible for two skilled people to control the entire ship. On that side of things, the running of the ship involves mostly steering from time to time and pushing the right buttons when needed. It wouldn't be exaggerating to say that *Sagara* could sail from Oban to New York with-out anyone on board. You just need to set the course, program it into a computer, start the engines, raise the anchor and away she goes.' Angus concluded, 'We considered hiring a crew but changed our minds. We value our privacy too much. We want to run the ship like a floating commune. Everyone has to do their bit.'

'Really? Will I have a job too?'

'Aye, Jean, you will,' said Angus. 'We thought you might like to work with Monica in the kitchen.'

'My suggestion,' said Monica, sitting to the left of Jean. 'How do you feel about that?'

'Fantastic! I can't wait to get started,' Jean gushed. 'Who does the cleaning?'

'We all do,' answered Angus. 'Everyone has to take care of their own quarters and the other areas we do in shifts. It doesn't require a lot of effort.'

'What will I be doing,' I asked.

'Well,' said Angus, after sipping from a glass of white wine, 'I thought you might like to learn a bit about how the ship works from Raj and study the ins and outs of navigation with me. Once we're out in the open sea, *Sagara* can run on automatic mostly, but someone has to program the automatic pilot first. I'd also like you to learn about our sophisticated radar system. It's best to have someone monitoring the ship's controls at all times. Don't want to cross the path of a supertanker in the middle of the night because of a technical error, now do we?'

'Certainly not,' I agreed. 'By the way, where is your friend, Captain Murphy?'

'Oh, he'll be back in a couple of days. He and Nina took their kids over to Glasgow. They wanted to go to a Lynyrd Skynyrd concert and check out a few relatives in their hometown.'

'I'm looking forward to meeting them,' I said, 'Murphy in particular. You've told me so much about him. What's he like these days?'

'Murphy?' Angus laughed. 'Murphy is one of a kind. I'll let you make your own mind up about him.'

'I like Raj and Alice.'

'That's good. You're going to be seeing quite a lot of them in the coming months. Life runs more smoothly when you like people.' Angus paused, then continued. 'Listen, Hamish, I've been thinking. We can give you and Jean a week to get ready before we set sail. Will that be enough time for you two to arrange everything you need to take care of?'

I thought about it for a few moments. 'Yes,' I said finally, 'I think we'll be able to manage that. It might get a bit hectic, but we'll have plenty of time to relax once we've sorted everything out.'

We both looked over to the stern. The sun was dropping toward the horizon, promising a glorious sunset.

'You can spend the night here,' Angus suggested. 'I can take you over to Oban in the morning.'

I agreed. It felt wonderful to be reunited with my brother.

On Monday morning I called Fergus Paterson into my office and sat for three hours with him, going over the duties that would become his responsibility during my absence. Fergus, a somewhat gruff Irishman in his mid-forties, had worked for me as a foreman for over ten years. He wasn't particularly popular with the men, but he was honest, hard-working, and diligent. At first, he was overwhelmed by the prospect of running my building company with over seventy skilled tradesmen to monitor but, when I informed him he'd be earning triple his current salary, he quickly took to the idea. When he left the office, I felt confident I'd made the right decision. What Fergus didn't know about the construction business probably wasn't worth knowing.

Jean busied herself with packing and instructing our cleaner about what she had to do, especially during winter when there was always a risk of pipes bursting from freezing temperatures. Jean shopped locally for items she thought we might need for the trip. She bought enough bottles of sun protector from the chemist to shield us from an atomic blast.

The waterproof cases for my laptops arrived on Friday afternoon. I'd ordered them from Amazon as a precautionary measure to protect my two computers from salt-laden air.

We had a farewell lunch with my three daughters and their families. Tavis, my youngest grandson, didn't take the idea of our imminent departure very well. The four-year-old was convinced he was never going to see Granny and Granda ever again. When I lifted him onto my knees, he was crying his heart out. I managed to allay his fears by promising to bring him a giant panda bear as a present upon my return. 'An alive one?' he'd asked, looking up into my eyes. It was an innocent question that almost succeeded in breaking my heart. I'd nodded and that seemed to do the trick. Wee Tavis didn't leave my side for the remainder of the afternoon.

On Saturday night, I went downstairs to the basement garage and disconnected the battery cables in our two cars. By Sunday afternoon, we were back on board *Sagara*.

I was sitting with a plate of warm pumpkin soup in front of me when I first laid eyes on Captain Murphy. He strolled into the main dining salon, dressed in a navy-blue, gold-braided uniform. There was a peaked cap on his head and, most surprising of all, a stuffed green parrot attached to an epaulette on his right shoulder. The captain fired off a brisk salute and said in a gruff voice, 'Evening, crew.' Everyone present, including the four younger crew members, sprang to their feet, saluted, and said in unison, 'Good evening, Captain Murphy, *sir*.'

Jean and I exchanged a perplexed glance and then, seconds later, rising to our feet, we followed suit. 'Good evening, Captain Murphy, *sir*.' Our voices rang hollow in the silence that followed. Suddenly, everyone began howling with laughter. Jean and I didn't catch on at first. Then, the embarrassing penny dropped. We were the unsuspecting victims of a prank. We'd been set up. I turned to look at Jean. Her face was scarlet. Still chuckling, Murphy ambled over to us. He slapped me on the back and shook my hand. 'Sorry about that, Hamish, the joke was on you, man,' he said, in a voice that was pure, undiluted Glaswegian. He pulled me towards him and gave me a swift hug. 'Heard all about you, pal. Pleasure to have you aboard. You're a part of the family now.' He then turned to Jean, shaking her head in disbelief at having fallen foul of such a ridiculous hoax. Murphy held her by the shoulders and looked into her furious eyes. She stuck out her bottom lip in a show of ersatz unhappiness. 'Oh, dear,' he said theatrically, 'I can see an exotic bird's feathers have been ruffled.' He glanced at the stuffed parrot on his shoulder. 'Come on, Polly, don't be shy. Say hello to Jean.'

Jean stood back from Murphy, gathered the most scathing insults she could muster, and boiled them down to three words, *'You cheeky bastard!'*

Murphy bent and slapped the knees of his neatly creased trousers. When he stood up straight again, Polly the parrot bobbed on his shoulder. 'Jean,' he said with a grin, 'I can see we're going to get on like an ammunition dump on fire. Angus has told me a lot about you, and you're even more formidable and beautiful than he described you. I'm very pleased to meet you, darlin'.' He offered his right hand. Jean pushed his hand aside, stepped forward, and embraced him. She whispered loudly in his ear, her voice as brittle and cold as thin ice. 'You're smiling now, but you won't be when I get you back for that, you big galoot.' Murphy sniggered and said, in a theatrical whisper that assumed everyone present was stone deaf, 'Where have you been all my life, doll. I love you to bits.'

Nina wandered over with her two kids in tow. 'Hi, Jean, I'm Nina. Is this idiot flirting with you already?'

Jean nodded. 'He is indeed, Nina.' She produced her warmest smile and her dark eyes narrowed into a salacious slant. 'How on earth do you manage to put up with him?' she asked.

Nina shrugged. 'That's a question I've been asking myself off and on for over thirty years. He's good in the sack and that's about it.' They gave each other a warm hug, then Nina introduced her children. She yammered something in quick-fire Dutch to her daughter, who looked about twenty, with long fair hair and, like her mother, a lot of carefully applied makeup on her high-cheekboned face. The young woman stepped forward and said in perfect English. 'My name's Layla. I'm delighted to meet you, Missus MacLeod.' Jean gave her a quick hug and then the young lad stepped up. He was perhaps seven years younger than his sister and tall for his age. He had a thick mop of curly brown hair and a glint in his eye like his father. 'How you doing, Missus MacLeod?' he said in a broad Scottish accent. 'I'm Ziggy.' My wife shook his hand and said, 'I'm doing fine, son. Just fine. You can call me Jean.'

We sat down to dinner. There were thirteen of us and I knew in my heart it was going to be a lucky number.

It had rained during the night. Coastal mist shrouded the rising sun, a white disk drifting over the mainland. I stood beside Murphy and Angus on *Sagara's* bridge. In front of us were various illuminated dials and a line of daylight-readable, flat-panel monitors on a wide control panel. Murphy sat down in the high-backed captain's chair and shifted two levers with black plastic knobs on them. Thick steel chains clanked over pulleys in the prow's hawseholes as the ship's twin anchors were raised. Murphy slid a bigger lever forward fractionally so the motor yacht took the strain off the anchor chains.

Sagara headed off along the Sound of Kerrara in a southerly direction. I looked across the bridge to my left and saw Oban emerging from the mist. Unfamiliar emotions rose from my guts and flowered in my chest. On one side, I felt relieved to leave my old life behind. I'd grown tired of my daily routine. On the other side, I felt tentacles of worry leech onto my mind. I knew I would miss my grandkids, and I fretted that my business would run smoothly. After all, I'd spent most of my adult life nurturing my money-generating baby. I'd promised myself to leave my material affairs behind, but I was finding out it wasn't as easy to do as it sounded. The more I thought about it, the more intense my mental activity became. I turned to my brother and said, 'Angus, how do you deal with unwanted thoughts?'

Angus placed his hands on the control panel and leaned forward. His eyes remained fixed straight ahead as if observing the misty horizon in case of another ship's sudden appearance. 'Well, Hamish, that's a common enough problem you're enquiring about. Everyone suffers from identifying with thoughts, especially the ones produced by negative emotions, which are almost always lies. I'm purely selfish about how I deal with such mental activities. I sometimes ask myself, 'What benefit can result from entertaining such thoughts?' If the answer comes back, 'No benefit whatsoever,' I drop that line of thinking immediately. We have no control over the thoughts that enter our mind but we can choose whether to think them or not.' He pushed off from the console and stood up straight. 'It usually works for me,' he went on. 'Thoughts need feeding. If they don't receive any form of nourishment, like giving them your attention, they pass on and disappear. That's why you feel tired if you think too much. Thoughts feed off you. They consume the highest octane fuel your body can manufacture. I'm not saying you should ignore thoughts or try to repress them, because those are also forms of attention. Just note what you're thinking and stay neutral about it. If thoughts persist, you can always tell them to shut up. That should do the trick.'

I thought about it. 'Sounds like good advice. I'll give it a try.'

Angus chuckled. 'You do that.'

Something buzzed. Captain Murphy leaned forward in his seat and glanced at a circular screen, glowing neon green. 'Small craft to port about three kilometres away,' he said to nobody in particular. 'Probably a trawler heading for Oban.' He sounded the ship's horn. It was loud.

I turned and studied Murphy's profile. He had a greying goatee beard, his long hair tied back in a ponytail beneath a crumpled sailor's cap with a golden anchor badge pinned to it. He looked like a middle-aged hippy version of Captain Haddock, the Tintin comic book character. He was a strange but likeable man. Ruthless and deadly if he had to be, according to my brother's reports. I knew already there were hidden depths to Murphy, some very dark, but at that moment he exuded confidence and I couldn't imagine a more trustworthy person at the helm of a motor yacht that weighed over 1300 tons.

Kerrara was left behind. The captain turned the wheel to starboard and the ship began to move in a southwesterly direction. The sun rose higher in the sky and the sea mist began to lift. Off to the right I could see the Isle of Mull's rugged coastline, the contours of hills in the background. Murphy set a more westerly course and said, 'I'll swing past the southern tip of Iona, so you guys can check out where it all began.'

About an hour passed. Angus handed me a powerful pair of binoculars. I used them to view the small island where we were born almost sixty years ago. I could make out a few buildings and a jetty. In the background, I could see a tall stone structure that was surely Iona Abbey. Sunlight glinted on glass, reminding me of the story Angus had told me about smashing the ancient building's stained-glass windows with a catapult when he was a young lad.

The sea air was making me hungry. I went down a companionway in search of some lunch. I sat alone in the galley and ate three vegetable burgers and a plate of reheated roast potatoes.

By late afternoon *Sagara* was entering the North Channel, the body of water that separates Ireland from the United Kingdom. I sat beside Jean on a wooden bench, on a small deck in the ship's prow. Behind us were stored two white rib boats covered by tarpaulins. A fresh wind blew into our faces. The motor yacht was now cruising at her maximum speed of sixteen knots, which Murphy had informed me was around thirty kilometres per hour. It felt fast to me. We passed The Isle of Man. There was a bit of a swell, but the ship stayed pretty level as it cut through the Irish Sea, with little in the way of to and fro motion. I was surprised that neither of us felt seasick. Jean had been working out for a couple of hours in the ship's fully equipped gym and, when she felt cold, we went indoors, showered, chatted a bit in our bedroom, and then went for dinner. After our meal, we watched Ridley Scott's *Bladerunner* in the small Dolby-Surround cinema. It had been years since I'd last seen it, and I'd forgotten what a great movie it is. So there I sat with Jean, Angus, Lara, and two teenagers in absolute luxury, cruising along Saint George's Channel on our way towards the Atlantic Ocean, without the faintest idea what our first port of call would be. I didn't care, because Jean and I were having the time of our life. *Sagara* cruised on into the night.

By morning, we were crossing the Celtic Sea, a body of water I'd been unaware of until that point in my life. I spent the afternoon with Raj down in the engine room. The ship had twin engines encased in protective metal coverings. The engine room was a long way from how I'd imagined it might look. Illuminated by bulkhead lights, it was done out in matt-grey paint. There was a wall of blinking red and green lights and gauges with black needles, four flat-panel monitors and an ergonomic computer keyboard on a desk, a board with various tools and spanners neatly hung in designated places, and not a drop of oil to be seen anywhere. The place was spotless. There was a strong smell of diesel oil. The fuel tanks contained tons of fuel, which gave the motor yacht a range of 14,000 kilometres. The only thing I'd imagined that was accurate was the noise level. There was no clanking of piston rods, but there was a loud, reverberatory hum, which Raj told me could damage your hearing if subjected to it over an extended period of time. He supplied me with a pair of ear defenders. We only removed these if there was a need to communicate verbally. Mostly Raj used a felt-tip pen on sheets of A4 paper to draw simple diagrams and show what dial was monitoring what. The most important gauges measured engine pressure and temperature. Some dials gave digital readings. We sat down in comfortable swivel chairs, drank hot coffee from a thermos flask, and munched on digestive biscuits. Like his buddy, Murphy, Raj seemed right at home doing what he was doing as if he'd been born to it. He informed me we were bound for the Azores on our way to the Panama Canal, with a detour that would take us through the Caribbean. With the deep hum vibrating on my ear protectors, I gazed up at a bank of flickering green and red lights and felt like I'd landed in Man Heaven. Raj tapped me on my shoulder. I looked into his radiant blue eyes and he gave me a thumbs-up signal with a clenched fist. I returned the hand gesture, nodded my head vigorously, and laughed. Raj grinned from ear to ear. He had beautiful white teeth, a great sense of humour, and a heart of gold.

,

19

A MAN OF THE SEA

We encountered our first storm two days out from the Azores. I'd just finished dinner and decided to go up to the navigation bridge. I found Angus studying a map in the chart room at the back of the bridge. 'What's up?' I asked my brother.

'There's been a severe weather warning,' he said, looking up from the sea chart spread before him on an angled table. 'We're heading right towards a big storm system and we're still over five-hundred kilometres north of the Azores.'

'Are we going to be okay?'

'Depends how you define *okay*,' he replied. 'We're not going to sink if that's what you're worried about. But it is going to get a bit rough. We've already stowed all the deck furniture and secured everything that needs to be lashed down.'

'I could have helped with that.'

'No problem, Hamish, it wasn't a big deal. Listen,' he said, picking up a drawing compass, 'I need to concentrate on plotting our course. Go and give the captain a bit of company.'

Murphy was standing with his feet apart in front of the ship's wheel, quite small in relation to the size of the vessel it controlled. 'How's it going, captain?' I asked.

'Fine, Hamish, fine. We're in for a bit of a blow, according to the reports. They tend to agree that there's an intense low-pressure system moving up quickly from south of the Azores.' Murphy did not look at me as he spoke, staring ahead at the grey sea. Daylight was beginning to fade. The sea didn't look particularly rough. Gentle swells were rolling towards us from the south. The captain glanced at a small flat screen with a digital readout. 'Atmospheric pressure is dropping fast,' he said.

The weather began to deteriorate, with rain, gusts of wind, and an overcast scudding in low over the rising waves. Murphy switched on the wipers, the ship's running lights, and the bridge's red night lighting. When it began to get dark outside he turned on two powerful wide beam searchlights fixed to the superstructure above the bridge. The ship's engines were fully throttled up, but our speed was being diminished by the impact of three-metre-high waves. Murphy, seated in the captain's chair, reached over to fiddle with a grey laptop. A church bell began to toll. It was an ominous sound. Up ahead over the sea, lightning flashed. A crowd cheered in the background.

The bell tolled again. Murphy tapped at a computer key and the sound level increased so much the whole place began reverberating with the sound of the bell. I now realised what it was. It was the intro to a live version of AC/DC's 'Hells Bells'. I'd always felt slightly embarrassed about my love for the Australian rock band's music until I read that Keith Richards also liked them. The bell tolled thirteen times. Angus Young cranked his guitar up. A kick drum set the beat and rattled the windows. The ship's bow plunged ahead into the waves. Sheets of water splashed across the foredeck. Brian Johnson's voice roared out of the speakers set to each side of the bridge. Lightning bolts lit up the cloud-filled sky. The ship's searchlights shone on a wall of grey water. 'Here we go,' called Murphy. Angus staggered over to the control console and gripped a support handle. The ship rose at a forty-degree angle and plunged down into a trough on the backside of the wave. *Hells bells...* 'Woo hoo!' yelled Murphy at the helm. AC/DC thundered out of the speakers. *My temperature's high...* I ran a hand over my forehead. I was sweating. Heavy spray slapped against the windows. The ship rose again and plunged into another trough with a crash that shook the superstructure. *Hells Bells...* 'Yeah!' Murphy yelled again. I looked away from the sea. Murphy and Angus were staggering about the bridge, dancing around under a red ceiling light like a pair of fiery sea devils. *Hells bells...* The unmanned steering wheel spun. I began to worry the ship might broach and capsize. My stomach lurched as the ship began to pitch and roll. The ship heaved upwards and Angus Young blistered the paint with a red-hot guitar solo. *Sagara* slammed down into another trough. The foredeck was completely submerged under frothing water. The bow rose up again and ploughed into a ten metre wave. *Hells bells...* The music faded. Murphy quickly returned to the wheel. The motor yacht's motions were becoming difficult to predict. The captain steered the ship into the oncoming waves. I began to feel a little nauseous. Angus placed a reassuring hand on my shoulder and said, 'I'll go below and check how everyone else is getting along. You stay here with Murphy and keep an eye on things.' He hurried off, struggling to keep his balance on the thick-pile woolen carpet.

Keep an eye on things? Angus might as well have asked me to levitate. I was having a job keeping my eye on anything. Everything was moving up and down. I looked over at Murphy. He turned in his chair to face me and smiled, his hands gripping the wheel. He didn't seem to be in the least bit perturbed. He obviously had prodigious reserves of calm to tap into when required. The ship heaved to one side and my stomach lurched. I wished I'd skipped those deep-fried prawns and chips I'd had for supper. The captain cut the ship's speed a little. *Sagara* began to roll more heavily. 'How long is this going to last?' I called to Murphy.

He shrugged. 'A few hours. Should have blown over by dawn, I reckon. Do you like AC/DC?'

There was a loud crash from the bow and the ship's superstructure groaned a complaint. Water thudded against the windscreen. 'What?'

'I said, do you like AC/DC?'

'Yes... Yes, I do.'

Murphy chortled. 'Fuckin' great band.'

I looked up at the wall clock. *Should have blown over by dawn.* Murphy's words rang in my head. *Hell's bells,* I thought, *dawn is eight hours away.*

The ship tore into another wave and ploughed down into a deep trough with a resounding crash that sent a shockwave through my body. I glanced at Murphy. He was dimming the light emitted from the instrument panels and smoking a roll-up. 'I thought you'd quit smoking,' I said.

He glowered at me. 'Don't you fucking well start. I'll throw my tobacco away when arrive in the Azores.'

'Do you mind if I roll one?' The sound of the wind howling and whistling against taut cables outside was lifting my nervousness into fear.

Murphy tossed his packet of Drum rolling tobacco over to me. 'Help yourself.'

I rolled a cigarette with some difficulty. I lit it and inhaled deeply. Never had a roll-up tasted so good. Ten minutes later, I threw up in the toilet.

Angus returned to the bridge and reeled towards me. 'Hey, Hamish, you better go below and check out your missus. She's looking a bit green about the gills.'

'Oh, okay, thanks. I'll away and see how she's getting along.' I let go of a support handle and tottered over to the door, grabbing onto anything I could to prevent stumbling and falling flat on my face.

Sagara continued to rock-and-roll her way into the stormy night.

The ship's corridors were see-sawing up and down. The swaying passageways, with their dimmed lighting and closed cabin doors, gave those parts of the ship a uniform allure, not much different from that of a modern hotel. My unsteady steps were silent on the thick carpet. I nearly knocked myself out when I stumbled and my head banged against an oak-panelled wall with a sickening thump. I felt queasy. When I reached my suite's door, I pushed down on the brass handle and lurched inside. I caught a glimpse of Jean, lying prone on the king-sized bed with her hands covering her eyes and forehead. I wobbled into the bathroom and threw up over the toilet bowel, already splattered with diarrhoea and vomit. My body began to shiver. I splashed water on my face and looked in the mirror, framed by glowing white light bulbs. I looked pale, haggard and old. In some forward-planning part of my overactive mind, it registered that I might shave my head like Angus; he looked ten years younger than me.

I zigzagged over to the bedroom and collapsed onto the bed beside Jean, who was still fully clothed. She groaned and then mumbled, 'I feel like I'm dying.'

I tried to console her. 'It's okay, Jean, the storm will blow itself out in a few hours.'

Jean groaned again. 'A few bloody hours. If this doesn't stop soon, I am going to die.' She turned on her side and dry heaved, her stomach already empty. 'Oh my god,' she moaned. 'Why did I come on this bloody boat? I must have been out of my mind.'

I was thinking the same thing. There was a loud crash from the direction of the ship's prow. The room tilted. Jean moaned, groaned, and muttered curses like someone with a sore throat speaking in tongues. I lay on my back and closed my eyes. Bad idea. My head spun and I knew I was about to throw up again. Half digested prawns and chips gushed out of my mouth in a gastric eruption that cascaded across my chest. I fell asleep at some point and woke up in the damp sludge of my own vomit, realizing the ship was no longer heaving. I could hear the quiet hum of the ship's engines rising from below. The storm had passed.

Although neither of us had anything that remotely resembled an appetite, Jean and I wandered into the main dining area at eleven o'clock on the following morning. Monica was the only person around. She was sitting at the big round table, munching on a slice of buttered toast, drinking coffee, and reading a paperback copy of Howard Marks' *Mister Nice*. She looked up as we approached and took our places by the table. 'Good morning,' Monica said brightly, removing her reading glasses. She jerked her head and tossed her long grey hair out of her face. 'Survived last night's wee storm, I see. Coffee?' she asked, lifting a silver coffee pot towards waiting cups.

'Yes, good idea, Mona,' I said. 'I think I could just about handle a cup of coffee.'

Jean declined the offer and poured herself a glass of water from a crystal carafe.

'By the looks of you two, I'd say you didn't have a very good night.'

'Mona, my dear,' said Jean, pushing her black hair behind her ears, 'I thought I was going to die last night. I've never felt so miserable in my entire life. I can't bloody well wait to set foot on dry land again.'

Monica gave her a sympathetic smile. 'You'll get over it. I've never had a problem with seasickness, but I know it can make you feel dreadful.'

'Any idea when we'll reach the Azores?' I asked, sipping coffee from a dainty porcelain cup.

'Lara was telling me earlier that we should reach the island of São Miguel by tomorrow morning. We won't be there for long, though. The idea is to head for the island of Faial, where lots of yachts stop off when making the Atlantic crossing.'

'When will that be?' Jean asked.

'No more than a day I should think.'

Jean's face dropped.

By late afternoon I could see the outline of São Miguel on the distant horizon. I was feeling a lot better by this time. Jean had gone for a sauna. I leaned over the ship's prow and watched the bow cleave through the dark-blue water. The air was warm with only a few patches of cloud in the blue sky. Over to my left, I caught a glimpse of something big breaking the sea's surface and realized it must have been some kind of whale. I turned around and looked up towards the bridge. Behind the sky's reflection on a slanted window, I could just make out Raj, waving and pointing in the direction the whale had broken through the water. I looked back to the sea just in time to catch sight of a humpback breaching. It must have been a kilometre away. I glimpsed the giant mammal's white belly before it crashed back into the water. It was a very inspirational sight that made me wonder how it must be to live a whale's life, cruising the world's oceans in search of krill, plankton, and maybe a family.

I walked up a companionway and entered the bridge. Sitar music burbled out of the speakers at low volume. Raj was alone. 'How's it going?' he asked.

'Better,' I said.

He chuckled knowingly. 'Bit of a rough night, eh? I was down in the engine room the whole time. Not so bad to be in the belly of the ship during a gale like that. Alice is still in bed recovering. She was as sick as a dog. The kids loved it. They're already asking when the next storm's coming.'

'I hope not any time soon,' I commented.

'How's Jean?'

'Complaining as usual.'

'Tell me about it. Hey,' said Raj, suddenly changing the subject, 'Did you see that whale?'

'Yes, I did.'

'Fucking amazing, man! I just don't get why people hunt them. It's not as if we need blubber and oil for our hurricane lamps anymore. For me, whales are a symbol of freedom. Unlike us humans they don't build houses, don't need supermarkets and don't leave nuclear waste or clouds of toxic smoke behind them. You know, those guys have been around for fifty million years. Five hundred times longer than humans. Think about it. As far as they're concerned, we're the new brats on the block, leaving piles of plastic rubbish and oil slicks behind wherever we go. Only been here for a short time and, man, have we fucked things up big time. You know why whales shoot out of the sea like that?'

I shrugged. 'Looking for a mate?'

'They are communicating.'

'With us?'

'Of course.'

'What are they saying?'

'Enjoy a good swim in the ocean and stop making such a fucking mess of this beautiful planet.'

I laughed. 'You're probably right.'

'I was just thinking while watching you down on the deck, would you like to take the helm for a while? I need to take a shower. I haven't slept in twenty-four hours.'

'What? Me steer the ship, you mean?'

Raj gave me a curious sideways glance. 'Yeah, why not? If you have a nervous breakdown or a heart attack, hit that big red button over there.' He pointed to a red alarm button mounted beside a panel of blinking lights. 'I checked the radar. There's nothing afloat within a forty-kilometre radius of us. See that black needle there?' He nodded at a big dial to the left of me. 'Try and keep that on zero. Just keep her dead ahead. If you see Blackbeard or Captain Pissgums in the prow of a pirate ship heading towards us, give 'em a broadside. If that doesn't work, get ready to repel all boarders.'

'Eh... What?' I asked, completely bewildered.

'Somebody will be up to relieve you before it gets dark. We could put her on automatic but, as you are about to find out, this is a lot more fun.' Raj stood back from the wheel and looked at me. 'On you go then.' I stepped forward, sat down in the leather captain's chair and took hold of the wheel. Raj gave me a gentle pat of encouragement on the back. 'See you later, Hamish,' he said, before walking to the door at the back of the bridge and closing it behind him.

The soothing sitar music stopped playing in the background, to be replaced by the low hum of electronic equipment. I suddenly felt very alone. I gripped the wooden wheel, horrified at the thought of making some kind of terrible mistake. My shoulders tensed up. I took a few deep breaths. I realized I wasn't actually doing very much, apart from gripping the smooth wheel so tightly that my knuckles had turned white. I stretched my hands out one at a time. After about ten minutes, I'd built up enough confidence to begin experimenting. I turned the wheel a fraction to the right and immediately *Sagara's* prow veered a little in that direction. I was amazed at how responsive the ship was. I looked at the needle on the guidance system and, sure enough, it was pointing four degrees to the right of zero. I moved the wheel back to its original position and the big black needle edged back towards zero. *Great!* I was beginning to enjoy myself. I looked over the sea towards São Miguel. The island was still a long way off, but I was sure it appeared bigger than the last time I'd looked. To the left of São Miguel, I began to make out the shadowy outline of a smaller island. I looked down at the console in front of me and checked a digital readout. The ship was speeding over the depths of the Atlantic Ocean at exactly fourteen knots.

Time passed, the sun set and twilight turned to darkness. I remembered the switch controlling the bridge's night lights and flicked them on. Dim red light illuminated the bridge. I began to worry everyone had forgotten that a man was steering the ship, who hadn't a clue what he was doing. I heard a door open behind me. I looked over my shoulder and saw Jean. 'What are you doing here,' I asked.

She cleared her throat. 'Oh, I'm visiting the red light district and I seem to have forgotten where I parked my Mercedes.'

'What?' I asked, rising to my feet.

'What the hell do think I'm doing here? I came up to see how Admiral Hamish is getting along. I can leave if my presence is disturbing you.'

'No! Don't do that. I'm sorry, Jean, I was getting worried that they'd forgotten I was up here, steering the ship into the darkness.'

'Murphy told me that he'll be up to relieve you soon. I have to switch on the running lights.' She flipped a switch at the far end of the control panel. A red and a green light immediately blinked on down on the fore deck's beams. 'There,' she said. Jean came over and slipped an arm around my waist. 'How does it feel to be in control of the ship?'

'Amazing. I was scared stiff at first, but I have the hang of it now.'

'Clever boy.'

I turned to look into her mischievous eyes, a few inches lower than mine. Her face glowed lime green in the dim light thrown up by the instrument panel. She gave me a peck on the lips. I tasted lipstick. We looked out the window. Stars sparkled in the sky ahead of us. Jean's arm tightened around my waist. There was a pinprick of light flashing from São Miguel's direction. 'Must be a lighthouse,' I commented absently. We stood on the bridge for another twenty minutes, saying nothing, happy to enjoy each other's company in silence. Just the two of us. The unique and intimate situation created a memory that I would cherish for the rest of my life.

The door opened behind us and Murphy entered with his son Ziggy. 'Everything fine up here?' he asked, stooping to check something on the control panel.

'Just grand, Murphy,' I said. 'I hadn't realized how responsive the ship is to the wheel.'

'You get used to it. You can stay where you are if you like it so much.'

I shook my head. 'No, but thanks for offering. I've had enough of this for one day.'

'Hey, dad, can I steer the boat?' Ziggy asked eagerly.

'Yeah, sure, go ahead,' said Murphy to his son, who was tall enough to look out the window.

I stepped aside. Ziggy sat down in the captain's chair and took ahold of the wheel, immediately spinning it to the right. The ship veered so sharply I almost fell over.

Murphy grabbed the wheel and steered the ship back onto an even keel. 'You little shit,' he growled playfully to his son, 'I've told you not to do that. Do it again and you're banned from the helm for a week. You hear me?'

'Aye, dad, I hear you,' said Ziggy submissively. 'I won't do it again. I promise.'

Murphy stood aside and once more his son took hold of the wheel. Ziggy looked up at his father. 'Thanks, dad. Look, I'm behaving myself now.'

Murphy nodded thoughtfully. 'Aye, so you are, pal. I wonder how long that will last.'

'Bit of a chip off the old block there, if I'm not mistaken,' I commented.

'Yeah, Hamish, you're right. Sometime the wee bugger worries me, but most days I think how lucky I am to have a wonderful boy like him.' The ship veered to the left. Murphy gave Ziggy a gentle slap on the back of his head and admonished him by saying, 'Pack it in, you little fuckin' squirt!' Ziggy sniggered.

Jean screwed up her face in mock distaste and I laughed. We wished Murphy and his son a good night and headed downstairs. I hurried in the galley's direction. My appetite had returned.

I awoke late the following morning. The ship's engines had fallen silent. I had a quick shower, dressed, and left Jean to sleep, while I went to see what was going on outside.

I hurried along to the foredeck, stopping to look over towards the island of São Miguel, partially shrouded in mist. I could smell the land, an aromatic blend of heather and freshly cut herbs. *Sagara* was anchored about half-a-kilometre from the shore, facing a curving breakwater enclosing a bay. The mist cleared a little and I could make out the edges of Ponta Delgada. It appeared to be a small town, mainly composed of whitewashed houses, their doorways and windows outlined in black. In the background were taller more modern buildings. I noticed the ship's tenders were lashed down and still swathed under their waterproof tarpaulins; solid evidence confirming there were no immediate plans to go ashore. A twin-prop passenger plane whistled by overhead, its landing gear down. A small trawler chugged out from behind the breakwater. Two fishermen waved from the stern as the boat passed to starboard, gulls wheeling over its wake.

By early afternoon, São Miguel was receding in the distance. *Sagara* was running at full speed, heading towards the island of Pico. I went up to the bridge and found Angus at the helm. About a hundred kilometres away from Pico, we passed a Portuguese frigate steaming from the opposite direction. The warship cut its speed as it drew nearer. Thick black smoke belched from a funnel as the grey ship cruised by close enough for me to observe a uniformed man standing on a platform outside of the bridge, scanning *Sagara* with a pair of binoculars. When I saw him looking towards our bridge, I waved and the sailor waved back.

A small pimple appeared on the horizon. Towards sunset the pimple had turned into a massive extinct volcano, with white villages dotting its base along the coastline. Pico's summit was circled by cloud, giving the island a fairytale allure. A sickle moon hung in the western sky. Angus steered the ship along the twenty kilometre-wide channel separating Pico from the neighbouring island of São Jorge. It was ten in the evening when the island of Faial came in to view. Lights shimmered on the water from the town of Horta as we approached a breakwater similar to that of Ponta Delgada. It was decided to anchor offshore for the night.

The following morning, one of the white tenders was hoisted down onto the sea. I accompanied Angus Murphy and Lara on the short trip into the Horta Marina, where we tied the semi-rigid up at the reception quay. There were dozens of yachts, big and small, berthed in the marina, flags and pennants flapping and cracking in the breeze. We entered a small office and were politely informed by a young Portuguese woman, in perfectly pronounced English, that we had to go next door to the maritime police and customs before *Sagara* could be assigned an appropriate berth. It took over an hour to fill in several forms at the immigration office. When everything was in order, we returned to the marina office, where we were told that *Sagara* could now berth behind the harbour wall, beside a rust-streaked freighter in the process of unloading its cargo.

By early afternoon, *Sagara* was tied up at the harbour wall. Everyone on board was in a hurry to venture into Horta in search of some lunch. Over the decades it had become a tradition for sea travellers to paint something on the walls or even the pavement in the harbour area to commemorate their visit. I could have spent the afternoon looking at those colourful paintings, but hunger steered me in another direction. The first suitable establishment we came to was Peter's Café Sport, which soon became our favourite watering hole over the next ten days.

From the outside, the Café Sport looked quaint. The facade was bright blue. Above the main entrance, the café's name was painted on a big plank of varnished wood, flanked by an artisan's impression of two white sperm whales made from raised cement. Inside, the café's wooden bar was backed by shelves of bottles containing every kind of strong alcoholic drink imaginable. Multi-coloured ships' flags hung from the ceiling and walls, alongside brass clocks, barometers, and anchors with examples of seaman's knots completing the nautical theme. Tables and chairs were shifted and rearranged to accommodate our relatively large group. Soon all thirteen of us were eating a variety of freshly caught seafood accompanied by a delectable salad, roast potatoes and grilled vegetables. Murphy kept ordering bottles of expensive wine, while everyone, except the kids, kept drinking them. By late afternoon, all the adults in our group were very drunk, myself included. The kids went off to explore the harbour and then Murphy ordered a bottle of the cafés homemade gin. It was potent liquor. I can honestly say that I've never been so smashed in my life. At one point I stood up and proposed a toast. I began to give a speech, my words slurred. Jean ordered me to shut up and sit down. Everyone present laughed. I didn't mind. I was having a wonderful time. Of course, the people running the place adored us. The bill was over two thousand euros. Murphy paid. How Jean and I made it back to our suite on *Sagara* will forever remain a mystery to me. I woke up in the morning with a hangover worthy of a place in the *Guinness Book of Records*. I swore I'd never touch another drop of alcohol for as long as I lived; a sincere resolution that would be broken within twenty-four hours. I never did figure out the person or persons responsible for shaving my head as smooth as an egg, while I lay in an alcohol-induced stupor, but I had my suspicions.

Horta was a small town mostly built from black volcanic rock. The majority of the houses were whitewashed and capped by sloping red-tiled roofs. There were no concrete apartment blocks to be seen anywhere on Faial. Angus rented a car. He, Lara, Jean, and I, spent a few days exploring the island. There were signs of volcanic activity almost everywhere we went. We bought chicken from a small supermarket, wrapped pieces in aluminium foil, and buried the packages in hot gravel by a pool of bubbling water that smelled strongly of sulfur. We returned an hour later and the chicken had been cooked to perfection.

The views of the surrounding ocean from Faial's higher regions were vast. It was often misty, but on a clear day, one could see, at a distance of about six kilometres, the island of Pico. Even though its peak was well over two thousand metres high it looked tiny in comparison to the Atlantic Ocean and the wide-open sky. Walls of hydrangeas, predominantly violet, separated the steeply sloping fields. The locals were friendly and, away from town, the menfolk rode sturdy horses as they went about their daily business.

On our last day on Faial, we visited a black sand beach, where a lighthouse that had originally been on the coast was now some distance inland due to a volcanic eruption over fifty years previously. Faial was an unspoiled place with little in the way of commercial tourism. Something, I hoped, that would remain unchanged.

It was a mild summer's morning in late July 2010. *Sagara* cast off from Faial. I sat with Jean in the stern, drinking coffee and watching the island recede in the distance. I had a woollen hat on to keep my shaved head warm. Jean liked my new hairless hairstyle and thought it made me look younger and more masculine. I decide to keep it that way. The next leg of our Atlantic crossing was underway. Angus had worked out our course and fed his calculations into the ship's navigational computer. We were moving in a southwesterly direction towards our next port of call, Nassau in the Bahamas.

My favourite time of the day had become the middle of the night. I'd volunteered to do the bridge's night watch, beginning at ten in the evening and finishing at dawn. One of the job's perks was that I was excused from cleaning duties. I've always had an aversion to house cleaning, and I felt the same way about ship cleaning.

Some nights Jean would come up and sit with me. Occasionally, Monica or one of the other female crew members would pop in for a chat, or bring me a mug of strong tea. The hours I enjoyed most were when everyone else was asleep and I just had *Sagara* for company. I'd fallen in love with the ship and, just like a lover, I found she had her moods and unique ways of expressing herself. I knew when she was running efficiently and when she wasn't, due to some minor malfunction in her fuel supply or being run at full throttle for too long. I was sensitive to the varying pitch of her engines and the impact of natural forces on her hull. I'd also come to understand many of the functions of the ship's brain. I knew how the gyrocompass worked in conjunction with gravity and the Earth's rotation, how the depth sounder operated by transmitting a pulse into the sea, how the GPS helped navigate and how the speed log took its readings. I was becoming a man of the sea, isolated and remote from the human world, connected to something bigger than myself, a vast emptiness where nothing is fixed as you glide across the endless ocean.

Late at night, I'd remove my laptops from their waterproof cases to catch up with my emails and, when I was done with that, I'd work on my manuscript. If I was up to date I'd revisit earlier chapters and revise what I'd written months before. It was an endless source of entertainment. I was quite amazed by how much I'd learned about the writer's solitary craft since I'd first taken up writing after my car accident, an event that now seemed to have taken place in another lifetime. Apart from my own pleasure, I felt the story I'd written was my way of sharing something intimate about my life. I sometimes imagined what my grandchildren would think as adults, reading accounts of their great-uncle Angus's criminal exploits and adventures and my own somewhat staid and normal life. That is, apart from sitting on a landmine in Cambodia, being blown up and living to tell the tale. *Oh well,* I reasoned, *I suppose I'll be dead and buried by the time my grandchildren get around to reading about that.* And then, one night just before dawn, I had an idea. I printed out my first chapter on the bridge's laser printer. The following morning, I handed it over to my wife at the breakfast table.

'What's this?' Jean asked.

I explained.

She said, 'I'll read it this afternoon, after preparing lunch.' She gave me a peck on the cheek. 'Thanks.'

After supper that evening, I was passing time before I went up to the bridge for the nightshift. Jean came into our bedroom. I was stretched out on the bed, reading a paperback copy of Ian McEwan's *Saturday*.

'You shouldn't tell people I was drunk,' she complained. 'They might think I have a drinking problem.'

'What?' I hadn't a clue what she was talking about. 'I didn't tell anyone that.'

'Yes, you did.'

Then I remembered what I'd written in my first chapter. 'Oh! I'd forgotten about that. Do you want me to change it?'

'Definitely! Can you not say I looked like a sleeping angel? You know, something poetic.'

My mind cringed at the thought. 'Yes... Yes, of course, I can. So what else did you think, apart from not liking my description of you collapsing onto a foam rubber mattress after drinking bottles of Tiger beer?'

She sat down on the edge of the bed. 'Not bad at all. I liked that bit about the cobra. How come you never told me about it?'

'Because it's not true. I made it up.'

'You did? Why?'

'To grip the reader's attention and hopefully suspend their belief system in preparation for reading a lot of unbelievable stories, which are true.'

Jean nodded. 'I see. Well, I believed your cobra story. So you can take that as a good sign. When do I get to read the next chapter?'

At that moment I realised I was writing something that might appeal to readers beyond the small circle of family and close friends I'd envisaged. I answered Jean's question. 'I'll print out chapters two and three tonight and give them to you at breakfast time.'

'Great.' Jean leaned over and kissed the crown of my shaved head. 'Who'd ever have thought you'd turn out to be a writer?'

I looked at the time on the bottom right-hand corner of my computer screen: 03:05. I clicked 'print' and the laser printer began making a snick-snick sound as it printed out the chapters I'd promised to give my wife. I gathered up the sheets of A4 paper and stacked them together. I'd just closed my laptop's lid when I heard a warning buzz from the long-range radar repeater. I leaned over the green screen to study it. There was a small contact registering on the screen. The bearing was 240°. The range was 38 nautical miles. There was no immediate danger, but I could see that if *Sagara* continued on her present course there might be a possibility of a collision. I grabbed a pair of high-power binoculars and went outside. The sea was relatively calm and the moon was almost full, providing good night-time visibility. I raised the binoculars and scanned the horizon. At first I saw nothing, but then I caught a pinprick of light over to my right. I lowered the binoculars and realised the naked eye couldn't discern the tiny light. I went back inside and, under the bridge's dimmed red lights, once more studied the radar screen. *Yes*, I thought, *the light on the horizon corresponds to the position on the radar.* The contact on the screen was now solid and clearly defined. I reckoned it was a tanker or container ship. I was surprised because I knew we were at least one hundred nautical miles west of the nearest shipping lane. I sat back in the captain's chair and thought about what I should do. There was no imminent danger, so there was no point in going below to wake Murphy or Angus. I didn't need help. I knew what to do. I switched off the automatic pilot. *Sagara* was cruising at a little over thirteen knots. I kept the ship on her previous course and let ten minutes pass. I went outside and used the binoculars again. I could now make out two lights, one green, one white, dead ahead. I returned to the helm and changed course by 15°. Some time passed and I could now see the distant ship's deck and bridge lights through the window, without using the binoculars. I checked the radar again. *Sagara* was well clear of the ship's path. I waited for another twenty minutes and then went outside again and raised the binoculars. I saw the outline of a huge ship. She was moving at an angle and I realised that, due to her hull sitting high in the water, it was an empty supertanker, probably off course on a return journey to the Persian Gulf.

The oil tanker passed to starboard at a distance of approximately ten kilometres. She was moving at quite a clip for such a massive vessel. I switched on the autopilot and the guidance system took over again. *Sagara* returned to her previous heading. I was feeling quite chuffed with myself, having dealt with the spontaneous maritime event in what I viewed as a professional manner. Captain Hamish at your service. Moments later, the satisfied smile vanished from my face, when something happened that I'd completely forgotten to take into account; the super tanker's wake. *Sagara* hit a series of high waves side on. The ship heaved from side to side, her lower decks awash with water. 'Fuck!' I quickly switched off the autopilot and spun the wheel to make the ship's prow veer into the waves at a 90° angle. The ship bucked and plunged a few times before it was all over. I worried that some of the crew might have been thrown out of bed and imagined a furious Murphy running upstairs to the bridge to find out what the hell was going on. Nothing like that happened. I breathed a sigh of relief and returned the ship once more to automatic pilot. I felt like smoking a cigarette. Much to my delight, I found one of the captain's half-finished roll-ups in an ashtray. I lit up the cigarette, took a long drag and exhaled a lungful of foul-tasting smoke towards the main windscreen. I felt dizzy and flumped down into the captain's chair. The coast was clear.

I returned to my laptop and brought my manuscript up to date. Before returning the computer to its waterproof case, I checked the time again. It was 04:57.

It would soon be dawn. The long-range radar repeater's alarm signal buzzed for the second time that night. I checked the screen. There was no hint of a contact glowing on it. A few minutes passed and then the buzzer sounded again. I caught a broad flickering about twelve nautical miles dead ahead. Then nothing. The nearest landmass, the Dominican Republic, was still about five hundred nautical miles away to the southwest. I went outside and scanned the vast expanse of dark water in front of me with the binoculars. There was nothing visible that set any alarm bells ringing in my head. I returned to the radar scanner and, sure enough, there was a flickering oval shape that must have been twenty kilometres wide. *Sagara* was heading straight for it and would reach its perimeter in approximately fifteen minutes if I didn't cut her speed. I eased the twin throttle controls back and cut the speed to seven knots.

The sky was lightening to the east. I began to wonder if the radar was picking up on a huge pod of dolphins feeding on a school of fish. I went outside again and raised my binoculars. This time I saw immediately what the ship was heading towards. Dead ahead lay one of those islands of plastic refuse that dot the modern world's oceans. I hurried inside and slowed the ship down to three knots. Minutes later the ship edged into a blanket of non-biodegradable plastic waste. It crossed my mind to seek assistance but I didn't sense any immediate danger. Once again, I committed myself to handling the situation on my own. My main concern was that the ship's propellers might become entangled with abandoned fisherman's netting or nylon rope. I cut the ship's engines. Apart from the electronic hum produced by the bridge's electronic equipment, it was eerily silent. The ship was drifting further into the plastic mass. I heard something solid clunk against the ship's prow. I looked out the window, but from my position on the bridge, I couldn't see anything significant. I hurried outside and strode down a companionway, the metal handrail glistening with dew. I ran along the foredeck. It was beginning to get light. I leaned over the edge of the prow. What I saw filled me with dread. A sea mine was nudging against the hull. It was about the size of a big swimming pool filtration unit and surrounded by oil-stained plastic bottles. Half-a-dozen round-ended spikes stuck out from its curved, rust-eaten surface. It reminded me of something out of a Second World War submarine movie. *Clunk!* One of the sea mine's detonator spikes bumped against *Sagara's* dark-blue hull. 'Fucking hell!' I cursed, pushing myself away from the prow. I had to get back to the bridge and manoeuvre the ship away from the mine. I turned and saw Angus in his underpants running towards me.

The sea mine exploded with a tremendous blast. *Sagara's* foredeck blew up and disintegrated, taking Hamish and Angus MacLeod's lives in the same furious instant. The explosion's shock wave swept over what remained of the motor yacht, blistering paint and blowing out windows. The ship tilted forward and began to sink. A minute later, *Sagara* slipped below the surface, taking everyone on board with her. There were no survivors.

EPILOGUE

I was on my honeymoon in the Dominican Republic when I found Hamish MacLeod's Toshiba laptop in its waterproof case, washed up on the beach at Punta Cana. It was November 2016. That bloke, Donald Trump, had just been elected the 45th president of the United States.

We'd been staying at our all-inclusive hotel for a week. I couldn't resist all the free grub that was laid on. I'd begun jogging every morning at dawn. I like to keep in shape. I didn't want to return home to Newcastle looking like a fat chump with a suntan. The beach was deserted at sunrise, a pleasant change from the afternoon when the beach is crowded with German tourists and noisy quad bikes tearing along the shore. When I found Hamish's laptop on the shoreline, my first impulse was to hand it over to the local dibble. I decided against that. I'd heard the Dominican police are dead corrupt and I was certain they would have just nicked it for themselves.

The laptop's battery was flat. I used my own computer's charger to recharge it. Hamish had employed a security password and therefore I had to wait until I returned home before I could bypass that problem. Luke, my best mate, just so happens to be good at cracking computer log-in passwords because he works in a mobile phone repair shop. It wasn't like breaking into the Bank Of England. It took Luke five minutes to get in. We were quite surprised to find that Hamish had only been using the laptop for writing his story. There were no emails or anything like that. Of course, once I opened the Word Document and started reading, I could understand why Hamish had used a password. His brother, Angus, was a right criminal and his mate, Murphy, had offed a few blokes.

I Googled Hamish's construction company's phone number. The next thing I knew, I had some Scottish bird, Doreen, on the line. I knew straight away from the tone of her voice that she was out of fettle. I told her that I'd found her boss's laptop in the Dominican Republic. She hears this, then goes proper radgie with someone in the background, like. Comes back on the line and says, 'If this is some kind of joke, it's not funny!' and then hangs up on me. *Very nice, thank you very much,* I thought.

I reads the whole manuscript from beginning to end and I enjoy it so much that I gets to thinking that it might be worthwhile trying to get the story published. I'm a sparky by trade and hadn't a clue as to how to go about doing such a thing. Out of my depth, I suppose you could say. I checked Amazon, ordered a book with publisher's and agent's names and addresses in it, and sent out a bunch of enquires. Right lot of good that did me. Nobody was interested in it.

One night, I'm down at me local with Luke, having a few pints as one does. We gets to discussing the manuscript and Luke says to me, 'Mitchell, I think we should let my missus have a look at it.' Liz went to university and teaches kids at the local primary school. An educated woman, you might say. Speaks posh, a bit like Victoria Beckham.

Turns out Liz loves the story and suggests we approach a small press publisher, or just fork out some cash and self-publish. She thought that we should publish the book using a *nom de plume*. I looked that one up in the dictionary. If you are reading this, you know Liz's idea panned out.

I might add that it was Liz who wrote the last three paragraphs of Hamish's story. I think it was a good idea, making that up about a sea mine and all that. Kind of like rounded the story off good and proper. *What?* I can hear you thinking. *Some woman in Newcastle made up the end of the story?* Of course, she did. Once Hamish was out of the picture somebody had to finish the story for him. Doesn't matter to Hamish now that he's dead and gone, now does it? Rest in peace, mate. From what I gather you were a nice enough bloke while alive. A bit henpecked by the sound of it, but aren't we all, mate? Aren't we all? My better half is always on at me. Goes with the territory, I suppose.

Liz thinks I sound like a right Geordie when I write but thought that it would be okay, because it makes what I'm saying sound more authentic, like. I don't know if it does. I've always talked this way. If you're ever up in Newcastle look me up. We can go out for a pint. You can drink as much as you want because you will be paying for the drinks. Ha-ha! That's a joke, like.

Seriously, though, I've been thinking a lot about something Angus MacLeod said to his twin brother. 'It's only the mind that interprets life's events in terms of good and bad. In reality, there is no way of knowing what is, in fact, a blessing or a curse. All we can do is live through whatever is happening – here and now.'

You know what? Angus was dead right.

ACKNOWLEDGEMENT

The inspiration to begin writing The Tyro Series came after a narrow escape from the tsunami in Sri Lanka and accidently wandering into a minefield in Cambodia in 2004.

I am grateful to the following individuals for their support. Prita L Freytag, Helen Mitchell, Om Shivaom Freeman, German Hari (RIP), Mr P and my extended global family of friends.

A special word of thanks to Helen Gosch for lending her patience and editorial skills during the early days.

My eternal thanks to my spiritual teachers Osho, H W L Poonja, Nisargadatta Mahraj, Timothy Leary, Mr G, Mr O, and, last but not least, Maurice Nicoll.

'Lately it occurs to me what a long, strange trip it's been.'
                              Truckin'. Grateful Dead.

ABOUT THE AUTHOR

Luke Mitchell

If you wish to contact the author you can email. thetyroseries@gmail.com

BOOKS BY THIS AUTHOR

Mind Bomb

Borderline Dreamtime

Sagara

Printed in Great Britain
by Amazon